Dawn of a Dark Age

Jane Welch was born in Derbyshire in 1964. After working in Heffers Booksellers and running her own small business, she and her husband, Richard, spent five winters teaching skiing in the Pyrenees where she completed her first novel, *The Runes of War*. After HarperCollins made an offer for that and the rest of the Runespell Trilogy (*The Lost Runes* and *The Runes of Sorcery*) writing took over. Her second trilogy, The Book of Önd, (*The Lament of Abalone, The Bard of Castaguard* and *The Lord of Necrond*) was published in 1998 by Simon & Schuster.

She lives in Somerset with Richard and their two very much adored children, Harriet and George.

Jane Welch's web site address is: www.janewelch.com

BY JANE WELCH

The Runespell Trilogy

The Runes of War
The Lost Runes
The Runes of Sorcery

The Book of Önd

The Lament of Abalone
The Bard of Castaguard
The Lord of Necrönd

Voyager

JANE WELCH

Dawn of a Dark Age

Volume One of
The Book of Man

HarperCollins*Publishers*

Voyager
An Imprint of HarperCollins*Publishers*
77-85 Fulham Palace Road,
Hammersmith, London W6 8JB

www.voyager-books.com

A Paperback Original 2001
1 3 5 7 9 8 6 4 2

Copyright © Jane Welch 2001

The Author asserts the moral right to
be identified as the author of this work

A catalogue record for this book
is available from the British Library

ISBN 000 711249 1

Typeset in Goudy by Palimpsest Book Production Limited,
Polmont, Stirlingshire

Printed and bound in Great Britain by
Clays Ltd, St Ives plc

For Richard, Harriet and George
with all my love.

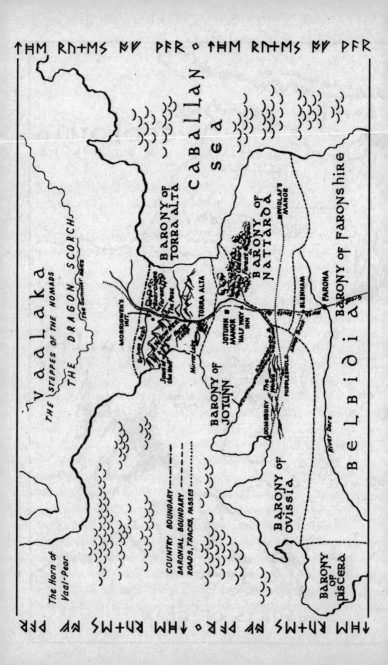

Prologue

Blood trickled from his shoulder, the dark liquid sliding from his brilliant golden scales and sizzling on the rocks at his feet.

Wriggling up through the crevice to the surface, he sniffed the air, seeking his best route of escape. The man had not followed him down through the tunnels; surely, it would take the two-legged creature some time to crawl up to the Tor and pursue him overland. He had time to draw breath before staggering to the river's edge.

Closing his claw around the trinket, he grimaced, his tight toothy grin biting back on his pain. The leaping water of the river at least cooled the deep cut under his wing and eased the stabbing pain radiating out from the barb of steel embedded in his shoulder. He bent his neck round, frantically twisting and stretching, but he couldn't reach the javelin. Dropping his great snout into the babbling waters, he allowed himself time to drink before stumbling on.

He must get back to the cave where the great golden queen bided her time, too big now to fly for the squirming new brood fighting for room in her bloated womb. Already, she had eaten her smaller mate to feed the huge litter that threatened to split her underbelly. Secretly, he feared that she would love her new offspring more than him. He, Aurek, could not risk losing her love; the trinket he had stolen from the Old Nest would prove his worth to her.

The act would be a clear sign, proof that he would soon be strong enough to reclaim their ancient and rightful home from the naked creatures that now infested the old rock. Then, she would always love him beyond all else. Certainly, he had already proved his courage. He grinned with deep satisfaction at the golden trinket; his mother loved gold.

But he was hurt and he needed her; her fire raged with a white heat that would burn to nothing the vile creature that pursued him. He was beginning to feel light-headed and his great lungs rasped with effort. He coughed, spits of blood dribbling from his nostrils. All the while, he clasped that snippet of gold in his great claw and vowed he would never let it go until he offered it into her hands. He ached and was tired but he would bring it home. The gift to his mother would prove that he had, at last, found a way back into the ancient home. One day . . ., he swore to himself, one day, he would sit atop that rocky Tor and scream out his name to the world, declaring that he, Aurek, was the great lord of the canyon.

Head low, drooping from the pain that scythed through his shoulder muscles, he limped on, squelching through the fine mud lining the river and then stumbling onto stony ground as he worked his way into the mountains.

His ears pricked and he sniffed the breeze. The two-legged pest must be mounted; his nostrils tingled with the strong scent of horse mingled with man. It had been a while since he had eaten and his wound was draining his energy; horseflesh would be good. If only he could spread those wings and fly, but the barb stuck in his right shoulder pierced the muscle and he could not spread his glorious golden wings to cast his terrifying shadow over the land.

He struggled on, his two hearts pounding their double beats in his heaving breast. The wind swirled within the steep valley and he could no longer smell the scent of horse. Horses; traitors to the animal kingdom like the hounds that ran with them! Aurek snorted angrily, forgetting his pain for a moment and drew in a sharp breath, ready to scream out his rage at all treacherous creatures that would side with man. But the movement sent stabs of pain arcing out from the javelin point. He dropped his great armoured head to the ground and took quick, shallow breaths until the spasms eased.

Once he tried to draw strength by sucking in a low deep breath, but the pain was excruciating as his lungs pressed against the barb of the javelin embedded in his flesh. He would not try that again. It was not a deep wound that the puny two-legged creature had inflicted on him, nor was it immediately life threatening; it was simply that he could not breathe deeply nor fly back to his mother; and he was not built for walking. Despite the pain in his shoulder, he proudly ruffled up the scales about his neck that were a deep golden colour inherited from the dazzling she-dragon.

He had his gift hooked tightly into his claw; one little man would not stop him getting to the caves to offer his gift that was just a tiny speck of gold, a cup barely big enough for him to stick the tip of his forked tongue into; but it would please Mother. It would prove he had breached the Old Nest.

Slinking along a valley bottom, he tried to keep out of the marshy fields, which sagged beside a stream, in an attempt to avoid leaving too marked a trail. It would have been better to clamber over the scree slopes and the rocky ledges above him but he was too exhausted. Despite his best efforts, he left deep long footprints amongst the spongy moss and mud of the upper courses of the mountain stream and knew he would be easy to follow.

A swathe of trees, pocketed into a depression just below the head of the valley, blocked his path; he sat back onto his haunches and groaned. He did not like trees. All his kind were wary of trees. The branches snagged on their wings and it was impossible to hunt within the woods. Disgustedly, he stared at the vegetation and then up at the steep sides of the mountains that cupped the valley. He would have to go through the trees; the climb was impossible since his weight would dislodge the scree and, without the use of his wings, he would slither and crash helplessly to the valley bottom.

Reluctantly, he pushed his way between the stout holly

trees; a low branch scraped at his back, snagging at the javelin. He snarled and snapped his jaws, trying to stifle the howl that was willing itself up from his gut. Lashing out, he uprooted a holly that barred his way before squeezing out between two more trees to reach the pass. His breath rasping, he clambered to the top. The cave was not far ahead now, on the far side of the next valley.

Aurek gave out a low moaning call.

The queen's answering cry shuddered the rocks about him but, to Aurek, it was like the sweetest of songs. Soon she would have this barb out from where it was wedged beneath his scales. Soon he would be able to breathe and fly once more.

He could see her now, the high noonday sun glinting off her flanks, her scales gleaming more brightly than an open casket of jewels. He staggered forward, his legs suddenly shaking and weak beneath him. The back legs that supported the bulk of his weight buckled and he sat back, stretching up his long snaking neck to call out again for her help.

As he approached the head of the pass, the wind swept up cleanly from behind. He snorted and stiffened, trumpeting out a warning cry to his mother whom he knew was too full-bellied to fly or protect herself with ease. He could have stumbled on faster if he had been prepared to relinquish his gift; but that was the very last thing he would do in this life.

The smell of horse was pungent and with it came the sickly scent of man. He could smell the oil on his sword, the tangy scent of polished metal and the sickly sweet aroma of sweat and pale flesh. Aurek knew now that he could not flee fast enough and must turn and face this wretched man, who had already caused him so much pain. He slithered down from the high rock, chucking first one leg forward and then another with that distinctive wide-legged gait of a great lizard. Waggling his tongue back and forth, he tasted the air.

The scent of horse wafted towards him and he managed to

spume a jet of flame. The fiery blast burnt a black path before him but the pain it caused in his chest and shoulder was so great that he coughed and sputtered and the next burst of flame was little more than a yellow flicker of candlelight.

Birds took to the air, squawking in fright. His mother's howl filled the mountains, shrieking out that she was coming for him. At last! Now he must just have patience. He knew she would be a little while since she was slow to move at all, her belly so swollen with her new litter. He had been the only one of twelve to survive her last and after the great queen had eaten his father, he and she had been sole companions. A creature so vast and powerful as a dragon was not an easy beast to recreate; it took a long terrible year of a mother's pain as the embryonic dragons swelled within her.

Aurek jolted back and sank onto his haunches, instinctively tucking down his neck to protect himself: the charging horse was suddenly before him. The man's armour banged and clattered as he galloped, great throwing knives, an axe, a mighty sword and four javelins strapped and buckled to the creaking leather of his saddle.

Aurek heard every sound. He noted every movement. Though in deep pain, he raced to face the attack. He tried to draw that belly-deep breath that would allow him to melt his armour and burn this knight to a splinter of charred bones, but the javelin between his shoulder blades stabbed at his lungs as he attempted to fill them. The pain was unbearable.

Head down like a bull, caparison flapping around the feathered legs, and plates of armour clanking, the horse charged on. A ton of steel and muscle thundered towards him, the point of a lance lowered at his breast.

With surprising agility, the dragon leapt aside and twisted his body sharply, lashing the horse in the chest with his barbed tail. The charger's hooves sparked on the rock and the horse was flung back onto its haunches by the force of the blow but, miraculously, the knight kept his seat and flung the first of his throwing knives. The blade clattered harmlessly against the dragon's armour of golden scales.

Enraged, Aurek screamed his challenge at the knight, who, to his bewilderment, cast off his helmet as if in contempt of the dragon's lethal strength. Humans were hard to tell apart but he judged him to be more solid than most with sleek black hair that he only noticed because it gleamed in the sunlight. With extraordinary courage, the man screamed back at him. Aurek fancied the yells might be words of speech but he had no understanding of the squeaks and yelps of man.

Hoarsely, he roared in retaliation, the air shaking with the thunderous bellow of his voice. 'I'll have my home back!' he shrieked, lashing out with his claws and trying to get close enough without letting the knight's lance jab up at the soft spot beneath his throat.

'Aurek! My son! Get away!' Mother was bellowing from across the valley, her wings outstretched in ungainly fashion to help her struggle across the rocks and heave her huge bulk towards him.

Aurek focused on the man and swept forward, claws open, his long sharp talons raking through the air. But the man was quick. Though Aurek's gaping snout stabbed forward and snapped perilously close, his injuries meant that he didn't have the speed to harm the man. The horse, though heavy, was light of foot and danced and darted to and fro while the man kept him at bay with his lance.

'Get back, Aurek!' his mother shrieked.

Flattening his short pointed ears, Aurek ignored her; he would prove to his mother that he could stand up to a lone knight. Angrily, he lunged forward with a claw but roared with frustration as, again, he sliced through thin air. Instinctively, he was wary of the gleaming sword in the man's right arm and he flicked his tail round and forward to draw the man's guard before lashing out at the knight's left side. For some reason, the knight seemed unable to bear a weapon in that hand.

6

At last, Aurek got a claw to the horse. The raking blow ripped open its chest, tearing away the flesh to show the pulsing red of the muscle beneath. The horse stumbled onto its knees and the rider was flung over his ears.

Aurek was about to crush him but, rather than backing away, the knight somersaulted forward over his raking claw and rolled beneath him. Something sharp pressed into the open wound beneath his wing and drove deep into his body.

'Mother!' he screamed. 'Mother! Save me!'

Twisting awkwardly, he blindly scraped beneath his body, the tip of one talon slicing into the man's cheek, but there was little power behind the blow as his pain overwhelmed him. Frantically, he tried to claw and shred at the long thorn in his side but the knight had twisted the javelin shaft and the barb had hooked deep into his muscle. Now the man had manoeuvred around to his rear and was hacking at his tail.

Aurek tried twisting to swat at him but the action threw him off balance. He was falling and not even his attempts to spread his wings could save his fall. He crashed onto his side, his own weight finishing the job that this man had been unable to complete; the javelin was driven deeper, stabbing between his ribs to reach one of his hearts.

Head twisted on its side, he watched the knight flee while he lay helpless and still, blackness dulling the edges of his vision. The all-embracing, cramping pain in his chest screamed through his entire body as he listened to the slow and steadily weakening thump of his remaining heart. Too weak to move, his head slumped onto the cold rock, blood oozing from his nostrils.

No longer able to smell the scent of the man, he could do nothing but wait, hoping that his magnificent mother would soon be with him to take away his terror at the sense of utter loneliness that engulfed him. Cold spread rapidly through his body.

But Mother was a long time coming. His eyelids grew heavy

and sagged, every breath excruciating. Within moments, his nostrils flared; a sour, acrid smell swept into his snout and his ears twitched at the sound of scraping. Something small poked its round head out from behind a rock and warily approached on two legs. The creature prodded his flank but he could do no more than grunt in protest and weakly drag open his eyelids to see a mud-brown hob hoot with glee. With a rusty sword, it set about trying to lever the golden trinket from his still clenched claw.

With a huge effort, Aurek snapped his jaws at the creature. The hob leapt back in fright, black blood pulsing in the huge arteries about its face but he did not run. The creature watched Aurek silently for a while before raising its sword, which was longer than its own rangy body. Boldly, it stepped forward.

In disbelief, Aurek watched helplessly as the creature swept the blade sideways, slicing under one of the scales of his legs and cutting it away. Then in one swing, the hob smote downwards on his raw flesh, striking rapidly again and again until he had hacked through a joint and cut through tendon and gristle. Finally, the severed limb fell away, the trinket still clamped between curving talons. Jets of deep red blood spurted from the wound.

The goblin sprang after the trinket and claw as, together, they slid down the steep rock and rolled away between two huge slabs of dark stone. Before the creature was lost from sight, it snapped round its pointed chin, taking one glance up the valley to where the golden queen bellowed and roared.

The young dragon's eyes sagged. 'Mother . . .'

After what seemed like an eternity of pain, she was at last standing over him, singing out the dragon's great song of loss. Then she was licking his face, her warm breath caressing his cheeks.

'Son, you'll mend. You are strong! Fight the pain. The blood of the great golden dragons of old runs hot in your veins. Do not leave me. Get up! Open your eyes; see the life in me!'

8

But he was too weak even to raise his head in response. All he could do was grunt softly. 'Mother, Mother I tried to bring you . . .' He could barely speak, his words hardly louder than the *bump-bump, bump-bump* of his remaining, overburdened heart.

He clenched his great strong jaws together, finding the strength to fight off the soft blanket of apathy that sought to claim him. Hot steaming tears hazed his darkening vision. 'I had a gift for you, Mother,' he hissed, knowing that one last burst of effort to speak was too much for his ruined body and that he could say no more. The sound of his pulsing heart was loud in his ears.

Mother, don't leave me, he willed, listening to the thump of his heart. *Bump, bump*, then *bump*. All was black and cold, a cruel biting cold. *Bump, bump*.

'Aurek, I love you,' he heard her murmur.

He wanted to answer, wanted to raise his eyelids to look into those huge loving eyes once more.

Mother, I have failed you, he thought. *All I wanted was to show you how strong I had become, that soon I would be able to win back our home. I had proof, had it in my claw. But I lost it. All I wanted was to prove that I could regain what was ours. I wanted to win the Old Nest for you and cry out from the great Tor, 'I am home!'*

Bump . . . bump. Bump . . . bump. His heart pulsed faintly. *Now I shall never be home.*

'Aurek, don't leave, me. Son, I love you. I love you. Speak to me; answer me!' his mother implored.

He was vaguely aware of her snout butting against his head, trying to make him lift it, but he had no strength. 'I love you, Aurek.'

Mother, I am scared. He could hear singing now and, though the pain of his body was numbly receding, he was terrified of the sense of loneliness sweeping through him.

Bump . . . Bump . . .

'Aurek . . .'

Bump . . .

Mother! I shall never forget you, he pledged, gripping only that thought as, with a wrench, he was suddenly free of the world and soaring through skies of deepest blue.

Chapter 1

Rollo stared upward, his thick red hair tumbling back from his young freckled face as he squinted against the glare of the snow. Had he really journeyed across half the world just for this? Wiping the sweat from his cheeks that were just beginning to sprout a soft adolescent down, he scowled at the great towers of Torra Alta, the long icicles dripping from the turrets and the snow devils rising from the towers where the bitter north wind whipped at the freshly fallen flakes. Men patrolled the battlements, tiny black figures against a grey sky.

The stern towers snagging at the brooding clouds filled him with a wary sense of unease; in fact the entire canyon that cut like a dark scar splitting the Yellow Mountains was, to his youthful eyes, gloomy and threatening. Flashing his father a sour look of resentment, he decided that he had been deliberately misled; his father had always described Torra Alta as a glorious place.

To add to Rollo's annoyance, his father, Baron Caspar, estranged lord of Torra Alta, seemed more radiant at the sight of the ancient fortress than he had ever been to see him. Sitting silently on his red roan stallion and marvelling at the view, it was as if he had totally forgotten his son. Unexpectedly, Caspar reached across and gripped his arm.

'That, Rollo, is home! That is Torra Alta!'

The young lad, who looked as if he would soon outstrip his father in height, wrinkled his nose. 'That! But . . .' He snorted in disgust as he sought a suitable insult. 'It's just a shack compared to Mother's palace, a thimble compared to the frontier towers she raised against the Empress.'

Caspar looked at his son in despair. 'Yes, but one day this will be yours. Your home. Your castle. Nothing that your mother commanded can ever be yours. You did not inherit your mother's powers over the bears; that gift went to your sister. You have always known that the law of Artor, the Bear Country, dictated that Imogen would inherit. Don't fight against something that you cannot change. Enjoy what you have. You have to admit that Torra Alta is fine!' Caspar sighed in appreciation at the sight.

'Ha!' Rollo scoffed, unable to think of anything more expressive.

'I miss your mother too; I wish you would believe that. But I can't change what has passed. Life goes on, Rollo, and we must make the most of what we have. Now, go on, look at that. Look at that tower of rock!'

He pointed at the jagged spire of bedrock that lanced up out of the canyon floor. A narrow road cut about its huge girth and spiralled upwards to the giddy heights of the frosted towers. 'We don't have carpets or silk-draped settles heaped with cushions; we have keen steel and the finest archers in the world. We have a castle of solid stone, an honest stronghold built by our ancestors to repel northern attack: a warrior's castle.'

'Ha!' Rollo snorted again, finding that he had no admiration for the incredible engineering employed to build such a structure upon the towering pinnacle of rock. In fact, he despised it though, at that moment, he could not account for the strength of his feelings.

Caspar gave him one of those thinly veiled looks of despair that so annoyed Rollo. 'Why is it that you are no easier to please now than when you were a young child? Haven't I done my best for you? I even trained up Chieftain for you though you know your mother didn't approve. I had to argue long and hard to persuade her that you could manage such a strong-willed mount so long as you were given the opportunity to learn.'

'But you still wouldn't let me ride Firecracker.' Rollo watched his father's face, knowing in his heart that he would avoid answering him; it was how Caspar always dealt with him.

Indeed, the Baron did look away. Thoughtfully, he stroked his old faithful horse that, even in Rollo's home continent on the far shore of the Tethys Ocean, was still unmatched for his speed and mean temperament. Even the bears of Tethya had kept a respectful distance from Firecracker's powerful rump and sharp teeth. Finally, Caspar smiled at his son. 'I love you too much, Rollo, to allow you to come to harm. Believe it or not, it is the truth.'

Rollo was saved from answering by a clarion call to muster, blasting out from above.

'That, my boy, is for us,' Caspar said with approval, his eyes gleaming.

'But they don't know we're coming. You sent no word,' Rollo objected.

'I had no need. Your grandmother knows. She will have sensed my homecoming. Fifteen years!' The corners of Caspar's mouth lifted. After breathing in deeply, he let out a long sigh, his breath steamy in the cold air. 'Fifteen long years.'

It was the first time since his mother's death that Rollo had seen his father smile. But it didn't make Rollo smile. He glared at the slope before him, snatched at Chieftain's reins to drag him to a halt and then, with a cry of attack, plunged his spurs into his horse's flanks and charged the slope as if it were an enemy of flesh and blood.

The Baron was quick to respond. Firecracker was over twenty years old but still showed little signs of ageing and had no trouble catching up with the Tethyan high-stepper. Despite their speed and showing remarkable horsemanship,

13

he grabbed his son's reins, quickly bringing both animals to a safer pace.

'Steady lad, it can be a treacherous slope in winter.'

'I can manage,' Rollo growled. 'Do you think I am afraid?' he challenged.

'Of course not,' Caspar said calmly. 'I have never thought you afraid of anything. To the contrary you are, perhaps, too brave and reckless for your own good.'

'It's not going to work, Father. I know why you are dragging me here. It won't change me.' Rollo growled between gritted teeth.

He had known that his father hoped their long journey might have eased his temper and drawn them closer together. The knowledge that he could be so little respected stirred blackly within him. People thought less of him because of his fiery temper. He knew they talked of the raging fire in his soul that could not be quelled and, worse, they whispered of his affliction.

Rollo kicked Caspar's hand and wrenched his horse's head around to break his father's grip. With sparks flying off Chieftain's hooves, the butter-white beast attacked the road. This time, Caspar let him go, keeping a non-provocative distance behind. 'I should have been tougher with him right from the start, just as everyone said,' he muttered into the rushing air.

Rollo raced on, his horse blowing hard as it heaved itself up the Tor. The road snaking around the pinnacle was, in places, little more than a narrow ledge, the stone surface both smooth with use and slippery with ice. Rollo refused to show that he was daunted by the steep drop, yet could not stop himself from imagining that the slice of rock beneath his mount might sheer away, leaving them to fall to the jagged jumble of scree below.

Chieftain was also less than happy and eyed the drop. When faced with a section that was narrower than the rest and shrouded in shadow, he finally drew to a stubborn halt and shied from the way ahead. Rather than calmly urging his horse forward, Rollo slapped at Chieftain's neck with the end of his reins.

'Rollo!' His father's tone was sharp. 'Stop that! Tell him you are not afraid; win his trust and confidence. Sit firmly; be confident and stop flapping.'

'He should obey me, obey me without question!' the youth snarled arrogantly, and jabbed his spurs viciously into Chieftain's creamy sides.

In response, the horse leapt up the road only hesitating at the final approach to the castle's barbican. Deep wagon tracks grooved the stone and a post with pulleys and long ropes had been installed at the top to help wagons up the last section though, clearly, it was not prudent for vehicles to attempt the climb in such slippery conditions. Rollo cursed the cold weather; he sorely missed the lands of his birth.

For the briefest moment, he, too, hesitated, craning his neck out to the side to stare down at the great drop from the rock to the stables at the foot of the Tor, now tiny squares in the canyon below. He flicked his gaze determinedly back to the road.

'Wretched animal, do not shame me,' he shouted in loud, unrestrained frustration, kicking his steed hard in the ribs.

Chieftain shied and sat back on his haunches and, for one moment, Rollo thought the animal would lose his footing. Shouting abusively, he drew his dagger and pricked his flank with the point; the animal burst up the last section of the slope, hooves slithering on ice that choked the cracks in the rocks, before finally overcoming the approach to the castle.

The road levelled off before the barbican's raised portcullis. Here, Rollo drew to a halt, waiting for his father who was following calmly, allowing Firecracker to pick a more careful path up the steep and slippery climb. Caspar said nothing to him. Showing no concern for his son's welfare, the Baron simply stared up at the whinstone walls and towers above them. Ballistas and huge catapult engines peered over the crenellated battlements. Clearly, the castle had been recently repaired, for the walls of the north tower stabbed up high above the rest, the stone brighter.

Baron Caspar nodded at it. 'I'd say that was a good twenty foot higher than it was before the last siege.' He grinned to himself. 'But should I really be surprised at Hal's need to build something greater and more obvious than his ancestors?'

Twisting in the saddle, Rollo looked high up at the overhanging battlements and, stretching back his neck to scan the shining whinstone walls that glistened with ice, he glimpsed two small faces peeking out from the crenellations. Much to Rollo's annoyance, since he felt the gesture was undignified, his father raised a friendly hand to wave. The faces instantly vanished.

The portcullis was already raised in welcome, the opening beckoning them in. Caspar reached out a hand to touch the huge blocks of stone forming his home as if in welcome as they passed under the arch of the barbican and into the cobbled courtyard beyond. Barely blowing from the climb, Firecracker stood up on his back legs and screamed at the sea of faces arrayed within the courtyard. His cry was met by the salute of a trumpet blast. Caspar raised a hand in acknowledgement, his feisty steed snorting, tossing his head and cantering on the spot, hooves clattering and sparking on the cobblestones.

Forming two lines to let the Baron and his son move forward, the men raised their caps and cheered.

'I'm home!' Caspar breathed, drinking in the atmosphere.

Never before had he felt so deeply touched. His son pressed up close beside him and gave him a rather surprised look at their reception and even a half smile. Caspar had the vague impression that he might have actually impressed his boy for once and ruefully reflected how Rollo had never held him in any high respect, having only ever viewed him in the shadow of his mother, Ursula.

The troops formed an avenue that led them to a stand draped in blue and gold bunting. Caspar halted in joy at the sight of his own mother, the high priestess Keridwen. However, he drew a deep regretful breath that his father would never more be there to meet him. While he had been away all these years, he had found it possible to believe that his father still marched through the echoing halls of Torra Alta. He shook his head, trying to oust his feelings of sorrow. To affirm his sense of continuing life, he looked to his strong, tall boy whose skin was deeply tanned, his young white teeth bright in his reddish-brown skin. He wondered whether Rollo would ever hold him in the same high regard that he held his own father.

With restrained dignity, Keridwen nodded her welcome but did not burst forward to embrace him, her only child, as he knew she must yearn to do, just as every fibre in his body cried out for her touch. Instead, she looked to Hal, Warden of Torra Alta, who had overseen the castle in Caspar's absence. Caspar understood the need for protocol.

His cerulean blue eyes welcomed his kinsmen though he kept his expression steady and calm, while his mind whirred. Already, he had noted much about his mother and Hal and in both instances was surprised. Keridwen, high priestess of the Trinity, the oldest of the three women who represented the mortal embodiment of the Great Mother, looked no older than when he had last seen her. She was still extraordinarily young and vibrant for her age, her flame-red hair, twisted into a knot on top of her head, showing no sign of grey, and her body still appeared lithe and strong.

Caspar turned his attention to Hal, who though only three years his senior was, in fact, his uncle. The man had gained in weight, being thicker set about the waist, and his chest and arms were more heavily muscled. His raven hair, however, was still as sleek and striking. All this was much as Caspar had expected, but what surprised him about his uncle was that his face no longer bore any trace of the youthful recklessness

17

and impudent good humour that he remembered. There were also the scars. Hal's thick arms, visible to the shoulder, bore the marks of many violent encounters. Even his handsome face was scored by a deep white scar contouring his left cheek. The injuries did not detract from Hal's undeniably handsome features but only served to make him look more impressive.

His eyes flitting about him into the crowd, Caspar noted the high number of men with severe wounds and amputations; the men of his homeland had suffered in his absence. Slipping from his stallion, he marched with all dignity towards the Warden of Torra Alta. Though he was choked with tears at the thought of hugging his mother, he knew that, for the sake of the garrison troops and the sense of solidarity amongst the nobles, he and Hal must first publicly embrace.

'Welcome home!' Hal cried out loudly above the muffled whispers of the crowd. 'Welcome home! Lord Caspar, Baron of Torra Alta!' The raven-haired nobleman took from his finger a blocky ring and held it up for all to see. 'As warden of this barony, I hereby return the guardianship of Torra Alta into the rightful hands of its lord.'

Caspar knew he should have prepared some great speech with which to impress the men but he had none and, for the moment, he could think of nothing to say. Through blurry eyes, he stared at the great ring that he, himself, had taken from his father's hand. It was too big to fit snugly on to his little finger and so, sliding it on to his ring finger, he turned to face those assembled in honour of his homecoming.

His eyes fell on one, two, three and more that he recognized; Orwin, Alief, Brock, Sergeant Tupper and a fine young man standing high up by a huge pile of shot that he guessed must be the young lad Pip now grown into manhood. His eyes scanned the ranks, searching until he found a tall, thin old man with a hooked nose; the Captain. Caspar nodded and the soldier nodded back with a quiet, welcoming smile. The estranged Baron drank in the encouragement.

'Men,' Caspar began a little too quietly and so stopped to clear his throat. 'Men,' he repeated more forcefully. 'Stout hearts of Torra Alta, though I have crossed the great Tethys Ocean and lived and raised my family,' he nodded at Rollo who was scowling at the strangers around him, 'far from these noble towers of my birth, I promise that not one day has passed when you were not in my thoughts. You have been always in my heart and it is good to be home and amongst you once more.'

A single cheer broke out from the back of the crowd, gained a supporter and quickly spread through the throng. But it was short-lived, subsiding into a curious silence as the men waited to hear what their hitherto absent overlord would have to say next. Caspar looked about him, wondering what more he *could* say.

At the midst of the crowd there was much loud whispering. 'I guess I was only a youngster then but he's more than a jot smaller than I remembered,' one man murmured. 'And why does his son look like he wants to bite our heads off?'

'Pound to a pinch of snuff, they'll be on their way and out of here as soon as they learn of the troubles afoot,' another grumbled.

After hearing the gist of the guarded murmurs, Caspar was even more lost for something rousing to say. He knew that Hal must have ordered these men into the courtyard to give him a fine welcome, but few knew him so why should he be dear to their hearts? Hal had always known how to muster the men's spirits and unite them under his banner, whereas Caspar had come to recognize his lack of ability in these matters. Still, he hoped that his actions would win their support and, though it would be slow, he would have to content himself with that.

Rollo cringed in embarrassment while his father spoke before

19

the men. He struggled to rise above the situation by staring disdainfully at the gathered Torra Altans. Their bearskins were threadbare, their gambesons worn and there seemed almost no distinction between ranks. The Captain, whom his father had always spoken about with great respect, was noteworthy only for his height. But he had to admit that Lord Hal was immediately an imposing figure; to his angry shame, he found his gut tighten at the very sight of him. There was something deeply unsettling about this man. The blood rushed up into Rollo's face and for a second he feared he might be overcome and suffer one of his fits. He drew deep breaths, struggling to remain calm.

Staring at Hal, he was determined to get the better of his emotions and, in an effort to do so, tried to judge him impartially. He was not so tall, though he was at least a head taller than his own father. Broad-shouldered with extraordinary black hair, he had smouldering olive-green eyes. Despite the cold, his arms were stripped bare, which emphasized the hardiness of his musculature. This brazen exposure made Rollo somehow accept the fact that the man's thick forearm on the left side ended at his wrist, a steel cap covering the stump.

He wore no insignia, fine clothes nor even armour. Rollo found that this conflicted with the image he had expected, implanted by his father who had passed many a long winter's evening telling them tales of his homeland. Rollo was sure he had described how Hal had always wished for fine armour. Clearly, his father had been wrong. But despite Hal's lack of grand attire, he had a commanding manner and all looked at him with respect.

Rollo bit his lip. Caspar had finished mumbling about how glad he was to be home and was standing looking awkward. The youth was deeply relieved when Hal saved him from further embarrassment by sweeping forward and slapping Caspar heartily on the back.

'Spar! Come on inside out of the cold. Your freckled face

makes me think that you've lost the hardiness to endure a Torra Altan winter,' he said affably.

'I'll have none of that,' Caspar retorted light-heartedly, prodding Hal's midriff. 'You'll find me tougher than the leathery stomach of a man that's doused himself in Caldean Red for half his sorry lifetime and, besides, I have already waited too long to greet this fine lady.' He turned to his mother and at last fell into her arms, hugging her close.

Rollo stiffened, a memory suddenly flooding back to him of the sweet smell of his own mother's hair and her warmth and comfort; but all that was gone forever.

After a long minute, Caspar pulled away from Keridwen and turned back to his son. 'Rollo, get over here and meet your kinsmen.'

'Hush, don't hurry the boy,' the priestess said kindly. 'It's a lot to take in. There's few that wouldn't be overwhelmed at their first visit to Torra Alta.'

'Overwhelmed!' Rollo echoed in disgust, looking down his short nose at his grandmother. 'This is but a mere shack compared to my mother's palace.'

'And a warm welcome to you too!' Keridwen said, her eyes half-laughing though her voice was stern. 'Do you know whom you are addressing?'

'Should I?' the youth defended himself haughtily.

'How dare you disgrace me like this!' Caspar snapped at his son.

'I see you've sired more than your match there,' Hal spoke with a wry laugh.

Caspar threw his eyes heavenward. 'And don't I know it! That's why I came home. I thought Rollo was sorely in need of some sobering time at Torra Alta amongst the men.'

'I thought you came home because of my message,' Hal remarked with surprise.

'What message?' Caspar asked, his voice suddenly tight.

'You didn't get my message?'

Caspar shook his head. 'No, I came to bring my son home

so that he might grow up knowing his inheritance. Perhaps we left before your message reached me.'

Hal paused for a second, raising a dark eyebrow in consideration. Shrugging, he drew in a deep breath as if trying to contain and gather all his thoughts, preparing to divulge them in a fluent manner. 'Well, we'd best get inside. There is much to tell.'

Aware that all had dismissed his presence but not knowing what else he could do, Rollo followed. Glaring at the deformity of Hal's hand, he felt a rising sickness well up from his stomach. The more he looked at Hal, the more a deep inexplicable sense of loathing churned within him. His vision darkened for a moment and he stumbled, his emotions getting the better of him. For fear of suffering one of his shameful attacks, he took deep breaths to calm himself, but they were less effective than the act of his grandmother looking round and smiling at him. Somehow, her gaze raised his spirits though he only allowed himself to scowl back at her.

Their boots struck loudly on the cold stone flags as they progressed through the lower halls and up a broad winding staircase until they finally reached the upper keep. A servant swung open the doors to the baronial rooms and Rollo craned his neck up to look over his kinsmen and see what lay within as the heady scent of mulled wine filled his nostrils. Side tables were set with steaming flagons ready to fill the pewter goblets on the long central table. A crackling fire filled a huge stone hearth and gave out a roasting glow into the hall, the dancing light giving life and movement to the tapestries lining the walls.

Once they were inside the room, Rollo moved slowly round, noting the lances and swords pinned to the lime-washed walls. Ignoring the yapping dogs that pressed up against him, sniffing his boots and breeches, he slowly took in his surroundings. He continued to step round until he was looking up at the entrance. He froze. Bile flooded his throat. His palms began to sweat and he felt the skin on his face go clammy and cold. With an open mouth, he stared at the trophy above the door. Leering down at him was a huge skull with vast curving teeth; a dragon's skull.

Staring into its gaping eye sockets, panic swamped him; he thought he was choking. It was as if a hand were being stuffed down his throat, reaching into his lungs and trying to wrench them out. He fell to the floor, spluttering, choking and clawing at his neck until the blackness claimed him.

'In the name of the Mother!' Hal exclaimed.

'Just give him room,' Caspar ordered, running to his son and gripping him tightly, waiting for the spasms to pass. He would never grow used to the fits. Every time it happened, it was as if a part of him died in terror of his boy failing to recover.

'What's the matter with him?' Hal asked softly, his voice full of genuine concern.

'It's not as bad as it looks,' Caspar assured everyone, intensely relieved when his mother knelt down beside Rollo and soothed her hand over the rigid muscles of his face now purple with blood. 'It soon passes. It usually comes when he gets upset.'

Keridwen sat back and hastily searched through a leather pouch that she kept tied about her neck; the smell of sweet herbs filled the air about her. 'Gortan valerian,' she stated. 'It will relax him but I'll need to mix it up with a sleeping potion. Oh, where are Brid and Isolde when I need them? Don't worry; I'll be back in a moment. I just need to fetch something from my rooms.'

She was back in minutes with a vial containing a syrupy liquid that she trickled into Rollo's mouth. Within seconds, the spasms began to lessen and the jerks of his muscles eased. Finally, his head flopped into his father's lap. Caspar hugged him close, the love for his child overwhelming his every thought. Scooping the boy up with some difficulty since Rollo had grown much over the last year, he carried him to a couch and laid him down. The youth was groaning softly and Caspar heaved a sigh of relief that his mother had a way of helping him.

The rest of the company had withdrawn to the fire, giving them a little space, while he and Keridwen sat with the boy and waited for him to come round. The priestess looked anxiously at the vial in her hand and he was uncomfortably aware of her uncertainty. Sick with fear, he wondered if she was questioning whether she had administered too much potion. Seeing his expression, she hastily gave him a confident smile and reached across to squeeze his hand.

The Baron looked about him, trying to take his mind off his fears. He noted at once the new tapestry hanging above the fireplace, which depicted the Trinity of the Crone, Mother and Maiden. The needlework of the tapestry was very fine and it was easy to marvel at Keridwen's likeness. Beside her in the picture was Brid, who looked comfortable in the role of the mother. It was the image of Isolde, however, that engaged Caspar's eyes the longest.

He was shocked. Surely, that could not be the girl he had left behind when she was no more than a baby? Her hair and eyes were as he had imagined after fifteen years. She had long strawberry blond hair, streaked with copper, curls floating down to her waist. And her eyes too were as he'd expected, a unique green with glints of gold that leapt out of the needlework. But all else about her was not at all as he had anticipated. The mouth was small and sadly morose; there was an apologetic stoop to her bearing and the gaunt cheeks spoke of a nervous disposition. This was not the happy, bubbling infant he had left in Keridwen's care.

'That's Isolde?' he asked, his voice still strained with concern for Rollo.

Keridwen followed his gaze, sighed and nodded. 'The women who stitched her likeness didn't capture the image of her soul very well,' she said with a shrug.

Caspar nodded. He hadn't seen Isolde since she was a tiny

child. Though only a baby, her happy, carefree disposition had warmed his heart and helped him through those tragic times. He sighed, longing to greet her after all these years.

He wondered where she was. He thought it strange, since everyone else had been mustered to give him an official welcome, that both Brid and Isolde had chosen to be absent. But he was not offended; no doubt, they had more pressing business.

Keridwen was stroking Rollo's forehead when the boy began to stir and groan. Caspar noted her heave a sigh of relief. 'I shouldn't think he'll sleep more than half an hour; he looks as if he has a very strong constitution. Now, Spar, you need to get yourself out of those damp clothes and get some warm food and wine inside you.'

Caspar nodded at this and relaxed, knowing that his son was in good hands. He stood up and immediately Hal stepped forward.

'He's all right then?'

Keridwen nodded.

'Good! That's good.' Hal opened his arms to Caspar and enclosed him in a warm embrace.

Hugely conscious of the cold hard steel of the cap covering Hal's stump that pressed into his back, Caspar hugged his uncle back, aware of the man's solid body and broad shoulders. For a moment, they looked at each other intently before bursting into laughter.

'It is good to see you! So good to see you home!' Hal enthused.

Caspar laughed more and turned from his uncle to scoop up his tiny mother and sweep her round in an arc that lifted her legs high off the floor.

'Spar!' she scolded, 'I'm an old woman; don't do that to me!'

He placed her lightly down beside him, stooped to kiss her silken head and was warmed when she raised her hand to smooth his cheek. 'Oh my only son, how I have missed you!'

25

She ran her finger down to the point of his stubble-covered chin and then pushed back his thick auburn hair that was streaked with gold by the eastern sun.

Unable to contain himself, Caspar again wrapped his arms about her. He had been separated from his mother throughout his childhood and it had always left him with a sense of vulnerability. He relished and always yearned for the sense of well-being that her closeness imbued in him.

'Now off with you and get into some fresh clothes before we talk more. Don't fear, I will not leave your boy,' she assured him.

'Are you feeling a little bit better now?' the woman with eyes as piercing and as blue as his father's was saying.

Rollo didn't answer as he sat up. She was pressing a goblet of clear water into his hand and, despite himself, he took a sip. He had not wanted to comply without a show of protest, though he had to admit that the water did make him feel better.

'What you need is a little food,' his grandmother was telling him. 'What do you fancy? Cook's made apple pie if you don't feel up to meat.'

'I'm not hungry,' he lied, watching the woman's response and wondering how she was going to persuade him to eat. He knew he was being perverse but he couldn't help it.

'That's fine,' she shrugged. 'The rest of us are going to eat. You just rest a little while longer and see how you feel later.'

Rollo grunted in dissatisfaction. He had thought she would have tried harder. And he could smell meat. All were hurriedly making their way towards the long table as boards of boar and venison were carried into the room. He looked at the empty chair beside his father and grudgingly decided that it would be easier to join the company now than wait until later.

'Bring the Baron food,' Hal boomed loudly over the excited chatter that filled the hall.

Much to his chagrin, Rollo noticed his father cringe at the title. He could not believe he had been dragged across half the world to suffer this embarrassment.

'We cannot discuss these latest developments on an empty stomach. And get some of these dogs out of here!' Hal ordered; stumbling over a large blunt-nosed terrier. The dog was intent on catching a spider that was creeping in and out of a crack between two of the broad floorboards. It took a moment for Hal to recover his temper and Rollo noted how he continually looked with irritation towards the door as if he had long been expecting someone. He then nodded at the large oak chair placed central to the long side of the refectory table. 'My Lord,' he addressed Caspar, 'take your place so the rest of us may be seated.'

Caspar flashed him a quick, uncomfortable smile before easing himself into the large chair. Rollo watched his father's fine-boned fingers stroke and grip the worn carvings of the great oak arms and wondered at his unease. Once the wood must have been whittled into a delicate carving of warring dragons though much of the detailing had been worn smooth over time by the many hands that had sat in that great chair.

He glanced sideways at the Baron, just a flicker of sympathy in his heart as he considered his father's feelings. The man was thirty-six, a similar age to his dear mother, if she were still alive. Ursula had worn the mantle of command with ease but Caspar fidgeted uncomfortably, and clearly was not used to the attention. His father's nerves, however, seemed to recover as further trays and platters were brought forth. Even Rollo could no longer suppress a smile at the aroma from the steaming meat puddings that were set before them.

Caspar clapped his hands in delight. 'There have been many things I've missed about Torra Alta and, though I love you all deeply, it's the food I've missed the most. And how is Cook?'

'Oh, she's well,' Keridwen said, laughing and wiping away

the tears pricking at the corners of her eyes. 'Mind, she's twice the size that she was. She says, if there was ever another siege, she would be prepared to last a full year without food.'

Hal grunted, his face set stern and the vein at his temple pounding. Suddenly, he thumped the table with his metal-clad stump and bellowed at the nearest servant. 'You, find Guthrey and Quinn and don't come back without them this time. I expressly told them that they must be present to greet their baron.' The servant scurried away and Hal grumbled more quietly, 'And where's Brid? I can't believe she's not here either.'

A servant filled Rollo's goblet with water and he took a long draught that at least cleared his head a little. He noted that his grandmother was sitting opposite him and, after a while, she looked up and gave him a faint encouraging smile. He was glad that she didn't ask him question after question as he'd expected. He was vaguely aware of Hal telling his father that they would talk of more serious matters anon but, for the moment, Hal began asking Caspar about their journey and the horrors of sailing between the ice-floes.

Keridwen nudged a heavy platter laden with slices of pink venison towards him. 'Take some.'

Though he was glad that she treated him this way, he still felt deeply resentful about being brought here and had no intention of being civil. He grunted and speared five slices with the point of his knife. Dripping with juice, he lifted them onto his plate and ate ravenously.

Once his plate was empty, Keridwen lent forward across the table. 'The apple pie is excellent, you know.'

'I don't want any.' Rollo replied flatly, just as there was a lull in the conversation and his words carried further than he had intended.

Eyebrows pressed low in a disapproving frown, Caspar broke off his conversation with Hal. 'Rollo!' he snapped in exasperation and embarrassment. 'Keridwen is not only your grandmother but a high priestess, One of the Three.

If you cannot think of something fitting to say, you ... you—'

'Hush, Spar,' Keridwen gently chided. 'I'm not made of glass. The boy won't break me that easily.' She smiled at the youth. 'There's plenty of time for us to get to know one another, now isn't there, Rollo?' She inclined her head knowingly at him and then, much to Rollo's relief, rather than persisting in focusing the conversation on him, turned to Hal. 'I think we've eaten enough,' she said meaningfully and gave him a long hard look.

'Yes,' Caspar agreed. He took a sip from his ale and also looked over his tankard at Hal. 'So tell all.'

Rollo was aware that this man had carried his father's responsibility commanding Torra Alta and the fifteen years had been long ones. There was no smile on Hal's lips as he rose to pace the heavily worn floorboards before the crackling fire.

Chapter 2

'Don't listen to him!' a soft voice spoke from the doorway. 'He just wants the opportunity to tell everyone, *yet again*, how many dragons he's slain.'

'Brid!' Caspar jumped to his feet and ran across the room. He swept her up in his arms and spun her round, immediately conscious of the increase in her weight and roundness of her belly, which had not been obvious under her loose gown.

'It has been noted,' Hal said in a deep rumbling voice, 'the fervent welcome you have given my wife. Now, unhand my woman,' he added with mock ferocity.

Brid scowled at this, took her husband's hand and nodded towards the arched doorway through which she had just entered. 'You'll be pleased to know I've found them,' she said, pointing at the two youths, who stood just within the threshold. Their chins were raised arrogantly, their faces, hands and clothing muddied and their eyes glinted with defiance. Caspar could see that he wasn't the only one having problems rearing children.

'Please tell me that you haven't been down in the well-room or clambering on the battlements fiddling with the catapult engines again?' Hal growled at the two boys.

Caspar couldn't help but smile as he thought how he and Hal had, so often, been in trouble for very similar crimes. He dragged his chair nearer to the fire and sat back, putting his weary feet up on the firm back of a thickset terrier that wagged his tail in delight at the attention. With mild amusement, he waited to see how Hal was going to deal with the situation. It was Brid, however, who saw to most of the scolding.

Her long, soft brown hair, streaked with glints of copper, sprayed out as she swung round on the two boys, who already stood head and shoulders above her. She moved a little awkwardly, clearly some way into her pregnancy but, to Caspar, she was still the most radiant woman on earth. He had loved his own wife dearly and they had been happy, but he still could not help feeling a race of excitement at the sight of his first love. Brid was magical!

She had pulled the two lads forward before the fire and was now brushing vigorously at their clothes as she tutted over them. 'I'll have you cleaning the stables out for the next week if I have any more of this disobedience.'

'You won't, Ma,' the younger one said scathingly. 'You can't make us.'

Brid smiled knowingly at them. 'Your overlord has returned and he can make you.' A triumphant smile stretched her ruby-red lips, revealing the even whiteness of her teeth.

The two boys looked at Caspar; the taller one with interest and the younger one with undisguised suspicion.

'He's not my liege,' the younger, dark-haired boy snapped. 'Everyone knows he walked out – abandoned us all and left Father with all the problems. He has no right to just march back in here and order us all around!' He turned to his companion for support. 'Has he, Quinn?'

'He's Lord of Torra Alta, isn't he?' the tall boy replied more affably.

Caspar had no difficulty deciding that the younger boy was Guthrey. Much of Hal's good looks and arrogant disposition swathed the looks and manner of his son. Brid's first born, Quinn, on the other hand was not so strained in his bearing and his dark brown eyes, unlike the olive eyes of his half-brother, lingered more searchingly on Caspar and Rollo. His attire was indistinguishable from any common archer save for the mysterious black gemstone hanging from a chain about his throat.

Leaving a muddy trail from his boots, Quinn strode across the floor and offered him an honest and open hand in welcome. Caspar rose to meet him, offering his own hand that was gripped and squeezed in friendship.

The Baron patted him firmly on the back and laughed. 'I see you have the grip of an archer there, Quinn!'

The youth looked pleased for a moment but then shifted his gaze towards Rollo who stood behind and to one side of Caspar, the muscles in his cheeks flexing as he anxiously worked his jaw.

'Rollo, step forward and meet your cousins,' Caspar ordered in a coaxing voice, his eyes willing his boy to obey.

Smiling broadly, Quinn reached out a hand but Rollo did not take it nor was he looking at him; Rollo's gaze was fixed on Guthrey. His eyes were slits and the heavy frown of his brow spoke of suspicion and dislike. Hal's son stood, legs astride and arms folded, glaring back.

'This is not your home,' Guthrey said bitterly. 'Go back to where you belong.'

Caspar could not decide whether he should intervene or leave his son to fight his own battles but, before he could come to a decision, Hal had taken the initiative.

With his one good hand, he lifted the boy by his collar. 'How dare you speak out like that. How dare you speak like that in front of the Baron? You are a man of Torra Alta and you should be honoured that you have any place in this castle. Rollo will one day be your lord, just as Caspar is mine and, however much you dislike that, you must learn to live with it. There are enough troubles here without you adding to them. Now get out of my sight.' He tossed his son to the floor and turned his back on him.

Guthrey leapt up and stared at Hal's back resentfully. Caspar had fully expected the youth to flee the room, red-faced, but was impressed by the quickness with which the thirteen-year-old composed himself. Rollo was of a similar age and he would not have credited his son with such restraint. Guthrey now raised his chin, shrugged and nonchalantly crossed to a sideboard where he began to pile a plate with food.

'He'll only cause more trouble after such treatment,' Keridwen chided Hal in a lowered voice.

'He has to learn obedience. Where would we all be without discipline in this castle?'

Brid raised her eyebrows at this but said nothing. She merely glanced anxiously towards Guthrey, who was studiously ignoring the adults and eyeing Rollo, a sneer claiming his expression.

So those had been the two faces Caspar had seen peering over the barbican. As far as he could tell, what these youngsters needed was a stag hunt or a trip into the Boarchase Forest rather than a shaming. They needed to run off some of their youthful exuberance and temper. There had been no boar hunting in the Bear Country, which in his wife's tongue was called Artor, and he had missed the thrill of the chase. But what did he know of rearing children, he thought regretfully as he glanced at Rollo.

Brid flopped into a chair and put her feet up on a stool. 'I'm sorry I was late to greet you, Spar, but I've been searching high and low for Isolde. Cook said she was in the stables, the stable master said she was with the bailiff. He said she had gone to the foot of the Tor to search for a particular flower she needed for Keridwen. The grooms in the stables below said she'd been there much earlier today but that she had specifically said she was going to help Cook with the preparations for your welcome. But Cook said she'd not seen hide nor hair of her.' There was a hint of concern in Brid's soft voice. 'I can't believe she's slipped out beyond the castle when she knows that even armed men have been seized by the great ravenshrikes or ambushed by hobs.'

'It's a full moon tonight, and she has no fear of the forest,'

Keridwen said quietly. 'I think perhaps we should make a wider search; she's worse than the boys. At least their impishness is predictable.'

'I'll get Pip onto it,' Hal growled and snapped his fingers at a servant behind him. 'Summon Lieutenant Piperol for me.'

'Lieutenant Piperol?' Caspar asked, fully realizing that it was not going to be easy to wrestle the reins of command from Hal who, though he had welcomed him with open arms, showed not the least sign of waiting for his word on any matter. For the sake of his son, he knew he must do something about the situation.

'Indeed, Lieutenant Piperol,' Hal said with a laugh. 'Pip couldn't take being called Lieutenant Pip and who could blame him? But he's Isolde's only true relative and he'll do anything to make sure she's safe.'

Caspar was impressed when the Lieutenant arrived. He was now in his mid twenties and could only be described as a great bear of a man. He had a determined set to his jaw and his clear, deep brown eyes spoke of a forceful and honest character.

Brid hurried to him. 'Pip, Isolde's missing again. Have you seen her?'

Pip shook his head, his peppercorn-brown hair swinging about his face. 'No, my lady. She would surely not have left the castle in this weather and not since Gromo returned with half his arm missing after a ravenshrike attack. And I repeatedly warned her that three men had gone missing only last month. Taken by hobs, we think, sir.' The last part he addressed to Caspar with a courteous tilt of his head. 'Welcome home, sir!'

'Good to see you, Pip!' Caspar enthused but was given no more opportunity to talk to the young man.

'It's a full moon,' Keridwen interrupted, reminding the Lieutenant of the matter at hand.

'I should have kept a better watch on her but there was much to be done with all the preparations for Spar's homecoming,' Brid said regretfully and looked down at her rounded belly. 'It's the child. Every time I am with child, I become hopelessly forgetful,' she informed Caspar with a self-mocking grin on her face that was no less beautiful than he had remembered.

'It's our third,' Hal said proudly, giving Brid a wink.

'Don't look so pleased about it.' his wife chided him though clearly she was equally proud. 'You're not the one who has to go through all this.' She nodded down at her belly before turning her attention to an apple, which she had fetched from the table.

'And congratulations to you both!' Caspar exclaimed, watching in fascination as Brid took a small knife from beneath her gown and sliced the apple in half through its girth, opening the two halves to reveal the five-sided star.

'A blessing from the gods,' he murmured.

Their eyes met and held for a brief moment before Caspar turned his gaze back to his uncle who had returned to the table and was chewing at a boar steak. He had speared the great slab of meat with his sharp knife and was tearing at it with strong white teeth.

'Hal, let us leave the matter of the young ones to others; you and I have more pressing business,' Caspar prompted.

The one-handed nobleman finished his mouthful, took a swig of ale and sat back. 'Did you get any of my messages?'

'Of course. I had the wonderful news at the birth of your son and daughter and even the sad news of Trog's death.' Caspar glanced round the room and noted the three rotund, blunt-nosed dogs lazing in front of the fire. They had pushed the larger deer-hounds off the thick rug and now lay pink-bellied and panting in the heat from the hearth. Caspar smiled at the memory of the beloved terrier.

'The dragons; you had those messages?' Hal asked, seeking the point of time from which to commence his explanation.

'Indeed. You said that, alone, you killed five.'

Hal smiled. 'You should have been there to see it, Spar;

I was magnificent,' he said quietly. From any other man it would have sounded like a boast but, from Hal, it was just a statement of fact. He nodded towards the great skull hanging above the door on the bare wall opposite the fire. 'Throughout the other baronies,' he raised the metal-capped stump of his left arm in mock triumph into the air, 'they call me Hal, the dragon-slayer.'

'Yes, my sweetheart, we know,' Brid said with mock impatience but turned at the sound of pattering feet. A young girl of perhaps five, with glorious black hair, came running to her and climbed into her lap.

Hal nodded at the child. 'This, Spar, is the most adorable and precious girl in all the world. Brannella, say hello to the Baron.'

The girl looked at Caspar and blushed, her long black eyelashes framing her wide, trusting eyes.

'Hello, Brannella,' Caspar said in a soft tone. His attention evidently overwhelmed the girl, however, because she buried her face in her mother's clothing, which did not quite muffle her giggles.

Hal beamed from ear to ear. 'My greatest treasure,' he announced. 'And you're quite proud of your old father too, aren't you, Brannella?' Hal prompted, returning to the previous subject. 'Spar, you cannot believe what strength and skill it takes to slay one of those great beasts. The force needed to thrust a blade between its scales and drive through its flesh . . . None of you have any idea—'

'No,' Brid conceded with some exasperation, easing Brannella from her lap, who ran to play with one of the dogs. 'No, we are all ignorant though you have told us a thousand times. Now just get on and tell Spar of our real problem.'

Hal nodded. 'Very well, my acid-tongued lady.' He dipped his head towards Caspar and murmured, 'She'll be a lot more pleasant when the baby is born.'

'Oh just get on!' Brid barked good-naturedly.

'Stop squabbling like children!' Keridwen ordered, her

voice soft but full of power. 'In my opinion, Hal doesn't fully understand what's happened so I shall tell the tale myself.' She swirled around, lifting her arms so that the light cloak that hung from her shoulders fanned out and cast a shadow about the room. The fire dampened down to produce a deep red glow that lit only the centre of the room where she stood. Darkness spread its gloomy cloak about the gathered Torra Altans, the light turning away from the windows as if by her command, though no doubt it was merely the heavy snow cloud that now overlay the castle.

'With the release of the monstrous creatures of power from their exile in the Otherworld came, also, the return of many less obviously dangerous but far more sinister beasts. They have crawled out from their hiding places in the unpopulated deserts of the earth and now seek a home in the more fertile regions of the world. And there are none more hospitable than Belbidia, as it was.'

As it was! Caspar thought in alarm but did not dare interrupt his mother. Her voice swelled like a choir filling an ancient cathedral and her eyes flashed in the half-light. 'If you had come through the low country you would know! The Baronies of Piscera and Ovissia have fallen to Blackthorn's people; the hobgoblins have taken over much of the mid-shires of Belbidia's heartland and we are cut off from the capital.'

Caspar nodded gravely at this, now realizing the need for the catapult engines, renewed and harnessed to Torra Alta's wall, and the high piles of stone shot standing at the ready.

'This problem has been swelling over the last decade,' Keridwen continued steadily. 'The hobs breed quickly and their young develop fast. Within just ten years, they are strong enough to bear arms. This we have struggled against for some years but now we have a new problem.' On small, light feet, she glided soundlessly across the bare boards of the hall to a low, age-blackened casket; it was banded with steel and secured by a heavy padlock. She took from her pocket a crudely wrought key that, nevertheless, worked the lock with ease. The muscles in her arms bulged as she lifted the casket's lid and eased it back. Dipping her hand within, she drew out a long thin object, which she solemnly carried to the table and laid down before Caspar.

'What do you make of that?' she asked.

The Baron shrugged and then looked up at the expectant faces around him. 'Where did you find it?'

'The great golden dragon returned. She had left us in peace for many moons but, suddenly, she swooped out of a moonless sky to feed on our livestock,' Hal began. 'The next morning I went after her, tracking her cry east into the Yellow Mountains. I reasoned that, after such a feast, she would find a spot to rest, and I would have my opportunity. Indeed, I found her fast asleep, steam waffling from her great nostrils. I'd been waiting for this chance from the day you left and I nearly had her,' he said in exasperation. 'I was close when, out of the bushes, came three hobs, big gnarly creatures, fully mature males – a rare sight up until recently. They came at me, swords drawn; even with my runesword, I could barely protect myself.'

Caspar looked up at his raven-haired uncle in amazement. He had felt the terrible power of Hal's runesword and how it imbued a dreadful sense of invincibility and bloodlust. He had seen it shatter enemy weapons with a single strike and plunge through armour and bone as if they were no more than butter.

Hal continued, 'The great runesword should have shattered their weapons and sliced through their gristly bodies in one clean stroke but their swords held. Thankfully, Pip chanced on the mêlée and used his bow. He killed one right out, injured another and the last turned and fled. The injured one hobbled after him and we were left with the dead one still clinging to this sword.' He nodded down at the crude weapon lying before Caspar.

'Had I not been holding the runesword, I would not have stood a chance,' Hal added heavily.

'I was always of the impression that hobgoblins knew little of craft and have never heard them lauded as swordsmiths,' Caspar complained. 'Dwarves, yes, but never hobs.'

'Absolutely,' Hal confirmed. 'They rely on huge numbers and care little about their own casualties to achieve a victory. They are not learned enough to forge a weapon that can resist the power of one of the world's greatest swords. Their iron melts at such low temperatures they cannot force out the impurities, leaving it brittle and flawed. Nevertheless . . .,' again, he cast his eyes on the pitted weapon before Caspar, 'they had three such swords.'

The Baron looked at it in bewilderment. It bore none of the marks of power; no sigil of victory, no rune of war. It was a plain sword with a dull uneven finish from which he deduced that it had been fashioned in haste rather than by the slow methods of the master swordsmiths. As he would have expected from a hobgoblin's weapon, it showed signs of pitting where the owner's neglect had allowed it to rust. The grip was uncommonly thick to accommodate the long fingers of a hob, and the hand guards crude.

Fashioned and maintained in such a way, the metal should be brittle and easily fractured, yet, not for one second did Caspar doubt Hal's tale of its power. He knew that, in the past, his uncle had been prone to add a small hint of drama to enhance a good story but he knew this was not the case now. Although the weapon before him looked crude, he sensed its ugly hum of power. He made to touch the hilt and felt a jarring shock of energy seize his fingers and lock them solid into a claw. Gritting his teeth, he pressed his hand down, fighting against the jarring pain, and at last grasped the hilt.

His face contorted into a mask of rage as a fearful surge of bloodlust flooded his veins. His mouth arid, he glared into the sea of faces about him that became a swirling blur as he raised the sword. The faces shrank back until only one shadowy figure remained, her voice clear and commanding. 'My son, the love of the Great Mother is not in that sword; let it drop.'

The throb of blood in his temples was so great he could barely think. He wished to kill, to appease the sword and learn all that the weapon promised. He was no one until that moment; a misfit, a stranger. But now, holding this sword, he felt what it was to be a lord of men.

His mother's voice suddenly sang loudly in his head. 'You are the sword's slave. Nothing but its slave!'

For a second, he saw her vividly, the glowing violet aura of the Goddess about her, and the sword clattered from his grasp. 'Ma . . .,' he murmured and sagged to his knees in exhaustion.

'It has horrifying similarities to the runesword entrusted to Hal by the Great Mother; the difference is that the runesword is an artefact of the Great Mother and so is bound to Her service. It is a cruel weapon of destruction but it cannot be turned against Her ways. This sword, however, was devised only for evil.' Keridwen sagged slightly as if the thought had weakened her. For a moment, she even looked her age.

Caspar stared at the sword and stepped back, distancing himself from the power that it still emanated. 'The hobs were protecting the dragon from your attack?' he asked, trying to make sense of the situation. 'And using swords that they should not have the craft to forge?' He looked to his mother and uncle for confirmation.

They nodded grimly and Caspar looked back at the sword. 'But why? But how?'

'Why is too difficult to guess at. How is, I'm afraid, too easy,' Keridwen said with a sigh and smoothed her small neat hands across the rough board of the great oak table. 'The Chalice of Önd.'

Caspar nodded, remembering the large golden cup that Brid had retrieved from the depths of a distant forest in

Ceolothia. His mother said no more and, frowning at her, he said, 'I still don't understand.'

She sighed in exasperation and sank into a chair. 'The Chalice absorbs the energy, the essential life force within any magical artefact it comes in contact with and, under the right conditions, can transfer that energy to another object dipped into it.'

'I know that,' Caspar interrupted. Following Keridwen's example, he slumped into a chair by the table and took a soothing gulp of ale. 'But what does that have to do with these swords?'

'The Chalice is missing and the last artefact of power that entered the Chalice before it went missing was Hal's runesword.'

'Missing! What do you mean it's missing?' Caspar found the muscles on his chest tightening. 'What? You just left it lying around?' He glowered at his uncle.

Hal stared hard back, his olive-green eyes darkening. 'Have you so little respect? Keridwen and Brid discussed it at length and we decided to have it locked within a casket beneath the lower dungeons, hidden amongst the old catacombs. We—'

Keridwen interrupted. 'We thought if anyone were looking for it, they would come to our rooms and search our sacred chambers. But—'

'Something got in from below!' Caspar anticipated her explanation. 'I thought you had secured the lower approaches to the castle,' he exclaimed, scanning the floor at his feet as if some hob were about to burst up from the floorboards.

'I had all the extremities of the tunnels blocked and huge metal grids set into the foot of the well entrance. But it wasn't enough to stop a dragon.'

Caspar stared at her. 'A dragon,' he repeated glumly.

'It took the Chalice. That was only a year or so after you left, and nothing came of it. But now the hobs must have it.'

Hal continued. 'We assumed that the great, golden dragon

took the Chalice from the young dragon's dead body and then hoarded it. There was much else to occupy our thoughts so we did not think more of it until we discovered these swords. Only then did we guess that somehow it had fallen into the hands of the hobs – Blackthorn's people. Either a hob stole it from the dragon's hoard or took it from the young dragon's claw before the great queen got to it.'

'A brave hob,' Caspar amended.

'Indeed!' Keridwen affirmed, rising from her seat. 'And we must retrieve it at all costs. Only the Mother knows what will happen if the hobs forge more of these weapons. If they have the power to destroy, they will use it.' Her eyes fixed on Caspar's and he knew now why they had summoned him; not to take up his rightful command and inheritance, but to scour the dark and sinister places of the world to recover the Chalice of Önd from the hobgoblins.

'I have cast the runes three times and, each time, the same runes tumbled into the circle of divination.' She held out her clenched fist and uncurled her fingers to reveal three runes: ᛖ ᛗ ᚱ. 'Nuin, the tree rune of the ash tree; Man, the rune of mankind; and Rad, the rune of seeking, which long ago Morrigwen, my predecessor, declared as your rune, Spar.'

'So you summoned me here from the other side of the world to seek the Chalice?'

'You are the Seeker; you alone have the Great Mother's blessing on this matter,' Keridwen insisted.

Caspar pushed back his thick auburn hair and rubbed his crooked nose before answering. 'Actually, I assumed that you had summoned me to take up my birthright and the baronial reins.'

Hal laughed. 'Now why would I do that, little nephew?'

Something snapped inside Caspar. He knew that his uncle was only teasing him but, if he let the jest ride, he also knew he would never establish any respect within his own castle. 'I entrusted you with Torra Alta; I didn't give it to you,' he said coldly.

Hal stared in surprise at the sudden, unexpected nature of this response. The veins in his temple throbbed as he paused for a brief second before replying, 'I love Torra Alta above all other duties,' he declared loudly. 'My father, Baron Brungard, filled my veins with the desire to love and protect her mighty towers. How dare you so slyly accuse me of treachery against Torra Alta! And you of all people! You who have held so many other duties higher than the responsibility to your home.'

Caspar felt the blood well up into his face. Already, Hal had out-performed him. Trembling, he rose to his feet and pointed an accusing finger at his uncle before he found the words to return the attack.

'Stop it, both of you!' Keridwen said in a low icy voice. 'There will be no castle left at all if you fight amongst yourselves.'

'All right then!' Hal said, a forced smile tight on his handsome face. 'I alone shall find the Chalice. And when I come home to find the castle singed to a crisp and a great fat golden dragon filling the lower halls with her wriggling infants, we shall all know whom to blame.'

'If you can fight dragons, then so too can I!' Caspar challenged through a tight throat. His collar was wet with sweat and his complexion deepening to a hot red. 'I trusted you, Hal; I did not know you would turn against me.'

'Turn against you! How dare you! It was you that forsook your duties. You gave me no choice. I thought you would be gone at best a year. But fifteen years, Spar! Fifteen! You can't expect to just swan back in here after fifteen long years and say "it's mine!"'

With a huge effort to retrieve self-control, Caspar smiled serenely. 'Oh but I can, Hal. I can. Because it is! I am Baron Branwolf's one and only child. It is mine and, in turn, it will be my son's!' His voice cracked and he thumped his tankard down on the table, much of the frothy brew slopping out over his white-knuckled fist.

Silence filled the room. His mother was looking at him calmly and smiled faintly, infusing him with confidence. And to his surprise, so too was Brid.

'Well, in that case, *Baron* Caspar,' Hal said stiffly, 'if you have now decided to change your principles and take up your office as Baron above the task bestowed on you by the Great Mother, I shall see to it that I am ready to leave in the morning. And I shall leave with a hundred of *your* men – by *your* leave, naturally – so that I can find the Chalice.'

He rose sharply; toppling his chair and letting it crash to the ground. Without a backward glance, he marched towards the door. 'Let's see how well you fare after fifteen years in a woman's pocket. We shall see how a man who fits so well into a pocket can fill the great boots of Baron Branwolf himself,' he sneered, and without a backward glance, was gone.

Caspar was struck with sadness. He had always been aware of his uncle's simmering resentment towards him but had never dreamt that it would swell into open hostility. He loved Hal. He looked at Brid and she shrugged apologetically. Caspar smiled back weakly and let out a deep breath to steady himself in readiness to give his first command as Baron of Torra Alta. He was about to speak when he heard angry shouts and the clatter of hooves below in the courtyard.

It took him a moment's glance around the room to note that Rollo, Guthrey and Quinn were no longer present and his heart leapt into his throat. By the Mother, what was his son up to now?

'Rollo!' he bellowed as he sprinted for the door.

Chapter 3

Rollo watched the two Torra Altan youths as they slipped from the hall. Already the arguments and discourse of the adults had turned into a drone and he was no longer interested. All that turned in his heated mind were the feelings of disdain and resentment that had emanated from his cousins; he didn't like it and he would not allow them to get away with treating him like that.

Seeing that no one, bar the affectionate terrier that he had been stroking, was paying him any attention, he also slipped from the room. Stealthily, he followed Guthrey and Quinn, taking care to muffle his footfalls on the winding back stair that spilt him out into a low unfurnished hall with three exits. But he must have kept too wary a distance because there was now neither sight nor sound of his cousins and he had no way of knowing which route to take. He looked at the three stone arches and decided that, naturally, he would not choose the middle road. The first son of Ursula the Revered, Queen of Artor, would never opt for the safe middle path; he was too courageous.

Ignoring the opening to his left, he crossed to the remaining arch, which was also the farthest from the stairway. This way led him down a long and low corridor that ended in a door. The door opened onto a stair that led up as well as down. He guessed that upwards would lead him to the battlements where the boys had probably gone back to explore the war-engines. But an odd compulsion drew his eyes downwards. It was gloomy, only a little natural light coiling down the worn steps, but that was the way he chose.

Picking his way carefully, his hand running along the wall to steady himself, he descended. With each turn of the spiral stair, it grew darker and darker. He had reached perhaps ninety steps when his hand felt the opening to a side passage. He broke off along that for a time with the thought of finding something to light his way before returning to his exploration. The great age of the stairway intrigued him, calling him downward to the secrets at its foot, though he could not explain why.

He had only gone a short way before he found a torch slotted into a bracket on the wall. He lifted it from its nest and trotted further along, looking for some means to light it. He was in yet another of Torra Alta's bewildering maze of corridors connecting many small rooms. The doorways to each were arched and surprisingly low. Peeking through, he saw bedclothes and general belongings within. The air was cold and the fires that burned down from the previous night had not yet been lit for the coming evening. Clearly, the men that normally slept here were busy about their duties at present.

At last, he glimpsed a still smouldering fire in the grate of one room and, after glancing in to check no one was about, he trotted in and plunged the torch into the embers until it caught the flame.

He made his way back to the stair. The red and yellow glow and warmth of the torch made him feel more relaxed than he had felt all day. He loved fire. In fact, it was his love of fire that had finally goaded his father into dragging him away from his friends and homeland. Rollo had taken five huge torches from the stable courtyard and set them up on the walls of his private rooms. Unfortunately, one of the drapes had caught fire. No doubt suspicious, as always, about what he was up to, his father had walked in at that precise moment, hollered for servants to bring buckets of water while he beat at the flames. Caspar had been too outraged even to scold him but had merely hissed that he must get his belongings together because they were going on a long journey on the morrow.

Rollo ground his teeth at the memory. First his mother had been taken from him and then his home. His eyes smarted as he stared into the fire and saw, again, the dancing flames of his mother's funeral pyre. Rollo believed that his father had abandoned the memory of his mother. She had been such a fine woman.

The smell of sulphur wafted up from below, pungent and clawing at the back of his throat. He breathed deeply; strangely enjoying the smell as if it reminded him of freshly baked bread though the notion was ridiculous; sulphur had a vile stench to it. Someone must have opened an outer door above him because he could suddenly hear a bustle of activity; wheels grinding on cobbles, someone shouting, a horse clattering nervously as it slipped on the smooth stones polished by the winter frost. He picked his way further down but halted when he heard voices.

'I thought that lily-livered coward was following,' he heard a young haughty voice declare loudly, the sound drifting down to him from above.

'He'll have got lost,' another voice said more jovially.

Rollo forgot the lure of the underground world and remembered his mission to ensure that his cousins were taught to respect him. So they hadn't gone up to the battlements after all, and he had not been as stealthy as he had hoped. He turned upwards towards the noise, passing close by a muffled whirr, clank and roar coming from a chamber behind a thick wall of rock. Soon, he was hurrying up the narrow flight of steps towards an open door that led out into a square courtyard.

As he suspected, Quinn and Guthrey stood smugly in the courtyard, the wind ruffling the thick fur of their bearskin cloaks, the air around them sparkling with tiny particles of snow. Rollo rose up from the dark stairwell and stood there, unaware of the chill of the air. Staring disdainfully at them, he wondered how he could insult them without any loss of his own dignity. Their eyes flickered towards him before they hastily turned away, muttering in low tones, heads pressed close. Slowly and deliberately, they marched away from him towards the stables.

Rage boiled up into Rollo's head. How dare they dismiss him like that! Determined in some way to impress them, he sauntered after them, a grin spreading slowly across his broad face. So they had chosen to lead him to the stables. Well, he could out-master them where horses were concerned; there was no doubt. Chieftain had been trained by his father and, although Caspar disappointed him in many ways, he was proud of his father's unquestionable ability with horses; Chieftain had been trained remarkably well.

As the two youths reached the high arch over the entrance to the stables, they turned and glowered at the sound of Rollo's approach.

'And where do you think you are going?' Guthrey demanded. 'Strangers are not permitted to wander freely around this castle. You'd get lost in a hawk's stoop, and waste valuable manpower as they searched for you. Haven't you heard these are difficult times? What are you doing troubling us anyway?' the younger of the Torra Altan youths spouted a torrent of accusations at him.

'I'm following no one! I was merely going to see that my horse was properly cared for and then . . .' Rollo was unsure of what he was going to say. 'And then I'm going out for a ride.'

'A ride?' Guthrey snorted in ridicule. 'Don't be absurd; the sun's going down. And you can't ride out alone, even by day. Didn't you hear what Lord Hal was trying to tell your father? The countryside is filled with hobs and the sky's alive with the great black ravenshrikes; many men have gone missing in the past few months. And you never know when the dragon will come back.'

'I'm not frightened of a dragon,' Rollo declared, deepening his voice to add conviction.

The taller boy laughed but the younger thicker-set youth dismissed his comment with a flick of his hand and goaded, 'It would be most irresponsible of you to ride out alone and Father would be livid. He's already had to send Lieutenant Piperol after Isolde and he won't want to send out another rescue party for you. Just imagine how ashamed you'd feel!'

'I would not get lost. This is a very small, tame country compared to my own,' Rollo said acidly, feeling his raging-hot anger rise and the blood vessels in his neck swell.

He marched between the two boys towards the great round rump of his horse, which he could see poking out from the end stall. Chieftain's tail swished as he was vigorously groomed by a red-faced stable-hand. Without any kind word, Rollo bluntly ordered, 'I need my horse; saddle him now.'

As he spoke, he heard similar cries at his back from the two young Torra Altan nobles as they summoned grooms to carry out their commands.

The red-faced groom straightened and turned to stare at Rollo, 'Now, young lad, this horse has just ridden in. His pasterns are a little warm; he needs a rest and—'

'I'll take Firecracker then.'

'Now, lad, for a start I have no authority to allow you and you're a mite inexperienced to go getting up on a beast like that. He's a nasty temperament on him that one, very nasty.' He glanced ruefully at a fresh crescent-shaped bruise on his forearm.

'My father lets me ride him anytime I want. How dare you question my orders?' Rollo puffed his chest out and drew himself up to his full height.

He could wait no longer so he snatched up Firecracker's tack and marched stiffly to his stall. He was relieved to see the brute tethered by two separate ropes to keep his head still; evidently, the grooms had found the old stallion more than difficult. Rollo was proud of the horse: Firecracker gleamed like burnished copper and, though the stable was full of magnificent war-horses, he was quite the most handsome beast amongst them.

As Rollo's feet rustled through the straw in the stallion's stall, Firecracker lashed out sideways but failed to connect with flesh; Rollo had already anticipated the attack. Having failed once, the old stallion persisted to bully the youth by squashing him against the boarding of the stall, his great hot body pressing out the air from Rollo's lungs with each movement. Still, he was not put off and thumped the horse hard in the shoulder to make him move. Firecracker was quicker this time and took a vicious cow kick, his sharp hoof nicking Rollo's leg just below the kneecap. Rollo stifled his yelp of pain and retaliated with a fast slap across the horse's muzzle.

The stallion squealed in protest and dipped his haunches ready to rear. For a moment, Rollo feared that the brute would snap free from his head-collar as the leathers were strained and twisted by the animal's strength. Snorting and bellowing out the air from its lungs, the horse gave one last stamp before finally standing still as if prepared, just for the moment, to tolerate the boy's authority.

Rollo seized the opportunity to throw the saddle over Firecracker's back and cinch the girth. He then lifted the bridle from a hook, determined to brave the horse's mouth. Firecracker's teeth were clamped shut. He had to admit some whisper of trepidation when dealing with his father's horse. The animal had bucked him off many times during his childhood and never missed an opportunity to lash out at him. He gritted his teeth; if he were going to impress anyone, he would do it with this horse.

Already, Quinn and Guthrey had their horses saddled and were jeering at his ineptitude. His hands quivering with frustration and anger, he positioned the bridle, ready to ease the bit up into the stallion's mouth but those vicious teeth were still clamped shut against the bit.

However, Rollo had learnt a trick or two. Holding the bit ready beneath the brute's mouth, he kneed the horse in the chest. Firecracker opened his mouth, ready to snap at him and, in that instant, Rollo yanked the bridle upwards, pulling the bit into place. He knew it would have been kinder to use some titbit to entice the horse's mouth open but he didn't have time and he didn't care all that much.

He backed the horse out of the stall. Firecracker swung round and danced on his toes, shying away every time Rollo got a foot near the stirrup. At the third attempt, he managed to vault clean up onto the horse's back but had no time to adjust the stirrups. With the stirrup irons banging against Firecracker's side, he clattered out into the courtyard only to find Quinn and Guthrey barring his way, mounted on their own shorter but heavier beasts.

Rollo raised his head and rode stiffly towards them, his legs tense, gripping Firecracker's sides as the horse jittered beneath him.

'Call that a war-horse?' Guthrey sneered.

Rollo didn't wait for a reply. He had been trained by the warriors of Ash. The people of Ash were an illusive race whose females were tantalizingly beautiful and whose males were giants standing to over seven feet tall, possessing enormous strength as well as a voracious appetite for battle. A number of these magnificent warriors had formed his mother's personal bodyguard, and he had learnt all he could from them. Rollo was quick to move his hand to the hilt of his sword. Standing high in his stirrups, a rush of adrenaline overcoming his trepidation, he plucked his sword from his scabbard.

Shrieking and snorting, Firecracker charged, his hocks dipping beneath him as he leapt forward in powerful bounds. But Rollo was not quite skilful enough to control the hot-blooded horse and, before he reached the two youths, the stallion began to crab and dance. Rollo lurched to smite his kinsmen but the movements of his horse made it impossible for him to hit his mark. He was uncomfortably balanced, the swing of his sword unbalancing him further. Struggling in an ungainly manner to stay seated, he was forced to snatch a fistful of mane in his left hand to stop him slipping from his saddle.

Guthrey roared with laughter.

Quinn pulled back and sat quietly on his horse, watching aloofly, as his half brother drew his sword. Twisting it so that the blade caught the flat rays from the last of the winter sun, Guthrey sent a stray beam to dazzle Rollo's eyes. The light flicked away and Rollo's focus narrowed onto the boy's arrogant face before him. Guthrey's full lips lifted into a mocking sneer as he laughed loudly. Immediately Rollo became oblivious to the soldiers shouting at them to stop and of their hollering for someone to fetch Lord Hal and Baron Caspar. He was aware only of his cousin's sneering grin and how he was going to smash it into a pulp.

For the first time in his life, he felt the horse beneath him become one with his spirit, their combined movements fluid and united. The animal sensed his intent, his focus and concentration. This time he did not have to yank the stallion's head round; already, the war-horse was pawing the cobbles, sparks flying from his hooves as he struck the hard stone and manoeuvred for attack.

Guthrey squared his mount up to the challenge, his laugh silenced and his face set hard, with eyes full of cold hatred. He raised his sword slowly but with confidence, jabbed his heels into his horse's side and bellowed, 'For Torra Alta!'

Shrieking wildly, Firecracker reared and Rollo was forced to lower his guard in order to cling on. By the time the stallion's hooves had crashed down and he had regained his seat, Guthrey was nearly on top of him, sword raised high in threat. Rollo twisted awkwardly and, as if time had slowed, watched as the blade sliced through the air towards his chest. He was poorly positioned. In automatic response, he tried to raise his arm to block the blow but was unused to fighting on horseback and the pommel of his sword snagged in the loose end of his reins. A wide-eyed look of glee brightened his cousin's face and Rollo sensed the youth's lack of restraint; Guthrey was out to mark him.

The horse saved him from the second pass of the blade by leaping back off all four hooves with the agility of a cat. Though Rollo never felt the cold bite of the steel, the sword had only nicked the back of his raised hand.

He was at once mindful of a furious bellow from his back. A man grabbed his reins and another his leg, hauling him from his snorting steed. Someone, a large man in an old leather hauberk and thick bearskin, brushed past, striding out for Guthrey. By the blackness of his hair and forceful bearing, he recognized him as Hal and a new surge of loathing welled up from the pit of his stomach. Still, he struggled to lunge up and fly at Guthrey but the men were too strong.

Whilst pinning him by the arm, one laughed into his ear, 'I know it's not right to go around trying to kill your cousin and all but it's fine to see that the lords of Torra Alta are still breeding lads with spirit!'

'You wretched boy! I'll have you flogged for this!' Hal roared at his son, lurching for the boy's reins.

But Guthrey was quick. He jabbed his spurs into his horse's ribs and wheeled her round, the rump swinging into Hal who stumbled before regaining balance. Guthrey sped towards the yawning hole of the open portcullis and halted just for a moment. His eyes flashed at his father, then beyond him to Rollo who glared back. Then, with a squeeze of his legs, Guthrey galloped out into the twilight.

'I'll have you flogged!' Hal roared as if he were a deranged boar, his breath coming in grunting puffs. With his one hand, he yanked Quinn out of the men's grasp and, holding him by the collar of his cloak, shook him vigorously. 'What is the meaning of this?'

The tall youth took one look at the man and then slithered out from his cloak. Quick as a hare, he leapt for his horse. Before any could stop him, he was away after his brother.

Rollo, alone, was left to face the ring of angry faces. Hands were on him, yanking him upright. He struggled, the rage still boiling within him, though, at the back of his mind he was aware of his father's shouts and the snorts of the stallion as he clattered wildly about the courtyard.

'Do you think you can come here and attack my son and get away with it? How dare you!' Lord Hal was yelling in his face.

Rollo felt physically ill at the sight of the man. He had always resented authority but this treatment was worse because this man had no rightful jurisdiction over him yet dared to yell at him like this.

'Spar, get over here and deal with your offspring!' Hal shouted furiously.

Hal and Rollo stared into one another's eyes for the few seconds it took the Baron to cross the courtyard. Caspar's face was scarlet with embarrassment and anger.

'How dare you do this! How dare you attack your cousin; it's unthinkable! You could have both been killed. You know I've forbidden you to ride Cracker.'

Rollo cared little for the blur of faces around him or their angry sentiments. Nor was he in the least perturbed by his father's scolding; only two thoughts possessed him. The first was that he had to get away from Hal; he couldn't bear to be near the man. And the second was that Guthrey had got away. He and Guthrey had started something and he was going to see it finished.

Caspar was pulling him out of Hal's grip and, for the first time, Rollo became aware of a sharp pain and looked down to see the strip of red across the back of his hand.

'Look at me when I'm talking to you!' Caspar shouted in frustration but his tone softened. 'Look, you've hurt yourself. Let me see it!' His father's voice was concerned but Rollo didn't want sympathy, in fact it only fuelled his rage to the point that he could no longer think.

Too often in his life, his anger had so utterly possessed him that his brain cramped. Like a trapped animal, he began to panic. His vision swam and darkened and a heat frothed up from his belly, choking his throat. He wanted to maim or kill. Frightened and angry all at once, he was alarmed by the strange sound shrieking up though his tight throat. Some impulse made him want to stand on top of the battlements and scream his rage at the world, throwing back his neck and howling like a beast, but he was held too fast.

Rage coursed through his body, jerking his muscles so that he thrashed, bit and kicked. A heavy blackness had dulled his senses and it was only with a numb remoteness that he felt the hands grappling for him. Somehow he struggled free, ducking and weaving through the men to reach Firecraker. The feel of the animal's warm hide helped him regain focus and seconds later he was saddled and galloping out beyond the portcullis, the cold of the evening air gradually forcing the return of his senses.

He felt no fear as he rode recklessly down the perilously steep road that descended the Tor, the horse slithering on the runs of ice. His cousin had marked him. He dug his heels into the stallion's flanks, oblivious to the sound of Firecracker's hooves skittering on the icy stones and pebbles tumbling from the road's edge that triggered a further shower of scree onto the slopes far, far below.

His hand throbbed but he was focused on the chase. Guthrey had not had that much of a head start and, though he didn't know the lay of the land, he had every confidence in his father's horse. He must catch the Torra Altan and mark him back; honour compelled him.

Gradually, he realized that Firecracker's forequarters were sloping away from him at a frightening angle and that the saddle was riding up the horse's withers. He sat back and reined in a little, hoping that the horse would make his own way. Firecracker's ears were laid flat back and he puffed with the effort, steam blasting from his nostrils, but, as Caspar had always boasted, he was a magnificent horse and he did not slow. Heart alone got him down that slope, hindquarters squatted beneath him and forelegs stretched forwards as he slid and slithered down the steeper sections.

Rollo became increasingly aware of bruising on his upper arms and the taste of blood in his mouth. He had a vague recollection now of how he had fought his way out from the grip of the men. Guilt clamped about him, darkening his thoughts as he realised that, again, his uncontrollable rage had entirely possessed him.

Caspar's voice rang out from above, 'Rollo! Rollo, no! Be careful. Rollo, my boy!'

The panic in his father's voice had told everyone that he feared for his son's life on the treacherous road. The humiliation drove out Rollo's fear and enabled him to find a better seat. Lengthening the reins further, he allowed Firecracker his head so that he could move more freely and balance himself.

The wind rushing into his face slowly cooled his temper and Rollo found he was enjoying himself, revelling in the freedom, relishing the release of all his simmering emotions. Fleeing the oppression of his inheritance and losing himself to the thrill of the chase heartened him. He and Guthrey had started something. He had pitted himself against this youth and he was going to win!

Now, half way down the Tor, he was composed enough to look out across the darkening canyon and glimpse the black forms of Guthrey and Quinn, galloping across the smooth valley floor. They had crossed a narrow wooden bridge spanning the river his father had called the Silversalmon and were heading east towards the canyon wall. Rollo made out a thin ledge that zigzagged down the sheer sides of the canyon and calculated that they were headed for its foot.

As the slope lessened, he gradually increased his pace until he reached the canyon floor and again gave Firecracker his head so that the stallion might extend into a gallop. Rollo soon realized that his saddle had slipped round to the right. Circling the horse to slow him, he allowed the stallion to catch his breath while he shortened the stirrups. Once he had managed that, he stamped down hard into his left stirrup iron to pull the saddle straight. Firecracker bucked in protest. Rollo caught a fistful of mane and, with more respect now, pressed the horse forward.

He had never truly appreciated the beast until this moment. Now, as he swallowed the distance in great strides, the Oriaxian purebred pounding the frozen ground, nose stretched out and mane and tail streaming like banners, Rollo understood the power and heart of this creature. By the time he reached the foot of the canyon wall, the others were only just over half way up: it wouldn't be too long before he caught them.

Firecracker leapt up the rocks like a goat, fearlessly attacking the slope. Quinn and Guthrey's horses on the other hand were now carefully picking their way in the gloom. But they were out of sight when he reached the summit. Presumably, they had disappeared behind the stark crags of the Yellow Mountains to be swallowed into the heavy shadow in the ravines between.

Rollo halted and looked about, trying to decide which way they had gone. Firecracker dropped his head, his sides heaving like bellows, streaks of foamy sweat coating his shoulders. But in a remarkably quick time, his ears were up and his breathing was steady. Steam rose in columns from the stallion's back and shoulders, two jets of steam, like dragon's breath, coiling from his nostrils.

Rollo's own nostrils flared. There was barely a scent in the crisp winter's air yet the hairs on his neck tingled, warning of danger. The black form of an eagle skimmed the cliffs high to his right; he twisted his neck to see the great bird lazily riding the streaks of golden light that bled from the sunset. Its high-pitched peal split the air. In the aftermath of its cry, the silence was long and eerie until, from far away, came back another cry, three screamed notes, deeper and more threatening, that pierced the distance. Suddenly

57

the eagle plummeted as if it had been shot by an arrow but Rollo was certain that it was fleeing from that other predator of the sky whose cry still echoed through the chill twilight.

He saw it now, what looked to be a giant hawk, circling a distant peak. Rollo lifted his chin, to prove to himself that he wasn't afraid of the monstrous bird whose wingspan he judged to be at least three times that of the eagle's. At the same time, he unconsciously patted the hilt of his sword and was grateful for the throwing knives strapped to Firecracker's saddle. He was even more grateful, however, that the great bird was circling away from him.

Presuming that the two youths would have certainly veered away from such a predator, he headed south along a stony ridge at a steady canter, scouring the ground for their tracks in the snow. It wasn't long before he picked them up. At first the ridge was bare where the raw wind had swept away the snow and so they had left no trace but, soon, Rollo saw that they had dropped down from the exposed ground and trudged through the drifted snow below, leaving a distinct trail of black pockets pitting its surface.

Ahead of him, a distinctive anvil-shaped mountain came into view, its high plateau of snow catching the last of the sun. At its abraded foot there lay what he thought must be a small lake though it could only be seen as a perfectly smooth plain at the base of the wind-blasted crags, the even snowfield tinged red in the twilight. For a second, the mountain captured his imagination and he stared up at it, feeling remarkably peaceful.

Determinedly, he focused on the backs of the two youths, who were trotting away from him and dropping down into a gully. They had no idea that he was following them. It was a situation he would change immediately and gave out an ululating cry of attack.

The two Torra Altan's glanced over their shoulders and then spurred their horses on to where the gully widened and allowed them space to turn. With all the appearance of war-hardened discipline, they drew their swords.

Guthrey didn't wait to meet Rollo's charge but, standing high in his stirrups, and swinging his sword wildly about his head, spurred his horse through the snow towards the Baron's son. Rollo's tight grimace softened to a triumphant grin as he became certain that he'd have no trouble knocking the flailing weapon from his opponent's grasp. He focused only on that wide yelling mouth, and the red moistness of Guthrey's tongue. He was certain he could smell the boy's breath and hear the thump of his racing heart even though it wasn't possible at that distance. Rollo took in a deep breath and let out a bestial scream.

Guthrey's horse shied at the alarming and unnatural sound. Rollo's vision began to blur and he could smell the hot sweatiness of the beast as if his face were buried in its coat. The muffled thud of Firecracker's hooves in the snow became distant and he was aware only of the sharp wind whistling past his ears; he had the strangest sensation that he was flying. He focused on Guthrey, ready to strike whilst his opponent was distracted by the horse's panic. But the act of his horse shying had actually made Guthrey sit more deeply into the saddle and take a firmer grip on his sword. The Torra Altan managed to turn Rollo's sword away, jarring the prince's arm as it was knocked aside.

Both horses dipped their hindquarters low to keep their power beneath them as their great muscles worked to keep them steady. Blood trickled from the mouth of Guthrey's horse where he had yanked too hard on the reins to balance himself.

Rollo could barely see for the red cloud that swam before his eyes. But he could smell – smell with an extreme intensity. And he wanted only to kill.

The crash of metal rang back and forth, trapped in the tight confines of the gully. Rollo lashed out wildly, aware at the back of his mind that he was not using his training but acting on savage instinct. He watched for a weakness in Guthrey's swordsmanship but was distracted as the air was buffeted from above. Through his grunts of effort, he heard the distinctive whoosh of a vast wingspan. As if responding only to his thoughts, Firecracker twisted away from the combat.

'Look out! Above you!' Quinn yelled urgently, bursting in front of them and lashing the air with his sword. Both Firecracker and Guthrey's mount paced back to give him room.

Rollo glimpsed the next sudden movement almost too late as Guthrey stole around Quinn who was still frantically hacking at the air to ward off the monstrous bird. Without even a yell of warning, Guthrey attacked Rollo from behind his brother's back. Wildly, Rollo lashed out in response. How dare his cousin cheat in this way and attack in such an underhand manner!

Obsessed with rage, Rollo made no attempt at simple defence but thrust hard, plunging his sword at his opponent and feeling the resistance of flesh and then the jarring crunch as the blade stopped against bone. Horse and rider crumpled into the snow.

Chapter 4

The blow struck Rollo on his back, snagging his clothing and raking over his spine, ripping the cry of self-loathing from his throat and jerking his staring gaze from the horse and rider struck down by his own hand.

His arms locked around Firecracker's neck, holding him against the force that dragged his hips out of his saddle. His muscles strained and his arms twisted at the shoulder until almost wrenched from their sockets. Then, with a loud rip, the cloth of his jacket gave way and he thumped back down into his saddle.

Still clinging to the horse's neck, he urged Firecracker under the lee of the ravine wall to protect them both from the airborne predator. The enormous shadow swooped back, skimming over the edge of the rock and on towards Quinn, who was still in the open. The tall youth forced his horse skilfully left and right, galloping between several tall jagged rocks to prevent the bird with its immense wingspan coming in too close. Quickly tiring of this, it swerved away from Quinn and, thrusting its talons out and forwards, its great wings thrashing the air and sending up huge swirling vortexes of snow high into the ravine, it hovered above the scene of battle. Rollo's heart thumped in his throat. The great bird was descending on Guthrey's bloody form where he lay pinned beneath his horse.

'No! No! Guthrey!' Quinn shrieked and turned back too late for his kinsman.

The giant hawklike bird thumped the air with its wings

and sprang up, the lifeless forms of Guthrey and his horse swinging limply from its talons. The bird struggled to lift the combined weight, its wings thrashing the air and whipping the snow up into a white storm all about them until finally it powered itself and its burden free of the ravine. Rollo looked up in horror at Guthrey's swinging body and then down at the huge bloody patch on the once pure white snow.

He felt sick. Sagging forward onto Firecracker's withers, he slumped there for a moment before managing to raise his head and stare after the monstrous bird. Every vestige of his pouting honour was stripped from him. He looked down in deep remorse at his bloodied hands and blade.

'Why have I done this?' he asked himself. 'What sin have I ever committed that my life should be so beset by such vile deeds?'

'We must go after him,' Quinn was shouting at him. 'Ravenshrikes don't kill outright; they keep their victims alive in order to train their young. We must go after him. Gromo was taken and he managed to cut himself free. Others have escaped too.'

Rollo nodded cautiously, realizing that Quinn could not have witnessed him inflict the mortal blow that had felled Guthrey. Hastily, he sheathed his weapon, hoping Quinn had not noticed the blood. But Quinn was not watching him; he had already set off after the great winged beast.

Guilt dragged at Rollo's heart. He had murdered his cousin. Some madness had possessed him, but who would believe that? Of course he hated his cousin, but he still couldn't believe he had actually struck such a blow. His intent had merely been to prove his strength and his courage to show Guthrey that he was a worthy opponent. He looked down at his scabbard and felt revolted with himself for what he had done. Even if he had not killed Guthrey outright, he had disabled him so that he could not flee the great ravenshrike. It was all his fault and he must now do what he could to help.

Kicking his heels into Firecracker's ribs, he plunged through the knee-deep snow after Quinn. Once he reached the head of the ravine, he looked up into the mauve sky and saw the giant bird heading for the anvil-topped mountain above the lake.

Scanning the terrain ahead, Rollo made out the dark line of a narrow track stripped of snow by the wind. A few scrubby trees clung to the bare rock either side, but they did nothing to diminish the cutting bite of the raw wind. Firecracker danced and squealed as the wind tugged at his mane and tail and Rollo tensed as the horse half reared. His father was right; the stallion was not a safe mount and he did not relish the thought of being thrown onto the broken rocks.

The track led them to a steep incline up through a narrow gully and the going became increasingly difficult in the failing light. Even Firecracker struggled through the trapped snow in the gully, leaping and bounding like a deer. The two youths, their faces a whitish blue from the cold, gritted their teeth against the wind and battled on, their boots now drenched from trailing in the snow. The only noise that cut through the horses' grunts of effort was the whistling wind.

About fifty yards ahead, the ground rose up and the wind had lashed the snow from the exposed slope. It was not far but, suddenly, both horses stopped in their tracks. Rollo lurched forward onto Firecracker's ears. The snow was up to their bellies and the animals were evidently reluctant to wade deeper. Rollo fixed his eyes on the firm ground ahead. It was only a matter of yards before they would climb up out of this deep snowfield and reach the wind-blasted rock and scree on the far side.

Slipping from Firecracker's back, he plunged into the snow that soaked through his breeches, stinging his skin. Dragging at the reins, he began to swim and stumble through the snow, though Firecracker resisted, snorting and tugging back, only yielding the barest inches. Quinn followed suit with his own horse, anxiously urging him forwards. Rollo could barely think for the violent chattering of his teeth.

Just for a second, the two youths glanced at one another in shared frustration before both sets of eyes filled with alarm.

The ground gave way beneath their feet. The sudden shock of bitingly cold snow smothering Rollo's face muffled his cry. His grip closed hard about his reins and his feet kicked and struggled in thin air though his upper body was trapped in the snow. But his frozen fingers lacked the strength to hold his weight and the reins whipped through his grasp. Suddenly, he was falling. He twisted and reached about him for a handhold as he fell, tumbling and twisting, bouncing off what he thought to be the branches of trees that cracked and splintered as they gave way beneath his weight. With him fell sheets of snow.

He stopped with a jolting thud amidst a cushioning blanket of snow and branches, instantly aware that he was unable to move as his legs were buried deeply within the wet snow that set firmly around him. Groaning, he tried to dig himself out with red and swollen fingers and was thankful for Quinn who reached from behind, hooked him under the armpits and dragged him clear. They both sat in the near dark, staring at one another while Rollo ran frozen hands down his shinbones, feeling for injury.

Ruefully, he blamed himself for their fall. He should have trusted the horses' instincts; he had been very foolish. Painfully, he pushed himself to his feet and stared up at the crack of twilight above their heads, the air sparkling with falling snow. At the top there were scrubby bushes that might ease their way if they could have reached them but the walls of the shaft were bereft of anything resembling a handhold for at least thirty feet. They were trapped.

Stepping slowly round, Rollo scanned the gloom. He thought he could make out a number of dark recesses. A shiver ran the length of his spine; the recesses were tunnels. Surely, one would lead them safely out of here. Stepping forward into the dark, he peered closely at the openings.

Several were little more than scraped hollows but four looked worthy of further investigation.

It was dangerous to enter unknown tunnels and he had been told so many times by his parents. His father had also told him of the world before the new age of dragons. In a time before his birth, wyverns had existed in such small numbers that some people didn't believe in them at all, and gnomes and hobgoblins had not lurked at the back of every cave. He did not relish the thought of what might lie within these tunnels.

What he needed was light. At his feet lay plenty of brushwood and, with numb and shaking fingers, he scooped together a bundle, using the longer strands of the softer, more pliable wood to wrap it tightly together at the base to form a handle. Quinn hurriedly copied him. Rollo then felt about on the rocky floor until he found a chip of stone and then made a little pile of crisp shavings from the brushwood into which he mixed scraps of his torn shirt. Working smartly brought feeling back into his extremities, he repeatedly struck his stone against the rock by the shavings until he had a spark that ignited on the torn threads of cotton. He blew and poked the smouldering shavings with a twig until that caught sufficiently to light the makeshift torches.

His blood throbbing with anticipation, he held his torch up and stared as the glowing red light swam into the recesses. He chose a tunnel at random for he had no idea of direction without reference to the inaccessible world above their heads. The darkness swallowed his light, drinking its energy, and he paced cautiously forward. The tunnel stretched deep into the rock beyond the reach of his torch and, moreover, when he had gone a little further, forked out in several directions.

He should have felt afraid of a dark underground world where any devilish creature might lurk but, instead, he was strangely elated. With Quinn pressed up close behind him, he took a dozen bold steps. Just for a moment, he thought he could smell his mother's sweet breath and hear her steady and comforting heartbeat. He shook his head, telling himself it was quite absurd as he stepped around in wonder, staring at the yellow and red stains of mineral runs that were smeared over the smooth walls. Crystalline shapes glistened in the light where the water dripped from the roof onto waxlike mounds on the floor. He began to explore the hollow space, glad that the air was warmer.

Half in a daze and only vaguely aware of Quinn's tread close on his heels, he wandered further from the shaft, following the smooth-walled tunnel towards the sound of an underground river. Already, he had forgotten that he had thrust his sword deep into his cousin's breast. And he cared not that he had raced out of Torra Alta, leaving his father and the castle in disarray; or that men would have been sent out into the dark to find him. He was interested only in the rock. His heart thumped loudly in his breast and he breathed in the hot smoke that wafted back at him from the spluttering torch, feeling intoxicated by it. This was more thrilling than anything else he had ever experienced!

His father had told him of the excitement of looking out from the heights of the castle of Torra Alta and the splendours of the canyon that the stronghold overlooked but, surely, this world beneath the crags was the true wonder.

He came to another fork in the tunnel and, without hesitating to question his choice, took the opening on his right. It occurred to him that he ought to mark the way so that he might find his way back if this route didn't prove successful but, when he looked round, he found the notion absurd. Of course, he knew the way back. It was obvious. His mind was filling with a sense of security and self-worth that he had not known since before his mother's death.

'It's like the caverns beneath the Tor,' Quinn murmured. 'I'll be bound, this was once a dragon's lair!'

Rollo was so happy exploring the wondrous shapes in the rock that he didn't bother to answer. In fact, he was so engrossed that he did not at first notice the faint scratching sound about him.

Whilst clambering up the slippery sides of a moss-coated rock, he was finally became aware of the chattering noise and scurry of feet just ahead. Rats, he told himself. The tunnel led into a large chamber, one side of which was immersed in water. For a moment, he felt giddy and his mind was filled with a mournful song as if remembered from a long-forgotten dream. It was a powerful song about magic and bravery and fire but he could not fully comprehend its meaning. For a second, he thought he could smell the strong scent of animal and the scorched acrid smell of fire on flesh but it faded. He shook himself. Perhaps he had hit his head harder than he had thought when he fell down the shaft.

He picked out another tunnel that led him down in a spiral through the levels of the crag. The faint scratching sounds were all about them now but, far more distinctive was the sound of feet behind him. He stopped in his tracks.

The noise stopped instantly too and his throat tightened as he wondered that, perhaps, one of the two-legged creatures that lived below the earth was now on their trail. Then he realized that, of course, they must be Quinn's footsteps; in the excitement, he had forgotten about the youth on his heels. He was suddenly annoyed with himself for being so ridiculously jittery and nervous like a silly girl. After all, he, Prince Rollo, first son of Ursula the Revered, was not afraid to meet a creature in the dark.

'It doesn't feel right down here,' Quinn breathed into the gloom. 'Spar must surely have warned you about the underground creatures that now lurk beneath Belbidia. I think we should go back to the shaft and wait for Hal to come and find us. That is what he would expect us to do if he managed to follow our tracks.'

'What do I care what your father thinks?'

'He isn't my father,' Quinn replied flatly.

Rollo was suddenly intrigued. 'What do you mean, he's not your father?'

Quinn laughed. 'You don't know? I thought the entire world knew the infamy of my birth.'

'I think you hold yourself in too high regard. Evidently you are not so widely spoken of as you might wish.'

Surprisingly, Quinn laughed at this insult and Rollo found that he did not dislike this youth as much as he had first thought. He watched him look about warily into the deep shadows beyond the spheres of their torches.

'I assumed Spar would have told you about me,' Quinn repeated the statement and shrugged. 'But if he hasn't, all the better.'

Rollo was intrigued but did not want to appear anything but indifferent so he bit back on his curiosity. Quinn gave him a half smile in offer of friendship though Rollo would not smile back. He noted the tension and grief behind the Torra Altan's eyes but also the firm self-controlled set to his jaw. There was a calm ease about this youth that Rollo had not sensed in his other relatives – or in himself for that matter. Quinn was not about to collapse into hysterics and was clearly holding to his belief that Guthrey was still alive. Rollo concluded, yet again, that Quinn could not have seen him strike that fatal blow.

'Look,' Quinn said slowly, opening out his hands in a gesture of conciliation. 'We are stuck down here together so we shall have to trust one another. We have had our quarrel and it's over. We all know that none of us meant any real harm.'

Rollo's mouth twitched nervously. He had not in his heart felt any true hatred towards Guthrey yet no one had forced him to strike that evil blow. A sickening wave of guilt flooded through his body.

His thoughts were truncated by the sound of a muffled bark echoing through the tunnels. He spun round, seeking out its source. A distant tinkle of falling rock echoed from one of the long tunnels and he caught a glimpse of two red eyes deep in the blackness.

'I think we'd better return to the shaft,' Quinn advised, his voice unnaturally bright to disguise his trepidation.

'Ha! It was probably only a brownie or a gnome. You Torra Altans always fear the worst. I'm not afraid –'

'No, it's a hob. Disgusting creatures,' Quinn added vehemently, ignoring all taunts. 'And you've plenty of reason to fear them. They took three of our most promising foals in the spring. Just ate their heads and left the rest. And they take people, too!'

'The mighty Lord Hal should be hunting them out of Torra Alta,' Rollo said with disdain.

'You think he doesn't? I took half a dozen myself with a bow.'

Rollo raised an eyebrow in disbelief; but turned his head towards the sound that had so disturbed them. 'Indeed,' he said sarcastically.

'Indeed!' Quinn retorted firmly, not reacting to his sneering tone. 'And they breed faster than stoats. They are far more of a threat to us than the dragons.'

Quinn's tone was so calm and affable that Rollo finally softened towards him and thought that, perhaps, he might be able to trust him – if only just a little.

'Well, if we are not going back, let's get on with it and find a way out of here,' Quinn said with sudden decisiveness. Rollo had not yet accredited him capable of such character and was even more surprised when the youth pushed past him to lead the way.

Quinn's legs were longer than his and Rollo had to stretch his stride in order to keep up. To his satisfaction, however, Quinn hesitated at the first fork in the tunnel, unable to choose a route.

'The right,' Rollo offered smoothly.

Quinn glanced at him, eyebrows raised in query. 'Do you have a particular reason?'

'No,' Rollo conceded. 'But someone's got to make a decision.' He couldn't explain why he was so sure only that he was. Besides, they had to move fast; the sound of soft-soled feet padding on the rock of the tunnel behind them was growing louder.

'I think we'd better hurry,' Quinn said, flashing a grin at Rollo. 'I know you were spoiling for a fight but I doubt that even you would choose to fight a hobgoblin.'

Rollo couldn't help but grin back at him and they broke into a jog, their gasped breaths loud in the confines of the tunnel and their hunched shadows, cast by their torches, bobbed up and down on the rounded walls. Rollo could see another fork just ahead and knew that, this time, they needed the left-hand tunnel. He had just put a hand to the entrance when his torchlight was reflected back at him by yet another set of red eyes gleaming in the dark.

'Our path appears blocked,' Quinn whispered with remarkable composure.

'It's only one. We can take him,' Rollo retorted with bravado.

'There's never only one. Hobs always scurry around in gangs,' Quinn assured him.

'Really?' Rollo replied. 'We don't have so many hobs at home,' he excused his ignorance. 'The griffins prey on them and keep their numbers down.'

'You'd think our dragons would eat them too but it seems not,' Quinn said, his eyes fixed into the darkness out of which the two points of red lights came swaying towards them. Soon there were four and then eight as the first was joined by others.

'This way!' Rollo exclaimed, tugging Quinn into the right-hand tunnel. 'We'll run for it.'

He launched into a sprint, his torch leaving a spray of comet-like sparks behind him. Quinn had no trouble keeping up as Rollo selected a steeply shelving, narrow tunnel that dropped them into a small chamber with five exits. Without thought, he chose one and hastened along a low tunnel whose walls were perfectly smooth and glistening with seams of polished crystals. As they descended, his mind began to numb and all sounds became distorted. He was vaguely aware of Quinn's presence behind him, the sound of the youth's leather boots slapping on the wet rock, but he could no longer hear his own feet. Instead, he was aware of a heavy lumbering thump and an extraordinary rasping against rock, loud in his ears. Strange smells filled his nose and became increasingly pungent.

His heart raced, its booming thump loud in his chest and a giddiness accompanied his heightened senses. He felt sweat break out all over his body and a sickness welling up from within. He could smell hob and man as easily as if they were rotting meat and horse. Cold sweat drenched his clothing and bile filled his mouth.

At last, the steep descent ended and they burst out into a large cavern. He staggered to a halt. They were deep in the bowels of the mountains, the sound of water, loud and comforting, trickling down through the layers of rock above. His knuckles were still white about his sputtering torch and he held it up to look about him.

A stifled gasp from Quinn jolted his mind and Rollo was instantly alert. The long-legged youth had stopped a short distance behind him and Rollo looked around for the object of Quinn's concern. He could see nothing at first but then leapt back in fright as he disturbed something at his feet. Looking down, he saw he was standing with one foot in the cavity of a ribcage. He knew at once it was human and, as he stared all about the cavern, he saw that bones were heaped one on another, a jumble of arms, legs and crushed skulls filling the chamber as far as he could see.

He crept back to Quinn's side, who stood swallowing and staring, too shocked to speak. At last, Quinn broke the silence, his voice tense and high. 'This must be where the great golden dragon takes her victims.'

Rollo looked down at the splintered bones and crushed skulls but knew they were not the cause of his nausea. He could not empathize with their plight and the terror of their deaths but was only interested in the great golden dragon that Quinn mentioned. 'What golden dragon?' he asked.

'*The* dragon,' Quinn corrected his description. 'She has taken the Yellow Mountains for her own. She kills any other dragon other than her own that attempts to come near. She has produced many young and is responsible for most of our livestock loses. This is not a good place to be!' His torch flickered and he only kept it aflame by turning it on its side. 'We must get up to the surface before the torches fail.'

Rollo nodded dizzily. 'Yes, the surface . . .,' he repeated, still staring around him at the grizzly chamber. The flesh was gone but remnants of hair and leather clothing still clung to the dry bones. 'We've got to go through that chamber,' he said, wafting his torch towards a deeper blackness in the gloom, his head tilting to one side as he quizzically frowned at his own words.

'How would you know?' Quinn demanded sceptically.

Offended at constantly being questioned, Rollo thought to swat the Torra Altan's nose but, bewildered by the giddiness in his head, he thought better of it and looked down at his feet and then straight into the Torra Altan's eyes. 'I don't know.' He closed his eyes for a moment and drew in a slow deep breath through his nostrils. 'We need to go through that chamber and up a sloping tunnel. Then we'll come to a wide chamber with a swiftly moving underground river cutting through the middle of it,' he began.

Quinn laughed. 'You're making it up. You couldn't possibly know what lay ahead.'

Eyes slitted with a sudden burst of intense anger, Rollo snarled, 'Well, you can stop here and get eaten by the dragon or hobs for all I care.'

'Hey!' Quinn objected amicably. 'I meant no offence.

You've got to admit, though, that there's no imaginable way you could know these routes.'

Rollo was forced to concede that it did sound mad, yet he could not shake the conviction that he was certain of the way. His voice now calm, he tried to explain, 'I know it sounds ridiculous but, if I close my eyes, I can picture it.'

Quinn shrugged. 'Well, there's only one way to find out. Are you man enough to walk through all those broken bodies?'

'I'm not afraid,' he said, stiffening and raising his chin. 'My mother commanded armies of bears. All obeyed her merest word. I am afraid of nothing.'

Stepping boldly forward into the chamber, he soon found that it was so crammed with heaped bodies that it was impossible to pick his way between the skeletons. But he had to go on, his flesh creeping as the sole of his foot pressed down on ribs that gave beneath him and then finally snapped. Quinn leapt after him, taking as few strides as possible to cross the deathly chamber, before hurrying upwards through a narrow tunnel just as Rollo had described. They found themselves on a ledge above a huge underground river that swirled and eddied. Quinn raised his torch, the light reaching across the chasm to another rocky promontory jutting out above the river on the far side. A little way back from the far ledge was a black arch that presumably was the mouth to a further tunnel.

'How did you know?' Quinn asked. 'You couldn't possibly have known what was down here.'

Rollo felt equally bewildered. 'It was as if I'd dreamed it,' he murmured. 'It's as if I've known about it all my life.'

'You'd better talk to my mother about it when you get back.'

'To Brid?'

'Whom else?'

'Well, I thought that Hal was your father so I didn't want to make any more incorrect assumptions.'

73

'Nice of you, I'm sure,' Quinn retorted with mock hurt. 'So, in your dream, how did you cross this river?'

Rollo looked down at the roaring black water, that was at least some twenty foot across. It was too dark to judge the depth, but the narrow channel and eddies suggested it was considerable. The speed at which the current danced away downstream, sucking water deep down towards the riverbed, made it certain that even the strongest of swimmers would be mad to attempt to swim across.

'I could ...' Rollo's voice trailed away and he stared wide-mouthed at the chasm. 'I would fly ...,' he said, again not really knowing why he said it. He laughed nervously at Quinn's puzzled expression. 'This is madness, isn't it?'

Quinn looked more serious. 'I should never have let you lead us this way. We should have faced the hobs. We'll have to go back.'

Rollo was still looking around him at the chasm and noted that it narrowed to their left. They picked their way upstream until their torches eventually illuminated the point where the river burst out from beneath an arch of rock. Running near the lower edge of the span there appeared to be a thin broken ledge that might afford them just enough footing to cross to the far side.

'Look! We can make it,' Rollo said and, without waiting for Quinn's reply, picked his way towards the ledge to survey the churning river once again.

He had no illusions as to whether he would survive if he fell into the torrent. The whirlpools indicated a fast undertow and he was certain that he would be sucked down and pinned against the riverbed for all eternity. The going was hard and he had only one hand with which to hold onto the rocks since his other held fast to the smouldering torch. There was no joy in imagining what would happen to them if they lost the torches.

He had no need to look back to check if Quinn were following since he could hear his grunts behind him as he too, clambered towards the ledge. The moistness in the atmosphere made the rocks slimy and Rollo slipped and cut his palm as he put his hand out to save himself. At last they both reached the narrow end of the chamber and saw that the ledge they needed to work their way along was barely a hand's breadth. The drop was not great, only a matter of twenty foot, but the tumbling waters of the sulphurous river were alarmingly fierce.

Still, Rollo would not admit fear to anyone, not even himself. 'I'll go first,' he told the older youth. 'You'll have to hold the torches and then throw them to me when I'm on the other side.'

Quinn nodded. 'There seems to be no other way, and if you fall, I'll know to pick my way back the way we came,' he said with a shrug and a light laugh.

'Well, you have to agree this beats watching the women pick away at the tapestries!'

'I have to admit I do. And, Cousin . . .,' Quinn paused as if testing out the word, 'at least we'll have a tale to tell when we find Guthrey.'

Without acknowledging the Torra Altan's optimism, Rollo handed him his torch and edged out onto the lip of rock that stretched for fifteen feet or more across the narrowest part of the river as it burst out into the cavern. He slid one foot out and reached for a handhold, his heart thumping wildly. The worst moment was letting go of his firm grip with his left hand and sliding his trailing foot up alongside his right foot. Inching out again, he stretched forward his right hand, but found only smooth rock. He stretched a little further to the point of feeling perilously unbalanced and at last he had a handhold. After sliding his right leg forward, he shuffled the last few feet until he reached a broader ledge of rock on the other side where he could turn around.

'Toss me a torch!' he requested, only then realizing how difficult it was going to be to catch it.

'Ready?' Quinn asked and lobbed the first one.

It arced and twisted through the air, leaving a trail of golden sparks. Rollo fixed his eye on the arm of the torch, watching it twist and turn. He had a keen eye. The warriors of Ash had taught him well and one of the most important skills of close combat was to keep an eye on a sword, to watch its twists and turns, and he had grown up with the skill. The arc of the torch's trajectory dropped it down low to his feet. Stooping, he caught it and, twisting his face aside as sparks sprayed up, he quickly wedged the point of the torch in a niche between the rocks and turned, ready to catch the next one.

Quinn lobbed the next in a higher arc this time and it, too, twisted and began to plunge back towards him, the shower of sparks obscuring the handle of the torch. The lob fell short and Rollo needed to lunge towards it but could only get a finger to the tip of the shaft. He tried to knock it upwards and towards him but it flipped over and away. Helplessly, he watched as it spiralled down towards the river, hissing and smoking as it plunged into the waters and was quickly gone.

'Well, you're not such a good catch, are you?' Quinn said with a touch of annoyance.

'That was not such a good throw,' Rollo retorted, his restraint fraying.

'To be fair, you are right,' Quinn replied with disarming friendliness, whilst already edging his way along the ledge. What Rollo had found exceedingly difficult, Quinn appeared to be completely untroubled by.

'Last year I had a dare with Guthrey that he wouldn't follow me around the lip circling the outer turret of the north tower. It's a big drop and only a three inch ledge but we both did it,' he said, alighting alongside Rollo.

'Evidently,' the Artoran youth replied coolly, reaching for the remaining torch, 'otherwise you wouldn't be here.'

Quinn laughed. 'Now then, mysterious youth with the strange sight, lead on.'

Rollo laughed uneasily. 'I don't have any powers of sight. I'm not some sly soothsayer but Prince of Artor, though that means nothing here.'

'Who cares for titles?' Quinn interrupted him. 'Let's get out of here. Hal will kill us if we don't get Guthrey back. In times like ours,' he said as if it were a phrase oft repeated by his elders, 'there is no place for troublesome youths who need rescuing from their own folly.' There was a false brightness to his voice that did not disguise the slight tremor. Rollo was certain that beneath that calm, light-hearted exterior Quinn was crying out in anguish for his half-brother.

The lanky Torra Altan trotted on after Rollo. Again, his head had become fuzzy and the smells around him were intensifying. He could barely think for his guilt and wondered whether he should not admit to plunging his sword into Guthrey's belly.

'Not so fast,' Quinn panted behind him. 'It's harder to see with just the one torch.'

Rollo grunted in return. His mind was filled with flashes of silver and gold and glimpses of jewels. He was fully expecting to see a heap of treasure as he rounded a bend in the tunnel that widened into a long thin chamber. Instead, he saw only the rotting corpses of more than a dozen hobs littering the floor. Still grasped in one long-fingered hand was a gold amulet and, lying in a crevice, he spotted a necklace of amber beads.

'They must have fought over the treasure,' he murmured, certain that this hall had once been filled with spoils.

Quinn picked up the necklace. 'It will make a fine gift,' he murmured thoughtfully, his mouth broadening into a soft smile. 'Come on, Rollo. We must hurry. How much further?'

'Not far,' he murmured. 'There's just another tunnel that spirals up into . . . into . . .' He stopped. 'But we shouldn't go!'

'I'm beginning to think . . . That is to say, I was used to Isolde's strange ways but at least she was consistent.'

'There is death,' Rollo continued as if he hadn't heard. 'Death!' he repeated.

'Death is but a part of the cycle and you must not fear it. Brid will tell you – a hundred times a day when she feels like it. Death is but a step on the journey before we reach the Great Mother from whence we are reborn. There is no life without death.'

Rollo found he was looking at Quinn's mouth but was unable to comprehend the words that suddenly sounded like strange, aggressive squeaks. His head spun and a low drone filled his ears. For a second his mind seemed to float away, remote from his body, and he swayed on his feet.

Quinn caught him and the torch before it dropped from his failing grip. 'You're not well. Let me take the torch and lead for a while.'

Reluctantly this time, Rollo padded after Quinn as they began the long arduous climb just as he had described it. He shrank back as Quinn trotted on ahead. The tunnel evened out; before them, vast arching bones curved up from the cave floor, reaching high into the vaulted cavern. Quinn stopped and held the torch high. Rollo stumbled to his side and pressed close for support, fearing he would retch as they began to pick their way through the vast forest of bones.

'A dragons' graveyard!' Quinn said in amazement as they ducked and weaved through ribcages and scrambled past great skulls.

Rollo found that he was suddenly not so afraid as he thought he would be and gently let his hand run over the surface of a great white skull. Only when Quinn shouted at him to follow did he clamber on. Quinn was still some way ahead, awkwardly scaling one beast that was lain over another, and was having some difficulty crawling over an arching run of vertebrae. The spines were extremely long and pointed and must once have supported the armoured plates that protruded up from the dragon's back. He was halfway to the top when the pile of bones began to shift beneath his weight.

'Quinn! Look out!'

Rollo watched in dismay as Quinn struggled for a hold and then was falling backwards, the torch spraying out flame. The lanky youth gave a grunt and a cry but Rollo saw no more as the torch crashed to the ground in a spray of sparks to become a low smouldering glow. The light was just enough to reveal Quinn entangled and struggling amongst a thicket of spearlike bones. Then the torch expired and the light was gone.

Chapter 5

His bow at his back, Caspar raised the firebrand and called out into the tunnels, his voice raw with shouting. Urgent voices rang down the shaft into the sombre quiet of the underground world but no sound beyond his own echo came back at him from any of the tunnels.

'Now I know what Branwolf felt like when we went missing in the tunnels beneath Torra Alta,' Hal muttered.

'How could they have been so stupid? First galloping off into the mountains and now this.' Caspar looked at the ground, seeing no evidence of his son or the other two boys. Through the dark, they had tracked them into the mountains, where they had been deeply troubled by the large stain of blood they had found on the bluff above the canyon. He had fully expected to find his son's body broken at the bottom of this collapsed shaft and his one relief now was that the collapsed shaft was empty. 'Well, it looks as if they survived the fall.'

'Obviously,' Hal said stiffly, his voice taut with worry. He looked up as his wife was lowered down on a rope and gave her a weak smile. 'This is no place for a woman and especially not one in your condition. It would be best if you left this to us.'

'They are my sons,' Brid said firmly and Hal nodded his understanding.

Caspar's teeth were chattering and his hands shook with fear. Though he loved both his children equally, it was Rollo who had occupied his time during their early years.

His daughter, Imogen had always been capable beyond her years and he had never feared for her. But Rollo found life difficult.

'I'm sure we'll find them,' Hal said, spreading his shoulders and drawing in a deep breath as if sucking the optimism of the words deep into his soul.

Caspar nodded but found it easier to listen to Pip who was muttering about hobs. Hal had sent for the Lieutenant the second the youths had galloped off.

'Where do we start looking? Every one of us will get lost down here without a plan,' Caspar fretted.

'We just need to be systematic,' Hal assured him and Caspar was glad of his uncle's calm authority. Right now, he no longer considered the fact that it lessened his own. 'Brid, I think it best if you stay here at the foot of this shaft with these men to guard you. Spar, you take one party, Pip another.'

Pip looked as if he were going to say something but then saluted smartly.

Hal grunted. 'Captain, we'll also take a tunnel each. Search until you can go no further and then return to Brid, who will co-ordinate and liaise.'

She nodded at this and then smiled sweetly at Caspar. 'Don't fear! We shall find them. Quinn is not so reckless and he'll look after them.'

Hal growled deep in his throat. 'This is the last trouble any of our boys are going to cause in Torra Alta.'

He strode off and Caspar was left with fifteen men looking at him with quiet expectation.

'Not too nice a home-welcoming for you, my Lord,' one of them said softly.

Caspar shook his head. Raising his firebrand high, he led them off at a steady march, ordering two of his men, Gromo, with the missing arm and one of the older ones in his late twenties, to mark their route. They soon reached a dividing of the ways. Both tunnels were equally broad and he took the left, thinking to return and search the right if they were unsuccessful. For prudence's sake, he, himself marked the route in places where the tunnel branched, just to be certain.

The underground ways were full of twists and turns that led between broad-domed chambers. At regular intervals, he called out for his son and, every time they took a fork, he stood at the point where the ways divided and called into the gloom of the one they chose not to take, waiting for a reply before moving on. At last, the tunnels branched no more and they came to a chamber where golden sulphur-choked water tumbled down a tall chimney in the rock and splashed into a pool that fed the underground rivers flowing through the very roots of the Yellow Mountains. They had reached the extent of the hollow caverns at this point and could explore no further. He stood still, listening but, when he was met only with silence, shouted until the back of his throat was raw and his voice cracked. Still no answer came.

'Spread out around the cavern and search any ways leading in,' he commanded.

The rocks echoed with the peeling ring of the men's voices. Caspar's own voice was hoarse and his head hurt with the pain of worrying over his son but it was soon all too evident that Rollo was not here. Slowly, they worked back the way they had come.

As they commenced their search of the remaining tunnels, he prayed one of the other parties had already found his son but he could not shake the dark foreboding that grew in the pit of his stomach. At last, they reached the tunnel he had marked as the first major divide. Here, he thought it prudent to keep all his men together as, clearly, there would be a number of smaller tunnels to explore.

After only a short distance, the tunnel ahead narrowed dramatically, closed in by fallen rubble, and they could only just squeeze through one at a time. Broken scree and fallen boulders made the going hard. The tunnel floor and roof, where visible, were scored with deep cracks and the way was crooked; Caspar guessed that the earth had moved at some point, breaking the tunnel and leaving only this narrow opening. Once through, he halted, listening intently.

There was a smell here that he recognized at once; the foul smell of dragon. He took just a few tentative paces before burying his mouth and nose in his cloak to help filter out the stench. A few steps on, he rounded a gentle bend and the tunnel widened into a chamber. He staggered back. Huge piles of dung littered the ground. The dung in places was still moist and, by the pungent stench, it surely came from a dragon that had lately overindulged on meat.

He cast his smarting eyes hastily about the chamber but, once he had found no sign of the boys, he shoved his men back, gesticulating at them to hurry. They needed to get through the narrow crack in the tunnel fast before the occupant returned or caught scent of them. Running and tripping, they retreated, Caspar standing with his torch high and his sword drawn as the men hastened through the gap.

Once all were through, he rested on the far side, panting heavily. Slumping back against the cool stone of the tunnel wall, he tried to calm the rising sense of sickness within him. He told himself that Rollo would never have ventured close to that smell but, all the same, he could not shake the bile-inducing image of the dragon feasting on his son, for that dung was fresh. He steeled his mind against the image and, with a shaking hand, pushed himself upright off the wall and hurried after the men. Numbly, he put one foot before the other, trying not to listen to the men's excited chatter about the size of the dragon that evidently lived down here.

They jogged at a fast pace up the gently shelving tunnel, Caspar hoping desperately that Rollo would be waiting for him beside Brid. His blood pounded in his ears and he could barely think. He halted at every side entrance, sending men along them to explore the ways, but each search was fruitless. He called his son's name until the rocks shook with the echo.

'Hush! Listen!' one of the men exclaimed, stopping Caspar from calling yet again.

Immediately, they all stood still, ears straining to hear through the remaining echoes that wafted back at them, destroying the quiet.

'I didn't hear anything; I—' Caspar whispered but then stopped in mid sentence. Feet! He could hear the patter of feet. He was about to shout in wild ecstasy, certain that it must be his son. It was only then he realized that there were too many feet and the sounds slapped like flat bare feet rather than the tap of human boots.

Judging by the men's faces, they knew what caused the sounds. They looked at one another uncomfortably, firmly gripping their drawn swords.

'What is it?' Caspar demanded.

'Hobs,' one muttered. 'Great rangy, man-eating hobs. They must have been lurking in one of the side tunnels and got in front of us when we went down to the dragon's den.'

Caspar's heart thumped in his throat. The hobs were headed straight for Brid. 'What are we waiting for, men?' he exclaimed and set off at a run.

He ran hard but the sound of the footsteps still sped further and further ahead of him. What could he do? They would be on Brid in moments. Lifting his silver horn to his lips, he piped out three shrill notes of warning, hoping that Brid and the men guarding her would hear and prepare for the attack. He also prayed they would pull Brid straight up and out of danger.

He sprinted after the hobs, and driven by a greater desperation to protect Brid, he was soon gaining on them. However, the clash of metal and the shrieks of men were already ringing back down the tunnels. He sprinted on harder, until he had rounded the last bend and had the hobs in sight. Plunging his sword into the back of the first creature before him, he staggered into the chamber below the shaft. Through the sweat and torch smoke that stung his eyes, he took in the terrible scene.

The knot of men guarding Brid were fighting bravely against the great hobgoblins. They were taller and thinner than men, their naked green-brown bodies slimy with sweat as they raised short black swords and hacked into the guard. With relief, Caspar saw that reinforcements were slithering down the ropes but his relief turned to horror; they were being picked off one by one by a hob with a bow. Caspar raised his own bow and, despite his heaving chest as he gasped to replenish his starved muscles with oxygen, he loosed an arrow and split the hob's skull.

The creature squealed like a snared rabbit and crashed to the ground. In the seconds before his troop appeared at his back, Caspar loosed three more arrows, spearing a hob through the gut, spilling its purplish-black blood. Slinging his bow upon his back, he thrust his firebrand into the face of the next closest to him, lunged forward with his sword and clipped the shoulder of another. But he was horrified at the force with which the hob raised its short sword and slashed his own weapon aside. Though the power of the stroke spun him round, he had the forethought to keep spinning and swung his sword right around to slash into the creature's opposite shoulder. It bit deep and jarred against bone.

The creature roared and stooped away only to be replaced by another that hacked at the injured hob in his path, knocking him down to reach Caspar. This hob leapt at him, knocking his sword aside and pinning him to the floor beneath its weight. He thought he was fighting for his life but, instead, found himself bound and gagged. A thick sack was thrown over his head and he was heaved up onto the hob's bony back.

The long protruding spines that jutted out of the length of the hob's back stabbed against his body and face as the creature set off with long tireless strides. Caspar's head and shoulders banged against the rock wall as he was carried away.

He had no idea why or where he was being taken, how many of his men lived or who else was with him. And he still did not know whether his son was alive or dead.

They paused momentarily. 'Rollo!' he shrieked only to find that his ribs were punched by the hob's sharp knuckles to silence him. That was not nearly enough to deter him. But one more crack on his head, as the hob banged him against the sides of the tunnels, sent him swimming into a daze that at least spared him the torment of worrying about his son. He came round some while later, the scent of a fresh breeze and the crisp winter air bringing him to his senses.

Someone was dragging the sacking cloth from his head and he gasped in the sharpness of the cold air. He tried to sit up only to be kicked in the chest and sent reeling to the ground. With his hands tied, all he could do was roll over, his face stinging from the bite of frosted ground.

Gradually, he realized that he was a good distance from home. He had been carried out of the Yellow Mountains. Judging by the tall oak trees, frosted long grasses and the sound of lowing cattle – alarmed, no doubt, by the smell of hob – he guessed he must have been carried south into the neighbouring Barony of Jotunn.

He rolled over and was vastly relieved to see Brid sitting beside him. Since she could sit and apparently had full use of her limbs, he thought her relatively unharmed. She did, however, look a little grey with pain and there was an ugly gash to her face.

She nodded at Caspar, acknowledging his waking presence. He nodded back grimly and then looked beyond her to see whom else had been captured. Seven of the men were with them; Gromo, Marcus and Owain from his party and four more from Brid's guard. Only Gromo and Marcus approached him in age. The rest were in their early twenties and one looked little more than a boy. All had severe cuts and bruises. One had a particularly nasty gash to his forehead, the wound still dribbling around the sides of his face and the youngest was gripping his forearm, a trickle of blood oozing between his fingers.

'What do you want with us?' Caspar demanded of the nearest hob. It crashed through his mind that these creatures may have also stolen his son away from Torra Alta. The hope swelled in his heart that they might all be delivered to the same place though his mind told him that such thoughts were forlorn.

'I wouldn't waste your breath talking to them,' Brid lisped, her words indistinct from a cut lip. She was beginning to pale to a horrible white and Caspar feared for her.

'Are you badly hurt?' he asked anxiously, visually checking her over in concern, for the cuts to her face and hands seemed superficial and he wondered that she didn't have a more severe injury that he could not see.

She nodded weakly. 'But I'm afraid there's nothing you can do.'

In disbelief, he watched the tears begin to stream down her face. He had rarely seen her cry; Brid was far too self-possessed to show such a weakness. Certainly, the Brid he had known as a youth would never have cried from physical pain; he knew, at once, what was wrong.

'The baby . . .'

She nodded. 'He was just beginning to kick. They punched me in the belly and now he is still.'

'Dead?' he asked softly, knowing the answer. He stared at her belly that was still full and rounded, the infant still within her. He had seen hard times and knew that it could take days sometimes before a dead child was expelled from its mother's womb.

She nodded and curled up onto the ground, sobbing into the earth, and Caspar felt his rage erupt within him. He had not seen Brid in fifteen years but that had not diminished his love for her. Though his hands were tied and he was still dizzy from his own injuries, he scrambled to his feet and charged the first hob, ramming his head into its stomach and sending it bowling over. The men cheered.

Unable to punch with his fists, he butted with his head and, when leathery flesh pressed against his face, he bit and twisted his head back and forth to tear away a chunk. The hob shrieked and Caspar bit harder, refusing to let go when another hob squeezed its long fingers around his neck and another kicked him hard in the groin. He kicked back until the flesh tore away in his mouth and he fell back on top of the other hobs, who now laid into him with their bony fists and feet.

'Stop!' the tallest hob shrieked in the old tongue of the Caballan that Caspar well understood. 'We want them alive. All alive. Soon, we'll capture one that can tell us all we need to know.'

Caspar and Brid looked at one another through their pain; so there was hope that their boys were alive. The Baron smiled weakly at Brid, trying to offer her solace and, as he did, realized that she was now in a perilous condition. He knew that, over the next few hours or even days, her pain would triple as the dead child within her came away. He had watched his own wife die from an infection after losing their child. Ursula had been stronger and braver than any other woman he had known and the sight of Brid brought the ache of that memory flooding back.

He wondered what these creatures would do if they actually knew whom they had captured. Soon, they were moving once more, each of them trussed up and slung over the back of a hob, carried as easily as if they had been small children. Caspar's head lolled to the rhythm of the hob's stride and, after a while, he even became accustomed to its rancid smell. Though the creature was naked down to its spread web feet, it appeared immune to the cold, though, every now and then, the two coarse lines of hairs, which grew thickly on either side of the grossly protruding nodules of its spine, prickled and stood on end. Its long ears twitched, listening for danger.

They kept up the march for at least six hours without stopping; Caspar's head was thick with blood as he swirled upside down. He didn't know what these hobs wanted with them; he only knew that they must endure their treatment until they found an opportunity to escape.

Occasionally, they tramped tracks that once must have been smooth roads through the bountiful barony but now were no more than broken paving split by seams of weeds. Fallen trees regularly blocked their path but the hobs scrambled over them with ease. At last, they came to a point where the road dipped down towards a river that tumbled from the mountains of Torra Alta, south towards the heartland of Belbidia. The silvery waters flowed in a slow, easy spread beneath the shadows of the trees, the rage of its youthful energy spent as it lolled in the easy passage of the lowlands of Belbidia. The hobs hastened down to the water's edge where a shelving gravel beach dipped into the flow at an inside bend of the river.

Caspar was tipped unceremoniously to the floor and crashed heavily down, bruising his hip and ribs on the stones. He winced as Brid was also dropped in the same manner, as were the soldiers. Six of them groaned and cursed but the last didn't move. The hobs sniffed at him then kicked him hard, the sound of breaking ribs painfully loud. The soldier didn't flinch or whimper. Clearly, the man was dead.

Caspar wriggled over the gravelly ground to reach the water's edge and stretched his neck out to dip his face into the flow. They had been offered no food and he was desperately thirsty after his efforts to fight back the hobs. The winter flow was icy cold against his cheek and chin but it slaked his thirst and cleared his head.

Once he had drunk his fill, he turned to see that Brid had followed his example. The hobs rested and, to Caspar's unutterable revulsion, drew their knives and hacked up the body of the dead Torra Altan. Brid stared on blankly while Owain retched and the youngest soldier began to cry.

The priestess glared at them. 'Control yourselves. He is dead and feels nothing.'

Both soldiers drew closer to their older companions for comfort. The Baron looked at them grimly, knowing that there were no meaningful words of succour he could offer.

The hobs made short work of their meal and, appearing dissatisfied, three of them set off into the wood, their strange barks filling the trees and setting the birds to flight. They came back dragging a young oxen that was still kicking weakly and began to eat it alive, their pointed teeth and protruding fangs shredding through the flesh.

Caspar looked on and wondered whether they were going to be fed. By now he had no qualms about stomaching raw beef. But the hobs chewed away until their bellies were stretched taught and bulging then, without stopping to rest more, they picked up their captives and were on their way without offering them a single morsel. Caspar eventually fell asleep from exhaustion and it was dark when the hobs next stopped. He was slung to the ground and stared about him in amazement. Clearly, they were in what once must have been a small market town. The roofs of the houses had caved in and rubble littered the ground. Crisp stems of fireweed, which in the summer must have been a splendid array of brilliant red all across the town, now lay bent and withered like fallen soldiers on a battlefield.

The remnants of human artefacts littered the broken paving as if they had been tossed into the streets, pots and pans everywhere. Shreds of clothing were draped on walls or bowled into corners by the wind as if they had long ago been blown from a washing line. Caspar stared into the dark of one of the derelict houses and glimpsed small red eyes glinting back at him. Unseen creatures squealed and chattered as the hobs ranged through. Soon, the red-eyed creatures lurking in the houses began hurling rocks and other items, even broken chairs and a picture frame. Caspar only snatched a brief glimpse of these creatures but judged them to be half the height of a human. Nevertheless, he was intrigued to note that the hobs appeared wary of them.

'Holly's people,' Brid murmured. 'Belligerent, brave and dangerous but not so malicious as the hobgoblins.'

'What do you know of hobgoblins?' the hob leader snarled in the old tongue of the Caballan, jerking Brid's head up. 'We are not malicious. We are only trying to survive despite you despotic humans. You wretched creatures who never allow any space for other beings on this earth. You have used your magic to subjugate the other peoples but it is not so easy now. Now we have power. Straif, soon to be the greatest lord of the Otherworld and brother to our own earthly Blackthorn, led us to it. But it is a manmade power and not even the guardians are privileged with all its secrets. It is you wretched humans who will tell us how best to unlock its powers.'

'What are you talking about?' Brid hissed through her teeth, her face now bloodless. Caspar could see that the pain was beginning to grip her gut. 'We have no knowledge that you could possibly want.'

The creature laughed, his leathery hide rippling over his bony ribs. 'They all say that. But sooner or later we'll steal one of your kind that does.' He looked at her sideways, his sharp canine fangs pushing out through his thin brown lips as if he guessed there was something special about her. 'Gobel's minions will know what you know and then you will tell us. All succumb to Gobel in the end.'

Brid's dragon-green eyes glared back at him defiantly but she said no more.

Soon they were through the tumble-down village and working their way into thicker woods. Here, the black stems of the spiny blackthorn grew in profusion, spotted with sticky buds, promising an array of early blossom. Sloe berries littered the floor where even the birds had not dared come close enough to pluck them from the bushes. Caspar screwed his eyes up tight as they were dragged into the close-packed shrubby trees, thorns snagging his skin. One caught on his cheek and tore a deep cut back to his ear. Brid moaned in agony while the young soldiers made loud protests.

Once they were through to the centre of the thicket, the hobs swept aside a thatch of twigs covering a mound of earth. The mound was hollowed out in the centre, and dipped into a hole leading into the earth. It looked much like the entrance to a badger's set only very much bigger. They were forced down into a dank, dark world beneath the roots of the thorn trees. A thin light was provided by a number of squat, foul-smelling candles roughly moulded from hard tallow fat. Caspar looked down at his feet and the thick hide that carpeted the earth floor, coarse dark brown hair winding up around his ankles.

'Mammoth skins,' Brid murmured, her eyes black with pain.

The hob let her slump to the ground. Her face contorted into a bloodless look of horror and she began a low moan. Her dress around her loins and legs was suddenly soaked with blood.

At that moment, a number of female hobs pushed their way through the male warriors, chattering angrily and elbowing their men aside as they came. The hobs retreated rather sheepishly from their womenfolk who clucked over Brid and then scooped her up to carry her deeper into the chamber. Soon after, Caspar was surprised to hear the sounds of a crude lullaby welling up from deeper within the dwelling as the female hobs crooned over Brid.

One of the females re-emerged after a few moments, marched stiffly towards the nearest of the tall rangy males, and without warning, leapt up at him and bit his nose. He made no attempt to strike her down though clearly she hurt him.

'You made her lose her baby, you vile creature! Killing is

one thing but motherhood is sacred. You must have respect for new life,' the female shrieked.

Other females gathered around her, their red eyes stabbing out at their menfolk. Then, all at once, they turned and scurried away back into the earthworks save for the first one who had so aggressively attacked the hob. 'Bring the other prisoners,' she ordered. 'The blood of the males of her own kind may strengthen her.'

The hobs nodded uncertainly at her then one moved decisively to rip off Caspar's bonds so he could walk, and then pushed him forward, down the route that Brid had been taken. The other men were similarly treated but the Baron had little thought for them at the moment. He did not need shoving as he hurried into the lower chambers. He was pushed roughly through a small hatch into what seemed like a giant nest padded with all manner of fur and containing the knot of females attending Brid.

The Torra Altans were lined up and stood stoically still as each was ordered to bare their forearm. Caspar was relieved, now hoping that only a small amount of blood would be taken from each and he prayed, too, that the hobs' remedy would help Brid. After sniffing them over, the old she-hob selected just three of the men; Caspar, Marcus and the young lad. Caspar was proud of his companions when neither flinched as the creature bit deep into their forearms and collected the trickle of blood that issued into a small goblet.

With three huge hobs standing guard at the door, the she-hobs didn't trouble themselves about the Torra Altans, but turned their attention back to Brid.

The priestess was wide-eyed with pain and fear. Without thought, Caspar needled his way between the female hobs and, worriedly, folded her hand into his. The hobs did nothing to stop him. All thought of their other troubles was, for the moment, gone as he felt her tremble. He had never seen so much blood away from the battlefield and he was frightened for her. She talked bravely at first but then the pain deepened and she moaned and grunted like a wounded animal, curling up about her stomach and then, as she weakened, slumping back in exhaustion. Caspar stared into her glazed eyes and raised her limp hand to his lips.

'Do something! Do something!' he shrieked at the creatures around him.

The she-hobs tugged him aside and ordered him out of the way while they brought a rough-hewn wooden cup filled with a steaming brew, the sweet scent undoubtedly of bloodwort. To this mixture, the old female added the fresh blood. They sat Brid up and trickled the potion into her mouth. She coughed and spluttered but managed to drink most of the medicine.

Caspar tried to help by cupping her head but he was pushed aside and pressed down by a big hob. One of the females stood over him. She was naked bar a thin metal band around her minuscule hips from which dangled a skirt of leather thongs. Her breasts were small and wrinkled and she looked very much like the desiccated corpse of a dead child.

Her big red eyes fixed on Caspar. 'It would give me pleasure to watch one of your kind die. For too long, you have driven us out of the sun and the lush lands of this earth. And, when it is time for us to kill you, have no doubts that I shall laugh at your agony and be the first to eat your entrails. But I will not desecrate the sanctity of motherhood. This woman has had her child killed within her womb and I will make amends by ensuring she lives. But that is the only concession I make to your kind.'

'I am grateful,' Caspar said bitterly, staring over at Brid's ashen face.

Once Brid had drunk a little more of the potion, the females retreated, leaving three big hobs to guard the mouth of the chamber. Marcus and the other soldiers looked anxiously at Brid and then turned to Caspar for guidance.

Wide-eyed, the youngest asked fearfully, 'Are they going to eat us?'

Caspar shook his head. 'Of course not. They wouldn't have dragged us all this way if that was their only intention.'

'But—,' the soldier protested.

Caspar waved down the youngster's gibbering. He was intent only on Brid. Why was it that such terrible things happened to everyone he loved? It seemed his love was cursed and brought only doom and despair to those it touched. He missed Ursula so much and closed his eyes, remembering her sweet face. Then he remembered his daughter, whom he had left in her native Artor, and his heart gave out to her, wishing his love to her across all those thousands of miles. At least she would be safe amidst the protection of her people.

'But . . . but . . .,' the young soldier stammered. 'What if she dies?'

'She will not die,' Caspar said with such conviction that he almost believed his own words. 'She is very strong and more courageous than any other woman alive. Besides, the Great Mother will not let her die; she is too precious.'

'What do you know of her?' Gromo looked resentfully at Caspar. 'You've been gone fifteen years; you know nothing of what happened here in Torra Alta. You weren't here when the dragons belched their fire into the turrets, burning the men alive. You weren't here when the unicorns stole away our best brood mares. You weren't here when the first hob raiders came pouring up out of the ground and poisoned our waters. You weren't here when I lost my arm. Where were you when we all fought and suffered for Torra Alta?'

Caspar stared back at the man and could think of nothing to say in his defence. He was not eloquent enough to speak in a way that would win over these men, as he knew his uncle had done, and he saw little point in arguing. Only time and his own actions could prove his worth. He smiled a sad smile, wondering what to do next. But the men stood there staring expectantly, waiting for his lead, and he knew that he must say something.

'I don't know what I can say,' he said gently. 'You will

judge me as you see fit but I was born here and belong here. Torra Alta is my birthright; she is everything to me.'

The men averted their gaze from his deep blue eyes and, shuffling to Brid's side, knelt to pray. Caspar sighed and then joined them, crouching close beside Brid's head.

'Morrigwen would have told you that it was part of life and the circle,' he spoke softly to her. He could not bear to see her distress and was grateful that she slept. At least this merciful stupor into which she had slipped saved her the torment of grief.

He understood that torment. Ursula had lost their child and he had wept with her and then had wept alone when his wife had also died. Caspar swallowed back his memories and stroked Brid's forehead, drawing his own comfort from the action.

He was glad when the men drew back and allowed him to attend to Brid alone. He dozed on lightly through the night, waking and holding her when she woke to moan and writhe and, now, was almost glad of her cries of pain; they, at least, proved she was alive. When she lolled back into a listless stupor he was terrified that, at any moment, she would fade and slip away entirely.

The sudden chatter and croaks from the hobs, which burst into activity as abruptly as birds into their morning chorus, made him jump in alarm, and he realized he had dozed into a deeper sleep than he intended. Looking into Brid's face, he searched for signs of life. With relief, he saw that she was breathing calmly and that the hobs' potion must have had a strong effect.

'Brid,' he murmured in her ear. 'Brid, wake up.' She didn't stir and he began to panic, vigorously shaking her hand. At last her fingers weakly squeezed his.

She blinked her eyes open but, too weak to speak properly, merely grunted, 'Friend,' before closing her eyes again and drifting back into sleep.

Caspar sat there all that morning, holding her hand, waiting to see what the hobs had in store for them, and brooding on how they might escape. The men were already chattering anxiously amongst themselves.

'Listen, Sir,' Marcus whispered stiffly to his overlord. 'There ain't that many hobs out there. We can take the female hobs with very little difficulty and then, with one charge, we'll have a good chance of breaking through the male hobs above.'

'Just us seven? And carrying Brid. Don't be—'

'We should try. It would be better to die trying than to rot here.'

Brid grunted and opened her eyes. Evidently, she had been listening though she had been lying utterly still, apparently asleep. Now she made the supreme effort to stir herself. 'Marcus, listen to your baron,' she croaked angrily. 'He will steer you right. Believe me. We must wait.'

'Hush! Be still,' Caspar urged her, firmly pressing her down before turning back to his men. 'Now is not the time to escape. First we must find out what these creatures are scheming and whether they have Quinn, Guthrey and Rollo. They stole us for a purpose and so, may also have also captured the boys.'

The men shook their heads but the young lad shuffled closer. 'Sir,' he said in a hushed tone that even bore a hint of respect for his overlord. 'What will they do with us?'

Caspar smiled reassuringly. 'Don't worry, lad. Clearly they want us alive.' He could think of nothing more positive to say to keep their spirits up and so began to sing one of the ancient ballads of Torra Alta. This one had thirty-three original verses and the men were eased by his fine voice and relaxed back to listen.

He laughed to himself, thinking that they might not accept him as their overlord but they did, at least, accept him as their minstrel. A light smile covered Brid's face as she weakly sat up and took a sip of the brew that the hobs had left beside her.

A faint noise behind him made Caspar snap his head round to face the narrow entrance. A large hob poked its face in through the small earthy hole. Caspar recognized him at once as the leader of the troop that had captured them since his nose was sliced with deep red cuts where the female hob had bitten him.

'You are summoned!'

Caspar tried not to react though his mind raced. Summoned? Summoned by whom? He had little time to dwell on the matter, however, as the hobs poured into the chamber and snatched them up by heels or wrist, depending on what came to hand, and dragged them up out of the earthworks.

Caspar pulled himself upright and looked about him. With their curved knives drawn, a ring of hobs stood circling them, preventing escape. He turned, looking for Brid, who was hauled out into the open and tossed down onto the grass. Caspar scooped her into his arms.

With her head lolled against his chest, he sat as he was ordered. The men followed suit, Gromo still grunting in dissatisfaction and muttering that Torra Altans shouldn't just sit down and take orders from hobs. He and Marcus even glowered at Caspar as if this entire situation were his fault. It had been his worst childhood nightmare that, when he one day took command of the castle, he would not have the authority to lead his men or win their respect; now his fears were being realized.

The curved swords of the hobs bristled about them, catching the wispy light of the winter dawn. A shift in their stance caught Caspar's eye and he looked upward, drawing Brid's frail body tight to him, cradling her protectively as if she were a child. Within the thickest heart of the blackthorn trees, hunched together in intense debate, were two figures. The stretched fingers of their hands touched to form a circle and a golden light shimmered within. Caspar had no idea who they were but he sensed the throb of spiritual power heavy in the air.

'Brid,' he murmured, trying to rouse her so that she might witness this sight. 'Brid!' he shook her more vigorously. But she did not stir.

Chapter 6

'Where is she?' Hal roared as he cleaned his blade and stepped back from the dark pool of blood at his feet. 'Where is Brid? Get the injured out of here and have these hobs burnt! What happened here?'

No one had an answer for him and fear raged within his head. He could not lose Brid; he would die without her. The moment he had heard screams and the clash of swords, he had run as fast as he could back down the tunnels to where he had left his wife. But he had been a long way away when the first sounds of battle reached his ears and his heart had shivered when he heard the distinctive, harsh cry of the hobs.

'Brid,' he cried, thumping the pommel of his sacred sword against the stone of the cavern wall in anguish. He kicked over the remains of the hobs that he had cleaved and split, remembering to severe their hands to make sure that they could not cause any more harm. He had learnt from bitter experience that hobs took much longer to die than humans, as if their souls were more deeply rooted in this earthly life.

Even if they had appeared fully dead for half an hour, he had still seen a few suddenly leap up and strike. There was no sign of Brid and, though there were many bodies strewn on the cavern floor, some of her guards were missing too. Hal could not make sense of it.

'Bring more light. Lay out the bodies so we can account for the men,' he ordered, still holding a bleeding hob in his fist. It choked and spluttered up dark and foul-smelling blood. He had already severed its hands, but he guessed it would live long enough to tell him what he wanted to know.

The men scurried around him, helping the wounded and laying out the dead. Hal studied the grim faces but his thoughts were broken by Pip's party returning.

'My lord,' he saluted and then gaped at the dead bodies. 'Oh blessed Earth, what has happened here?'

Hal took a deep breath, trying to steady his nerves. 'Brid is missing. Beyond that, I'm not sure.' He turned and called across the cavern to a tall thin man with a hooked nose. 'Captain, see what sense you can make of it.' The man had been head of the garrison under Caspar's father, Branwolf, and Hal had come to rely on his balanced counsel.

He felt sick; Brid and Guthrey missing – and Quinn too, he reminded himself. Though the boy was not his own, he knew in his heart that he loved him. For one thing, he was so much more affable than his own son. Clearly, he and Caspar had both passed on some unwanted traits to their respective offspring.

He stood back and drew deep breaths, knowing that he would not help any of his family if he let emotion get the better of him. He had to keep calm. And thankfully, the Captain was seeing to it that the four fittest hobs were securely tied. They would surely answer their questions.

He staggered back for a moment, wiping the last traces of dark blood from the great runesword that had been entrusted to him in his youth. The sword's song, which rang through his mind, gloried in the spilt blood, but its magic did not bolster him. He had but one thought.

'Brid,' he murmured. 'Brid, I swear if these hobs have harmed you, I'll kill every one of them until the Silversalmon runs black with their blood.' He felt sick with the terror of what might have happened to her and stared into the shimmering reflections in his brilliant sword. Pursing his lips, he shook his head to clear his mind. It was no use being emotional; he must simply get her back.

Action was needed! And needed now! He turned to see that the Captain had not been idle and was questioning the men in an attempt to ascertain exactly what had happened. They were gathered about two bodies in particular.

The Captain drew Hal aside. 'These two men were in Spar's party.'

Hal swallowed at the implications. Clearly, Caspar's party had been the first to return and must have found Brid and her guard under attack. Many had been killed but, since the bodies of several within both parties were not to be found, the survivors had either pursued the hobs, which was unlikely, or had been captured.

Hal felt sick. Rollo, Quinn, Guthrey, Brid and Spar all missing within the day. He had been worried for the three boys, naturally, but had felt that Quinn would see that no harm befell them and that the whole thing was little more than childish high spirits. But first the blood on the mountain and now his wife and Spar . . . He closed his eyes on his anguish and bit his lower lip, trying vainly to rein in his fears. But his sheathed emotions finally exploded; he swung round, drew back his sword and plunged it deep into the belly of one of the defenceless hobs that the captain had trussed up.

'What do you vile creatures want with them? Where have you taken them?' the nobleman yelled into the hob's scream, stirring the creature's guts and jerking his sword to make the creature respond. 'Tell me! Tell me!'

The hob screamed on and on but the raucous song of the runesword's magic was loud and triumphant within his head, filling Hal's soul with the lust of death and destruction. 'Fear me! I am a terrifying enemy! Harm my kin and I shall not rest until the severed heads of all your kind are impaled along all the roadsides from here to Ceolothia,' he roared. 'Fear me!'

The hob stared up at him with contempt, its eyes black with fresh bruising, a trickle of thick blood wriggling out from its mouth.

'We have risen again.' He spluttered in the old tongue of the Caballan. 'We are stronger than your kind. We have returned to our ancient guardian, Blackthorn, and he has united with Straif, his lordly brother of the Otherworld.'

Hal shrank back, dragging out his sword, the tip trailing across the creature's side.

As if reconsidering his action, he knelt down. 'You will shortly die without help; trust me,' he hissed into the hob's gristly ear. 'You have nothing to lose now and everything to gain. Tell me where they have taken them and I shall help you. We have great healers. You do not have to die. Your kind is strong and we can mend you,' he lied.

'Yes, yes,' the creature croaked. 'Can speak . . .' His words were lost in the gurgling of his throat.

Warily, Hal bent closer. 'Tell me. Tell me and you shall live.'

'They . . . they . . .' The hob's voice was failing and Hal could barely hear him.

He pressed still closer, desperate now to grasp at any straw that might lead him to Brid and Spar.

'They have taken –' Its words mutated into a sudden snarl.

Hal tried to leap back as an excruciating pain tore into his ear. 'Get this thing off me!' he shrieked, snatching up his dagger and plunging it upwards into the creature's rangy ribcage, fighting for the narrow gap between the bones so that he might reach into the soft tissue beneath. But he could barely think for the acute pain from the hob's pointed teeth that were clamped tight about his ear. Finally, he twisted the short blade and found a way through the thick cartilage. He stabbed hard, and felt the creature go rigid beneath him before it slumped away.

Hal clamped his hand to his ear and felt the wet blood flood out over his fingers. 'Get these men and these creatures to the surface,' he snarled through gritted teeth.

One of the sergeants was trying to take a look at his ear

and offering him a hand but Hal shoved him away. The pain was gone for the moment; all he felt within him was a boiling heat of rage. 'Get them to the surface,' he roared again.

'But, sir, you can't abandon the boys down here. The hobs . . .'

'We've searched thoroughly. They would have heard us calling. The hobs have them too, and they are long since gone,' Hal said with certainty, struggling up the ladder ahead of the rest. He still couldn't think properly, his head filled with vile images of the hobs crawling all over Brid. Did they know who she was, who Caspar was or had it just been unhappy misfortune that the creatures had taken them?

After being hauled up by a rope to the surface, he staggered a few paces in the grey light of dawn, his lungs cramping from the sudden bite of the cold. He felt giddy and looked around him at the wounded, dying and dead.

His first impulse was to race straight back into the tunnels but hobs were at home underground and may have taken any number of routes to reach the surface. The only thing he could deduce was that they had most probably taken one of the tunnels allocated to Caspar's search party since none of the other parties had run into them. Moreover, hobs travelled fast and tirelessly. They would never catch them in the tunnels nor even be able to track them since they would have left no spoor on the smooth rock of the tunnel floor. Most probably they had already broken out into the mountains and, from there, they could have taken his wife almost anywhere.

Grunting to himself, he tried to think of a more practical plan. The surviving hobs surely knew where Brid had been taken and it was better to extract the information from them than search hopelessly.

'Get the injured home,' he ordered and then detailed others to guard the captured hobs and take them down the difficult climb to the canyon and back to the castle.

Keridwen was waiting for him at the portcullis, her face

taught with worry. 'Where is she?' the Crone asked through white lips. 'Brid: what has happened to her?'

'Gone,' Hal croaked, slithering from his horse and allowing the woman to take his arm and lead him through the courtyard to the lower hall of the keep.

'Sit!' she commanded, pointing at a stool and then, turning, clicked her fingers at a young girl who stood nearby. 'Boiling water and towels! Now!' she ordered quietly but firmly before turning back to Hal and reaching inside the loose layers of her gown to draw out a scrip of herbs.

While waiting for the water, Hal growled his orders at the men who entered. 'Get the hobs to the guardroom and see that the injured men are brought here to the lower keep where they can be tended.'

'Hush!' Keridwen urged, firmly cupping his head and twisting it to take a better look at his ear. 'The Captain has already seen to it.'

The girl soon came scurrying back with two pitchers, one steaming. Tenderly, Keridwen began the task of cleaning Hal's ear. He barely winced, oblivious to the physical pain for the anguish in his head.

'You must be careful with this,' she mumbled as she licked the end of a piece of thread and, with perfectly steady hands, threaded a fine needle. 'A hobgoblin wound turns bad very easily and he's shredded your earlobe – well, what was left of it anyway.'

Impressed by Keridwen's composure in the circumstances, Hal rubbed at the stump of his left hand, trying to concentrate on that rather than the needle pricks to the flesh of his ear.

'Keep still,' Keridwen complained.

'You're taking too long!' Hal snapped back at her.

'It takes as long as it takes,' Keridwen retorted in her usual unruffled manner.

'I need to get out there. They need me. My boys, Brid, Spar! All gone! I have no time to just sit here.'

'Brid and Spar are both strong; they will look after one

another – and the boys, if they are with them. We must think hard before we act.'

Hal suspected she was talking as much to herself as to him. 'But Brid's pregnant; she's in no condition to cope with . . . with . . .'

Hal's words seemed to drain Keridwen's resolve. Suddenly, she looked drawn and pained. After taking a deep breath, she wearily let her shoulders drop, staring down at the ground, motionless for a long minute.

'I cannot sense either Brid nor Spar's thoughts in the channels of magic; it is hard to direct and focus because of my fears for them all. But it means nothing; they may well be safe.' She put down her needle and smeared a thick honey-based paste over the wound before wrapping his head in a bandage. 'The honey will draw out the evil poison in the hob's spit,' she told him.

Hal wasn't listening. 'You must try harder to seek them with your mind. And seek Guthrey too. Tell me where they are. Try harder,' he commanded tersely, not caring that he was yelling at a high priestess.

'Not even I have strong enough powers to do what you ask.'

'Do whatever you can. I'm going to see what I can wring from those hobs.'

'Let the Captain do it, Hal,' Keridwen replied with calm authority. 'He won't get his ear bitten off.'

Hal growled in his throat, already planning how he was going to gouge out the information from these creatures and organize the men to scour the land. Aware of Keridwen's quiet footsteps just behind him, he marched out of the keep and across the courtyard, throwing open the door into the guardroom. The air was heady with the pungent smell of hob gut. Sergeant Tupper had made a messy job of carving one of them up in order to scare the other two into talking but, by the look on the Captain's face, the method had been ineffective.

Keridwen was at Hal's shoulder but did not wince at the mess of blood or the cruel treatment of the hobs. 'What have they said?' she asked quietly.

'Nothing, my lady!' the Captain replied respectfully. 'They don't seem to know whom they have taken.'

'I'll have my wife!' Hal roared. 'I will not let them threaten my family. These creatures shelter in the roots of blackthorns, is that not so? I order every one of theses trees burned.'

'And I override it!' Keridwen countered.

'You cannot! I am commander of Torra Alta!' Hal roared.

'No, Hal, not any more,' Keridwen said quietly. 'My son has returned. He is Baron of Torra Alta now. He would never allow such idiocy.'

Hal glared at her and then, snapping away his stare, erupted at the trussed up hobs. 'Where's my woman?'

'We'll tell you nothing,' one snarled in the old Caballan tongue that all from Belbidia understood well enough.

'You are in no position to refuse,' Hal hissed back, aware in the corner of his vision that the Captain had taken a long poker and was stirring the fire with it. 'Tell me where they are or you will suffer.'

'Tell us how to use the golden cup and promise to set us free and we shall tell you what you need to know,' the other hob bargained.

Hal was sick, revolted with the idea of carving these creatures up in order to draw out knowledge from them, but he had to do it. 'Just tell us what we need to know and your pain ends,' he roared. 'Where have your people taken them?'

'We shall not lead you to them,' the hob snorted, blood bubbling from its nostril.

'I'm going to cut out your kidneys and stuff them down your throat if you don't tell me. Where are they?' Hal roared until the room shook with the sound of his voice.

The nearest hob looked at him sullenly and then spat a thick green gob of saliva at him. 'You will not win, little man.

Soon my people will capture one of your kind who will tell us all we need to know.'

Enraged, his nerves strained to breaking, Hal drew the runesword and smote at the neck of the first hob. With one stroke he cleaved straight through the creature and on through the neck of the last remaining hob. The two heads thudded to the ground.

The Captain looked at Hal and said very calmly, 'Well, Sir, they aren't going to tell us too much now, are they?'

Hal shrugged. 'They weren't going to tell us anything however brutal we were and it was debasing to persist with such vile cruelty.'

Turning on his heel, Hal marched from the guardroom out into the cool, crisp wintry air.

'I thought they knew how to work the magic of the Chalice.' He looked to Keridwen for an explanation.

'The Chalice will only pass on the essential energy of an artefact a number of times before that energy becomes lessened. The spell must be renewed. Clearly they do not know how to do that.'

Hal nodded and drew a deep breath, trying to find the courage and hope to drive out his fears. Throwing back his shoulders, he gritted his teeth, clamping back his emotions only to crumple inwardly when his little four-year-old daughter came trotting out from the keep. He ran to her, scooping her up before she had a chance to see what had happened in the guardroom.

'Pa, I heard horrible noises. Pa, what's happening? Ma said she wouldn't be long; she promised to make a dress for my new doll.' The raven-haired child held up a rather ragged-looking object for Hal to inspect.

The tears sprang to his eyes. Though Brid was extremely accomplished in many ways, she was not an artist with a needle and thread. The sight of her unskilled handiwork made his heart burst with grief but he smiled at his beautiful daughter who looked entirely like him and not one bit like her mother. 'Brannella, my little one, Ma won't be long. She's out, looking after your Uncle Spar.'

Keridwen drew close and Brannella held out her arms for the woman and clung close. 'Keridwen, will you make my doll a dress?'

The woman kissed her forehead and, dipping her head, rubbed her nose against the little girl's. 'Yes, of course I'll make your doll a dress but there's something I have to do first. I'll help you if you'll help me. Will you?'

Brannella nodded eagerly, her tiny hand weaving firmly into Keridwen's fingers.

'Good girl,' Keridwen praised her. 'We've got to pound up a few herbs because some of the men are not well today.'

'Oh,' said Brannella brightly. 'Can I pick flowers with you?'

'It's winter, pet. We can choose some of the dried herbs from the herbarium.'

'Can I mash them in the bowl?'

'Of course you can, sweet one.' Keridwen cuddled her close and glanced over her shoulder to give Hal a reassuring nod.

'Thank you. I . . .' He smiled and nodded back to her, deeply grateful. If something did happen to Brid and, though his own soul would be torn asunder by it, at least Keridwen would mother his children; he had every faith in her.

Keridwen took the child off into the keep just as a slight girl slunk in through the portcullis. A tall black wolf paced at her side.

Hal kept his eye on the girl while ordering the Captain to prepare a search party immediately. She halted at the gates to the castle, and the wolf sniffed the air, turned and was gone. Her quick green eyes flitting about her, the girl crept into the courtyard, keeping tight to the shadows. Hal noted how she paused to stare long and hard at the guardroom, her head tilted slightly back as if sniffing the air, before hurrying on towards the keep.

'Isolde! Where have you been? Isolde!' Hal summoned her,

the anger in his voice barely veiled. 'You know how dangerous it is beyond the castle walls yet you persist in going out alone. I've had men out looking for you.'

Though her demeanour in general was meek and self-apologetic, she fixed him in the eye, square-on, and gave him a calm smile that was well beyond her sixteen years. Hal was uneasy at the sudden rise in the girl's aura of confidence. He had seen her hidden core of steeliness before, it seemed she reserved this side of her character solely for altercations with him.

'You are not my Master, Hal,' she said through her smile. 'I am One of the Three!'

The arrogance with which this slip of a girl treated him galled Hal to the pit of his stomach. How could such an unassuming, nervous creature find the strength of character to stand up to him?

'You might not be for much longer. While you've been roaming about the countryside, Brid's been taken by hobs.' He spoke harshly, not caring that the news would distress her.

He did not like the girl and made no bones about it. She did not like him, paid him no respect and was far too clever for her years. Moreover, she caused trouble between his boys and most annoyingly, though she had barely past her first birthday when Caspar had left, she had never forgotten him. She spoke often of his fine spirit, his courage and loyalty and how he, Hal, could learn much from his example.

'Brid! You've let hobs steal Brid! How could you?'

'We were looking for Quinn, Guthrey and Rollo.'

'And they're missing too?' She sniffed at him before running straight towards the lower keep in search of Keridwen.

Hal stared after her. He hated the fact that Brannella doted on Isolde; in his opinion, the girl was not to be trusted though, naturally, Brid did not hold with his views. 'Brid . . .,' he moaned in anguish just as the Captain appeared from the guardroom and marched towards him.

'Captain!' Hal hailed him, pleased to see that a troop of

three score men, bulky beneath their heavy bearskin cloaks, were hurrying from the keep, carrying packs and weapons. Grooms were bringing out horses, their breath steaming in the cool morning air. The courtyard rang with the clatter of hooves on cobbles.

Chapter 7

Caspar stared, his arms closing protectively about Brid's limp body.

Though the two figures stood upright and had the bearing of any normal human, obviously, they could not be. Humans did not produce a visible aura about their bodies, nor did they exude a strangely intense presence. Their ragged hair was tangled with moss, burrs and ivy, their long graceful hands like the limbs and twigs of winter trees and their skin was dark and gnarly. Caspar knew by his black skin and the wreath of thorns about his head that one was Blackthorn. Snarling and growling, there was an impression of cruelty about him that was not present in the other.

Opposite Blackthorn stood a far more beautiful being. The air smelt so sweetly of her scent that, though he had never seen her before, Caspar felt certain she must be Old Woman Honeysuckle. He stared at her and, just for a second as the sun came out from behind a cloud, he glimpsed perhaps half a dozen of her people. They were a quarter of the size of a human and all fair of face with wide set eyes and tiny sharp noses. Membranous wings fluttered at their backs.

'Fairies,' he breathed, enchanted by Old Woman Honeysuckle's magical air. Like Blackthorn, she was one of the ancient guardians of the speaking races that Brid had told him so much about. Graceful and intensely sweet-smelling like honeysuckle, she was the immortal guardian of the fairy people.

Thoughts swirled in his mind; fairies in negotiation with

hobgoblins. Dread welled up from a cold pit in the bottom of his stomach as he wondered just what these two races were plotting.

Blackthorn and Honeysuckle broke out from their glowing circle and came over to stare down at the eight captives as if they had heard the thoughts of Caspar's questioning mind.

Gesturing at his hobs and Honeysuckle's fairies, Blackthorn spoke to the prisoners. 'Here are two of the original twelve peoples who trod the Mother's soil from the very first and you,' he looked at Caspar, 'are the thirteenth. In the beginning there were only twelve but out of an unnatural marriage between the peoples of Ash and Yew came forth Man. Though a short-lived race, he reproduced at such a rate and was so callous towards all other children of the Great Mother that, soon, he chased out the other peoples from the good lands. Twelve speaking races was enough; thirteen is too many.'

Blackthorn leant heavily on his crooked staff. 'We, the old ones, the guardians, are of a different time and a different creation to the peoples of earth. The Great Lord in the sky gave of his own belly to create the Earth, and then he created us and, at the very same moment, formed also the Otherworld and our brothers, the ealdormen, who maintain order over the souls that pass through it.'

Blackthorn thumped the ground with his staff. 'Your kind sought to destroy the others and have hounded them from all but memory. Now we, the guardians, shall see to it that you will never again harm our people.'

'Put their leader in the circle!' the large hob demanded, snapping his bulging eyes in Caspar's direction. 'He will tell us what we need to know.'

Hastily, Caspar thrust Brid into the arms of one of the men before his wrists were snatched up in a hob's powerful grip. The ancient eyes of Blackthorn and Honeysuckle looked at him curiously as if they suspected there was more to him than met the eye. He was grateful that Brid had swooned again,

113

her powers therefore latent and so less detectable by those with a sense for such things.

'What do you want with me?' Caspar demanded. 'My people have been no trouble to you and merely want to live in peace in our own castle.'

'In peace! You creatures understand nothing of peace,' he spat. 'You want everything for yourselves. But now my hobs have something of yours and you will help us to unbind its magic. You may as well make it easier for yourselves by speaking forth now.'

Caspar shrugged. 'I know nothing of such matters. I am a warrior not a priest. I am but . . .' He stumbled for something plausible to say that would keep them alive. Looking anxiously around him, he realized that, as soon as these foul-smelling beasts had wrung all they could from him and his men, they would most probably be slaughtered.

His skin prickled and he dug his nails deep into his palms, his mind racing. 'I mean, I know nothing of some things but perhaps a little of others.' He wished only to buy them time. Hal would surely track them down, and Caspar was sure he would be leading a force strong enough to effect a rescue.

'You will tell my hobs how to use it,' Blackthorn snarled.

'Use what?' Caspar asked reasonably. He had no wish to antagonize the creatures further.

Blackthorn gently tugged at Caspar's hands and looked deep into his eyes. He turned his hands over and examined the thick calluses worn by a bowstring. 'You are more than a common soldier. Though you have fought hard and your body shows many scars of battle, your nails are clean and your clothes are mended. You will talk to spare your men.'

Caspar looked back blandly into Blackthorn's dark gnarly face. 'I shall tell you anything I can though I am sure my understanding will be slight compared to your own.'

'Tell the hobs of the Chalice of Önd! Forged by man, the knowledge of its magic is within your lore. I know you Torra Altans understand its powers since it was taken

114

from your castle. Tell us and I will spare you and your men.'

Although Caspar had guessed that was the artefact in question, he felt his flat smile quiver and his eyelids blink in rapid succession as he tried to still his pulse and calm the flush that he felt flooding up his neck. He stiffened his lips and drew in a deep steady breath, trying to keep the flicker of emotion from his eyes, and maintain a look of innocence. 'I have not heard of this chalice,' he protested.

Silently, he cursed Hal for letting so valuable and dangerous a possession slip from his grasp. As the thoughts formed, he noted how Honeysuckle peered at him more intently and remembered Brid teaching him many years ago that honeysuckle was the tree that represented hidden secrets.

He stepped back, withering from her stare, and tried to fill his mind with thoughts more appropriate to a common sergeant rather than those of a baron. He tried to imagine a simple mud hut, a mother with warts on her nose stirring a cauldron of porridge. He invented for himself lots of brothers and sisters dressed in rags, watching him and cheering as he and his ale-swilling friends practised the bow at the village butts. Clearly, Honeysuckle could not quite read his mind but she surely sensed that he was hiding a secret.

'There's more,' the wispy old woman murmured in a silky tone. 'Much more than he's telling.'

Blackthorn seemed to brighten at this knowledge. 'The woman,' he ordered. 'Slice off her ear and then let's see how he co-operates.'

Old Woman Honeysuckle looked at him doubtfully. 'There are better ways of finding the truth—'

Old Man Blackthorn thumped his staff down on the ground by her feet and she leapt back, the beautiful lines on her face tautening into an expression of apprehension. The flitting fairies sprang close to her side.

'Your ways are weak. I—' Blackthorn's snarling words stopped short in his throat.

115

A moment later, Caspar was no longer wondering what Blackthorn was about to say; he felt the ground tremble. A terrible trumpeting roar quaked the forest. Birds scattered into the air, squawking.

Honeysuckle and her fairies fled like dandelion clocks caught in a sudden gust of wind.

'Bind them,' Blackthorn ordered the remaining hobs.

No sooner was the task completed than the hobs turned and ran for their homes buried deep within the earth. Caspar lay where he had been left and watched as Blackthorn stepped into the thicket of the trees and disappeared from sight. The Baron wriggled and squirmed to get alongside Brid's still body and covered her as best he could with his shoulders to protect her from whatever crashed through the trees.

The ground shook with each approaching footfall; whatever it was, it was huge. The great thumping slowed and the huge trumpeting cry blasted out once more. He twisted round but could see nothing of it. Trees creaked and snapped as they were trodden under its great weight.

Then the giant beast rose up on to its back legs and thumped down, pummelling the trees at the edge of the clearing with its forelegs. Caspar felt himself being bounced off the ground with the shock. He could see vast white tusks that shredded trees and a huge hairy trunk. The creature was in panic, its small eyes rolling as it swung its head from side to side, confused and uncertain as to where to run.

What could frighten a mammoth, Caspar could not imagine. He gritted his teeth and, doing what he could to shield Brid, cringed as its feet trampled all about them, the mammoth as oblivious to their presence as he might be to an ant in his path. Owain shrieked in agony and Caspar twisted round to see that the man's leg had been crushed beneath the great weight. He feared that it might turn to trample the rest of them but it set off deeper into the thick of the blackthorn bushes. It had not gone far when the earth subsided beneath its weight. Muffled screams filtered up from the collapsed earthworks.

The mammoth screamed in alarm as it stumbled and tripped in its efforts to scramble free of the treacherous ground. At last, it heaved itself past the extent of the tunnels and crashed away into the woods. Only then did Caspar see the spear embedded deeply in its flank and realize that it was being hunted.

He twisted his arms, trying to work his hands free but the rope was too tightly knotted. Looking about at his men, he tried to figure out how they could free themselves before any surviving hobs extricated themselves from the earth.

He was also unsure of what might be hunting the mammoth, and he struggled frantically, rolling and twisting in one last effort to worm his fingers out of the knot. Straining to the point of dislocating his wrists, he thrashed and struggled but then ceased, suddenly aware that the hunter had entered the clearing. He wasn't exactly sure what he had expected but it certainly wasn't this magnificent black charger, or the ordinary man seated upon its back.

The horse carried a large number of gruesome-looking weapons. Caspar's eyes skimmed over the sword, heavy crossbow, double-headed axes and spears with huge broad barbs and others with sharp piercing spikes. Lengths of rope were coiled and looped over the back of the saddle.

He couldn't take more in as he slumped back, exhausted by the effort of his frenzied struggle against his bonds. The horse stamped closer until its feathered legs and heavy hooves were standing foursquare, uncomfortably near to his head. Though Caspar had faith that the animal would not wittingly hurt him, the iron-clad hooves were unnervingly close. To his relief, it did no more than dip its muzzle towards him, its prickly whiskers feathering over his nose and cheek. As the horse lifted its head away, he noted that the browband of its bridle was decorated with a series of unusual runes.

With delicate and surprising precision for one so heavy and

muscular, the horse stepped between the bodies of the men until it was flank on to him. Muttering to himself, the man on its back stared down with a degree of frustration before looking to the path trampled by the fleeing mammoth.

Caspar guessed that the man was trying to decide whether to help them or pursue the mammoth. 'There'll be other mammoths. Save us. For pity's sake, save us.'

'There are always people to save on this earth; I cannot save them all,' the man replied, unmoved.

'What kind of a monster are you if you choose not to save those right before your eyes?' Caspar tried to appeal to his sense of honour. 'Look me in the eyes and say you cannot save us.'

The man stooped lower on his horse, his long hair tumbling forward. His skin looked unwashed and was marked with scars. His eyes were a soft green that seemed out of keeping with his rugged face and his teeth looked strong and white. Although he still hesitated, Caspar could see his mind had been swayed. But the Baron was forced to fight back his impatience as the mammoth-hunter took his time, looking down at the men, before sliding from his horse.

With surprisingly quick hands, he slit the bonds on the injured Owain, who had passed out from the pain and lay on his side, breathing shallowly. Hastily, the stranger moved through the rest of the men before finally freeing Caspar and Brid.

The mammoth-hunter glanced anxiously towards the collapsed area of ground where the hobs' moans and shrieks filtered to the surface. An arm was already wheedling its way out through the soil and Caspar didn't think it would be long before the hobs dug their way out and were after them.

Once free, Caspar struggled upright and stared up at the long-haired man. 'Your horse. We need your horse to carry the wounded man and the woman away from here.'

'I've helped you; isn't that enough? That,' he wafted his knife along the crushed path of trees in the trail of the mammoth, 'is the biggest bull I've seen on this continent and I nearly have him. I've been hunting him for many weeks. I've bloodied him. You cannot expect me to forsake him.'

'You cannot forsake us. The hobs will soon be free and they will hunt us down if we cannot get away now. Your horse, sir! I demand it! We cannot out run them with two injured amongst us.'

'Leave your injured behind. They will surely die anyway. What will two more matter when so many others are dying across the face of this world?'

'Help us! It is in your heart to help others. I know it!' Caspar said, desperately hoping that such a statement might drag an ounce of decency from this dour man.

'What are you? A soothsayer? The last thing this world needs is another seer filling men's heads with omens and forlorn hopes.' The man's eyes swept past him and paused on Brid. For a brief second his brows knotted together as if a sudden thought had sprung to his mind. He turned back to Caspar, awaiting an answer.

'No,' the Baron said in some frustration. 'But please do what you can to get us out of here.' As he spoke, he saw the stranger's gaze flit to the collapsed earthwork behind him. Instantly, Caspar had his hand on his knife, spun round and flung it directly into the gut of the hob emerging from the soil.

'Take the horse! Take Raven!' the man said, stepping forward with his sword in one hand and a light-weight battle axe in the other as three hobs, soil clinging to their hands and faces, wormed out from the loose soil.

Caspar lunged for the stranger's horse and snatched up a hatchet and a knife before standing beside the mammoth-hunter. 'Take the horse and get out of here,' the Baron ordered his men. 'Get Brid and Owain to safety.'

'But Sir!' the youngest protested.

'Do as I say. An order is an order!'

To his relief, his men obeyed, lifting Brid and the injured

119

soldier onto the black mare. Now, at least he could concentrate on the advancing hobs. Though hobgoblins were large and much stronger than humans, Caspar was not afraid. He had fought men twice his weight and knew that skill and speed were easily as important. The stranger seemed to have both and did most of the work to cut down the hobs as they emerged.

Caspar slashed and cut, but the blow that should have gashed deeply into muscle and splintered bone failed against the thick hide. He discovered that a double-handed blow to the thin joint of the elbow was most effective but the hobs soon anticipated his stroke and knocked aside his weapon. One moved in at speed, its blade slicing upwards and dragging through the flesh of his thigh before he could twist aside. The stranger saw he was in trouble and, smiting with his axe, cleaved the hob's head.

Though pulped brains were dribbling out from its split skull, the rangy creature still managed to take one last swipe, which Caspar barely deflected. It was yet another few seconds before the creature toppled.

The mammoth-hunter was pressed up close to the Torra Altan, his sword against a hob's throat. The hob's long fingers were tight about his fists, wrestling for control. Another hob charged in, ready to stab at the wrestling stranger. Caspar flung his hatchet, and to his satisfaction, pierced the hob clean between the eyes. The creature fell, its knife still clutched in its hand as it stumbled against the mammoth-hunter, dragging the weapon through the man's calf. The stranger barely winced as he concentrated on the hob who held his hands, his arms shaking with the effort of struggling for his sword. At last, he dropped his weight to his knees, twisted the blade free, and without adjustment to his own position, stabbed upwards through the creature's leathery jowls.

The hob's mouth screamed open and a jet of blackish blood spumed into the mammoth-hunter's face. He staggered back, coughing and spluttering, wiping at his face in a frenzy as if he had been sprayed with quicklime.

Caspar caught him and dragged him back, stumbling, into the undergrowth. The two of them did their best to run, hobbling on their injured legs. Caspar refused to feel the pain. He concentrated only on putting some distance between them and the nest of hobs. Their blood would leave an easy trail and he needed to find water so that they could wash and bind their wounds.

The mammoth-slayer was stumbling awkwardly and Caspar had to grab his arm to stop him falling.

'My eyes,' the stranger yelled. 'Don't let go of me!'

Caspar gripped him firmly. 'Do not worry. A Torra Altan never leaves a friend behind.'

'So noble!' the man managed to mock through his pain.

They ran on deeper into the wintry woods that were entangled with travellers' joy and ivy, the dark green leaves of the holly trees hanging low to the ground, scratching at their faces as they went.

Caspar felt that the trees objected to their presence and worried that they would take their sudden entry into the holly woods as an act of aggression.

'Peace!' he shouted. 'We wish you no harm but are fleeing from Blackthorn's people.'

He could have been mistaken but, out of the corner of his eye, he thought he saw compact, green-skinned people drop down from the trees, waiting for their pursuers to appear. Imaginary or not, he drew strength from their help.

It was still another mile before he found water and by then he was utterly exhausted. Stumbling into the stream, he let it wash up over his boots. But he had not forgotten his new friend, cradling him in the water and sloshing it over his face to cleanse away the hobgoblin blood.

At last, the man caught his hand. 'Enough! Enough! First you make sure I lose the mammoth and then you try and drown me!'

Caspar smiled at him, glad of the water about his legs that cooled the raging heat in his wounded thigh. 'Can you see?'

The man blinked. His eyes were red raw and sweating tears but he nodded.

Caspar looked hard at him. 'Good. I have to say you look a sight better for a wash!'

'I've been in the forests a long time. A man doesn't need to wash when he's in the forest. Now, let's get onto the far bank and get my boot off so I can see what the damage is to my leg.'

They crossed the stream and, from the stillness of the forest, guessed that the hobs had not yet followed them if, indeed, any more had managed to crawl out from their underground home.

Wincing from his own wound, Caspar helped the man sit back and then heaved at his boot. He watched the stranger's face contort into a grimace of pain though not a sound escaped his lips. With gritted teeth, he looked down at the long jagged tear in his leg.

'Messy business fighting hobs,' he grumbled.

'Let the river wash it a while and then I'll do what I can for you,' Caspar assured him.

'So if you're no soothsayer, you must be a healer.'

'I'm no healer,' Caspar said indignantly. He would have thought it obvious by his actions and his skill with a weapon that he was surely a warrior, and wondered that the man did not recognize the fact.

Exhausted, his injured leg stinging, Caspar sought through his pockets for the wallet that contained items essential for survival – beyond, of course, his bow and a good knife. Unfortunately, he now lacked his bow. Opening the wallet, he saw a flint to strike a flame, a fish hook, silk thread and a needle.

'Let me have a look at the wound then,' he said calmly.

The stranger grunted and lay on his back while Caspar pressed the skin together and began to stitch the wound. To his surprise the stranger's calf muscle didn't even twitch as he pricked the skin. Impressed with the man's self-control, Caspar finally packed mud around the wound to draw out any impurities and then bandaged it firmly with a strip of cloth from the man's own shirt.

The mammoth-hunter looked at him now with intelligent but cynical eyes and was about to say something when, far in the distance, they heard the trumpeting roar of the mammoth. It was a cry of both rage and despair. Caspar watched the man's face tighten into an expression of frustration.

'This is what comes of helping people. The mammoth gets away, my horse is being mistreated by a bunch of ham-fisted soldiers and my leg's in pieces.'

'Your leg is not in pieces; it'll mend fine. And I'll give you another horse, another ten horses if you think she's been spoiled,' Caspar said generously but meaning it. He glanced at the man sideways. 'But you haven't lost your horse. You'll get her back as soon as we catch up with my men.'

'And the girl . . .,' the long-haired man added with surprising sharpness.

Disturbed by the man's tone, Caspar turned away to attend to his own wound. After wriggling out of his sodden breeches that clung to his legs, he looked down at the long curving gash to his thigh.

The man stared. 'I'm sorry. I didn't realize you were hurt too,' he said with genuine surprise.

'We Torra Altans don't like to make a fuss over an injury,' Caspar said lightly though his heart was heavy with fear for Brid. Quietly, he sat down to wash and stitch the tear.

'Torra Altans! How can anyone claim to belong to any region now? Nothing is ours any more. They have taken all,' he said heavily. 'I have lost . . .'

His voice died away as if he was not ready to speak about it yet. Knowing what it was like to lose loved ones, Caspar nodded and allowed the man his privacy. Besides, he had too many troubles of his own to become involved in other people's.

'So, Torra Altan, what is your name?' The man finally broke the pensive silence.

'Spar,' Caspar told him, offering no more than that.

The man nodded and offered his hand. 'Silas, the mammoth-slayer.'

'I'm honoured,' Caspar said, suspecting that Silas was not really the man's name since he had blinked too hard when he gave it. 'Are you rested? We must move on and find Brid. I have to get her home.'

'Home,' Silas muttered wistfully.

Caspar guessed it had been many years since he had been home.

'You say that Torra Alta is your home yet you do not live in these parts,' the man said at length as the pair limped through the forest, the tall man shortening his stride to keep close to Caspar. 'It's midwinter here and your skin has too much colour.'

'I've been away a long time.'

The man laughed. 'You are not old enough for anything to have been a long time.'

'And you are?'

Silas flashed him a quick smile and Caspar wondered if he had misjudged him. 'For me fifteen years away from Torra Alta is a long time. My soul is in that land and the land is in my soul,' the Baron added flippantly.

Silas burst into a deep booming laugh and Caspar felt suddenly humbled in his presence. He didn't know quite what to say for fear of ridicule.

They stumbled on through a forest criss-crossed with all manner of foot-worn paths. Caspar examined the narrow prints in the frozen soil, human in shape but much smaller, and guessed they had been made by either Holly's or Hazel's people. The two races were not dissimilar in stature, though Hazel's people had gentler features, lacking the taut

124

aggression characteristic of Holly's people. He was still not yet familiar enough with them to know them by their tracks. In his wife's domain of Artor, the land had been plagued by monstrous beasts rather than the smaller races of legend that now roamed the fertile soils of the Caballan.

Silas chose their route through the trees though Caspar felt they should be heading further to the north to arrive back at a point where they might pick up the trail of his men. But the mammoth-slayer seemed so confident of the way that he didn't question him for quite some time.

'Do you know where you are taking us? They did not flee in this direction.'

'Of course I know. Raven will take them to only one place; she knows where it's safe in this forest and will go there and nowhere else, whatever your friends try to persuade her to do. And if they have hurt her, I will kill them all,' he added with sudden savagery.

Caspar limped after the man, wondering what to make of him and hoping he was right to trust him. He needed to get Brid home, find his son and then retrieve the Chalice of Önd. His mind dwelt on the thought of Rollo and he bit his lip, trying to squeeze down the sense of dread that his son was dead. 'Oh Mother, protect him. He is wayward and vulnerable and he needs Your love.'

The idea that his tough aggressive son was actually vulnerable seemed laughable but he knew it was true. He understood that Rollo felt confused, abandoned and resentful towards him. The knowledge deeply saddened Caspar and yet there had never been anything he could do to persuade Rollo that he cared deeply for him.

The midwinter's day was gloomy and sapped of colour. Mists drifted up from the brooks where platforms of ice spanned out from the banks and hovered an inch or so above the rushing water, bearing testament to a higher water level that had since subsided. The ground crunched beneath Caspar's weary feet and he feared for both Brid and his son out in this weather; Brid because she was weak after losing her baby and his son because he had so little experience of this cold climate.

At last, Silas made his way to a single yew around which the mists clung tightly, the old boughs lazing on the ground. Breathing in the heady scent from the old tree's foliage, he saw how the air was still beneath its shelter. Caspar had a peculiar sense that time also moved more slowly about it.

Silas drew down one of the springy branches and, with his knife, cut off a long thin length to make a staff. The man stooped to strip the fine long lengths of bark from the wood and then paused for thought, glancing very briefly at Caspar, before carving runes onto the bare reddish wood.

'Silas, the mammoth-slayer,' Caspar grunted feeling a little light-headed from his injury and lack of food, 'you know much about runes.'

'So, Spar, you, who claim no greater name nor title, you recognize runes when you see them, is that not so?'

Caspar nodded guardedly. 'You have written a rune of strength to help you walk. Not a great spell but a spell nevertheless.' He also noted that Silas had carved other runes onto his staff of which he did not know the meaning but he didn't emphasize his ignorance by admitting to it. He had noted, however, that they were the same runes which had adorned Raven's bridle.

'Why would anyone use a great spell when a simple one is so often more effective,' Silas said with a light smile.

Caspar shrugged his shoulders in agreement. 'Too true, friend.'

'You are too free with your offer of friendship,' the man chided him again with a grin.

In an unguarded moment, Caspar warmed towards the man, but at the back of his mind, he was aware that Silas watched him all too carefully, studying his response. The Baron had a small but unshakeable feeling that he was being manipulated or tested in some way. The more he thought on it, the more he decided it was likely that Silas had cut the runes to test his knowledge.

The ground rose steeply and Caspar had to take it slowly for fear of splitting open the wound on his thigh. Silas, however, helped by his staff, strode on with ever more fluid strides.

At the top of a hill the strong wind had kept the saplings low and sparse. In the far distance, Caspar could just make out a hazy spire rising out of the shady forest. He recognized it at once as the spire that topped the cathedral in Farona, Belbidia's fine capital that was now an enclave within the hobgoblin forests. Hal had explained that, though word had occasionally come through of King Rewik's whereabouts, there was little hope that he could unite the nation now that the barons had ruled themselves for so long.

Belbidia had long been a powerful nation, its economy rooted in agriculture and the resultant international trading. The country was divided into seven baronies. The King held the Barony of Faronshire in the heart of the continent. It was a region ideal for wheat production and was responsible for much of Belbidia's wealth.

Jotunn, lying immediately south of Torra Alta, was home to Baron Oxgard and his herds of beef cattle. He had long quarrelled with his eastern neighbour, Old Baron Wiglaf who raised herds of dairy cattle.

During Caspar's youth, his uncle Gwion had colluded with the Vaalakans, a barbaric tribe north of Torra Alta, to topple Belbidia. The subsequent war triggered the release of the fearsome animals of legend, such as the dragons, taurs, hobs and griffins into Caballan. The old order had crumbled. Overrun by hobs, King Rewik was unable to assert his authority over the kingdom and the baronies were now independent states under the rule of the Barons.

Caspar lowered his gaze from the distant spire and frowned at the undulating landscape, mists swirling in the hollows. He rubbed his eyes uncertainly. He must be more tired than he thought because he found it impossible to focus, the distances blurring and merging. One second he could see wrinkles of valleys lying between him and a prominent rounded hill; the next minute the valleys smoothed and merged, the distances shortening.

The sense of disorientation only increased as they set out for a village they had seen from their vantage point. The tightly huddled dwellings set about a frozen pond had seemed close-by and yet it took an extraordinarily long time for them to hobble towards it as, after each rise, they were met with another unexpected one. He frowned and rubbed at his temples, wondering what had caused this distortion of his senses.

At last, as evening drew near, they pushed through a thicket of hazel and hawthorn trees to find they were suddenly right amongst the deserted buildings. Ivies scrambled over the houses and clawed off the roofs that were dipped and sagging like horses too old for the saddle. Silas led him towards a low-towered church overshadowed by yew trees and standing atop a small knoll.

Silas smiled. 'She is here.'

'Brid?' Caspar asked, his heart leaping into his throat.

Silas shook his head. 'No, no . . . though indeed she must be as well. No, I meant Raven. She is here; I can smell her. I have always been able to smell her. She is here.'

Caspar, himself, was devoted to his own horse but he had never met anyone quite so obsessively fond of his mount and his eyebrows rose at the man's peculiar words. They hurried on, slipping between the interwoven boughs of the trees. At once, Caspar felt a light-headedness overwhelm him as the sweet, intoxicating smell of yew filled his nostrils.

The mammoth-hunter used his staff as if he were wielding a double-handed axe to cleave a path through the misty air and push back the interlocking branches. Caspar did not like the look of the mist though it parted before Silas, and they limped through it without any ill effect.

While the long-haired stranger strode ahead, Caspar hobbled up towards the church where the yews were even more tightly packed. The sudden caw of a crow made the hairs on the back of his neck stand on end and he stopped short to take stock of the eerie surroundings. The great double doors at the west end of the church were banging in a stiff breeze and, for a moment, he fancied he could hear the moans from the graves that were packed tightly together in the courtyard. So many deaths, he thought – and so many lives. He stepped onto the stone-flagged threshold of the church and halted in alarm.

He had expected to see a font, pews, a pulpit and an altar but there was none of these things. Instead, the church was filled with mist. Caspar blinked. 'This is no shrine to the New Faith.'

Silas the mammoth-slayer laughed. 'You are acutely observant,' he mocked.

The strange man lowered his staff into the mist and Caspar suddenly sensed an ageless wisdom within this being. Again, the mists parted. Caspar was certain that, now, he would see the normal interior of a church but, instead, the mist seemed to dissolve away the stone fabric of the church walls that melted away into the semi-circle of yews at his back, revealing an airy glade before him. He felt soft grass at his feet and looked down to see a dark green lawn thick with all the lushness of spring. Within the glade bubbled a font of clear water that filled a shallow pool, the pebbles and water a golden hue reflecting the light of a bright sun overhead. The mist still lapped around the pool's edge and curled about the edges of a large slab of flat stone.

Caspar looked at Silas in bewilderment. He did not know what to make of this and thought, at first, that they might be at some gateway to the Otherworld. He feared he would be sucked into the dimension beyond life. Taking a deep breath to regain his composure, he said steadily, 'This place is not real.'

'So many things in life are not what they seem,' Silas said obscurely, stepping forward.

As the mists swirled and drew away from the edge of the pool, spilling over his calves and thighs, Caspar saw that there was a huddle of people resting beside the waters, their backs leaning against the sides of the low stone.

Immediately, he broke out into a run, oblivious to the pain in his thigh. 'Brid, Brid,' he shouted and stopped short as he saw her cradled in a nest of bearskins, one of the young soldiers stooping attentively over her.

Caspar staggered to a halt before his men and flung himself down beside her. 'Is she well? Tell me she has stirred.' he said, clutching hold of Brid's hand.

One soldier nodded and was about to speak but was silenced as Brid slowly turned her head and blinked her eyes open.

'Hush, Spar,' she murmured, a flicker of a smile on her pale lips. 'I'm as well as I might be,' she said drowsily, her eyes only half opening and her grip weak against Caspar's hand. 'I've lost my baby, Spar. A part of my soul has died with her.' She slumped back and closed her eyes, breathing heavily.

Caspar sat, looking into her face, wondering what must be done now. He sent the young soldier to fill a gourd with fresh water and drew hope that, with some help, Brid was able to sip a little before slumping back down in exhaustion. Knowing that he had done everything he could for the moment, he looked to his men. Owain, whose leg had been crushed, lay still, wrapped in a blanket and Caspar guessed he had been dead a few hours. The others looked wan and frightened but shuffled up closer.

'You came back for us, my lord. You didn't desert us,' Gromo said as if he were surprised but also intensely relieved. 'You came for us even into this misty world of nightmares.'

'Of course I came back for you. We are all men of Torra Alta, are we not?'

'Indeed, sir,' he saluted smartly. 'What are your orders, sir?'

Caspar was relieved that the resentment and suspicion that the men had held towards him was beginning to ebb but he had no idea what he was supposed to do now.

'How do we get home, Sir?' Marcus asked. 'Lord Hal will be sending out further search parties and more men will be lost if they trace us here.'

'We shall go home through . . . through the . . .' Caspar looked behind him and raised his hand pointing to the archway that had been filled by the great double doors at the west end of the church but in their stead stood two yew trees.

'We're lost.' Caspar unwittingly let the words escape his lips and then immediately regretted it. He looked to his men. 'Do not worry; Silas, the mammoth-slayer, will lead us out of here, I'm certain. Silas will . . .' But where was Silas? He looked west across the glade towards a rank of trees and noted the sleek black mare. She was grazing warily at the very edge of the glade, her ears laid flat. As he watched, she threw up her head and trotted off smartly into the trees. Silas was running after her, evidently trying to catch the horse. But she was not to be trapped.

'Silas! Silas!' he shouted but the man vanished into the trees. Caspar was about to send one of his men after the stranger when he decided against it. There was something about the mammoth-slayer that he still could not trust and he thought that they were probably better off without his help.

The Baron sat down heavily. Putting his head in his hands, he rubbed his temples, trying to rid himself of the confusion and self-doubt that this disorientating world forced on him. 'No matter, I am sure I can find the way,' he said, turning to squint at the yew trees that were gradually becoming black shapes in the growing twilight. He couldn't quite focus his mind to work out how to proceed. Surely, the way was just beyond the trees.

His men were looking at him expectantly and he realized he had not given them adequate guidance. He smiled reassuringly. 'It's just the other side of the yew trees. Go and take a look.'

The men shook their heads. 'No, we've already looked and it's too easy to get lost. In fact, the young lad still hasn't returned.'

Caspar groaned. There were ways of organizing search parties and procedures to follow, and losing men was not one of them. The throbbing pain in his leg was spiking up his side now and he wondered if his injury was having an adverse effect on his mind. He looked to Brid but she was in no fit state to help.

'I'll go and look myself,' he said. 'I've just come through the solid doors of a church so I know it's there.'

The men nodded and followed a couple of steps behind as if expecting the eyes of their overlord to perceive far more than their own had been able to do.

Caspar limped up to the yews and stared. He was still hoping to see the double doors but, instead, he saw a pleasant vale that gently dipped and rose, and a glassy lake lying in a hollow. White cattle with long horns were grazing at the water's edge, their shadows long in the failing light. To the east, the ground rose up to where nine barrows dominated the skyline.

'I told you, sir,' Gromo complained. 'There ain't no way out of this unnatural place.'

Chapter 8

The strong sweet smell of blood curled up from below.

She groaned in pained frustration. Muscles twitching, her wing tips quivered as she restrained herself from gliding down to take her fill. Snapping her mouth shut, she shook her neck, the ruff of scales at the base of her head fanning out and glinting in the golden sunlight.

The scavengers of the night skies had been at work on the plains below; she trembled with rage that she must allow such creatures to live but then placated herself with the thought that she would slay them once they had fulfilled their purpose. She had little time now to hunt down and destroy the ones that dared intrude upon her mountain territory but, naturally, would slaughter them if they crossed her path. But those on the plains she must let live: they helped Gobel. Soon he would find one with the knowledge to make his kind strong enough to oust the thieves from the caverns of her home.

If she had nested in her true home, then her boy, her magnificent Aurek would still be alive; the only golden dragon to be born since the Return. Red dragons! She spat in disgust. That was all she had borne since and many of those she had eaten in revulsion at their puny struggling. She reconciled herself that at least they weren't green, like the scavenging dragons on the east coast but, still, they were not worthy of her. She missed her golden son. Her mighty son! After so many years the grief still raked through her.

Looking disgustedly over the plains, her sinuous, armoured neck stretched forward and her barbed tongue flickered out, tasting the air. A ball of rage exploded in her gut and tore up her throat, becoming a roar of dreadful ferocity that turned the crisp air to a misty fug; below her was a feast that she could not join. So much blood. Spilt blood. Putrid guts. Her particular favourite was to press her claw slowly down on a man's skull until it cracked open so that she could lap up the brains. But she must remain up here in the clouds and stay hungry. The wars must go on; she was not strong enough to oust the usurpers alone. No, Blackthorn's people must do it for her; they were weak, wretched creatures but they were numerous.

Gobel's warriors must grow in strength as she had promised Blackthorn. Her great bulk stooping out of the sky would not help them find the ones with the knowledge they sought. No, she must be satisfied with the offerings. Dead meat! No joy of the kill! But Gobel insisted that it incited more terror amongst the quiet hidden ones than indiscriminate killing and she believed him. If the wretched hob could find no one amongst the usurpers then, surely, the hidden ones would find the knowledge. Gobel's warriors were too weak without it.

She wondered why Gobel had taken so long to visit her today. Where was the creature? She snarled savagely, wondering how long her temper would hold. She did not like him particularly but he was a means to an end and she wouldn't make the mistake of trying to eat one of his kind again; the taste was terrible. And since she couldn't eat him, she was happy to join with him to attain her purpose.

'Gobel,' she snarled, the vapour from her flaring nostrils shimmering the air before her. 'Bitter little creature, where are you?'

Her nostrils sucked in air to get a whiff of his sour smell. She sighed and relaxed. He was coming. She hoped he brought news. There was no other pleasure for her now. Smacking her tail into the wall of rock beside her to relieve her tension, she pushed her great rump into the air to balance herself as she stretched her neck down and forward. Rocks crashed about her and loose scree gave way beneath her immense weight. With claws spread wide, she gripped firmly to the brink.

'Gobel,' she purred as his spindly hand appeared at the base of the rock. 'Where are they? Have you not found one yet?'

She knew at once by the over-stretched smile on his narrow leathery face that he had failed her. He had merely a gift, some trinket in his long bony fingers. Sharply, she sucked in her breath, thinking to spume flame at the miserly creature and vaporize his hand and the trinket but she managed to swallow down the ball of flame.

To Gobel's credit, he had not flung himself down on the ground to tremble and puke like any other two-legged creature would have done in her presence. Instead, he stood his ground, his teeth clenched and his brownish lips now grey and bloodless. The trinket dropped from his trembling hands but he did not crumble.

'Brave creature,' she hissed at him, her long neck snaking forward to sniff at the gift.

With remarkably precision for one so large, she thrust out a long claw and snagged the offering. Dropping it at her feet, she sniffed at the gold disk with the design of a rampant lion wrestling a serpent on it and then fixed her black eye on him, her eyelids blinking upwards. The lids bore no eyelashes but were merely leathery hoods, scraping over the glistening, beady balls of her eyes.

Despite her disappointment, she gave Gobel a wrinkled smile, long yellow fangs protruding irksomely from her jaw. 'So, my little two-legged friend, this by the smell of it is the token of a proud and mighty man. His people are destroyed, I hope.'

Gobel allowed a lopsided smile to crease his face. 'He was a great man. We destroyed his armies and ripped this from his grasp. We have his lands and left his people nothing.'

She reared up, threw back her head and filled the bladder at her throat before giving out a great bellowing roar that echoed between the cloud-shrouded peaks. 'What do I care about this man?' She tossed the trinket aside. 'He has not stolen my home.'

'No, no, but we are still looking and there are new plans regarding the hidden ones,' Gobel struggled to appease her wrath.

'Plans! There are always more plans and they always come to nothing. All I get is cold meat.' A grumble churned in the beast's great belly.

'Ah, but this time you can you can use your fire.'

The dragon snapped her head up and then snaked it down towards the mud-green hob and let her tongue slide out to lick his face. 'Will I get to hear them scream? Shall I taste fresh blood?' A pleasured gurgle rippled through her long throat.

The hob grinned smugly and nodded. 'And there are a number of humans that must be destroyed. Just the males though,' the hob began but the monstrous lizard had lost patience with lengthy explanation.

Delightedly, she snapped her jaws. 'We shall have them all soon, Gobel.' Her tongue coiled about her four protruding fangs and ran along the razor edge of the incisors at the front of her mouth. 'You have done better than I thought, Gobel. Much better!'

A half-smile flickered onto the hob's narrow face but was instantly gone as the great queen's snout snapped in front of his nose.

'But if you could take so much from such a powerful man, why can't you reclaim my nest for me? It is all I want. It is mine and I shall have it!' She crashed down and the little creature was knocked to the ground. 'You are failing me. I should knock you right off the mountain. I want my home back. I want my son back! Straif has promised me! He is one of the great lords of the Otherworld, master of souls, and he promised me!'

She twisted round, her great tail flailing out and the barb skimming over Gobel's head as he flattened himself to the ground. Snarling, she crept back into the cave. Once alone, she curled up around a single claw half the length of her own and nestled her head against the split grey nail. It was all they had found of him.

'My son, my sweet son. You will sit on the throne yet!'

Chapter 9

'Quinn! Quinn, are you all right?' Rollo hissed into the sudden gloom of the cavern. 'Quinn!'

A groan rose from the direction that he had last seen Quinn and he stared into the dark, afraid to move. With hands stretched out in front, feeling his way through the thick blackness, he edged slowly forward.

Each new step brought him confidence; though he could not see, his sense of hearing and touch were suddenly acute enough to compensate. His hand touched a huge bone the thickness of a heavy branch and his head swam with the image of a crested golden dragon, its scales gleaming in a crisp bright sky. The winged beast twisted and spun in the air like a hawk enjoying the freedom of the heavens, diving, swooping and gliding with magnificent skill.

'I am lord of the heavens,' he felt the words burst from his mouth. 'I am the son of kings.'

'Rollo, what is the matter with you? Help me!' Quinn called to him, the edge to his voice betraying his pain and fear.

Rollo remembered himself and took a deep breath to calm his giddy head, only to be overwhelmed with the scent of man and blood. Nostrils flaring, he picked his way through the skeletons and stooped down, beside Quinn.

'I am sorry I lost the torch,' the Torra Altan said, his voice strained with the effort of suppressing his pain.

'It was burning low anyway,' Rollo said kindly. 'Where are you bleeding?' he asked, the smell strong in his nostrils. He was more frightened by his heightened senses than he was by their predicament.

'Bleeding? I don't know! It's just my leg,' Quinn groaned. 'It hurts!'

Rollo felt for Quinn's thigh and slid his hand down onto the blood-soaked leather until his fingertips stopped up against a thin spike of dragon bone that had broken off a dragon's spine. Gingerly, he felt all around and discovered the entry and exit point of the spike just above Quinn's knee.

Quinn was sucking in his breath through his teeth, evidently in considerable pain though he did not whimper.

Rollo was impressed. 'I can't pull it out here in the dark,' he admitted. 'It might make the bleeding worse. I'll strap it and you'll have to limp on it like that. Can you do it?'

'I can!' Quinn insisted stoically. 'Now just get us out of here!'

After doing his best to bandage the wound with a strip of his shirt, Rollo pulled the youth up, gripping his arm to steady him. Carefully, they picked their way through the debris, the bones like a forest about them, creaking and stirring.

'I'm sorry I lost my temper with you,' he apologized, trying to keep his companion's spirits up. 'And I'm sorry I got you into this mess.' With his fingers, he had determined that the splinter of bone skewering Quinn's leg was wedged up against the youth's kneecap; he had to be in excruciating pain though he was limping along without complaint.

'I'm sorry too,' Quinn grunted through clenched teeth. 'Lord Hal will slaughter me if I come home without Guthrey.'

'No. He'll be pleased that at least you are safe,' Rollo said with encouragement, forcing the horrible truth from his mind that Guthrey was already dead at his own hand. There was something about Quinn that made him feel comfortable about himself and he felt less need to air his more caustic nature in the youth's presence.

There was a long silence that Quinn eventually broke.

'No,' he breathed into the darkness. 'He'll be pleased to be rid of me.'

'Why on earth?' Rollo asked.

'I told you; I'm not his son. I don't even know who my father was.'

'So Hal married Brid even though she already had a son by another man!' Rollo blurted.

'Hal loved my mother enough to forgive her. He tolerates my presence only because of her.'

'No one could fail to love your mother,' Rollo admitted. 'She is very beautiful and her eyes are almost frightening yet full of hope.'

'Isolde is like that too,' Quinn murmured, leaning heavily on Rollo, 'though few see beyond her meekness.' He grunted with pain. 'We must have been walking all night. Do you think it's far now?'

'I don't think so,' Rollo said plainly. He had forgotten that he could not see. Somehow, he was able to form a picture in his mind of the smooth tunnels around him. He stopped abruptly at a point where they felt a sudden breeze gushing in from a side tunnel and leapt back, dragging Quinn with him.

'But that must be a way out to the surface. I can feel the fresh air,' Quinn complained.

'Quiet!' Rollo's nose twitched and his mouth flooded with a bitter taste that made him want to gag. 'Hobs,' he warned.

The two of them pressed themselves back against the rock and Rollo concentrated on calming his breathing. His mind was confused. It was insane but part of him wanted to race out and attack. Part of him thought no more of the hobs than if they were rats infesting his home. The other part considered them lethal and treacherous and he struggled to listen to this more sensible part. At least the wind from the surface was blowing towards them and carrying their scent away from the hobs.

The hobs moved on and the sound of their cackling and

140

low barks gradually faded away. Now that the way was clear, Rollo and Quinn staggered on as quickly as Quinn's injury allowed. The ground sloped upwards and within minutes they were approaching the surface. Rollo felt his keen sense of smell leave him and the strange images that had filled his head retreated like the tide as sunlight lit the tunnel ahead. He looked at Quinn and noted the grim lines of his mouth as the Torra Altan girded himself against his pain and looked down gravely at the horrible point piercing his knee.

An intertwined thatch of juniper bushes clogged the mouth of the tunnel and Rollo pushed ahead so that Quinn could have a clear path. The sun was high overhead and more time had passed than he had reckoned. It was then with great surprise that, once through the juniper, he found himself face to face with a young girl. Her bright golden-green eyes gleamed at him from a heart-shaped face framed by reddish blond hair that curled luxuriously around her cheeks and neck. She wore a simple dress that might once have been emerald green but was too mud-stained to be worthy of that description.

'Isolde! Issy, I don't believe it! How did you get here?' Quinn gasped.

She shrugged, patting the yellow-hearted ruby strung about her neck. Rollo noticed immediately that though hers was a bright, dazzling jewel and the stone about Quinn's neck was a dusky grey, they hung from identical chains. Rollo wondered what their significance was and what the girl meant by her gesture.

'You are never hard for me to find and I knew I had to get to you before Hal did.' Her head tilted to one side and she flashed Rollo a nervous look of suspicion, before fixing her gaze back on Quinn. A relieved smile relaxed her nervous face as she reached forward, offering him her hand for support.

'You'll need more than a wound like that to avoid Lord Hal's wrath,' she teased softly. 'He's likely to sling you from the top turret this time.'

'Oh, Issy, he'll do worse – and I'll deserve it – when he hears about Guthrey,' Quinn said heavily.

'What's happened?' Isolde's wide green eyes blackened in alarm.

'A great ravenshrike,' Quinn said gravely, not needing to say more.

'Did they take him alive?' the girl asked, her eyes urgently searching Rollo's face. 'A few have escaped their clutches before now.'

Rollo felt his stomach knot; a very small part of him wished that the unfortunate youth was already consumed so that all evidence of his crime was completely destroyed. Yet, at the same time he wanted his cousin to be alive and safe. He did not want to be guilty of killing his kinsmen; but there was no possible way to undo what he had done.

The girl's lower lip was beginning to tremble and the colour ebbed from her hollow cheeks.

Quinn clutched her hand. 'I know,' he said softly, clearly unable to express his distress. 'But there was nothing Rollo nor I could do. We simply have to hope he is still alive and that we can find him before it's too late. Oh, Issy,' he squeezed her hand tight, 'I thought we would be lost under the earth forever, but Rollo somehow knew the way.'

'Rollo . . .,' she echoed, studying the young prince guardedly, her head shyly lowered. It was all the welcome she seemed capable of making.

'I didn't really do anything; it was just luck,' Caspar's son said hastily, still fearful of the strange things that had happened to him down in the dark.

'Let me look at your leg,' Isolde begged Quinn, ignoring Rollo as if he had suddenly ceased to exist.

He looked back at her and thought that, despite the grubby face and apologetic droop to her head, there was true loveliness there. Her whole presence seemed to swell to fill his vision and he was dazzled by the light reflecting off the jewel strung around her neck.

'Sunlight,' he murmured stupidly, the exertion of the last few hours suddenly catching up with him. Feeling more exhausted than he had ever felt in his life, his legs gave way and he folded down into the crisp cold of the frosted grass.

'Everybody's looking for you. Well, that's not true,' she amended. 'Everybody *was* looking for you.'

Quinn grunted. 'So Hal has given up on us already?' There was a touch of hurt in his voice and Rollo felt for him. He understood that Quinn wanted Hal's approval as a father. He, too, wanted Caspar's approval but could see no way of winning it; his father had done nothing but criticize him his entire life.

'No, no, that's not true. It's just ... just ...' Isolde faltered, all lightness gone from her voice and it was as if a hundred candles had been blown out with one breath. 'Hal is looking ...' Her voice trailed away. She swallowed and at last managed to say, 'He's looking for your mother.'

Quinn went white and Rollo understood all too acutely the Torra Altan's shock. His words came hoarsely, 'What do you mean, he's looking for my mother?'

Isolde took a deep breath and looked at her hands. 'She was with the search party that followed you into the earth. She and Baron Caspar were taken by hobs.'

Rollo felt as if a spear had been jabbed into his side. 'Father ...' The blood drained from his head and he flopped down onto his hands, clutching at the ground to keep himself steady.

'Hobs,' Quinn repeated stupidly.

From where she was kneeling by his impaled knee, Isolde looked up and sniffed at him, her thoughts unfathomable. She shook her head and spoke in that very soft voice of hers as if talking only to herself. 'Many have been taken by hobs in the last months. Though the wretched creatures have stolen the Chalice, it appears they were able to work its magic for only a short time before its spell ran dry. They seek out people, trying to force them to divulge the secrets of the

Chalice. Perhaps it was their intention to capture Keridwen, Brid or even myself in the hope that we would give them the knowledge they seek. At any rate, they have Brid.' Her lip trembled and she bit it hard. Stiffening her shoulders, she focused on Quinn. 'Now, if you can, I need you to lie on your side so I can look at the back of your leg.'

Once the long-limbed youth was looking away from her, she gestured at Rollo to help her by firmly holding Quinn's leg down on either side of the knee.

'I'm just going to cut away some of your breeches,' she said, though she didn't reach for a knife but placed her hand on the thicker end of the sharp bone and nodded at Rollo, warning him to be ready. With remarkable strength for so slight a girl and with brave determination that Rollo would not have guessed she possessed, she pulled hard, ripping the dragon's bone from his leg.

Quinn gasped and doubled up to clutch his leg, his face puce with agony, his scream swallowed in a series of groaning gasps. Panting, for self-control, his breath hissed through his gritted his teeth.

'Hobs,' he squeezed the word out. 'What will they do to her? If anyone harms Mother . . .' Clearly, no words could express his feelings.

Still pressing Quinn down so that Isolde could work to clean the wound, Rollo struggled to think clearly. He wished he had some of his sister's skill. She would have been able to find Brid and Caspar in moments. She would peal out that extraordinary cry of hers and every bear for miles around would rush to do her bidding. But he was not the one born with the gift; he was just a plain ordinary youth whose birthright was to inherit the cold, wretched barony of Torra Alta – a region infested with treacherous creatures and where everyone hated him.

Having done her best to clean and bandage the wound, Isolde sat back onto her heels and wiped the blood from her hands on the hem of her dress. She looked pensively at the knee, gazed north into the mountains and then south to where they dropped away, green slopes stretching out beneath the snowy caps.

'We must have travelled much further than I thought,' Quinn managed to force the words out through his gritted teeth.

Isolde nodded. 'We're much closer to Jotunn here. I suggest we head for Baron Oxgard's new stronghold on the Jotunn border. The wound may well fester and it'll be very hard going back through mountains crawling with hobs. And the smell of blood will draw the ravenshrikes quicker than anything.'

'But Guthrey; we have to go after Guthrey,' Quinn protested.

'I'm afraid we have to get you mended before we can head after him,' the girl objected.

Guilt rose like bile into Rollo's throat but, still, he had no intention of going after Guthrey – he knew there was no point. His priority was his father.

'No!' Quinn protested.

'But your leg, Quinn. First—' the young priestess argued.

'No, Isolde, we have to find Guthrey and then my mother!' Quinn interrupted her and she shut her mouth tight. Her eyes, however, flitted quickly over her hands and Rollo had the sense that her mind whirred behind those mysterious eyes.

'You must get to safety,' Quinn urged the young priestess. 'The hobs will want you just as much as they want Brid. If you divulged—'

'I would never divulge anything,' she said with hurt.

'Not even to save Brid? I wonder,' Quinn retorted and Rollo saw the girl uncomfortably reconsider her position. She didn't seem to know what to do or say. Quinn continued, 'For all our sakes we must take you to Jotunn.' The injured youth nodded south towards the wooded plains. 'You are right; we cannot risk the mountains with my leg like this, but we shall get help there. Baron Oxgard will send men to look for Guthrey.'

Rollo chewed at his tongue, his thoughts tumbling, twisting and knotting together in a hectic jumble. He wanted to go straight after his father but could see no way that he could do that without a guide. Silently, he admitted to himself that he must stay with Quinn and Isolde. They needed him as much as he needed them.

'I don't know how you're going to walk on that leg,' he said, just to emphasize the fact.

'I'll walk,' Quinn grunted determinedly. 'Both my mother and Guthrey are in peril; you think a little pain is going to stop me walking.'

'You won't need to walk. I found your horses; they're tethered in the valley close by,' the young girl explained.

Rollo looked at her in amazement. 'You mean a girl like yourself handled two war-horses in terrain and conditions like this! You managed to lead Firecracker?'

'The red one?' Isolde asked, offering her hand to help Quinn to his feet and letting Rollo support him under his other arm.

'Yes, the red one!'

'Oh no, he wouldn't be led. I had to ride him and lead the other one.'

'You rode Cracker!' Rollo exclaimed, wondering how the girl had really managed to bring the horses to this point.

She ignored his sarcastic tone and, together, they struggled to help Quinn down a narrow gully and through a small wood. The floor was crunchy with pine needles and fir cones under foot before they broke out into a snow-filled valley to see the horses.

'Do you think you can ride?' Rollo asked Quinn

Quinn looked at him as if such a question were an insult. Isolde held Quinn's horse still while Rollo pushed the youth up into the saddle. Quinn winced, but, after a moment, he sat firm, teeth gritted hard. Once he was settled, Isolde nimbly climbed up behind him, taking care not to knock his injury.

Rollo was left to take Firecracker who snorted at him in sudden alarm. He knew the animal was difficult but he had never known him to be quite so aggressive towards him. The horse half-reared, lashing out with its hooves.

'He smells the touch of the dragon on you,' Quinn guessed. 'You'd better swap with Issy until the smell wears off.'

Rollo was humiliated. He was furious that the horse would not obey him but quickly realized he was not going to win and would make less of a fool of himself if he capitulated now.

'Are you sure you can manage him?' he asked the girl.

Slipping from Quinn's horse, she cast him just the briefest look of indignation, her eyes unwilling to make contact. Then, she focused her attention on the stallion, and began murmuring softly. The Oriaxian purebred stretched out his nose to snuffle her hand.

Rollo watched the girl swing herself effortlessly up into the saddle, impressed that she was not in the least unsettled by Firecracker leaping to the side and bucking. He would have expected any girl to fling her arms around the horse's neck and squeal but she merely laughed and soothed Firecracker's neck. The unbecoming look of self-doubt that haunted her face vanished as the horse strutted and danced, the great power in his hocks appearing to make him float as he covered the ground.

They had to pick their way carefully through the valleys, the horses labouring through heavy snow. Soon, they were beneath the canopy of tall trees and, although it was gloomier in the wood, at least it broke the chill wind. The wood stretched on southwards. Here, the ground was only recently claimed by the forest and the trees were no more than whippy saplings. After a while, Rollo realized that shapes were flitting through the young trees and undergrowth that smothered what once must have been pasture. He leant forward to whisper into Quinn's ear.

147

'To our right and left,' he warned. He had seen the movements amongst the shadows and was perplexed that the others hadn't noticed it.

'Only wolves,' Quinn dismissed them with the barest of interest, his teeth gritted against his pain and his eyes strained and distant.

Once on flatter ground, they picked up the pace, Firecracker stretching ahead. 'Shouldn't we be concerned about wolves?' Rollo asked, shouting above the thump of the horses' hooves and the bellow of their lungs. He didn't want to appear afraid when the others clearly were not but, all the same, wolves were wolves!

'Oh, they're always with Isolde.' Quinn dismissed them without a thought. 'They follow her everywhere. Hal worries that she'll turn them into scavenging pests but Brid encourages it because she says the wolves will keep her safe. They say she was a wolf in her last life.' He laughed. 'How does anyone know what they were in their last life?'

Rollo had never even considered the question and it barely penetrated his conscious thoughts now; all he knew was that he was himself and was intensely aware that he was different to others. His mind, however, was diverted from the wolves by an extraordinary sound like the strangled note of a deep bugle.

'What was that?' Quinn muttered, his hand fumbling for his sword as he swayed slightly in the saddle.

The hairs on the back of Rollo's neck began to prickle. 'Mammoth!' he answered. He had seen mammoths before and he didn't particularly relish the idea of ever seeing another.

Isolde drew to a halt and pointed at the trail. Huge round prints crossed their path; saplings to either side were crushed and broken. Following the mammoth prints were those of a lone horse. The waifish girl cocked her head sideways at the prints. 'The horse is carrying a fairly heavy rider.'

'That's a brave man hunting a mammoth alone,' Rollo remarked. His father had chased mammoth off their lands

148

two winters ago now. They had had come south during a particularly cold winter and caused havoc in the outlying villages. It had taken a party of fifty men and bears to drive the beasts off. He couldn't imagine what one man alone could hope to achieve following a mammoth.

'Let's hurry,' Isolde urged. 'Quinn needs help and it's getting late. I don't want to be out in these woods come dark.'

As if to emphasize her point, a great cackling broke out from a thicket of hazel. Urged by their tired riders, the horses broke into a fast trot, weaving through the woods until they abruptly stumbled on to a track. They hastened along it until the path joined a paved road, the trees to either side hacked back. Rollo was relieved. As he looked along the road, he could see signs of civilization. They broke into a gallop and were soon thundering towards a rather cobbled-together castle, the ruins of a large roofless farmhouse lying in its shadow.

The curtain wall about the bailey was of wooden construction, parapets and towers linked by narrow bridges to facilitate the deployment of men. The portcullis housed within a high stone barbican was raised and men were driving bleating and lowing livestock through to keep them safe for the night. Rising above that, at the very heart of the complex, was a conical motte topped by a plain circular keep built from pale stone. A hasty construction of wooden towers thrust up from the stone of the fortress from which a watchman blasted out a note at their approach. They thundered across the drawbridge and into the bailey, the horses' hooves echoing back from the walls of the keep before them.

'We seek shelter and aid,' Rollo called out. 'One of our number is injured.'

Quinn managed only to groan and slumped forward onto the horse's neck while Rollo supported him about his waist.

Men crowded round, easing Quinn down from his horse, while several others scurried away to find someone of authority. Presently, a young but heavy man strode out from the keep. Behind him, the sound of hammering was still in progress, the men working into the evening by the light of blazing fires. He approached at a fast march, chain-mail clinking beneath a shaped breastplate; a thick woollen cloak, emblazoned with the insignia of a bull's head, swirled about his calves. The soldiers stood smartly aside to make way for him. He stopped before the party of three youngsters and sighed at their state. With fingers heavy with chunky rings, he offered his hand to help Quinn.

'Look at the state of you, Master Quinn. What trouble is there in Torra Alta that you are running about on your own so late?' He didn't wait for an answer but looked to Isolde and bowed his head. 'You, my lady, are most welcome. Come, let's get you safely within my halls before the ravenshrikes take to the dark skies.'

'Thank you, Lord Oxgard,' Quinn groaned as he was supported between the nobleman and a burly soldier.

Rollo dropped back a pace, his palms sweating and his vision beginning to tinge red at the edges. He wondered what was wrong with him.

'Get those beacon fires up,' the Jotunn nobleman roared. 'And, Sergeant, the men are slow in with the pigs. See that they get them safely within the bailey. I will not have any more lost to the ravenshrikes, you hear?'

After crossing the busy bailey, they found themselves before the solid keep. The only entrance that Rollo could see was a double door of wood girded with bands of steel. The nobleman helped Quinn towards it and shoved open the doors that led into an empty hall. They passed through that and through more studded doors that led them into an inner courtyard.

Rollo looked up to see that they were within the hollow heart of the keep, a circle of walls rising high all around him. After crossing the courtyard, they passed through a smaller door to a simple wide hall. A low arched ceiling spanned overhead and, welcoming them in, was a vast roaring fire.

Children sat dangerously close, wriggling their chapped toes in the heat.

A long refectory table bowed under the weight of half a cow but, beside that, there was little to eat beyond barley bread twisted into a variety of a shapes and heaps of mashed root vegetables. Rollo was not in the least interested in eating vegetables. Mashed turnips were not suitable fare for a prince!

Men, women and servants filled the hall and all rose from their meal as the bedraggled party entered the room. Rollo was gratified that they commanded such respect but he quickly saw it was not offered to the sons of the great Lords of Torra Alta. No, he and Quinn were of little note. Their attention was focused on Isolde who seemed less than comfortable with their adulation.

'It may not be so grand as the produce we once offered, but the troubles, you know,' Baron Oxgard, apologized for their simple fare. 'I wish we were back in the old manor at the heart of Jotunn where we could offer you comfortable lodgings but we were lucky to escape at all. Now, tell us what brings you here.' He clicked his fingers at a servant. 'Bring a physician to see to Master Quinn's leg.' He looked to Rollo. 'Friend, are you unharmed? Are you in need of attention?'

'No, *Friend*,' Rollo retorted a little sarcastically. 'Quinn needs help but beyond that we seek news of Lord Hal of Torra Alta. He has ridden out in search of Baron Caspar. And also we need a search—'

'Baron Caspar has returned to these shores! That is news!' Oxgard interrupted.

'Returned only to be taken by hobs,' Rollo explained, sensing that the moment was not quite right to explain about Guthrey. Now he was feeling annoyed that his father should have been so inept as to allow himself to be taken. The ignominy of it! Rollo was determined that he would find him before Hal did.

'Caspar missing!' Oxgard exclaimed.

'And Brid,' Quinn added, weakly.

Oxgard leapt up, knocking the great carved chair over behind him. 'Brid taken! Oh by the Great Mother, our end is near! I have lost most of my family and now this. I promised my father on his deathbed that I would keep his lands but they are being eaten away by the power-hungry manor-lords that have already overcome Wiglaf. He was weak. I scoffed at his weakness but I am no better myself. Already, we have fled our home and have been forced north to where my brother thankfully had the forethought to start building this castle. They are coming for us! Very soon, they will be here. Where is my rune-singer? Where? What must I do to keep this plague back?'

Rollo suspected that Oxgard was relatively new to the notion of command and was not entirely comfortable with it.

An old fat woman with sagging dark skin beneath her eyes, stamped forward and reached up to soothe his shoulders. 'My son, there is no need for rune-singers or any other diviners. The ravenshrikes will come again as they have on every clear night. We must simply be ready for them. Have courage. Take hold of your father's sword and grip it fast.'

'It did him little good,' Oxgard despaired. 'This should have been Thane's task not mine. I once had three strong brothers. Thane and Oxwin fell in the battle against Gwion; my father and Boris in the struggles against the taurs. I am the last and all I ever wanted was to be a farmer.'

'Sit, drink and be hospitable,' the old woman said firmly and Rollo could see from where the Barony of Jotunn drew its strength. The dowager nodded at Isolde. 'I never welcomed any of you women of the Old Faith and I still believe that, if none had listened to you, these troubles would not beset us now; but I am alone in these thoughts here and so, out of courtesy to my family, I acknowledge you. Please be seated at my table.'

Isolde appeared to lack the wherewithal to supply a suitably face-saving remark. She looked anxiously at Quinn and gripped his hand. 'He needs me,' she stammered.

'How can you say such things, Mother?' Oxgard snapped at the old woman. 'Be more civil to Lady Isolde; she is a high priestess!' Oxgard turned to Isolde. 'Please excuse my mother, she's suffered a great deal.'

Lady Helena snorted in disgust. 'I'm too old to be civil. I remember how all this came about. Torra Altans have always brought trouble with them. Now, son, sit and talk. The men know what to do and you may as well rest before the ravenshrikes attack.'

'It seems we would have been in less danger in the woods,' Quinn said brightly, despite the taught grimace on his face as the physician washed his wound.

Oxgard gave out a half laugh. 'You'd have been dead by midnight. The woods are crawling with hobs by night. Wretched beasts. We were all worried about dragons and wyverns but the great beasts have been less trouble than the smaller creatures that swarm in vast numbers. But enough of that. Tell us your tale,' the Baron of Jotunn nodded at Quinn, ignoring Rollo. The burly man had recovered some of his composure and carved himself a large juicy chunk of meat from the cow.

Quinn took a draught of beef tea and Rollo was impressed at how quickly the youth mastered his pain. The tall Torra Altan made a point of not looking at his wound as the physicians worked on it but, instead, turned to the Jotunn nobleman. 'Rollo came home with his father,' he began.

Until this point Baron Oxgard had not paid the least bit of interest in Rollo but now fixed him with an inquisitive look. 'Apart from the red hair, you do not look a bit like him. So the heir to Torra Alta has returned? I have no doubt that Guthrey was pleased about that.'

Quinn's head dropped. 'Guthrey was snatched by a ravenshrike just before we fell into some underground caves, an ancient dragon's layer as it turned out. We heard hobs and hurried deeper to hide from them but then lost our torches and . . .,' Quinn looked thoughtfully at Rollo as if he had only just remembered this point, 'we would have been lost there only Rollo knew his way out.'

Everyone stared at Rollo in disbelief though he was convinced that accusation stabbed out from their Belbidian eyes. 'It wasn't my fault,' he snapped. 'The ravenshrike just dropped out of the sky.'

'It's all right, lad,' Oxgard reached across the table and gripped Rollo's fingers in a gesture of support and comfort. 'We know you did your best, but what could anyone do against one of those gigantic birds?'

Rollo looked down at the table, wondering how he could bear his guilt.

'We shall have to go after him!' Quinn grunted, clutching his thigh just above the knee, his lip trembling a little.

'Poor Guthrey!' Oxgard said with sincere grief. 'A few have escaped the clutches of the great ravenshrikes before now. I shall send men out to look for him at first light. There is hope. And, Rollo, at least you got Quinn out alive,' he added kindly.

The undeserved sympathy mixed with his secret guilt and enraged Rollo and, glaring down at his pewter plate, he stabbed at his meat with his knife. 'I just want to go home,' he murmured to himself, blinking back the hot tears of shame and rage.

'I don't know,' Quinn was saying. 'I don't know how he found his way out but he did.'

Rollo was acutely aware of Isolde's searching gaze, her bright golden-green eyes darkening to points of black as she tried to read him. Rollo looked up at her and stared back until she flicked her gaze away.

'He seemed to smell his way out!' Quinn exclaimed, laughing at the absurdity of the notion. His voice was growing louder as the physician's drugs began to crush his pain.

'If I may be permitted,' the physician excused his interruption, 'I would suggest that his father, Baron Caspar, had been to those caves in his youth and must have told the young lord about it in a story.'

'No!' Rollo said emphatically.

'It would seem most probable that you inherited the knowledge from your father,' the physician presented his hypothesis.

Isolde looked at the man as if he were mad but said nothing.

'It wasn't like that,' Quinn began to argue but no one was listening. Oxgard was already moving towards an arrow-slit that looked south-west towards Baron Wiglaf's lands.

'They are coming,' he murmured.

'I don't hear anything,' Lady Helena said, dismissively. 'Don't be so jumpy.'

'You are too old. I can hear them.'

Rollo strained his ears. There was the sound of a brewing wind such as might happen at dawn with the rising sun stirring the air currents. The sound was not uncanny in itself but it was a still night, the stars bright and clear. Then, through the noise, came the faintest notes of a thin, high-pitched cry that grew and grew until Rollo's ears were pounding. He was aware of little else happening around him as the piercing sound invaded his brain. Oblivious to the shouts for all women and children to get below to the deeper chambers, he heard only the high-pitched scream. Quinn was gone, Isolde was gone and someone was tugging at his arm, trying to drag him towards a door. But he would not go.

Ravenshrikes, Oxgard had called them, but he had a different name in his head, though, when he came to pronounce it, he could not. His thoughts were panicked with notions of disease and young being eaten, torn from their mothers midst terrible cries. Scavengers, hyenas of the skies, he thought unable to think of a better word for them.

Ripping himself free from the man's grip, he began

scrambling up a winding staircase and out through a trap door to join the men on the battlements above the keep. Now he could see them, a black cloud against the starry sky. He yelled and pointed and the men looked up.

'Where?' one cried, trying to angle a great catapult at the patch of black sky that Rollo was pointing at. 'Where?'

'There!' Rollo shouted. 'Can't you see them?' He squinted into the dark. Perhaps he had not seen them but he knew they were there. He could smell their sharp scent.

He stared until his eyes ached then suddenly the darkness took on an outline that blotted out the stars as they passed. When they were close enough, the light from the beacons reflected from their black feathers and Rollo could clearly see their long, stabbing beaks jutting from heavy, crow-shaped heads. The streamlined creatures were about the size of a large goat, supporting wings with a span over twenty foot.

'Pull!' a sergeant yelled and the twang and crash of giant catapults drowned all other noise. The castle walls shook with the impact of the engines' throwing arms slamming against their crossbeams. Rocks and splinters of metal were hurled into the sky.

Rollo stared as the creatures deftly weaved to avoid much of the shot. 'Fire,' he murmured. 'Fire . . . Burn them . . .'

'Look out on the turret!' a man cried as three ravenshrikes stretched out their talons to perch on the wooden structure above the stone keep. The wooden turret creaked beneath the weight. Long barbed tails dangled down, thrashing at the men on the battlements below. From their perch, they took it in turns to mock the men within the castle and those that were still struggling to get the last of the livestock into the bailey.

Red-hot anger boiled up into Rollo's brain. He didn't care that this was not his fight. He grabbed one of the braziers, ran to the catapult engine and stuffed the torch in amongst the shot. The flame was catapulted into the sky, spraying out a magnificent trail of fireworms that tumbled, twisted and spiralled in the winds.

The creatures leapt into the air, squawking like a flock of terrified pheasants, but quickly regrouped when no more fireballs were hurled at them. Another black cloud swooped in and headed straight for the barbican and the housing of the portcullis. Wings outstretched, the birds clung to the masonry with their talons. With great beaks they drilled at the mortar and then scrabbled with their claws to loosen great blocks of masonry.

'Loose fire at them,' Rollo screamed, incensed with loathing for the birds.

No one heeded him, merely hurling javelins and catapuling more shot. He grabbed two torches and leapt up the stone steps cut into the edge of the walls and began to brandish his flame at the creatures' dangling tail feathers. It was only then, when he was close to them, that he saw the men riding on their backs. He could not believe it. Surely they were hobs or another race of the old kind that had banded with these strange creatures. But just as a dog knew its own, Rollo could feel in his bones that these were men.

That moment of hesitation stayed his hand and the nearest long tail whipped out and caught his wrist, cutting deep. Something stung his face. He flung one torch and then charged in with another, singeing the creature's tail. It screamed and leapt into the skies followed by the rest and, as suddenly as they had arrived, the ravenshrikes were gone. Rollo held his wrist, breathing steadily. It was only then that he realised he had burnt his hand where the brand had wafted back at him, and that his face screamed with pain as if the skin had been lacerated. He raised his good hand to his cheek and was amazed to find it was bristling with thorny spikes embedded in his skin.

Stumbling to his knees, he stared stupidly at the singed skin of his hand and grimaced from the mounting pain. 'It burns,' he mumbled in vague confusion.

He remembered little else until he came to, lying in a chamber within the keep. Isolde was looking down at him.

'Is he awake?' Oxgard's firm voice spoke out above the general groans that filled the room.

Isolde nodded and the Baron of Jotunn drew closer and stooped over Rollo. 'We are very grateful to you. We chased them away with relative ease once we used the firebrands though a few others have been burnt like yourself.'

'There was a man,' Rollo said with difficulty, his face smarting, the skin tight and swollen. 'Men were riding on their backs.'

'No, lad,' Oxgard soothed. 'Those creatures eat humans; they do not carry them.'

'Nevertheless, I saw men on their backs,' Rollo insisted.

'A hob, no doubt.' Lady Helena was dismissive. 'Listen, Rollo, you are young and the young often get over excited and can easily be confused.'

Rollo felt his temples throb. 'I know what I saw!'

'Yes, dear.' The noblewoman disregarded his words.

Rollo's fists clenched but he was distracted from his rage by a cool touch running down the length of his fingers. 'Hush, son of Caspar,' Isolde's very soft voice murmured. 'Pay them no heed. Know what you know and believe in yourself.'

Rollo looked at her and wanted to smile only she nervously dropped her gaze and returned to tending his hand. After a moment's awkward pause, she asked gently, 'What were you thinking? How did you hope to drive them off alone?'

He looked into those golden-green eyes and it was as if he looked into a different world. She had the most beautiful eyes he had ever seen. His father, much to his mother's disgust, had always claimed that Brid had the most beautiful eyes in the world but he had been wrong.

Lady Helena sniffed at the girl as she stooped over Rollo's hand. 'Not so brash and bold as the other priestesses, are you little mouse?' The old lady snorted in disgust, years of pent up anger making her voice tremble. 'I knew! I knew all those years ago that your kind would bring us trouble.' She looked at her son. 'If it weren't for her and the others of her faith, your brothers would still be alive, Oxgard.'

As Rollo had expected, Isolde made no attempt to meet Helena's gaze but what he didn't expect was for a quiet smile to spread across the priestess's face. She seemed to be laughing inwardly as if she were somehow remote from all this drama and that it touched on her no more than a feather brushing against the hoof of a great destrier.

Helena stamped her foot and Rollo was most surprised to see Isolde raise her chin and stare at the noblewoman. 'Woman, you know nothing of me,' she said icily.

For the first time, Rollo noticed Quinn sitting close by. He smiled a brief welcome before closing his eyes and shutting out the world. He was too exhausted to listen anymore. Comfortably aware of Isolde's presence close by, he slid into a soothing sleep and dreamed he was back with his mother, snuggled up against her as they rode on a great shaggy bear at the northern extremity of Artor. The dream was taken from the time when, together, they had looked out on the wastelands beyond the border that belonged to the Empress of Oran.

He had shuddered as he gazed over those bleak lands laid waste by the Empress to fill the hungry stomachs of her ever-growing army. Ursula had patted his hand and told him not to be afraid; she would keep him safe from the Empress.

His mother had felt strong and warm and they had sat close. He remembered her lean strong arms around him and he had felt totally safe and complete. It had been one of the few blissful moments he had shared with her without having it interrupted by his oh-so-important sister. He had been two when his sister was born, his great and powerful sister who would forever push him from his mother's lap.

In his dream, he forgot that his mother was gone. He drew his knees up under his chin and felt her curl around him and then, as dreams so often do, there was a subtle change

159

in his dream-world. He was still with her; he was certain of that because nothing else could provide the same feelings of well-being and love, but he could no longer see her because he was too close up against her and Ursula's soothing voice had turned to sobs.

Her face was nuzzled up against his, great tears dripping and rolling down her cheeks onto his. He tried to speak but had no voice; he tried to tell her not to be afraid for him because he would be safe; the Great Mother had called him and would look out for him. Gone was the soft caress of her skin and, instead, Rollo felt only a coldness. Frowning in his sleep, he tried to manipulate his thoughts so that he might feel how his mother's touch should be. It was as if he were forgetting her and he could not bear that thought.

She was crying for him. 'My sweet, sweet boy, don't leave me! Don't leave me!' Her voice faded further and further away.

Rollo came round with the cry ringing in his head, the sound gradually blending into someone singing. Immediately, he was intrigued and overwhelmed by thise passionate sound that had filtered into his dream and excited every inch of his body. His eyes flickered open.

Wearily aware that his pain had eased, he turned his head and saw who was singing beside him. A heart-shaped face with wide eyes and magnificent curls of golden hair pressed close, but Rollo no longer cared for her looks; he was gazing through her eyes into her soul. 'Isolde . . .'

'Rollo,' she murmured back. 'You are with us again.'

'Of course,' he grunted. 'I've only been asleep.'

A door opened, letting in a cold draught that carried snatches of a conversation taking place just outside the room to Rollo's ears. He learnt that Guthrey had still not been found and they were deeply worried for him as well as concerned for Rollo; he heard his name as if it belonged to another. Then suddenly there was a loud voice amongst them.

'Awake now? Well, I never!' Lady Helena's voice was shrill and easily recognizable. He heard footsteps approaching. 'I would have sworn he was dead. Been dead for three days. It's most unwholesome to be dead like that and come back to life.' She drew closer and sniffed at him. 'Still, lad, I am glad, I am very glad of it. We owe you a debt of gratitude. Your daring act with the fire may have nearly cost you your hand but you've shown us a way to drive them off.'

Rollo found it very hard to focus his thoughts. Isolde put a cup to his lips and he sipped at the liquid that was both sweet and biter at the same time. After a few minutes, the potion did something to ease the pain in his hand. He wondered vaguely why he had been such a fool.

He might have wondered more if Isolde's potions had not, at that moment, taken hold, pushing him back into his dream. All he could hear was a faraway voice that rang on and on. 'Do not forget me; never forget me. I love you.'

Hot tears scolded his cheeks. 'Mother,' he shrieked. 'Mother! I will never forget.'

Chapter 10

Miserably, Caspar concluded that the night had already worn away any of the new-found faith that the men had placed in him. The dark hours had been cold and long and his joints ached. He looked at Brid forlornly. She had stirred briefly during the night but had hardly moved since, and he was terrified that they would lose her.

The men watched him suspiciously. Gromo cleared his throat. 'Lord Hal will come for us. He would never let his men down and he would see the sky in flames and the earth rent asunder for Lady Brid; do not doubt it.' They all nodded in agreement at this, their mouths clamped sourly shut as they looked at Caspar, clearly thinking him inadequate.

And they were right, he admitted to himself; so far he had proved totally impotent in the face of their plight. Hunching up over Brid's quiet body, he pulled the bearskins more tightly about her and bit his lip.

She looked so peaceful now, asleep in the milky light that preceded dawn. It was still winter in this deep valley but Caspar sensed there was a greater warmth here that did not come from the energy of the sun but welled up from the very heart of the Earth itself. Pleasant though the warmth was, it wasn't going to help him get home. He wondered whether he shouldn't have pursued Silas last night after all.

Staring at the surrounding landscape, he waited for the long fingers of dawn to thread their way into the shadows of the trees, and suddenly realized he could see the black outline of the mammoth-slayer's horse. The hope that Silas was still nearby slowly grew within him. He wondered at the man's lack of skill to catch Raven and also at the horse's persistence in staying close to them.

Rubbing his fingers to encourage the feeling back into them, he returned his attention to Brid, wondering how best to carry her. His thoughts were interrupted by a soft whicker and a short drum-roll of hooves on turf and he knew that the black mare had been disturbed by something. Turning, he saw her at the edge of a small copse of holly trees, now discernible in the growing light, that stood some two hundred yards from of a mixed wood of holly, oak and beech. She dropped her head to nuzzle the grass, delicately nipping off the fresh shoots, but shortly lifted her head and trotted on another score of paces.

By the look of the horse's alert ears and the way she moved, Caspar guessed that she was still being stalked by Silas, who must be somewhere in the trees. The Baron mused how that was no way to catch a horse, when he was suddenly alarmed by the mare's change in stance. Her head jerked and she froze in fear.

Caspar immediately knew something was wrong. Trembling, the mare stared east into the sun that was now pushing up out of the earth behind the nine barrows, which lay like sleeping giants on the horizon. The mist was thin, clothing the hills like a grey cloak, before the sun touched it and turned it to flaming orange.

Suddenly, the mare squealed and bolted away, sending up chunks of turf from her heels as her great weight thudded west across the soft ground and into the trees. He could see no reason to be alarmed beyond the reactions of the horse but instinct urged Caspar to flee with her.

'Run!' he shouted at his men. 'Run!'

They looked at him askance but none obeyed him. What was he to do? 'Brid! Brid, sweetest Brid!' He scooped her up in his arms, glad that she was small and light. She had lost much of her pregnancy weight during the last few days, far more than was normal in her efforts to survive the trauma and replace the lost blood; he was almost thankful since it enabled him to carry her with ease.

He could do nothing about his men. Brid's safety was his priority. He ran hard, Gromo shouting in protest that he had so roughly snatched up Brid. It was only as he splashed through an icy stream that he glanced back at the spot where they had been standing by the low flat stone. The men were making a half-hearted attempt to follow him but kept turning to stare at the compelling sight of the deeply red dawn.

Was it his fault that they did not respect him enough to obey his command and instantly flee to save themselves? They should have obeyed him without question. In their minds, he had betrayed them by his absence and now they looked back to welcome what they perceived as the greatest of the Primal Gods. But the sun was growing too large and did not radiate primal power. Far greater was the primal power of the earth beneath his feet. Knowing that his priority now was to save Brid, he ran.

Hefting her up onto his shoulder, he looked around for signs of the mare. Common sense told him to follow the horse; Raven knew what she was running from. He caught a glimpse of her dark shape threading into the trees. With Brid lolled over his shoulder, he did his best to run from the deep glow spreading behind the barrows, and fled towards the close-packed boughs of holly and hazel. He must reach the trees.

For a moment, he halted to shout again for his men. 'Run! To me! To me!'

But they would not listen to him. He was not angry. How could he be angry? It was his own fault; he was the one who had failed to inspire their trust, a trust that all men should feel toward their leader. Thinking his lungs would burst, he forced his legs to pump beneath him. He could hear now, above his own breaths, a vast pair of lungs sucking away the cool atmosphere and breathing out steamy heat.

At last, he reached the shelter of the trees whose whippy branches lashed his face. With little room for Brid's limp body on his back, he squeezed between them and turned. They were not yet safe; he would have to drag her deeper but he had missed the path taken by the horse and found himself twisted and entangled amongst holly bushes. But at least he had a moment to draw breath and time to turn and see what was happening.

He did not yet know what he would see, only that it would be terrible. He wondered now at Silas's reasoning behind bringing them there and why the mammoth-slayer had seemingly deserted them. The glow of the sun suddenly became a vast glare that flashed out to fill half the sky. Instinct forced Caspar to duck his head but, to his amazement, the light didn't strike the earth but was deflected. It was as if they were protected by an enormous shield, he concluded, seeing how the energy was swept aside and curled around what appeared to be an invisible dome way above him. The flare of light dwindled and was sucked back to what looked like the sun though it was too deep a red.

Soon, the sky around the sun began to darken and char. The edges of the dark hole began to blister, peeling and curling like scorched parchment in the heat of a candle. Caspar caught a glimpse of a cloudy sky beyond the brilliant blue above him. Then, in horror, he shrank back and ducked down, shielding Brid in his embrace as a great snout thrust through the tear in the atmosphere. Ripples shivered and spread right around the sky, curving back down towards the horizon. A sheet of flame jetted forwards and burst through followed by a claw that ripped aside more of the deep blue sky before a huge monster squeezed through. The weight of the beast shuddered the ground as it landed.

Caspar could not help but stare up at the strange tear in the sky that revealed the grey of a wintry world beyond. That was his sky, the sky he had left behind before entering the church.

His gaze leapt back to the great golden dragon that now stood above his men. Marcus, a brave Torra Altan to the core, held up a knife, which he must have prudently taken from Raven's saddle.

Caspar wanted to close his eyes and weep for their fool-hardiness. Why couldn't they have listened to him? If he had come back, maybe even just one year earlier, they might have listened to him. But he had been gone fifteen years and was all but forgotten by the men. He had lost their respect and now they were the ones who would pay for his mistake.

For an agonizingly long minute, the huge golden she-dragon stooped over them, sniffing, before she threw back her head and bellowed her bloodthirsty roar. She shook out her huge golden wings, the leathery skin transparent and the light of the true sun illuminating a web of bulging blood vessels pumping blood to her clawed wing tips. Nostrils flaring, her head curled tightly down to protect the soft spot at her throat. A forked tongue flickered in and out of her red mouth. With one sudden movement, her claws whipped at Marcus's bravely upheld knife, snagging the weapon and sending it cartwheeling up into the air. For a spilt second, her entire body was taut and utterly still before her long snout darted forward like a snake and her tongue lashed out, twisting around the man's neck and flicking him up into the air.

She caught him in her jaws, the great teeth snapping shut, crunching clean through his neck and shoulder. His head and the upper portion of his chest were gone, swallowed whole, while the rest fell to the ground. The monster thumped a proprietorial claw down on the legs and torso, which squirted blood into the soil as if from a spilled cup. Then, like a great bird, she pinned down one leg and tore off the other with her long snout.

The other men stood and stared, transfixed in horror. Only when one started to run did the dragon react, sending a jet of flame scorching along the grass to envelop his legs and then his whole body. His hands clawed the air as if trying to pull himself free of the furnace on invisible ropes. At the same time, the beast's tail whipped round and stabbed downward, pinning Gromo through the belly before he had gone more than two paces. Her jet of flame spumed again and the last man was shrivelled in her flames. The dragon didn't bother to inspect those that had been incinerated but turned straight on Gromo who squirmed on the ground, impaled by the barb on the end of her tail.

The huge beast was as flexible as a cat, her long sinuous body curving round on itself. Caspar's face was tight with horror. There was simply nothing he could do as he watched the great beast pluck its tail out from its victim, raise a claw and place it firmly over the man's ribcage. Slowly, she lent forward, transferring her weight until the bones snapped. She then bit off the man's head and, as if she were a monstrous terrier with a rat, shook what remained before tossing it aside.

Stretching her neck up, she raised her golden crest and ruffled up the armoured plating on her neck, the scales rattling in the sudden silence. Snorts of steam squirted from her nostril, her long tongue flickering forward, tasting the air. She was still searching.

Trying to still his trembling hands, Caspar drew low over Brid, hauling her back into the trees, his arms shredded by the long holly leaves. Once he was through the trees, it was easier. The canopy of branches lifted as he moved into the airier woodland of oaks and beeches. Throwing Brid onto his back, he began to run, her arms trailing down and bumping softly against his back.

Overhead, the sky darkened as a shadow spread across the land and he glanced up to see the vast spread of the dragon's wings as she soared across the forest. Clearly, she was unwilling to land as she would become entangled in the trees. The monstrous lizard swooped lower, fire spuming from her mouth and singeing the treetops. Caspar hoped that, whilst expending energy on flying, the dragon did not have enough to spout flame as well. He prayed that she could not continue to roar out such heat without grievously depleting her strength.

Stumbling to a stream that wound beneath a rocky over-hang, he decided that it was here he would hide. He scooped up a cupful of water into his palm to slake his thirst after his frantic run and froze as a terrible cry rang out over the forest. At first the sound was so violent and great that he perceived it only as a roar but, as the notes echoed and rebounded, he heard within them distinct words.

'Burn! Burn, fire burn! Flesh sizzle!'

Caspar gasped. The dragon spoke! It was unimaginable. Dragons could not speak yet it was roaring out discernible words in a deep and terrible voice that made the air tremble and shake. The monster twisted and tumbled in the air, apparently in gleeful delight, using her thick tail like a club to swipe at the treetops, before she roared out again, 'Fire!'

Caspar could not understand all that she said but it terrified him. An animal that spoke had intelligence.

No, this was absurd. Dragons did not speak. They were simply huge flying lizards. It was his imagination. He was probably just asleep, and this, no matter how horrifyingly real it seemed, was no more than a nightmare. This world could not be real.

Again, the dragon roared and he felt Brid stir and clutch him close as if she were a child in her mother's arms. Without thinking, Caspar kissed the top of her head and she whimpered softly and snuggled up against his chest.

'Brid! Brid! Wake up,' he begged.

The dragon roared out again, the sound now becoming distant. 'Fire, burn!'

Brid jerked upright, her big green eyes blinking in con-fusion and dismay. 'What was that?'

'A dragon.'

'Dragon's don't speak . . .' Her eyes flitted about her, taking in her surroundings, and then they looked down at her flat belly. Her lips whitened; her face fell in despair. 'I didn't dream it . . .'

Caspar nodded sympathetically. 'I am sorry, Brid. Truly, I am. He held out his arms to her and she fell against his chest, tears soaking through his shirt. Cupping her head, he held her to him, wishing there was some way he could comfort her and take away the pain.

'Hobs!' she sobbed. 'They killed my baby.'

Her sobs became shrieks of anguish and Caspar was fearful that the dragon would return.

'Brid, Brid, stop that!' He shook her vigorously. 'You'll get us both killed.'

He was still shaking her when her cry failed and she went limp in his arms. She sagged against his chest and he was fearful for a moment that he had shaken the life out of her. 'Brid!' He hugged her close and kissed her eyes, hoping that they would open.

'They took my baby, Hal,' she said so quietly that he almost did not hear. 'Hal . . .'

'It's me; Spar,' Caspar said inadequately. 'I'll get you home to Hal, don't worry,' he reassured her softly, cupping his hand and scooping the cool water to her lips.

If he managed to get her to drink, she might regain some strength and lucidity. She sputtered and gasped but soon sagged back into his arms and he knew that he must find help for her.

Carrying her on his back, he staggered on until noon. He would have continued despite his injured leg but Brid was in need of rest and water. Setting her down by a small stream, he wrapped her in his bearskin cloak. She looked peaceful and he couldn't help wondering how different life might have been if she had chosen him instead of Hal. As it was, he had found happiness first with May and then Ursula. But both May and Ursula were dead. Perhaps the Great Mother was protecting Brid from him; his love was surely cursed.

He would never love like that again; to love was to lose and he had lost more than he could bear in one lifetime. Tears pricked at the corner of his eyes. And where was Rollo? Had he lost him for good too? His son . . .

He stared into the swirling patterns of the clear water and drew Brid close, taking a guilty but nevertheless intense pleasure in the proximity of her body. He kissed her cheeks. 'You are the Mother of the Trinity,' he soothed. 'You are the life that walks the earth; you are the most precious being alive and I love and worship you with all my being.'

The pain of his leg and the exertion of the last few days caught up with him and, for a moment, he allowed himself to close his eyes and rest. Drawing Brid even tighter to him to keep them both warm, he dozed lightly.

The smell of smoke wafting through the trees woke him up with a start. He was hugely relieved to see that Brid was also stirring from her stupor. Hastily struggling to his feet, he looked about him but could see nothing from the forest floor. Stooping, he wrapped his bearskin tightly around Brid's shoulders as she stared, blinking at the sky.

'Lie still and keep warm. I'm just going to take a look,' he told her.

Choosing a smooth-barked beech tree at the edge of the glade, he swung himself up into the lower branches and quickly climbed high up its trunk, thankful for the lack of leaf, which afforded him a better view. There was little to see, for the land was undulating and thick with trees, but what he could see was a huge tower of black smoke rising to the west. He leapt down at great speed, painfully catching his thigh on the point of a broken branch.

It seemed foolhardy to head towards the smoke but instinct told him that smoke meant people; right now he needed people. Someone would surely be able to lead them out of here – even that treacherous Silas, the mammoth-slayer, if he could lay his hands on the man.

He began to limp back to Brid and staggered in his stride.

She was sitting upright and, at the sound of his approach, she raised her head. Her eyes were bloodshot with tears but she was calm now, as if the madness of her grief had finally left her.

'Where are we?' she asked weakly.

'I don't know exactly. A man, he called himself Silas, saved us from the hobs. He lent you his horse and you and the men came to this strange land where the sky is not real. He and I found you but then he disappeared while looking for his horse and we were attacked by a . . .'

'. . . a dragon? I remember a dragon that shouted words!'

Caspar nodded. 'It came out of the sun. The men wouldn't flee. The sun turned into the dragon's fiery breath and the creature tore its way into this world; only you and I got away.'

Brid briefly closed her eyes on the dreadful news before raising her hand, asking to be helped to her feet. 'This simply cannot be. You are misperceiving things.'

He wrapped his arms about her. 'I should carry you,' he insisted.

'I'm weak,' she conceded. 'A part of my soul has been ripped from me and I am weak. You must help me, Spar.'

He bowed his head. 'You are One of the Three and for that reason alone there is nothing that I would not do for you.'

'You've changed little in all these years.' Brid raised a light smile and allowed Caspar to lift her into his arms.

Aiming for the column of smoke, he found it very hard going through the woods but, at last, he reached a break in the trees. He halted in dismay at the sight. An entire village was laid waste, bodies strewn everywhere, legs and arms ripped from their sockets and heads bitten clean off. The circle of simple houses was engulfed in flames and black smoke as the timbers fed the fire. Nearby, the thatch of a barn was pocketed with circular fires that were rapidly spreading to form a flaming mat, the straw spitting and crackling in the intense heat.

The dragon attack had been savage. Caspar swallowed in horror. He was distressed for these people before him but also felt a deep stab of guilt as he suddenly realized that Hal had witnessed such atrocities many times in his absence. He had been in another continent when the people of his barony had needed him.

'You must see if there is anyone left alive,' Brid told him.

'But I can't leave you.'

'I'll be all right,' she insisted. 'There may yet be someone trapped or hiding; you must at least look.'

He took his cloak, knowing that it would protect him from sparks, and ran forward around the perimeter of the village but could see or hear no one. Eyes smarting from the smoke and sickened by the sight of so many children crushed or burnt to death, he was about to turn back when he heard a thin cry.

Raising his cloak over his mouth and nose, he pushed into the heat and smoke. Turning the corner of a stone wall, he stared in horror, his stomach turning, and he was glad that Brid was not with him to witness the sight. A charred carcass hung from a stake. Clearly, someone had been tied to the post as an offering to appease the dragon. Sadly, the villagers must have believed the legends that told how a dragon could be bought for the price of one maiden. Strips of singed flesh hung from her like crisp, black parchment.

Heaped high around the staked carcass were the remains of more women, young and old, each one cut across the chest or throat with a claw and left to bleed to death. He turned the bodies over, pulling the upper ones aside to look for signs of life in any beneath. There was no hope that any of the men were alive; they were torn limb from limb, remnants of their bodies lying across the green. The dragon must have attacked them first before turning on the cowering women.

Turning the bodies over one at a time, he searched their horror-struck faces for signs of life. Their mouths were filled with blood that had flooded up from their ruptured lungs. At last, he heard a small noise from somewhere in the heap and heaved aside a large woman to find a small girl, beneath. She blinked up at him in utter terror, her hands clamped around the body of the woman.

'Don't worry; I won't hurt you,' Caspar told her very gently. 'Come with me.'

'No! I won't leave Nanna,' she screamed. 'Nanna! Nanna!' Her face crumpled up into a mask of horror. 'Nanna!'

Caspar prised her fingers away from the dead woman. The girl arched her back and went rigid in his arms, screaming uncontrollably. There was nothing he could do other than hold onto her and drag her back to Brid. But he had lost his grip on the child by the time he reached the priestess. She struggled from his grasp and fell to the ground where she lay shrieking.

'Let her cry,' Brid said wearily, her compassion muffled by her own grief and exhaustion. 'She needs to cry. You cannot imagine what she feels,' she told Caspar.

'But I can,' he retorted. 'I watched as my own father was consumed in the fire of a dragon.'

Brid nodded. 'But you cannot imagine what it must be like to be a child and watch your mother – everything to you in all the world – burn like that.'

'Her grandmother or nurse, I think,' Caspar softly corrected her and only then realized that Brid was thinking about herself and the unspeakable trauma of her own childhood. 'She called her Nanna.'

The priestess stroked the child's cheek. 'Your Nanna still loves you and will always love you,' she assured her.

The child's sobs of anguish lessened very slowly and she curled up on the ground around Brid's feet for comfort. 'My Nanna,' she moaned pitifully.

Caspar watched in amazement as Brid seemed to grow in stature. Her wan face flooded with colour, the grey returning to the healthy bronze that she never lost even in winter.

She let the child cry for several minutes and then at last

tugged her up. 'You will always love her and never forget her, just as I will always love the child I have lost. Nothing will ever replace them and we must both grieve. But do not imagine you are alone. You and I shall care for one another,' she said quietly, kneeling down and cradling her. The child continued to cry but, at last, wrapped her arms about Brid and clung on.

'She must be very hungry and thirsty; we must find food,' Caspar said. Carefully, he pulled the child from Brid's arms, knowing that they must move from this spot. 'Can you walk?' he asked the priestess. 'I'll have to help the girl so can you manage?'

Brid nodded but, in truth, could only stumble forward very slowly, clinging to Caspar's arm. Fortunately, despite her grief the girl could stagger along helped by the Baron but they made slow and weary progress. Caspar studied the close-cropped pastures around and noted heaped piles of horse manure and the occasional hoof print and deduced that these pastures had been grazed by horses though there was no sign of them now.

They stumbled onto a track, which at last took them to a lone house that was entirely shuttered up. Leaving Brid sagging against the gatepost, Caspar banged at the front door and then the back.

'They must have fled from the dragon,' Brid said, stumbling to a window and easing back its shutter. 'Look! Food!' she exclaimed in triumph. 'Go in and get it for us, Spar.'

'I'm not a thief,' he protested.

'Oh everyone is a thief!' she retaliated waspishly. 'You've been away too long. Since the country has been split up, everyone has stolen from someone in order to survive. If it makes you feel better, leave some money. And get on with it! We shall perish if we don't eat. This poor girl is starving.'

Caspar nodded and wriggled through the unglazed window. Leaving behind a handsome number of coins for whoever owned the house, he filled a tablecloth with food and knotted the ends together. They sat in the deserted vegetable garden of the lone house, eating solemnly for several minutes, none of them saying a word. Even the little girl ate a little between her sobs.

Caspar studied her uncomfortably. A piece of stale bread crushed in her tense fist, her hand was shaking vigorously. She was older than he had first thought, perhaps about the age of his own daughter, her misery making her appear younger than her years. Caspar didn't know what he could do to help but Brid overcame her own depleted strength to rise to the occasion. She gripped the girl's hand tightly.

'The dragon,' the girl sniffed. 'Silas promised he would save us from it. He promised he would bring the offering of a mammoth!'

Caspar started at the mention of the name and wondered what had happened to the man. A pang of guilt stabbed through him. If it hadn't have been for him, then Silas would have had his mammoth and this child's family would still be alive. 'I'm sorry,' he murmured under his breath.

'He promised . . .,' the girl wailed and Brid gripped her hand tighter.

'What's your name?' the priestess asked gently.

The girl paused for a moment, looking hard into Brid's eyes as if looking for any deeper reason that she might ask that question. She cleared her throat. 'Leaf. My name is Leaf.'

Caspar thought it a strange name. 'I'm Spar,' he told her, patting his chest, 'and this is Brid.'

'Well, Leaf, do you have any other family we can take you to?' the priestess asked huskily.

Leaf sniffed, looked at her sideways, her eyes narrowing in suspicion. She took a while to answer as if deciding what to say. 'The next village . . . Nanna's brother. He's the village elder.'

Caspar had a sinking feeling in his stomach. They must hurry. 'How do we get there?' he asked.

The girl nodded along the dry road, the grassy verges still short from the previous autumn of heavy grazing.

Caspar kept wondering where on earth they were in this strangely quiet place. The wind was too still for the dun clouds scudding over the horizon. He squeezed Brid's hand, offering her comfort and then lifted the girl up onto her feet. She whimpered when separated from Brid's grasp but finally, limp and exhausted, clung to Caspar's hand as he tugged her along.

The pace was slow. Every now and then Brid stumbled and clutched at his arm to save herself. He knew she was constantly thinking of her lost child; her eyes dull with sorrow, she would draw herself up and suck in a deep breath whilst casting her eyes at Leaf. All the while tears rolled down the little girl's cheeks.

'Child,' Brid said huskily as if talking to herself, 'it is part of the cycle. Without death there is no life.'

The road wove its way gently up the slope of a hill. As they neared the top, Caspar instinctively pressed down and crouched low onto his haunches to avoid becoming distinctly visible on the skyline.

Below him, crowded about a ford through a quiet river, lay half a dozen houses under yellow thatches. The houses were timber-framed, the limed beams a soft grey against the pigs'-blood-pink of the walls. A few glazed windows reflected the light in the lower stories of the grander houses, the small panes glinting like sparkling crystals. The doors to a barn were banging and one was already torn off at the upper hinge. Doves fled from their holes in the dovecote built into the eaves of the barn. At their approach, chickens ran squawking in panic from the barn but there were no immediate signs of human activity.

'They must have run,' Leaf murmured. The sight had stemmed her tears and she was suddenly alert, surveying the scenery. 'They must have fled when they saw the smoke from my village.'

Caspar agreed with her, mildly surprised at her level-headed thinking after her trauma. They looked into the barn and the girl doubled up and began to retch; even Caspar staggered back but Brid was steady on her feet and stared at the carnage. There were tiny pieces of cow everywhere. A head and neck were draped over the rafters, legs and stomachs spread all across the floor. There must have been half a dozen beasts tethered within the stalls ready for milking, Caspar judged, noting the buckets of spilt milk now pink with blood.

Strips of torn hide dripped blood from where the cows had been tossed against the barn walls and landed to break their necks on the floor. One was skewered by a scythe, another had landed on the blade of a plough that had cleaved clean through the skull. Caspar's muscles tensed as he heard distressed breathing coming from near the end of the barn. He picked his way through to find the source of the noise.

A young heifer lay on her side with one leg half-bitten clean off. The animal's eyes rolled fearfully as she saw him and he quietly took his knife and stepped round behind her head. Kneeling down, he soothed her ear before sliding his hands down and quickly slitting her throat. Hurriedly, he picked his way back out of the gruesome abattoir and wiped the sticky blood from his boots on the crisp grass outside.

'At least the people seemed to have got away,' he grunted. 'What animal kills like that? Kills for the sheer love of killing?'

'No,' the girl shook her head. 'She killed as a warning – a warning to anyone that might dare fail to provide her with an offering.'

Caspar looked at her intensely, suddenly aware of the acuteness of this little girl's reasoning. Taking in steady breaths to cleanse himself of his remaining queasiness, Caspar raised his head to look about him. The vales that spread before him were dotted with villages and he looked in dismay at the five columns of smoke that leapt up into the sky. His eyes followed the smoke as it coiled and billowed into the blue and then suddenly he saw her as she soared up from the far side of a distant hill; the golden dragon.

Curling and twisting in the air, she was as agile as a swallow. For a second, she spread her golden wings wide and hung in the air, her underbelly black in the shadow of her wings. Then she beat those wings furiously, powering herself up into the sky before suddenly furling them close to her body. With her head thrust forward like an arrow and her cry splitting the quiet, she fell into the glare of the sun and was gone.

Leaf began to shake. 'She will come back for us. Soon, every last one of us will be dead. There will be none of us left on the face of the earth.'

'She's only one dragon. We can get men to hunt out just one dragon,' Caspar assured her.

'Here, there's only Silas,' Leaf said enigmatically. 'Only Silas can do it.'

'What do you mean, only Silas can do it?'

Leaf looked at him sideways with eyes that made him feel unutterably stupid. 'Who else is there?'

'I am Lord of Torra Alta; I shall see to it that this dragon is hunted out. I have men specially trained for the task.'

Leaf smiled at him. 'They can't come here. Your men would be as dangerous to us as the dragon.'

Fixing her with a quizzical eye, Caspar wondered vaguely what it was that he did not understand.

Brid, who had slumped down weakly onto the ground, was holding up her hand and feeling the air as if drawing thoughts from it, her face knotted in concern. She then touched the ground and scooped up a pinch of mud in her fingers. After dribbling it into her open palm, she drew circles in it with the forefinger of her other hand. 'This is the soil of the Mother.'

'Oh, yes, this is the soil of the Great Mother,' Leaf echoed. 'And we love Her. She is the great provider.' The girl sighed.

'But the dragon will take all from us.' She stared up into the sky, shielding her eyes from the glare of the sun. Forlornly, she dropped her gaze and began to sob again.

Brid took her hand and pressed the handful of earth into the child's palm. 'How long have you been hiding?'

Caspar wondered what on earth she was talking about but, as they struggled to the top of the next hill, his question stopped on his lips. Blinking, he raised his hand to shield his eyes from the sun. 'But it's beautiful. This can't exist; it isn't possible.' He stared towards the horizon at the distant glint. 'There is no such city so close to home; I would know. I thought the great beasts and the outlaws were tearing cities down, not allowing them to be built.'

'Oh do be quiet, Spar,' Brid protested, folding her hand into his and managing to give it a weak squeeze.

The Baron felt foolish and confused. His mind was exhausted by worry as, over the next hour, they closed on the city.

'Down!' Caspar suddenly warned as he saw the birds take to the wing.

The sun swelled and throbbed, deepening to a bloated scarlet, and Caspar knew that the monstrous flying lizard was on her way back. The sun continued to swell and deepen in colour until it suddenly burst, leaving a crisp black hole in the atmosphere. A huge claw thrust through, tearing aside the sky as if it were a blue gossamer sheet, the entire heavens rippling and shimmering under the stress of this elemental disturbance. After the claw came the great snout and then the entire body of the huge dragon as she squeezed through the hole and tumbled and twisted in the air high above them, her terrifying cry chilling the air.

She thumped down onto the ground a little distance from the gleaming city walls and roared out her challenge at the golden gates. Oxen and horses were being dragged through the gates and chained to huge stakes. Cries of fear and hysterical despair wailed out from the city. Caspar, too, felt drawn into their wretched gloom and struggled against it. To despair was to give up and no Torra Altan gave up on anything.

'Have they no ammunition, no war-engines, no spears?' he wondered out-loud. 'A lucky shot . . . Just one shot; it's always worth a try.'

Leaf looked at him in disgust. 'Spears! Don't be so ridiculous. Our men cannot handle spears.'

The dragon's great weight shook the ground as her ponderous legs thumped forward. She glared in disdain at the chained oxen, her stomach already bloated with food. Caspar wondered why a well-fed beast should come to scavenge at the city gates.

A horn blast piped out from the east, sounding out towards them from along a straight wide road that led to an empty plain. Unlike all the other roads leading to the city, Caspar saw no mills or houses that way. The road faded very gradually into a flat landscape that became grey and milky and, finally, indistinguishable from the bank of cloud resting on the horizon. A huge shape gradually took form, rolling out from the milky haze. At first, Caspar thought it to be far in the distance but soon saw that the mist had deceived his eyes and that the approaching black shape was very close indeed.

Cantering ahead of the shape, skirted in mist until his outline took on definition and colour, rode a man. The horse was the hue of midnight and was stepping with such a high and beautiful action, head tucked down towards the chest, that Caspar immediately recognized her as Raven. He had the extraordinary perception that she carried Silas with a mixture of devotion and resentment; he was certain of it. He shook himself, wondering how he could think such a ridiculous thing when there were so many other serious matters at hand.

Stiffening, he strained to interpret what was making that great grinding noise behind the rider. Slowly, the huge dark shape became more distinct. First, Caspar picked out a train of at least twenty draught horses dragging a huge platform, which ground on low solid wooden wheels. There, at least, was the source of the noise. Slumped into the platform was the body of a great tusked mammoth that was nearly half the size again of the dragon.

The crowd on the city wall gave out a heart-felt cheer. The city streets echoed with shouts of, 'Silas the Saviour, Silas the Mammoth-Slayer, Silas the Deliverer.'

Why not Silas the Dragon-Slayer, Caspar thought. He could not understand that, if he could manage, single-handed, to kill a mammoth, why he could not also kill a dragon.

His concentration was snatched by the dragon rearing up onto her hind legs, head tucked in tight to protect the soft spot at her throat. Then, in a display of victory, she spread wide her wings to cast a great shadow over the mammoth. The men with Silas stood stiff with terror as the great beast, like a tyrant queen, marched between them and began to nudge one or two aside with her vast nose as she made her way about the mammoth. Her tongue flickered out, licking the mammoth's furry face and then sliding her rasping tongue down its neck to its chest. Cobralike, she drew back her neck and struck forward, her head like a spear burying deep into the mammoth's ribcage.

Her front claws scrabbled and ripped at the flesh to widen the wound. The sound of huge bones cracking and splintering was clearly audible as the dragon's great neck worked back and forth while her buried head wrenched at the innards. The splintering sound was replaced by a squelching of innards and then by the sound of ripping and snapping of tendons, ligaments and blood vessels as the huge lizard withdrew her bloodied head, a huge red heart clamped in her jaws.

Completely unperturbed by the men all about, she threw back her head and swallowed her prize whole, the bulge in her throat large as the great heart was slowly drawn down the long neck into her stomach. She put her spread clawed foot onto the mammoth's breast, pressing down, forcing a spurt of blood out from the wound.

Leaf gripped Caspar's hand all the tighter. 'Save us. In the name of the Great Mother, save us.'

Her words were silenced as, from her perch on the mammoth's back, the dragon drew back her head and howled up at the tear in the atmosphere that had not yet mended. Instinctively, Caspar drew Leaf and Brid down into the grass. Within seconds, more claws appeared at the hole and then six much smaller dragons, red in colour, slipped through, one by one, to land beside the golden dragon. She greeted them with a waffle of warm air from her nostrils and Caspar guessed these smaller beasts were her brood. They each snatched a limb or some other part of the mammoth and then, with huge effort and vast beats of their wings that sent dust rolling across the landscape, they hauled the mammoth into the sky.

With curving talons, they clung to the edges of the charred hole in the atmosphere as they dragged the carcass through. Once they were gone, the hole slowly smoothed over to return to a seamless blue. Caspar blinked, his eyes dazzled by the now bright sky.

While he was still staring up in disbelief, Brid was already attending to Leaf. 'You poor girl,' the priestess soothed. 'Losing your family and now having to witness this.'

Leaf nodded solemnly. 'I loved Nanna very, very much. I had been living with her ever since I reached the age when I could read the sacred letters so that I might understand the arts of the inner circle. They thought I would be safer with her in the village.'

Brid looked at her more intently. 'The dragon didn't pick that village at random then? It knew? It knew you were there . . . ?'

Caspar looked from the woman to the girl and saw both acknowledge in the other something that each respected.

'You understand much for a woman of the outside world,' Leaf commented.

'And you understand too much for any girl,' Brid retorted, her voice weak and strained. 'You had better take me to your mother.' There was a hint of a scolding in Brid's tired tone and the girl seemed to understand that.

Leaf led them down the slope, merely glancing sideways at the huge bloody platform, keeping her head down, and only eyeing Silas the mammoth-slayer out of the corner of her eye. Caspar was, himself, distracted by the horse and he could not explain it. He found her a most intriguing creature yet she was only a horse. Half-rearing, she sat back on her haunches, frightened by all the screaming that had gone on and yet she, too, seemed aware of his presence. The only explanation he could find was his affinity with horses; they had always understood him whereas people had not. Though he knew they had little intelligence, he had the intense sense that their instincts were in tune with the realities of the world around, whereas humans were too easily deluded and led astray.

With a snappy motion, Silas cocked his head on one side and, for a moment, appeared surprised at Caspar's approach. 'So you made it!' He looked anxiously over Caspar's shoulder and nodded in relief when he saw Brid. 'And the fair lady too!'

'You left us there to be eaten by the dragon,' Caspar accused.

'Eaten . . . I . . . no, I was merely running for my life,' the man protested, clearly caught off guard. 'But you are safe now, Friend. Come, the people of this city will help you. I shall help you! I see your lady is somewhat recovered.'

'Who is he?' Brid asked under her breath but Caspar did not reply; he was wondering why the man now actively offered his help whereas before he had been so reticent and elusive. Not knowing what else to do, Caspar merely grunted but was glad when Silas offered his horse to Brid.

Once through the tall city gates, the mammoth-slayer snapped his fingers at the watchman, who shouted behind him for guards and, almost immediately, a number of young men stepped out smartly from a guardroom built into the thick wall. Caspar looked at them sideways. He had been expecting soldiers or guardsmen of some sort, but these men were dressed in light fabric jackets and soft woollen hose. They wore soft-soled shoes with curling tips and they were extraordinarily clean for guards.

The young Baron glanced at his own hands that gripped Leaf's soft wrists and was aware of the rough calluses against her smooth skin. Though a nobleman, he had used his hands all his life, either handling a bow or horses. The demeanour and appearance of these men, however, spoke of a soft indoor life.

The girl squirmed and wriggled nervously so he slung her up behind Brid, where she clung to the priestess as if desperate for her reassurance.

Caspar looked up at the towering city as the gates clanged shut and suddenly realized why these people where so utterly terrified of the fire-breathing beast. Their city that had gleamed in the beautiful sunlight was built mainly of wood. He had expected such fine architecture to be stone. The roofs of the grander buildings were clad in strips of copper, now green from exposure to the elements, but on the lower houses the roofs were of thatch. One breath from the dragon and they would all have perished.

Staring up at the huge and complicated structures, Caspar forgot their troubles. The basic structure of each building was a central tower banded by an external spiralling staircase. Halfway up the central column curved struts fanned out to support broad platforms encircling each tower. From these platforms, more towers grew. Bridges arched between the towers, creating a network of paths above their heads. It was an extraordinary feat of engineering and he was amazed that something so refined could be built out of wood. He also wondered at the lack of foresight to build in such an insubstantial way; it was as if they had no belief in the future.

Men and women with large frightened eyes poked their heads out from behind doors and many exclaimed with delight at the sight of Silas.

'We are saved!' the cry went up, filling the street. 'Silas is here.'

The extraordinary man reached out and shook hands with them. Several tried to press gifts into his hands, bunches of flowers, offerings of food, coins and, strangest of all, books, lots and lots of books.

To Caspar's surprise, Silas accepted none of them. He smiled and clasped hands and nodded his thanks but pressed the gifts back. 'The dragon is gone again until the next offering is due,' he exclaimed. 'Gone!'

'May the Great Lady always love you,' the town's folk exclaimed.

At last, they approached a circular lawn where a lone majestic leafless tree grew at the very heart of the city. The houses fronting this central green were even more remarkable than the ones on the outskirts of the city. Narrow towers supported wide disc-like structures. Many were linked to neighbouring structures by rope bridges and each circular platform was roofed with a gently sloping blanket of turf. Many of the towers had several such structures at different levels.

'They look like trees,' Brid said slowly. 'Tall trees with green canopies of grass and moss. The trees . . .' She looked about her thoughtfully.

'What is it?' Caspar asked.

Brid shrugged. 'I don't know. I can't quite believe this is real and I certainly can't believe I didn't know of its existence. What manner of race do you suppose they are?'

'What do you mean?' he asked, still staring giddily upwards.

'Well, they are clearly not like us, are they?' Brid said with a hint of exasperation.

'You mean they are not human?'

Brid snorted at his slowness. 'Of course they're not human.'

185

'How can you tell?' Caspar asked sceptically. He had met many races over the last fifteen years since the ancient creatures of the world had been freed. He had made strong friends amongst the men of Ash, had found the little kobolds mildly amusing, had always been wary of the few cantankerous dwarves that it had been his misfortune to rub shoulders with, and, of course, he had now met enough hobs to last a lifetime.

Brid ignored his question. 'And they're not wizards either,' she said with surety and relief. 'At first I feared they must be because they are the only other people that look like us, but wizards would have had little trouble defending themselves from dragons.' She turned to look at the lone tree in the middle of the green and Caspar followed her gaze and guessed at her thought.

'They are the People of Beech,' he surmised.

'Of course,' Brid said wearily 'The People of Beech; Phagos the tree of learning and knowledge.'

Now the excitement of the dragon was over, people were pouring out from their homes with piles of books, paper and parchment under their arms and were choosing a spot on the green to sit and study as if for leisure. Many chose to sit in circles of up to a dozen and passed parchments back and forth whilst others remained in deep discussion.

Brid, however, was not interested in this. Her eyes were on Silas, who was approaching the largest of the wooden houses. He took Raven's reins and handed them to a man in attendance before gesturing to Caspar to follow. The Baron lifted first Leaf and then Brid down from the back of the mare and put his arms around Brid, helping her to walk. Leaf thankfully no longer needed his assistance as they began their laboured climb up the staircase that coiled around the central pillar.

At last, they reached green doors set into the side of the column. In a stiff, jerky manner, Silas rapped at the doors with his staff. The doors half opened. 'Tell the High Lady Zophia that I am home and shall await her within,' he commanded.

The doors were opened wider and Caspar, Brid and Leaf were ushered in and again led up a short flight of stairs that opened into a broad circular room that they had seen from below as a huge disc spreading out from the narrow tower. They were led to one of the windows and looked in wonder over the city. Caspar was acutely aware of being extraordinarily close to the sky and looked up. It was almost like looking through a film of water that was somehow hanging in the air above their heads.

'It's as if we are trapped within a huge glass jar,' he commented to Brid.

She nodded weakly, her face a little green, and he realized that the effort of the climb had sapped her strength. Brid croaked, 'I don't know how we entered this secret world. I don't understand how it is possible.' Her breathing was heavy and she was sweating.

Closing his arms around her for support, he eased her head onto his shoulder. There was nothing more he could do for the moment so, to distract himself from his concern, he turned his attention back the to sky. As he stared into it, he could see minute crystals soaking up the sunlight. Sparkling shapes momentarily formed and, for a second, he thought he could make out spellrunes within the glinting droplets in the atmosphere.

He pointed but had no need to explain to Brid what he thought he saw.

She followed his finger. 'Whatever else these people of Beech are, they are very scared people. Very scared indeed.' She held out her hand as a sparkling light, like a snowflake, drifted down from the heavens and in through the unglazed windows. The flake landed clear into her palm and Caspar looked to see it was a tiny sparkling rune that appeared to be cut from pure silver.

He did not know the rune's meaning and so looked to Brid for an answer.

'Runes of protection,' she murmured. 'Millions upon millions of them.'

Chapter 11

The High Lady Zophia was just as Caspar had imagined. She had rich brown hair piled high on her head, ringlets and curls spilling out from the delicate circlet about her brow. She was tall and slender, her skin white and flawless with just a hint of soft pink to her cheeks and lips.

Sitting upright on a slender chair, she wore a blue dress under a white robe that cascaded from her shoulders. Her delicate feet were clad in red slippers, one foot tapping on the dais upon which her chair was set.

'Why have you brought these people here?' she asked Silas in a slightly nervous tone.

'I would not willingly endanger your people,' Silas said evasively. 'I believed these outsiders lost to the dragon. I knew the golden queen would come again soon, so my priority was to kill a mammoth for the offering. What would you have had me do, dear lady? Would it have been better if I had failed to bring the offering that turned the dragon away from the gates of this beautiful city?'

A general wide-eyed look of alarm spread amongst the assembled servants and guards. Horrified murmurs circled around the broad low chamber.

'But what is to be done with them?' the High Lady demanded.

'Done with us?' Brid murmured into Caspar's shoulder. The exertion of the climb had been too much for her and she was very pale. Beads of sweat had formed on her forehead and he was worried that an infection had taken hold. It was not uncommon even after a normal birth and he had known many who had died in such a way.

Bracing her in his arms, he spoke out, 'You can do nothing with us but let us go home. We wish you no harm and your world is deeply hidden from us. We would soon forget our way here. I must get Brid home!'

'Forget?' Zophia said uncertainly, her eyes now flitting past Brid to the little girl at her heels. Leaf raised her arms in greeting and the High Lady suddenly leapt to her feet, her eyes widening in sudden recognition. She held out her hands and ran forward, dropping to her knees to hug the child. 'Leaf! Leaf! Is that really you? What happened? Why are you here? You know it's not safe in the city. You should never have left the village. You have grown much in two years and I didn't recognize you!'

'It has been too long, Mother!' Leaf said with great sadness. 'I was forced to leave. The dragon came. The dragon came and burned them all. I was only saved by Nanna who protected me with her own body though I nearly suffocated and couldn't get out from beneath her. It was only by chance that this young lady and her man came by and pulled me out.'

'But, Silas, you said she would be safe!' Zophia wailed, hugging her daughter tight, her face now white and her hands shaking.

Seeing that the attention had been diverted away from them, Caspar took the opportunity to ease Brid down onto a couch at the side of the room.

'The exertion,' Brid murmured, her eyelids flickering as they slowly closed. 'And the pain is worse.' She pressed at her belly.

'Indeed,' Silas continued to address the High Lady. 'I thought she would be safe but the mammoth got away and I was late with the monthly offering. As you saw, the dragon went wild with frenzy and anger. Until now, we have been lucky in that the hard winters have driven the mammoths south so that they are easier to hunt but it is not always so easy. We were fortunate that I could return in time to save the city.'

'You are not fortunate at all. You cannot just keep paying off the dragon,' Caspar warned them. 'You must defend yourselves.'

They paid him no more than a brief glance. The frustration made him curse under his breath as he struggled to find patience. Rather than repeat his warning, he watched and listened, all the while soothing Brid. But she barely responded and he despaired as he watched her slowly slipping back into her stupor.

The High Lady had her arms wrapped about Leaf. Her composure vanished as she checked her daughter all over, peering into her eyes, examining her face and hands and stroking her long dark hair. They were not an unattractive people, tall and lithe-limbed though not extraordinary, and, to Caspar's eye, they were perhaps a little plain about the face. Yet, their demeanour was different to the average person. They looked at each other in a calm and thoughtful manner tempered with great sorrow. Caspar sensed a collective emotion of profound regret.

'What should we do about them?' Zophia again asked Silas while nodding at the two Torra Altans.

Caspar felt Brid stiffen and squeeze his hand as if warning him to be vigilant for their safety. He looked round, wondering why Zophia was so concerned about Silas's views. If he were just a hunter, as he claimed, then she should not hold him in such high regard. He noted that Leaf looked sideways at her mother and suspiciously at Silas, though the mammoth-slayer smiled openly enough as he answered the lady.

'It is not my position to govern, dear lady. But you know what the law is regarding people who find their way here and jeopardize the safety of your people. The woman, however, is clearly ill and we owe the man a debt of gratitude. Perhaps you

191

should be lenient with them,' he suggested, his eyes lingering on Brid.

'I am not sure . . .' The High Lady blinked rapidly and her eyes searched the palms of her hands as if the answer were written there. 'I am responsible for the safety of all and we do not know—'

'Lady Zophia,' Caspar hastily interrupted, 'we wish no harm, only to go home.'

The High Lady peered at him through slitted eyes. 'Oh we all wish to go home. We have wished for a great many years.'

'Mother,' the girl said quietly, 'are you worse? You seem . . .'

'I am but weary.' She smiled. 'Very weary. I think we must put this to the Council.' She nodded as if trying to decide whether this was the right thing to do before rising unsteadily, her arm tight about her little girl. I do not want you to grow old: it is not good for us. We cannot grow old and wise as we used to. There are so few of us now. I can't remember all the things I used to know. They write . . . Our scholars try so hard to write it down but more knowledge is being lost day by day. The knowledge of how it was is all but lost. How it was, how it is and how it should be; we had the answers once.' She sighed heavily.

Caspar did not need Brid's training to sense that Zophia was very sick indeed.

The High Lady snapped her fingers. 'Music! I must have music to take away the pain. I must.'

Silas took her hand and helped her to walk unsteadily to a door in the central column, a small man with a set of pipes dancing merrily after them. The mammoth-hunter nodded at the guard next to him and then cast his eyes back towards Caspar. Instantly, the guard paced towards Caspar and urged him politely but firmly to follow; he had no choice but to obey. Lifting Brid into his arms, he strode after the sound of the pipes and ascended a flight of steps that led into a narrow corridor; the roof arched and the walls curved in on them.

The corridor sloped steadily down until it opened up into a low broad chamber divided by rows of laden shelves and huge wooden desks. Caspar stared in amazement. It was a library the like of which he had never seen. The large room was divided by screens with corridors and small antechambers and, everywhere he looked, open shelves were crammed to the ceiling with books. The pipe music faded away as if in respect to those within.

For a minute, Caspar was so amazed that all his fears and worries were gone. Never had he seen so many books nor so many people interested in them, heads down, their noses almost brushing the pages. All were dressed alike, men and women, in grey cloaks. They muttered in low voices to one another in between frantic spurts of writing or tortured puzzling over the heavy tomes they studied.

Brid stirred in Caspar's aching arms and he longed for somewhere safe to lay her down. She groaned in pain and then managed to murmur, 'Look at their faces, Spar.'

Pulling Brid tighter to his chest, Caspar looked about him, wondering what she meant. The people seemed quite content, their faces furrowed with deep concentration but, as he studied them for a little longer, he began to wonder at their obsessive studying.

'They are mad, aren't they?' he whispered in Brid's ear, aware that she was sticky with sweat and that her breathing was fast and light.

'Beware the fool,' she murmured, distractedly, 'because he knows not what havoc he wreaks.'

'They aren't dangerous; all these people can't keep one lone dragon at bay.'

'Oh Spar, I'm too ill for this. Can't you think for yourself?' Brid complained, her eyes sagging closed. 'This entire realm cannot stop one dragon yet Silas can . . . Silas can . . .'

Caspar adjusted Brid in his arms, lifting her a little higher to ease the strain on his muscles. She needed help and he prayed Zophia would soon grant his request. Following after

Silas and the High Lady, they wove around the ranks of desks. Caspar glanced over the shoulder of one and was perturbed to note that the man had abandoned his quill and, instead, was continually dipping his finger into the ink pot, painstakingly drawing row upon row of circles rather than forming proper characters.

Caspar lowered his head to the side to read the title of one of the books on the neighbouring desk. The runic script was intricately drawn and it took him a moment to decipher the lettering. *The Book of Runic Elements, volume one: Runes of Ice, Sky and Fire.*

It was only when Caspar saw one man licking the letters of a page and another with the book against his ear that he became totally aware of Brid's assertion. He was impressed that, even in her present condition, she had the lucidity to see what was going on around her. Eyeing the scholars warily, he followed the High Lady as they progressed through the library, Zophia nodding respectfully at the older men and women as she passed.

'I used to feel so annoyed with them,' she murmured to her daughter. 'I was angry with them for forgetting but now I am only sad for them and I fear for the rest of us because I, too, am forgetting. It will happen to us all.' Suddenly her eyes were burning with intense clarity as she turned on her heel and fixed Caspar in the eye. 'You must understand. We have to find a way to remember.' She screwed her hands up into tight balls, the muscles in her neck strained and prominent as she stared at him. She only relaxed when she became aware of Leaf tugging at her sleeve.

'Oh Mother, oh Mother,' Leaf soothed. 'Be strong. Your time is not yet. You must guide us a while longer.'

The girl's composure and strength of character impressed Caspar. She was very young to shoulder such a calm head.

Leaf turned to Caspar and touched Brid's sleeve. 'She must help us. I have not yet drawn on the knowledge of the ancients. I know that, by the time I am mature enough to be initiated, I shall be within just a few years of the disease overwhelming me. There is never enough time.'

Caspar looked at her, his eyes begging. 'But Brid is ill. It is she who needs your help. *You* must help her otherwise she will never be able to help you. There is no need of ancient knowledge to understand that!'

Leaf nodded solemnly.

Beyond the library, they came to a darker, lower chamber, the ceiling set with the carved and painted images of suns, moons and stars. Two concentric rings of men and women sat about the chamber. The outer circle sat on an elevated circular dais. Sitting on their haunches in front of them, was a younger group huddled tight about a mercurial pool at the centre of the room. The outer circle were still and calm and so didn't draw the eye but those of the inner circle were working hard with their hands, their mouths moving in silent chant.

'What are they doing?' Caspar whispered reverently, looking in amazement at the extraordinary sight.

They seemed to be dipping their quills into the pool of mercury and then, in the finest characters, inscribing runes onto clear crystals about the size of his hand. The crystals were then placed into stone bowls and pulverized with small gold-headed hammers. The fine dust that remained was scooped up and tossed out of the windows where the winds caught them and snatched them up, lifting them up to join the distant glaze that sparkled over their heads.

Brid groaned in his arms. 'Runes of concealing, runes of protection, runes of healing and safety but the combinations and additional runes . . .' She grunted and her eyes closed again. 'I feel . . . I don't feel well, Hal. Terrible pains . . . The baby. I can't feel her kicking.'

Caspar was deeply concerned that she no longer even knew him. She was turning a sickly grey with blotches of heightened colour about her cheeks and was clearly confused and forgetful. She needed help.

'It's very simple really,' Leaf was explaining about the rune-carved crystals. 'When they smash the crystals, the runes are broken down and divided until their qualities are imprinted onto the very particles themselves. The particles are so light they can be borne up into atmosphere and carry the runic message into the sky.'

Caspar turned his attention back to the scholars and noted how those at the centre worked the hardest, writing as fast as they could. Those of the second row worked more slowly, taking a little longer to think about what they were doing, one or two rubbing at their brows in consternation. One girl who had stopped work, was dragging at her hair and then suddenly flung down her mortar in a rage of frustration.

'Oh Great Mother, spare me the torment. Spare me!' she wailed.

'It is worse for the scholars, they say,' Leaf said softly. 'Their minds are so keen and they work so fast but, when they lose their powers of retention, they find the ensuing confusion more unbearable than those that are not so gifted. It is a terrible thing for them.'

Silas looked to the High Lady and cleared his throat as if to prompt her into action. 'Lady Zophia, is it not time you addressed the Council to determine what should be done with this man and woman?' He then grinned tightly at Caspar and spoke more softly. 'Do not worry; I shall see to it that they allow me to take you back along the roads; it is only fair. You did not wish to come here. State your case and allow it to be considered; they will listen and appreciate good reasoning.' He raised his hand to silence Caspar who was about to speak. 'Better, I shall state your case for you.'

The tall man with the long hair nodded about him at the ring of scholars who raised their faces to him, their eyes bearing a faraway look. They were not simple or vacant, Caspar decided; they were unspeakably sad, as if they had lost something irreplaceable.

Silas began, 'This man was fleeing from the hobs that we

work so hard to keep out of the realm. I saved him by chance but was injured in the process. He then helped me and, if it were not for his skill, I would have been for evermore unable to bring you offerings with which to appease the dragon.'

There was a murmur amongst the people, which Silas allowed to die down before he continued, 'He served me well; he should be rewarded.'

The older ones were nodding enthusiastically and Caspar was alarmed to see how easily they were swayed by this one man. Then one of the younger ones laid down his pestle and stood up.

'Yet he knows the ways to our realm. My mind is not as acute as it was but I am sure that no race should be trusted with the fate of another. We cannot let him go, however innocent he may be.'

'What if I promise to return with men to destroy this dragon?' Caspar argued in his most reasonable of voices. 'If you let us go home, I can help you.'

One of the older members of the council spoke forth, 'We cannot accept the word of an outsider. Besides, what you propose would be worse than the dragon. Think of it; soldiers here in our realm! It could only lead to our destruction.'

'I must get back to my son. Please listen to me,' Caspar begged. 'I could destroy the dragon in my world. Anything for my freedom! I must get home for my son.'

'The cup!' the councillor bargained. 'We must have the Chalice.'

Caspar's blood ran cold and his mind screamed within his head that something was wrong here but he could not imagine what. 'A chalice?' he asked with feigned innocence. 'What chalice?'

'You know perfectly well: The Chalice of Önd.' The councillor stood up from his chair and Caspar could see that his hands were shaking violently. 'We cannot keep ourselves safe much longer since more and more of us are falling ill by the day. If you bring us the Chalice, our very finest minds will be freed from the labour of forever reforming the spell that keeps our lands concealed. The Chalice would replicate the runes for us, so releasing our scholars. Then they could work on the problem of our sickness and find a way to save us.'

Silas nodded at this. 'I would help you find it,' he offered Caspar with enthusiasm. 'You saved me; it would only be fair.'

His gaze flitted between him and Leaf who surreptitiously shook her head just the tiniest fraction, warning him not to listen to the man.

'I know nothing of this Chalice. How can you expect me to find it? You must let me go! For pity's sake, let me go so that I might find my son.'

As the scholars debated their fate, he wondered if he hadn't, at times, seen the Scholars of Beech in his own world but never noticed them since they were so unremarkable in looks. Even the High Lady had a plain face and a common shade of brown hair.

'We cannot let you go! You must remain here until you change your mind and agree to help us!' the councillor announced.

'But—' Caspar began to protest but the councillor waved him down. 'We shall do what we can to help the woman of course. Our physicians are skilled.'

Caspar did not resist as Brid was lifted from his arms. He knew he could do nothing to help her himself and had no reason to doubt that these people would do all they could for her. While Brid was carried back towards Zophia's quarters, he was led down a tight stairway and out onto the soft carpet of green grass footing the city buildings. Silas followed one or two paces behind, still trying to persuade Caspar to let him help him.

Courteously but firmly, he was ushered towards the edge of the city where there was a neatly tended garden set at the edge of a fenced paddock. The garden was surrounded by a wattle fence and a solid wooden gate. At the centre of the garden was a small circular hut with a thatched roof and many large ornate windows. He realized that he was expected to stay within the simple garden though it was by no means secure.

'They are not a violent people,' Silas assured him, 'but they have ways of keeping you here.'

Caspar was led into the hut, which contained a table, a chair and a bench. Women hurried in with simple fare of nuts and bread, and water was provided in a pitcher. There were also blankets with which he could make himself a bed. No sooner were the goods deposited than he was alone.

For a moment, he stared at the closed gate before deciding to test how effectively he was contained. Rubbing at his thigh, which was still sore and slightly swollen from his injury, he walked slowly towards the gate. He was limping slightly and paused to adjust the cloth that covered the wound. When he looked up, the gate seemed further off than he had expected. He started off again, more quickly this time.

But the faster he walked, the longer the garden path became and he got no closer to his goal. He halted and decided that he must take another approach. Turning away from the gate, he began to amble down one of the paths, hoping to curl his way round to it but, no matter which way he turned, the boundary to the garden came no closer.

Remembering Silas's staff, Caspar realized that the runes the man had cut onto it must have allowed him to counteract the disorientating spell. For over an hour, Caspar paced round and around the garden but still could not find his way to its edge.

In utter frustration, he returned to the hut. Sinking down into the chair, he let his head fall forward onto the table. He thumped his forehead into the wood, trying to clear his thoughts. Swallowing hard, he remembered his son and immediately cursed his own stupidity for taking the boy from the country of his birth.

He clenched his fists against the torment of his thoughts.

He had become a father young in life and that trial, more than any other, had catapulted him into adulthood. Fourteen years of serene happiness with his wife had restored his faith in humanity and love but he was not happy now and had not been since her death.

Angrily kicking the table over, he stooped forward and stared at the beaten earth floor that was packed down to a smooth finish. Finding a piece of wood had broken from the table, he used it to loosen the soil, niggling away at it, letting the senseless act of destruction ease his frustration and facilitate his thoughts. Imprisoned by mad men, he thought in despair. I can do them no harm and yet they are afraid of me. But it was no good just sitting here. After taking a swig of water and tearing off a hunk of bread, he resolved to explore the garden again.

Staring up at the hazy sky, he now realized why it was so much warmer here; it was like being in the solar room of some airy manor. The filtered sunlight made strange patterns on the lush grass, which the gentle breeze caressed. A feathery shade was created by the bare beech trees that grew profusely across the meadow spreading out at the rear of the garden. Eyeing the ring of hurdles, he struggled to think how he was ever going to escape from here.

He sat staring into the field and then suddenly stiffened at the sight of Silas's beautiful black mare being turned loose at the far end of the meadow. At first, she bucked and kicked her heels, galloping along the far perimeter of the paddock as if she were also seeking a way out but, eventually, she contented herself by lowering her head into the lush grass alongside a quiet brook. Her ears twitched occasionally and her full tail lashed her flank to ward off any flies that crawled amongst the streaks of crisp sweat at her shoulders and rump. She had been ridden hard in the last hour, Caspar surmised, plucking up a piece of grass and twiddling it to ease his frustration.

He found the animal strangely intriguing. Having a great love of all horses, he had spent as much time as he could in their company, taking huge pleasure in training selected colts for his children. This horse, however, drew his interest far more than most. He had the distinct impression that she was watching him but not in the wary, curious way that an ordinary horse might. Perhaps living with these strange people within the security of their world had changed her.

The piece of grass he had in his hand was now snapped into twelve tiny pieces. Letting the last piece drop, he picked up a pebble, turned it over and then attempted to fling it as far out into the meadow as he could, not in the least surprised to see it land no more than a few paces in front of him.

'Tell me how I get out of here,' he demanded of the thin air.

A little voice whispered behind him. 'I can get you out.'

The surprise made him jump for he had thought himself alone and was certain that he would have seen anyone approach. His eyebrows raised as he wondered how his young visitor had arrived so surreptitiously.

'Leaf!' he greeted her, hiding his surprise in a warm smile.

'I would have come sooner but I had to see Father. He would have let you go but he is sick and has no say. My mother barely visits him – she listens too much to Silas.' She sighed ruefully. 'I don't understand what is going on but it was Silas that suggested I stayed in the village. I'm sure he wanted me out of the way.'

Caspar nodded, prompting her to go on, and was not aware of the horse slowly nibbling her way through the grass, taking one slow step after another and making gradual progress up the slope towards him.

Leaf looked down at her feet, studying the cracked leather of her shoes. Caspar guessed that she had news he did not want to hear. Her hazel eyes met his.

'I was too long with Father; by the time I got back, Mother told me that Silas had persuaded the Council that Brid should be released. He insisted that she must be helped by our physicians and given something to make her forget her time in this realm so that he could return her to her own world.'

'Silas took her?' Caspar asked in horror, gripping Leaf's shoulders and staring hard into her face. 'They let him take her?'

Leaf reached out to hug him, the tears finally welling up into her eyes. 'Spar, I'm so scared. I barely know you; I only know that Brid understood. She was our last hope and now she is gone. Silas took her right away but must have left her somewhere just over the borders of our realm because he is back already and gone straight to my mother.' She clung tightly to him. 'You must help us. I have tried to walk out of here before now to get help but when I reach the crystal curtain I daren't go beyond for fear of the terrors of the outside world.'

Caspar knelt down to her level and closed his arms about her. 'It is true that there are hobs and dragons beyond your haven but you are at just as much at risk from dragons here, if not more so.'

Leaf shook her head. 'I'm too young to know what it was like when we openly shared our world but my ancestors must have had a very good reason for hiding themselves like this.'

Caspar had no doubt that their reason had been to protect themselves from his own kind. He wondered how it had come to pass that man had become so feared. He could understand if it had been the cold-hearted hobs but he could not understand why, with all his principled ways and high morals, man was so destructive.

He kept his counsel and smiled winningly at Leaf. 'You could come with me. It is my world on the outside. Believe it or not, I am a powerful man. If you lead me out of here and help me find Brid, I will do all I can to help you and your people. We will find this dragon and hunt it down for you, delivering your people from its menace.'

'And from the menace of Silas?' Leaf added. 'They don't see. Since Father's malaise, Mother has command but she isn't thinking clearly either. Silas has won my mother's confidence. But she is a good woman, you know.' Leaf's voice cracked and the sobs filled her throat again. 'She means well but she is losing her reason. Only two years ago; she was so bright and quick and certain but now she is forgetful and hazy. And soon this will happen to me too! I must do something to save my people. I must, and now, before it is all lost forever.'

Caspar patted her small pale hand. 'Indeed, you must. Child of this hidden realm, I will look after you and be your protector,' he vowed, 'if you will only lead me. I must find Brid and my son.'

'We have a pact,' she said, her tight sad mouth at last widening to a smile. Still clutching her hand, Caspar straightened up, aware that Leaf's hand trembled in his. He saw that this girl possessed caution of knowledge far more steady and more contemplative than a human child.

'My father is the High Lord of this land,' she murmured. 'I must get him back to where he belongs as leader of my people before we are destroyed entirely by this dragon.'

'Let's delay no longer,' Caspar said with forced brightness, hoping to keep Leaf's spirits up. 'Get me out of here!'

He sighed at Leaf, his heart going out to her; she reminded him of how much he missed Imogen. 'How do we get out of here?' he asked, focusing on his present dilemma.

'Simple,' Leaf replied. 'I have the key.' She unclasped her left hand and Caspar saw, not a key, but a small amulet carved with runes. He thought the runes looked similar to the ones he had seen on Silas's staff and the headband of Raven's bridle.

He laughed dryly. 'So that's how he did it. Come on, let's get out of here before anyone comes looking for me.' Not once did it flicker through his mind that Leaf's motives were for anything but the best.

Tugging him by the hand, she led him along the gravel path through the tilled beds of the herb garden. Low lavender hedges lined the paths, their frosted green virtually the only plant showing its greenery so early in the year. Within a few minutes, they were at the gate. Here Caspar paused; the horse had suddenly whickered as if calling him.

He turned and she raced across the turf, head high, clips of earth flying up behind her and her tail streaming out like a banner. She skidded to a halt before the fence, her front hooves digging deep into the soft sod, her head tucked down towards her chest. Then, very much to Caspar's surprise, she wheeled away to give herself a short run up at the fence before leaping neatly over and approaching with slow purpose, her shining eyes rolling in fear and every muscles trembling.

Alarmed that a horse should behave in such a manner, Caspar stood, legs astride, ready to face up to her in case she decided to run them down. But the animal appeared confused and fearful as if driven to approach him by an unnatural instinct that she didn't understand. The Baron had often seen fear in animals. Fear was a basic and pure emotion shared by all living things and was quite natural in a horse. But he also thought that he saw sadness in her expression and frowned, staring back at the horse while Leaf struggled to unbolt the wooden gates that led out of the idyllic garden. The black mare dipped her head and then stretched out her neck towards him, snuffling at his hand, her nostrils flared, drinking in his scent.

'There, girl,' he soothed, hoping to calm her. He took a slow but firm step forward to show he was not afraid. However, he prudently leapt back as she stood up on her hind legs, whether in fear or aggression he could not tell. She dropped down onto all fours again, and raked the ground three times with her foreleg, gouging the ground with each strike of her hoof.

'Quick!' Leaf hissed. 'It's open. Come on!'

Once through the gate, Leaf carefully bolted it behind

them to leave the appearance that nothing had been disturbed. 'What did you do to that horse? All that squealing will bring Silas faster than a trumpet blast. What were you thinking of?' she scolded him.

'I didn't do anything!' Caspar protested, wondering why he felt so inadequate and apologetic in front of this little girl.

She looked hastily about her. 'As soon as they discover you have gone, they will presume that you will run back along the paths you know. That is always the way of your kind. We'll get a good head start on them if we do the opposite and first go deeper into the city. Don't worry; we shall be safe.'

Leaf led him back towards the main city and into a series of rose gardens laid out in peaceful, regimented lines that were not particularly imaginative but pleasing in their ordered symmetry. Caspar decided they gave insight into the mind of these people.

'My mother's garden,' Leaf confirmed. 'She tends it herself whenever she can. No one will notice us if we just walk through calmly. Thankfully, your looks do not set you so much apart from our own people.'

Tightly clipped yew hedges led them into another part of the garden and Caspar was immediately alarmed. Clearly, this garden had been laid out to the same design of shaped hedges and raised beds as the others but this one had been decimated. Weaving his way through the overgrown garden, where crisp, wintry weeds poked up through the gravel and overgrown shrubs created the effect of a small wood, he clambered over a thorny rose tree that lay across their path. It had been staked to grow out of the bed and along the path and others had also been dragged out of the perfect design.

'Your father's garden,' he guessed and Leaf shook her head.

'No. No, alas, it is Mother's. It was so beautiful once, absolutely perfect in its symmetry. But, even two years ago, she was starting to cut the buds off her roses before they flowered.' She looked away and jerked her head up as if forcing herself to face up to the enormity of her problems.

As they pushed their way along the path, the garden about them became more and more overgrown until the brambles completely smothered the path and they were forced onto the beds that were thigh-high in fireweed. Caspar wondered at the sadness of it all. The once neat and orderly minds that had shown their reverence for symmetry and logic in creating these wonderful gardens were now shaping chaos.

Leaf led them through another garden. 'I must give the key back to Father otherwise they will blame him when Mother eventually remembers that he still had one. I cannot let anything more happen to him; you do understand? I know it will take longer but I must.'

Caspar nodded, wishing that his own children held him in the same high regard. When they reached a solid wooden door, which was beginning to rot at top and bottom, Leaf worked hard to fit a conventional key into the old rusted lock. At last, she leant against the wood and it swung outwards on loose hinges. Caspar was about to follow her, when he was distracted by the distant distressed call of a horse that seemed to plunge deep into his soul as if it were a primeval call from his ancestors.

The shouts and calls of men were came from the distant meadow and he knew it wouldn't be long before Silas and the High Lady organized a search.

Leaf tiptoed through the door into a walled area that Caspar could not truly describe as a garden. Rooted logs lay between pieces of old broken benches, planks plunged into the ground and withered stems of plants wrapped around the top in mimicry of a tree. They worked their way through the dense cover until they came to the centre of the enclosed area where Caspar saw a man who was nearing the end of his middle years.

He was stooped over an area of cleared and tilled soil, a bundle of freshly picked bluebells tucked under one arm. He appeared to be trying to plant the cut flowers back into the soil and clearly had been doing this for some while because, though there were several rows that stood upright, there were others behind that were beginning to wither and, beyond that, others that had wilted entirely. The man appeared deeply perplexed by all this and kept hurrying back to them and trying to make them stand up.

'Oh why do you always die on me? You used to thrive all over my garden at this time of year but now you die. Don't die, pretty people.'

Leaf coughed and the man spun round in alarm, evidently surprised by their presence. At first, he looked confused and wary, distractedly wiping a tear from his eye that had no doubt been shed for his bluebells. Caspar felt intensely sorry for him.

'It's only me,' Leaf said softly and trotted up to him.

He took a step back, no welcoming smile on his face, and simply frowned at her. She seemed unperturbed by his lack of greeting.

'I must give you back the key,' she explained, stepping very slowly forward as if not wishing to frighten him. Caspar wondered that a girl so young could have the sensitivity and understanding to treat the man with such gentleness. 'I must leave you, Father, and get help for us all. You are a good man and I love you dearly.' She pressed the amulet into his hand.

He didn't look at it but simply put it into his pocket as if conditioned to do so. 'I don't know you, stranger,' he said to her gruffly. 'Now hurry along and stop messing up my garden. You can't play here; you'll ruin the roses. I can't have that. I have the finest rose garden and must have the finest blooms ready for my sweet lady. She loves roses. She'll visit me soon, won't she? Tell her, child, that she must come and visit me. I am lonely without her. I'll pay you well.' He reached down and plucked up one of the withered bluebells.

The little girl clutched the flower. 'That is what I mean

to do, Father, though it may take a little while.' She closed her fist around the bluebell and then stepped back tugging at Caspar's hand. 'Come, we must hurry.'

'Wait!' the man commanded in a voice suddenly deep with dignity and ringing with the power of command. 'Young man, do not forget where you came from. She is calling to remind you. Calling to you,' he said, already his voice losing its moment of lucidity. 'She needs your help. You must not forget her. Forget . . .,' he repeated and then frowned, and looked down at his feet, his muttered words dying in his confusion.

Caspar nudged Leaf onwards. 'We have no time for this now; which way?'

Sniffing and still clutching the withered bluebell, Leaf trotted down one of the meandering paths. They had nearly reached the open gate at the far end of the garden when she glanced back, a smile brightening her face as she saw the old man staring after them, his hand partially raised in a half-hearted gesture of farewell.

'Somewhere in his mind, he still remembers me,' she managed to croak through her tight throat.

'Remember!' the man called out! 'Remember otherwise we shall all, in the end, be lost.'

Chapter 12

Her lungs cramped with cold.

Exhausted, her will alone kept her trembling muscles working. She managed to force an irregular beat from her wings, the propulsion lessening with each lame stroke. Through blurred vision, she desperately sought a place to land.

Dragons liked mountains; there was always some outcrop or peak on which to alight, but here upon the foggy plains trees grew in profusion.

Wings stretched wide, she glided, lacking the strength to do more. The man had asked too much of her and still had not brought her anywhere near her reward.

There were large trees below but she had no choice. Her strength was spent and the muscles along her chest and back that worked her wings would no longer respond to her will. All she could do was glide and shut her eyes against the impact.

Instinct forced her to draw her legs forward and stretch down with her toes, the tops of trees thrashing against her. She dipped the lower portion of her wings, trapping the air, and drew her neck up and back to balance herself. For a moment there was space beneath her as she passed beyond the taller trees and dropped towards a swathe of saplings, the young trees scraping and snapping against her belly. She skidded to the ground, twisted and jolted by their youthful strength and pecked forward, her jaw crashing into the frost-hardened earth.

She lay for some time without moving. The wind had been

knocked from her lungs and her vision was black. Sharp pains ran along the underside of her belly where the broken spines of the saplings had ripped at her scales. She was cold, so, so cold.

It was not right that one of her kind should be forced into the skies at this time of year. She should have crawled down into a comfortable nest deep below ground and kept herself warm through the winter. And she would have done so if only she could have curled her long, strong body about the adorable warm mass of her son. She would have licked his face and brought her wing up to cover them both. She would have been lulled to sleep listening to the bump-bump, bump-bump of his hearts. Her dreams would have been soothed by the lullaby of her love for him. But that comfort had been taken from her.

Now all love was gone. The cold sapped her strength that had been dangerously depleted by bellowing out the fierce heat from her belly to spit fire at those villages and then going back to struggle with the massive weight of the mammoths. The depth of her hatred kept her going but she had misjudged her stamina and not allowed for the strenuous effort of breaking out through the curtain of crystals that surrounded the warm land. With so much of her fire disgorged, she was perilously cold and weak.

With the last of her strength, she drew her wings about her body and, exhausted, slipped into a trancelike sleep.

The scent of horse filled her nostrils; the dream was so luscious that she even chomped her great jaws in her sleep and was reluctant to stir from the pleasures of her slumber. The horse snorted in alarm and she slowly raised one eyelid, suddenly aware that it was no dream. She blinked but could see nothing but trees. Almost imperceptibly, she slowly tensed her aching muscles in readiness and inched up her neck in preparation to strike. Had the creature sensed that her fire was spent and so dared to come so close? Her claws flexed.

She then blinked her other eye open and grunted in disgust.

'Gobel,' she groaned and allowed her head to thump back onto the earth.

'You look tired, old queen,' he sneered at her, sliding down from the saddle and struggling to cling onto the reins of the iron-grey horse that she eyed greedily.

She knew it was unwise to let the little wretch see her vulnerable state of weakness, yet she was too weary to play such games.

'Well?' she croaked irritably.

'He needs you,' Gobel replied laconically, his head jerking left and right in a manner that was common to hobs.

'He needs more of me? That man has asked too much already yet I still see no evidence that he keeps to his side of the bargain.' The effort and her pain were now immense but she knew that, even if she were to die a thousand times, it would be worth it to be reunited with Aurek.

'He asks me to assure you that very soon—'

'Soon? Soon!' she growled in her throat. 'All I ever hear is soon.' One day, she vowed, she would bite this hob's head off, however foul he might taste. She deeply resented the fact that she needed him. But she would do anything to have her son and the lords of the Otherworld had promised her they would render his soul to her, if she would help the wretched man that this hob spoke for. Cold smoke waffled up from deep within her and drifted from her flaring nostrils. 'What does he want this time?'

'It is but a small task, oh greatest of queens,' the little hob hissed. 'It is the small matter of a human female.'

'He has a woman for me to eat?' The great dragon managed to raise her head and her tongue slid around her long dagger-sharp teeth. The soft sweet flesh of a woman was better than any other meat and her mouth was instantly awash with saliva that slid in drools from the points of her great fangs. The excitement stirred the dwindling flame within her belly.

Struggling to hold his horse, Gobel hastily stepped back, his breath whistling between his jagged teeth, his nostrils flaring wide to show the glistening gristle within. 'Let me explain,' he began.

'Very well,' the dragon agreed once he had finished. 'It is an easier task than the mammoth. And next time, tell him, I need one where I can land. I cannot alight in the thick of the trees.' She spread wide her wings and showed the tear in her scales beaded with red where the tree had caught her. She drew her neck up and back, her tongue flickering out at the hob, suddenly angry that he and his master had shown her so little respect. 'You understand me, don't you?'

The scrawny hob took another step back and she noted with satisfaction the way he trembled. 'I understand.'

'I do not like to let creatures like you live,' she hissed. 'You make the world smell sour. You can tell your master that I will do as he asks but you shall go to him on foot.'

Trembling, the hob tugged at the reins to draw his quivering mount to him.

Drawing her legs up beneath her, the giant lizard sprang like a cat. With satisfaction, she saw the look of alarm on the hob's face as her great mouth closed about the horse's head. She jerked her jaws to the side and felt the vertebrae snap. Closing her fangs tight, the head came away and the warm, salty brew of blood swilled down her throat.

One eye on the stammering hob, she tore out another chunk of flesh from the horse's breast as she clawed her way in towards the warm offal within its ribcage. With shards of flesh hanging from her jaws, she swung her heavy head back around and blinked at Gobel lugubriously.

'My horse!' the hob stammered. 'My horse!'

'It did not suit you. It made you look like a man.' Already, she could feel the warmth flooding through her body and the blood beginning to pump to the outer extremities of her great wings. She belched, glad of the food. 'Besides, I was hungry.'

Chapter 13

Brid awoke, bewildered, alone and in darkness.

A strange and bitter taste filled her mouth. She ran her tongue around the inside of her mouth and it was a moment before she recognized the vile taste. Someone had poisoned her with henbane! That, at least, accounted for the sense of hazy forgetfulness and the strange dreams that had filled her sleep.

Feeling sick and disorientated, she could remember nothing of recent events. But the deep gnawing ache in her belly could not be obscured. The henbane had failed to steal one particular memory from her; she knew her baby was gone. Curling up and rolling onto her side, she cradled herself in her arms and sobbed, not caring that it was dark and cold and that she was lost and alone. She didn't know how much time passed, but, slowly, the recollection of fiendish hobgoblins came to her. She remembered the cruel punches that had killed her child but nothing beyond that. The memory of it pillaged all sensible thought and she screamed into the earth until she could scream no more.

The ravages of grief eased as her tears became hot and dry and her throat hoarse. Somewhere in the back of her mind, a voice told her that she had three other children who depended on her and that she must get herself to safety.

Finally aware of the numbing cold, she stretched out for the cloak that she had flung off in her grief and wrapped it tight about her. The movement brought the return of the pain within her belly but the deep discomfort cleared her head. Slowly, she eased onto her side and, from there, pushed herself up into a sitting position. Blinking, she stared about her but could see nothing in the pitch darkness. Realizing that she could do little until she could see her surroundings, she endeavoured to make herself more comfortable while she waited for the dawn, drawing her legs beneath her for warmth. Only then did she become aware of the heavy coldness about her ankle. Her trembling hands felt their way down her shinbone to a cold metal ring clasped about her lower leg. The ring was icy to the touch and rough, as if heavily rusted. Feeling it over, she discovered that the ring was attached to a heavy chain.

Stiff with cold, her hand closed tight about the chain and she yanked it as hard as her weakened state would allow, only to feel it snap taught. She pulled again, this time leaning back to increase her force. Lights danced and swirled, teasing her brain into thinking she was spinning. She pulled even harder but the chain did not budge. The effort had exhausted her but she fought off the urge to curl up on the cold ground; she knew she must force herself to follow the chain.

She didn't know where she was or why she was there. Though it was dark, she closed her eyes and drew a deep breath, trying to focus on her other senses. By the smells and muffled sounds of rustling leaves and small creatures creeping through undergrowth, she knew that she was outside. Opening her eyes wide, she stared upward. Not a single star spangled in the darkness above. She could smell earth and, combing her fingers over the ground where she sat, she felt dry pine needles and twigs. Yet the ground was beaten hard to a firm pavement and was too smooth for the natural forest floor.

Spreading her fingers wide, she felt around, scooping together a nest of pine needles and scraps of bark and twigs. She needed light. Just the smallest flame would help her. Feeling for the herb scrip that hung her from a cord about her neck, she rummaged inside for the wallet that contained a few small items that most Torra Altans carried on them. She felt for two chips of flint and then fingered the hem of her skirt until she discovered a thread of cotton. This she snapped off.

It was extremely difficult working in such darkness and she struggled to concentrate and hold herself upright. She needed to strike her flint and at the same time keep the thread of cotton placed to catch the spark. Dangling the thread from her teeth so as not to lose it, she hunched herself up over the flints. Fortunately, the cotton was eager to catch the spark and it took her only a few minutes to strike a spark large enough to crisp the tip of the thread. Soon it was aglow.

She huddled over the tiny glow of orange, nursing and coaxing it into a viable flame. For a moment, it sputtered and darkened and she thought she had lost it, and it felt as if it were her own life dwindling, on the point of being extinguished. She held her breath and cupped her hand around it, hoping, praying, watching as it brightened once more and she had enough flame to tease one of the pine needles into catching alight and then another. Soon, she had a little nest of fire just hot enough to light a twig.

Working in the tiny light that the twig offered, she gathered more twigs until she had a small bundle. Stripping some bark, she wove it about the ends to form a handle. After lighting her makeshift torch, she held it up high. It was only then that she realized she was in a pit, high shored walls all about her. Looking up, she could just make out the outlines of branches twenty feet above her. She raised the torch a little higher and saw that the pit was sealed over with a heavy covering of pine branches. The smoke began to curl down towards her, trapped within the pit.

Now that the urgent struggle to create a flame was over, Brid realized that she was in a perilously weakened state. Swaying on her feet, her arms sagged and she slumped back down to the cold ground and glared at the chain. She kept from her mind the thought of who or what had secured her as bait in what could only be a trap for a large predator. For now, she had to concentrate on getting free. With shaking hands, she examined the chain. It was, as she had thought, thickly crusted in rust but now she could see how each link was crudely welded together.

'Hob,' she muttered to herself. 'Hob iron.' Her gaze hastily slid along the chain, her eyes fell on a huge ring fixed into wooden shoring on the side of the pit. She snatched up the chain and pulled with all her strength, hoping that perhaps it might come free but she succeeded only in hurting her hands and exhausting herself further.

Shivering and sweating at the same time, she stumbled through the treacherous criss-cross of branches, which must have fallen from above, to examine the ring.

'Two stout branches,' she said to herself through chattering teeth. 'That's what I need.' Though she spoke of practicalities, her brain was still focused on the conundrum of what she was doing here. She remembered the underground tunnels and being attacked by hobs, and had the vague memory that Caspar had been close by. She wondered what had happened to him. He would never forsake her. And neither would her Hal. With all Torra Alta's skilled men and with Hal's determination, surely, they would find her. Hal would never rest until he had rescued her, she was certain. And yet, where was he? Cold fear for the safety of those she loved hardened her resolve.

She worked hard. First, she wedged her torch between two fallen branches and, struggling to raise a large piece of wood up alongside the ring to act as a fulcrum, she then lifted another to act as a lever. Pushing the end of the post into the ring, she then pressed it back against the shored up wall, hoping to prise the ring from its housing; but it remained solid. All too soon, she was exhausted. Her hands slipped and the post fell from her grip, thumping onto her toe. That sharp pain became the one thing that was too much for her and she sagged into the folds of her cloak and wrapped her arms around her, despairing of what she should do. Angrily, she glared at the chain.

But a chain was only as strong as its weakest link. Of course! Why hadn't she thought of it before? She must find it; she had to get free.

Hob metals were notorious for being poorly crafted. They melted at low temperatures and were filled with carbon and sulphurous impurities that made the resultant steel brittle.

Dragging the chain behind her, she gathered as much of the suitable wood littering the floor of the pit as she could reach and built up the fire until the flames were bright. Starting with the link at her ankle, she drew the chain through her fingers, examining each one. Surely, one would be thinner, cracked or crooked. Surely, one would offer her hope of escape.

She worked her way right back to the ring fixed into the shoring of the trap but the chain was remarkably uniform for one made by hob fingers. She had hoped she might find one link cracked or in some way imperfect so that she might lever it open but luck was not with her. Still, there had to be something she could do. Far off, she heard the low of taurs and the croak of a lequus that would be drawn to the trap by her scent. The muscles tightened down her spine as she thought of the fearsome beasts. Both were hybrids; taurs bore the head, shoulders and feet of a bull, but the body of a man, whereas lequui were far more powerful, being half horse and half lion. The mix of two animals created a conflict within their natures, resulting in unpredictable and violent temperaments. She stopped and listened, trying to judge whether they were coming closer.

Returning to the fire, she sunk to her knees, staring forlornly at the chain. At least, the fire brought her warmth and more feeling to her fingers, and the dancing flames gave her the glimmer of an idea. Carefully, she dragged the chain round so that it ran through the very centre of the fire. Fixing her gaze on the metal, she watched the colour slowly brighten and hoped that the impure metal might melt sufficiently for her to then lever the link apart. While she waited, she sought about for two stones, which she prised up from the firm bed of the pit to act as a crude hammer and anvil.

Occasionally adding more wood to her fire, she waited. The smoke and flame should keep a night predator away and she faintly enjoyed the groggy feeling it gave her as it numbed her fears and grief.

Why was she here? Where was Hal? What had happened to her boys? The questions churned round and round in her exhausted mind. She stared down at her hands, a long thread of hair twisted about the button of the cuff of her sleeve. The single strand was thick and black and had come from a horse's mane. She frowned, wondering how it had got there and, searching the rest of her garments, she saw that there were short black hairs from a horse's coat caught in the fabric all across the front of her dress. It was as if she had been slung across the withers of a horse.

She stared back into the flames, pleased that the metal was now beginning to glow. Her lids blinking over her smarting eyes, she kept on staring. While she waited, she ran her tongue around her dry lips, still puzzled by the bitter taste of henbane. Who had given her such a medicine? Surely not the hobs; it was well known that they left their injured and sick to die and so could know nothing of herblore or they would tend their wounded and infirm. But perhaps they knew something of poison?

Her patience breaking, she decided that the metal might be sufficiently hot and malleable. Dragging the chain out of the fire, she positioned the brightest portion over the larger of her stones. After wrapping her hand in a length of cloth torn from her skirt, she picked up her second stone and began to beat it down on the chain. The stone skidded off the chain, springing to the side, having made no impact on the metal at all.

Using her feet to hold the cool portions of the chain on either side of the glowing links taut and firmly in place, she pounded it again and again but the metal was cooling rapidly and she had not managed to fracture it in the least.

Not yet prepared to give up, she dragged the chain back into the fire and, only then, admitted to herself that she simply did not have enough wood to make a hot enough fire to melt even hob iron. Once she was no longer distracted by having a practical task to achieve, the hopelessness of her situation returned. What good was she to her missing boys, chained up here as live bait for some monster? The thought quickened her pulse. She had to get out.

The misery of her situation and grief at her loss slowly claimed her weakened body. Sick with hunger, confused and alone, she could feel the tears threatening to storm her cheeks. Yet, she would not give in. To surrender to despair was to admit that her boys were already slaughtered. She would not accept that. But, what could she do to save them?

I am the Mother, she told herself, barely believing it and feeling no more than a miserable child. She was lost and confused and was haunted by the vague sense that days had passed of which she remembered nothing. The flames slowly dwindled and the chill of the night returned.

Exhaustion dragged her down into sleep, where she dreamt she was surrounded by gibbering kobolds. The noise eventually drew her from her slumber and she realized it was only her own chattering teeth that had disturbed her. Curling up, she resolved to try and sleep again. If only there had been kobolds. The people of Old Woman Willow would help her, Brid was sure. For Quinn's sake . . .

Screwing her eyes up tight, she tried to force herself into sleep but it was so cold that even the bearskin cloak made very little difference against the harsh winter chill. She managed only to slip into a half-waking nightmare, every sound in the forest loud and unreal. She was startled by a deep bark that rang through the forest. Animals shrieked in alarm and she could hear them scampering away in search of refuge. The forest above was suddenly silent. Her pulse pounding in her ears, Brid froze, listening intently for what had disturbed the creatures of the night. A moment later, another bark boomed through the trees and soon the forest was filled with answering calls.

'Hobs!' she gasped, her hand reaching for one of the large branches of wood she had ready for her fire. They were coming for her. Doing her best to keep the chain from rattling, she crept to the edge of the pit and pressed herself up against the shoring. Above her, the sound of a single hob expelling a yelp of excitement was swiftly followed by a cacophony of bloodthirsty cries. Fear pounded blood through Brid's veins.

Great Mother, hear me! Keridwen! Isolde! She marshalled her resolve, her mind concentrating to form their images within her head. *We are One; we are the Trinity. Be beside me; be with me; do not let me die alone at the hands of these creatures that have already stolen my baby. Keridwen, I know you can hear me.*

She felt the power swell within her and rejoiced: Keridwen had sensed her need and willed her energy over the miles. But she felt no similar flow of energy from Isolde. Brid's hopes dwindled. Two joined in will was not enough. There had to be three to invoke the awesome power of the Great Mother.

Isolde, she despaired. *Why can't you hear me? What did we do wrong that you do not believe in yourself and your power? You must believe.*

The flickering energy within her surged and swelled for just a moment before the power ebbed away and she was, again, nothing more than herself. Overwrought, Brid's clenched fist thumped into the walls of the pit. They had all held such high hopes for the youngest of the Trinity. Isolde had instinctively grasped the principles of life and the balance of nature but she had not prospered under their tutelage and had gradually turned from a bright and happy child into a cowed girl.

Moreover, she had shrunk from the responsibilities entrusted to her as Maiden of the Trinity.

Brid couldn't help being angry with the girl, yet, at the same time, she knew it was her own fault. She had loved her but, perhaps, not enough and maybe had expected too much of her too soon. Keridwen had told her not to fret, that all would work out in the end, but Brid didn't know how. It was impossible to make the girl study. She barely knew the fundamentals of runelore beyond which letter each rune represented, understanding nothing of their magical qualities. Moreover, the girl had not trained her mind to reach that mystical level where the spirit is freed from the body, enabling extraordinary perception and clarity of thought.

Brid was acutely aware of how hard the training was. Her own perception was at times clouded by her temper and arrogance and she had striven hard to overcome her shortcomings that she might better serve the Mother's will. She had always struggled to improve herself, unlike Isolde, who always seemed to run from such mental battles.

Staring at the blackness above her, she prepared herself. Her knuckles were white on the length of chain that was all she had to defend herself. She gripped it tighter, her muscles freezing at the sound of branches being dragged aside. A slither of starry sky appeared above her partially obscured by three narrow heads. Six eyes glowed red and blinked as they stared down at her.

She gritted her teeth, trying to prepare herself for the worst. All her thoughts centred on the greatest sadness that now she could do nothing for her sons. And what would Brannella think when she failed to return? She had promised she would make a dress for Brannella's doll. She could not bear the thought that she might fail any one of her children.

A snarl gurgled at the back of her throat. If these creatures were going to take all that happiness from her, she would not die without inflicting some dreadful hurt on them. But

221

they did not leap down into the pit but rather dragged the branch back in place to cover the pit. In her frustration, she smashed the length of chain against the wooden shoring on the side of the pit. What did they want with her?

The hobs were babbling above her and she wondered at their behaviour. She had expected them simply to fall on her and rip her limb from limb. She started as one gave out a deep barking cry. Her flesh shuddered at the sound. Instinctively, she knew that the hob was calling for assistance as answering barks rattled back through the forest. The cries must have disturbed a mammoth since they were immediately drowned by a raucous trumpet blast, the fearful sound shuddering through the night.

Brid stared upwards, her head pounding with the rush of blood as she tried to work out what was happening. The trap was certainly large enough for a mammoth but they couldn't be using her as bait for one; mammoths were not predators and her presence in the pit would surely alert the beast to the presence of the trap? So why was she in the trap? She crawled to a corner and pressed herself deeply into it, sure of her reasoning but still fearing that the mammoth might fall in and crush her.

The trumpeting grew louder and the pulse of enormously heavy footfalls was so strong that the ground shook with each beat. Even now she could hear the hoots and yells of the hobs as if they were trying to drive the creature from its chosen path. Brid could barely guess at what was happening; she only knew that the ground and shoring about her shuddered with the footfall of the great beast and that bits of twig and branch were dislodged and falling onto her from above as it pounded closer. The cries of the hobs suddenly became more urgent and changed in pitch as the mammoth's ear-splitting call rang out, now alarmingly close.

The hobs sounded as if they were running. The mammoth seemed to have veered away a little and she could hear a third sound; hooves galloping fast – perilously fast for the black of the night in a moonless forest. Then came the sound of a man's cry amongst the barks of the hobs. It sounded like a cry of attack and Brid prayed that, whoever he was, he was driving the hobs away.

'Great Mother, be praised,' Brid murmured with real hope at the sound of the hobs' cries growing fainter as they ran off into the night.

She had barely allowed herself to draw one deep breath when her heart leapt into her throat as something crashed through the branches above. Instinctively, she curled into a ball, covering her head with her hands, aware of something crashing to the ground amid the harsh sound of splintering wood.

Soft starlight gave form to the world about her and, peeking out from behind her hands, she made out the writhing shape of a struggling horse and the form of a man entangled in the stirrups and reins. Although he was being kicked and yanked cruelly by the animal's frantic movements, he seemed uncaring of his own safety and was attempting to soothe the animal with steady words.

Not thinking of the danger, Brid skirted around the flailing hooves and grabbed the horse's bridle in an effort to keep the animal still. It strained against her and, though she had little weight with which to pin it down, she did what she could to help the man disentangle himself. He made no acknowledgement of her help but simply knelt by the horse's head, stroking the white blaze upon the animal's forehead, which was brilliant in the starlight, and smoothing the shaking muscles of its chest.

The fall of branches from above had smothered her fire to a smouldering glow, which gave out only enough light to define gloomy shapes in the darkness. Naturally she would do what she could to help the unfortunate man who had fallen into the trap but one thought was uppermost in her mind: he could help her. For the first time since she had awoken in the pit, she had hope of escape.

223

For several minutes, she worked to rekindle the fire until, once more, an orange glow illuminated the interior of the deep pit. Only then did she view her new companions. A large man, made to look even larger and more fearsome by the horned helmet on his head, was stooped over his horse. The animal was breathing more calmly now and had ceased to try and drag itself to its feet and so Brid had a chance to run her eye over its body. The lower part of the near foreleg appeared to have an extra joint in it, the cannon bone just above the hoof jutting forward at an unnatural angle. The horse trembled with pain.

'Your horse is badly hurt,' she said quietly, knowing that the animal should be put out of its misery. 'She's suffering and . . .'

'Those devils!' the man croaked through his grief. 'They crept up on me and tried to steal her. One even took a bite clean out of her rump. I should never have chased them.' He pressed his head against his horse's muzzle. 'Oh Sorrel, I'm so sorry. I'm truly sorry.' His eyes widened in horror as Brid raised the torch over the injured animal and the man craned his neck to look at the mare's dislocated lower leg. With his face set rigid, he shoved Brid out of the way as if she were a drunk who had come between him and his woman. Stroking the mare's muzzle, he murmured soothingly to her, praising her for all the fine deeds she had done.

'Sweet, Sorrel,' he choked, 'you carried me through a dozen battles and across three continents but for what? To end like this in a miserable pit in the middle of . . .'

Brid sensed that the man seemed unaware of what to do and appeared abnormally shocked by the animal's injury. Clearly, he had witnessed death and destruction before now since the ground was littered with weapons that had fallen with him, indicating that he was a man of warfare and action. Surely, this knight had seen many animals destroyed in battle.

To her surprise, the stranger suddenly turned on her, his eyes black with intense anger. 'Together we have fought in the greatest of battles, stood up against the Emperor of Athell himself. Only Sorrel's brave heart kept us up and fighting while all others were cut to pieces. They very nearly had me and one got close enough to rip the brooch pin from my cloak but her strength enabled us to plough through their numbers. I have come from a distant corner of the world and crossed three continents and fathomless oceans to reach this mean little country and for what? She cannot end here in this pit.' His lips trembled with grief and it was a moment before he was able to steady himself. 'You must help her. You must get help.' His words were spoken savagely and Brid was taken aback by the madness in his eyes.

'How?' she asked, slumping to the ground.

The sudden shock of the man and his beast falling into the pit had lent her strength but now she felt drained and weak. She looked helplessly up at the sheer sides of the pit walls surrounding them, the shoring stretching twenty foot above her head. She had thought it too smooth to climb but, perhaps, with this man's help, she might be able to use his weapons and perhaps some of the horse's harness to make an escape. Despite her own plight and exhaustion, Brid wondered at how a knight bearing such an evil array of weapons had become so sentimental over his horse.

Reaching over, she put her hand on his shoulder. He shoved her hand away. 'What do you know? What do you know of my grief? Get away from me, woman!'

Brid felt a trickle of blood ooze from her mouth and realized that the tip of one of his nails had clipped her lip. Trembling with cold and feebleness from lack of food, she found it hard to think clearly and it took her a long time to rise to her shaking feet. She was alarmed at the man's reaction but, realizing that he was her only hope of getting out of here, she knew she had to bring him to his senses.. In frustration, she watched as he sat down by his horse's head and, once more, began to stroke the snow-white blaze of her chestnut face.

'Oh Sorrel, it was my fault, all my fault. Why did I let this happen to you? Why? And when we are finally so near our journey's end. You cannot die now when, at last, we have nearly caught up with him.' His voice was choked with tears. 'Not now! Not when we are so close! I cannot believe you are dying because of three lousy hobs.'

To Brid's astonishment, the man crumpled forward onto the horse's neck, closing his eyes on his distress. Knowing that she risked further injury but unable to stop herself, she crept to him and put her slender arms about his great shoulders. 'Hush, it is but a part of the cycle. You will not be separated; she will merely go on before you.'

'Death!' the man exploded, swivelling round and clutching both Brid's wrists before she could pull away. His grip closed ever more tightly until her hands began to go white. 'Believe me, woman, death severs us from our loved ones. Death steals all joy. Death murders all hope. You think you know, but you know nothing!'

Despite herself and her conviction about the everlasting soul, Brid shrank from the utter terror and misery in the man's eyes. His soul had lost all hope. The warrior tossed her aside and she fought to assuage the rising faintness that threatened to overwhelm her.

'Sweet, Sorrel, I will not let you die. We cannot let them beat us. Not when we are so close. I cannot do it without you,' the man's voice cracked and he slowly let his head hang forward until his chin rested against his chest.

Brid watched him for a moment and then decided she must act. They could not risk remaining in the pit a moment longer. Sad though it was, they would have to see to the horse quickly before finding a way of escape.

'She is suffering. There is no way to get her out of this pit and we cannot leave her in such pain. A dislocation like that is more painful than a break,' Brid said softly but firmly as if she were talking to a distressed child. 'It can only be a kindness to end her misery. If you cannot, then I will do it for you.'

The stranger gasped in horror. 'No!'

Brid looked in dismay at the animal's heaving sides and then at the man's heavy, grief-laden features beneath his horned helmet. There was something so utterly final in the set of his face and it would be a waste of time to argue with him. If he wasn't going to allow the poor creature to be put out of her misery, she must to do something to help. The frustration screamed within her. The hobs would soon return and it was scant conciliation that she now shared her fate with this strange, heavily armoured warrior. She looked at him and groaned inwardly. He appeared in no fit state to fight.

There had to be something she could do. Taking a deep breath and, despite her conviction that the kindest thing for Sorrel was a swift end, she forced her exhausted body into action and moved around to the horse's injured leg. 'Try and hold her head still,' she ordered softly.

Already certain that the joint just above the hoof had been dislocated by the impact of the fall, Brid tenderly ran her hand up the bone of the lower leg to see if it had been broken. Though clearly in considerable pain, the horse was remarkably calm at her touch and it took her just a moment to determine that, bar the odd scratch from the branches through which she had fallen and a deep bite on her rump, the dislocation was the only serious injury.

Withdrawing beyond the range of the horse's sharp hooves, Brid took her herb scrip from around her neck and, with fumbling fingers, teased open the ties. A strange mixture of sweet, musty smells wafted out as she poked around, looking for the coils of grey willow bark that she had carefully collected. She pinched out as much of the bark as she could find and handed the shavings to the distressed knight.

'It's willow bark. Grind it up in your fingers and put it under her tongue. It may not be much but it will help her pain.'

The man nodded and dutifully did as he was bade, his fearful eyes flitting the whole time between Brid and his mare. 'Can't you do more?' he demanded.

Brid raised a hand to stay his questions while she searched through her herb scrip for something that might help; it was going to take a lot of force to pull the joint back into place and they needed help. The task would have been hard enough to perform on a man but on a heavily muscled horse like this . . . she plucked out a red stem that had small withered leaves still clinging to it. Just to be certain that, in the dim light, she had the right plant, she bit the end of the stem and grimaced at the bitter taste

'Stagbush,' she announced confidently as a worried expression spread across the man's face. His expression did not change but he seemed resigned to her help and continued to soothe his horse. Brid noted with relief that the willow bark was already having an effect; the animal's wild frightened eyes had ceased to roll and the terrible shuddering of her body had eased considerably. She looked thoughtfully at the stem of stagbush. The plant would relax muscles and this was necessary if they were going to have any chance of heaving the joint back into place. She needed to extract the juice and, since the horse could not be relied upon to chew away at the stem, she had to do it for the animal and then spit out the masticated pulp before feeding it to the stricken mare. It took longer than she hoped but, at last, it was done.

'Now what?' the knight demanded when he had finished easing the pulpy mash into the horse's mouth.

'We must wait for the herbs to take effect. Her muscles are still in spasm and will resist any attempt we make to straighten the joint, hurting her more. With numb fingers, Brid felt through the thatch of twigs and branches that had fallen from above and found two sturdy pieces of wood that she placed either side of the horse's leg to support and stabilize the joint once it was reset. She then unbuckled the reins from the bridle and took the stirrup leathers from the saddle. Using the reins to bind the splints above the injured joint, she set the stirrup leathers to one side ready to help bind the splint once the joint was realigned.

While the man soothed the horse's muzzle, Brid sat cross-legged, her forehead slumped onto her crossed arms that rested on her knees. She waited and focused all her energy, trying to form the image of a pure white light in her mind. She wanted to drive out all thoughts of despair and misery from her mind. If she let them invade her thoughts, she would collapse entirely. Only when a suitable time had passed for the stagbush to take effect did she rise and move closer to the horse.

'Now,' she turned to look into the warrior's eyes. 'You must take her hoof and pull her leg straight while I bind the splint in place. You must be strong in your action because, if we fail to reset the joint and ease her discomfort with the first attempt, she will not allow us to try again.' He nodded grimly and Brid closed her eyes, drawing in deep breaths to prepare herself for the exertion.

She nodded at the man to proceed.

The horse kicked and squealed with the pain as, with one smooth but powerful movement, the man heaved at her hoof.

'Harder!' Brid urged, using her own weight against the horse's shoulder to resist the warrior's pull. 'Harder, much harder!'

The warrior was purple in the face and grunting with effort but, at last, with a sudden snap, the joint popped back into place. Swiftly, Brid lashed the end of the splints firmly to the leg. Only when the joint was stabilized did the man ease his hold. On all fours, he crawled slowly forward, anxiously noting the horse's heaving breaths and her snorts of distress.

Despite feeling numb and weak from chewing the stagbush herself, Brid did her best to finish the splint with a cloth bandage. Using dirt from the floor of the pit, which she mixed to a slurry with spit, she marked the runes of healing onto the bandage. This done, she slumped down, her head dropping down between her knees as she sucked in breath to give her strength. It was a moment before she found the presence of mind to search through her herb-scrip for something to restore her own strength.

'Bloodwort,' she murmured in satisfaction, as she pinched a sweet-smelling sprig between her fingers. At least the herb would help sustain her until she found food.

'Thank you,' the man said, his voice thick with the croak of tears. 'I can never thank you enough.'

'She still may not survive,' Brid told him matter-of-factly, wiping cold sweat from her brow and struggling to keep her focus as faintness swelled up and threatened to swamp her. Anxiously she wondered how long the bloodwort would take to work. 'Animals die easily from the shock of an injury.' For a moment, she was forced to sit completely still to fight off the giddiness. With her head still slumped between her knees and her hands shaking, it occurred to her that she had been lucky to survive the loss of her child. Panting, she forced out her words. 'If no blood vessels are damaged or trapped within the joint, the pain will lessen now that the leg is realigned.'

He nodded and grunted, oblivious to Brid's physical distress. 'You can help us. You must help us get out of here.'

Brid looked at the bulk of the horse and then blankly at the man, before gazing up at the sheer walls imprisoning them, noticing the thin lilac dawn creeping into the sky above. After a moment or two, she nodded. 'Yes, we must get out of here. If I climb onto your shoulders, I might just be able to reach something to help me climb out.'

'And then what?' the man asked darkly. 'You couldn't pull me out let alone Sorrel and I'm not leaving her. You don't look as if you could walk more than twenty paces, even if I did have some rope to climb out with – which I don't.' He sat, readjusted his cloak and spread it over the animal to keep her warm.

Brid looked up at the high, shored walls and decided that this was not hob craftsmenship. The engineering was too exact and too advanced since the walls were straight and uniform and the shuttering smooth. The stranger was right; she couldn't climb out. She sat back against the mare's back, offering her own body heat to keep the animal warm. There was nothing she could do other than pray that the Great Mother would guide Hal to her.

'I'm sure help is coming,' she said reasonably, trying to disguise the doubt in her voice, but relieved that at last the giddiness was receding and her strength was slowly returning.

The man grunted sceptically. Chewing at his lip, he kept looking up anxiously, as if waiting for the hobs to emerge and finish them off. 'Don't worry, Sorrel,' he told the horse reassuringly.

Brid sniffed at this and drew out her rune scrip for comfort. It was a small leather pouch that chinked with the sound of smooth tablets of bone knocking one against another. She opened the ties and sorted through the runes in the hope that, even if she couldn't find solutions to her plight, she might at least find courage.

Sifting through the runes, her mind rolled over her problems. Miserably she wondered how she had neglected her duties. How could she have allowed Guthrey to become so arrogant and conceited? And what of Isolde? She certainly had not done well there either. She fingered through the runes made from the bones of the ancient priestesses that had preceded her. Before she had died, Morrigwen, the last crone, had assured her that some of the bones in her scrip were more than seven hundred years old. Caressing the most yellow and cracked tablets, she tried to feel through their bones for the presence and wisdom of the ancient priestesses.

Morrigwen had been Brid's tutor and she sighed, remembering how she had sat at the old woman's feet as she displayed each of the runes to her. At first, Morrigwen had told her little of their meaning. Instead, Brid had been asked to carry each rune around with her until she felt its import. Many years later, when she was fully conversant with the meanings and spell-casting properties of the runes, Morrigwen had taught her how to feel for the knowledge in the bone itself.

'Are we trying to reach this woman's soul?' Brid had once asked.

Morrigwen had shaken her old head. 'No, child, her soul will have long ago passed on through Rye Errish to be one with the Great Mother in Annwyn and, thence, reborn into the great cycle of life. It is her essence, her energy imprinted on the bone that you seek. You must learn to feel for it.'

It was not until long after Morrigwen's death that Brid had actually experienced the sensations that the old woman had described. It was only after the birth of her first child, Quinn, that she was enlightened with the true understanding of the cycle of life. Within hours of the boy's birth, she had felt power grow within her and felt infused with the understanding of how life was all part of a single thread. It was only as she fully understood how her life was in Quinn that she could feel the presence and the power of the generations sweeping back into time before her.

Now, with eyes closed tight, she stroked each rune, emptying her mind of thought until she saw only a sleek blackness like the velvet of a starless sky. Then, within that blackness, the faint round outline of the moon appeared and, from that moon, developed a face. She touched another fragment of bone and then another and, each time, a different face took shape in her mind's eye as she sensed the energy of the priestess from the fragment of bone taken from their shattered skull.

When she had first achieved the skill of seeking out the imprint of human touch in the bone, she had discovered that, for each priestess, death had been painful, dark and frightening. She had shuddered at the pain and the terror of passing into the unknown through the disembodied ether to reach the Otherworld of Rye Errish. Even though time and time again the souls took that journey, they were all capable of losing their way, at risk of disappearing into the nothingness of thought in the blackness of the universe.

Her hand cupped one bone that was longer than the rest and Brid felt reluctant to put it down. She opened her eyes and looked at it: R; the rune Rad. She frowned. But that was the rune Morrigwen had picked for Caspar many years ago. It represented a long journey and Morrigwen had claimed it was a questing journey and that Caspar was the seeker. She wondered what the Great Mother was trying to tell her. Was Caspar in trouble now? Was he seeking her? But that was ridiculous; he would naturally be seeking his son.

'Dear Spar,' she murmured. 'Dear Spar . . .' She placed the rune at her feet.

'What are you doing?' the warrior demanded gruffly. 'Is there nothing more useful you can do than play with bits of old bone?'

'I seek answers,' she said stiffly. Her muddied nose tilted upwards and a look of disdainful authority hardened her otherwise very beautiful face. She did not have the strength to argue so she simply intended to keep him at a stiff distance.

'Silly letters won't give you answers to a problem like this. We must use reason to get out of here. I have never solved any problem by studying symbols or heeding omens. Once I thought as you, but I was wrong. So wrong! I even persuaded my liege to follow the mystic path. We tried to talk and write our way out of our difficulties with the Emperor but it was a mistake.' He pointed at his own chest. 'And now, I'm all that's left to save them.'

'Well, your weapons haven't got us out of here and you don't appear to be doing anything useful, so perhaps a little calm thought won't go amiss,' Brid told him firmly, wondering what atrocity this man had suffered.

Snorting disdainfully at him, she returned her concentration to her runes. Leaving the rune of the seeker at her feet she scooped up her other runes, tossed them back into the scrip and shook them vigorously. She knew now that she was meant to do something about this horrible world they had found themselves in. She had been too wrapped up in her own personal problems and had not given the world its due attention. With renewed determination, she tried to clear her mind again and listen to the winds whistling through the channels of magic.

As she began to empty her mind, her senses dulled but it was hard to reach the calm that would enable her to block out the grunts of pain from the horse and the sighs of grief from the knight. She could hear the clink of his plated armour capping his shoulders and covering his breast, and the creak of his leather gambeson. She could smell his sweat, his fear and the stench of his aggression. It crossed her mind that Hal would be perturbed that she was stuck in a pit with this man. It would be beyond Hal's belief that any man could be so obsessed by a wounded horse to ignore her charms.

A sigh parted her lips. Was she certain that all these strange happenings were part of a greater plan? She wanted to believe that she was glimpsing just a corner of the pattern and would somehow, from that, figure out the whole.

At last, her thoughts dropped calmly into the darkness of a trance. Without conscious effort, she reached into the scrip and drew out a fistful of runes. She tossed them into the air and they fell into the circle drawn around the rune Rad. She looked and stared, wondering at the significance of the four runes R ▤ M ✛ that now lay in her circle. The tree rune Nuin and the rune Man, were the very same runes that Keridwen had continually cast in connection with Rad. Now, joining them, was the rune Nyd, representing need.

Leaving the runes, she rose to touch the shafts of dawn light that felt for her through the sparse tangle of branches above the pit. Instinctively, she knew there was a larger plan, though she didn't know what it was. Surely, that was what the rune Nuin was telling her since Nuin was the ash tree representing the link between all things within the universe. Her eyes flitted about her and it was as if she were viewing everything through a film of tears. This huge trap, the strange man and his obsessive love for his horse, became somehow remote and yet of vital importance; the apparently unrelated events were connected in some way. She sensed a thread.

While the warrior hunched low over his horse, she raised her hands, stretching up for the light, hoping that the full meaning of her casting would come to her with the first of the sun's rays. She loved the light and watched it coil round her fingers. Allowing herself to become one with the world, she was no longer conscious of herself, only of the completeness of nature around her. She was aware of the aura of the elements and all the beings about her, how their energies mingled and flowed from one to the other. Then suddenly, her attention was acutely focused on the warrior.

Her mind spiralled down towards him. As if separated by a sheet of ice, she stared at him as he stooped over his horse. She noted his sword, heavily engraved with runes, his battle-axe, chipped at one corner, and his barbed mace. Knives jutted from his belt, one ornately carved with a lion wrestling a serpent. A curious ivory figurine hung from his belt alongside a silver horn. His cloak was fastened by a wooden brooch that looked very plain compared to the silver disc of his belt buckle, which again bore the emblem of a lion and serpent. She thought that slightly odd that he wore a wooden brooch on a cloak so obviously made for a wealthy man. It was dyed a rich blue but was grimy with Belbidian mud that was also thickly caked about his spurred boots.

Something about this man shouted at her. At first she thought it was the runes on his sword but she decided she was wrong. What she felt from him was immense power blended with a gentleness that seemed incongruous with his battled-hardened appearance. She knew men of battle and was under no prejudice that they were cruel by any means. They mostly went to battle for worthy reasons, for love more than hate, to protect and fend for their loved ones. There was no crime in being a warrior yet there was still something inglorious about this man and she found it hard to believe that such a sense of power was emanating from him.

She gazed up again, hoping that the warmth on her face might inspire her. She remained staring upwards for many minutes until, finally, patterns formed and began to swirl in her mind and she started to sway. Fancifully, she thought the twigs above her formed a design of interlacing runes, the oak and the ash speaking to her, but she could not hold her position long enough to read them. All profound thought was suddenly gone.

It was not her body swaying, above her the branches were moving. A vast taloned foot plunged through the branches, sending a fall of timber tumbling down around her.

The curving talons were spread wide as they reached for her. Though she ducked and tried to shield her head from injury, the huge talons closed around her shoulder and dug in. She felt the great claws pierce hotly into her flesh, hooking into the muscle in an unshakeable grip.

Brid screamed as she had never screamed in her life.

Chapter 14

'Are you sure this is safe?' Caspar whispered in Leaf's ear.

It seemed ludicrous to trust in so young a child but he found himself compelled to believe in her. Besides, what choice did he have? He was at least free of the garden but he still had to get free of this strangely hidden world under the jurisdiction of the High Lady Zophia. Still, it seemed madness to hide right in the heart of the city above the High Lady's roof itself. They had climbed stair after stair and finally approached a lone tower that rose up above the rest of the city.

What Caspar liked least about this plan was that there was only one way up and one way down from the highest point. If they were discovered, they would be trapped. He sucked at his upper lip and bit it thoughtfully. Still, he had to put his faith somewhere and Leaf seemed to have a cogent perspective on things.

She tugged at his arm. 'Now, come on, Spar. This is the safest way. They'll search every nook and cranny of the city but they won't find us here. This is a great place to hide and from here, I can return to my rooms and be seen with the Lady Zophia until the fuss dies down. They won't suspect that I've helped you so they are less likely to look to me in order to find you.'

'How long do you want me to stay up here?' Caspar asked, his throat tight. 'Brid is gone! My son is missing! I don't have time to hide.'

Leaf patted his hand as if he were a child and she the adult. 'I know,' she soothed. 'We shall be able to see from here what is going on. Silas will turn the place upside down and it is better to wait safely just a little while longer than to rush out only to be taken straight back to where you were.'

Caspar nodded at the reasoning behind this as he followed Leaf up the winding staircase.

'Hello!' the girl called out softly.

'Hello!' came a reply from above.

Again, she called out her greeting in her carefree voice and the same reply came winding down to them. The voice sounded amused and, by the slight quaver to it, Caspar judged it belonged to a woman of great age. He was a little perturbed as the floorboards creaked and shifted beneath his weight as if there was very little left holding them together. 'I wouldn't like to be up here when there's a storm blowing,' he remarked.

'There are no storms here,' Leaf assured him brightly.

At last, they reached the top and stood on a small landing before a rickety door. It was slightly ajar, the wood bare and unpolished and the surface furry with spiders' webs. Leaf knocked at the door and pushed it slowly open. There, inside, dominating the room was the most enormous spinning wheel Caspar had ever seen. A little old woman was sitting at it, her foot paddling away at the tread that turned the wheel, her hands working as if she were feeding in fleece to be twisted and stretched to make wool. Though there was no wool, the woman, deep in concentration, persisted with her work.

'Hello!' Leaf repeated more forcefully.

The old woman stopped her make-believe spinning and pulled her glasses down her nose so that she could peer over the top of them at her two visitors. She was smothered in a heavy black woollen garment. Her fingers were swollen with arthritis and her back was stooped. Though she was heavily wrinkled and her hair crisp and fuzzy, there was an essential beauty still apparent in her high cheekbones and large, teasing eyes.

She appeared to live entirely in this one room. There was a

238

bed against the far wall, a bright sky-blue quilt heaped on top of it and matching drapes hanging from four bed posts. Built into the solid stone that housed the spiral stair was a small hearth in which a fire smouldered. Large iron hooks hung from the lintel and on one of them hung a blackened kettle that was singing away merrily as if it had been left for a very long time. The room was not tidy; old books were heaped up in rickety piles and tired parchments, covered with faded ink marks, lay scattered about the floor. Some of the books were placed as stools or steps and Caspar finally noticed that the old woman was sitting on a pile of heavy tomes.

'Well, well, well, a visit! I hope you don't think you've come here to get in my way, young lady.' The old woman stared at Leaf and only looked at Caspar through the corner of her eye. 'What purpose do you have in bringing a man up here, child? I haven't had need of a man in . . .' She dropped her gaze and looked at her fingers as if to count the number of years. 'In . . . in . . . it's longer than I can remember.' She frowned a little and then looked back at her work. 'Goodness me! Goodness me! I won't get it done in time. You'll have to make yourselves comfortable; I'm so busy I haven't got time for the usual hospitalities.' She turned back to her wheel and set her foot on the treadle, her hands, as before, working away as if feeding in the fleece.

Nodding, Leaf pushed Caspar towards a pile of books beside the fire. 'Now sit down and make yourself some tea otherwise you'll upset her. I must hurry to my mother.'

Caspar snatched her hand just as she pulled away to head back down the stairs. 'Are your sure this is wise, Leaf? Who is this woman? Won't she tell the authorities?'

'She is the authority and, of course, she won't,' Leaf replied, enigmatically and confusing him all the more. 'She's my grandmother and no one comes up here except me. They won't think of looking for you here as it would be madness to hide up in a turret with no escape – unless you suddenly sprouted wings, of course. Lastly, Silas has no knowledge of Xanthia's existence.'

'But why not?'

'The High Lady never talks about her.'

Caspar raised an eyebrow, prompting Leaf to expand on this statement.

'Xanthia is Father's mother and she never liked Mother. Apparently, Xanthia told Zophia that she was not good enough for her son and, to show how much she disapproved of the match, Grandma took herself off to her rooms the moment they were married and hasn't come out since. Father visited often and took me to see her and she's always been lovely to me though she's never had one good word to say about my mother. So, you see, she won't inform Zophia because she won't to do anything to help my mother. Poor Mother!' Leaf sighed. 'I don't think she deserved all of Grandma's scorn but it may help us now.'

She turned to the old woman. 'Now, Grandma, you won't say a word about my friend here, will you? Zophia is looking for him so if any soldiers come knocking at your door you won't let on, will you?'

'Zophia! She's after this man?' the woman's voice was instantly high and strained.

Leaf nodded. 'Oh yes. He came to help Father.' She handed the old woman a little handkerchief with her father's initials on it. 'But Zophia wouldn't let him.'

'My son! This man is here to help my son and Zophia doesn't like it?' Leaf's grandmother was outraged. 'Soldiers indeed! If they come anywhere near my rooms, I'll have them out of the window in a trice. A trice, I tell you!'

Leaf nodded, apparently satisfied and then turned towards the stairs. As if a sudden thought had come to her, she beckoned Caspar to her and indicated the bolts on the inside of the door. 'I think you had best make it fast behind me,' she advised. Beaming a bright smile full of hope, she turned and sped away down the creaking stairs.

Once he had shot the bolts into place, Caspar sat in front of the fire, wondering why the old woman didn't seem quite as forgetful as her son. But what conversation could he make with someone who was spinning thin air? Perhaps it was prudent not to make conversation at all and so he stared into the embers, trying to keep his thoughts calm. Trapped here and powerless to do anything, his thoughts immediately turned to Rollo.

'It's not polite to sit and stare,' the woman grumbled. 'Now what you must do, young man, is to make yourself some tea. And it would be nice if you poured some for me too.'

Caspar was not entirely sure what flavour of tea he poured but it had a pleasantly fruity taste. He took a second sip and sat back, realizing how very tired he was. It was a moment before he became aware of the woman watching him; he gave her a brief uncomfortable smile.

'It would also be polite,' she chastized him, 'to mention how fine my spinning is.'

Caspar hastily composed himself, 'Why, yes, of course. Where are my manners?' He stared at the empty spindle and the wheel and wondered what he should say to please the woman. He coughed. 'Why, yes, of course. I am not an expert in these matters naturally—'

'Naturally,' the woman interrupted. 'No, you are a soldier, not a man used to examining woman's work.'

He nodded at this, his eyebrows rising as he wondered how she knew. 'Absolutely,' he said more happily now. 'but I am most impressed by the consistency of your thread. To spin so fine a thread and yet to make it of such an even texture is an art in deed.'

The woman hooted with delight. 'Oh how droll, how very droll. And what a perfect thing to say. Absolutely perfect. Go on!'

Caspar smiled rather sheepishly. 'You'll have to help me here. What more can one say to praise someone's spinning?'

241

She seemed also to enjoy this answer and chortled away to herself. 'It's for a wedding, you know.'

'Indeed?'

'Yes, it is for the bride. It will be a winter wedding so she must be kept warm and so this fabric will be ideal. It is silk woven in with wool – as you can well see,' she emphasized.

'Absolutely,' he confirmed. 'I was going to remark on how difficult it must be to keep the tension just right when working with two different materials.'

She grinned. 'You are too clever for a man! Too clever! But you can't guess who the bride is to be.'

'That I can't,' Caspar confessed. He was certain the woman was completely mad and yet felt she was toying with him.

'I don't know what Leaf is up to,' the woman abruptly changed the subject, 'but she's all of me that goes on into the future generations and she's a very fine girl indeed despite her mother. Never liked that woman. Never!' She began to tread a little harder.

'Madam, I would be careful; you'll spoil the thread,' Caspar advised.

Xanthia laughed again. 'Yes, yes, my boy, you are right. You are absolutely right. And we couldn't have that now, could we? Not after all the effort I've put into it. The cloth is only as good as the quality of thread it's woven from. Where was I?'

'Zophia?' Caspar suggested.

'That creature! That female! Ha! And she thought she was good enough for my son. How ridiculous!' the old woman exploded.

'Your son is very fine indeed,' Caspar soothed, suddenly worried that the woman might get too over-excited. He was finding her more unpredictable than he had expected and he did not wish to upset her.

'He is! Yet again, you are absolutely right. I told him not to marry Zophia, you know. A king should not marry a scholar. No, he should marry some pretty little thing that has clandestine liaisons with half the court and prattles away to the merchants and travellers. It is not expedient to choose from the scholars. She'll plot him right off the throne, I told him, I did. Can't go around having a queen that can think for herself. She'll be running the court in no time, and she was. The only blessing was Leaf and she could outshine the brightest diamond. My little Leaf! Now have you guessed yet?'

'Guessed?' Caspar asked helplessly.

'About the wedding.'

He was about to reply when Xanthia raised her hand to silence him. 'Now am I going a little deaf or can I hear noises? Oh dear, young man, it seems they are looking for you already.'

She seemed to Caspar to be rather too pleased at this idea and he decided that Leaf had made an error of judgement.

He strained to hear and, at last, recognized the sound of voices someway below, the opening and slamming of doors and things being moved around as if someone were searching a cluttered area.

'They'll be up here soon,' the woman continued, seemingly amused. 'Shall we play a little game?'

Caspar didn't like the idea of this at all but didn't see what option he had. 'I love games,' he said politely

'You have charming manners. I would never have guessed that a man of such high breeding as yourself should have such charming manners. I would never have guessed it. Never!'

Wondering how she knew anything about him at all, Caspar smiled, trying to grit back his teeth on his frustration. There was absolutely nowhere to hide and it sounded as if the soldiers below were gradually drawing closer.

'Now for the game. Yes, of course! You must guess who the bride is,' the old woman laughed lightly and even ceased her spinning for a moment to look into Caspar's face and judge his reaction. 'Tell me who the bride is.' She nodded slowly, her grey eyes twinkling. The sunlight falling in through the windows cast shadows across her heavily lined face, highlighting several hairs sprouting from her chin.

Caspar suddenly guessed her game. 'Let me see if I understand you correctly. Unless I guess who the bride is, you will give me away to the guards – despite Leaf's wishes?' he asked, his voice edged with disbelief.

She clapped her hands. 'Indeed! And you are quite remarkably sharp; I would have never thought it of your kind. Yes, that is very much the game. It is rather exciting, don't you think?'

'But you promised Leaf,' Caspar reminded her, mustering all his self-control to keep his tone calm and reasonable.

'I did, didn't I?' the woman seemed to reflect on this technicality for a moment. 'But she is half Zophia's and half my son's so I can only do half of what she wants? Besides, it gets tedious up here alone and it is so nice to have a game to play. You have three guesses naturally. It is always the way with games; there has to be three guesses.'

Caspar could hear banging from bellow. 'Could it be a wedding dress for Leaf?' he asked hastily. Leaf was the most obvious choice since she was the old woman's granddaughter.

'Is that your first guess?' the woman asked formally.

Caspar nodded. 'Yes, it's my first guess,' he confirmed, trying to keep the impatience from his voice.

'Well, it's not a very educated guess, now is it? Leaf's wedding indeed! I sincerely hope not! The poor creature that takes her is in for the shock of his life!' She snorted at the idea and Caspar rather thought that this old woman's husband had probably also suffered for his choice of bride.

Xanthia snorted in disapproval. 'Leaf! The very idea! How old is the girl now? I thought you would be very much better at this game, young man, but it seems I might as well open the door and call the guards straight in. Use your head. You know Leaf is far, far too young. Besides, I have no intention of living to see her wedding. She'll make the most dreadful choice and I have no doubt she won't listen to my advice. No one listens to my advice and it costs them dear. Very dear. Now think a little harder, man, and make your second guess.'

Caspar racked his brain whilst inwardly cursing Leaf. 'How could she have penned him up here in a mad woman's room with absolutely no escape and nowhere to hide? Leaf's grandmother was looking hard at him and was clearly enjoying his torment.

The shouts from below were getting louder. 'You go back down and take the turret on the right; I'll keep on heading up here to the old dowager's rooms; it won't take long to search there. You'll find the old apothecary rooms that way, plenty of places for him to hide in there. When I've finished up here, I'll come and join you.'

Caspar knew he didn't have long before he was discovered. He looked to the old woman, his eyes imploring her co-operation.

She ignored his look. 'Come on, come on, what's your next guess?'

'I'm at a disadvantage, my lady,' Caspar said as politely as he could. 'I am a stranger in this delightful realm of yours and I have not had the pleasure of meeting too many of your kith and kin.'

'Indeed!' The woman smiled slyly at him. 'Yet we have struck our little bargain and I will have my game. Now guess again. Guess again! You have all the information you need.' She paused as if waiting for him to absorb that fact. 'That's a clue in case you didn't know. You obviously need a little clue. Now guess. Tell me the name of the bride.'

'Zophia!' he blurted. 'It must be Zophia.'

'And why?' the woman asked suspiciously.

'You do not like her, that is plain. So if she were to divorce your son, you would be delighted, in fact, so delighted that you might sew her a very fine gown in expectation of her finding another and in celebration of your son's freedom.' Caspar stared expectantly at the woman's face, hoping for a positive reaction. 'Since Zophia is already married you thought I would never guess the right answer but I have won the game, have I not?'

The woman smiled quietly. 'You have not! You have not! What a preposterous idea! If she divorced my son, I'd be busy spinning a noose for her neck not a wedding gown. I never liked the woman – she's too sly – but I don't want her to hurt my son any more than she already has. The ignominy of divorce and the way people talk would be the death of him.'

Too sly, Caspar thought ruefully to himself.

'And that was not such a clever guess and I don't believe you had thought out your reasoning before you blurted her name either. I think you said her name because Zophia is the only other female you know in our realm. Would you give away your life so easily? Would you? You must learn to think. There is more in your mind than just idle thoughts. Make it work. Oh, I know how it pains you but you are capable of so much more if only you will try just a little harder,' she urged him. 'Now you have one last guess.' She held up a knobbly finger. 'Just one.'

Caspar stared at her tight lips and his mind raced though he could think of no plausible answer. He could hear, now, the creak of boots on the stairs.

The old woman was looking at him intently. 'Have you no answer, man? What a shame. And I was so enjoying your company.'

'My Lady Xanthia,' a voice called without and Caspar's heart missed a beat.

The old woman looked at him. 'It's your last chance. Just one more guess. One more.'

How could he guess? This was utter madness. He could hear the footsteps without, the rickety old stairs groaning under the weight.

'Come on! Do not let fear steal your brain. You must think. You can see the answer right before you. It is here in this room yet you are too stupid to realize it, far to stupid,' the old woman scolded him in lowered tones.

But there could be a thousand answers within this room, Caspar silently protested looking at the many books. There were hundreds of books. Anyone of them might tell of a girl for whom Xanthia whimsically fancied making a dress. There was a fire, a kettle, a bed and one proper chair, and a window out of which he could see a brilliant sky.

Suddenly a thought struck him. Could it be that the sky was the answer she was seeking? Perhaps that was where her madness had taken her. Was it a marriage between earth and sky? Only the sky would wear the most beautiful of garments that was lighter than air. But this notion made little sense because the earth was female and so the sky would be the male partner and would not wear the dress. He could feel his pulse pounding in his head. How could he possibly compete against such madness?

The latch rattled and Caspar stared at it, willing the unseen hand behind to go away.

'Answer!' the old woman hissed in his ear. 'Play my game. Humour an old woman. You must reach down into your heart and answer from within. The guard is here, right here at the door. Answer me now!'

The hand knocked on the solid wood of the door. 'Madam Xanthia, I have orders to search every room.'

'I will just be a moment,' she croaked impatiently. 'You can't hurry old bones like mine.' Slowly, she rose and began to shuffle towards the door, her stick tapping on the floorboards as she went. She drew close to Caspar on her way and breathed into his face. 'Now is your very last chance.'

He swallowed hard, glanced once towards the door, once back at the spinning wheel and then back into her silvery grey eyes. Suddenly, he knew there was only one answer he could give.

'No one! There is no bride. There is no wedding because there is no thread on that spinning wheel.' He watched her face, waiting for her reaction.

The door latch rattled again.

'Hide in my bed!' the woman hissed at him. 'Quick, quick now.' She then smiled. 'Well done, young man. I think Leaf is right in thinking you worth rescuing.'

Caspar dived for the bed that was clad in a thick quilt. After wrinkling up the covers to make it look like the bed had never been made and so helping to disguise his form, he dived under the bulky layers and wriggled to the bottom of the bed. He listened intently as the woman opened the door though the sounds were somewhat muffled by the stuffy quilt.

Xanthia spoke, 'What, young man, do you think you are doing rattling at my door and dragging me out of bed? I hope you're bringing wood for the fire. It's cold up here. I've not been able to get out of bed all day for the cold.'

'Madam, I have orders to search your room.'

'Orders? Orders from whom?'

Caspar could hear the door bang against stone as it was flung wide against the wall.

'Take a look for yourself right now. Bursting up to an old woman's room and demanding to search it! I've never heard such rudeness. What a to do!' Xanthia's voice softened and became suddenly thoughtful. 'Unless you are searching for mice. Now look you here, I have something to show you.' Caspar could hear footsteps as the old woman and the soldier crossed the room. He presumed she was showing him the crack in the plasterwork alongside the chimney-breast. 'Is that what your looking for? As soon as my back's turned, they're all over the place. Now what do you intend to do about it?'

The man coughed awkwardly and shuffled his feet. 'Madam, I'm not here about—'

'Now, I'm going back to bed because my feet are cold. You see to it that those mice are dealt with. Why haven't you brought a cat with you?' Caspar braced himself as the woman's weight pressed down on the covers above him. 'What sort of a fool comes to kill mice without bringing a cat? Now, I won't

248

be having poison here in my rooms, you hear? I won't have it. Where's the cat?'

'Madam Xanthia, there's no cat,' the man protested in confusion.

'What!' the woman squawked in annoyance. Caspar heard a clatter as her shoes were kicked off. She then wriggled her legs under the covers. Her feet were indeed cold. She gave him a playful kick as if she were rather enjoying this game of charades. 'What do you mean there's no cat. Are you completely incompetent? What's the name of your superior?'

'Madam Xanthia, there's no cat,' he said placatingly, 'because I didn't come here about the mice. I came here looking for a man.'

'I'm not interested in men. I'm much too old for that sort of thing. If you want a man that's your business but it doesn't help me. I want something done about these mice! Mice you hear? There's a big difference. I need a cat. Are you going to fetch me one?'

'No, Madam, I—'

'What do you mean, no? Are you disobeying me?' There was a coldness to her tone that was heavy with threat.

'Madam, no, of course not. It's just that I'm under strict orders to search the towers for a man that's escaped.'

'Well, why didn't you say so?' she thundered at him. 'Have a guard put at the foot of the stair. Is this man dangerous? You'd better hurry and find him then, hadn't you? And when you've found him return with a cat. A cat not a man, mind, and I prefer the ginger ones. They are the best mousers.'

There was a thump of boots on the floorboards followed by heels rattling on steps and the creak and groan of the stairs as the guard retreated hastily from the tower room. The old woman stayed put where she was for a few moments longer and then withdrew her cold toes from Caspar's ribcage.

'Now, young man, get yourself out of my bed. I can't have strange men in my bed, you know. Think of the rumours!'

Caspar elbowed his way out, glad of the air. He smiled his thanks at the old woman. 'That was most kind of you. Thank you.'

Xanthia wrinkled her nose at him. 'Now, look at the mess you've made of my carefully spun yarn. Look at it! You'll have to help me.' She pushed him down onto a pile of old books and plucked up his hands so that he held each up either side of his chest. 'Now, keep them like that. It'll take me hours to get all of this straight. Absolutely hours. Hold that in your thumb,' she ordered, pressing thin air into Caspar's hands.

He dutifully played his part and watched as she scooped up an imaginary tangle of yarn from the floor and began to wind it back and forth around his fingers.

But the old woman hadn't finished complaining. 'What a bother! It's just like Leaf to cause such a bother. It's her mother's influence, of course.' The woman grumbled on like this for quite some while and Caspar was amazed to think that Madam Xanthia, who had played such a lucid game with the guard, appeared now to be quite mad again. He wondered if it were all just another game.

His arms were beginning to ache and he was tempted to ask her why they were going through this charade when she had already admitted that there was no dress to be made and no materials with which to make it. However, he resisted the urge for fear of displeasing her. She could, after all, recall the guard at any moment.

Presently, there was the light tap of footsteps on the stairs below followed by a breezy, 'Hello.'

The old woman echoed the greeting and then leaned forward towards Caspar.

'Now, you tell Leaf that you've had a fine time and that I've treated you well otherwise she'll be cross with me. Be kind to an old woman,' Xanthia implored him gently before saying in a loud imperious tone, 'Keep your hands up. I want to get this thread straight otherwise I'll never make the dress in time for the wedding.'

Caspar sighed.

The door pushed open and Leaf stepped brightly inside. 'The guards have been and gone, I hear. Well done, Grandma!' She ran over and kissed the old woman's wrinkled brow. 'I heard them say they searched your room. I knew you'd look after him for me. Thank you, Grandma.'

The old dowager gave her a wink. 'Well, young lady, I have to say I haven't had so much fun in ages. The guard didn't know whether he was coming or going. And I haven't had a man in my bed since . . . since . . . well, I really can't remember. Oh yes that's right—'

'Grandma! Now really! Stop that!' Leaf protested.

'Would you deny an old woman a little amusement?' Xanthia complained.

'Can I put my arms down now?' Caspar interrupted.

'No, of course not,' Xanthia said sharply but Leaf intervened and pushed his arms down for him.

'Grandma!' she scolded the woman. 'There is more pressing business with which to concern ourselves.'

Leaf took Caspar's hand and led him to a thin window. The ill-fitted glazing let a sharp draught blow between the lead kames and the glass. The glare from the crystal-filled sky was bright and Caspar shielded his eyes from it. 'I came back the minute I heard that Silas was gone.'

Caspar swallowed, trying to take it all in. From the tall tower, they could see all across this green and lush land. In the far distance, a milky white mist hid the edge of the realm. The roads wound from one windmill to the next, finally fading into the mist but, though Caspar had a good view, he could see no sign of Silas. Hastily, he ran from one window to the next until he had checked every direction. From each vantage-point, he could see the same idyllic view and none of them showed a single glimpse of the mammoth-hunter.

'I should have been looking out then I'd know which way he went.' Caspar cursed himself for his lack of forethought. 'How could I have been such an idiot?'

'Because you're only a man,' Xanthia taunted, watching his reaction with interest before returning her attention to her spinning wheel. 'You would never have seen him anyway. The mists are very confusing at the edge of the world.'

In exasperation, Caspar turned to Leaf. 'Which way do we go? How do we find Brid?'

The child didn't answer but continued to study the scene below. At last, she tapped the glazed pane. 'Look there!' she exclaimed. 'That has to be the way.'

Caspar stared over her shoulder but could see nothing. 'Where? What do you mean?'

'Look into the mist,' she said and pointed again. 'There! Look!'

Caspar squinted. Beyond a still windmill that stood beside the thin line of a dusty road, he could just make out a swirling disturbance in the base of the mist. He closed his eyes for a moment, trying to cope with his fears. 'What has he done with Brid?' he asked Leaf.

She didn't answer and Caspar looked at those sad intelligent eyes, knowing that she feared something was wrong.

'I must leave immediately,' he told her.

Chapter 15

Rollo lay rigid on his bed, staring at the ceiling. The bandages rimming his eyes itched and his face stung but he barely noticed. The dream from which he had woken had left him full of fear and loneliness.

He had often been lonely growing up. Though there had been many children of his own age, they had never sought him out and he had found it easier to keep to himself or to seek his mother's company. But he could never be with her again and the year-long grief was still sharp, the sense of abandonment intense.

He tried to banish the memory of the dream but his mind continually swung back to it. Like so many dreams he had experienced lately, he had been searching for his mother amongst a crowd of women, frantically running between them, checking their faces. He could no longer remember her face! The realization that he was gradually forgetting her filled him with self-loathing. How could he let her down in this unforgivable way?

He had always been too proud to cry and yet now he could not stop himself. The salt tears seeped under his bandages and stung his swollen cheeks.

They had left him too long. Nobody cared about him; nobody wanted him. Miserably, he thought how little his father must care for him to bring him to this wretched continent.

A storm of anger brewed within him, rising up to overwhelm his thoughts. He gritted his teeth against it, only for his rage to escape into more sizzling tears. He could bear the emotions inside him no more. Rolling over, he beat his bandaged fists into the bed. When that failed to make him feel any better, he leapt up and flung himself against the wall, unaware of what he was doing, only that he wanted to hurt someone badly. Anybody. Even himself. Someone must suffer. The terrible rage within him flared into a burning ball of pain. His vision darkened and the smell of the pus and blood of his wounds became chokingly thick in the air as the bandages unravelled.

Exhausted, he sagged back onto his haunches and glared at the hooked swollen claw that once had been his hand. It was the claw of a monster! It was as if his true self were emerging from his body. All would see him now as he really was. It was as ugly as his uncontrollable rage.

His father had always been so patronizingly understanding of his moods; and told him, oh so soothingly, that he would grow out of them. Why should he? Why should he change to be like everyone else? They didn't understand him. No one understood him! His hand accidentally knocked against a painted vase, spinning it from the table on which it had stood. The vase shattered, the sound of destruction deeply satisfying, and he looked around for something more to destroy.

Through the blur of tears he became aware of a black shape standing at the door. The figure, he was certain, was staring at him, mocking him, laughing at his disfigurement and the stupidity with which he had flung himself at the ravenshrikes. With a great roar of rage, he charged, grabbing and flinging whatever came to hand.

Something struck him hard on the forehead and he sank giddily to his knees.

Everything was terribly wrong, he told himself. It should be impossible for him to fall like that. As he plunged into blackness, a terrible pain swam up from his chest and he could not draw breath.

*   *   *

254

The next time he awoke, he felt calmer. The screams and shrieks that had so troubled him before had died down. Now, he could smell something beautifully sweet. The sound of a quiet voice filled his mind with tranquil and beautiful images. He blinked his eyes open and found himself looking into a pair of bright golden-green eyes.

'Isolde,' he murmured but she did not reply. She barely seemed to notice him as she concentrated on her painstaking task of plucking out, one by one, the burning thorns from his face with a pair of fine bone tweezers. Her expression puzzled, she looked at each thorn as if it were quite inexplicable as to how it had got there.

'Remarkable!'

'What is?' he asked, his voice hoarse.

'I don't understand it. I do not have the skill to heal like Brid yet your skin has recovered remarkably. I have seen these wounds before but never have I seen such resistance to the acid in the thorns. Remarkable!' she said again. 'There must be something in your blood,' she joked.

He frowned in puzzlement.

'Not having Brid's skill, I thought I would have trouble healing you,' she confessed to him. 'But your skin is barely infected. I cannot believe that my herblore alone has healed you so well.' She cocked her head on one side and Rollo couldn't fathom whether she found this an intriguing conundrum or whether she was actually struggling with the emotion of being pleased with herself. He wondered at her unnatural shyness and guessed it was a result of being brought up by that arrogant bastard, Hal.

Again, the growling pit of anger swelled within him. It was at times like these that he missed the people of Ash, the only people who didn't despise him for his uncontrollable rage. He had even overheard his father suggesting that he be given a calming potion to ease his rage, and had hated his father for not accepting him as he was.

'I am a prince,' he said suddenly, unaware of why he said

it. 'I deserve respect. My father should have shown me more respect.'

Isolde nodded. 'And I am a priestess and, as such, it is presumed I should be respected by all,' she said in a sad whisper.

Rollo gazed into her golden green eyes and saw a profound pain. 'You are very pretty,' he murmured, the terrible rage within him gradually subsiding. Though it was too painful for him to smile, he hoped his eyes were smiling at her.

She smiled back awkwardly, not knowing how to accept his compliment. Her hand nudged up at her nose, her eyes peeking out shyly over the top. 'I am simply as the Great Mother made me; there is beauty in all life.'

She returned to the laborious task of picking out the barbs and Rollo did his very best not to wince. He was determined to impress this girl.

Isolde extracted yet another thorn and held it quizzically up to the light.

'What do you make of these thorns?' she asked calmly, holding one too close to Rollo's eyes for him to focus on.

He pushed her hand away and squinted at the thorn. It was nigh on an inch long, black with a long tapered point. 'It's a thorn. Too long for a hawthorn. I would guess it's blackthorn,' he said matter-of-factly, though he could barely believe it.

Isolde nodded. 'Blackthorn. I knew it was blackthorn.'

'So why did you ask?' Rollo queried, bemused by the girl's lack of conviction in her own opinion.

Isolde looked at him sideways, her eyes slitted as if she were unable to decide what to think of him. 'I ask because I don't understand what happened. You were badly burned, but your burns have healed even more quickly than the injuries caused by the thorns. And ravenshrikes don't have thorns.'

'Ah ha! Here is something that the revered Maiden does not know.' He tried to laugh but the chortle pained his tight chest. 'I told you there were men on their backs and they flung their staffs at me. Do you believe me now?' He grinned at her, determined to offer his friendship even though it pained his cheeks.

The girl ignored his attempts to tease her out from her mantle of reserved indifference. 'A man on the back of a ravenshrike?' She sniffed but made no further comment.

Rollo had the impression that she did not believe him but lacked the nerve to say so. He would normally be affronted by such doubt but he was more concerned by her inability to speak her mind. The corners of his lips crinkled into a smile.

Immediately, Isolde withdrew from him. 'You are laughing at me,' she accused, her lips pursing.

'No,' Rollo said with uncharacteristic gentleness, regretting that he had upset her. 'You are too beautiful and too kind to be so defensive about yourself.'

'And you, stranger, are too dangerous to be trusted,' she said, lowering her guard slightly as she tended the wounds to his face. 'Do you feel any better? I gave you a soothing potion of ground willow bark to ease the pain.'

Suddenly, he remembered breaking the vase and marvelled that she behaved so uncritically towards him after witnessing his uncontrollable fury that was occasionally so intense that it triggered a fit. The shame of it!

'Where's Quinn?' he asked, his eyes still hot and swollen against his eyelids as he tried to look around the chamber. He was lying on a day bed within a circular chamber warmed by a large fire. On the far side of the chamber from an arched door were three curtains, which, he presumed, sectioned the day chamber from sleeping quarters.

'He's been trying to talk to Oxgard.' The girl looked towards the door as if expecting him to enter at any second. 'It's near dark; he should be back with news by now.'

'News?' Rollo asked, gradually feeling a little better at the warmth of the brew that the girl raised to his lips.

'Of Guthrey,' she confirmed.

Rollo suddenly felt twice as ill as he had done a moment

earlier, the pain in his hand and face nothing to the gnawing anguish of his guilt. 'Guthrey?'

She nodded, her eyes brightening. 'There is hope. Yesterday, Oxgard's men rode out to where we last saw the ravenshrike and they managed to find its eyrie. But the nest was devastated, torn apart by some larger creature.'

'And that means there's hope for Guthrey?' Rollo queried her logic.

'I am certain he has escaped.'

'I don't understand; what makes you so certain?' Rollo squeezed out the words, his heart throbbing in his throat, praying to the Great Mother that his dreadful secret would not be revealed.

'The ravenshrike had a deep nest where they stored their food. It was broken apart and they found many partially maimed animals that had crawled some distance and then died. At the foot of the eyrie, they found the remains of Guthrey's horse, its stomach and chest pecked clean, but no human remains. He must have got away. Oxgard was extending the search and trying to get word to Hal but had not located him yet.' Lips atremble, her hands were twisting up into knots.

'No news of Brid and my father then?'

Isolde shook her head and pushed her hands back up through the curls of her thick golden hair. 'No. If Brid is . . .' Her voice cracked and she hastily looked away.

The sound of the door being unbolted drew Rollo's attention and it was only then that he realized they were locked within the chamber. He was about to demand why when Quinn appeared, ushered in by an escort of three men.

Pallid and strained, the long-legged Torra Altan looked fixedly at Rollo. 'You're awake.'

'An astute observation,' Rollo retorted, aware of the cool tone in the Torra Altan's voice. He glared back and only then, as Quinn stepped forward into the halo of light cast by the candles, did Rollo note the Torra Altan's ugly black eye. 'You've been in a fight,' Rollo said light-heartedly.

'An astute observation,' Quinn echoed with snapping sarcasm. 'I take it you don't remember.'

'Quinn,' Isolde gently interrupted. 'Don't be too hard. He was ill. The pain . . . He couldn't see properly.'

Rollo felt the horrible canker of his guilt and shame twist up within him as he realized that he must have lashed out at Quinn during a fit. First Guthrey and now Quinn! It was not safe to be near him. Rolling over, he closed his eyes, trying to shut out his thoughts. The sound of the door being bolted again brought him sharply to his senses.

Quinn appeared resigned to the fact that they were locked in and didn't even turn to test the handle. Rollo couldn't bear the idea. His instincts urged him to fly at the door but, in trying to leap from his sickbed, he caught his burnt hand in the blanket. Clutching his wounded limb to him, he doubled up, swallowing back the pain.

Isolde pressed him gently back down into his rearranged bedding and offered him another draft of her brew. She then turned to Quinn. 'Well?'

'Dragons,' Quinn blurted. 'They found three of the young ravenshrikes' bodies on the ground alongside a heap of dragon droppings. One was burnt and the other two had their heads ripped off. The mother ravenshrike they found a little further off, disembowelled by a large claw. The bird had remnants of clothing still hooked around its claw; it had been carrying Guthrey.'

Isolde sat down quietly on the bed. 'A dragon would have killed him instantly.'

Quinn's voice was high and excited. 'It wasn't after food, only after destroying the ravenshrikes. Dragons are fiercely territorial. Guthrey may still have got away; he could be out there lying injured, waiting for help. Oxgard won't send any more men. He says the ravenshrikes will be back soon and he can't spare men to search after someone who, he now insists, must certainly be dead.'

Rollo was inclined to agree with this but said nothing.

'We shall have to go ourselves,' Quinn said with decisiveness.

'What about Brid and Spar? What about your mother, Quinn? Shouldn't we look for her?' Rollo asked.

Quinn took a deep breath. 'All Torra Alta is looking for Brid and Spar but no one is looking for Guthrey. We shall have to break out of here and find him.'

By this time, Rollo had finally worked himself to his feet. Gingerly, he began feeling his way from the couch to a chair and tried to take the last few paces that would carry him across to the door. He swayed on his feet for a few moments but, slowly, the giddiness ebbed and only the pain remained. It sharpened his thoughts.

'We're locked in. Why has Oxgard locked us in?'

Quinn sat down – and all too calmly, Rollo thought, considering the circumstances.

The Torra Altan let out a heavy sigh. 'To start with, Oxgard didn't want any more of his men attacked by you. Then he insisted that we must be kept here in safety and that Lord Hal would wreak a worse vengeance than the ravenshrikes on him if he allowed any of us to come to harm. We are being held here for our own safety, I am informed.'

'No one is deciding my destiny for me!' Rollo roared and then regretted it; his throat was extremely sore.

Quinn gave him a lopsided smile. 'Believe me, I've tried but Lady Helena will have none of it. She promised that Oxgard would see us escorted back to Torra Alta the minute he could spare the men, whenever that might be.'

Rollo growled his indignation, 'I am a prince. Oxgard will obey me!'

Quinn's lips crinkled in amusement. 'No one cares about princes here. It matters not whether you are a prince or a yeoman, only whether you have the wit to fight for your own.'

Isolde stepped between them, raising her small hand to quiet Rollo who looked as if he would fly at Quinn at any moment. 'Rest, Rollo; you will need your strength.' Isolde straightened up and stood trembling between them, her green eyes darkening as she girded herself to speak out. 'If Oxgard will not let us go, we must simply slip out. If your wounds continue to improve, we shall go at first light.'

Her voice was very quiet and she looked anxiously between them as if searching for their approval.

'Surely it would be better to go now under cover of dark,' Quinn argued.

Rollo nodded at this. If they were going to escape, they should do it while the castle was watching the skies for ravenshrikes. 'And, if the door is kept locked, how do you propose we escape?'

Isolde shrugged helplessly, her busy fingers fretting with her very long hair as if she were trying to think. 'We have to get out of here.'

Quinn snorted. 'I suggest we break out of here the moment the ravenshrikes attack again.'

'Yes, but how?' Isolde asked.

Quinn held up his dagger. 'We chip out the masonry around the grill in the bottom of the garderobe.' He nodded at the blue curtain behind him. 'Then we just drop down through the hole.'

'I'm a prince. I don't crawl out through cesspits,' Rollo objected.

'Well, you can remain here and be a prince all by yourself,' Quinn told him.

Rollo thought about it for a second and grunted that he would come.

As if by a common accord, Quinn took Isolde's hand and Rollo's good one, though he had to tug it away from his side. Isolde gingerly felt for Rollo's other arm, gripping it above his injury. The three of them now formed a circle. They were linked as one: Isolde, the Maiden, Rollo, reluctant heir

261

to Torra Alta and the bastard, Quinn. From that moment Rollo knew there was something very different about the three of them.

All three faces were grave as they looked at one another, absorbing the moment and marking it as special. Finally a muted cheer broke from Rollo's raw throat as he felt, for the first time since his mother's death, that he belonged. He gripped Quinn's hand fiercely and smiled at Isolde until they suddenly all burst out laughing.

Isolde's eyes sparkled. 'We have made magic,' she said, her nails pinching Rollo's arm in her excitement. 'I thought Keridwen, Brid and I were the only ones but look! Look within the circle.'

Rollo felt a degree of uncomfortable apprehension. He could feel heat emanating from the space at their centre and saw the air shimmer. Though he could draw no rational reason for what he saw, he sensed its import.

'We have power,' Isolde said calmly, her eyes twinkling with joy.

Quinn, too, was staring at the shimmering air. 'What is it?' he asked in bewilderment.

'I told you, it is power,' Isolde scoffed, her excitement overcoming her apologetic nature.

'And how do we use it?' Rollo asked.

'Not everything is there to be used,' Isolde mumbled without looking him in the eye.

The light that hovered between them seemed to swell and grow. All three watched and stared, their excited breath shallow and fast, before Rollo shook his hands free and the light was gone. 'We waste time. Come on, Quinn, get this grill out.' He was suddenly feeling much better.

Isolde pulled aside the heavy blue curtain and they squeezed into a small bare room, a cool draft blowing up from below. At the back of the room was a recess into the keep's thick wall, a hole at its foot set strategically over a steaming midden twenty-foot below. It was not a wide opening but, once they had the protective grill free, they would be able to drop down.

Since his hand was too sore, there was little Rollo could do to help for the moment. He watched as Quinn chiselled away at the mortar around the grill at the back of the garderobe. The task was taking far longer than Rollo expected and so he turned his attention to Isolde, who worked hard shredding and knotting the bedclothes to form a rope. He noted that she still eyed him with some suspicion.

'Why were you not at the castle to greet me and my father?' he demanded.

'I couldn't face him,' she mumbled, her eyes averted.

'Why ever not? What has he ever done to you?'

She said nothing for a moment and Rollo was about to ask her more forcefully when she suddenly blurted, 'He left me. He abandoned me. How could I face him after that?'

'What do you mean, abandoned you?' Rollo asked suspiciously.

'He cared for me from the beginning. I was only weeks old when my mother died and he loved me and nurtured me. He was a father to me and then he left.'

'A father!' Rollo felt deep anguish welling up within him; the ever smouldering fire of his temper was instantly ablaze. 'A father to you!' He scowled angrily and drew back from her, feeling intensively jealous of his father's love. No wonder Caspar had brought him here. It wasn't for him at all. No! Now it was clear that his father had wanted to return for Isolde.

The priestess didn't answer him but merely stared fixedly at the sheets she was knotting together.

'Ha!' he exploded and sank back into brooding silence. To calm his churning mind, he focused on the present.

Quinn straightened his hunched position and rolled his head from side to side to ease the tension in his neck, before giving Rollo a quizzical look. When the Artoran gave out no further expletive, Quinn sat back to nurse his injured knee.

'Once we are out of here, we head north into the mountains until we find the eyrie and then search for any trace of Guthrey. We'll have to get through these woods first, of course, and that'll be the hardest. Despite Oxgard's attempts to get rid of the hobs, he tells me they're a real threat.'

Quinn fell silent again as he concentrated on his task in hand and, at last, tugged the grill free and dragged it into the room. 'Now we wait till the ravenshrikes come. We'd best get some rest,' he advised.

Rollo watched Isolde as she slid behind the central curtain to her ante-chamber. Only then did he retreat to his own sleeping quarters. He thought he would never sleep, but despite the pains in his hand and face, Isolde's potions began to ease his troubles and he drifted off. He awoke when it was still fully dark though he had an instinctive sense that it would soon be morning.

He knew at once, what had awoken him; he was acutely aware of Isolde's presence in his room. He could smell that sweet fresh smell of her hair but, more alarmingly, he could hear her heartbeat. His own heart thumped at the realization that it should be impossible for him to do that. It took him a moment to calm himself and still the swirling lights that filled his mind. Gradually, he became focused and rubbed at his eyes to clear the sleep.

'It's near morning.' She was fidgeting with her hands in that nervous manner of hers. 'The ravenshrikes still have not come so don't you think we should grab something to eat and make a break for it while we still have some cover of darkness?'

Rollo eased himself upright. He had slept in his breeches and so needed only to wriggle into a fresh shirt. He stretched out for a boot that lay at the foot of his bed and began struggling with one hand to pull it on.

'Do you want help?' Isolde offered, immediately stooping down.

He held up his bandaged hand to ward her off, relieved that

it no longer pained him as much as it had. 'I can manage. Let's have some of that bread left from last—' Suddenly he leapt up. 'They are coming!'

'Who is?' Quinn demanded.

Rollo leapt towards the tall narrow window and scrambled onto a chair to look out. 'The ravenshrikes!'

'But I don't hear anything,' Isolde protested, climbing up beside him, her breath warm on the back of his neck.

'I can hear them,' he hissed, 'screaming on the wind.'

The other two hung over his shoulder, their breath held as they listened.

'I hear nothing,' Quinn said dismissively.

'Nor do– no, wait. Listen!' Isolde murmured excitedly. 'A thin, high wail.'

Rollo found it extremely difficult to think for the sound and it was only Isolde tugging at his arm that goaded him into action. They ran to the garderobe and peered out into the drop above the midden.

Rollo was still unimpressed by their plan. He was extremely reluctant to lower himself into such a foul pit but they had to get out of Oxgard's stronghold. One by one, they dropped into the midden, leaving behind the white flag of sheets that had reduced the drop to little more than ten feet. Isolde had saved most of her bedding rope for the drop down the far side of the curtain wall.

Heads low, they scurried across the open bailey. Above them, the sky was bright with flame as the men of Jotunn swung their great torches and used their catapult engines to hurl flaming, oil-soaked rags into the air. Rollo looked up and saw with alarm how men were picked off the battlements and carried away screaming.

But he had no time to dwell on it as they made straight for the barbican farthest from the ravenshrikes' assault, and crept up a flight of steps cut into the wall. As Quinn had predicted, no one noticed them in all the yelling and shouting and soon all three looked over the wall into the dark of the woods beyond. Hastily, Quinn found a post to which he could fasten their makeshift rope and tossed the length of knotted sheets over the wall.

Conscious and regretful that he was leaving Firecracker and his weapons behind, Rollo went first, slithering down and using his one good hand and the crook of his elbow to spare his injury. Once at the bottom, he held the rope firmly, first for Isolde and then for Quinn, to prevent them from knocking into the wall. Heads down, they ran for the woods.

As they plunged into the dark, Rollo saw two red eyes blink at them and then vanish, light feet leaping away through the forest. At first, he was alarmed, thinking that it was a hob but Isolde put a hand on his arm. 'It's only the wolf,' she reassured him. 'He would never do anyone any harm if they were with me.'

It was too dark to pick their way through the undergrowth so, for a while, they hid in the bole of a long-dead oak tree, waiting for the first grey wisps of dawn to provide enough light; then they moved off. Consciously keeping tight to Isolde's side, Rollo ran at a steady pace, amazed that Quinn managed to run at all as he limped along just behind them. The early light was just enough for them to see by until they were deep into the woods where the branches smothered the sky and stilled the wind. Panting, they drew to a halt.

Though he would not say it aloud, Rollo still had doubts in the back of his mind that they were doing the right thing. They had heard the grunts and moans of night predators as they travelled and he wished that he had a sword. He reached for Isolde's hand and felt her tremble.

'Which way?' he hissed at Quinn, trying to keep his voice steady as the grunts of a large animal a little way off to the right rumbled through the forest.

The noise was alien to him and so alarming. He was only certain that it wasn't a bear. His own country had a dense population of giant bears and, as a result, was relatively free of predators that might have preyed on man. Here, however,

266

there was only man to keep them away and the herds of Jotunn cattle attracted them in large numbers.

Their anxiety slowly lessened as shafts of thin light filtered down through the trees and the deep grunts and bellows tailed off. They made faster progress now and Rollo noted that Isolde and Quinn seemed quite at home in the woods. The girl in particular was less tense. The two Torra Altans easily stooped, twisted and weaved around the gnarled, moss-covered branches, whereas he tripped at every opportunity in his efforts to keep up.

He had to admit that he was impressed by Quinn's instinctive knowledge of the lie of the land. He also knew how best to keep downwind of large animals, when to hide their tracks in a stream or when to take to the trees to avoid the predators.

Rollo looked on with reluctant admiration. 'How did he know about that lequus?' he asked Isolde, his heart still pounding in his chest. Quinn had been aware of the fearful beast and directed them downwind of it long before they had seen the savage creature. Half lion half horse, it was tearing at a bullock it had brought down. Stealthily, they had crept around the edge of the glade without the beast being aware of them; Rollo had felt his life was entirely in Quinn's hands.

'He spends all his time with the huntsmen in the woods, learning their art. Lord Hal is not too impressed by this and would see him turn his skill to archery or swordsmanship but Quinn is not being groomed to be a lord, so they care less what he does,' Isolde informed him.

Rollo was immediately alert as Quinn motioned towards a large oak and gestured that they should head to the left of it. The tall youth hissed, 'Taurs! We must head down into the marshy hollows, away from these grassy glades.'

Following his line of sight, Rollo glimpsed only the rounded shoulders and pale horns of cattle poking above the ferns. Grunts and the contented munch of grazing animals came to his ears. Though suspecting that Quinn was over-reacting, he followed the instructions despite his better judgement. He disliked heading into the damper places where the large trees of oak and ash gave way to elder and hazel and finally into uncomfortably large numbers of blackthorn. He brushed against one and, immediately, a dark red line of blood sprang up on the back of his hand where he had been raked by a thorn.

'Hob country,' Isolde warned, her voice trembling.

'I know,' Quinn hissed. 'But isn't that better than taurs?'

'I don't know! What do we do?' Isolde said, glancing nervously back the way they had come and then at Rollo and Quinn.

The three looked at each other in indecision, not knowing which was the better route to take. All the while, the steady munching of busy mouths grew louder.

'It might be better to risk the taurs,' Quinn said at length. 'They rarely move in groups of more than a half dozen, whereas, if you stumble across one hob, you can bet a golden hawk that there will be a huge gang of them close behind. But there's no sign of any hobs yet. I say we head for the blackthorns,' he contradicted himself.

A cloud of alarmed birds burst from the nearby trees and the air was suddenly filled with their angry cries. The ground began to tremble with the sound of stampeding cattle. Something had frightened the taurs.

Quinn snatched Isolde's hand, attempting to drag her forward, the sense of urgency clearly driving out the pain that had previously slowed him. But Isolde stumbled and could not keep up with his long-legged pace. The sound of thundering hooves and beasts crashing into trees was growing louder and Rollo feared that, at any moment, they would be trampled.

'You hide,' Quinn instructed. 'I'll run on to try and draw the taurs off.'

Rollo understood his plan. An oak tree lay on its side where the great bole of the tree had been split by lightning. They scrambled over it and Rollo pulled Isolde to him, crawling as far as he could under the fallen trunk. Pulling his head down into his chest, he lay hunched over the priestess as the small herd poured around the log or leapt over it, the ground shaking as they pounded the earth. Two leapt over them, their hooves rattling on the wood, and he was virtually bounced off the ground as the beasts thumped to the ground.

Once the herd, which sounded as if it were considerably stronger than a mere half dozen, had passed, he peered through his fingers, shocked at the sight of the curious beasts. He could just make out Quinn, who had pulled himself up into a tree some way ahead, and the strange sight of the taurs charging by underneath. He was about to raise his head tentatively when he saw Quinn wave him down. The youth hollered and Rollo ducked as two blurred shapes skimmed over his head. The creatures veered away from the rest of the herd to chase after Quinn. Sprouting from their cleft hooves were the thick legs and lower torso of humans that supported shaggy shoulders and the great neck and head of horned bulls. Their heads lowered ready to gore Quinn's back.

Rollo gave out a great shriek of rage to lure the taurs back, but then yelped in alarm as Quinn vanished from sight. The two taurs disappeared right behind him amidst the sound of shrieking and snapping twigs. Rollo sprinted after them, coming to a halt before a deep dent in the earth. Branches and vegetation criss-crossed a dark pit. The taurs were bellowing furiously from somewhere far below but Quinn clung to a branch that had been caught in some long trailing brambles and that alone prevented him from falling into the pit.

Already, Isolde was trying to reach Quinn, who was scrabbling for a better hold. Rollo flung himself to the ground, stretched out and grabbed Quinn's wrist. His gaze fell deeper into the gloom below as the taurs bellowed up from the deep pit. Despite the pain in his scorched hand,

Rollo managed to drag Quinn clear and they rolled over onto their backs in relief, both panting heavily.

'Are you all right?' Isolde asked anxiously.

The tall Torra Altan youth nodded. 'Just a graze. One of them caught me across the back of the shoulders, that was all.'

They stared down in trepidation at the animals below, aware of what might have been. They also knew that the sound of the taurs' bellowing would draw large predators and whoever built the pit, all too soon.

'We've got to get away from here,' Quinn panted.

Isolde seemed momentarily distracted and did not react with the urgency that Rollo thought expedient. 'Why in the name of the Mother would someone build so deep a pit out here?' she muttered.

'Isolde! Come on,' Quinn urged her impatiently. 'We'd better get out of these blackthorn bushes as fast as—' The words were stilled by Rollo's hand on his lips as the sound of a snorting horse broke through the trees.

'What do you think you are doing tampering with my trap?' demanded a deep voice as a man with long, ragged hair rode out of the gloom, impressively tall on his sleek black horse.

Chapter 16

Rollo stepped back as the rugged-looking stranger brushed past him on his horse and peered down into the trap. As anguished bellows rang up from below, the black mare shrieked and shied away from the edge until the man thumped her neck, swearing at her to hold still. His muscles straining to raise his weighty crossbow, he slotted a thick bolt into place, wound back the mechanism and pulled the trigger.

One of the animals in the pit gave out a squeal of pain that sent the other into a frenzy of terror. Rollo cautiously peered over the edge of the pit to see that one taur was running in frantic circles about the body of the fallen beast. In its frenzied efforts to escape, it had pulled away several lengths of the stout wooden shuttering. Entangling itself in the long timbers, it had broken one of its legs below the knee. The animal seemed unaware of the flailing limb as it crashed on, its awkward movements making it hard for the stranger to hold his aim. When he finally loosed his bolt, the long heavy barb struck the animal just forward of its left ear, driving fully two hands span into the bull-like skull. The taur charged on until it crashed against the pit walls. A trembling shudder ran through its strangely formed body as its legs buckled and it fell amongst the debris of the pit floor.

Satisfied that the beasts were dead, the stranger turned his attention to the three youngsters, observing each in turn before finally speaking. 'So tell me, what exactly are you three doing running about so far from your homes? You've been out all night by the looks of you, which isn't exactly recommended in these parts. Short of leaping off a cliff, that's got to be the fastest way to get yourself killed.' His eyes flickered over them while he waited for their response.

Isolde crept behind Quinn. 'I don't like him,' she whispered.

The stranger curiously studied each in turn as they stared back in glum silence. 'Speak up then! Are you lost? Do you need help? What brings you to this unlikely spot?'

Quinn edged slightly forward. 'We might ask the same of you, sir,' he said stiffly. 'But we won't! We have no need of assistance.'

The man guffawed at this. 'Indeed not! Three youngsters chased by taurs and all but falling into a mammoth trap! Oh, yes, you seem right on top of the situation,' he laughed, stooping low on his horse, his long hair tumbling forward. His skin was unwashed and marked with many scars. His eyes were a milky green that somehow looked too soft for his rugged-looking face. His teeth were strong and white but his smile was thin.

Rollo was unsure of Quinn's ability to deal with the situation and decided a smoother, more confident tone was required. 'Whatever brought us here is of little matter. We are here now and have misjudged our route. By the look of things, you are familiar with these woods and so I'm glad you stumbled on us. Do you know how we can safely head north out of these woods?'

Again, the man laughed though Rollo had the sense that his eyes were not mirthful but were studying them thoughtfully. He peered around Quinn to look at Isolde with too much interest, though that was barely surprising. As Rollo had observed many times at court, there seemed nothing quite so attractive to old men as a girl on the verge of blossoming into womanhood.

The stranger lounged back in his saddle. 'You just stick close by me. That's the only safe way out of here. Once beyond the woods, you'll be as safe as anyone can be nowadays.'

Now that the cries from the taurs were silenced, the man's horse ceased to play up. On a loose rein, the mare moved in closer, whickering softly and snuffling the air around Quinn and Isolde.

The mare seemed to be studying them with as much interest as they studied her rider. She was sleek black with a very long mane and tail, and a small, pretty head that she kept tucked in tight to her chest. The soft glow of the early morning sun glistened in the sweat on her coat like miniature jewels. In fact, she was one of the most magnificent horses Rollo had seen – withstanding Firecracker and his progeny, naturally. However, he found the way she watched them most unnerving; it was quite absurd to think that a horse might find them intriguing.

The man dropped down from his black mare and peered into the pit to satisfy himself that the taurs were dead. While his horse nibbled at the grass growing in the glade, he set about repairing the trap. He took an axe and a rope from his saddle and worked hard, selecting and chopping down long leggy saplings to span the pit. These he covered with an interlocking layer of leafed branches. All the while he worked, he continually cast his gaze towards the three youngsters as if trying to make up his mind what he thought of them.

Recovering their strength, Rollo, Quinn and Isolde sat on the grass, likewise, eyeing the man. As the morning sun rose higher, allowing more light to break through the twiggy branches overhead, the young prince of Artor considered the stranger's appearance. His hair was unusually long for a man and his teeth, although bright, were rather short and blunt. He had a quick smile but the look in his eyes was reserved and his brow was deeply furrowed.

What surprised Rollo most of all was that he treated what was clearly a very precious horse with undue harshness. She

273

did not wander as the stranger worked but tore up the ferns, one foot looped through the reins that had slid from her neck and trailed in the earth. It was obvious that she was worth a fortune. She was pretty as well as strong. Rollo had at once noted her ostentatious gait, her heavily muscled, feathered legs stepping high and clearly demonstrating her power and stamina. Now, as she grazed, he saw that her flanks were striped with red scars and he immediately associated these with the pair of angry spurs jutting arrogantly from the heel of the man's boot. It surprised him that anyone would treat so fair an animal with such cruelty.

He was not overly sentimental about horses and so was not appalled by such brutality but merely thought it strange, unnecessary and unwise. His father had been able to tame the wildest of beasts but never used harsh methods; Rollo wondered why this man resorted to such means.

He leaned towards Quinn and tugged at the youth's shirt. 'Do you think we should wait for this man's help? We know nothing about him.'

'He's surviving in the wild of the forest, isn't he?' Quinn retorted.

The horse's ears pricked back as if listening to their conversation. Rollo chided himself for becoming overly imaginative, a quality for which he had no respect. Life was about practicalities not dreams.

'I've nearly finished here,' the man called to them. 'If one of you will help me with this last branch to cover the centre of the pit, I'll share my bread with you.'

Quinn nodded and pushed himself to his feet. Still limping, he helped the man heave the branch into place and then gratefully accepted the offer of food.

They ate standing up and in silence. Only when the meal was done and the stranger had finished wiping the crumbs from his stubbly face did anyone speak.

'I'd best be pointing you in the direction of home,' the stranger said. 'These woods are no place for children. Now where are you from and I'll set you on the right road?' Again he appraised the three youngsters while he waited for one of them to answer.

Isolde nudged Quinn, urging him to speak for her, and Rollo wondered why this girl, who had so much power, was so reserved. Her eyes, he considered, were darkly guilty.

'We just need a route that leads towards Torra Alta,' Quinn said firmly, his hands clenched with determination. 'We're looking for someone and—'

'Oh, you were out here alone looking for someone? Was there no one better suited to the task than you three youngsters?'

'We are not as hopeless as you might assume,' Rollo said indignantly. 'I have been trained by the Warriors of Ash themselves and could outfight a man twice my weight.'

'Only because he would fall about laughing,' the man chortled. His mouth twisted into a smile but his eyes continued to flit suspiciously between the three companions.

'Well now! Three children deep in hob country is, to say the least, slightly surprising; we're near the Oldhart Forest here. You must be desperate or you wouldn't be here.'

'Of course we're desperate,' Quinn retorted, his face taut with pain. 'My brother is lost.' He simplified the facts.

The man looked at him, eyebrows raised. Rollo was becoming increasingly anxious; this man was too curious. He had a sudden compulsion to kick Quinn and keep him silent but it was too late.

'Three very finely dressed young gentlefolk, if I'm not mistaken. Your father must be someone of high standing.'

Quinn shrugged and to Rollo's relief said only, 'Just an archer.' His words, however, were spoken a little too brightly.

Rollo could not believe that the youth was so inept at lying. It was clear by the weight of the woollen clothes beneath his bearskin cloak and the newness of his boots that he was of some status; and Rollo noted how the stranger's eyes flitted over Quinn and gave him a wry smile.

'An archer, eh?'

'Yes, an archer!' Quinn repeated with indignation. 'I could hit a chosen mark at a hundred paces.'

'I don't doubt that. The nobles of Torra Alta are reputed to be the finest shots in all the Caballan,' the stranger said with enthusiasm.

Quinn nodded. 'We are indeed. And—' Quinn stopped short, clearly realizing that he had already said too much.

Rollo felt that he could have smoothly covered this mistake if only he had kept on talking but Quinn's face had gone a deep shade of red. Rollo had inherited his father's dark red hair and freckled skin and he, too, was prone to colouring with emotion, but it was something he had learnt to suppress. He had always longed for his mother's dark skin simply because it gave less away.

'So, Torra Altan, aren't you and your friends a little far from home?'

'I never said we were Torra Altans,' Quinn objected.

'Mmm.' The man nodded his head but clearly disagreed. 'Perhaps not. But even I can recognize a Torra Altan – the openness of the expression, the trusting eyes, the longer length to the hair, the brown bearskins.' He nodded at Isolde and Quinn's cloaks. 'The winters must be harsh up there in your mountains, harsher even than in these bitter woods.'

Quinn laughed. 'Bitter! This is but a mild spring. If you want to see angry weather, a midwinter's storm in Torra Alta will take the skin off your face in less than five minutes. Isolde and I are used to it but Rollo, here, is not so used to the cold weather, are you, Rollo?'

Rollo's heart sank. How could Quinn be so naïve as to talk so openly with this stranger? He had made the classic mistake of believing others trustworthy and well-intentioned just because he was. How the youth had remained so personable when he had been brought up by Hal, Rollo could not imagine.

'Now, you shouldn't go around telling strangers all about

yourself,' the man laughed at Quinn just as if he had read Rollo's thoughts. 'So what disaster befell your brother, sending the three of you out into the woods? Like as not, you'd have been eaten by taurs within the hour if I hadn't chanced on you so you may as well tell.'

'We were travelling north of here and Quinn's brother got separated from the rest of the party,' Rollo hastily improvised, hoping to speak before Quinn divulged even more about them. He certainly did not want explain their unfortunate fight.

'Travelling, eh?' the man repeated, his eyes inscrutable, and Rollo could not decide whether he believed him or not. 'And what happened to the rest of your party?'

Rollo hastily flicked back his hair, distracting the man's gaze from the flush of colour rising up his neck. 'We were attacked by hobs. The men ran off to lead the hobs away from us and they never came back.' Rollo dropped his voice to a whisper and stepped closer to the man. 'I didn't want to say in front of the girl but I think the hobs must have caught them. Still, until it's proved that there's no hope, we shall have to keep on looking. Have you seen or heard anything? A man like yourself surely knows how to watch and listen while keeping hidden himself.' Rollo attempted to flatter the man.

'All I know about hobs is to stay well clear of them,' the long-haired stranger said casually, scraping off the muck on his boot with a stick. 'Doesn't the sun ever shine in this wretched country?'

Rollo very much agreed with his sentiments about the weather. He was also beginning to feel more comfortable in the stranger's presence now that the man seemed mostly concerned about the grizzly climate. Perhaps, he was a simple hunter after all.

'It's winter!' Isolde suddenly snapped, her tone irritable. 'What would you expect? Now please, sir, we are cold and hungry and worried for our friends. Can you help us or not?'

Rollo was quite surprised to hear Isolde speak out with such venom. She spoke rarely and when she did, it was usually with soft apologetic words. He found himself quite impressed by her outburst.

The man was nodding. 'Well, it seems I'd best get you to safety as fast as possible. So, it's back to Torra Alta then? I was thinking about heading that way myself. So you'll be best sticking with old Merrit,' he told them jovially, patting his chest. He looked at them sideways for a while, his mouth raised in a tight grin. 'Come on, I've got kills to make to fill the larder but my conscience won't let me rest until I've set you three on your way home. There's just a couple of tasks I have to complete first that won't take us too much out of the way. And nor will they take long,' he added hastily reading Quinn's impatient expression.

Merrit, as the man had called himself, gathered his belongings together. The axe and rope were loaded back onto the horse where they nestled alongside a collection of whips, a large number of javelins, a heavy box of bolts and the remarkably weighty crossbow with which he had despatched the taurs in the pit. Strapped to the back of the saddle were a roll of bedding and a number of leather satchels, tightly buckled down. Dangling from the high pommel of the saddle was a coiled brass horn. Rollo had never seen such an extraordinary instrument.

He also considered that, if the man were civil he would have told them more about the tasks he needed to fulfil but Merrit showed no such inclination. The youth decided that perhaps he was being over-cynical and shrugged away the man's behaviour. Adults often treated youngsters with disregard and, in that way, the stranger was no different from any other man.

Musing further, Rollo decided that, in fact, no one had paid him any attention from the moment his sister had demonstrated her inherited affinity with bears. All had bowed and scraped to her, passing him over as if he were no more important than a lapdog. As a very young child, he had been aware of how his parents had pinned their hopes on him, watching him expectantly for signs of his mother's ability to communicate with the great bears of Artor. The young boys of the castle had flocked to him, eager for his friendship as they all awaited that moment when he would finally speak to the bears. But that moment had never come.

Imogen had been born and, as his sister, he had loved her. She was a happy delightful girl whom everyone adored. 'Look at those wonderful curls,' one would say. Or, 'My, what a smile! Rollo, have you ever seen such a fine smile? Aren't you just so proud of your sister?'

And in a way, he had been. He had known right from the start, before anyone else, that Imogen had inherited the skill. It was not until she was about five that it became apparent but he had known from the very beginning that she possessed it. The moment that strange ululating cry burst out from her small body and everyone saw the bears flock to her side, the friends he had made deserted him to follow his sister.

His mother had explained that these deserters were not real friends since they had only valued him for his status. But it did not make him feel any better. He had enjoyed their company and he was intelligent enough to realize that it meant that none of them had ever really liked him. It was a hard truth for a child of barely seven years. Perhaps that was why he liked Isolde. She, too, knew what it was like to be alone. Yet, she sought solitude; it had been thrust upon him. Moreover, she did not need his friendship; she had Quinn whereas he had lost Imogen. He suppressed a sigh. His sister had never shunned him, and though she had been the cause of his sudden unpopularity, he had never blamed her. She had always seen him as her older brother and he missed her. It seemed that everyone was lost to him now.

Without even thinking about the direction they were taking, he traipsed after Merrit as the man set off through the scrubby woodland. Observing the curious man, he considered that at least he had weapons and could save them from the taurs if they were to appear again. What had Quinn been thinking of dragging them out into the woods? The youth was mad! He scowled at Quinn's back and began to lag behind, kicking at the dirt as he went. His head was beginning to throb but he ignored the warning signs. He could have a headache just as anyone else, couldn't he? It was quite normal.

For a time, Rollo let the steady sway of the horse's hindquarters calm his mind but soon the sores on his hand, hot beneath the bandages, began to irritate. He tried to think of something else. Thankfully, the throb in his head had eased and he was no longer concerned that the stress and strains of the last few days were going to force yet another seizure on him.

Ahead of him, Isolde was looking about nervously, her gaze lingering on him and he could see her smooth forehead gradually wrinkling into lines.

'We're going the wrong way,' she whispered to Quinn, her hand in his. Rollo scowled at their sibling-like affection.

'What?' Clearly, Quinn had not been taking any heed of their direction but was absorbed in studying Merrit's high-stepping horse.

'Don't worry,' the stranger said over his shoulder. 'I know, you are eager to get home but I have traps set all about this edge of the Oldhart Forest and I really must check on them as we are so close. It won't take us very much longer. Soon, I'll see you to the road that will take you clean to Torra Alta. I promise.'

Rollo stopped in his stride. 'What was that noise?' he demanded, hearing in the distance what he took to be a fanfare. 'Do you think that's Hal?'

Isolde shook her head but said nothing.

'Hal wouldn't announce himself with a trumpet blast,' Quinn explained for Isolde.

'But it might be! What if he's calling us to him?' Rollo

objected, suddenly aware that Merrit's eyes were fixed hard on him. What was he doing? He had mentioned Hal by name! Angry with himself, Rollo wondered if his own feelings were putting his companions in danger. Certainly, he had no wish to be back in Torra Alta with Hal. What was going to happen to him when they discovered that it was his fault that Hal's beloved son would never be coming home?

The trumpet blasted again and, this time, Rollo knew instantly what it was and couldn't understand how he had been able to mistake it for a trumpet call. 'Mammoth,' he grunted. 'Is there no end to the beasts roving this country?' he despaired, kicking at the dirt.

Isolde swung round at him, the big eyes in her gaunt face suddenly narrowing to suspicious slits. 'You blame me too! Everyone blames me!'

'Blames you for what? For mammoths?' Rollo laughed at her. 'You may be able to pull a rabbit or a blind toad from your cauldron, or whatever it is you use, but an entire mammoth? Now, really!'

She smiled at him sideways and he gave her a lopsided grin back; there was something about her oddity that made him warm to her.

The trumpeting was drawing nearer and Quinn glanced over his shoulder before trotting up level with Merrit. 'Wouldn't it be wiser to head away from that noise?'

The stranger shrugged. 'I know she's coming at us but she'll head away any moment now. There's an old canal between us, hidden in the trees and she won't risk crossing something like that. A mammoth can't take the risk of falling. One broken bone in their giant bodies and they never get up again.'

He seemed calm though his horse twitched and shied at the mammoth's blaring. Eventually, he reached out to snap off a stick from an overhanging branch and thwacked her hard across the rump with it. She bucked once in protest but then settled down as the man hissed, 'You know what'll happen if you let me down.'

The horse tossed her head and Rollo had the absurd notion that, any moment, she might speak.

'I hate to spoil your plans but we really are heading entirely in the wrong direction. We're heading south and the Great North Road surely lies to the west,' Quinn said loudly. He looked to Isolde for confirmation and she nodded.

Merrit twisted his head round rather too sharply than was natural and Rollo knew something was wrong; it was just that the movement had been too snappy. He felt intensely uncomfortable about this man but still he didn't know quite what else they could do.

'I know exactly where we are,' Merrit said hotly but soothed his tone before continuing. 'I told you, didn't I? I have to see my traps on the way. There's one just a little way south of here. I have to check my traps regularly. No good otherwise. They always need repairing.'

Without further protest, the three youngsters followed on after the man. Rollo was too lost in the worry of his thoughts to notice much about his surroundings. However, the one thing he did note was that many of the taller trees looked sick, their boughs split and dark with rotten wood. A profusion of winter honeysuckle that was already bursting into bloom smothered the ground between the trees. Rollo looked harder and suddenly noticed little lights like fireflies jumping unnaturally about the flowers.

Isolde clutched Quinn's arm, her fingernails digging deep into his skin. 'Brid said she saw them only last summer but I've never seen them before. Aren't they beautiful?'

'I can see only lights,' Rollo grunted. It was a strange phenomenon, certainly, but there must be a reasonable explanation. He could hear the steady thump, thump of the mammoth's footfall and the shrieks and calls of the birds that flocked into the sky. He felt his heart race as he imagined the monstrous woolly mammoth on their trail but reminded himself that Merrit was right; a mammoth would not attempt to cross a disused canal.

The walk was making him hot and the exertion was pumping the blood to his sore hand, making it throb. Unable to bare the prickling heat from the bandages anymore, he ripped them off, hoping that the fresh air might heal the scabs faster. Though, the skin was indeed, very much healed, the flesh was still tender. Naturally, he did his best to cradle the hand but the discomfort was distracting and he found it hard to listen to Quinn who was now limping close beside him.

'I'm telling you, Rollo, this is not right,' Quinn hissed conspiratorially. 'We can't afford to waste any more time. Any delay could cost Guthrey his life. I'm sure we shouldn't be going deeper into these woods.'

'If you're so sure of where we are, why don't you make the decision and lead us to the Great North Road yourself?' Rollo hissed back in frustration.

'We need him,' Quinn excused his lack of action. 'He's right; the taurs nearly had us.' Quinn stopped to rub at his injured knee before setting off again, his face tight with worry. Despite the injury, Quinn strode past Rollo and seemed intent on drawing level with Merrit on his black mare.

Isolde fell into step alongside Rollo. Looking down, he winced at the sight of her bare feet on the cold ground but said nothing. After many minutes of silence during which time he critically observed Quinn, who was trying to break into conversation with Merrit, Rollo hissed, 'What was Quinn thinking about? How could he have been such an idiot to say so much about who we are?'

Isolde's slight hand moved to her neck and she stroked the dazzling golden-hearted ruby that hung from a thick chain. Most of the while, she kept it concealed but now had drawn it out from beneath the layers of her clothing as if she needed to touch it for comfort. 'I— I—. Well, what else should he have said?' she asked timidly.

'Anything would have been better. Anything!' He snorted.

Isolde did not reply but lowered her gaze to the torn and ragged hem of her mud-stained dress. She was like a discarded rag doll, Rollo decided. But why should he trouble himself with her woes when he had so many troubles of his own? Quinn was still talking to the stranger and Rollo found he was fearful of what the youth might be saying to the man. It just didn't seem prudent to talk with strangers in this unstable world. He sighed and wished he were home. If he had been home he would have never have met Guthrey . . .

His cousin's name roared into his thoughts and, like a firework bursting at its zenith, filled his mind with crackling emotion. The intensity of the moment was brief but the bright image of the thrust that had killed Guthrey drifted to the black void of his imagination. He felt sick and his head pounded. The events of the last few days had driven the thought from his mind but now it came back. Guthrey was dead. He had killed him. He had killed his cousin. Even now, he could still feel the jarring shock of his sword striking bone. His father would disown him for such a vile crime and Hal would probably kill him if he ever found out. But no one must ever find out. And the longer they were lost in the woods the better because, then, there would be less chance of finding Guthrey.

He chewed on the idea. But what if Oxgard's men found him first? What if they realized that the wound that had killed him could only have been made by a sword? Rollo imagined the half-rotten corpse being dragged forward while all accusing eyes fixed on him.

But it was self-defence, he persuaded himself. It was Guthrey who had attacked him. He had not meant to kill him. The thoughts churned in Rollo's troubled mind and he felt the pressure of blood building up within his brain. But it had been his fault! He remembered distinctly the hot queasy feeling that ran through his mind prior to one of his fits. Rage had possessed him, shameful rage, and in that state, he had murdered Guthrey. He glared down at the lumpy scabs on his scorched hand.

If only Guthrey had killed me and not the other way

around, he thought to himself. 'I am a monster!' he croaked, gritting his teeth on his pain and self-loathing. With a start, he realized he had spoken out loud.

Isolde was staring at him. 'What did you say?' she asked. 'I'm sorry, I wasn't listening.'

'Nothing,' Rollo said hastily, feeling the colour flood his cheeks.

At that moment, the long-haired man drew to a halt at the edge of a glade and sniffed the air. Waving to the others to keep still, he dismounted and paced forward towards a level area of ground overlain with a criss-cross of branches. He shifted one of these aside and peered beneath it, grunting in dissatisfaction. 'I must have one. It will undo so much otherwise. I must keep their trust.' He sniffed the air again, obviously distracted. When he focused on the youngsters, he gave them a hasty smile as if he had momentarily forgotten their presence. 'Well, if I must nursemaid you three, you can help me. Rip up some bracken and toss it over this trap, here.'

'What are you trying to catch?' Quinn asked, obeying without protest.

'Mammoth, of course.'

'Why, of course? I would have thought that a mammoth was a most dangerous creature to trap,' the youth stated sensibly and Rollo was glad to hear that Quinn had at least some degree of scepticism.

'Oh, how little you youngsters think beyond what affects you,' the man sighed.

Rollo thought such philosophical words rather curious coming from a man of such obvious hard living.

Merrit continued, 'I achieve much by trapping the mammoth. First of all, I save homes from being trampled. The mammoth herds have been moving steadily south and they can do more damage than an entire family of dragons. What they don't eat they trample.'

'But what concern is it of yours?' Rollo demanded. 'You are a foreigner; why not help the people of your own lands?'

'Who are you to talk of foreigners? By the colour of your skin, you're no native to these cold shores. And you ask too many questions for a young lad,' the man snapped at him. 'I may be one man alone, but I can do my bit to help others against the troubles that have befallen us all since the great beasts gained their freedom and plague the world.'

Isolde looked sharply away at this, her head dropping.

'Don't worry, Issy,' Quinn said gently. 'I'm sure we'll find him and, if we don't, Hal will. Hal would never rest until his wife and his only son are brought home.'

Isolde smiled at the tall youth and ran to slip her hand into his. She was a few years older than Quinn but there was something childlike in her shrinking manner that made her seem younger. Quinn put an arm round her shoulder and then turned back to Merrit.

'If it wouldn't be too much trouble, could you point us on our way? We really must hurry.'

'I would be a poor friend to send you off alone. It'll be dark before long and I don't think any of you would survive the night out here in the woods alone. Perhaps in the morning . . .'

'Our journey is terribly important. Please, just tell us the quickest way to the nearest road,' Quinn implored. 'You see, we have to find my brother. He was stolen by a ravenshrike but he may still be alive.'

Rollo flashed Quinn an angry glance. What was the youth doing telling this perfect stranger about their disaster?

'Ravenshrikes?' the man queried. 'Well, now. He could still be alive as you say.'

'But I don't understand it at all,' Rollo blurted, deeply distressed by the turn in the conversation. 'What possible purpose would ravenshrikes have to keep humans alive? It would have killed him days ago. It makes no sense to me. Guthrey is dead and we should think of our own safety now. At least then, we can stop Hal and my father from sending out needless search parties to look for us.' Rollo's voice trailed away and he looked between his quiet companions and the dark face of the stranger whose eyes were fixed on his lips, drinking in his every word. Now it had been him and not Quinn who had blurted out their status. In times like this, those of noble blood would be worth a fortune in ransom.

'Ravenshrikes are voracious hunters,' the stranger explained. 'They are obsessive about the act of hunting and attack. They like their food alive and invariably take too much of it. Live food has a tendency to get up and walk away rather than hang around a ravenshrike's nest, waiting for the birds to get hungry again. Come on, then,' he said brightly, dismissing the whole conversation. He nodded wisely to the three youngsters and then nodded in the direction of the track, urging them onwards.

Rollo began to wonder whether he wasn't just being a little paranoid. The man had shown no great joy at learning more about them and appeared only interested in his giant mammoth traps.

'I've got three more traps to check in this direction,' Merrit informed them. 'Then we'll be nearing an old drove track that goes south through the Oldhart Forest. I know it's the wrong direction for you but it'll be quicker in the long run because this way we can reach the Dairy Track that links Nattarda to the Great North Road. The Dairy Track is one of the few roads in these parts that's still passable. You can head on alone from there. I thinks it's sheer folly to travel alone but if that's what you children want, then so be it. I have too many worries of my own without troubling myself with saving you.'

They trudged on, Quinn still limping on his injured knee though he never complained. The trees grew sparser, which pleased Rollo. It allowed the sun to filter down and warm the back of his neck as he stared down and kept on marching.

Merrit suddenly yanked his horse to a halt and waved to the three youngsters to be quiet. 'He's here. I can smell him!'

'Smell what?'

'I told you to be quiet.' Merrit was suddenly intensely agitated and glanced over the three of them as if wondering what should be done with them. 'Your job is just to keep quiet and keep out of harm's way. Do you understand me?'

Quinn was nodding but Rollo scowled. He didn't like being told what to do by this man even if they did need him to guide them through the forest.

The long-haired stranger was looking beyond them at a broad glade sunken into a hollow and surrounded by a number of graceful beeches. Threads of wheat still grew up through the grass of the clearing showing that this was once ploughed land, the older trees spiking out of what must once have been hedges. Two of the great silvery-barked trees had grown to twice the height of their offspring. Like an old couple, they stood pressed up close to one another, only two arm's lengths separating their great trunks. Sliding from his horse, the stranger grabbed Isolde roughly by the wrist and pulled her towards the trees whilst shouting at Rollo and Quinn to follow.

'Just stand here between the trees and don't move a muscle. You'll be safe in that gap. Quite safe. I'm going to have him this time!'

Chapter 17

Merrit unhooked the horn from the front of his saddle as he scanned the sweep of the glade. The open ground was refreshingly bright and airy in the midst of the scrubby forest. A bronze haze of wheat shimmered between the overgrown hedges. Copses dotted the ground and, standing tall above the ragged shrubs within the hedgerows were older beech, oak and ash trees that must have sheltered the field for hundreds of years. Three bare oaks stood within the field itself and another tree lay uprooted, ivies and grasses scrambling over it as if trying to draw it down into the soil. Nearby a thatch of cut pine branches lay on the open ground, covering what Rollo presumed to be another trap.

Leaning back against one of the great beech trees, Rollo scowled, distrustful of the situation. His gaze returned to the long-haired stranger who was licking his finger and holding it up to test the direction of the wind. His assessment made, Merrit nodded thoughtfully.

'What's he doing?' Isolde asked. 'He seems to be taking an age. Can't we just keep on going without him?'

'We can't. We're lost and he knows better how to defend us from the predators of the forest. We need him,' Quinn said reasonably. 'If we're hoping to get home, we're going to need his help.'

'We're going home then?' Isolde asked, evidently pleased by Quinn's decision. 'I thought we were going to try and hunt out the ravenshrike's nest.'

'I know that's what we intended but we're going home

now. We haven't even been able to look after ourselves properly so how do you suppose we could rescue Guthrey even if we found him? Besides . . .' His voice trailed away. 'Besides, however much we want to believe that there is still a chance, it is now too absurd to believe he's still alive. We'll just have to go back and explain it all to Hal and take what's due to us.'

'It wasn't your fault,' Rollo said quickly, trying to hide the guilt in his voice. 'Why should you blame yourself?'

'The blame is mine for encouraging Guthrey to continue in such a silly quarrel.' His lip was trembling and Rollo could see that he was battling to hold down his distress over Guthrey and his mother. The youth stiffened up his shoulders. 'We must return home. It's the only thing to do,' he repeated, his voice tapering off as he watched Merrit. 'What on earth is that man doing?'

'The poor horse doesn't like it!' Isolde whispered as Merrit led his mount to the centre of the sweep of grassland and then tied its reins to the roots of the fallen tree that lay just upwind of the pit. The man tugged at the knot to make sure it was secure and, when he was satisfied, moved to the rear of his horse, removed his javelins and began to sort through the rolls strapped to the back of the saddle. He patted the smallest satchel, which had a wolfskin cover, as if to reassure himself that it was safe and another he unbuckled and unfurled. The roll contained a huge red sheet, which he shook out and spread over the mare's back, tying it about her neck. The loose ends, lying over her hindquarters, flapped in the breeze.

He then plucked from his pack two short sticks with strips of cloth attached to one end. These flapping pennants he fixed to the horse's bridle. Finally, he unwrapped a number of small metal discs, pierced through their centres, which he threaded on a single string. As soon as they were unwrapped, they clanged and clattered together, making a horrible din. Attaching the string to the horse's bit, he hastily retreated as the startled mount reared and snorted in protest.

Merrit then strode to the edge of the glade, halfway between the three youngsters and the pit. Here he planted six javelins into the soft earth before nodding in satisfaction at his arrangement.

Rollo was about to ask Quinn what he thought the stranger was trying to achieve when, to his amazement, he saw that the youth was crying softly. Somehow, he had assumed that Torra Altans were devoid of sentiment. As the Barony was a dark cold, stern place where the wind howled through the high-walled canyon, he had presumed that the character of the Torra Altans would reflect this.

Isolde pressed her head against Quinn's shuddering shoulder. 'You must not give up hope,' she murmured. 'Brid and Guthrey would never give up on you and so you must not give up on them.'

'I just don't believe it any more,' Quinn sniffed but his words were lost as an extraordinarily deep-noted bellow erupted from Merrit's coiled horn. The man had left his javelins and had returned to the horse. He stood now with his horn in his hand, drawing in another deep breath. Again, he blew the deep note.

The noise frightened the horse, making her rear and tug at her reins and then strike the trunk of the fallen tree with angry hooves in a frantic effort to break away. Rollo could see real terror in the animal and was angered at Merrit's treatment of so fine a beast. The red sheet was flapping and the pennants about her head beat about her laid back ears. Steam rose from her back and flecks of sweat darkened the red cloth. Rollo fancied he could even smell her fear.

He watched as Merrit reached into his cloak and withdrew a vial, the contents of which he sprinkled about the horse. He then began a series of blasted notes on his horn, varying the length and hastening the cry, each blast louder and louder until Rollo was forced to put his hands to his ears to block out the sound.

'What is he doing?' Isolde exclaimed between blasts.

'Calling the mammoth,' Rollo suggested knowingly but he hadn't really any idea. At that moment, the scent from the vial wafted to his nose and he clamped his hand over his mouth and nose to try and filter out the concentrated stench of musk.

'Very clever,' Isolde murmured. 'I think he's enticing the mammoth to him with a mating cry.'

Rollo nodded. 'Certainly, he is trying to draw the mammoth but it's not a mating cry. It's a challenge. He's impersonating the challenge of a bull mammoth. And the smell is the scent from a male mammoth in must.'

'In must?' Isolde queried.

'It's what happens to a bull mammoth during the mating season. Mammoths aren't like dogs where only the females go on heat; the males sweat a horrible smelling secretion from their glands and Merrit has been able to gather the stuff from somewhere. It'll drive any other male mammoth wild and my guess is that a bull will try and kill it.'

'The horse?' Isolde asked anxiously. 'The horse is bait?'

'Well, since it's drenched in so much of the stuff, that's my guess.'

Isolde stepped behind him and he was aware of her warm breath on his neck. 'Where did you learn such a thing?' she asked softly, her chin resting lightly on his shoulder, her eyes on the extraordinary scene before them.

'I told you, we were plagued by mammoths in Artor. Merrit is a brave man, a very brave man. I wonder why he does it? It seems strange that a foreigner would . . .'

'Perhaps he's married a Belbidian woman and has Belbidian children,' Isolde suggested, and Rollo looked at her sharply. Her teeth were beginning to chatter. He turned to see Quinn, who had now sagged to the ground and was thumping at the tree with a clenched fits. Rollo half wanted to comfort him but how could he? Quinn's grief had been caused by his own hands. He was relieved when Isolde tugged at his arm and inclined her head towards his.

'Leave him alone a while, Rollo,' she whispered into the silence now that Merrit had paused his trumpeting. 'It's very hard for him. He and Guthrey have always been very close. And on top of that, there's his mother . . .'

Rollo didn't take much persuasion to leave Quinn to his thoughts as Merrit, again, started up his extraordinary blasting noise on his coiled horn. He kept on for half an hour by which time the three youths had slumped between the two beech trees.

A beechnut still clinging to the tree suddenly dropped at Rollo's feet and then a couple more. The ground on which he sat shuddered and he pushed himself to his feet to see what Merrit was doing. The long-haired man gave out three more blaring notes and then hastened to where he had placed his javelins. Here, he paused, listening to the thundering crash of the fast-approaching mammoth.

The pounding footfalls slowed and the air trembled an answering challenge of the mammoth. Then, steadily, the crashing footfalls began to speed up. The sound of splintering timber rent the air and Rollo couldn't help but shrink back as he glimpsed the animal's huge white tusks coming through the tree on the far side of the glade.

It still puzzled him that one man would even attempt to fell a mammoth. It was no easy task for a well-organized troop yet this man stood his ground; the notes now sharp and angry, a regular blast of insults directed at those huge tusks that swayed towards them. Young trees were stamped aside. Then there he was.

'Mother!' Rollo breathed. His hands went limp and his legs drained of energy. The beast was huge, trampling aside the smaller trees. The long brown trunk covered in a shaggy mat of brindle hairs uprooted one tree and used it like a staff to smash aside other trees around.

The horse shrieked in fear. The bull mammoth discarded the tree, curled up its trunk and swung the tip delicately from side to side, sniffing the air. Its thin tongue poked out from the beard of hair covering its mouth, and licked the air. The scent was strong and the bull gave out a bellow of rage and scuffed one of its round feet over the ground, raking away grass and brambles in its anger. The ears poking out from the woolly mass of its high-domed head waggled furiously. Rollo wished he was anywhere other than here. He knew there was a pit between him and the mammoth but it now seemed a very small pit and there seemed a lot of ground for the mammoth to approach around it. Rollo looked anxiously at the array of javelins planted in the ground, ready for Merrit to pluck up and hurl.

'Those javelins won't pierce the mammoth's woolly hide far enough to do any real damage,' Rollo said hoarsely, trying to keep the squeak from his voice. This was madness. He was witnessing the actions of the insane. Yet Merrit was behaving calmly as if he knew exactly what he was doing. Surely, he did not work entirely alone. He could never have dug those traps and, once the animal was killed, how did he intend to drag it out of that pit? He could not cut it up; it would take a man a week to carve up a mammoth and by which time every scavenger in the area would be wanting a share.

The mammoth took a couple of giant paces forward, throwing its weight from one foreleg to another and, in a display of strength and anger, turned its bulk toward a large, old oak that stood nearby. It thumped its huge skull against the tree and Rollo's eyes widened as he heard the timbers crack. Then it made its first charge. Rollo was appalled to find that he screwed his eyes up at the sight and, by the time he forced them open, he discovered that the mammoth's charge had halted prematurely as if to test the reaction of his opponent.

Terrified, Merrit's horse reared, bucked and began to try and shake itself free of the jangling bridle. Twice the mare stumbled down onto her knees. With the red sheet flapping wildly, flags fluttering and the metal chimes jangling, the horse was bewildered and terrified.

The mammoth bellowed at the display and charged in earnest. The horse screamed in panic and, finally tripping in its harness, sprawled to the ground. It was then that one of the leather straps of the bridle snapped and the mare was suddenly free. Stumbling, she pushed her nose against the ground and then was up again, running wildly, skimming past the beech trees and heading for the thick cover of the copses beyond.

The mammoth charged headlong after the horse, taking a path that would lead it directly toward the trap. Though reason persuaded him that it was impossible for the mammoth to reach him because, at any second, it would crash down into the pit, Rollo's emotions told him that it would skim over the light covering of branches, avoid the horse and run straight at him, all the while trumpeting, 'Murderer! Murderer!' before impaling him on those great tusks.

Off to Rollo's right, the mare suddenly reappeared from the edge of the glade, running fast, the red cloth flailing in her wake. The mammoth was only a few yards from the edge of the covered pit, but the beast swerved, his trunk swinging in pursuit of the bolting horse. Pieces of turf flew up into the air as the mammoth skidded and dropped onto one knee in its efforts to change direction. One of its hindlegs thrust out sideways and dipped into the pit. The creature screamed in alarm, dragged itself upright and continued, unharmed, in pursuit of the horse.

But the woolly mammoth had lost valuable time and space. The horse had bolted past the shrubby copses and galloped for an area of heavier, older trees amidst the sapling forest and, though the mammoth could break its way into the tight confines of the old wood, it rapidly slowed him up. Not so the horse, which, like a racing current, weaved through the trees as if they were boulders in the bed of a mountain river.

The mammoth charged on a few more yards, blowing and puffing, producing enough steam for a herd of cows a hundred strong. Then it drew to a halt and swung slowly round. Its trunk sniffed the air as if it realized that not all was what it seemed. It took one pace and then another towards them. Seeing this turn of events, Merrit ran forward to where his horse had been tethered. He jeered and howled defiantly and, with a suddenness of movement that even surprised Rollo, he sprinted forward and hurled his first javelin.

Good throw though it was, the javelin barely grazed the animal, striking as it did the hardness of the mammoth's leg before falling uselessly to the ground. Rollo wasn't even sure that the beast had felt the javelin's sting.

Merrit was backing slowly now towards the scant safety of a great beech tree only twenty yards from the pair that sheltered the three youngsters. Rollo was scared. He thumped the sides of the beech beside him, wondering what to do as he looked across the glade at the size of the oak that the mammoth had managed to crack simply by leaning its great bulk against it. The two beech trees on either side of him suddenly looked very slender and for the first time he realized that, even if the trees were strong enough to withstand the mammoth, they could not prevent the animal's trunk curling between them and snatching one of them away.

He wondered if, like Merrit, they shouldn't be slowly retreating. He even took one pace back, his eyes fixed fearfully on the mammoth, hoping that if he moved slowly it would take no notice. He took another pace. Perhaps they could make it. He was about to whisper to Quinn and Isolde to follow when he noted a subtle change in the mammoth. It had been swaying from one foot to another, swinging its trunk but now it was stiffening up.

Rollo could feel the rising tension and stood stiff himself, watching, waiting. Even though he had been expecting it, he felt his knees buckle as the mammoth finally charged. But it was running at Merrit and not him. The man reacted

296

without delay, hurling one javelin and then another. The huge beast bellowed as the point stabbed into the soft tissue at the corner of its eye. It shook its great head, sending blobs of blood splattering across the glade.

With remarkable calm, Merrit continued his retreat to the nearest large tree and flattened himself against the trunk before slithering round to the far side of it and out of the mammoth's sight.

The towering beast reared up and thrust both its forelegs forward, thumping down with all its weight against the side of one of the great beech trees. Wild with anger, it rattled its tusks against the trees and did exactly as Rollo had predicted. Using its trunk, it felt around the sides of the tree.

Rollo turned to his friends. 'We've got to make a run for it,' he hissed. 'He'll tear his way to us if we don't. On the count of three. Ready?'

'No!' Isolde was shouting. 'No, no!'

Rollo thought she was shouting at him but very soon realized that she was shouting at Quinn who was running out into the open in front of the mammoth.

'Run!' Quinn yelled. 'Rollo, take Isolde and run!'

Grabbing Isolde's wrist, Rollo began to drag her through the undergrowth and towards the trees behind them. His fear and urgency was such that he did not even feel the pain in his scorched hand. The creature's bellows rattled the forest and he could barely think for the noise. 'Come on!' he snarled at Isolde's resistance.

'No! I'm not leaving Quinn.'

'You idiot girl!' Rollo was furious. Perhaps he should just leave her and run for cover himself. Surely, the mammoth wouldn't bother with him, once he was hidden amongst the trees. But he kept his grip on Isolde. Quinn was doing all he could to save the girl and he needed to make it up to the young Torra Altan. He had stolen Quinn's brother from him and he had to make amends somehow. If this was what Quinn wanted, then he would do it.

Isolde was not only small but also thin and he was able drag her with relative ease but it was not so fast as he would like. He cast over his shoulder to see that the bull mammoth was swaying from side to side, deciding which way to charge. There was no sign of Merrit, who had clearly done the sensible thing and fled, leaving his javelins planted in the soil. The mammoth curled up its trunk. One jab from the huge tusks sent the great ivy-covered trunk skidding across the ground. He put one huge foot on it and bounced his great weight down, driving the fallen log deep into the ground.

The trees! Rollo urged himself and dragged Isolde after him. 'Stop screaming, you idiot girl! Do you want to attract his attention?'

But it was too late. The mammoth came on, snorted at the great pit in the ground and picked its way round the side of it before approaching the largest gap between the beech trees of the old hedge. Its side banged into the thick trunks as it passed, and the trees rocked and shuddered but managed to stay firm. The next tree it hit gave out a resounding crack as the heartwood split.

'Come on, come on!' Rollo yelled.

The mammoth was gaining on them, but then gave out a grunt and a roar. Looking back, Rollo saw that Quinn had hurled one of Merrit's javelins into the mammoth's flank. Though Quinn had not managed to inflict a serious wound, he had managed to distract it from its charge just for a moment. In the next second, Rollo made the copse of closely packed trees. Though they were clearly visible, he hoped the mammoth would have little chance in reaching them.

Panting, he wrapped his arms about Isolde and held her forcibly to him.

'Let go of me! I must help Quinn!' she shrieked.

'Quinn is safe. He's trying to look after you,' Rollo protested, wondering how long he could keep from losing his temper with the girl. Why were some people so determinedly stupid?

298

His attention was snapped away from Isolde by the tearing sound of splintering wood and a sudden crack. The first of the oaks in the copse toppled beneath the mammoth's force. The creature's trunk wormed its way into the trees and blasted out hot air that swept the hair back from Rollo's face. Isolde screamed back at the beast. Then the next tree came down and, this time, two great tusks pierced the voids between the trees and rattled back and forth.

The tips of the white tusks were only yards away and Rollo dragged Isolde towards the rear of the copse. The great beast stamped around the outside, trampling down the smaller birch and hazel, crushing saplings until it was closer to them. Again, it reared up and thumped its forelegs against the upper bowl of a sturdy oak, rocking the tree back and forth until it suddenly gave, crashing towards them. Rollo ducked, dragging Isolde down beneath him as branches crashed all about them, the falling timber hacking through the standing trees, snapping off boughs and slicing deep into the copse.

One of the tips of the branches jabbed into his back and snapped off. He waited for one to impale him but he was lucky; the tree had been stopped in its fall. They had been protected by a single sturdy branch that had deflected the worst of the falling timber.

'I can't breathe,' Isolde gasped. 'Rollo, you're crushing me . . . Rollo . . . Rollo are you alive?'

'Barely,' he grunted. His back felt sore and his face felt hot where the very tip of the twigs had struck him. The mammoth was still smashing its way towards them.

He wondered whether they should try to outrun the beast; but he had seen how fast the mammoth could move. Their only hope was for Quinn to distract it again. Clearly, that was Quinn's intention as he pulled back his arm, ready to hurl one of the javelins.

The missile fell uselessly away and the mammoth ignored the young Torra Altan, thrusting his tusks deeper into the wood. It was now harder for Rollo and Isolde to move.

They were tripping in the fallen branches and forced to scramble over the interwoven network of timber. Rollo's trousers snagged on a broken branch and held him just for a moment. Then something heavy thumped against his leg and twisted round his ankle. He found himself being dragged back through the undergrowth at high speed; his body scraped over roots and branches. The mammoth had him! He felt his end was close until the mammoth bellowed and suddenly released him from the coil of its trunk.

Rollo ran to Isolde, who stood trembling in the centre of the flattened thicket.

'Quinn! Oh no, Quinn!' She was pointing at the youth and Rollo's eyes followed her trembling finger. Quinn was standing on the fallen tree in the middle of the glade, howling and hooting to draw the mammoth's attention. The great bull was slowly turning to face him, a javelin sticking into its shoulder.

It trod heavily back towards the glade, snorting at the ground and waggling its short ears as it prepared to charge Quinn. The youth remained on the log, waving his hands frantically. Then the giant beast charged in earnest.

Quinn dropped his last remaining javelin and ran, heading away from Rollo and Isolde, and sprinting and hopping with his injured leg across the open ground toward another copse of closely packed trees beyond the opposite side of the glade. Rollo was certain he would never be able to cross the open sweep of grass before the mammoth knocked him down.

The animal crashed against the pair of beech trees, which had first sheltered Rollo and Isolde, and stumbled. This brought Quinn a moment of time and he sprinted on, out of the glade and beyond the tall oaks and beeches. But now, the great beast's strides swallowed the distance and it was gaining on him fast. Rollo's heart sank.

The mammoth was slowed down as he brushed against an oak it had crashed against earlier, when entering the glade.

The tree had given out a resounding crack as the heartwood had split vertically but had not fallen, as it had been held in place by a swaddling of grape ivy. But now, as the mammoth's shoulder thumped into it, the tree gave way. It splintered half way up and the interlacing of branches and twigs came crashing down towards Quinn.

The mammoth snorted loudly as it thudded to a halt. For a second, the only sound was the animal's great heaves of breath.

'Here! Hey! Hey! Get away from him! Leave him alone!' Isolde yelled wildly at the mammoth, her compulsion to save Quinn much more acute than Rollo's.

He looked around helplessly for something he could do as the mammoth began to tramp through the fallen branches of the tree, its long trunk wafting back and forth, trying to smell out the youth that was undoubtedly crushed beneath the fallen timber.

Isolde was now running across the glade, tears streaming down her cheeks, and their seemed to be little Rollo could do but run after her. She was running for the javelin Quinn had dropped. It was hopeless; the javelin had done nothing to stop the mammoth. Rollo couldn't understand why Merrit had attempted to use javelins in the first place; they were obviously hopeless. It was crazy, absolutely crazy!

Isolde was now standing on the log in the middle of the glade but the mammoth, still intent on Quinn, was not interested in her. It half reared and thumped its legs down on the branches, the entire fallen tree bouncing off the ground and then crashing down again. The beast raised one gigantic foot and thumped it down and then another, picking its way into the fallen canopy and rattling its great long tusks against the timber.

Rollo picked up a branch, thumping it against the tree as Quinn had done to distract the mammoth; but this time it had no effect. From this angle, Rollo caught a glimpse of the muddy blue of Quinn's sleeve. He was flat on his back, not moving, branches the thickness of a man's thigh overlying him.

The mammoth took another pace forward, causing the branch over Quinn's body to press down further. There was another crunch and splintering of wood as the massive animal took a further step closer to Quinn. Two more paces and the beast would be on top of him.

'Rollo! Rollo, do something!' Isolde shrieked. 'Do something!'

But what could he do? Running back, he snatched the javelin from her grip. It was worth nothing but he could at least show her that he was willing to help. Taking the javelin, he ran at the mammoth and hurled it for all he was worth, only then aware that the art of throwing such a weapon was a skill that he did not possess.

The javelin dropped feebly to the ground, a long way short of its target. Totally unaware of this failed assault, the mammoth raised its leg ready to smash it down again. Rollo's eyes flitted between Quinn's prone form and the huge round shape of the mammoth's foot. There was nothing he could do.

Chapter 18

Rollo caught his breath as a blaring clarion blast rang through the forest.

The mammoth rocked back on its haunches, easing its weight off the tree that pinned Quinn to the earth. Its trunk swung up and the great bull raised its head, looking wildly about. Retreating another two paces, its huge legs stamped round amidst the fallen branches of the tree's canopy.

Rollo caught a flash of red in the trees ahead. A moment later the horn blasted again, the notes angry and rousing.

The bull mammoth bellowed back in protest.

Merrit had returned; Rollo could not believe it. Neither could he believe it when Isolde ran forward to help Quinn, the great flanks of the mammoth towering above her. Rollo despaired that he had let her escape his grasp. How could he have been so slow?

Merrit's magnificent horse charged straight at the mammoth but then swerved hard to the right. The massive bull tried to follow her and face her straight on but, entangled as he was amidst the branches, his movements were cumbersome. The mare's lungs pumped with the rhythmic snort of an overworked horse, her legs far out to the side as she turned sharply. Rollo wondered how she kept her footing.

He was also amazed by Merrit's agility and skill in such conditions. He was manoeuvring a weapon in his grasp. Everything was moving so fast that it was hard for Rollo to make it out at first but then he recognized it as the crossbow, which Merrit levelled at the mammoth. The horse slowed fractionally and, just as she approached a tree and was about to race round the far side of it, Merrit loosed his first bolt. But it was not just a bolt that was fired. With it came a length of rope.

The bull screamed as the quarrel pierced its hide. Rollo was impressed by the man's aim. A mammoth was no small mark but Merrit had been nearing a gallop when he loosed the bolt. Nevertheless, the quarrel had buried its nose into the animal's knee joint and there it had stuck. But it was what happened next that most impressed Rollo. The man did not continue in the same direction but dragged his horse to a halt and raced back to the tree. He flung himself from the saddle and, gripping the other end of the rope fast, circled the tree a number of times, ducking under the rope that secured the mammoth and wrapping a length of it about the tree. Skilfully, he secured it with a knot. A second later, he was back in the saddle and galloping around to the far side of the shrieking mammoth, its great legs backing towards Quinn.

'Rollo! Rollo, help me!' Isolde was shouting. 'You've got to help me!'

He ran to her side. The mammoth was only yards from them as it used its trunk to try and drag out the quarrel from its hide. It then squealed in pain and suddenly thumped down to its knees. Rollo could not see around the great hump of the mammoth's back but he guessed Merrit was aiming another quarrel and rope at the far side of the bull. But he had no time to think about that now.

It was the echo of his father's voice ringing in his ears that finally goaded him to act. 'We never leave a friend behind, Rollo. That's what makes us feared and that's what makes us great. We never give up.' Stumbling and tripping, he fought his way through the fallen branches. He knew the sentiment to be foolish. Many men could die saving one and that was ridiculous; it made no sense at all. But what had made sense to him now was that Quinn had done everything he could to save him and he could do no less. Anything less was cowardice and, whatever he was in this world, he was not a coward.

Her hands about Quinn's limp wrists, Isolde was trying to drag the youth free. The mammoth was still crashing through the branches of the fallen tree and there was no way of knowing which way it would stumble next. It bellowed again, the roar so loud it seemed to pound his brain. The air whistled with the sound of another quarrel being loosed from the crossbow. Accompanying the whistle was the unusual whirr of rope being rapidly unravelled as it was slung forward with the bolt.

The great mammoth staggered down onto its rump and, kicking frantically, managed to jerk itself up again. Rollo feared that, at any moment, it would topple and crush them all. But he couldn't get Quinn out. He and Isolde were pulling with all their might but his leg was trapped beneath a branch and the mammoth's weight was pinning it down. Rollo tried to lift the branch but that was utterly hopeless. The shadow of the beast plunged him into gloom. Its tail whipped round and flicked across the back of his neck, sending him sprawling, but he scrambled forward hastily; he had seen the branch bounce off the ground just for a second as the mammoth had adjusted its weight.

'Isolde! Isolde! On my say so, pull!' he ordered.

The girl's tear-stained face looked up at him and she nodded. He was suddenly amazed at her composure. He rummaged amongst the fallen branches until he found a stout stake. This he positioned so that its tip butted up against the branch pinning Quinn. Then he watched and waited for his opportunity. The branch remained pinned to the ground and quite immovable but he did not take his eyes off it; he would have only a split second in which to act. At last his moment came. The mammoth stumbled again and the branch over Quinn fleetingly lifted. As quick as a cat, he rammed his makeshift prop under the branch and yelled at Isolde to pull.

But Isolde was barely strong enough. The mammoth bellowed again and reared up, unbalanced, the first rope, now twisted about its leg, pulling it sideways. One of the quarrels buried in the mammoth's hide must have been suddenly plucked from its gory bed as, like a whip, the free rope lashed through the air overhead. The quarrel thumped into a tree trunk and buried itself deep into the wood.

Rollo wasted no time. He hurled himself down beside Isolde and heaved at Quinn's arm with all his might. The mammoth was falling.

Quinn's limp body came free with a rush but he was still a heavy weight to drag. Muscles tearing in his back, Rollo heaved him clear of the snagging branches and was able to pull him more rapidly across the slick grass. As he did, the earth shook with the weight of the mammoth crashing down to the ground. The noise of splintering wood was coupled with the cracking sound of breaking bone as the animal's own weight crushed its ribs. The great bull lay on its side, lungs heaving in gasps of air as its massive chest rose and fell.

Rollo looked from Quinn, who was face down in the earth, to the great mammoth and thought it was prudent that he pulled his friend further off lest the mammoth managed to stumble up or swing its head round to strike at them with its tusks. While Isolde did her best to help, he dragged Quinn by both wrists and, when he had reached what he thought to be a safe distance, he stopped and gently rolled him over onto his back.

Rollo had no energy to do more than flop down beside him. Half dazed, he stared at the sight of the injured mammoth. Merrit had fired six bolts and five had held. The ends of the ropes he had woven about the trees and these held the animal fast. Rollo had wondered how a man would make a clean kill of a mammoth but now realized that, of course, it wasn't going to be a clean death at all but a slow agonizing one. The pits were designed not to trap but to maim the beats.

Merrit rode triumphantly forward on his strutting horse. He

slipped from the saddle and then bravely marched towards the mammoth whose vast belly was like a small mountain as it lay on its side. To Rollo's amazement, the man pulled himself up the giant's back, using the great thick hairs as handholds. Once at the top, he stood upright, looking like a midget on the creature's belly, and gloated down on the mammoth's blinking eye.

'I have you! You are the mightiest of creatures, the very largest, the very strongest, but I have conquered you. I have outsmarted you. One man alone, I have brought you to your doom. One man alone!' He threw back his head and laughed.

Rollo could almost forgive him for the madness in that laugh. He, too, felt insane with relief and exhaustion; he knew that they had been lucky to pull Quinn free in time before the mammoth had crashed down. He knew it could so easily have been different.

Isolde was stooped over the youth beside him, her expression taut. Perhaps, after all, it was all too late.

'He feels cold,' Isolde croaked. 'Oh why didn't I pay more heed to Brid's teaching? I cannot let her son die; I cannot bear it. Guthrey and now Quinn,' she wailed. 'Oh, Brid, help me. I don't know what to do.' She flopped forward onto Quinn's chest and began to sob, her hair splaying out over the youth's face.

Rollo jumped; Merrit was standing over them. He stared down, his expression enigmatic. He looked old and exhausted after the exertion but still the elation of his triumph glinted in his eye. He pulled the girl away and in stark contrast to the way he had gloried over the mammoth, said calmly, 'Ease him over onto his side and let him breathe. Smother him like that and he won't stand a chance. Now, let's have a look at him.'

Trembling, Isolde shrank back 'But he looks so grey . . .' Her voice choked.

Rollo slipped his hand into Isolde's and squeezed it tight.

No one spoke as Merrit loosened Quinn's clothing and leant forward to press his ear against the youth's chest.

'Is he breathing?' Isolde's voice was strained and scratchy.

'Hush! I can't hear a thing with you talking,' Merrit scolded irritably and closed his eyes, intent on listening for any signs of life from the boy.

'Well?' Isolde demanded after a long ten seconds had passed.

The man sat back. 'He's breathing – just. He has had a bad knock to the head,' he pointed to a purplish bump on Quinn's temple and began systematically to examine the boy's body. 'He has an injury to this knee but he may also have deeper injuries. Let's keep him warm; that's the first thing. Now, Isolde, get yourself busy collecting firewood. Rollo, use whatever you can to make him comfortable and I'll see what medicines I have in my pack.'

'Thank you,' Rollo managed to say and gave Merrit a faint smile. He was too exhausted to do more than that but he felt the man deserved his gratitude since, after all, he had come back and risked his own life for them. Clearly, he had misjudged him. He had disliked him from the moment they had met. He had not liked his manner, didn't like the fact that he was out alone in the woods and certainly did not approve of the way he had treated his horse. But Merrit had come back for them and that showed he had courage.

He looked around to see the mare grazing warily at the edge of the glade, her ears laid back against her neat head and a thick crust of sweat coating her chest. Whip marks lined her sides. There was even a beading of blood. He found it extraordinary that the man should have whipped his horse for bolting from a mammoth, especially after being tethered and adorned in jangling chimes. Any animal would have bolted; Merrit could hardly have expected otherwise.

Isolde returned with plenty of firewood. She looked at Quinn long and hard, closed her eyes and took a deep breath as if trying to draw in strength from the air.

When she opened her eyes, she smiled at Rollo. 'At least we got him free and that was down to your quick thinking. I hindered your rescue; I'm sorry I was totally useless.'

'Useless? Don't be daft!' Rollo retorted not so much out of sympathy but more out of surprise.

'I'm always useless,' Isolde continued forlornly.

'But you can't think that! No one thinks you're useless. In fact, from what I've seen, everyone loves you. Look how Oxgard spoke to you, for instance.'

'Hush! It's best not to speak so openly,' she whispered, nodding at the long-haired foreigner who was bent over Quinn, checking his breathing. 'We still know nothing about Merrit and, though I'm grateful that he came back to help us, I'm still unsure of him.'

Rollo nodded in agreement. When Merrit had finished tending Quinn, he sat back to see how they fared with the preparations for a fire, and nodded approvingly. Rollo was glad of the man's praise. Normally, he scorned the praise of others, finding it belittling and patronizing. But the praise of this man, who had felled a mammoth single-handed, was worth something. Caspar would never have achieved such a task. Rollo considered the thought. Never.

'We're very grateful, Merrit. You were clever the way you brought that monster down. I was certain we were all dead but you did it. It was amazing!'

'Clever, eh?' Merrit focused on that particular word. 'Yes, I must admit that I was. But it was the crossbow and the strength and lightness of the rope that did it.' He nodded at the packs on the back of his grazing horse. 'It took me a long time to get the design of the bolt and the weight of the rope just right to work effectively but I did it. And the quarrel has to be heavy and sharp enough to pierce the creature's tough hide and to travel deep into the joint and yet it needs an effective barb so that it's almost impossible for the mammoth to pull it out again. Oh, and it all has to be light enough to be fired from a crossbow that I can draw with my own hand.

Once I've got the mammoth anchored, it's just a matter of how many ropes I can get in it. Now, Rollo, go and fetch some water. I've found bloodwort and a twist of hyssop; if I had some melilot we could make a potion that would be sure to heal Quinn.' He smiled warmly at the two youngsters and Rollo was very glad of his authoritative company.

'I have melilot,' Isolde announced quietly.

'My! A girl that carries herbs about her as she travels through the forest. Do you possess knowledge of their use?' he asked.

She shook her head. 'Regretfully, I only gather herbs – it is wonderful to go deep into the forest and seek out their delicate colours. I am by no means a herbalist.' She sighed. 'There are so many herbs and I do not have a good memory for such things.' She put her hand into her herb scrip and drew out a small dried sprig with frazzled yellowish brown petals that must once have been a deep yellow when they were first picked.

Isolde crouched expectantly beside Quinn, watching the shallow rise and fall of his chest. Once the fire began to warm them and Merrit had set a pot to boil with the infusion of herbs, he did his best to examine the poor youth more fully.

'I see he already had a nasty injury to his knee,' he commented. 'It looks pretty recent.' He fell silent for a moment as he carefully prodded Quinn's legs and arms and then concentrated on the area where the branch had pinned him across his calf. 'There's more damage to his leg at the ankle but it's not serious beyond some pretty heavy bruising though I imagine he'll be pretty sore when he comes round.'

As he spoke, Quinn made his first attempt to move and then groaned. Opening his eyes and seeing everyone looking down at him, he attempted to sit up. 'Oh my head. My pounding head. What happened?' he asked, gingerly lying back down and touching the bruise at his temple with the tips of his fingers.

Isolde laughed delightedly at the sound of the youth's voice. 'Quinn!' she exclaimed and shuffled closer on her knees and clasped his hand in hers. 'Quinn . . . I was so worried.'

'Issy, please don't shout in my ear,' he groaned, 'otherwise you'll finish me off. What hit me?'

Isolde gabbled excitedly about the mammoth and the tree while Quinn, after several more attempts to sit up, evidently decided it was more prudent to lie still and keep his eyes shut. 'I remember now; the mammoth . . . What's happened to it?'

Both Rollo and Isolde stared at the mountainous mass lying amid the crushed saplings and broken branches.

'He's dying . . . slowly.' Isolde looked up sadly at the mammoth and then at Merrit. 'I know it's not my place to say but shouldn't you do something to put him out of his misery? Poor thing.'

'Poor thing? How can you say poor thing when it nearly killed your friend here?' Merrit seemed quite taken aback by the idea.

'But he's suffering,' Isolde squeaked and, unable to look the man in the eye, lowered her head before continuing in the quietest of voices, 'I know that mammoths are savage and dangerous but that is only their nature. I— I—' she stammered helplessly, clearly unwilling to speak out.

'You think I should end its misery?' the man questioned.

Isolde nodded shyly.

'Well, I'd like to know how you intend to kill it. It would take half an hour of hacking with a knife to get through the hide at its neck to slit its throat and I'm certainly not going to struggle away for that long. You're welcome to the task, but I warn you, you'll most probably get knocked by one of its tusks and that would probably take half your skull off. I don't know why you're worried. It normally takes three days for it to die in the pits.'

Isolde looked at him in open-mouthed horror and then hastily turned her attention back to Quinn.

Night came early in the forest. It was late winter, the days were still short, and Rollo was very glad of the fire. He was even more glad of Merrit's presence and was certain now that they would have perished without him. Quite certain. The man had helped him build a ring of fires about their camp to protect them from the creatures of the night. He breathed in the wood-smoke, and exhaled, his breath steaming in the chill air. Pulling his cloak tight about his shoulders, he slumped back against the ivy-covered log and tried to find a way to sit that lessened the discomfort of all the knocks and bruises about his body.

Isolde offered him a cup of the medicine that Merrit had brewed up for Quinn. 'It'll help soothe some of the pains,' she told him.

He grunted ungraciously, suddenly feeling angry with both her and Quinn. Their closeness and understanding of one another irritated him; it left no space for anyone else. With his head on one side, he furtively examined Isolde. He liked her quiet manner; most girls he knew were far too bold. Isolde was real. There was nothing affected about her, nothing grand or pretentious. But she also got in the way of any friendship he might have with Quinn. Still it was absurd to think of being friends with Quinn when he had slaughtered his brother. He clenched his teeth on the thought, his guilty secret making him feel queasy with regret. It was a new sensation; he had never regretted anything that he had done before in his life.

He took a long draught of the bitter medicine and drew up his cloak about his ears. Though he was uncomfortable and longed for a warm bed, he was soon asleep.

He awoke to the sound of an axe thumping against flesh. Blinking, he stiffened upright and was horrified to see the great mammoth's legs jerk with pain. Merrit had clearly been up some time and was hard at work. He was standing before the mammoth and was using his axe to hack a gash into its face. He then shoved a wooden spike into the wound he had opened up and used his war hammer to drive in a spike, smiting down with tremendous force. The creature jerked for the last time. The heaving ribcage shuddered and sagged and Rollo watched its last breath sigh out. The suffering was over.

Once the mammoth was dead, Merrit began working twice as hard and hammered away for all he was worth until Rollo heard the dull thump of the spike turn to a resounding ring as it struck solid bone. The man then hurried to his pack and withdrew a crow bar and mallet and, climbing up on the pulp that had been the mammoth's face, he thrust the bar into the bloodied mess and began to work it back and forth. Then he used the hammer to ram it deep into the crack between the tusk and the skull. After working it back and forth, he hammered again until there was a loud cracking sound as a section of jawbone splintered. He continued to toil away in the same manner for quite some while, working around the root of the tusk, hammering and breaking bone in his efforts to free the ivory.

Rollo stared on in morbid fascination and was not aware that Isolde was standing beside him until she spoke.

'Be damned in thy beauty,' she murmured.

'What does that mean?' Rollo asked.

She shrugged. 'It is never safe to be beautiful and noticed. It is preferable by far to be plain and unadorned. If the mammoth did not have such wondrous tusks, he would still be alive.'

'That is hardly the mammoth's fault since, to him, the tusks are not a thing of beauty. To the mammoth, they are a thing of power and strength used in battle to overpower other mammoths and protect the herd. They are functional and it is only man that finds them beautiful,' Rollo corrected her.

Merrit now lifted one of his ropes from his saddle and

wrapped it about the curved end of the tusk until he had secured it tightly. He then harnessed the loose end of the rope to his horse's saddle and whacked the black mare hard across the rump.

Dutifully, the high-stepping charger paced forward, taking up the slack in the rope that tugged backwards on her saddle. The strain was transmitted to the breast band that stopped the saddle slipping backwards, the leather cutting deeply into her muscled chest. She leant hard against the strap, the muscle being squeezed over the top of the breast band. She kept on, head down, straining. The mammoth's head nodded a little as she tugged and then, with a slurping rush and a snapping sound the first tusk came free. The mare stumbled forward onto her knees.

It was another half an hour before Merrit had freed the remaining tusk by which time the youths had built up the fire and managed to find some bread in Merrit's open pack, which he had left by the fire.

The man busied himself, tying the tusks together and lashing them to the back of the mare's saddle. Clearly, the horse was going to have to drag them though the harness was totally inappropriate for such a burden.

Merrit returned to the fireside, his quick eyes seeing the food. 'You've been in my packs!' he accused. He jerked his head sharply round to glance back at his horse and seemed relieved to see that it was just the one pack that they had rummaged through.

'I, I, I'm sorry,' Isolde stuttered.

'We didn't think you'd mind,' Rollo said hastily at the sign of disapproval on Merrit's face.

Quickly a smile lightened Merrit's expression. 'Of course, I don't mind that you found food. I just didn't want you to hurt yourself, that's all. I've sharp tools in my packs. I've got traps and knives that could take your hand clean off. Just don't go in them again. All right?' he warned.

All three nodded.

By this time, Quinn was sitting up and looking remarkably well considering his ordeal. But when he tried to stand it was a different matter. He couldn't even pull his boot onto his left foot; the ankle was too swollen.

Isolde looked at it and pouted. 'Oh Quinn, what are we going to do with you?'

'I'll just have to manage,' he said stiffly. 'If you could find me a stout stick, that might help.'

'You're being quite ridiculous,' Rollo interrupted them. 'You'll just have to ride Merrit's horse, won't he, Merrit?'

The tall man flashed him a sharp look and then a tight smile stretched his lips wide over his short teeth. 'Of course! That would be the natural thing to do, wouldn't it?'

Rollo thought it a strange reply but did no more than raise an eyebrow. Merrit, however, noted his questioning look and their eyes met, holding each other's gaze in suspicion. The long-haired stranger was the first to break away and, from that moment, Rollo was certain that he had to be wary. He was why; after all, Merrit had gone to great lengths to help them, but he knew he had to be cautious.

They broke camp and, as they walked, boots crunching on beechnuts and acorns underfoot, Rollo quietly expressed his concerns to Isolde.

'We should be heading back to Torra Alta as fast as possible. We know so little about this man and he's just left that mammoth there. I don't understand it. You don't make a kill like that and just leave it behind.'

'But it's not easy to move it, though, is it?' Isolde pointed out.

'Precisely! I thought it was impossible for one man alone to kill a mammoth. I admit I was wrong, but how is a single man going to move a huge hulk like that? It makes absolutely no sense. He must be working with someone.'

'Perhaps he doesn't try to move it. Perhaps he just leaves it there,' Isolde suggested.

'You think he's just trying to clear the woods of the

mammoths in order to protect the people hereabouts?' Rollo queried, at last aware of the pain in his injured hand. He nursed it as he walked but was pleased to note that it was still healing well and he could flex it with ease now.

Isolde shook her head. 'No, I think he only ever intended to take the tusks.'

Rollo chewed on his lip. He couldn't quite make sense of Merrit. 'He tackles mammoths single-handedly yet he's using pits that one man alone could not have dug. He has no qualms about hacking at the creature's face when the animal is still alive yet he is generous enough to feed and protect us.' The red-haired youth thought on this point.

'Perhaps he's lonely,' Isolde guessed.

Rollo was about to tell her she was being ridiculous when he noted that Merrit was talking to Quinn. The lanky youth was clearly in some pain from his ankle, which made him vulnerable and perhaps not so quick-witted. Rollo quickened his pace to draw alongside.

Merrit asked Quinn, 'You were travelling north, you said? Well, it'll be colder up there but you look as if you're dressed for it.'

Quinn grunted in a non-committal manner and Merrit persisted in trying to make conversation. 'Isolde knows much of medicine for one so young, I am very impressed. It's an important skill. Still, she doesn't seem so impressed with herself,' he said casually

Quinn nodded. 'No, she's always been a little shy.'

'Are you brother and sister?' Merrit asked nonchalantly.

Quinn laughed at the idea. 'No, no, it's just that Brid is—'

'Look! What was that?' Rollo exclaimed, hastily interrupting.

'What was what?' Merrit asked gruffly, flashing him another hasty look of distrust.

'I thought I heard another trumpet blast from a mammoth! I'm certain I did,' Rollo insisted. He knew it was a ridiculous thing to say but he couldn't think of a more original way of interrupting them before Quinn blurted something important. Why did the youth have to be so nice?

'You're imagining things, lad,' Merrit said with a belittling tone to his voice.

'Am I?' Rollo said stiffly. 'So Merrit, tell us? Where are you from?'

The man smiled. 'Ah! So the surly young lad wants to make conversation now, does he? Interesting!'

'I don't see that it's interesting at all. I was simply wondering,' Rollo defended himself and now felt thoroughly put out of his stride. It took him a moment to come up with another question. 'So how many more traps do we have to check before you can start taking us to the Dairy Track that we can follow to the Great North Road and so to Torra Alta?'

'Three,' the man replied without pausing to think.

'And what do you do if the trap has your required mammoth in it?'

'Do?'

'Yes, do? How do you get the mammoth out and what do you do with it?'

'You're full of questions, aren't you?' Merrit laughed at him. 'Anyone would think that you weren't the least grateful to me for saving your friend's life.'

'Of course, we're grateful,' Quinn interrupted. 'Rollo, what on earth are you getting at?'

Rollo smiled sarcastically at Quinn and made a promise to himself that he would thump the youth very hard just as soon as he had the opportunity. How could anyone be such an idiot? So brave yet so stupid. He snorted derisively and then turned his attention back on the stranger who strode alongside his high-stepping horse.

'Go on, Merrit, do tell us. What do you do with the mammoths? Why did you risk life and limb and then just leave them there?'

'Oh I don't leave them,' the man laughed. 'I get very good money for them.'

'How?' Rollo demanded.

'Now would I go round telling the likes of you? I'd only have to turn my back five minutes and you'll have stolen my job. Isn't that right?' The man laughed and, to Rollo's annoyance, Quinn laughed too.

'Don't be absurd,' Rollo retorted sulkily. 'You don't honestly think that we'd be idiotic enough to risk our precious young lives trying to kill mammoths? I for one would be very pleased if I never saw another mammoth for the rest of my days. But why is it that you won't tell us what you do with them?'

Merrit laughed again. 'My, we do have high opinions of ourselves, don't we? I was only joking of course. It wouldn't cross my mind for more than a second that you would ever consider trying to slay a mammoth. It is an art, a skill learnt over many years and the very idea that you might consider yourself up to the task even once you were fully grown is quite absurd!'

Rollo scowled and felt the blood beginning to rise up his neck. He clenched his fists and dug his nails into the flesh of his hand in an attempt to control himself. 'I didn't say that. The idea is also ludicrous to me. I just don't understand what you do with all that meat.'

'You don't understand very much, young lad. The trouble with youth is that you only ever see things from your own perspective. I make a fortune of course. Food's been scarce hereabouts for quite a time now. The scrubby forest supports a lot of predators and the skirmishes between landlords and barons have brought disruption to the farmers and villagers. Many have given up altogether and left their crops to rot in the fields. Naturally, there's not enough food. A mammoth can supply a village with sustenance for an entire winter. And they pay well for it.'

Rollo thought this through and decided it did not seem

so unreasonable. 'Hmm, but how do you get the mammoth to them?'

'Ah well, that's another story.' Merrit laughed out loud but did not answer that question. 'The danger and the skill are in the killing. The people in the villages are not skilled in the art of hunting and have little idea what to do. Which reminds me; I must say how very impressed I was to see your composure, most impressed.'

Rollo couldn't help but smile at this praise but was less pleased when Merrit continued, 'And I was most impressed with this young man in particular.' He nodded up at Quinn. 'Imagine charging in there and throwing a javelin like that when he didn't have the first clue as to what he was doing. Impressively brave, most impressively brave!'

'You know, you still haven't answered my question,' Rollo persisted, still convinced that the man was hiding something.

'Oh yes, that's right, the question of how I get the mammoth to the villagers. Well, obviously I don't,' he laughed. 'The villagers go to the mammoth.'

Rollo scowled. It was obvious of course and yet he had not thought of it. Deciding that he had said too much he contented himself with keeping quiet. He trudged along behind the others, nursing his hand.

Every once in a while, the great tusks got caught on a root or the ropes snagged on one of the many saplings. Then Merrit would go into a frenzy of swearing as he backed the mare up, hitting her hard across the muzzle if she did not immediately obey his command.

Rollo noted that Isolde was beginning to look more and more perturbed and kept casting her eyes up at the sun and then along at Merrit. But, though her frown grew, she never once said anything and, at last, Rollo's impatience snapped. He snagged her hand and tugged her to a halt, indicating with his eyes that they should wait until the others had moved on out of earshot.

'I don't trust him,' he hissed.

'But we still need him; what else can we do?' Isolde murmured. 'We'd have been dead long ago if it wasn't for him. We should never have left Jotunn.'

'Are you saying it's all my fault?' Rollo asked, his tone full of bristling affront.

'No, of course, I'm not. I'm sorry; I was blaming myself. I thought I would find the way but it seems I overestimated my abilities,' she sighed. 'See how wrong I am? I would swear we needed to head further south in order to meet up with the Dairy Track. We're going too far to the east and heading in almost entirely the wrong direction again.'

'What?' Rollo exclaimed. 'You should have said something. Why didn't you say so earlier?'

'What was there to say?'

Rollo thumped his head with the flat of his hand. 'You two! Between you and Quinn . . .,' he began in exasperation but he could not think of anything insulting enough to say. He kicked the dirt to relieve some of his frustration. So where was Merrit taking them and why? His instinct was to vacillate between slavery and ransom. He was fairly certain that they hadn't said anything too incriminating as to their noble birth and therefore hadn't publicized their high ransom value so he considered that slavery was the more likely. At the first opportunity, they needed to lose this man though it occurred to him that it would be fairly handy to keep the horse.

He began to consider how to break away from Merrit but knew, at once, that their first problem was that Quinn was hurt and would struggle without a horse. It was a large problem but, nevertheless, they must do something. Perhaps when they stopped to have something to eat there might be an opportunity to make a run for it. They would surely stop soon.

However, Merrit made no such suggestion and they were now taking a more easterly route. Isolde was convinced that the Dairy Track was due south and he wondered why they were now veering away from it. He pressed close to her. 'Tell me, are we heading even further east now?' he hissed.

She mumbled too quietly for him to hear.

'Speak up!' he demanded in frustration at her poor communication.

'Yes, we're heading further east,' she confirmed.

Grunting angrily, Rollo could think of no other course of action other than to query the situation with Merrit. 'Why are we going east?' he asked. 'I thought you were going to help us find our way to the Dairy Track so that we could start heading back towards Torra Alta.'

'You're not a very trusting soul, are you?' Merrit said sharply. 'I don't know why I'm bothering with you at all especially since my horse will probably be lame by the end of this since she's had to carry your friend's weight as well as drag the tusks. Don't you think that's hard for her?'

Rollo grunted, not knowing what to say. 'Yes, but we're still heading further east than we should be,' he complained lamely.

'Oh, an expert tracker, are we? And, of course, you know this area like the back of your hand. After all, you were never lost out here and nearly trampled to pieces by taurs. I've never known a more ungrateful lot. When I find your parents, I trust they will be a little more grateful than you are. One would expect a pretty good reward for bringing home such a surly crew of troublemakers. Ruined my week you three have. Ruined it.'

'You got the mammoth, didn't you?' Rollo reminded him. 'You couldn't possibly count this as a bad week. Those tusks must be worth twenty times the amount you'll get for the mammoth meat.'

'First you know everything about tracking and now, from the way you talk, a man could only presume that your father is a great merchant too,' Merrit taunted.

'No, no! He— I— I didn't mean that.' Rollo managed to stop himself from saying more. 'But that's not the point. Why won't you tell us why we're not going the way you said you would take us?'

'Two reasons,' the man said, grunting to heave the tusk off from a root where it had jammed. He clicked his tongue, ordering the mare to move on again. 'Firstly, everyone,' he emphasized with almost adolescent enjoyment of taunting Rollo, 'knows to stay away from what was the village of Granham. It's full of nasties in there. Holly's people mainly. They may be small but they'll eat you for breakfast, eyeballs first.' The man shuddered. 'Then there's hobs to the north and east of us in the pines. We have but a thin line that we can safely take. Oh, and the other reason I'm heading in this direction is that I need to sell the tusks and the mammoth meat. I have to earn my keep, you know. I said that I'd help you find your way home but I didn't say I'd put myself out. I'm not a pilgrim doing penance, you know.'

Rollo smiled weakly. Everything Merrit said made sense. Still he didn't like the man and yet there didn't seem to be anything he could do about their predicament. Again, he dropped back with Isolde who was fidgeting with the radiant jewel about her throat. She jumped when Rollo spoke.

'You were miles away,' he commented.

'I know; I was thinking about Quinn. He's in pain but worse is his grief over Brid and Guthrey. It's eating him up. I know he's been hoping that Hal will have found his mother but no one knows about Guthrey. He knows we've got to go home but he feels like a wretched coward crawling back to Torra Alta without Guthrey. He feels responsible. He's always been the concerned, sensible one and he's always the one charged with looking after us. And, if you didn't know, Guthrey is the absolute apple of Hal's eye.'

Rollo was quite surprised to hear this remark and his eyebrows rose.

'Oh, he is,' Isolde confirmed, evidently having read his expression aright. 'Hal wants him to do well for himself and hates to see him getting into trouble. And Guthrey, of course, resents the attention and the pressure Hal puts on him, so they argue. It's a hard burden to carry someone else's hopes and dreams. Nobody expects anything of Quinn, of course and he can be exactly who he is, though no one is too sure what that is. But Quinn thrives on it. Happy as a hare he normally is.' She sighed. 'But he won't be after this. Hal will never forgive him and, if Brid is lost too, he'll probably throw him out.'

Rollo's face fell and he stared down gloomily at his boots. The leather was cracked where he had trudged through rain and snow to get to Torra Alta. His toes were cold where they were pressing up against the end of the boots. Evidently, he had grown somewhat since they had been made for him.

Merrit kept casting his eyes heavenward. Rollo wondered what he was doing and, seeing his expression, Isolde muttered, 'He's worried about the time.'

'Why would anyone worry about the time out here?' Rollo queried.

'It must be that he's got a prearranged meeting,' Isolde concluded for him. 'He's been hurrying us along for a while now and he's been getting crosser and crosser with his poor horse.'

Chapter 19

The shock was so sudden that it was a moment before the pain hit her. At first, Brid was swung into the shoring on the side of the pit and then dragged upwards through the broken branches. It was yet another few seconds before she was aware of the full intensity of the terrible, crushing pain about her shoulder.

A huge talon pierced her flesh and hooked into her upper right arm and shoulder. She dangled helplessly, the wind tearing through her clothing and whisking away her screams. A warm moistness of blood oozed down her back and side.

As she was whipped up through branches, she looked down for a second on the injured horse and the warrior within the deep trap. The man stared up at her forlornly, one hand raised, as if somehow hoping to claw her down.

As the pit was lost from sight and the trees became small distant blobs of dusky colour far below, Brid's next fear was that the dragon might drop her and that she would be smashed and shredded on the trees. As they soared higher, she ceased to struggle.

She was barely able to breathe for the wind rushing into her face and the cramping spasms around her shoulder. Her hair tangled around her face, momentarily blinding her and increasing her panic. The pain in her shoulder was excruciating, yet her fear and desperation to live drove it from her mind.

The steady beat of the creature's golden wings quickened to a frantic pulse as it climbed. Only when the world was a tiny map far below did the monstrous lizard tuck its legs neatly up behind its belly, stretch its wings wide and glide. The air was strangely still where Brid was now clutched against the dragon's bescaled golden belly. The huge muscles of its legs were like lumps of granite in front of her and she stared helplessly at the two-foot long talon that gripped her shoulder.

There was no point in struggling and she forced herself to overcome her fear, blotting the pain from her mind in order to think. Trying very hard not to look down, she stared in awe at the spread of the creature's huge wings. Full of blood, muscle and gut, the animal was heavy and she was amazed at the creature's power to lift itself from the ground. Exhausted by her pain, she focused only on the rhythmic sweep of those huge wings.

They were still climbing, circling up on the rising air currents, and Brid was miserably aware of the increasing cold. Numbly, she wondered if her shoulder muscle would tear away, letting her fall. But the dragon's grip held firm and they swept into the clouds, the vast wings stirring the vapours and leaving behind a vortex of swirling mist. The massive wings pumped them higher and higher until they broke above the clouds. All around them, the most spectacular colours that Brid had ever seen curved up from the surface of the cloud in the form of a rainbow. The dragon raised its head and, like a dart, shot through the extraordinary spectrum.

Brid had not thought it possible; in her experience, rainbows were elusive and unattainable. She was amazed by the dazzling beauty, the brightness and the intensity of the air as they swam through the bands of colour and sparkling light. The moisture in the atmosphere was wet on her face and clung to her eyelashes like sparkling jewels.

An enormous sense of power rippled through the rainbow and she felt the vital essence of sentient beings all about her. At first, she saw only wisps of vapour but, as the colours of the magical world intensified, she saw delicate bodies dancing and laughing all about her. From her learning, Brid recognized them as the Ondines of the air, who danced and spun about in frivolous abandonment, uncaring of the misery of the world below.

Full of gaiety, the spirits swam about her, intrigued by her sudden intrusion. Hands snatched at her hair and others clung to the dragon as if enjoying the free ride and the surge of power that catapulted them up to the very heights of the indigo and violet of the bow. Here, they let go of their hold and tumbled and twisted down, spiralling like falling feathers back into the warm colours of the rainbow below.

'I am the Mother,' Brid called back to them. 'Save me!'

She heard only laughter. What did it matter to them whether she lived or died? Their world was up in the sky beyond the reach of mortals. Nothing altered their beautiful life in the dazzling world of the rainbow.

She looked ahead into the deep blue of the cold sky as the dragon dragged itself free of the rainbow and soared out into the sharp clarity of the air beyond. The wind roared in Brid's ears as the great golden dragon thrust its head forward and thrashed the sky with its huge wings, the tips touching at the top and bottom of each stroke.

Brid blinked. Giant snowflakes the size of her palm swirled in the air around her. Each flake that whipped into her face was bitingly cold and she gasped at the sting of their touch in the thin, freezing air. It was only the heat from the dragon that kept her alive. In fact, the creature drew her closer up to its belly where thick veins bulged with the heat of its raging blood. It even once dropped its head and curled it back towards her, breathing warm air from its giant lungs over her body.

Brid barely cared anymore. She was disorientated with cold. Her mind was slowly slipping from consciousness as the thin air starved her body of oxygen. She wasn't even sure if she were dreaming or not. She was no longer even aware of the pain in her shoulder as the numbing cold stole all sensation from her.

After a while, she must have slipped entirely into a dream world because, suddenly, she was alert, the pain in her shoulder acute. They were lower now and she could breathe though she still felt sick from the effects of the altitude and the loss of blood from the wound to her shoulder. Weakly, she wondered how much more her body could take. Her reserves were already depleted; she was in no condition to survive the rigours of altitude and cold.

Again, the dragon twisted its neck round to warm her with stinking hot breath. Choking in the stench, Brid was, nevertheless, glad of the warmth. Steeped in a moment of self-pity, she bemoaned the catalogue of catastrophes that had recently befallen her. Even now, she could not piece together the trail of events missing from her memory. Had she been chained into that trap to lure the dragon? Or had the person or creature that had chained her there simply thought it a good prison until they returned to fetch her? Without her memory of the preceding few days, none of it made any sense.

The dragon suddenly banked hard to the right and she was almost torn from its grasp. A high pitched scream wailed out from below and she glimpsed the greenish-brown streak of a griffin launching itself from a crag and spearheading up for the dragon. Evidently, they had passed over the griffin's nest and the creature was outraged at the intrusion. Another, larger griffin was darting in from their right and dived at the dragon, mobbing its head and raking at its neck.

The dragon barrelled over in mid-air and Brid shrieked as she was flung upwards, her skirt and cloak splaying out and her body pulling terribly at her pierced shoulder. The dragon lashed out with its front claws, catching one of the griffins and sending it tumbling down through the air. But the other one used the opportunity to dart in at the dragon's long thin neck and clamp its great beak over the pale golden windpipe.

327

Suddenly, locked together, they were spiralling down. The dragon scrabbled frantically at the griffin, scratching with its claws and then kicking like a rabbit with its free back leg while the other one steadfastly held to Brid. She was shaken vigorously, though it seemed that the dragon was trying to spare her by keeping her held well out of the way. At last, its great claws tore through the griffin's backbone and the attacker fell away.

Fearfully aware that they were tumbling through space, Brid could almost smell the earth below as it swooped towards them. At any moment, she would be crushed flat as they hit the ground. But the dragon flipped itself over in mid air, spread wide its wings and Brid felt her stomach being left behind as they soared upwards again. The monstrous lizard steered left, banking away over a leafless oak forest and then out towards the grey-green of the Caballan Sea. Weakly, Brid hung there, hoping that whatever fate her boys were suffering it was not so cruel as this. She glimpsed the smooth coastline of eastern Jotunn caressed by the quiet waters of the almost landlocked sea.

White sails caught the wind as the merchant ships rode the seas. She even saw the humps of a sea serpent rippling through the waters. The dragon followed the coast for some distance before swerving inland at a point that Brid reckoned to be southern Nattarda, the Barony belonging to Wiglaf. Perhaps, the golden beast had been avoiding the territory of the green dragons reputed to live in the north.

Nattarda's meadows were churned by winter mud, the grass stripped bare by the herds of taurs that roved eastern Belbidia. Swathes of scrubby trees sprang up across the moorland and the roads that had fallen into disrepair were only recognizable by the avenues of brambles that now formed a sprawl of vegetation along the thoroughfares. To Brid's surprise, the dragon did not immediately select a place to land but appeared to be scouring the ground. The great lizard steered clear of the woodlands and skimmed over the open moors and plains, her vast shadow darkening the land as she glided over a herd of cattle.

Bellowing, the beasts stampeded, steam rising off their backs and pouring from their mouths in their frightened exertion. The dragon circled, lowered her snout and effortlessly snatched one up; her long teeth piercing its ribcage. The cow kicked and struggled. The dragon wrenched her head rapidly from side to side and the cow was dead, its neck snapped.

The huge lizard alighted on a prominent rounded hill, stumbling awkwardly as she kept her near hindleg high in the air to protect Brid on landing. Nevertheless, the priestess was jolted severely, bit her tongue and her head whipped forward, tearing neck muscles. The dragon shook her free from its great claw and let her slump to the ground.

With its great wings hooded over its head as if to hide its prey, it began to snap and tear at the carcass of the cow, using one claw to rip open the belly and drag out the offal. Hungrily, she gobbled up the soft tissues and then began to crunch through bones, all the while, her dark glistening eyes fixed on Brid.

Brid stared back. Surely now, while she was on the ground, she should try to crawl away; she might never get another chance. Brid tried to stretch out an arm to haul herself through the stiff grass but she was more weak and cramped by pain than she thought. The dragon was still watching her as if curious about how much the frail human form could withstand. Then her leg snapped forward and Brid cringed as the great talons thumped down with precision right before her face, the tip of the heel talon just grazing her eyebrow.

Gently, the creature spread its claw about Brid, scooped her up and dragged her back, its eyelids snapping shut and open as it watched her. Brid shrank from the intelligence in the creature's eyes. The dragon croaked and grunted and the priestess had the horrible sense that it was trying to talk to her. Unable to move her left arm for the injury to her shoulder, she tried to drag her cloak up around her to keep her warm and for the sense of security provided by the thick fur.

The dragon let its head droop to one side as it quizzically watched her and then tentatively raised a claw and gently tugged aside the cloak. The creature nudged Brid in the back and she was flung to the ground, the wind knocked from her lungs. She thought that her end had come as a leathery tongue rasped across her back but the dragon did no more than lick her. Though still in shock and weak with cold and hunger, she realized that the dragon was cleaning her shoulder, the warmth easing the wound a little. She then screamed as a sudden burning pain coursed from her shoulder into her chest. A second later, she collapsed and slumped to the ground.

When she came round, the light was beginning to fade. Her back and upper arm stung with pain. She stared up at the dragon, hating it for the terror it instilled in her. Never before had she felt such fear and she was determined that she would not succumb to it and die snivelling.

'If you are going to kill me why don't you just get on with it? What have I ever done to hurt you? What do you want with me, you vile, overgrown toad?'

The monster drew back its thin snout and cocked its head to one side as if listening and Brid pushed herself to her feet and resolved to end this torture once and for all by charging the beast. It was a ridiculous plan but she could take no more. Only as she began to push herself to her feet did she feel how easily she could move her shoulder. It was then she realized that the dragon had not been trying to cause her pain, but had used its saliva to cauterize the wound and purify the flesh. The creature was deliberately keeping her alive. The exertion of standing made her head swim and, clumsily, she sank back down.

The dragon tossed her a slab of meat. What may have only

been a small morsel for the dragon was an enormous amount to Brid. She was hungry beyond words but the meat was not easy to eat. The dragon watched and then slowly dragged the meat back. Dropping its snout, it effortlessly tore off a smaller strip and nudged the more manageable slice back towards the exhausted priestess.

With trembling hands, she picked up the flesh and began to suck it. The meat was warm and still bloated with blood. She chewed a little at the slimy, raw flesh but it was hard work for blunt human teeth.

The dragon purred at her and Brid glared back.

'What do you want with me?' she snarled and suddenly flung the strip of meat back at the dragon's face. With alarming speed, the dragon opened its jaws, caught the morsel and darted forward, pressing its great snout up against Brid's face.

The priestess did not flinch but stared back into those liquid eyes. The dragon pressed closer, gradually toppling her off balance. She sensed the creature's restraint and was fully aware of how easily it could kill her – yet it did not. Instead, it sat back on its haunches, its long thin neck snaking up into the sky, and let out a pitiful wail that silenced all birdsong within earshot. Slowly, its neck coiled down and its head swung closer to Brid. The creature grunted softly and again Brid had the distinct impression that the creature was trying to speak to her.

Its claw snatched forward and closed about her waist. Brid was clutched to the dragon's breast as, suddenly, the monster sprinted forward on its huge rear legs before leaping into the air and spreading wide its wings labouring to soar in the cooling air. Slowly, they spiralled up into the evening sky. Flickers of flame jetting from the dragon's nostrils bright in the twilight.

They climbed higher and higher and, as the sun began to plunge into the earth of the western horizon Belbidia was shrouded in night. Brid was aware that the beast was having to expend much more energy, beating its wings far more rapidly than it had during the day, to climb the cool of the night sky. High above the earth, they still caught the thin red beams that tipped upwards from a sun just below the horizon.

Then, out from the blackness below came a high-pitched scream that grew rapidly louder as something darted towards them. Similar creatures sped towards them from all four winds. Brid closed her eyes, certain that the dragon could not defend itself against so many. She knew at once that they were ravenshrikes. They were not nearly so big as a dragon but they were fast, their teeth were sharp, their claws powerful and they hunted in large swarms.

Brid found herself clinging to the claw of the dragon; she did not want to be dragged from its grasp by these beasts nor did she want to plummet to the earth far below. But the dragon had decided her fate as it rifled up through the air, twisting at an impossible speed and gaining height. The beast turned over, belly-up under one of the ravenshrikes, and thrust Brid up into its clutches.

Brid's ears rang with the shrill notes of the ravenshrike's high-pitched scream. She was expecting to be ripped apart by its claws or shaken until her neck broke but, instead, she was clutched tightly in the pincer-grip of its talons. At once, she noted that the creature was not so strong as the dragon and, clearly, had to compensate for her weight. All about her, other ravenshrikes drew close until she was at the heart of the dense black cloud.

Unanswerable questions stormed through her mind. Why would the ravenshrikes have been so foolish as to attack the dragon and why had the dragon failed to fight for the prey it had so clearly coveted? Brid could not believe the obvious answer that the dragon had deliberately handed her to the ravenshrikes. It was as if the magnificent golden beast had been waiting until dusk for the ravenshrikes to emerge. She could not believe it. A dragon had no more intelligence than a lizard.

Far below, she could make out the lights of the occasional village. There was even a lighthouse and the swaying lanterns of a ship at anchor as they dropped lower. Everywhere, campfires were burning.

Slowly, they glided towards a ring of flames. Again the ravenshrikes began their high-pitched screams as if announcing their approach, and Brid could barely think for the noise. The air rushing in her face, she felt as if she were falling out of the sky as the great black birds plunged towards the black heart of the fiery ring.

Here, a new sound assailed her ears as she was dropped from twelve foot above the ground and thumped onto earth. She rolled over, her mouth full of blood and mud and her tangled hair momentarily blinding her. She had fallen on her wrist and had distinctly heard it crack before her mind was totally absorbed in the fearful noise that surrounded her.

Deep-throated barks mixed with a cacophony of hoops and yells cackled all around. Slowly, she pulled her head up from the mud and stared at the ring of standing stones illuminated in the light of the fires. Atop each obelisk was a hob brandishing a burning torch, their eyes glowing red in the dark. Even from where she lay in pain on the cold ground, she could smell their fetid breath that rose in pillars of steam from their mouths.

The crescent moon was resting just above the shoulders of the earth and, bathed in its silvery light, a hunched figure lurched towards her from between two of the tallest standing stones.

Chapter 20

Rollo lagged behind as Merrit urged his horse to push through the tangle of undergrowth. Dried brambles and wispy legs of traveller's joy had claimed the way ahead. At last, they broke through onto a wider path, one trod by larger beasts, where Rollo was able to pick out the imprint of a lequus hoof in the frozen mud.

Merrit looked relieved as they pushed into a faster pace. Every now and then, he flicked his head up, searching for the sun to judge the time. Rollo nodded at this, deciding that Isolde was almost certainly right. Merrit did, indeed, look expectant and worried as if he were concerned that he might not make a rendezvous.

He drew level with the nervous girl. 'If he is hurrying to a prearranged meeting, why hasn't he just left us and gone on alone? He would cover the ground more quickly without us slowing him down.'

Isolde's head dropped to one side as she studied the horse and its burden in front. 'Well, not a lot faster as his horse is dragging those great tusks, though, I agree, if the poor thing wasn't also carrying Quinn, it might help her a little.'

'Aren't you at all worried about being in this man's company? You have to admit that what he does and says doesn't quite add up.'

Isolde nodded thoughtfully and then shrugged, her brow wrinkling into a look of consternation. 'Yes, of course, I'm worried. But, he has javelins and a crossbow and the skill to use them, which is a lot more than can be said for us.'

A sudden deep bark chilled Rollo's spine and he halted in his tracks. 'What in the name of the Mother?'

He didn't need an answer; he knew what it was and the chill of dread spread through his body. Quinn jerked upright; he had obviously been dozing in the saddle and the noise had shaken him from his rest. Isolde pressed herself close against Rollo. Merrit, however, barely flinched and merely looked to his horse as if checking that all his weapons were ready to hand before waving them on.

There was nothing else they could do. Sweat broke out on his forehead and the palms of his hands. Once or twice, he was conscious of something on the trail behind them but, when he saw Isolde surreptitiously looking round and smile to herself, he wondered if it wasn't the same black wolf they had seen in Jotunn.

But the wolf never came out into full view and it was only a little while later that Rollo became aware of the sound of feet padding through the woods and the odd bush stirring and rustling more than the light breeze warranted. Still, Merrit did not flinch and so he presumed that they were safe from whatever it was that tracked them.

A series of strangulated cries far to their left burst out from deep within the northern block of forest. It sounded like the yelling of hounds at the culmination of a hunt, horrible, savage and cruel. The hairs on the back of Rollo's neck were standing on end and he felt the cords in his throat tightening.

Merrit nonchalantly cast his eyes in the direction of the cry but seemed untroubled. Rollo wondered if that was because he was confident in his own skill to defend himself or whether he knew that the cries came from something that was no threat to them. He wished he had such confidence and, again, found himself admiring the man. Why couldn't his father be as worthy of his admiration as this lone hunter? It came as a shock to find hot tears pricking at his eyes. He was at a loss as what to do and felt confused, bewildered and ashamed all at once. 'Dear Mother, Great Mother,' he tried to pray but thought only of his real mother and saw in his mind's eye the flames of her funeral pyre.

His throat tightened and he rubbed at his stinging eyes. She had told him so little of her early life. She had always said that she would tell him of it when he was old enough to understand. But she had died before that, died giving birth to a child who had not lived. Her death made no sense then or now, and Rollo knew that, if he had been able to choose, he would wish it were his father who were dead and not his mother. On his journey to his father's homeland he had dreamt of the time before his mother was with child. In his dream he had learnt presciently the cause of her death and went by night, dagger in hand, to assassinate his own father and so prevent the conception that would kill her. He found them lying together, their bodies coupled as one. In a rage, he had lunged, stabbed and fought until the tip of his long thin blade was buried deep but, in the darkness he could not tell whom he had killed. The memory of the dream shook him now as it had done then.

He was shaken from the misery of his thoughts by a light touch on his arm.

'Rollo, are you all right?' Isolde asked gently. 'You seem a little—'

'Yes, of course I'm all right,' he snapped. 'Who wouldn't be a little down lost in this treacherous country and wondering what's happened to their father? Why are you always so full of idiotic questions?' he demanded, wishing that he had said something less harsh as he saw the hurt that his words induced.

'I thought you were different,' she said, looking down to avoid his gaze. 'I thought you understood what it was like.'

'What do you mean?' he asked gruffly, though he was genuinely concerned.

She shrugged and looked away but suddenly her eyes flicked up at him and she fixed him with a cold, steely look that pierced right through him. 'You are a selfish boy who brings harm to yourself and all those around you. You look to blame anything and everyone for your wretched life rather than see that it is you who is the cause.'

Shocked that Isolde could show such venom towards him, Rollo could not contain his anger. 'The trouble with you, Isolde, is you don't like yourself,' he said cruelly. 'Why would anyone want to talk to you when you don't even like yourself? You're always apologizing and it's annoying. Annoying, you hear? Anyone would think you were eight the way you go on. You say nothing and yet you dare to give disdainful looks as if you could have done everything better.'

The girl took a deep sharp breath, her eyes wide with shock, and he thought for a minute that she would retaliate with something equally cutting, but slowly her chest deflated and her shoulders sagged. 'I think you are right,' she said at length.

She even managed to give him a nervous smile, which made Rollo all the more annoyed with her. His father had promised he would like Belbidia, assuring him that the country was full of beautiful girls. Naturally, he had scowled at his father's words though, secretly intrigued by the idea. But, as usual, his father had lied. The only girl he had met was this annoying willow-wand, Isolde.

The scrubby forest was slowly turning to regimented lines of apple trees. Many of the boughs were split or snapped where, over the years, the neglected trees had grown wild and borne heavy crops of apples that had weighed down and broken their leggy boughs. Thick grass grew beneath their feet. Before long they came to the top of a smoothly rounded hill and, for the first time that day, Rollo was able to look across the land they had travelled through. From here, he could see how the sapling forests had spread over the hedged fields, regimented boxes of thicker vegetation and taller trees dividing up the juvenile forest.

The trees grew vigorously, enjoying the lush fertile soil of

337

the plains. He wondered if the men had fought for their land as they had done in Artor and even in Torra Alta. He snorted, thinking how ironic it was that the Torra Altans would fight so hard for what was nothing more than a barren rock and a filthy, cold climate whereas the lowland Belbidians had walked out and left lush grazing pasture and fat fields of wheat to the giant predators. Perhaps the people of this once so civilized land just didn't have the stomach to stand up and fight for what was theirs.

Following Merrit's gaze to the right, he saw the tall skeletal shapes of bare poplars. Amongst them, he glimpsed a thread of smoke. As his eye focused on the spot, he made out a collection of tiled roofs and a tall chimney.

Civilization! The thought of a warm soft bed to rest his bones and proper food leapt into his mind. Surely Merrit would be able to point them on their way now. A collection of buildings like that was surely on a road that would lead to the Dairy Track. But of course, they could not stop there. They had many hours of daylight left in which to travel and should use every moment of it to make their way to safety. The thought struck him that then Quinn would raise the alarm about Guthrey and the memory of his evil deed stung his mind. He didn't know how much longer he would have to keep up this charade, but the consequences of being found out tightened his empty stomach, forcing bile up into his throat.

Angrily, he glowered at Quinn. Already he had admitted there was little chance of finding his brother alive, yet he was foolishly clinging to the absurd notion that there was still hope. It would be Quinn's fault if anything were to happen now, for even if Guthrey had been alive when he was taken by the ravenshrikes, no one could survive this long. He shook his head at the stupidity of the Torra Altans.

Merrit pulled on the lead rein to turn the horse towards the distant tiled roofs and Rollo was hopeful that a good meal and a soft bed might still be forthcoming.

Quinn, however, protested. 'Surely, you can just point us in the direction of the road now?'

'This is the direction of the road,' Merrit snapped. 'The mill, there, is right on it. As soon as we reach it, you can get off my horse and limp along on your own.' The man's face wrinkled into a teasing sneer. 'What is it about the impatience of youth? Why is it that you always think you know better?'

Quinn shrugged away Merrit's jest. 'I'm sorry. It must be my ankle making me a little crotchety. I am grateful for your help and I apologize if I offended you.'

Merrit smiled. 'And so you should. You are lucky to have fallen in with a soul as generous and caring as myself. There aren't many that would bother with three troublesome youngsters in times like this. You've taken advantage of my soft heart.'

Quinn laughed. 'And we're very grateful for your soft heart, Merrit. Now I've already said I'm sorry. What more do you want?'

The foreigner had no answer for him.

The air puffed from their nostrils like dragon smoke as they descended into the chill of a hollow. A mist was gathering as they ambled through the over-grown orchards down towards the collection of barns about the mill that stood tall out of the black waters of the millpond. A huge wheel turned very slowly in the flow of the millrace, leaves choking the paddles and inhibiting the flow. The only sound above the movement of water was the clank of the tusks and the swishing of the grass as the heavy cargo was dragged through it. They waded through the wet grass a little way until they came to an outgrown hedge of hazel and elder. A track led to an old rickety gate in the hedge. The ground around it was rutted and puddles lay in the hollows.

Merrit fixed the three youngsters with a hard look. 'Now listen up, you three, you're to stay here. I don't want any of you to move more than an inch from the horse, you hear?'

He looked at their eyes and waited for each of them to nod a solemn agreement.

Even Rollo managed to force his chin up and down and to fill his face with a look of wide-eyed obedience. Merrit grunted in satisfaction and turned to remove the smallest pack from the back of his saddle. The horse's ears were laid flat back as if nervous of the environment, her sides heaving a little from the effort of hauling the tusks.

'Now stay here,' Merrit repeated before climbing over the gate and marching stiffly towards the mill, the coveted pack slung over one shoulder.

The three of them watched his back for the short minute it took him to disappear out of sight. The horse shifted her weight beneath Quinn and then ambled towards a puddle, which she snuffled and then drank from. Quinn slipped his feet from his stirrups and stretched his legs forward.

'Let me see your ankle. Is it any better?' Isolde asked with concern.

'Oh, don't fuss, Issy,' Quinn complained. 'But, yes, it is.' To prove it, he swung the leg over the saddle and slid down from the horse though Rollo could see him wince as he landed and guard it as he limped to the gate. He rested against the railings.

Rollo's nostrils twitched; he smelt something strange in the air. Climbing onto the first bar of the gate, he craned forward until he could catch a glimpse of the mill and the cluster of barns on the far side of a millrace.

'Are you sure your leg is better?' Isolde asked Quinn suspiciously.

'Quite sure. It's much better.'

Rollo snorted. 'Probably just a little stiff from lack of use, but nothing a Torra Altan can't handle,' he purred sarcastically. The young prince was enjoying himself and was trying to think of something else to say when he noticed the deep, reddish brown rump of a horse just visible at the far side of the mill. Clearly, this was Merrit's rendezvous.

'I'm going to take a closer look,' he announced.

Quinn shook his head. 'Merrit wouldn't be pleased; we said we wouldn't move.'

'I didn't. He told us not to move and I merely acknowledged his statement; that's not the same thing as agreeing to it. Who is he, anyway, telling me what to do? I am a prince. No one tells me what to do. I'm going to find out what he's up to.'

'Wouldn't you suppose that he's up to just what he said? He's meeting someone to get a good price for the ivory,' Quinn remarked.

Rollo thought for a moment. 'Perhaps. But we could take the horse and the ivory! We could just ride out of here with it.'

Quinn laughed. 'And how far would we get? He'd be on us like a hawk on a rabbit. Don't be absurd. He knows we wouldn't take the tusks. We wouldn't know what to do with them even if we could get them out of here.'

Rollo lowered himself back down and rested his chin on the gate. There was no doubt that Quinn was right but he still wasn't happy. 'I just want to know what he's up to. We're putting our lives in his hands. Don't you think we're being a little bit too trusting? Shouldn't we be slightly more cautious?'

Isolde nodded at this. 'But, Rollo, if you don't mind me saying, we still don't want to upset him. That wouldn't be helpful.'

'I don't care if I upset him. I want to know what he's up to.'

Despite strong protests from the other two, Rollo slunk down towards the mill, aware of the soft whicker from the horse behind him that was almost like a warning. Merrit had crossed the millrace by a bridge but that route would leave Rollo exposed to view and he thought it more prudent to keep in the lee of the overgrown hedge as he approached the dark strip of water. He turned round just to check on

341

the others and noted that Isolde was already trying to do something to ease the sores on the mare's breast caused by the thin harness digging into her flesh.

He admired her gentle consideration yet, not wanting to admit to such softness himself, he crept on, his mind focused on the task in hand. The rump of the brown horse he had glimpsed was not the hindquarters of a common draught horse. The sun had glinted on a sleek cloak that came only with good food and expert grooming. Clearly it was not the chattel of a common man. His suspicions were soon confirmed. Pressing himself against the thick wrinkled trunk of a willow, whose roots dipped into the millrace, he leaned forward and was able to see around the side of the mill. At the corner was the horse he had glimpsed, a strong bay. The animal carried a high-cantled saddle over a red saddlecloth bordered in gold. Definitely the horse of a wealthy man, there was no question. Rollo was pleased with his observation skills. Leaving the concealment of the willow, he crept closer, now sharply aware of the sound of iron-shod hooves on the stone of the cobbled yard. He was close enough to see the motif on the bottom corner of the saddlecloth. It meant nothing to him but he made a mental note of the design just in case Quinn and Isolde might know to whom the emblem belonged.

To not recognize family crests was most disconcerting. If he had been in Artor, he would have been able to name the family of any of five hundred emblems. And if he had been in his own continent, he would have been back home by now regardless of what troubles he had run into. That neither Quinn nor Isolde could find their way home in their own country did not surprise him but simply confirmed his low opinion of Torra Altans.

Cosseted and nannied, they had not yet learned how to stand on their own two feet. He snorted to himself and looked ahead, deliberating how best to get close enough to overhear what Merrit and the owner of the bay gelding were saying.

To his left at the head of the millrace was a narrow dam

controlling the flow to the mill-wheel and he decided that it would provide the best route to cross the water and reach the back of the stable. He was half way to his objective when he heard a rider approaching from the far side of the mill. Pressing himself down into the wet grass, he waited. The rider that came into view was clad in a grimy coloured hooded cloak that hid his features and his horse did not have the same fine looks as the bay animal. It's flanks were covered in lacerations and weals and Rollo could almost smell the festering sores from where he was crouching.

What was wrong with Merrit and his colleagues that they had to mistreat their animals so badly?

Anxious to hear what they were up to, he crept tentatively onto the stonework of the narrow dam and, standing in the shadow of the mill, watched the third rider dismount. He was tall beneath his sacking cloth and, when he slid from his horse, he glided like a ghost across the cobbles, his boots silent on the rounded stones. In fact, Rollo could see no boots at all since his cloak trailed along the ground.

He swallowed hard as he felt a light giddiness rising into his brain. He cursed to himself, taking deep breaths to try and clear his head. The symptoms were all too familiar. Lights flickered and danced at the periphery of his vision and he could feel the first pulsing throb of a headache.

He must calm himself. There was never a good place to have a fit, he told himself as he stared at the thin ledge on which he perched above the millrace, but this was definitely one of the worst. The pool was deep and he could see the strength of the flow as the water churned and was drawn deep down into a culvert and sucked out through a grid on the other side, deep within the millpond. One slip and he would be dragged against that grid never to rise again.

Drawing a deep breath, he cursed his weakness. He gritted his teeth. He couldn't really understand what was upsetting him so but decided it must be the smell from the horse's sores that penetrated his brain. On top of that, there was another smell that made him want to vomit. He couldn't quite put his finger on what it was as he hastily shuffled to the edge of the thin dam. Hurriedly, he crept up to the side of the nearest barn where he could hear Merrit arguing with the two other horsemen.

'Of course, it's worth it!' Merrit was adamant. 'They know something. They know far more than they are letting on but they're too frightened to do anything at the moment. They're terrified of the forest creatures so I think this may well be the best way.'

Rollo flushed; was Merrit referring to him, Isolde and Quinn? His pulse pounded.

'But it's too slow and we need results,' one of the others hissed.

Merrit continued to argue but Rollo was focusing on that second voice. Its intonation had struck a cord in his subconscious, sending shivers right through him. His arm began to ache and he looked down at the cramped fingers of his forearm that had suddenly spasmed.

'It's slow but more reliable,' Merrit was saying.

'As you wish,' a smooth Belbidian voice agreed to the plan. 'Do you want me to take the tusks from you? That'll be a simple matter and I'll get a good price for them. I'll help you fetch them and we can all get away from here.'

'In just a moment,' Merrit told him dismissively, asserting his authority. 'There's still the matter of the mammoth.' He turned to the lean cloaked figure. 'I want you to tell her where it is. I'll need her to load up the cart; it's impossible without her. The clearing is big enough, so she won't make the fuss that she did last time.'

The cloaked figure made a strange clicking noise in his throat as if he were very much disturbed by the fuss that had been made.

'When you have taken the message, hurry back to the arena,' Merrit continued. 'And don't worry about me; I know what I'm doing with them. You don't think they'd outsmart me now, do you?'

'I don't think anyone would outsmart you,' the figure in the cloak replied with a cackle in his voice.

The sound of the man's voice made the hairs on the back of Rollo's neck stand on end. He pushed himself hard against the wall as he watched the cloaked figure return to his horse. The animal was tethered to a ring in the wall and, though it pulled toward a water trough, its master would not let it drink. The youth rubbed at his eyes; his vision was beginning to blur. The wind shifted to come to him straight from the mill and he stiffened in alarm.

Though he knew he was a little confused, that stench was distinctive enough. He would recognize the smell of hob anywhere. If Merrit were dealing with hobs then they were all in danger. The pain at his temple eased and he congratulated himself for avoiding the fit. He had been right and the physicians wrong; he could control his fits! He also congratulated himself on being aware from the start that there was something suspicious about Merrit.

Rollo shuddered and felt the full rush of the blood to his head and a hazy blackness swim into his mind. Unfocused and confused, he staggered as fast as he could back towards the thin dam at the head of the millrace but, now, the wall of rock in the water seemed to be squirming as if it were a live snake before him. He thought he would retch and took deep breaths to steady himself but to no effect. The anger was rising up within him at his stupidity in allowing himself to be led by Merrit. A man who would trade with hobs was capable of any atrocity. He had to get away.

Dropping onto all fours, he crawled out onto the dam. His fingers gripping the greasy stones, he watched his reflection in the silvery bow of the water before it was dragged down into the depths below. His reflection arced and curved and his face grew long and hideous. Then suddenly his reflection was lurching towards him and he realized his balance was gone and that he was slowly toppling.

'Steady, now,' a quite voice murmured. 'Just slide one hand forward. Come on, slide it forward and look at me.'

Rollo forced his head upward to see three images of Isolde slowly revolving around one another.

'Come on, Rollo, just slide your hand forward. Think only about your hand and look into my eyes.'

Looking up, he found there was just one thing that he could focus on and that was the glorious colour of Isolde's eyes. He didn't know how he did it but, a moment later, he managed to hold himself steady and inched forward to reach out for her. Then her small hand was around his, pulling him towards her. He kicked forward and, with a rush, was beyond the dam and rolling on top of her. Her touch steadied his mind, as did the act of trying to tell her what he had heard. Keeping low and to the hedge, Isolde helped him stumble back to Quinn who was waiting anxiously with the horse.

'We can't stay . . . We can't . . . We have to go now,' Rollo panted.

'Steady now and take a breath so that we can hear you properly,' Quinn was advising him.

Rollo looked hastily back towards the mill and could see that Merrit and the well-dressed man on the bay horse had rounded the mill and were still in deep conversation. 'Hob,' he gasped. 'Hob!'

'There's no hob,' Quinn objected. 'I stood on the gate to see. There were two men. That one,' he nodded towards the mill, 'and the one that left.'

'Yes, him. The cloaked one,' Rollo gasped.

'So? He's cloaked. What's the mystery in that? It's very normal at this time of year,' Quinn said reasonably, tugging at his own cloak.

'Didn't you see the way he moved? Didn't you smell him?' Rollo insisted.

'I saw him all right, Rollo. The trouble is you're not seeing straight. You couldn't even walk back here unaided.'

'But I was seeing straight then. I know what I saw.'

'You couldn't see anything beneath that cloak. Stop imagining things.'

'I'm not imagining anything,' Rollo insisted. 'I was right about the dragon's graveyard and I'm right about this. That creature down there talking with Merrit was a hob. I would wager this ring on it.' He tapped his neck where his mother's ring hung on a chain. 'The cloaked man was a hob. And a man that deals with hobs is not to be trusted. He wants something from us and I'm not waiting to find out what it is.'

'What could he possibly want with us?' Quinn dismissed this argument though, at last, there was a hint of concern to his voice.

'Well, it doesn't take much imagination, does it? He's been trading in ivory. Clearly, he's a merchant with a lot of shifty connections doing deals in all sorts of clandestine places. If he were honest, he would have met these people out in the open in front of us. And then there's the matter of the other man. He was clearly of note and even had an insignia on his saddlecloth. Men of money don't trade in out of the way places unless there's something shifty about the deal.'

'What was the insignia?' Quinn asked.

Rollo waved his arms about, trying to describe it. 'It looked a bit like a pair of scales. Like scales at a market, you know. A thing with pans on either end.'

'Two milking pails,' Quinn corrected him. 'It's a yoke for carrying milk and it's the emblem of Nattarda. It must have been Baron Wiglaf's man but more likely it was his horse that a ruffian had stolen.'

Rollo shrugged, thinking the matter unimportant. 'Whatever, but my guess is that Merrit's disarming Belbidians and selling them as slaves to the hobs. It makes perfect sense and explains all the oddities. Well, I've not travelled half way across this world, ripped from a country that I love, only to be enslaved by hobs. I'd rather get gored by taurs or trampled by mammoths. I'm leaving right now, whether you're with me or not.'

Much to Rollo's amazement, Quinn was nodding. Isolde said nothing but watched Quinn's reaction as if waiting on his decision and then she, too, nodded.

'We should get the tusks free and take the horse, then,' Quinn directed.

Initially, Rollo thought that was the obvious thing to do but then decided against it. 'If we take his horse, which is clearly a valuable animal, he'll pursue us until we drop, whereas, if we flee on foot, he just might not bother with us. Look.' Rollo leaned out over the gate, pushing aside the bare branches of elder so that he could peek between the twigs. 'He's still deep in argument now and we may get a few minutes head start.'

'He won't have any trouble tracking us though,' Isolde pointed out.

'Yes, but don't you see? Rollo is right,' Quinn argued. 'It may be too much trouble for him to track us, especially dragging a cargo of ivory. But, first, let's just make our odds a little better before we go. He rummaged in Merrit's pack and took out a leather sheath containing an ivory-handled knife.

'Why don't we take more?' Rollo asked. 'An axe could come in handy.' Before Quinn could answer him, he raised a flat hand to silence him. 'No, you're right; the less we take, the less reason he has to come after us. I doubt that he'll trouble himself about a knife though.'

Quinn nodded. 'I meant to do a little more to improve our chances of escape.' He moved to the mare's foreleg and slid a hand down past her knee to her pastern. Obediently, she lifted one of her heavy hooves and Quinn worked his knife into the shoe. It took him a long valuable minute to work the shoes loose enough so that he could be sure it would very quickly come free when the man set off after them. Rollo agreed that one loose shoe would be enough to slow any pursuit yet not look so suspicious and inflame Merrit's anger towards them.

Isolde, all this while, had been stepping slowly round as if to divine the best route. 'We can't head north otherwise we'll be in the depths of the hob-infested forest. And if we head too far to the south we'll be on the road. That would be good but we would be too conspicuous and Merrit would certainly check that direction first. What if we try to take a parallel course to the road? Do you think that's possible, Quinn?'

The youth smiled at her. 'Yes, Issy, that sounds right. If we keeping heading west until we skirt the edge of Granham, we should then be able to safely join the Dairy Track.' He sheathed the knife, tied it to his belt and then put his hand on Rollo's shoulder. 'I'm sorry to burden you with this but I'm going to need your help. My leg is maybe not quite as strong as I thought.'

Despite himself, Rollo flashed Quinn a quick smile. It was rare for someone to solicit his help.

They struggled back up the track, through the orchard and were soon under the cover of the forest, striking a course that ran parallel with the road. Rollo was aware of Quinn's laboured breaths. He had realized, of course, that Quinn was in pain but he was alarmed at how slowly he could move. Perhaps the idea of leaving the horse behind had been a bad one after all. Perhaps they should have chosen a more suitable opportunity to run, but now it was too late.

'Perhaps Merrit will think that some monster swooped out of the sky and plucked us away,' Quinn joked.

'I don't see that that's funny. Do you have to find everything funny?' Rollo snapped.

'Well, if you don't find life funny then you tend to find it painful,' the youth retorted.

Rollo grunted under Quinn's weight as he helped him along with Isolde doing her best to assist by supporting him on the other side.

'It was madness to leave the horse,' Quinn said after a few minutes.

'We've been through that already,' Rollo said with some exasperation.

'I know, I know and I still think it was the right thing to do. But I think now perhaps we should split up. You and Isolde would travel a lot more swiftly without me.'

'That's oh-so-noble-of-you, I'm sure, but we'll be a lot safer sticking together.' Rollo said stiffly.

Panting hard, they struggled as fast as they could for over half a mile in silence. Looking back, there was no sign of the mill or anyone in pursuit and so they began to ease their pace. They trudged another full mile and there was still no sign of Merrit. Fearing that it would tempt fate, Rollo refrained from mentioning the man by name and it seemed the others were of like mind. Instead they concentrated on the way ahead and began as best they could to trace a path through the tangled woods.

It was a curious wood for there were very few older trees. Most were saplings that had not yet grown big enough to blot out the light and so the grasses and undergrowth were particularly thick.

Quinn now spurned their assistance and, hobbling with the aid of a stick, he repeatedly lagged behind. Rollo was frequently unnerved since, when he looked round to check that he was there, he often found the Torra Altan exceedingly difficult to spot against the flecked background. Despite Quinn's injuries, they appeared to be making good time and Rollo admired the youth's courage. He was less impressed when he heard Quinn ask Isolde whether she still sensed Brid's living spirit in the ether.

At first, Rollo wanted to snort at this idea but then decided that he would be wrong to belittle such a notion. He had known precisely when his mother had died. The memory still clutched at his heart, squeezing it painfully. He had been sent out hunting with one of the warriors of Ash and had unexpectedly slumped onto his horse's neck, suddenly finding it hard to breathe. The moment was brief but it coincided exactly with the time of his mother's death.

'Rollo, come on, what's the matter?' Quinn was dragging at his arm. 'You've stopped. We've got to keep going.'

Rollo was about to step up the pace when he was suddenly aware of a new smell that was vaguely familiar. It was sweet and juicy and reminded him of a late breakfast after an early morning's hunt. Bacon and fresh bread, he decided, the bread still slightly doughy. The idea was absolutely absurd and he was becoming increasingly unnerved by the extraordinary bouts of heightened senses he had experienced since arriving in Belbidia. He could not possibly smell breakfast here in the woods.

He sniffed again, his brow wrinkling into a frown. But the smell was not bacon and bread! It was now a smell of ale and oil which, certainly, should not have reminded him of breakfast; he must still be suffering the after-effects of the mild seizure he had experienced at the mill. But he guessed where the smell was coming from and he lent forward to warn Isolde and Quinn.

'Careful,' Rollo whispered. 'There's—'

Before he could say more, a group of figures stepped out from the trees. He had been wary of hobs and thought that, if they had been travelling in the middle of the day, they would probably be all right, but he had not expected to see *these* creatures. Short and stocky, only a fraction taller than little Isolde, they stood before the youths, bearing large circular shields. Several brandished short swords while others held picks and axes.

Rollo wanted to laugh. But they were dwarves! Short little men with long beards, neatly brushed, they reeked of beer. All notion of breakfast was quite gone from his mind at the sight of them. They had dark black boots and very grubby clothes. Thick cloaks lay heavily on their backs and they seemed familiar with the weapons in their hands. Surly eyed, and heavily laden with baggage as well as weapons, Rollo feared that they had the sly, hungry look of either looters or fugitives.

'Get them!' a gruff voiced snarled. 'There's a smell of money about them.'

Isolde made the first move. Opting for the sensible thing to do, she ran.

Chapter 21

'Run for it!' Quinn shouted at Rollo, shoving him away. The lanky Torra Altan spread his legs wide, the knife that he had taken from Merrit firmly held up in readiness to face the dwarves' attack. 'Get her home, Rollo. Promise me you'll get her home.'

Rollo ran. He knew it was cowardly but he had no weapon and he knew that Quinn was thinking about Isolde. He ran wildly after the fleet-footed girl, determined to catch her and equally determined to flee the dwarves.

He didn't know much about dwarves. His father had said that they were far more civilized than they were generally reputed to be and were highly skilled craftsmen turning their hands to whatever they set their minds to; silversmiths or swordsmiths, musicians or artists; they were always masters of their craft. However, every other reference he had ever heard said that they were troublesome, easily offended, greedy and very dangerous. And, the bunch that had ambushed them were as roguish and as rough a band of troublemakers as Rollo had ever seen. They sported cuts and bruises and wore various tribal cloths about their waists. The cloths were of different clans and the desperate, greedy look about their eyes had immediately convinced Rollo that they were outcasts.

A string of ivy creeping between the trees tripped him. He wanted to get out of these woods. It was country he was unaccustomed to and, often over the past few days, he had felt that they were going round and round in circles. It was as if the trees were bewitched.

He scrambled up just in time to glimpse a speck of blue as Isolde sped away. How could she run so fast on bare feet? The very thought of all those brambles underfoot made him shudder.

But he was catching her. The ground was beginning to rise and the trees were thinning as they made their way up into heath-land. When he was far out into the open, he stopped. There were no signs of pursuit and, as he looked about, he had the first glimpse of hope in days; in the far distance to the south the heath dropped away and he could see the brown line of a road. Roads went places. A road could take him home.

Rollo steadied his breathing and set off after Isolde. He hoped that Quinn had also got away. It was unthinkable that he hadn't and Rollo had to console himself with the fact that, at least, he would be helping Isolde to safety though, in truth, she was probably not even aware of his presence behind her. At last, he was closing on her. Finally, she came to a halt at the top of a small rise from where, she looked back at the scrubby woodlands that they had left far behind.

Her intriguing eyes met his as he drew to a halt beside her. Doubling over, he tried to catch his breath and ease the stitch in his side. 'Where now?' he gasped. 'I saw the road. Look; over there.' He pointed. 'And is that Granham?' He pointed to the west at a group of crumbling roofs perched on rubble and held up, it would appear, mostly by ivy. 'They can't have followed us. Quinn's plan must have worked.'

Isolde was no longer looking at him but was staring back into the woodlands. 'You go on then,' she said softly. 'I'm not leaving Quinn.'

'He'll stand a better chance without you.' Rollo pointed out reassuringly. 'It was what he wanted. And he made me promise to take you home.'

'Quinn needs me. He doesn't stand a chance without me,' Isolde said coldly and somehow Rollo had the impression that she was not solely referring to the present situation. 'There has to be something we can do. Think of something,' she demanded, her clenched fists shaking, the muscles on her thin neck taught and her mouth drawn.

'I have! We head back to Torra Alta now.'

'Not without Quinn.' Isolde's voice was trembling. Quite suddenly, she flew at Rollo and was beating him about the face, thumping his chest, as he tried to fend her off. At last, he managed to get a hold of her wrists and pin her wiry arms to her sides but that meant she only resorted to kicking and biting instead.

Tears were streaming down her face. 'Do something!' she yelled at him. 'You do something. This is all your fault. All your wretched fault. You have to think of something.' At last she fell against his chest and began to sob. 'I can't go on without Quinn.'

Rollo hugged her close, uncomfortably aware of the sweet scent of lavender and rose about her hair. It must have been days since she had washed yet the scent still lingered. She was grimy from head to toe, trickles of blood running about her bare ankles where she had scratched herself in the undergrowth. Her tears made miniature creamy rivers down her otherwise muddy cheeks. He looked at her, calmly amazed at his own self-control in the face of her outburst of emotion.

Normally, if someone had hit him like that, even if that person had been a girl, he would have hit them back. He hugged her a little tighter, feeling bigger and tougher from the contrast of being pressed against the slightness of her willowy body. It was no wonder she could run fast; there was nothing to her. She was little more than a feather.

'Rollo, oh, Rollo,' she gasped, her breathing constricted in his clutch. 'What do we do?' she asked, her sudden reliance on him making him feel the older of the two and very much more responsible than his scant thirteen years.

He looked towards the road. He knew what his answer should be; every bone in his body told him what he must do yet he could not refuse this girl. A minute ago, he would have walked away and his conscience would have been none the worse for it. He would have decided that she had brought it all on herself and there was no point saving anyone from themselves because they would never thank you for it. The fact that she had broken down on him, sobbing and pleading, had made little difference either. What had swayed him was that she had lost her temper. At last, he was with someone who needed him.

He sighed. 'Well, what do you propose we do?

Isolde pouted. 'I— I don't know. I assumed you would know,' she said, her voice croaky. 'Quinn always had good plans.' She suppressed a sob. 'It was always the three of us. Guthrey would say what he wanted to achieve – that we must build a dam or scale a tree or catch a boar even. He was always so full of bravado. But it was Quinn that had the mind for planning. He would always sit and think everything out for us.'

Rollo's eyebrows rose. 'Well, he didn't have time to think this one out too clearly.'

'It's kept us free so that we have an opportunity to think. And Quinn, of course, could not run,' she said defensively.

Rollo thought on their problem. 'We don't know that he didn't escape but, if he didn't, perhaps they'll let him go when they realize he's of no use to them.'

'No use? Quinn? They'll take one look at his hands and know he's an archer.'

Rollo laughed at the girl's innocence. 'What would a dwarf want with an archer? There's only one thing that a dwarf wants and that's money. They'll either sell him to the hobs, which is probably too much bother, or try and fetch a ransom for him though that's doubtful too. He looks like he's worth . . . Well, I'd say he looks as if he's worth no more than you or I. Look at us! Downtrodden ragamuffins. We look like we've lived rough all our lives.'

'We do? Ha!' Isolde sniffed at the idea. 'Don't be ridiculous.' She flicked back her hair with a nonchalant swat of her hand in a manner that instantly annoyed Rollo.

'I'm not being ridiculous. We're caked in mud, you've no boots even and our clothes are torn and stained.'

'All right, so you're a little dirty,' Isolde conceded. 'But take your hair: it's been cut evenly all round with scissors. It hasn't just been hacked off with a knife like the hair of a common woodsman's boy would have been. Scissors are hard to come by in Belbidia now. And Quinn's hair is a good deal neater than your own. Secondly,' she reached out to touch his hands and turned them over, 'have you ever seen a woodsman's hands?'

'Well, of course I have.'

'No, I mean have you seen them close up?' Isolde clarified her question. 'A hand can tell you much about a person. The dirt on a woodsman's hand is so thick that it's deeper than the very grain of the skin, and the fingers are thicker and the palm distinctly callused from wielding an axe. Now look here.' She pointed to his palms. 'You have a little bit of thickening from carrying reins and mainly in your left hand – which tells much about you,' she added. 'Such marks on your left hand,' she repeated, 'indicate that you carry a weapon in your right, I would say. Not too many woodsmen do that now, do they? And then you even have a slight bump on the top of your middle finger made by writing.'

'How did you know that?' Rollo asked, turning his right hand over to examine it and saw that she was absolutely right.

She laughed. 'Because I look for such things. But Quinn's hands are even more obvious. He has the thick calluses of an archer on the inside of the fore and middle finger of his right hand. They are highly distinctive. He also has marks on his body from light combat. Now there are not so many that carry the marks of battle at so young an age. Only those born into noble families, trained from the earliest years and pitched against sparring partners gather such scars. The wounds are old too. He got the first when he was six – a sickle cut to his upper arm. It's no more than the thread of a white scar now but it tells a tale about him. And every telltale sign sings out that he is high born.'

Rollo was impressed with her reason and observation skills. 'I see there are advantages to being so quiet,' he commented though he was not really intending to put the girl down. 'However, there is one flaw in your argument. It is quite remarkable that you have managed to note all these things about Quinn and myself. Most remarkable! Isn't it quite possible that the dwarves lack your remarkable skill? Surely, they will see only a grubby boy just like everyone else would – apart from your own quirky self that is?'

Isolde looked at him sideways, her large golden-green eyes flooding with tears, her gaunt cheeks bruised and muddied, her long golden hair a tangled mat about her shoulders and her simple dress a ragged cloth. Rollo could see nothing in her that would cut her apart from a woodcutter's half-starved daughter and he didn't imagine that he or Quinn looked any better.

But looking into Isolde's pleading eyes, he could see they would have to go back for Quinn. He didn't know what they could do but they would have to do something. He slumped back down onto the grass, plucked up a strand and proceeded to strip the seeds from it. 'Well, the only thing we can to is make our way back and see whether he's escaped or not.'

'He hasn't escaped,' Isolde said flatly. 'I know Quinn. He would have stayed there to the bitter end just to give us the best chance of getting away.'

Rollo looked up from the dried winter grass on which he sat and stared back the way they had come. It was some time before he could think clearly for the muddled churning of his mind. How could he have let all this happen? He should have refused to leave home. He should have run away to the lake villages in the north of Artor where, at least, he understood the customs properly. But he had obeyed his father and left Artor. If only he had not allowed himself to be so riled by Guthrey. In fact, he wondered why he had been. Reeling with guilt, his mind took him back to those first moments entering the castle.

Instantly, he knew what had upset him. It had been the sight of the dragon's skull above the door. But that was absurd. It was only a trophy; there was absolutely no reason why that would upset him. It wasn't as if it were a bear. His sister, Imogen, once vomited at the sight of a killed bear and he wondered at his family's weakness. It was surely all Caspar's fault. He grunted in disapproval.

'That skull, that dragon's skull,' he said out loud.

'What dragon's skull?'

'The one over the door in the hall of the upper keep of your home!'

'What? But what does that have to do with Quinn?' Isolde asked in surprise. 'I don't understand.'

'I was just thinking that the dragon skull had been the start of my—'

He broke off. Something was moving through the hazel copses far to their right. Hastily, he scanned the rest of the scene. They were moving to his left too and soon they were closing in on the rise of the heath. He caught the glint of the sun bouncing off metal and his heart leapt into his throat. He crouched to the ground, hoping they were not too discernible against the heath.

'Isolde,' he murmured. 'They are coming for us.' High above their heads, a crow cawed out its taunting cry as if drawing attention to them, pointing out to all the world that they were there on the hilltop. And what a ridiculous place to be! They could be seen for miles around by anyone who cared to look.

He looked down the far side of the hill and saw the dark line of a stream marked by the thick band of trees that crammed its banks. From here, it was clear that the stream led back into the thicker dark green of fir trees and he wondered whether they should run to hide there. He dismissed the idea at once.

They should head for the road since, sooner or later, that would lead to a village. But Isolde had been faster to make up her mind; against his better judgement, she was racing down the hill, heading north for the thicker cover of the pine trees. He had no choice but to follow.

They crouched low, making sure that they could not be seen, Rollo's breathing loud in his ears as he ran. Soon, they made the stream and Isolde cast quickly behind her before pushing her way through the dense vegetation and leaping into the shallow waters.

'Quick!' Isolde urged. 'It'll be better going in the stream and they won't see us here.'

The cold water stung Rollo's toes as it seeped through the stitching in his boots and made his socks sodden. He winced at the very thought of Isolde's bare feet as she skipped along the gravelly bottom of the stream.

For a short while, he thought they had outrun the dwarves. He couldn't believe that such stocky men could run so fast, and so it was with surprised consternation that he heard the shouts close behind them. The gruff voices sent a shiver down his spine. He could have sworn that they had kept themselves safe from view. Surely, the dwarves had not seen them run for the stream. But obviously they had. Again, he rued their stupidity in resting on the top of the hill.

Tripping on a jagged stone in the riverbed, he stumbled, sprawling headlong into the flow, the cold water stinging his face. Pulling himself quickly to his feet, he did his best to catch up with Isolde. But his breeches were sodden, and they were dragging on his legs, making running very much harder. At last, Isolde halted, looked about her and indicated that they should head off to the right, taking the opportunity to use a jetty of rock that dipped into the river to hide their footprints.

Tiptoeing, she stepped out of the river and onto the smooth slab of rock, her feet red with the cold. Once she reached the end of the rock, she looked about her and then leapt across to a fallen log, picking her way carefully along it until she reached its end. Then she turned and beckoned Rollo to follow, indicating that, he too, should make his way along the log. 'We don't want to leave any footprints close to the stream,' she whispered.

They were now well into the thick vegetation of the pine forest and, by the orderly lines of the trees, they knew that this must once have been a plantation though, already, seedlings choked up the uniform spaces between the lines of timber. Rollo followed her, balancing along the log as she indicated and then picking his way from one log, tree root or stone to the next to keep their feet out of the impressionable mud.

Once they had travelled like this for fifty paces, Isolde halted. 'I can see an old firebreak ahead. If we can reach that, it'll be easy going and we'll outrun them. But let's try not to leave any prints until we get there.'

He nodded in agreement.

Once they reached the firebreak, which ran like a green swathe through the plantation and kept clear by grazing deer and hogs, they paused for a moment, doubling up and drawing breath.

Isolde looked up and down the open tract that cut through the trees. 'They would never expect us to head back to where they have left Quinn. He may be guarded by only one or two and it might be our best chance to rescue him. If we go south along the firebreak and then cut into the trees again, we could circle round behind and find our way back.

Rollo smiled. It was a simple plan and simple plans were usually the best. They jogged south along the grassy sward of the firebreak, making good time, and Rollo was almost beginning to feel hopeful that their scheme would work. Then he became aware of a pricking sensation running up his spine. Someone or something was also running through the trees alongside them.

Isolde did not cast her eyes in that direction but Rollo noted the subtle lengthening in the rhythm of her stride to match the stride pattern of the flickering shadow. Then the shadow vanished and Isolde jerked to a halt, her body motionless as she listened.

'They're still searching for us. I can hear them.' She pointed to her right. A moment later Rollo, too, was aware of the cries and shouts from the dwarves who seemed to make no effort to cover their noise as they crashed through the forest.

'They've come away from the stream already,' Rollo complained, annoyed that their efforts had been in vain.

'Here, into the woods before they see us. Quick!' Isolde pulled his sleeve hard and they ran into the trees where it took a moment for Rollo's eyes to adjust to the shade. While all was shrouded in gloom, he smelt wolf and caught the glint of two red eyes. But as his eyes grew accustomed to the dark, the strong scent diminished.

Isolde ran straight towards the glinting eyes of the wolf but then suddenly stopped as if some thought had brought her up short.

'How are they doing it?' she whispered, turning and gripping Rollo's arm until it hurt. 'Of course, they are using Quinn!' Her hand flew to her breast and she pulled out the deep yellow-hearted ruby, which had been tucked inside her garments, and peered into it. 'I would never have imagined they could do something like that.'

'Like what?' Rollo was confused. 'Shouldn't we keep running?'

Isolde's hand sagged to her side. 'No, they will always catch up with us. They can detect us.' She gave out a puff of despair.

'But how? How can they see us?'

'The stones,' Isolde explained.

'But I don't understand. How?'

The priestess stared into the heart of the crystal but, when Rollo followed her example, he could see nothing.

'I can't see anything.'

'No, but I can. Look into my eyes,' she instructed.

Rollo bent down so that, when Isolde stared into the crystal, he could see the image of what she saw reflected in her pupils. Quinn was being dragged by the hair by a dwarf. The dwarf was pulling with one hand and holding something small and dark in the other.

Isolde leapt back in fright and covered the sunburst ruby with the palm of her hand. She then looked around her in panic. 'My ruby is drawing him to us. He has managed to read Quinn's stone,' Isolde yelped in dismay. 'Oh Mother, oh Mother what do I do with it? Rollo, help!'

The youth was quite alarmed at her sudden panic and wasn't at all sure what she was talking about. 'Get rid of it,' he said instinctively. 'If the ruby is drawing them to us, we must get rid of it.'

'But how?'

'Just throw it away and we'll run as we were before. Quick!' Rollo moved towards her, ready to snatch it from her.

'No! No, I can't throw it away. No!'

As he lunged for the jewel, she swung round to flee him and Rollo only managed to grab her hair. He yanked back harder than he had meant, pulling her off her feet. 'If that ruby's going to get us all killed, just get rid of it.'

'I can't,' she whimpered. 'Rollo, you're hurting me.'

He was furious that she had not told him of the risk that the jewel exposed them to, and he genuinely thought he would thump her at any moment if she continued to thwart him. He gritted his teeth, restraining himself as he struggled to grab the jewel. Then suddenly he stopped as a snarl thrummed in his ear. From behind the nearest tree stepped out a great black wolf, its pink gums clearly visible as its lips were pulled back to bare its large white teeth.

Rollo's blood ran cold. He had no idea that a wolf would

be either so big or so terrifying. His eyes fixed on that evil-looking jaw and he let Isolde slip from his fingers. She was coughing and spluttering and he had the horrible realization that his fingers had been about her throat. He went limp, realizing that he had not even known what he was doing.

Staggering to her feet, she cast him a dismissive look and stepped towards the wolf. 'Of course!' she whispered hoarsely, her attention fixed on the wolf as if she had completely forgotten Rollo's uncontrolled rage.

But Rollo could not so easily disregard his actions. What was the matter with him? He should just fling himself into the jaws of the wolf and be done with it. All of this was his fault. Guthrey would be alive; his father and Brid wouldn't be missing; Quinn wouldn't have been captured and he wouldn't have nearly strangled Isolde. He was a wretched human being. Slowly, his mind was drawn back to Isolde who seemed to have totally dismissed him.

He had expected some form of admonishment from her or for her simply to run from him but, instead, she was creeping towards the wolf and singing in a very soft and lovely voice, the words strange and poetic. Clearly, the wolf enjoyed the sound as he slithered forward on his belly, wagging his tail.

'Brother wolf,' Isolde murmured and sat down by his head.

The creature dropped his muzzle into her lap and she stroked back his soft ears. Then, she lifted the sunburst ruby and its chain from around her neck and slipped the chain about the wolf's neck before testing to see whether it was secure. Taking the leather thong from her herb scrip, which she then stuffed into a pocket, she knotted it about the chain, ensuring it was doubly secure.

'Begone with you!' she commanded. 'Away!'

The wolf snuffled her hand and then, suddenly, turned and fled north in the direction she had pointed. Isolde gripped Rollo's hand and pulled him hastily towards a large log that lay half buried in thick ferns. She wriggled down into the ferns and pressed close to the log. Rollo did the same, shrinking down into the dirt and trying to still his breathing.

The sound of his pulse roared in his ears and he felt sick with the pumping of his heart that seemed to have leapt up into his throat. The dwarves came crashing into the plantation. He could hear their shouts and the thud of angry axes splitting wood as they vented their frustration on the trees.

But he could also hear Quinn who was shouting, 'You'll never find her. She is of the water and the air and the wind. She is not of this earth and can vanish as easily as a sunbeam at the first touch of a cloud.'

There was a thud of knuckle against jaw and Quinn was suddenly silent. The dwarves soon crashed past their hidding place. Rollo lay still beneath the canopy of ferns, aware of the intense smell of leaf-mould, heightened by the dampness in the air. He wished he could just lie down there where he was and rest for a while. All he wanted to do was to close his eyes and hope that the world would simply disappear.

'They've gone!' Isolde said loudly in his ear, making him jump and open his eyes.

'Are you sure?'

'Of course I am! They've gone after my jewel.'

'You mean the wolf?' he asked.

'Well, yes, they're following my ruby,' Isolde corrected. Her hand clutched to her chest. 'I feel naked without it.'

Rollo was unable to stop his imagination following that train of thought. Too skinny though, he decided. Too skinny and too nervous. When he had first seen her, he had thought that at least she had beautiful hair but that could hardly be said now; it was ragged and dirty. She was breathing hard and looked rather like a terrified rabbit.

Taking a deep breath, he wondered whether he should start by apologizing to her but then decided he couldn't face that.

It would only make him look more stupid. Isolde, however, didn't seem in the least concerned about him.

'So which way now?' he asked.

'We still have to help Quinn and m—m—my . . .,' she began to stammer. 'My ruby!'

'What does a ruby matter at a time like this?' Rollo said stiffly.

'We must follow them. Perhaps when they stop to rest, we'll have an opportunity to help Quinn escape,' she suggested and set off up the trail after the dwarves.

Rollo hurried after her. 'I still don't understand. I don't understand how they could follow us or what the jewel has to do with it. Is it something like a lodestone?' he asked. 'There was a lodestone on board the ship that brought me and my father to Belbidia. It pointed continually to the north.'

Isolde flicked him a brief glance. He could see that she was limping heavily and that her legs were covered in scratches and bruises.

'Stop and sit down for a moment,' he ordered smoothly. 'We've got to do something about your feet and we'll make better time if you stop now.'

Reluctantly Isolde obeyed. Sitting back, she raised one slender ankle at a time for him to examine the bottom of her feet.

'They're covered in thorns! No wonder you're limping. Why didn't you wear shoes?' Rollo berated her in amazement.

'The wolf doesn't wear shoes so why should I?' she retorted, wincing as Rollo plucked out the thorns one by one from the soles of her feet.

'If you ask me, the bottom of your feet should belong to a wolf not a girl. They're just one great thick pad of hard leather. Don't you ever wear shoes?' he asked.

'No, they are noisy and clumsy.'

'Yes, but they keep your feet warm and dry and stop the thorns,' he told her, only then realizing that he was shivering

366

himself. But there was nothing that he could do other than shiver and bear it. He was grateful though for the tall trees all about them that stilled the cooling wind. When the last of the thorns were removed, he pulled her to her feet. It would be best to keep moving, and at least the trail was easy to follow since the dwarves had hacked their way through the undergrowth.

'I've never seen dwarves before,' Rollo said by way of conversation and so avoiding the silence with which he was less than comfortable. 'My father met several when we put into port at Negraferre on the western coast of Tethya – that's in the Empress's very own lands. Apparently, there are dwarves all over Negraferre, a very large number they say. They're interested in the iron smelters and the Negraferre metal itself. Father wouldn't let me off the ship. He was afraid that I would either run back home or might somehow pick a fight.' Rollo laughed at the absurdity of the idea. 'Anyone would be mad to pick a fight with one of those brutes.'

'I never met one either,' Isolde added, limping on as they followed the trail.' I hadn't really given them much thought before today. Brid said they were a difficult people. She said that they had rigid protocols and would anger quickly if their customs were even unintentionally disregarded. Apparently, they are most hospitable to travellers if you join them when they've finished work for the day and begun preparations for their nightly feast. They cannot, however, bear to be disturbed during their working hours.'

'Well, they don't seem to mind breaching our customs,' Rollo commented.

'No, it seems not.' Isolde managed a small laugh.

'I can't believe we're so important to them, can you? Surely, we're not worth the effort of charging through the forest like this?'

'I still don't understand how they are doing it. What has that strange stone of yours got to do with it? And your eyes, Isolde; that was very eerie,' Rollo exclaimed with a shudder.

The girl glanced at him as if checking on his expression to see whether he was horrified by her not. Clearly, she decided that she could still trust him. 'I see visions in the stones. It's a long story. My father, you see . . .,' she began and then stopped. 'No, you won't believe it. Nobody believes it but perhaps your own father will tell you about it one day. He saw it all, right from the beginning. But as I said, I can see images within my sunburst ruby and the vision is attracted most readily to Quinn's black jewel. The two gems have an affinity for one another. If he is wearing his jewel, his black onyx, I always know where he is.'

Rollo nodded, remembering how she had found them when they climbed out of the dragon's lair. 'But how can the dwarves see your ruby using Quinn's gem? Do you suppose that they have the same power as you?' he asked quietly, finding himself frightened by Isolde's unnatural gift. She seemed so reserved and unassuming; she possessed so little presence that it seemed remarkable that she had any special powers.

'I don't suppose for one second,' she muttered back, sounding almost affronted by the notion.

'How do you know?' he argued.

'Believe me, I know,' she said heavily. 'I'm the only one in the world.'

'Unique? How very presumptuous!' Rollo mocked though he had often felt that way himself.

She flashed him a cold look but made no attempt to contradict him as she scrambled on through the forest. At last, they came to a clearing and Isolde stopped short, craning her neck back to look straight up above her. 'An ancient silver fir,' she said, staring up the reddish bark into the giddy heights of the canopy far above them.

'What of it?' Rollo was puzzled that the tree had caught her attention.

'We shouldn't just stumble on through this manmade forest, simply hoping for an opportunity to rescue Quinn.

We should make our opportunity. I should climb the tree and see what there is to be seen. From up there the world will look different. It will give us a different perspective.'

'Us? Well, I'm certainly not climbing up there,' Rollo grumbled.

Isolde bent down and picked up one of the tight cones that had fallen at the tree's foot. She nodded up at the tree and then across at him. 'And nor am I. Brid would have done it of course. She can climb any tree in any wood. I even saw her climb up the great silver fir in the Boarchase and that was twice as high as this one; but I couldn't do it.' Suddenly, she crumpled to the floor and began snivelling quietly to herself.

Rollo wasn't sure what he should do. Tugging at her shoulder, he said awkwardly, 'Come on. It's no use sitting there. Come on, Issy,' he said, trying to be friendly by using Quinn's name for her. 'I couldn't climb that tree either. It doesn't mean we've failed. There are plenty of other ways to track Quinn. We can second-guess where they are going, can't we? Perhaps we can even take a quicker route. 'Where would the wolf go?'

Isolde smiled. 'You called me Issy. Quinn's the only one that's ever done that before.'

'Look, stop feeling sorry for yourself and think. You can't just lie there sobbing.' He pulled her to her feet. 'We simply have to keep going.'

'It's long gone midday. If we're not careful, we'll be stuck out in the open come dark,' Isolde whimpered. 'We're utter fools, trudging about alone like this. But, assuming I've remembered my lessons correctly, the dwarves should stop before nightfall. Dwarves are inflexible creatures of habit is what she said. And I'm fairly sure Brid said that they always stopped whatever they were doing for a good evening meal after which they told stories until well into the night. Apparently, they eat so much that they need the time to let the food settle before they sleep. But I probably didn't remember it right. I'm afraid I get a lot of things wrong, so I've probably got that wrong too.'

Feeling very much at a low ebb himself, Rollo wasn't sure how much more he could take of this and suddenly snapped her round by her arm and gripped her by the shoulders. Shaking her vigorously, he half growled and half snarled at her. 'Just buck up! We're going to get Quinn out of this mess if it kills us. It's bad enough about Guthrey but we won't lose Quinn too.'

Isolde's head flopped alarmingly and he was suddenly worried that he had actually hurt her. Often he had been told that he didn't know his own strength. Hastily, he let her go and watched her sag through his fingers, her eyes black and accusing as she sank to the floor. Disgusted with Isolde and himself, he began to trudge on alone, hoping that she would follow.

He had gone some way and was beginning to think he would have to go back for her when, at last, he heard a twig snap behind him and realized she had been close behind him for some time.

Rollo made no attempt at an apology. 'Where would the wolf go?'

'I don't know for sure,' Isolde said uncertainly. 'He's a wolf, a wild wolf. He could go anywhere.'

'But where do you *think* he would go?' Rollo persisted. 'And don't tell me he's wild. As a rule, wild wolves don't follow girls about; he behaves like a dog so think of him as one. Now, my dog . . .,' he began and then swallowed his words, remembering that he had left the old hunting hound behind with Imogen. Caspar had said he was too old for the journey and that it wouldn't be fair on the hound. He coughed to clear his throat and started again. 'Now, if it were my old dog, I would know where he would go. He would always trot around the palace grounds of an evening, taking exactly the same routes and sniffing at exactly the same spots. Now wouldn't your wolf do something predictable?'

'No!' Isolde replied stiffly. 'I told you he is a wild wolf and, beside, he's a long way off his territory and he now has a precious gem about his neck.'

'Which he accepted freely to help you? Oh, a very wild wolf indeed!' Rollo said with heavy sarcasm.

Isolde sniffed but said no more, keeping her eyes on the crisp forest floor.

'I'm hungry,' Rollo complained after they had continued like this for more than an hour. The woods were gradually beginning to thin and they were following a track that, by its rutted surface, had been frequented by carts. Clearly, people still came to this part of the forest to collect timber.

The broad booted prints of the dwarves were visible in the mud, leading them into a vale with steep sides that rose ahead to a high escarpment. Rollo was still wondering when it was that they had last actually eaten when, far to their right, he saw smoke winding up from the chimney of a log cabin. It was set low in the valley directly beneath a prominent, overhanging rock that rose up out of the bony ridge of the escarpment running along the northern boundary of the valley. The cabin beckoned to him but the dwarves had taken a path to the left towards the lower-lying end of the ridge.

'Of course! Come twilight, the wolf will head for the high ground to welcome the moon!' Isolde said with a smile and waved her hand up towards the escarpment. 'Oh Rollo, I'm so sorry I took so long to think of it, especially when it was so obvious.'

The red-haired youth looked up at the cloudless sky, felt the sharpness of the winter chill in the air and guessed that the moon would be very bright that night. He also presumed that, therefore, they would be very cold.

'He'll head up to the peak above that cabin,' Isolde said with certainty, pointing. 'See that outcrop of rock? That's just the sort of place he'd look for.'

'Are you sure?' Rollo queried, familiarizing himself with the landscape ahead. 'The dwarves have gone to our left.'

'No, but that's my best guess. You see, he certainly won't go near the cabin. He'll take the long route round and skirt out way to the left, keeping to the scrub of the high-ground and well away from the vale. That's why the dwarves have headed that way.' She nodded to her left. 'Come nightfall, he'll head up to that prominent rock where he can sit and howl and his voice will carry for miles through the stillness of twilight for other wolves to hear.'

'We could head straight through the valley and then lay in wait under the crag for the dwarves to come,' Rollo began to formulate a plan. 'That way, at least, we'll be rested when they make camp for the night.'

The whole scheme sounded reasonable, especially since it meant they could rest for a while. Surely, this time, they wouldn't be spotted by the dwarves and so would stand a chance of finding a way to steal Quinn back. With growing hope, they crept past the log cabin and found themselves a spot just beneath the escarpment from where they could look down into the valley. A small copse of birch trees grew in the shelter of a bracken-filled hollow, offering them shelter, and Rollo urged Isolde towards it.

'I'm hungry,' the girl complained in a strained whisper.

They had found water in a cool stream to slake their thirst but Rollo had to eat.

'Wait here,' he urged and slipped back towards the cabin.

He crept beneath the boughs of an old apple tree that was entirely stripped of leaves, the fruit long since harvested in the autumn before. He could see a chicken coop but knew there was no point trying to steal a chicken. For a start, it would raise the alarm but, also, they couldn't light a fire to cook it. In the end, he decided to slink to the back of the vegetable patch. Whoever lived here was keeping warm by the fire. He crept to the square of tilled earth, the patch of dark bare earth distinctive in the paler grey of the grass, and looked down at the withered offerings.

Carrots, nothing but carrots. He found a stick to help him

dig and began to pull them up. He managed to drag out about half a dozen before deciding he had left Isolde long enough. Hunched up over his prize, he ran back to the little hollow by the birch trees and found her fast asleep.

He couldn't believe that, with all the worry, she was actually sleeping but he was glad for her. The priestess was curled up in a little ball as if she were a tiny child. He sat down beside her and pulled her cloak up round her. Tucking her arms in, he noticed, with alarm, how cold her hands were. He then checked on her feet; they were like ice.

'Oh Isolde,' he murmured.

He didn't know what else to do so he crawled deeper into the hollow and pulled her onto his lap, tucking her feet under his jacket. He winced from the cold as the chill of her flesh drew the warmth from his body but, worried that she would lose her feet to frostbite, he gritted his teeth on the discomfort. She hadn't even stirred when he moved her. Closing her cloak tight about both of them to keep them warm, he wrapped his arms about her small bony body. Although he had gone to the trouble of fetching the carrots, he most certainly couldn't be bothered to eat any now.

'Poor little Isolde,' he murmured. A moment ago, he had been cursing this world and thinking how wretched things were when he, a prince of the fair land of Artor, was reduced to stealing carrots from a peasant's vegetable garden; but, now, he was no longer concerned about himself but only about this thin, helpless girl.

He wondered about the girl and her strange nature. His father had spoken highly of her and had told him how the three high priestesses were the most important people in all the world. He could imagine that to be true of Keridwen and even smiled at the thought. Apart from his mother, of course, Keridwen was undoubtedly the most wonderful person he had ever met. He had immediately found her to be strong and kind and not one bit like his father. She wasn't worried or judgmental. He had felt it in his bones that Keridwen had been concerned only about his happiness.

He wondered how Keridwen and Brid, who were so confident and authoritative, had managed to choose someone as weak as Isolde to be the Maiden. He could not understand it; she was a mouse, a terrified rabbit. She belonged in the fields, gleaning corn after the men had done their work. Or perhaps she would be happier still as a hermit.

Worrying that she was still too cold, he tightened his grip around her. His next concern was that he would fall asleep himself. It was growing rapidly colder as the sun dipped towards the distant horizon, sinking into a pool of mist on the flat skyline. His eyelids were beginning to sag and he kept jerking his lolling head back to keep himself awake.

The next time he snapped his eyes open it was suddenly dark and he realized to his horror that he must have actually fallen asleep. He shook himself and regretfully moved to wake Isolde. It seemed a shame and, for a moment, he wanted to let her sleep but, if they were going to find Quinn, they would have to move now. He soothed back the hair from her face and she groaned and pushed his hand away.

'Issy,' he whispered.

'No, go away,' she murmured and then suddenly she was bolt upright and wide-awake, staring at Rollo. 'What are you doing? What's happening? It's night! The moon!' she exclaimed, evidently taking in the scene all at once, looking at him and then herself and seeing how she was all curled up on his knee.

'You were cold,' he said by way of explanation. 'I was trying to keep you warm.'

She eased herself off him but not, he thought, with indignation at his closeness. Apparently, she was thinking only of one thing as she looked to the crag above them.

'He is there,' she murmured.

'I can't see a thing,' Rollo hissed, immediately missing the warm close comfort of the girl's body.

'He's there,' she insisted, drawing herself up to crawl out of the hollow and look out into the gloom. 'And if he's there, the dwarves won't be far behind. She eased herself up and crept forward to look down the long bony approach to the escarpment that skirted the perimeter of the dale.

Rollo crawled out of the hollow and peered through the branches of the birch trees. The dwarves had set up camp some distance out to their left far from the cabin and high up on the long approach to the craggy rock selected by the wolf. 'Well, Issy, it looks as though you were right after all,' he said with some relief. 'Well done you.'

Isolde seemed uncomfortable at being praised. 'Brid told me that was the way of dwarves. They do not cheat the night-time hours as men do. They have to sit and sing their songs and drink. Since the wolf is keeping still, they will assume that they can catch us in the morning.'

Hunkering down and keeping his head low, Rollo studied the dwarves, noting the four small campfires at the edge of their camp and one larger one at the centre. With the wind teasing Isolde's hair, which looked silvery in the moonlight, she stared down at the camp, her hands at her throat and her fingers clenched in tight knots of anxiety.

The dwarves' song wafted up on the wind just as the wolf rose from the ground and became a distinctive silhouette on the skyline behind them.

In days gone by, we loved our mead,
And all of us were merry.
But times are hard, the honey scarce,
So we drink wild elderberry.

If we can't have mead, it's ale we want
And ale we'll get tomorrow.
But as times are hard, the barley scarce
It's elder for our sorrow

No cider, stout nor frothy beer
And no pears to make sweet perry.
But if we can't have mead nor frothy ale
We drink the elderberry.

Rollo laughed. 'They can't be very dangerous if they sing like that.'

'I don't hear Quinn singing,' she said and silenced his humour.

Once it was fully dark, they crept towards the camp, Rollo now impressed by the girl's composure. The dancing fires made the surrounding shadows deeper. Rollo halted as the nearest of the four fires suddenly exploded in a shower of sparks that lessened to a more controlled and continuous display of dancing, coloured lights. He was enthralled by the flashes of bright colour as the three other fires likewise erupted into a shower of fireworks. Blues and greens sprayed out in garish fountains as each of the four dwarves on sentry duty tipped powders into the heart of the flames.

Chapter 22

Leaf's tears dripped onto the wilted bluebell that she still clutched to her breast. 'I shouldn't cry,' she sniffed. 'There's no point in crying,' her voice was hoarse and tight.

Caspar didn't really know how to comfort her. On one hand, she was no more than a child and yet, she seemed somehow superior to him. He wanted to pick her up and hug her but he held back, fearing that such an action might offend her.

'You will help me,' she told Caspar. 'You have to! The Great Mother brought you to me, I am sure of it. And there is so little time. There is no one else and I do not have the strength to do all that is needed alone.'

She looked up at Caspar, her straight brown hair sliding back off her shoulders, her eyes wide and imploring, the tears running freely down her face. She had changed out of her dress and was now clad in boy's clothing that made her look even younger. Perhaps it was because she was leaving her world for the first time that her precocious confidence was gone. She kept glancing back at the spires of her people's city and stroking the withered bluebell her father had given her.

'Poor Father. What will they do to him without me? I still don't know if I should leave him. Someone has to protect him.'

Caspar stopped and pulled her round to face him, taking both her hands in his. 'The Great Mother has, indeed, brought us together for a purpose; we need each other. I shall help you and you will help me.'

'You will keep to your promise?' she sniffed.

He nodded calmly. 'Of course. And there's no point staying by your father's side if you cannot find the cure for the ailment that afflicts him and all your people. I am sure he would rather suffer if it means that you find a way to help his people.'

'When we have found your son, you'll help me rescue my father, help me find a way to save my people? They are dying; he is dying.' The sobs turned to a flood of tears and she fell against Caspar.

Her little bones felt so small beneath his touch as he eventually hugged her to him. He knelt down and pushed the wet strands of hair back from her damp face. 'Leaf, don't despair. I promised I shall help you and I will keep to my promise. Now, that is the word of the Baron of Torra Alta and no Torra Altan goes back on his word. There has to be an answer, a cure for the disease and I know many people who have great learning in such matters. They will find what is causing it.'

'Silas is causing it,' the young girl said bitterly.

'How can Silas be doing that?' Caspar asked reasonably. 'It's more likely something you are eating or something that's got into the water supply. Ragwort has such an effect, I believe.'

'Ragwort also makes people tremble and induces a state of fear. That is not the case here,' Leaf told him, demonstrating her knowledge.

'How do you know?'

She smiled in an almost patronizing manner at him. 'It was the very first thing we checked. We screened all our foods for poisons and tested our water supply. No, it is from within us that this disease emanates and I am certain that Silas is preying off it. I don't know what he's up to but it's just too incredible that, single-handedly, he continues to produce the mammoths to appease the dragon!' She laughed as if the idea were utterly ludicrous.

'But he does, doesn't he?' Caspar asked, a little confused.

'Oh, yes, he does. But how does one man lift a mammoth onto that contraption of his?' Leaf asked. 'He comes striding back as if he's our sole saviour and so graciously accepts our lavish gratitude. But one man alone to do that? It's not credible. How does he do it?'

'Pulleys, ropes and horses?' he suggested.

'That's what everyone tells me but it makes no sense. Even Mother told me that but, that was when it was just the great taurs that he brought back. Now it's mammoths!'

'If everyone tells you so, don't you think that perhaps they are right?' Caspar suggested.

'No, because it doesn't make sense! Why does he bother to keep on bringing the offerings to deter the dragon? Why doesn't he just go to a safer part of the world? He doesn't have to help us.'

'Well, actually, Leaf, that's not so hard to understand,' Caspar said and smiled at her, thinking that she was actually far more naïve than he had judged her to be. In a way, that made him feel better and he felt less in awe of her intellect. It had been rather unnerving to feel in the shadow of a little child.

'There is nowhere now that is exactly safe,' he explained. 'Dangerous creatures rove all the corners of the world and there is no escaping them. Somehow or other, we all have to find a way to feed ourselves and put clothes on our backs. And Silas, however he does it, has managed to find a way to become very important indeed. He has a country indebted to him. No doubt, he dreams of having a palace built for himself and servants and an endless supply of money. He'll say to Zophia that he can't protect her people without this and without that and sooner or later he will deliberately be late with an offering just to be sure that everyone knows how important he is to them.' Caspar paused and thought about what he had just said. 'Or perhaps that is what he has already been doing. Perhaps that was why he let your village burn.'

'He let my village burn to be rid of me. He knows I'm

coming to an age when people will take heed of me, yet am not old enough to be suffering the effects of the disease. He wanted me out of the way. It's as simple as that. Which means, of course, that he had some means of luring the dragon to my particular village.'

'But the dragon burnt about three or four villages in your vicinity. It did not burn just your village.' Caspar protested.

Leaf pouted. 'Probably to make it look less obvious that she was after me. But it has struck terror into my people's hearts and so they will value Silas's help all the more.'

Caspar laughed. 'And you're telling me that a dragon had the forethought and intelligence to help in all that!'

The young girl shrugged and fell silent as the road took them past a lake cradled in the bottom of a green vale. White cattle were grazing down by the water's edge and one or two had waded in up to their knees to drink, their reflections rippling as their breath caressed the water. Crocuses and early bluebells danced beneath the trees.

'It is very beautiful here.'

Leaf nodded, wiping away her tears. 'I know; that's why I'm afraid to leave. Here it is peaceful and calm. I could sit by the lake and read or play the flute with no fear that some hob or taur is going to leap out of the woods at any moment and snatch me away. It is safe. I do not want to go out there.' She nodded to the road that stretched on past the windmill that they had seen from Xanthia's tower.

'It's not so bad,' he murmured, his mind already beyond the confines of the secret realm.

Once they passed the windmill, there was a subtle change in the atmosphere. Caspar didn't notice it at first as he stepped into the shadow of the mill whose sails turned so very slowly in the quiet breeze. But once beyond it, he noted that the air was distinctly cooler. Drifts of lazy mist seeped down the slopes of the vale about them and rolled down towards the road. Gradually, the mist grew thicker, the air even cooler until, before he knew it, Caspar could see no more than a few yards in any direction.

He took Leaf's hand and tugged her on. 'Come on, into the mist we must go,' he said with forced confidence. 'Please tell me that you know the way.'

She nodded. 'Yes, of course I know the way. And I have Mother's amulet. While you were with Grandma, I wasn't just changing my clothes; I had time to collect a few things.'

To prove her point, she drew out a small charm from within her shirt. In the time she had been away, she had been able to find herself a pair of boy's breeches, a stout pair of boots, a heavily starched shirt, a leather jerkin and a cloak. She carried a woollen jacket and a very long scarf but it was too warm to wear them at present. She looked a little like a pixie with her hair now scooped up into two knots on either side of her head. Her thick woollen cloak was fastened with a heavy brooch pin that looked far too valuable to be so openly worn. Still, she looked well-dressed enough to survive the chill on the far side of the barrier protecting this peaceful land.

The amulet was dangling from a fine chain, which she held aloft. She allowed the pendant to swing forward and back, wafting it into the mist, which stirred and parted, slowly opening up a channel through the murky vapours. Caspar stepped boldly forward, uncomfortably conscious of the dampness of the air and the way it crept into his lungs making breathing difficult. As they paced forwards, the mist swirled behind them almost as if it were alive. He fancied the fingers of a giant spirit were closing in about them and drawing them into its grasp.

The dampness soaked in through his clothing, making his flesh cringe at the cold touch. Leaf hastily slipped on her jacket and scarf beneath her cloak. Nervously, he reached out and snagged the edge of Leaf's cloak.

'I think we should be very careful not to get separated,' he warned her. 'Keep close; I can barely see you.' Particles of icy dust were floating into his eye. Suddenly he bumped into Leaf who had stopped right in his path. 'What's the matter?' he asked anxiously.

'I don't know,' she said uncertainly as she swung her pendant into the mist, which now cleared only the narrowest path ahead. 'It doesn't seem to be working as well as it should.'

Caspar groaned inwardly. But, worried that Leaf might lose her nerve altogether and, with it, her reason, he tried to keep as calm as possible. 'What makes you think something is wrong?' he asked nonchalantly.

'The mist should part more easily. Definitely, it should.' The girl swiped at the icy particles before her eyes.

Caspar brushed his crooked nose to stop the particles tickling him. 'They are thickening, I agree,' he said matter-of-factly, though he was struggling to remain calm.

Leaf nodded and to Caspar's dismay, she began to sob. 'I don't understand. The amulet should work; I took it straight from Mother's jewellery box. This is the one that unlocks the doorways through the mist. I know it is.' She turned, put her arms about Caspar and began to sob against his belly. 'Spar, help me. I'm scared.'

'Hush, don't be afraid. No magic works well when you're scared. You have to believe in it and since you know that—'

'But it isn't magic,' Leaf protested. 'It's just a key that unlocks the way.' She snatched at the mist and opened her hand. 'Look at it, Spar. Look! What has he done?' She was quiet for the briefest of moments before clapping her hands together and answering her question for herself. 'He's altered the formula on the amulet; that's what he has done. He knows I might find a way and he's changed it so that I might be lost in here forever.' Her face whitened at the prospect.

Caspar was staring at the plain gold amulet dangling from the chain. 'Perhaps we can work out the answer together. Let's have a look at your amulet.'

Obediently, Leaf dropped it into the palm of his hand. He

blinked at it, noting that there were a number of interlocked runes etched into the plain bar of metal. 'What does it say? Is it possible that these runes have been written only for your mother or for Silas?' Caspar asked.

Leaf shook her head. 'I don't think so. It doesn't have my mother's insignia on it. It just has the mark of my people.'

'Where? Show me the mark,' Caspar requested.

Leaf indicated the lowest design on the configuration of characters. 'That, there, is the mark of the quill; it is the insignia of the scholars.'

He nodded thoughtfully whilst trying to make sense of the other symbols etched into the gold.

'Do you know what the rest of the markings mean?' he asked hopefully.

Leaf shook her head and Caspar sniffed, dropping his head and trying to think. It was then that he noted the faint blue of the sky overhead. 'I wonder if I lifted you up onto my shoulders that you might be able to see above the mist,' he suggested.

Leaf nodded. 'It is certainly worth a try.' Her hands were cold on his skin as she clambered up and positioned herself on his shoulders. 'Ha!' she laughed in delighted triumph. 'You are right, Spar. That was so clever of you.'

Caspar was beginning to find it troubling that both Xanthia and Leaf had described him as clever that day. It was very rare that anyone had credited him with those credentials of late. Even his wife's advisors had kept him at arm's length, always saying that he did not understand the people of Artor.

'What can you see?' he asked anxiously.

'I can see just the tips of a tree, a huge white poplar,' she related.

'Great!' Caspar breathed, deciding that their troubles would shortly be over. 'Just keep steering me towards it. This mist can't go on forever.'

'Head left a little,' Leaf ordered, kicking her heel into

his chest in her excitement and tightening her grip about his throat.

Caspar grunted in complaint. 'I am neither a horse nor do I wish to be throttled.'

'I'm sorry,' she said tightly. 'But can't you hurry?'

'I'm doing my best,' he protested, stumbling on though he found it most disconcerting walking into a wall of white. He coughed once or twice, disliking the way the dampness sank into his lungs. 'We'll both have pneumonia,' he complained.

'Right a little, now,' Leaf urged him, ignoring his moans. 'We're getting closer. Hey! Look out!'

Caspar had stumbled and reached out one hand to save himself while desperately trying to cling onto Leaf with the other. He kept upright and saved her from tumbling to the ground but not without first pulling a muscle in his shoulder. It hurt and made him feel slightly sick but there was nothing for it but to carry on.

'Are you all right?' he asked her through gritted teeth, hoping that, if he kept moving, the pain would ease.

'Just about,' she grunted in acknowledgement.

'I tripped on a log, I think,' Caspar explained, moving on a little more slowly now.

He brushed his feet forward and decided that he must be moving through ferns or rushes by the sound of things. His eyes were beginning to ache from continually staring into the whiteness that surrounded him. He edged on and was further alarmed by the distinctive sound of a splash. He had stepped into a puddle and could feel the firm earth give as his boot sunk into mud.

'Can you still see the tree?' he asked Leaf.

'Yes, yes,' she urged. 'You're exactly on the right track.'

He muttered to himself and halted. 'What's the matter?' Leaf queried his action.

'The ground's wet.'

'Oh,' she commented, apparently understanding his dilemma

at once. 'Try going on just a little way and see if it's just a puddle or if it gets deeper.'

Caspar took a step back, reluctant to follow this advice. 'I think we had better think about this. I don't wish to walk into a swamp.' He eased Leaf down from his shoulders and noted that she was shivering 'I think we should work our way round the edge of the water,' he suggested.

'But that could take forever,' Leaf immediately argued. 'Here!' She handed him one end of her scarf. 'You take hold of one end and wade in while I hold the other. Then we can keep in contact and you'll be less likely to stumble. Perhaps it's no more than a few feet across.'

Caspar nodded. Leaf's plan seemed perfectly reasonable. 'Have you got a firm grip on your end?' he asked.

'Very,' she assured him.

'Good!' With one hand tightly on the scarf, he took small tentative steps forward across the sodden ground. 'It's not too deep yet,' he called out after he had gone just a few paces but Leaf's form was already no more than a shadow in the haze. 'You can follow me in a little way and see how far we get.'

'Right!' she called back.

Caspar took another step and then another until he was at the extremity of the scarf and probably no more than six feet from Leaf though it felt like a mile. Already, she had been utterly swallowed by the blanketing cloud of crystalline particles. With each step, the mire was getting just a little deeper and was now dragging at his boots. But there was still a firm footing and he thought it safe to tread a little further.

'Keep talking to me, Leaf,' he implored, disliking the eerie quiet of the mist and the sense of loneliness that being unable to see induced.

'I'm right here,' she said. 'Just keep on going. But go steadily,' she added.

Caspar took another three steps and was pleased to find that it was no longer getting any deeper. He hoped that they were managing to keep a true course and were still heading straight for the poplar, which was their only landmark. It certainly didn't feel as if he had veered off course.

Very quickly, Leaf's attempts to talk failed and so he thought to provoke her into conversation. 'Your grandmother, the Lady Xanthia, she didn't really seem mad at all. It was just as if she enjoyed teasing me.'

'She liked you,' Leaf said though Caspar did not see the relevance in that statement.

He laughed. Despite all his difficulties he was quite gratified to have won the approval of the dowager. 'How do you know?'

'Oh, she said so just as we were leaving,' Leaf explained. 'She said I was to take care of you because, if the rest of mankind were like you, then they were probably worth saving after all.'

Caspar laughed again. 'She only liked me because I guessed the answer to her riddle.'

'Indeed?' Leaf actually sounded impressed. 'There's few that could keep you company in that boast. She used to annoy many of my people and they would say that her mind did not follow the clear thought-patterns of our kind.' Leaf dropped her voice to a conspiratorial tone that seemed hardly necessary where they were in the mist. 'She is not, of course, truly of the blood. I believe that is why she hasn't been so severely affected by the illness.'

'Then perhaps you too are less at risk.'

'I don't think so. After all, my father has been stricken, so whatever foreign blood is in Xanthia's veins was already diluted by the time it was handed down to him and, of course, even more so by the time it reached me.' Leaf's voice sounded faint through the mist. 'My mother is certainly true blooded. She is very much a scholar. Her father was the most revered scholar of his time and I am certain that there is no blight in her lineage.'

'Your grandmother reminds me of the people of Ash,'

Caspar said with certainty. 'They are a light-hearted people and extremely attractive. Xanthia was once remarkably beautiful, I am sure.'

'The funny thing,' Leaf went on through chattering teeth, 'is that Xanthia was always considered to be at a mental disadvantage, but now everyone else her age has barely a jot of sense left. The irony . . .,' she sighed.

'The ability to remember facts is not the be all and end all of intelligence,' Caspar pontificated, needing to talk about almost anything so long as they remained in audible contact. 'Some people have an instinct about things that can make them far more acute and knowledgeable than those who only learn from reading. The people of Ash, for instance, are very attuned to the subtle changes in nature and are extremely observant. Though they are not learned and barely read they are, in their own way, extremely clever.'

'Clever indeed! From what I've read, they are entirely strange. Sensitive, yes, I do agree with you,' Leaf answered thoughtfully as if she were a young lady rather than a child. 'But they do not know the things we know.' She sighed. 'Knew,' she corrected herself. 'Spar, my toes are cold. The water is seeping in through the leather of my boots. Do you think it's much further?'

'I hope not,' he answered, now worrying about how he was going to find Brid once they reached the far side of the mist.

'Do you think Silas will have taken Brid very far?' he asked.

His question was met only with silence and Caspar tugged on the scarf just to reassure himself that she was still there. It was so eerie talking to a disembodied voice in the smoky gloom. 'Leaf! Answer me.'

'I was just thinking,' she said defensively. 'Silas wasn't gone long the first time he took Brid. After showing his face back in the hidden realm, he must have gone back for her. He wouldn't have gone to all that effort to have her released specifically into his care, if he didn't want her for something.'

'What could Silas possibly want with Brid?' Caspar asked.

'What could Silas possibly want with my mother?' Leaf retorted by way of reply.

Caspar did not find her answer particularly helpful. 'I told you; she brings him power. He gets to save an entire city; he gets to be treated like a prince.'

Leaf sniffed. 'That is not a big enough prize. What is the fun of being treated like a prince by madmen? He is nothing but a prince of fools, a king of jesters. There is no future, no pride in that. No, what Silas is seeking is something more, I am sure of it.'

Caspar sighed; the girl was almost certainly right. He felt more as if he were talking to his mother than a girl of his daughter's age. Her arguments were conclusive and thoughtful and her manner far too calm for a youngster.

'Now,' she continued. 'Silas wasn't gone that long. His horse was sweated and he had ridden hard but he was gone no more than a couple of hours, which only gave him enough time to reach the edge of our lands and then return. Wherever he left Brid, it's not far beyond the other side of the mist. All we have to do is . . .' There was a pause in her speech.

'Leaf, are you there?' The scarf was slack and Caspar's heart was suddenly pounding in his mouth. 'Leaf!'

'Yes, I'm here,' she said somewhat closer to him now than before and he foolishly realized that he had himself stopped and that she had caught up with him a little. The water was now close to the top of his boots and, as she approached, he felt the wave created by her hurrying legs wash up and slop into his boots. 'This water is cold,' Leaf moaned into his back.

Caspar peered through the haze at her faint outline. 'You must be soaked right through,' he scolded her.

'I know but I didn't like being left so far behind,' she explained.

He grunted at her in disapproval. The whole idea of staying separated is that, if I get in to trouble, you can perhaps help me by holding on to that scarf. And if you can't, well, at least you won't be getting into trouble yourself and you'll be no worse off than if you'd never met me.'

'What are you talking about?' Leaf scolded him in return. 'You can't turn back the wheel of time. Maybe one day we'll work out how to do it but not yet.'

Caspar ignored her remark. 'Well, put your clever little brain to use and tell me how much further you think we should wade. It seems to be getting deeper and I can feel a current. In your estimation, are we crossing a narrow expanse of water and so will soon be rising up the far bank or do you think we're at the edge of a treacherous swamp?'

'How do you think I could know that?' she asked as if he were quite unthinking.

'That's precisely what I meant before. A woman of Ash would know the answer. She would dip her fingers into the water and sense her environment from it. But neither you nor I have that instinct. What I am trying to say, Leaf, is that I don't know what to do. Should we keep on going or should we retrace our steps and see if we can find a way round this marshy place?'

'If we retrace our steps in this fog, we're bound to end up going in circles. It's still shallow so there doesn't seem any sense in giving up just yet,' Leaf argued. 'Only . . .' She stopped short.

'Only . . . ?' Caspar prompted.

'Only it's so cold and I'm finding it hard to think straight,' she confessed.

'I'm sorry.' He reached for her tiny hand and squeezed it. 'As soon as we get through this, I'll light a fire,' he said, forcing himself to sound unworried. Her skin was icy to the touch and he feared that the coldness of the mist and the water would soon be too much for her small body to bear; he had to hurry and yet knew that he could not for fear of drowning them both. 'Stand still while I feel my way forward.'

'We should have picked up a stout stick so that you could probe the way ahead,' Leaf said with some regret.

'Well, it's no use thinking of sensible things now we're so deep into this. Have you got a good hold of that scarf?'

'Yes,' Leaf said firmly.

Worried that the young girl was becoming dangerously cold, Caspar waded on a little faster, becoming more and more concerned as the water began to slosh up around his thighs and soak his breeches, stinging his skin with needles of icy cold. This was an outrageously mad thing to do, he told himself. Suddenly, he was aware that the current around him was moving very much faster. The ground was less muddy and he was standing on crunching gravel that shifted a little beneath his feet. Clearly, they were in a shallow river. Perhaps they had finally reached the midstream.

He became aware of the noise of the water all around him as it played over the stone and of a distant roar as the river tumbled and twisted, perhaps through rapids or maybe over a weir or into a mill leat; it was impossible to say.

Taking one more step forward, he found the firmness of rock beneath his feet. He shifted his weight onto it but the rock abruptly twisted beneath him and he slipped down its far side. The riverbed was suddenly shelving away from him. He put his hands out to save himself as his feet were swept out from under him by the force of the current. His face plunged into black icy water. The dark and the cold were disorientating and frightening but nothing to the realization that he was being swept out into the fast flow of a sizeable river.

He thrashed his arms, immediately aware that there was no resistance from the scarf that he still gripped tightly in his fist. Instinctively, he stretched up for the surface though without success. Then his feet touched down on the gravel bottom and he was able to kick up, fighting his way towards the air. He gulped in a lungful but then lost his footing again. This time, as he plunged back into the water, his forehead knocked against rock and, for a moment, he saw nothing but a redness behind his eyes.

Air! He must have air, he told himself as he became more and more disorientated by the cold, the spinning current and his damaged head. His feet found gravel again and he managed to push himself to the surface where he was spun round and around in the fast-moving eddies. As he struggled to keep his head up, the roar of tumbling water further downstream steadily grew louder and louder.

Suddenly he was spinning along with the rushing current, the muscles on his face cramping with cold and his legs and arms barely responding. There was nothing he could do as the current raced him over a liquid arc before plunging him downwards in a froth of bubbles. His lungs were fit to burst when his hand touched something solid. Gripping on tight, he hauled himself through the water until his head was above the surface. The solid object turned out to be a long slippery beam that jutted from the bank into the water and it was that alone that saved him.

He gasped in air, his fingers having difficulty scrabbling for the bank as exhaustion loosened his grip. Coughing out the water, he crawled beyond the pull of the river and spluttered into the gloom. The mist was now much thicker all about him. Gratefully, he patted the slimy beam jutting into the water from the bank. Without it, he would have drowned. At last, he found the strength to drag his upper body up onto the bank that, here, was not so marshy as it had been upstream.

Shivering violently, his teeth chattering so loudly that he could barely think, he dragged his lower half forward until he was at last clear of the water.

'Leaf!' he moaned. 'Leaf!' He couldn't raise his voice beyond a moan and now realized his next problem was that he was alone and did not have the vaguest idea how he was going to find the girl.

He should move. He must move. But exhausted from the struggle and the cold, he barely had the will. He pushed himself up to his feet and then slumped back down onto his knees. He was just too cold! Shivering violently, he dropped his forehead back down to the ground. Perhaps he could just give up and lie here? It was just so difficult to fight off the cold. Then, very slowly, the image of his son calling out for him, begging him for help, swam into his head. If he didn't fight off this lethargy, if he didn't struggle to find his son . . . he couldn't bear to think on it. Rollo needed him! He must find Rollo.

'Rollo!' he called into the mist. 'Rollo! Rollo! I'm coming!'

How was he going to get out of here? The mist couldn't continue forever. If only he could get through it, he would get warm. If he just started to move, he would get warm. But where was Leaf to help him?

'Leaf, Leaf!' he croaked. He needed her; he needed her and her amulet.

Chapter 23

The guards posted at the portcullis shrank back.

Hal was aware of the flashes of terror in their eyes as he rode through their number. Had he really become so formidable?

The thought didn't trouble him for long as he hastened forward, his eyes scanning Torra Alta's central courtyard for signs of Keridwen. He could not see her but knew she would be watching. The thought deepened his frown. He was not unused to the feel of her critical gaze; she alone showed no fear of him but eyed him coolly, and often with disapproval.

He knew that most of the men remained loyal only because of her. She had won their trust through fifteen years of shared hardship. Her grief of course, was as acute as his, for he did not doubt the depth of her love for those who were missing, yet she was not devoured by it.

Though his boots were wet from the ride and his hands scratched to shreds by the thickets of blackthorns they had searched that day, he was not pleased to be home. He would never be pleased until the day he returned with his family. Thumping his heels into his horse's side, he clattered across the courtyard, not caring whom he knocked out of his way. Smartly, he dismounted and thrust his reins into the stable master's hands.

Nervously, the man glanced into his ill-tempered face and somehow managed to steel himself to speak out.

'Sir . . .,' the stablemaster said quietly.

'What is it?' Hal demanded gruffly, annoyed at being

delayed. His thoughts were on his wife and son and he felt his anger rise at the man's intrusion.

'Sir, I know it's not my place to say but perhaps it is that you don't know. I . . .,' the stablemaster began but then faltered.

'Get on with it, man, and tell me!' Hal bellowed at him.

The stablemaster was stroking the horse and would not look across at the nobleman but only at the sweated animal whose head was drooping down by his knees. 'We do not have any more horses to spare, Sir. She has carried you without rest for days and nights on end and look at her now, Sir. This animal will be dead by morning. Horses do not know when to stop. They will run until they drop. They place their trust in us and . . .'

The raven-haired nobleman stared at the sweat-soaked beast, her legs shaking beneath her as she staggered towards her stall. She was given a large bucket of water and was vigorously rubbed down but Hal could see she was not strong enough to drink. And if she did not drink, she would die as the stablemaster predicted.

Resentfully, he glared at the man. 'I will kill every horse in this stable to get my wife and son back,' he growled. 'You think, I care about a horse? Any horse? He took a deep breath and paused before adding quietly but no less vehemently, 'I will permit no chink of weakness within these walls. You are mistaken in voicing such an opinion and I will hear no more of it.'

Hal did, in fact, feel a degree of regret about the horse and admired the man's courage in standing up to him. But he was furious that the stablemaster should publicly blame him. It was not his fault: he had to do everything he could, however many horses died; all that mattered was finding his wife and his missing kin.

His frustration at his failure to find them pushed his emotions beyond his control and a growl burst from his throat. It was only his admiration for the stablemaster that stayed him from striking. With restraint, he turned his back but, unable to contain the sudden rush of venom, he snatched up a stable pitchfork and swung it with all his force against one of the stalls. With a satisfying crack, the pitchfork snapped. He hurled the broken shaft down at the feet of a trembling stable lad, who jumped back in fear and scurried away to the back of the stables, frantically busying himself with Hal's tack.

Drawing his trembling hand up to his brow, he fought to still the anguish within. All these men at his command and they had found nothing. He blinked, trying to steady his thoughts. He must eat and rest, otherwise, he would be no good to his wife. Soon, the other parties would be home – maybe with news. Soon, someone would hear of or find something that would lead him to his wife. He tried hard to force from his mind the thought of what horrors had befallen them, but could not help fearing the hobs had eaten them alive.

Dazed, he staggered through the twin doors of the stables and then stopped and tried to bring a smile to his face. Before him was a small child. Her hair in ragged knots and her face unwashed, she stood clinging to the little doll that she had not once put down since her mother's disappearance.

Hal swallowed. 'Brannella,' he murmured with deep, over-whelming love. The look of her tore at his insides; her beautiful face was streaked with tears and her eyes were red and swollen but she stood there bravely biting back her lower lip, a smile lifting her mouth as she looked up at him, full of hope.

Reaching down, he scooped her up and held her to him. 'What are you doing out here alone? I told you never, ever to leave Keridwen's side. Never!' he scolded, his tone harsher than he intended.

Hal regretted his actions. He did not want his little girl to hate him but he was terrified for her. The hobs had crawled in and taken everything else that he loved; when would they come for her?

'Pa, did you find her? You promised me you would find her,' she said softly, and with no sign of being alarmed at the harshness of his censure.

Hal held her all the more tightly to him, blinking back the tears from his eyes. 'Not yet, Brannella, but I shall soon. We will never give up.'

Looking up from the child's face, he saw with relief that, indeed, Brannella had not strayed far from Keridwen's side. The priestess was crossing the inner courtyard to greet him.

On seeing his expression, she nodded sadly and Hal knew there was no need to explain that he had found no trace of their missing loved ones.

'I see you've been taking it out on your girl, as usual,' the priestess said with bitterness. 'Don't forget that she is suffering just as much as you and I.' She didn't wait for him to defend himself. 'I've come to tell you, there's a messenger from Ceowulf waiting for you.'

Hal responded at once, thrusting Brannella into Keridwen's arms with a force that nearly toppled her. He ran to the keep, knocking aside two of his servants that stood in his way. Two at a time, he mastered the stairs and swung open the door to the great hall where the messenger was waiting.

Like most from the southern barony of Caldea, the man had thick black hair and his skin was darkly tanned. Caldea, which was joined to the rest of Belbidia only by a thin isthmus, was under the jurisdiction of Baron Ceowulf, who was perhaps the only man Hal could call his friend. Hal took a deep breath, gathering his composure as the messenger almost dropped his tankard onto the table and jumped smartly to his feet, hastily wiping the froth from his mouth before saluting.

'My Lord Hal, Baron Ceowulf sends his greetings and well-wishes in these troubled times.'

Hal stepped forward calmly. Though supplies were scarce of late, he was glad to see that his hospitality had been extended towards the messenger. 'Do not trouble me with formalities,' he said as he drew out a chair at the end of the table nearest the fire and nodded at the messenger to sit beside him. 'Tell me everything.'

'I had trouble getting through,' the man started hesitantly. 'Faronshire is impassable and your own barony is a perilous place in which to travel.'

Hal nodded. 'I know. I do not have enough men; and the hobs are numerous. The mountains are still ours but the border between us and Jotunn has become hazardous. I cannot get through to Baron Oxgard anymore. I have tried and will try again for I still hope that he has heard something of my family.'

'I had to take a boat and approach from the north,' the messenger explained. 'Baron Ceowulf is convinced that, if we are to fight off these hobs, we must first unite Belbidia. He is holding both Caldea and Piscera now. The Baron of Piscera has given him martial jurisdiction of his men but we have had no word from King Rewik.'

'I regret I can offer Ceowulf nothing until I have found my wife and my son,' Hal managed to squeeze the words through the dryness of his throat.

The Caldean messenger drew in a deep breath. 'I learned today of your loss. I do not speak my own mind but that of your friend's, Baron Ceowulf. He does not know of this new sorrow but he anticipated that you might seek only to defend Torra Alta and asked me to say that, whatever happens, you must keep a road open to the western coast. If not, you will be cut off within the month; the hobs are clamping their grip hard around the north.'

Hal sighed at this. How could he spare the men?

The messenger continued, 'Baron Ceowulf has tried to get word to Baron Wiglaf in Nattarda but he has had no word back and it is rumoured that the land is devastated by a plague of green dragons. We cannot reach Jotunn.'

Hal nodded. 'Yes, as I said, we have tried too. Baron Oxgard is in trouble. Like us, his supplies will be growing short.' He rubbed at the stump of his left hand that was sore from bruises and cuts. He had killed eight hobs that day; the memory of their dying shrieks still rang in his mind. He had not even had time to wash their blood from his hands and rid himself of his stinking clothes.

Without warning, he picked up the half full tankard of ale that the messenger had placed on the table and, standing, hurled it at the wall. But it wasn't enough to ease the torment in his soul and so he turned on one of the dogs that dared to come irritatingly close and swiped at it with a chair. The animal yelped and limped away. One of the fat Ophidian terriers sat up and bared his teeth at Hal, a soft growl gurgling in its throat.

The messenger had risen and taken one or two steps back in alarm and was watching him anxiously. Collecting himself, Hal smiled and calmly sat back down as if nothing had happened.

His head throbbed and he stared blankly at his good right hand; it was trembling. Clenching his fist, he willed himself to retrieve his self-control. 'Tell Ceowulf that I will keep a road open to the west, running between the Yellow Mountains and the Boarchase Forest. My men will see to it while I continue to look for my family. Ceowulf will understand.'

'He will send food and what men he can for your service. Some of the farmers from Faronshire and the other baronies have stout hearts and have come to him to offer their services,' the messenger informed him.

Hal nodded. 'That is good.' He snapped his head round at a sound behind him. One of his servants had tiptoed in with a plate of food and was timorously placing it on the table behind him. 'What is this?' Hal roared. 'Are we now such barbarians that you offer me food before my guest?'

'No, sir, no! I—I—' the man stammered, unable to express himself in the face of the nobleman's anger.

Hal was about to hurl the hot food back into the servant's face when he caught sight of his daughter standing in the doorway. As always, she was clinging tightly to her ragged doll. Hal wanted to burn it. Every second he saw that doll, it reminded him that Brid was lost, that his son was missing, and that Caspar, Quinn and Rollo were gone. His breathing was becoming faster and his hand trembled with rage at his sorrow.

Brannella was staring expectantly at the messenger. 'Is it word of Ma?' she demanded.

Unable to bear the sight of his daughter vainly raising her hopes, Hal thought he would burst. Choking back the rising cry of anguish in his throat, he tried to shake his head. He wanted to tear the doll from his daughter's hands. Thankfully Keridwen was suddenly there behind Brannella, stroking the girl's jet-black hair, her presence enabling Hal to think more clearly.

'No, sweetheart,' the woman murmured gently to the young child, 'he has no news of Brid.'

Brannella swallowed and Hal did not know how he was going to bear her disappointment. The girl looked up forlornly at Keridwen and then fled to her father, flinging her arms around his neck and kissing him.

'Don't worry, Pa, she's coming home.' Brannella sniffed back her sobs. 'She promised me and Ma would never break a promise.'

Hal buried his head in her hair that hid his tears and breathed in the sweet scent of innocent hope.

Chapter 24

Rollo eased forward on his belly and looked on the scene before him with wonder.

'Rollo, please! What are you doing?' Isolde hissed behind him.

Her hand slid around his ankle, but he was barely conscious of it; the fascinating fires and their wonderful colours were all absorbing. He had idled away the long, lonely winter evenings of his childhood, feeding the flames in the hearth in his room with various combinations of offerings in attempt to make the flames flicker with different colours. He loved fire; it was a wondrous magic! His pulse was beginning to race with excitement as a shower of green sparks sprayed out from the nearest fire. How were they doing that?

'Ow!' he complained under his breath as something sharp dug into his ankle and then realized that Isolde was trying to drag him back and had pinched him to bring him to his senses. Remembering himself, he slithered backwards to her side, shrinking from the sphere of light cast by the dwarves' fires.

'What were you thinking of?' Isolde asked, exasperation getting the better of her quiet nature.

'Thinking? I—I—' Rollo stammered, still mesmerized and confused for the moment about what he was supposed to be doing. 'It was just the fires.' Even though they had slunk out of their hollow and crept down towards the dwarves, they were able to talk quite freely for the riotous noise from the camp.

Isolde tugged at his arm. 'I can't see him,' she hissed. 'Where is he? Surely he should still be with them. Unless . . . You don't think they've . . .'

'Don't panic, we can't see everything from here,' the Artoran tried to reassure her, taking her hand as they crept around the edge of the camp. When they reached the far side, Isolde froze and put her other hand on Rollo's to halt him. She nodded towards what had appeared to be no more than a humped shape near the central fire but, even from that distance, Rollo knew the shrouded figure was Quinn. The hood of his cloak was pulled down low, and the light shone off his pale face. There was an empty plate lying in front of his crossed legs and it was a relief to see that at least the dwarves had actually fed him.

Rollo and Isolde retreated a little distance to formulate a plan.

'What do we do now?' Rollo fretted. 'We can't exactly walk right in there, can we? Even if we wait until they are finished with their storytelling, there are four sentries and Quinn's tied up with his hands behind him.'

Isolde chewed at her lip and cast her eyes up towards the moon before checking to see that the wolf was still perched on the rocky promontory. 'Somehow we need to draw them from the camp so that they leave him unattended.'

'And how do you propose we do that?' Rollo sneered.

Isolde did not reply.

Still at a loss for a feasible plan, they both stared into the camp. The most thick-set of the twelve dwarves was marching up and down, waving something small about in his hand. He wore a broad-rimmed hat that looked out of place coupled with a metal breastplate that gleamed beneath his tunic. He seemed fascinated by the object clutched in his grip and, when he held it up to the firelight, Rollo could see that it was a small black sphere.

Isolde made a low guttural sound of anger very softly in

her throat. Rollo thought the sound to be most unnatural coming from a girl. 'What's the matter?' he asked.

'It's Quinn's onyx. Look at that dwarf with his grubby fists all over it.' She snapped her teeth together in outrage and Rollo twisted round to stare at her, very much surprised by the vehemence of her action. Isolde shrank further back into the gloom and began tugging at her hair in frustration. 'I can't believe it. We've got this close and we can't think of a way to rescue him.'

He had no answer for her and looked back at the camp.

'How did he know?' she asked out loud.

'How did he know what?' Rollo asked, irritated by her inadequate communication. He waited a moment for her to reply but she was, once more, lost in thought and oblivious to his question. Sitting out here all night in the cold was not his idea of a good plan. He drew out two of the carrots from his pocket and offered one to Isolde. To his surprise, she took it, rubbed it vigorously to be rid of the dirt and began to chew.

'I thought you would be too upset to eat,' he remarked in some surprise.

She looked at him slightly askance but said nothing.

Shrugging, Rollo turned his attention back to the carrot, brushing off as much of the earth with his good hand as he could before taking a bite. It was surprisingly sweet and the process of chewing eased some of his tension.

'We wait,' he said slowly, at last coming up with the beginnings of a plan. 'Listen to them singing and see the amount they are drinking – mead by the smell of it. And mead is potent stuff. Even the sentries are drinking. Have you ever seen anyone drink as much as that? They'll all be sound asleep within the hour and too drunk to notice a thing. They certainly won't worry themselves about predators because no prowling beast is going to try and get past those fires.'

'You think we should wait until they are drunk and

then creep in?' Isolde asked, in an attempt to clarifying his sketchy plan.

'Well, not exactly,' he added hurriedly, hearing in her tone that she thought such a plan a little lacking in content. 'No, I'm sure they will leave someone to watch over Quinn so we'll still have to create a distraction. One of us should distract the watch while the other rushes in to retrieve Quinn.'

To his great surprise and gratification, Isolde nodded. 'That's half a plan, I have to admit.' She smiled at him.

'The question is, however, how do we distract him?' Full of thought, he took a further bite on his carrot. His eyes immediately fixed on the spit that the dwarves had set up over their central fire. Sizzling fat dripped from a crisping carcass and his mouth began to water. There were twelve dwarves in all but it seemed they were preparing to feast on an entire pig; it was most unfair.

They were still wide awake an hour later and, as the night grew darker, their singing became louder and more forceful. At first, they sung of gold.

> Bright gold under the sun,
> Silver by the moon,
> King and Queen of metals
> Be my fortune.
>
> Lead and mercury in the pot,
> Build the fire and make it hot.
> With beam of moon and ray of sun
> On winter's dawn the toil begun.
>
> With Beltane's fire, in goes zinc.
> Cobalt and strontium add to the drink.
> Then by the equinox of spring
> Gold, gold, gold my fortune bring!

The poem seemed mostly obsessed by the properties of gold,

which it listed in detail, and he thought the whole subject entirely dull and not worthy of a song at all. Bored with their song, his concentration was drawn to the change in watch as the dwarf pacing the perimeter of the camp relinquished his duty to another. The replacement paced slowly around the camp, a large tankard in his fist, steaming in the cold night air. At intervals, he stopped to drink from it before staggering on. A long time later, when Rollo was despairing of the dwarves' stamina, he changed places with another dwarf.

Though there was nothing they could do but shiver and wait, Isolde showed no signs of tiredness. Her eyes watched the replacement guard. Clearly, he had drunk considerably more than the last dwarf on watch as his circle was somewhat elliptical and, unlike his predecessor, he stopped to warm his great thick hands beside each of the fires that spat out coloured flames into the brooding dark of the night.

'The effects of the drink will continue to grow on them and we won't have to wait that much longer until he's next to useless. I'm sure it won't be long now,' Rollo commented and Isolde nodded though in a most unconvinced way.

She sat back and fell into silent vigil and Rollo presumed she was trying to improve on their plan. He fell to watching the fires and sighed to himself, wishing that he could be closer to the flames.

'It won't be long now,' he repeated optimistically, rubbing at himself to restore some feeling to his limbs.

'I don't know,' Isolde said through her chattering teeth. 'They're not showing any signs of flagging.'

Indeed, the dwarves were still in full song and still carving hunks of meat from the roasting pig. Rollo drew close to her and wrapped his heavy woollen cloak about them both. She went stiff for a moment as if mindful of his closeness but then relaxed and accepted the offer of his warmth.

'That one in the hat,' she murmured, indicating the broad dwarf who was now sitting hunched by the central fire, studying the jewel they had taken from Quinn. Every once in a while, the dwarf raised his head and stared straight up at the promontory of rock high on the escarpment. 'He's not as drunk as the others and he's spent much of the evening staring at Quinn's onyx. I'm amazed that they understood how to use it to locate my ruby. I wonder how he discovered it so quickly.'

Rollo was frustrated. 'Perhaps we should leave your philosophical problems until later. Surely the important thing right now is that he seems to have worked out that your ruby is staying still because he keeps looking at the stone and then up at the wolf. Since he believes that we are now stationary, I think we can safely presume that he'll soon finish his drink and then he'll sleep like the others.' Rollo looked around at the well-fed dwarves that, one by one, were dropping to the ground and curling up amid heavy cloaks. 'I presume he'll sleep . . .' Rollo worried about that point. 'But we could be waiting here all night.'

'You're right.' Isolde's lithe body snapped upright, almost knocking him over. She was at once bright-eyed with excitement. 'What if we can get my ruby to come closer? If he thinks it's just beyond the perimeter of his camp, surely he would investigate? Then that would give us the chance to slip in and grab Quinn while the rest slept.'

'Mmm,' Rollo considered her suggestion. 'He might, as you say, go after the ruby but, on the other hand, he might just rouse the entire camp.' He pointed out the flaw in Isolde's plan.

She shrugged. 'I agree. But they've drunk so much they would take some waking. He might just go and look for himself first before attempting to wake his fellows.'

'It's worth a try,' Rollo agreed and grinned at her. 'And I certainly don't want to spend all night waiting for nothing. It's definitely worth a try. Now what do you have to do to move the wolf?'

'You'll have to stay here,' Isolde instructed. 'If I go to him, I may be able to entice him down a little.'

'Are you sure you won't just be leading the dwarves to you by going near the wolf?' Rollo worried.

She shrugged. 'What choice do we have?' She studied the dwarf that was poring over Quinn's stone. 'I think, perhaps, we should wait just a little while longer, don't you?' she asked.

Rollo nodded. He was watching the steaming tankard beside the dwarf with the hat and was wishing that the squat fellow would drink a little more of it. A distant moan and bellow from a far off lequus drifted to them on the wind, but the dwarf paid no heed. He was intent only on studying the black gem.

'Silver!' the dwarf suddenly shouted. 'Silver!' He tossed the black gem into the fire.

'Oh no, look what he's doing to it!' Isolde yelped under her breath.

Rollo was fascinated to see how the flames suddenly leapt up and burnt a brilliant silver colour.

Isolde looked as if she would faint. 'No! Quinn needs it. I need it!'

'It's like dragon flame,' Rollo gasped. 'Have you ever seen anything so wonderful?'

Isolde scowled. 'Now it's in the fire, he won't be able to use it to locate the ruby so we won't be able to distract him with the wolf. What is he doing with it anyway?' Isolde was exasperated, watching in dismay as their only plan failed before it was even started. 'Now we shall have to wait until he falls asleep.'

But the dwarf showed no sign of needing rest and was busily stirring the fire and watching the flames leap up from around the black stone. He danced about the blaze and then inexplicably tossed a large hunk of meat onto the plate before Quinn as if he were rewarding his prisoner. He then untied his hands and pushed the plate towards him.

Rollo was still more surprised to see him eat.

'How could he?' Rollo complained.

'How could he what? Isolde asked.

Rollo was aware that, despite everything, he enjoyed being alone with this girl. She was laconic in her speech and not overly critical of him. When there were too many people about, she became reticent and glum with shyness but on her own she was quite companionable. 'How can Quinn eat?' he queried, pointing at the hooded figure in the centre of the camp.

'Torra Altans are well-trained and they know that they must always eat and drink whenever they are given the opportunity. When I was very young and we were first afflicted with the dragons, Hal organized many dragon hunts. The men were very inexperienced then and very nervous but they still were forced to eat a good breakfast before they went out. Hal ordered it.'

'Hal,' Rollo echoed in disgust.

Isolde smiled. 'I know what you mean. He's a bit over-bearing.'

Rollo hadn't even considered that. He just didn't like the man. 'Mmm,' he muttered non-committally. It was not a conversation he wished to pursue.

'During one harsh winter, he made us eat dragon meat. It was terrible. We had to keep the horses in the barns and the cattle numbers were halved overnight. We had to build up the stocks and so Hal ordered that we ate the dragons that we killed rather than cutting into the livestock. Never before or since have I eaten anything so tough and so disgusting.'

Rollo winced at the idea of eating dragon. 'Is that where the skull in the hall came from? Was it placed in the hall as a reminder of those times?'

Isolde thought about it. 'No, the skull in the hall belonged to a golden dragon. I was barely two at the time and people say I could not remember it, but I do; I remember it very well. Hal was injured and he came home without the dragon. But the next day they dragged it all the way home. Hal was different back then. Kind and full of charisma, he inspired enthusiasm in all those about him and the men of the castle would have gladly followed him anywhere. He might have left the carcass to rot where it fell but, because it was a young dragon and the gold of its scales was amazingly beautiful, he wanted it preserved as a trophy. I remember the sight of it to this day; how the sunlight glinted off those scales. Anyway, Hal wanted to have it stuffed as a trophy but he then he discovered that a claw was missing.'

The girl grinned at Rollo. 'Hal had a furious temper even then. His rage was such that I didn't dare be in the same room as him for weeks. He was so disappointed. The night before they went out for the carcass, he had told everyone how he was going to have the whole thing stuffed and mounted and made to lie beside the table in the great hall. Keridwen was appalled by the idea.' Isolde laughed as if she were fond of the story she was telling.

'She was even more furious with him when he brought the beast home,' she continued her tale. 'She said it was petty vanity, and a dishonourable way to treat the bones of so powerful a creature. It's never good to argue with Keridwen. She doesn't get angry or raise her voice but it feels as if the whole castle is three degrees colder if you displease her.' She laughed at this and Rollo decided that she must have been joking – surely!

'Anyway, Hal strutted around the house and said that since he himself had one hand missing, he couldn't have a trophy similarly maimed; people would make jokes. But I think that was an excuse; I think he didn't wish to continue because he valued Keridwen's approval.'

'So what did he do with the carcass?' Rollo managed to ask, feeling his own right hand go weak at the very notion of losing a limb. It was a terrible thought. He pushed both of his hands under his arms and pressed down with his elbows as if to lock them safely away.

'He had the head mounted and the rest he cast over the

east wall. The golden hue of the scales had faded before the end of the first day.'

'He didn't eat it then?'

Isolde laughed lightly. 'I was very young and didn't pay all that much attention to those details. I know that for a few years it hung there stuffed but Hal became suddenly angry about it. He didn't like the now muddied colour of its scales and complained about its eyes. Ah, its eyes! I didn't mention how they never lost the gleam of life. So he had the flesh stripped off and the skull boiled so that he could have just the bare white bones of the skull remounted and hung on the wall.'

Rollo nodded. He could almost imagine those eyes, those deep, deep green eyes of the dragon in its magnificent golden armour. Staring into the nearest of the dwarves' fires, he let his mind wonder and imagined that great armoured head and the powerful scaled body of the beast dancing in the colourful flames of the fire. Blinking to concentrate his mind on the present, he nibbled a little more on the carrot and saw that, by this time, Quinn's arms had been retied behind his back. He watched as the youth did his best to lie down to sleep.

'I can't believe he's going to sleep,' Rollo complained. 'It'll be very much harder to rescue him, if I have to wake him up.'

'He must eat and he must sleep. He will do what he can to survive. Quinn is very much a pragmatist. He's sensible and will do what is right though I wish he hadn't told us to run. He shouldn't have done that,' Isolde protested, heaving a sigh.

She then caught her breath as the dwarf beneath the wide-brimmed hat reached for one of the long thin pikes that his comrades carried and poked the fire with it. He then raked out Quinn's black gemstone from the flames and began to examine it closely. After a little while, he reached inside a bag that he had placed beside him and drew out several small wallets. After sprinkling a little something from each wallet onto the palm of his hand, he stirred the mix with his forefinger. Rollo couldn't really tell what he was doing but certainly the dwarf seemed very deliberate in his actions.

They waited and, presently, all but the watch and the dwarf in the broad-rimmed hat were wrapped in blankets and sleeping. Fervently clutching the black onyx in his hand, the dwarf sat back by his tankard and took a long draught from his mead. Grunting, he tipped out the cold dregs and rose to march over to the steaming cauldron. After dipping his tankard into the brew, he downed the entire quart of honeyed liquid within a minute.

Soon the watch changed again. Like the dwarves on duty before him, this one did not seem unduly concerned about monitoring the dark shadows beyond their camp. Certainly, their extraordinarily heavy, double-headed axes that lay at their sides looked as if they would do a huge amount of damage to anything foolish enough to threaten them. It wasn't long before he gave up pacing the perimeter of the camp and sat with his back to one of the fires. Rollo stared at him blankly for a while.

A sharp prod in the ribs from Isolde's bony hand made him realize that he must have been dozing.

'I'm going to wake Quinn,' she whispered and, before Rollo could stop her, she had slipped away.

Moments later, he heard what sounded like the distant howl of a wolf. He looked over his shoulder to see where the sound came from and whether Isolde's wolf had moved from the skyline. But he could still see the humped shape of the wolf, which was no longer watching the moon but had pricked its ears up at the sound of the cry. As smooth as a cat, its shape slunk off the skyline.

Rollo looked back at the camp and was relieved to see that the cry had not disturbed the dwarves But it woke Quinn.

He thought it quite extraordinary that, even in his sleep, Quinn had apparently managed to discern that the cry had come from Isolde as opposed to a real wolf. The youth was slowly pushing himself upright and even crept to the end of what Rollo saw, for the first time, to be a tether attached to his bound wrists. Rollo considered the ropes. He pondered on how he could cut Quinn free and decided that, the minute he managed to break into the camp, he would snatch up one of the dwarves' axes and use the edge to cut the bonds.

Without Isolde's ruby to give them away, they at least had hope of escape. He was relieved when Isolde returned. She nodded in satisfaction at the sight of Quinn now awake and alert.

'You sounded just like a real wolf,' Rollo praised her.

She shrugged. 'It's not the most worthwhile of accomplishments.'

'I don't know; it seems to have helped us.'

The girl drew a deep breath and sighed as if unwilling to accept the compliment. 'I would guess that the wolf will be making his way towards us soon. We'll meet him coming down. You had better follow me. And stay close,' she warned.

Isolde proved extremely difficult to follow. One moment, Rollo could see her and, the next, she had almost entirely disappeared. She moved silently; as silently as a wolf, he concluded. Her affinity with the wolf did nothing to deter his trepidation when the great shaggy beast, which looked coal black against the night, was right at their side.

But Rollo was distracted from the wolf's proximity by sudden activity in the dwarves' camp. The dwarf with the large hat had heaved himself up onto his broad feet. 'What's he doing?' the youth asked in frustration at their luckless inability to control the situation.

'I don't know,' Isolde said with a hint of irritation.

The dwarf had picked up one of the large round shields that they all carried. He laid the shield down and filled the flat dish of its interior with a viscous blue liquid from a smaller, second cauldron bubbling alongside the larger pot containing the mead. Stepping to one side, he let the moonlight fall on it and watched intently as he placed the black gem into the shield's centre. He looked over at the dwarf supposedly on watch, as if he wanted to tell him something, but the other dwarf had fallen asleep. Untroubled by this neglect of duty he returned his attention to the black onyx.

After a moment watching the dwarf, Isolde murmured, 'I think he's only trying to discover more of the gem's properties. Isn't he ever going to sleep? How are we going to rescue Quinn if he remains awake?'

'We'll just have to stick to our plan. If you call the wolf in close, perhaps the dwarf will investigate and then we might be able to find a way to slink into the camp while he's disturbed.'

'Excellent!' Isolde said with enthusiasm.

Rollo knew they were clutching at straws, though he wouldn't have thought it for the enthusiasm with which Isolde embraced their plan. She even pulled herself close to him and kissed his cheek. His spirits soared.

His elation diminished somewhat, when she murmured, 'Oh Quinn, sweet Quinn, don't despair; we'll get you out of there soon.'

'Now, listen,' she said more firmly to Rollo. 'I will call the wolf. You make a huge clattering row up here as if you're being attacked by him and I'll slink in close and get Quinn.'

'No, the other way around,' Rollo objected. 'You make the diversion. I don't want to be left out here alone with the wolf.'

'But, Rollo, are you sure you'll be able to creep in stealthily?' she asked tentatively.

'I'll have to,' Rollo said flatly. 'And don't argue. It's the only way.'

Isolde closed her mouth on her criticism and simply nodded.

Rollo looked into the dark pools of her eyes and felt the need to restate the plan since he wasn't convinced that she was clear on the matter. 'You cause the diversion and I'll slip in and release Quinn. Are we agreed?'

Isolde nodded. 'Yes, we are agreed. Count to one hundred slowly and I'll be ready.' She was gone without another word and Rollo could only hope that she had a sensible idea how to cause a distraction. He shook himself ready for action and began to creep as close to the camp as he dared while still remaining hidden. As instructed, he counted to one hundred and waited, mesmerized by the flames from the blue fire nearest him. He wondered again how the dwarves had achieved such a colour. Peering closer, he saw that there was a ring of metal aglow at the fire's base. The ring produced a violet glow, which coloured the rest of the flames.

His focus was jerked up and his eyes were suddenly wide open as he saw Isolde standing right beside the edge of the camp, the wolf pressed up against her side. The brazen boldness of it all shocked him to the core. She had appeared out of nowhere and must have used the cover of the wolf. Suddenly, she was upright, her arms spread wide, an ethereal presence in the ghostly moonlight. The dwarf with the hat turned towards her but didn't shout or cry; he just stared at her open mouthed. After perhaps half a minute in which time neither Isolde nor the dwarf moved, he reached for his weapon, rose and made an uncertain line through the camp towards Isolde.

'Idiot girl!' Rollo cursed and began crawling on his hands and knees, hood pulled forward and down to cover his face. 'What madness!' This was not his idea of a distraction at all. He had meant her to entice the wolf in close, not for her to reveal herself to these dangerous fellows. Now he would never get the chance. Now they would all be chopped into mincemeat and roasted on one of those brilliantly coloured fires.

He crawled faster. He had spotted a short throwing axe with a keen edge and aimed for it. There were only two dwarves to get past, their snores loud in the stillness of the night, and he needed to crawl between them to reach the axe. After that, he could make his way to Quinn. He even dared to look up for a moment to see what Quinn was doing and whether he was trying to free himself from his bonds; but Quinn was looking towards Isolde. The dwarf was swaying in apparent disbelief towards her. Rollo watched as the wolf rose up beside her to stand up on its back legs, the gem at its throat bright in the firelight.

The dwarf halted but continued to stare at Isolde. The orange firelight catching only the angular points of her body made her look skeletal-thin. Her big eyes were black like the empty eye sockets of a skull. Rollo's mind raced. To a drunken man, the sight of her would have been more than a shock and, indeed, the dwarf did look to his tankard as if wondering that the mead had not tainted his vision. The dwarf continued to move slowly towards her, his hand half raised, pointing at the bright jewel at the wolf's throat.

Rollo kicked himself for hesitating. He needed to move and wriggled on as best he could. Feeling his leg brush against one of the great humps of the dwarves, he froze, fearing that he might wake but, fortunately, the snores continued. He crawled on a little further, trying to keep his breathing as still as possible. It was not at all easy to worm his way silently through the camp for the number of tankards, plates, pots and pans but he knew he must to reach the axe.

But before he reached the weapon, his hand fell on a knife, the edge sharp enough to cut rope. Glad of his first stroke of luck, he smiled to himself and turned to crawl directly towards Quinn at the centre of the camp.

His optimism did not last but waned with each foot he progressed forward; he was surrounded by large heaps of snoring dwarves, their hands still clutching their spears, swords or axes as they slept. This was madness. How long would Isolde's scheme last? So far the dwarf appeared intrigued by the apparition but he could not be so afraid or curious as to remain silent forever.

The dwarf slowly looked round and back at his sleeping companions as if seeking their confirmation of what he saw.

Certainly, if he had not known who she was, Rollo would have been alarmed at the sight of Isolde standing there so still, her cloak thrown back, her bone-white arms bare and glowing in the moonlight. With the wolf standing up on its hindlegs, a tall and extraordinary figure, Rollo would have believed he was looking at a werewolf beside her. And with the mist swirling up around their ankles, it looked as if they were floating in mid-air.

Rollo froze, fearing imminent discovery, and hoped his cloak was covering him. In the dim light, he looked just like another bedding roll or pack. The dwarf took several paces back and grunted harshly at the one who was meant to be on watch. There was no reaction and so he kicked the slumbering dwarf hard in the side, who cursed angrily at being awoken and then gave a startled gasp as he looked up and saw Isolde. His battle axe was instantly gripped firmly in both his hands.

Rollo knew he had to move but he didn't know how he could without being seen now that both dwarves were awake. As long as he stayed still under his cloak, he felt he would most probably be safe but, sooner or later, someone would trip over him. Then he would be forced to act. Squinting from under his cloak, he could see that the dwarf with the hat was now holding a long pike, which he was pointing at Isolde.

The other dwarf was alongside him and thumped the heavy weight of his axe handle into the palm of his hand by way of a threat. The dwarves' forearms were as round as a man's thigh and Rollo was quite shocked at just how big dwarves really were. He had thought them to be a small people. Indeed, they were quite short, the tallest of them standing little more than five feet, but it was the weight of them, the sheer bulk of their bones and the size of their muscles on their short limbs that alarmed him. They were certainly bigger than any man Rollo had ever seen.

Gathering his courage, he urged himself to move. Lying

flat on his stomach and using just his toes and fingers, he inched forward until, at last, he was beside Quinn.

He was amazed that he had achieved this much of his task. Quinn's back was towards him and he could see that he was tightly bound to a short stake set in the ground near the central fire. Rollo elbowed his way forward a fraction more and reached forward to touch Quinn's hand. The youth jumped and Rollo hoped that the sudden movement hadn't attracted the dwarves' attention. Quinn's fingers wriggled to assist him as the Artoran prince struggled to turn the knife and push it between the twisted bonds.

He had hoped that the rope would cut easily. The knife was sharp enough but it didn't appear to be cutting. He wriggled a bit closer so that he could bend his arms a little more and get a better angle on the rope. All at once, the dwarves' snores seemed too quiet and his own breaths too loud and neither were loud enough to conceal the sounds of the knife sawing at the rope. Quinn was wriggling frantically to try and work his wrists free which did nothing but make the task more difficult for Rollo. Quinn jerked his wrists away and Rollo realized that he had nicked him with the knife. He was beginning to panic as the two dwarves were arguing and then at last one lunged at Isolde.

She gave out a little shriek and leapt back.

Rollo's heart stopped in mid beat. If only she hadn't shrieked; instantly her spell over the dwarves was broken. She had seemed ethereal but the cry was so distinctly human and the dwarves clearly had no difficulty recognizing that fact.

'I'll have you, woman! I'll have you and your wolf and I'll have that stone,' the dwarf cursed as she vanished into blackness.

'Hurry!' Quinn grunted as quietly as was humanly possible. 'We must help Isolde.'

Rollo threw back his cloak and knelt upwards so he could

use all his strength to work on the ropes. The wolf growled and snapped from somewhere beyond the glow of the fires. The two dwarves were shouting excitedly.

'This cursed rope,' Rollo whispered. The dwarves around them were beginning to stir; they had so little time. He flung the knife aside and lunged for the axe that he had originally sought and pressed its blade down on Quinn's bonds. It was a clumsy weapon but the edge was sharper than he had hoped.

'Get these ropes off me,' Quinn whispered through gritted teeth. 'Either get them off me or go and help Isolde.'

Sweat was pouring from Rollo's brow. It had all gone horribly wrong. It should have taken only a moment. Isolde's plan had been mad but it could have succeeded. What was he going to do? He couldn't leave Quinn, not now, when they were so close. There had to be another way. Hastily, he looked around.

'Untie it! Just work the bloody knot free.' Quinn's voice was high and strained in his effort to keep his voice quiet. Rollo stooped down and tried his best but the rope was exceedingly coarse and stiff and he was making no progress.

Then the wolf gave out a spine-chilling howl and all the dwarves lying in the camp were suddenly grunting and pushing back their bedding. One sat up and, at once, looked straight out towards the wolf.

Tears of frustration ran down Rollo's cheeks. Everything he did went wrong. Even though her plan had been mad, Isolde had managed to achieve her objective. He, of course, had failed on the very simple matter of cutting the rope. Suddenly, he could bear the frustration no longer nor could he bear himself and his incompetence. The rage burst up from within him and threw him to his feet.

At the back of his mind, he was vaguely aware of lunging for one of the long pikes, spinning round and whacking it hard into the belly of the first dwarf that had tried to stand.

417

Then he dropped the weapon and charged like a bull into the round belly of another, fists pummelling. He had forgotten about Quinn, forgotten about Isolde; he was aware only of his own failings.

Chapter 25

A searing pain clawed up Rollo's leg and jolted him back to his senses. Crying out in alarm, he rolled to the floor, aware that he had been shoved into the flames. Frantically, he flapped at his legs, relieved to see that his breeches were only singed. He sat still in resignation, breathing hard and conscious of the ring of broad brown boots around him.

He didn't bother to look up but, instead, scowled across at Quinn, who was still tied to the post.

'You're an idiot!' Quinn said in an exasperated tone.

'How was I to know the rope wouldn't cut?' Rollo objected.

'You managed to cut me easily enough though. You should have just slit my wrists and been done with it,' Quinn barked more sharply now. 'You are a menace, Rollo of Artor, an absolute, bloody menace.'

Rollo could think of no reply and refused to look up until one of the dwarves gripped his chin in a thick callused hand and yanked it upwards.

The dwarf bent forward, his eyes dark beneath his broad-rimmed hat. 'Haf compliments your conduct. That was quite a display. And to knock the wind out of a dwarf . . . Well!' He turned to one of his comrades. 'See here and learn, Lith. Look how small a mite managed to fell you.'

Lith stabbed his spear into the ground and kicked up the ashes of the fire into Haf's face, who laughed along with the rest of the company. Haf, who seemed to carry the most authority within the band, returned his attention back to Rollo, bending down low and sniffing at him.

He then thrust a burning torch into his face to get a better look.

'Well, I never! What have we got here? A common manling by the look of him. Nothing too special to look at yet he behaves like he's swallowed an entire tankard of flaming elixir!' The dwarf stood up, reached his hands into his pockets and drew out two gemstones. One was the onyx he had taken from Quinn; the other was brilliant red with a golden glowing hint of yellow at its heart.

Rollo's hopes that Isolde was free collapsed. Craning his head to look over the heaps of bedding littered about the camp, he saw her hunched up on the ground, sobbing over a dark shape at the edge of the camp. A dwarf stood over her.

Haf followed Rollo's gaze and, with a wave of his hand, signalled to the dwarf guarding Isolde. Picking her up by the back of her ragged dress, he dragged her through the camp and dropped her at Rollo's side. Though she was shivering, she made no attempt to pull her cloak around her and lay face down, sobbing into the earth. Rollo felt desperately sorry. He could see the body of the wolf more clearly now that Isolde was no longer bent over it. The hideous outline of an axe handle stuck up from its head. He continued to watch as a dwarf put his boot down on its head and heaved out the throwing axe from its skull. Diligently, the dwarf wiped the blade before smoothing the edge with a flat stone from his pocket.

Rollo knew it was all his fault for failing to cut the rope. He was responsible for their capture and the death of the wolf and he was responsible for Isolde's grief. The sight of her distress hurt Rollo as if she had struck him.

'I could have told you it wouldn't work, if you hadn't run off,' he snapped at her, spitefully. 'It was a stupid plan. Now look where it's got us all,' he said as hurtfully as he could to cover up for his own mistake.

Isolde didn't so much as glance at him but continued to whimper into the earth.

'Don't blame her,' Quinn hissed through his teeth as Rollo was dragged to his side and had his hands tied behind his back.

Next his feet were kicked away from under him and he was secured to the same post as Quinn. The two youths were forced to sit with their backs to each other.

'Isolde has done nothing wrong,' Quinn persisted. 'You should have known better than attempt such a hare-brained scheme. And worst, you left her to carry out the most dangerous part of your ridiculous plan. They might have thrown the axe at her rather than the wolf. They could have been pulling that axe out from *her* skull!'

'I didn't take the easier task. I was the one crawling through the camp, remember? I was the one brushing right up against the dwarves,' Rollo defended himself.

'Hardly brushing! Why did you have to go and hit one of them like that? You should have just run for it like I said. Were you trying to be a hero? You're just an idiot, an incompetent idiot.' Quinn growled.

Rollo tried to squirm round and kick him but he couldn't reach. So incensed with the Torra Altan for speaking to him like that, he twisted and arched his neck around in an attempt to bite him but still he couldn't inflict any injury on Quinn. He gave up and wailed, 'I was trying to cut you free. I was trying to help you. You were the idiot who got caught.'

'I cannot deny that but you, Rollo, were the one who said we should run from Merrit. Hasn't it occurred to you that it may have been your crazy imagination that dreamt all that nonsense up about him trading and scheming with hobs?'

'It wasn't!' Rollo howled in protest. 'It wasn't, I'm telling you. He was up to no good. He was talking about what plans he had in store for us.'

'I have only your word on that.' Quinn's lips were trembling. 'Anyway, it's been your fault all along because it was you who picked the fight with Guthrey.'

'Me! What do you mean me? I didn't do that. It was him.

421

It wasn't my fault!' Rollo's voice cracked in his anger and, finally, he managed to swing his leg round far enough for his toe to connect with Quinn's injured leg.

'You're a little wretch, a devil!' Quinn growled. 'That you could bring Isolde to this place is unforgivable, but how could you be so stupid as to put her in such danger?'

Though he tried to kick Quinn again, he was prevented by the intervention of the dwarves. They had tired of their bickering and dragged Rollo to a separate post so that Quinn was well out of his reach. Thankfully, one of the dwarves was kind enough to throw his cloak over him, which must have slipped from his shoulder in the skirmish. Now regretting his outburst, Rollo watched as Isolde was dragged to his previous spot and tied with her back against Quinn's.

The girl weakly mumbled, 'I'm sorry, Quinn; I failed you. I had it all worked out but we just didn't quite manage it.'

'Yes, well, I'm just as cross with you as I am with him,' Quinn grumbled more gently at her. 'What were you thinking of?'

'I–I– I don't know.'

'Yes, she does,' Rollo interrupted. 'She was thinking of you, Quinn, you ungrateful bastard.'

'Don't you call me that!' Quinn snarled back, his teeth barred and his body suddenly taut as he strained against his ropes.

Rollo realized that he had hit on a sore point. 'Bastard!' he reiterated.

Quinn glared at him, the pulse in his forehead throbbing. After a long moment, the Torra Altan's look softened and his shoulders dropped. 'I feel sorry for you, Rollo. You attack and criticize others solely to make yourself feel better. But it won't, you know. You should just learn to like yourself a little bit more then you wouldn't feel so ashamed of yourself all the time.'

'I don't!' Rollo's voice was high and surprised, caught off-guard by this notion.

'Don't you?' Quinn asked softly.

'Hush,' Isolde advised through her sniffs. 'We're all in this together; shouldn't we just be friends? We were only trying to help you, Quinn.'

There was a moment's silence as the taller youth thought about it then he said more gently, 'I'm only cross because I was worried for you, Issy. When I was alone in this camp, I believed you were on your way home. I was sure that Rollo would look after you and get you home. But, instead, you came after me. I'm not worth all of this, you know.'

'Of course you're worth it,' Isolde sobbed.

Amazed that the dwarves paid them little more heed, Rollo blinked at the strange fellows as they simply crawled back under their blankets and cloaks. Within minutes, all, save for Lith whose turn it was to be on watch, were fast asleep. Lith paced slowly about the camp, singing a song that seemed, to Rollo, to be far too beautiful to be coming from the dwarf's thick lips. As before, it was a song of treasure and gold. Lulled by the sound, Rollo sighed, almost forgetting where he was. Now, there was nothing left for him to do other than go to sleep, which even in this awkward position with his head flopped forward onto his chest and his arm muscles cramping, was not too hard since he was so utterly exhausted. Soothed by the sound of crackling fires and the dwarf's wonderfully melodious voice, he slipped into a doze.

It was near midnight when the watch changed next. The two dwarves exchanging words stirred Rollo from his slumber and he watched as the new red-bearded watch, who lacked the large pot belly common to the others, looked about the camp. At length he examined the prisoners and, to Rollo's surprise and relief released their bonds and then retied them at their front instead of behind their backs. Rollo was more than pleased as well as astonished to have a warm tankard placed under his nose.

'No point being uncomfortable,' the dwarf told them. 'I don't want to see you suffering but I do need to know that you're secure after all the trouble you've caused. Now, drink well and then sleep. Both will ease your sores and your troubles in equal amounts.'

Glad to be able to move his arms just a little, Rollo took one long draught and then nervously eased the tankard back from his lips. The guard was now some distance from them and it was safe to speak. 'You don't suppose it's poison,' he asked his companions.

Quinn laughed. 'They'd hardly go to the trouble of poisoning us. If they wanted us dead, they'd just give us a swift clout on the head from one of their great ham-like fists.'

Reassured, Rollo took another long draught and was intensely relieved to feel the warmth sink down into his belly. The tankard was very large by human standards but nevertheless, he drank every last drop. As the dwarf had promised, it did indeed make him feel much better. Soon, he lay down and stared into the flickering fires. The drink passed through his empty stomach rapidly and it wasn't long before the world was beginning to swim; he thought it most probable that he would be very ill in the morning.

He was tied to a stake and the ground on which he lay was both damp and cold and yet he felt surprisingly at peace. Thankfully there was no wind and the warm atmosphere near the fire seemed to cosset every inch of his bruised and battered body. The firelight reminded him of home and the huge stone fireplaces in his mother's rooms where he used to curl up on her knee while the minstrels sang. The dwarves' mead was truly remarkable stuff and with that thought he drifted off to sleep.

By morning, he was even more amazed at the wonders of the mead. The fires had died down a great deal but they still gave out warmth. He ached very little from his cuts and bruises but the most amazing thing of all was that he had no headache. After drinking a full quart of dwarven mead he should feel awful but, remarkably, he didn't.

Quinn and Isolde were also awake. Quinn nodded and

Isolde gave him a sad but supportive smile. He nodded back and then focused his attention on his captors, surprised at how well the dwarves treated them. First, they were taken one by one to a steam and untied so that they could wash and make themselves comfortable.

In order to make it easier for them to eat, the dwarves did not retie their hands but, instead, secured them for the time-being at the ankle, making it very plain that they would fare no better than the wolf if they attempted to escape.

'Given time, you would be able to untie the knot,' Haf, the broad dwarf with the large hat, told them. 'But do not bother to attempt such a foolish thing. If you do, we will chop off your fingers with an axe to stop you being so annoying in future. Do you understand?'

Rollo understood perfectly.

He returned and took his seat down next to Isolde and Quinn where they were offered a large breakfast of ham and unleavened bread that was hard on the teeth and heavy on the stomach, though it was exactly what Rollo wanted.

'What do you suppose they will do with us?' he spluttered through his crammed mouth.

Quinn shook his head and swallowed. 'I have no idea, though they are obsessively interested in the gemstones.'

'My sunburst ruby!' Isolde bemoaned her loss. 'The very finest, the very purest; it was cut at the height of midsummer's day when the sun was at its zenith and its power intense and pure.'

Quinn nodded grimly. 'The minute that dwarf caught sight of the jewel about my neck, he pulled it from my throat. At first, I thought he would discard it in disappointment because, to the unpractised eye, it looks little more than black, coloured glass and it certainly doesn't look valuable. But he noticed at once the tiny sliver of silvery thread at its heart and how that thread swivelled and spun within the liquid heart of the gem. It didn't take him very long at all to work out that the silver fleck was pointing always towards you. I couldn't believe it but he did. Neither could I believe the pace at which they pursued you. For such stout, short-legged fellows they certainly can move.'

He looked up as Haf stamped over and knelt down in front of them. The dwarf pushed back his hat before dangling the two contrasting gemstones before their eyes.

'Look at them,' he crooned in admiration. 'The sun and the moon. Two opposites. And do you know what the remarkable thing is about opposites? Do you? Well, I'll tell you. They attract. I have heard of these sunburst rubies, naturally,' he said, smoothing his thick thumb over the brilliant red gem with the yellow heart that looked as if a drop of sun was trapped within its centre. 'It is an alchemist's tease.' He turned to the dark jewel. 'But not this.' He shook the slim chain that held Quinn's gemstone. 'Now, tell me; where did you get this from?'

'They are common enough,' Quinn calmly lied. 'I have told you already that they are mined in the walls of the canyon within the Barony of Torra Alta. Perhaps, if you are interested in purchasing some, we could show you the way.'

'Haa, haa!' the dwarf laughed falsely. 'Do not think me such a fool, young manling? I am not just going to take you home and, besides, I know it's the sunburst rubies that are found at Torra Alta, not this murky stone. You are simply hoping that the fine Torra Altan archers will rescue you as we approach.'

'I thought no such—' Quinn had a chance to sound wounded before Haf interrupted.

'Now, it's no good looking at me like that. I know you're a Torra Altan. I've seen your hands and they are the hands of an archer so I think it's a safe bet to say you, at least, are from there. You think I am a fool. Just because my skull is twice as thick as yours doesn't make me stupid. Never underestimate the knowledge in a dwarf. We are far more long-lived than you silly little people who rush so quickly through life, believing you rule the world rather than realizing that you are simply a very small part of it.' He sneered in disgust. 'I have been in this country only a few months but it is long enough to know the reputation of Torra Alta. It is virtually all that is left of Belbidia now, apart from the very southern barony of Caldea. They say that's held under martial rule by a cruel baron but he seems to be the only one in this backward country that's prepared to take control and band men together. You are a sorry lot, you people of Belbidia. Do you think we dwarves would have been able to achieve such success if we hadn't worked together? Together, I say and not working with man or hob,' he added with feeling. 'I'll not be a party to that, however much he is offering. We're craftsmen and we'll work for ourselves. What do you say to that?'

'Er, I . . .' Clearly, Quinn could not think of anything suitable to say.

'Enough! Now, tell me all you know about this jewel.' The dwarf held up the onyx and looked at the three of them as if he were trying to read their minds. 'You first.' He pointed at Rollo.

'I know nothing about it,' Rollo replied calmly, determined to appear unflustered before his companions. 'I am new to this country and I don't know that it's anything beyond a black stone.'

The dwarf looked at him sideways and then turned his attention to Quinn. 'I've questioned you enough about your own gem so tell me now about the golden-hearted ruby.' The dwarf tossed the gem up in the air and caught it again in a possessively tight grip.

'It's called a sunburst ruby,' Quinn replied candidly but then lied, 'It is nothing but a pretty stone though they are said to be highly coveted by stonewights. They are found in Ceolothia and northern Belbidia.'

'Good, good,' the dwarf said dismissively and then turned very much more intently on Isolde. 'Now he has told me a little about the ruby, you tell me about the other gem. Possessing a stone such as this you must be an alchemist's daughter, are you not?' he demanded but didn't wait for her answer. 'A human alchemist. I never thought to see this day but, it is possible that you have discovered something that I have not. You will tell me.'

Isolde kept her eyes down. 'I am not an alchemist,' she said in a quavering whisper. 'An alchemist would have powders and liquids and would understand the ways of metals.' With shaking fingers, she opened her scrip. 'I have flowers and herbs. I am a no more than a gatherer of herbs.'

The dwarf nodded. 'Be that as it may, you know something of the black jewel. I know you do otherwise you wouldn't have tried to trick us with the wolf.'

Isolde shook her head. 'I know nothing of it. I do not even know what such a darkly coloured gem might be called.'

Quite suddenly the dwarf's patience snapped. His calm expression turned to one of purple fury. Without warning, he sprang at Quinn and gripped him by the throat. His hugely thick fingers, which sprouted black hairs and callused nails began to close around his windpipe. 'I am tired of you, boy. You'll tell me where you got this stone. Tell me its name and its properties. Where did you get it? Speak to me or I'll transfer my grip to the girl and rip her throat out.' The dwarf shoved Quinn away and picked Isolde up by the hair.

Rollo was amazed that, though Isolde was still trembling, she did not cry out.

'Stop! Stop it!' Quinn choked. 'Leave her be and I'll tell you what I know.'

The dwarf nodded in satisfaction and let Isolde slump from his grip.

Quinn gave her a long concerned look, coughed and said quietly, 'I truly don't know all that much about the stone, only that my mother gave it to me. She said it was a gift from my father. She said it was very precious but I do not know that it has any properties that are worth anything to anyone other than ourselves.' He nodded towards Isolde. 'She also had a precious stone and, when we were very young, we would sit and play with our stones together. We didn't know if they were like that from the start or whether it was something that had happened as a result of our playing with the stones but, one day, we were rolling them about in a game a little like giant marbles and we realised that they would always roll towards one another. On closer inspection, we saw how the hearts of each gem were pulled towards the other, the little slither of silver and a finger of yellow from the sunburst ruby moving through the fabric of the gemstone to point toward the other.'

'Very candid of you, I'm sure,' the dwarf said in his deep melodious voice that reeked of sarcasm. 'Though you're telling me nothing I don't already know. Tell me; what's two waifs and strays doing in possession of such playthings. The ruby alone is worth a considerable sum. And this one has possibilities.' He peeked inside his fist that was closed about Quinn's stone and then turned to his ruddy-faced comrades. 'I am thinking of the silver! The prize may be less but the probability of gaining it is so much more. Gold is the ultimate prize but we have been trying for thousands of years and still that knowledge is beyond us; but silver now . . .' He drew the hand holding Quinn's gem up to his heart and momentarily closed his eyes in delight.

'Now listen, boy, I need to know where you found this stone. Tell us more about it and be smart. I don't want to harm the girl but I will if you make me.'

Quinn sucked in his lower lip and then sighed heavily as if in resigned defeat. 'All right, I'll tell you. The stone comes from the roots of Torra Alta where the Silversalmon river dips around a special rock. The river drags the light down from the moon and seeps down with it into the dark rocks at the very roots of the tor. If the full moon coincides with the winter solstice, these rocks are formed.'

For a moment the dwarf's eyes were big and round as he listened with genuine interest and then they narrowed to slits. 'Listen, manling, I know this girl is very precious to you. If you lie to me once more with any story that suggests I should be taking you home to Torra Alta, then I shall cut off her ears. Do you understand?'

Quinn nodded. 'Yes, I understand,' he said huskily. 'I understand very well.' His hands fell open in a gesture of defeat.

The dwarf smiled. 'In that case, you tell me all you know about this gem.' He dangled the two jewels from their matching chains and watched them spin, one spinning with the direction of the sun and the other spinning counter to it.

'Aspects of duality,' the dwarf murmured reverently and grinned. Rollo was most surprised to see that his teeth were very short, yellow and thick and looked like those of a horse. Haf continued, 'This is a very interesting find. I have made my fortune all in one day and quite by accident.' He laughed and the other dwarves laughed with him. He tossed the black jewel up into the air and caught it again while looking sternly at Quinn. 'Now this time, tell me truthfully; where did you get the stone?'

His knife glinting in his hand, the dwarf moved to Isolde and gently lifted the heavy mat of her tangled hair from her slender neck before looking expectantly back at Quinn, his eyes daring the youth to lie.

'Don't hurt her,' Quinn said, his voice squeezing out in a croak through his bruised throat. 'Please, please don't hurt her. I'll do anything. I'll tell you anything you want.'

'Just tell me about the stone.'

The youth flapped his arms in despair. 'But there's nothing to tell. My mother gave it to me. She said it was from my father.'

'And where did your father get it?'

'I don't know. I've never met my father. Mother said it was tears from the willow.' Quinn's voice was beginning to crack.

The dwarves fell into deep discussion over this, chattering

amongst themselves, before the dwarf with the hat turned back on Quinn. 'Was it the sunlight on the dews of a willow leaf? Is it somehow formed from the hardened resin of the willow?'

Quinn shrugged forlornly. 'I really don't know.'

'And you have never seen another?'

Quinn shook his head. 'No, never, though I know there are many more sunburst rubies like that one.' He nodded at the bright gem in Haf's other hand.

'Yes, yes, we all know that,' the dwarf dismissed this information. 'You know, I do believe you are telling the truth. I am pleased with you for that and it will make your journey all the more easy. Bor, Arg,' he shouted at two of the dwarves, 'let's have them prepared to move out.'

'Where are you taking us?' Quinn asked.

The dwarf twisted his beard into a rope and pushed it over his shoulder so that he could more readily fasten his cloak. 'There are many different peoples here about that are paying a good price for Torra Altans. There is no mistaking that you are high born Torra Altans and so the price will be accordingly high. Of course we will not deal with the man who seduced one of our very best chemists to his service but there is a band of hobs who will pay. It is a cruel thing to do because I don't suppose you will fare so well with them. I don't believe they feed their prisoners and they certainly won't give you mead.' He laughed at the notion. 'We'll let you go with a bellyful of bread in your stomach to ease your pain a little but, honestly, there's not much more we can do than that.'

'You're selling us to the hobs!' Rollo struggled against his bonds but was immediately grasped by one of the dwarves. 'You treacherous, vile creatures. You can't do that to us?'

'I told you,' the dwarf said calmly. 'You are highborn Torra Altans; precisely what they want! Now, how much do you suppose a hob would pay a company of wily dwarves for such a prize? I'm guessing it will be very high, very high indeed.'

'You'll get double crossed by them,' Rollo warned. 'No one deals with hobs and comes away smiling.'

The dwarf laughed at him. 'The manling talks as if he were a sage. You expect us to listen to you who have lived but a speck of time? A mere speck. You have experience of nothing yet you expect us to listen to you?' He threw back his head and roared with laughter. 'Come on, let's get these three scrawny lambs to market.' He snapped his fingers at the dwarves about him. 'It is time to find that ugly hob that's trying to put money in so many people's pockets. I'm looking forward to this.'

However hard he kicked, Rollo was unable to deter the dwarf that pressed his fists together and retied his rope bonds. He was no longer surprised that, when he had first tried to cut through Quinn's tethers, he had been unable to cut through the rope for, in the morning light, it was easy to see the threads of metal woven into it. Clearly, the dwarves were very skilled in their crafts.

The dwarves broke camp quickly. Five of them loaded up the heavy gear onto their backs. They then put a pole through the handle of the larger cauldron and hoisted it onto their shoulders, the weight shared between two of them. The remaining seven strode out at the fore of the party, unencumbered by bedding and cooking materials, bearing only their weapons.

Haf led the way and Bor and Arg marched just behind, dragging the prisoners. The ropes binding Quinn and Isolde were tied about Arg's waist while Rollo was tethered to the black-bearded dwarf, Bor. There seemed very little hope of escape and Rollo could do nothing but stumble after their captors. Isolde, who had become forlorn and listless since the death of the wolf, trudged on, head down, as if she were marching to witness the end of the world.

Though limping heavily and clearly in some pain, it was Quinn who managed to break the silence. 'Talk about out of the frying pan and into the fire,' he exclaimed.

'Don't you dare blame me again for all this!' Rollo snarled.

'I wasn't,' Quinn said with exasperation. 'Don't be so touchy. I was just trying to talk. It seemed better than marching on in doomed silence.'

'How can you make light of this?' Rollo complained. 'We've got to get away.'

'I'm making light of it because there is nothing else we can do.' Quinn nodded at his wrists. 'I've tried for two days to get out of these dwarf knots and I can't shift them at all. We'll just have to wait for a more sensible opportunity to escape.'

'But don't you realize? Don't you see?' Rollo exclaimed in anguish. 'We can't possibly let ourselves be taken by hobs. Didn't you hear Haf? They specifically want Torra Altans. The only reason they could possibly want Torra Altans is to use us against our own people.'

Quinn nodded, suddenly much more solemn. 'I know, but I don't know what we can do about it. That was why I was so angry when you came back for me. I thought that at least you and Isolde were safe. I thought you might get her all the way home but, like an idiot, you came back.'

'It wasn't my choice, believe me,' Rollo assured him in the nastiest tone he could muster but Quinn merely shrugged and trudged on.

There was nothing Rollo could do. He tried leaning back against the rope to annoy Bor but it seemed to make no impact on the dwarf's progress. However, his tethers cut into his wrists, the coarse rope with its threads of metal like miniature razor blades against his skin. He soon gave up and, head down, watched his boots beat the firm path that slowly turned to a bed of pine needles. Glancing at the sun, he estimated that they were travelling east, back towards the plantation of pine trees. He distinctly remembered that Merrit had warned that the pine forest was riddled with hobs.

He was simply not going to be taken by hobs. They would have to chop him up piece by piece, if they were going to make him. Rollo couldn't help himself; his mind blackened and he felt himself falling.

The cold shock of liquid thrown in his face brought him round. He spluttered and choked.

'They don't pay us one bean for dead Torra Altans, young manling,' Haf complained in his ear.

Quinn and Isolde had withdrawn as far as their bonds would allow and Quinn was pressing Isolde behind him. The dwarves stood in an amazed circle, clubs in hand, so Rollo knew that he had done something to distress them. However, he couldn't think too clearly because he was in quite some degree of pain; he must have hit his head against a rock. His wrists were also bleeding where he had cut himself against the ropes.

Haf yanked his head back, holding him by his hair. He then snapped his fingers at one of the other dwarves. 'Lith, there's a vial in my pack; fetch it for me.'

Obediently, Lith unbuckled Haf's pack that was strapped to his back and produced a vial that, to Rollo's eyes, appeared completely empty. The Artoran youth continued to struggle and kick but, now that there were many hands on him, there was nothing he could do. His eyes almost crossed as the vial was brought up under his nose and the stopper plucked off. A hazy cloud began to rise from the vial and Rollo was briefly aware of a sweet smell that eased his mind. Jerking his head aside, he broke free from Haf's grasp. Seemingly concerned that he might lose the contents of his precious vial, the dwarf hastily withdrew.

'Come on, now, there's a good lad. You'll feel an awful lot better with this inside you. Can't have you dying on us. That really would spoil everyone's day and you wouldn't want to be responsible for that, would you? I've already counted my coppers on this one. I need the money. I've an investment to make.' He patted his coat pocket where he had placed the two jewels. 'I'll need a forge and a furnace . . . It'll take quite a few experiments until I pull this one off, I have no doubt.'

He looked wistful for a moment and then suddenly turned to growl at his colleagues. 'Now hold the youth tight. I do not wish to waste any more time on this.'

Rollo wrenched his head back and forth, trying to avoid breathing in the vapour from the vial. He didn't know what it was but he knew from the look on Haf's face that it would knock him out cold. No one was going to do that to him! His own father had suggested something similar, advocating that he should be drugged for his own good so that he didn't find life so stressful, so that he didn't suffer from these fits of rage or from the shameful seizures. But he would not be drugged. He would not be less than he was. If he were going to be torn apart by the hobs, he would be torn apart whole and in sound mind. He was not afraid. He was afraid of nothing but having the right to be himself removed.

Twisting his head from side to side, he fought off the dwarves but Haf grabbed his hair to keep his head still whilst bringing the open vial up under Rollo's nose.

'There, lad, that'll soon feel better,' the dwarf assured him. 'You won't be so much trouble and we'll still get our money.'

I won't let them do this to me, Rollo vowed to himself. *I won't.* Cross-eyed, he glared at the vial before his nose and held his breath. He could see the smile spreading on Haf's face and saw him relax a little, waiting for that moment when he would have to draw breath. Rollo took advantage of that lapse in alertness. With the speed of a cobra, he thumped his head forward, knocking the vial aside. Haf roared in alarm, which made Lith, who was holding Rollo down, slacken his grip. Rollo grabbed his moment and leapt straight at Haf's nose and bit it. Haf staggered back, clasping his face, but Bor, the black-bearded dwarf to whom Rollo was tethered, stepped in and tried to enfold him in his thick arms. But he was much quicker than these heavy-limbed men. His hand flew to Bor's belt and he snatched out his knife.

He didn't have a hope of breaking free but, still, he would

435

do what he could. It would be better to die here than be handed to the hobs. He jerked the knife upwards towards Bor's neck and managed to nick the skin but the dwarf slammed one great fist to his throat and shoved him back. Rollo made once last wild attempt to stab out and, this time, drew blood, a trickle running from the dwarf's ear.

The smell of dwarf blood stung his nostrils and flooded his throat. Instantly, he was brought to a frenzy and thrashed, tore and bit as if he were a rabid dog. Bor flung him to the floor and thumped down on top of him, knocking the knife out from his hand. He could hear shouts from Isolde and Quinn, who were evidently trying to distract the other dwarves, but he could not properly hear what they were saying since his concentration was focused on trying to bite the dwarf's thumb that was closest to his mouth. At last, he had it and bit hard, sinking his incisors in deep. The dwarf roared and raised his other fist above Rollo's head, drawing it back, ready to smash him to a pulp.

In that split second, Rollo was instantly calm and rational as he realized that, if that solid fist was pounded into his face, it would certainly kill him. Bor gave out a roar in readiness to put all his weight behind his punch but, just as Rollo heard a strange whistling sound and a heavy thud, he seemed to throw his entire body instead.

The dwarf's heavy bulk crashed forward, pressing down on his chest and lungs; he could not breathe. There were shouts and cries all about him as he strove to free himself from beneath the lifeless dwarf. After long seconds of desperate struggling, he managed to heave an arm off his face and was able to see a little of what was going on. Quinn was lying over Isolde, protecting her with his body as the dwarves raised their shields and threw their hurling axes, which made a terrifying whirring noise as they arced into the sky.

Three of the dwarves, including Arg, fell within one minute, crashing to the ground, the tails of quarrels jutting from their breasts. Isolde screamed as blood spurted from

Arg's neck over her face. Though she pulled to get away, there was no escape from the rope binding her to the slain dwarf. After another two fell, the remaining six broke their circle and fled.

Rollo wriggled out from beneath Bor's dead weight. But escape was impossible since he, Isolde and Quinn were still tethered to the slaughtered dwarves.

Quinn immediately fell on Arg's bloody body, struggling to untie the knots while Rollo looked about for the knife that had been knocked from his hand. When he couldn't see it, he strained to reach the body of the next dwarf lying face down in the mud but his rope was too short.

'Quick, Quinn, do something. Find a way to get us free!' Rollo insisted but then froze as a familiar voice spoke behind him.

'Do you need something like this?'

Rollo might have known. Until that second it hadn't occurred to him how someone had managed to pierce dwarf armour with a normal crossbow bolt but now he realized that the bolts were fired from a crossbow designed for hunting mammoth.

Merrit was as impressive as ever on his fine charger. He had in his hand an unusual-looking knife that he flipped over in a rather amused fashion as he laughed at their plight. He tossed the blade at Rollo's feet. Rather than metal, the blade looked as if it were polished glass.

As he touched his hand to the edge, it immediately drew blood. 'An obsidian blade! I haven't seen one of these since I left Tethya.'

Rollo cut their bonds with ease and then turned back to look at the man and his horse. The mare dipped her head and greeted them with a stamp of her hoof and a snort through her velvet nostrils. He allowed his gasped breaths to still before dragging himself up to his feet and pushing back his bedraggled hair.

Merrit looked down at them in despair. 'I was worried for

you. I couldn't think what had happened to you since you slipped away. You stole neither my mare nor the tusks so I thought something sinister must have happened. And I was right.' He laughed lightly. 'Taken by a rogue band of dwarves. It's taken me all this while to find you.'

Rollo swallowed but Quinn limped forward to the man. 'How can we ever thank you enough?' He stretched out a hand and gripped Merrit's palm, who looked somewhat taken aback by this gesture.

Rollo, on the other hand, did not share Quinn's sentiments. He still hadn't forgotten that they had fled from this man in the first place. Moreover, he thought it peculiar that a virtual stranger would track them all that way just to help them; the man was just too good to be true. He surely had a more meaningful motive than altruism.

'Sweet Isolde, I was so worried for you. After the days we'd been together, I didn't realize how much I would miss you,' Merrit said smoothly.

'Hmm!' Rollo snorted in indignation. No one would miss Isolde; most people would barely know she was there. It was only when she was spoken to directly that she offered an opinion on anything. Look at her! Bedraggled and exhausted, she had her arm round Quinn in an attempt to help him but her eyes were acutely fixed on the direction in which the dwarves had fled. She was, he presumed, still thinking about her precious gemstone.

She offered no words to Merrit but focused back on Quinn. 'Are you hurt?' she murmured under her breath.

He shook his head. 'No, no! I'm just desperate to get back home. All I can think about is my mother and Guthrey.'

Rollo felt the hot, spiky hand of guilt sear up his throat and squeeze his windpipe. Poor Guthrey! He hated himself for the atrocious thing he had done. He would give almost anything to be like Quinn. The Torra Altan youth was confident and accomplished in a modest way and Rollo was sure that he had other talents that he had not yet revealed.

'You had best get yourself back up on my horse,' Merrit told Quinn. 'It seems you've had an even worse time of it than when I found you last. I told you these wild regions were no place for three youngsters like yourselves.'

Without a word, Quinn dutifully obeyed but Rollo sank down, sat on the ground and stared. How could Quinn do that? It was all so neat and simple. 'Well, hang the lot of you,' he said flatly. 'You just go on home with that hob-smelling demon. I'm staying here.'

'Come on, Rollo, there's a good fellow. He came back for us. You'd have been dead two minutes ago if he hadn't. And well, quite honestly, at least he doesn't smell as if he's spent his life swimming in a dwarf's tankard,' Quinn said congenially. Rollo suspected this to be true but he still wasn't any happier about Merrit. 'You go to wherever it is you have to go. I'm not taking one pace with that man.'

The young prince was most surprised when they did actually turn their backs on him and start to walk away, heading, he guessed, back for the Dairy Track. Only Isolde looked back and, after a moment, reached out her hand, beckoning him to come with them.

Stubbornly, Rollo sat there on the cold earth and the others were long gone before he was suddenly aware that he was keeping company with the six dead dwarves. Now that wasn't funny! It would be no time before the ravens came and, after that, the wolves. He must move!

In no time at all, he was on his feet and sprinting after Isolde, Quinn and the strange long-haired man who gave himself only the name of Merrit.

Chapter 26

No one greeted Rollo with anything more than a tired nod, as if they had expected him to follow. He did not appreciate that.

Isolde was wrapping strands of her long, ragged hair round and round her little finger, gazing at the waters of a scurrying stream that swept alongside the Dairy Track. She had given him no more than the briefest of glances before returning to stare blankly in front of her. Quinn sat astride the horse while Merrit strode alongside, the pair chatting happily together as if nothing had ever happened to break up their happy caravan.

Falling in behind, Rollo stamped along, brooding quietly to himself. After stopping to refill their water canisters from a clear pool in the stream, they trudged on, dipping beneath the low branches of an old ash that were all but claimed by ivy, saucerlike flakes of fungi growing at the roots.

They were making good progress now towards the Great North Road and Rollo was beginning to feel foolish; perhaps his sceptical nature had forced him to misconstrue Merrit's conduct at the mill. Despite his misguided behaviour that had driven them into the perilous clutches of the dwarves, he began to feel that, at last, luck was with them. And so it seemed until they came to a halt as the stream plunged into the Barleytwist River that crossed their path. The ancient stone bridge had been torn down, bits of it poking out through the leaping waters of the churning flow. Angry and swollen with the winter storms, it was impossible to ford.

Merrit shook his head at the wreck of the bridge. 'That's a blow. And just when we were making such good time.' He looked up and down the flow of the river and then nodded north into the woods lining the Barleytwist. 'Well, there's nothing for it but to find somewhere else to cross. We'll carry on upriver; I've a friend in these parts and he's bound to know a way.'

After splashing through the stream, they passed into an ancient area of woodland. At last, they were free of the birch and hazel saplings that had dominated so much of Belbidia's lowlands. Presently Rollo thought he could smell wood-smoke.

Merrit gave him a rare smile. 'A spot of lunch wouldn't go amiss,' he said jovially.

All but Rollo nodded. He was feeling rather sick; the knowledge of how close he had come to being sold to hobs was only just becoming real to him.

'Hello!' Merrit called out into the forest. Dipping beneath a trailing branch, he picked up a narrow footpath and waved them forward. Quinn was forced to bend low onto the horse's neck so that he could pass beneath the low boughs as they followed Merrit along the track. Gradually, the way broadened, opening out into a swathe of lush grass amidst the regal trees whose bare branches rattled in the light breeze.

Rollo was quite taken aback to hear the sound of chickens squawking. A large boar was snuffling at the roots of a coppiced willow within a well-fenced enclosure. Beyond the pigpen lay an open-fronted animal shelter and four low huts with thatched roofs. Washing was strung on a line between two of them and there was the sound of a baby crying.

'Hello!' Merrit called again.

'Hey there! Hey everyone, it's Merrit!' a child's voice cried.

'Get the pot on, wife,' a deep voice ordered just before a man with the traditional Belbidian looks of brown hair and hazel eyes strode out from behind one of the huts. In one

441

hand, he held a length of hazel and in the other a short hatchet.

'Good man, Merrit! Welcome, welcome! You are always welcome here! Always. I was just saying to Sara that it had been a good many weeks since we had seen you and now, as if by magic, here you are. I've had a rabbit hanging for a couple of days. It won't take a minute to fry it up in the pan. I'm assuming you'll be staying for supper and the night?'

'That would be most welcome, John,' Merrit said warmly. 'Most welcome.'

'It's the least I can do after what you have done for us. I was saying to Sara only last week that it's nearly a year since you saved the boy from the mammoth. He would have crushed the lad if you hadn't arrived just when you did. I can still remember the sound of that horn of yours as you came charging through the trees.'

Merrit held his hands up as if defending himself from all this praise. 'Now, now. It's my job, after all, and I was just fortunate to be in the right place at the right time.'

Rollo stood at the edge of the glade, absorbing everything. Certainly, the farmer was genuine in his praise. Maybe, as Quinn had insisted, he had misunderstood what Merrit had said at the mill and read far too much into innocent words. He studied the man who was talking warmly with the grateful woodsman. Perhaps Merrit really did just want to help those unfortunates who couldn't help themselves in these times? After all, what reward could this woodsman offer beyond a plate of rabbit and a warm bed?

Merrit led his horse to a water trough and allowed her to drink. The boar grunted in indignation at this intrusion into his territory but did not trouble himself enough to break off from his foraging.

'And you have brought friends with you, I see. Sara, what food have we got stored in the saltbox?' John called out. 'Merrit has company with him. And they're in need of sustenance by the look of them.'

Rollo was not that familiar with the different Belbidian dialects but it struck him that this simple yeoman was not so simple as he had first appeared; the man spoke a little too well. His clothes were torn and muddy and his boots were cobbled together with inexpert stitching but he had a scarf round his neck that was made of brightly coloured wool and he had a silver buckle on his belt. Rollo must have been staring because the man gave him a hasty smile.

'Now, don't just stand there, lad. You look famished. Welcome to my humble abode and please share some bread with me while we await Sara's fine cooking. I managed to make some elderberry wine in the autumn and I hope you will do me the honour of tasting it. It's a little young and we shouldn't be drinking it yet but, though I say so myself, it's a fair taste and you may enjoy it.' He fell silent and looked thoughtfully at the three half-starved youngsters. 'Or perhaps you children are a little young to be drinking wine?'

'Elderberry wine can barely be described as wine!' Rollo sneered rudely and immediately regretted his surly words. John was only trying to be hospitable yet he had immediately been unpleasant to the man.

'My, we are fine and full of airs for one who's been lost in these woods,' John laughed at him. 'Well, there's no call for you to drink my wine. It sits just as well with me if you have water.'

'I'm sorry,' Rollo managed to mumble under his breath. 'I didn't mean . . . I'm just tired, that's all,' he apologized.

'Not to worry,' a rather portly woman waddled out from the hut, one hand around a baby perched comfortably on her hip and the other holding a large wooden spoon. She dropped the spoon into an empty pot as she passed and put her arm about Rollo's shoulder. 'Don't mind John. He's not used to the world the way it is yet and still longs for how things were. It makes him a little sharpish at times.'

'Dear Lady Wife, you have no call to speak about me like that in front of guests,' the husband snapped. 'Now come in

443

and rest your feet,' he addressed the weary travellers. 'I'll just pop out the back and fetch my wine.'

The words 'come in' clearly did not convey quite the same meaning to Rollo as the man had intended them to. Rollo presumed they were being invited into the rather rickety-looking hut but, in fact, they were invited only to its threshold and the rough-hewn benches that were placed on three sides about a firepit.

'Welcome to my kitchen,' Sara said enthusiastically and grinned. 'Take a seat.'

Merrit returned from beyond the animal shelter, bearing a leather pitcher and a number of goblets.

Rollo stared at the goblets. 'Pewter,' he remarked in surprise.

The woodsman grinned at him. 'Just because we live in the woods doesn't mean we are savages. Do you think a man like myself should not have pewter?'

'No, indeed.' Rollo tried his best to correct the impression he was giving of himself. He wondered why it was that Quinn and Isolde had kept on the right side of this man whereas he managed to offend him at every turn. It finally occurred to him that it was because the other two had barely said a word. He grunted in dissatisfaction at this state of affairs.

John poured them each a cup of wine. Rollo sniffed at it tentatively while Quinn took a polite sip and then placed it carefully at his feet. Isolde nodded her thanks and, though she had been too shy to talk to either of the parents, gave the child a playful wink.

The young boy giggled.

'Hello,' Isolde said warmly, stooping to pick up the wooden spoon that the woman had discarded. She stood it up on the bench and made it dance as if it were a little person. The child giggled in delight and ran to find another spoon that he, too, could make dance.

'Here, Merrit, let me help you with that!' John leapt to his feet as Merrit was preparing to attend to his horse. 'You take

444

a seat. I'll give your horse as good a rub down as she'd get in any king's mews.'

Merrit smiled but insisted on unsaddling the horse himself. He lifted down the heavy packs and let them rest against his saddle but the smallest pack he clutched to himself and, when he returned to the wooden bench, placed it carefully beside him and patted it thoughtfully, smoothing over the thick wolfskin that covered the satchel. Rollo watched as Isolde's eyes fixed on the pack, her nose wrinkling in disgust.

'Poor wolf,' she murmured huskily under her breath.

Rollo raised an eyebrow at her. He could not understand that she, who wore a heavy bearskin, could criticize someone for having a wolf pelt covering on their satchel. The Artoran could not abide hypocrisy.

Now that Merrit was seated, Sara served up the simple fare of rabbit and bread. Rollo was actually quite impressed as he tasted the succulent meat that had been hastily fried in sizzling fat. Dark berries swam in a rich juice spiced with the piquant taste of sorrel. There were no vegetables but the bread had a pleasant nutty flavour, though it was a little over-salted. He was thirsty and, seeing no water upon the table but not wanting to inconvenience his hosts by asking them to rise from their food, he had no option but to turn to the elderberry wine.

The words of the dwarves' song came back, and in agreement with Haf and his dwarves he wished he had mead or ale instead of elderberry wine. In his firm opinion, elderberry was not a suitable fruit for making wine. Moreover, before he had set so much as one foot in Belbidia, he had decided that any wine made in the region would be thin and sweet, not at all like the aromatic, full-bodied tang of the wines of Tethya. The children of Artor drank wine from a very young age and, when his father had told him that such habits were not the ways of Belbidians, he had decided that he would not like Belbidia nor its wine.

John's elderberry wine smelt of flowers and reminded him

pleasantly of spring. Quinn had already taken a sip and then took a longer draught as if pleased with the flavour. Rollo was encouraged to follow suit, took one sip and then pulled back in amazement.

'Not so scathing now, are you, lad?' John appeared amused by his reaction.

'It's wonderful!' Rollo exclaimed. 'I've not tasted the like even in Tethya.'

'Tethya! You are a long way from home,' the woodsman exclaimed.

Rollo ardently agreed that he was and held out his goblet for a refill from the pitcher. He considered that, if the man knew of Tethya, he was not a man that had lived in the midst of a forest all his life. He seemed a jumble of contradictions. Clearly, a great deal more thought and skill had gone into the preparation of his wine than had been spent on the repairs to his home. But perhaps he had the balance right; enough of this elderberry nectar and even he could live quite happily in the forest for many years. Rollo laughed lightly at the idea.

Isolde was beginning to smile. 'Elderberry wine,' she giggled to Quinn. 'What would Brid say if she caught me drinking wine?'

Quinn smiled back weakly. Clearly, the wine had not yet eased his fears for his mother's safety.

'I'd best fetch another pitcher,' John offered. 'When you encouraged me to make the wine, Merrit, I thought I would be wasting my time but I think it's the best thing that's happened since I lost my home. I've made many friends since.'

'That is good, John, good. There is nothing better in this world than friends. I think that is the message most of us have learnt over the last decade.'

Rollo looked at Merrit sideways, aware that he had only lost friends in that time. He noted that Isolde was not warmed by his words either but looked down at her grubby bare feet and wriggled her toes.

John trotted off and disappeared behind the draughty

446

animal shelter, grunting to lift up a large board set into the ground. He bent over, his top half disappearing into the ground before he emerged with two pitchers. Merrit rose and went to help the woodsman and, together, they stood apart from the table in deep discussion. Rollo had to agree that he was very glad of the hospitality and was almost enjoying himself now that his toes were being warmed by the fire and that his belly was aglow with the wine.

'You shouldn't be wandering around the woods with no shoes on, child,' Sara scolded Isolde. 'It's not healthy and it's a wonder that your feet aren't swollen with chilblains in this weather. Don't you put your toes so close to the fire either because if you haven't got chilblains already, you soon will.'

Isolde smiled meekly and pulled her skirts down to cover her toes.

'I could always fetch you some shoes. I think I might have an old pair that belonged . . .' The woman broke off and sighed. 'Well, let's just say they're no good to me now and you may as well have them.' Sara absentmindedly reached for her young son and gave his shoulder a protective squeeze; the boy indignantly pushed her hand away.

'That's very kind, of you, Sara.' Isolde spoke so softly that the woman had to lean forward to listen. 'But I couldn't possibly accept.'

'No, no I insist. They would only be going to waste.'

'Please, don't trouble yourself,' Isolde protested.

'It's no trouble at all!'

Isolde looked helplessly at Quinn and he nodded at her as if reading her thoughts.

'No, really,' the youth said more firmly. 'Isolde never wears shoes.'

'Well, why ever not? That's the silliest thing I ever heard,' Sara scolded as if she were talking to one of her own offspring and not a stranger.

Isolde shrugged and Rollo noted that there was a sudden

447

lull in the animated conversation between Merrit and John. The priestess nudged at her nose and looked suddenly embarrassed as all eyes were turned on her.

'It's nothing really. I just don't wear shoes,' she said as if annoyed by all the attention. 'And you know,' she added as if trying to distract everyone from her, 'chilblains are not made worse by the warmth of a fire, at all. They are caused only by cold and are really the very first stages of frostbite. People think they are caused by heat simply because they start to itch when they are warmed up and so you notice them more.'

'Well, I'm quite sure you must be the authority on chilblains,' the woman laughed. 'And nor do I pretend to be an expert on old wives' tales. But it seems to me that you're a mite too young yourself to be carrying that banner,' she chided Isolde. 'Shouldn't you be seeing to it that you find yourself a man before you start telling an old mother like myself how much of one's body should be toasted in front of the fire?' She slapped her stomach. 'Born seven children, I have. I'll grant you that only three lived beyond infancy and my poor sweet Clara didn't survive the attack. I don't care what penance you're doing but, if you're sitting in my kitchen, you'll have something warm on your feet or, I'll swear, I'll catch my death of cold just by looking at you.' She stamped away into her hut and returned shortly with a stout pair of girl's boots, the heels only slightly worn down.

Isolde looked at the boots with a hint of distaste but gave Sara a bright smile. Rollo read the hesitation but even found himself wishing that, for Sara's sake, she would graciously accept the boots. Clearly, they belonged to the woman's dead child and she wanted to see some good come of them. It would only hurt the woman's feelings if Isolde refused and he saw no good reason for her to do that. Sara had been kind and he felt sorry for her situation.

Merrit and John rejoined the company. The woodsman looked at his wife, who was now rather pink in the face and beginning to tell them all about the rather messy birth of their last child.

'Clearly, woman, we have been too long in the woods if you must tell such stories to perfect strangers. It is not the subject for the dinner table. Moreover, you have most certainly had too much wine. Far too much of my precious liqueur!' He dismissed his wife by turning his enthusiastic attention back onto Merrit. 'Now, sit, Merrit, and have some food. These youngsters will have eaten their share and yours if you don't hurry.'

The man chose to sit down alongside Rollo. The boy felt the bench creak and give beneath the man's weight so he prudently moved his feet from underneath it just in case it gave way entirely.

'Now, John, tell me what has been happening in this peaceful neck of the woods,' Merrit asked politely as he scooped up a spoonful of the sauce before attacking the rabbit. 'A very fine meal, Mistress Sara, I must say. Now go on, John, entertain a man while he eats.'

Rollo watched as John took a swig of wine and smacked his lips, raising his cup to his friend. 'Well, I must say one thing, Merrit, we've had a sight more company since you gave me the recipe for this wine. As you well know from the last time you visited, the bridge on the Dairy Track has been down a few months now so I've had a fair few passers by looking for a way to cross the Barleytwist. More often than not they drop by on their way back. It's not the quickest route but soon, I warrant you, they'll be a new track through here linking the old roads. And they're all coming in search of elderberry wine. It's very good for business.'

Rollo blinked, thinking that Merrit had definitely seemed surprised at finding the bridge down and yet, clearly, he had already known about it. He shook his head, trying to shake the fuzzy feeling that the elderberry wine induced. No, surely he had misheard or misunderstood.

'Excellent. There's nothing like a bit of wine to help

business,' Merrit enthused jovially, taking a small sip whilst encouraging John to refill his own goblet. 'Go on. You might as well enjoy what you can of it before everyone else drinks it up. So have you entertained anyone interesting?'

The woodsman shrugged. 'Met two brothers from the border of Nattarda and Jotunn who had lost their herds and were wondering whether there'd be work for them in Ovissia. I told them that Ovissians don't take kindly to cattlemen at the best of times and that, like as not, they'd fare better in Piscera if they were prepared to turn their hands to fishing. They looked at me as if I were quite mad and told me that they were too old to change their way of life.' John laughed at this. 'As if we haven't all had to make a few adjustments.' He waved his hands about him at his ramshackle collection of huts. 'I used to live in a three storey stone townhouse in the centre of Bleham. Busy town it was and there was a good calling for men with a good knowledge of the law.'

Rollo's eyebrows rose and John caught his look of surprise.

'You wouldn't take me for a man of the law now, would you, son? But I was until those wretched hobs stormed the town and tore down the houses. Sara and I wandered through abandoned fields for weeks. People were dying on the road. They were robbing each other, killing each other for food or clothes. There was so little food. Each town we went to was no better. We'd beg for shelter and occasionally a good-hearted soul would put us up in their barn but, sooner or later, the hobs attacked. It was the year the hobs first flooded into Belbidia and I thought that the very end of the world was coming with them. Then after what happened to poor Clara,' John croaked and blinked rapidly for a few seconds, 'Sara wisely said that we should head into the woods. And here we've been ever since and, but for the mammoth, we've been safe, though it's amazing what queer folk one meets wandering in these remote parts.' He gave Isolde a wry smile.

'There's been folk coming out from Nattarda and Jotunn quite regularly now and one or two that's set up home in the

450

forest like ourselves. Hobs aren't so keen on this part of the wood. Too many oak and ash trees, you know. I learnt that early on. But I haven't seen such rum folk as you in a long while,' he teased.

Isolde coloured up and hid her face in her cup of honey-sweet elderberry wine.

Rollo laughed. 'There's nothing strange about us.'

'Mmm.' The man sounded doubtful though there was an amused twinkle in his eyes.

Rollo felt a pleasing sense of warmth spread through his body and took another sip of the wine. 'Honeysuckle,' he murmured. 'It has a taste of honeysuckle.'

'You have a very acute sense of taste,' John remarked, impressed. 'Merrit suggested it last time he tested the wine and he was right; it makes all the difference.'

Sara was still staring at Isolde's now booted feet. Her cheeks ruddy with the sudden flush of alcohol, the woman demanded, 'So what penance are you doing, child? I can't believe one so young as yourself has sinned?'

'Sinned? I never said I had sinned.' Isolde looked hurt. 'No, I simply like to feel the warmth of the Great Mother at my feet.'

'It seems to me that the Great Mother is pretty chilly at the moment,' John laughed and, encouraged by the wine, Rollo found his joke a great deal more amusing than he should have done.

Isolde, however, took offence. 'You should not laugh at things you do not understand. If you want to learn about the world, you should feel the earth, smell the air and listen to the trees.'

'My dear, I've been in these woods eight years now and, believe me, the trees don't speak.'

'That's because you do not understand their tongue,' Isolde said with surprising loudness, the alcohol loosening her inhibitions. 'Brid thinks I haven't been paying attention to her lessons but she is wrong. I love the trees.'

451

Rollo noted how Merrit's eyes briefly widened at Isolde's words. Though the man studiously turned to examining his hand as if some sore or injury were bothering him, Rollo was certain that he was listening intently to Isolde's every word.

The priestess sighed. 'The ash tells us how all events in the world are linked and how we are but a part of the whole. The hazel,' she wafted her hand back in the direction in which they had recently passed and then at the wattle hurdle that John was crafting, 'speaks of intuition. All the trees have a message for us and, if we listen, we shall grow in understanding.'

'Seems to me man's learnt very little,' Sara snorted. 'He hasn't even learnt how to defend himself from hobs.'

Rollo lazed back and listened to them arguing. Sara had clearly been chosen by John for her beauty. The man was not handsome but had a sharp mind and discussed all the topics raised with interest, though the subjects were becoming less sensible by the second.

'So why do you know so much of trees and ailments?' Sara had persistently returned to the subject of chilblains. Though she would not admit it, they clearly plagued her own toes and Isolde had described in detail the very best treatment for them several times.

Rollo was vaguely aware that Merrit had not spoken for some time but was resting with his back against the wattle wall of the hut, the hood of his cloak pulled down over his eyes. Rollo leant back also and half closed his eyes, glad of the wine in his belly that eased the distress in his head.

Quinn also seemed to have forgotten all their troubles and was already demonstrating his skill with a bow. He had borrowed John's hunting bow and had no trouble piercing his target – a small square of white cloth that he had pinned to a distant tree.

Even Merrit's eyes flicked open at this display. He nodded to himself, his gaze running over the three youngsters before turning back to John. 'Tell us more of what other strangers you have seen.'

'One man from the east coast was saying that he was deeply troubled by the number of villagers that had been stolen away and all taken off to Nattarda,. Another said that Baron Wiglaf's been breeding these fearful ravenshrikes. What a story now! I don't believe it; no man would breed such vile beasts. Mammoths are one thing but these monstrous ravenshrikes are quite another. They swoop down at night and take men straight from their beds, so they say.'

'Ravenshrikes?' Quinn queried, leaping on the word.

'Indeed, ravenshrikes. There's been many, many people stolen away. It's put terror into the heart of any city still occupied by men and they are fleeing into the woods where, no doubt, most will starve.'

'So why do you think this is happening?' Merrit asked. 'Did any of the strangers have any idea as to why ravenshrikes should do such a strange thing?'

The man shrugged. 'No one knows. We can see that the hobs want our lands and that the likes of the taurs, the dragons and the griffins just want to eat but no one knows what purpose drives the ravenshrikes. The latest I heard on the matter was that a whole caravan of pilgrims was stolen off the North Road. And the same group were seen quite some while later carried over Jotunn, again heading for Nattarda, men and women, all still screaming and kicking.'

'I told you he was alive,' Quinn suddenly exclaimed with delight. In his exuberance, he attempted to perform a cart-wheel though only succeeded in tripping over a bench and toppling one of the wine pitchers that Merrit caught, saving its contents.

'Sit down, lad, before you do some real mischief! John, go on; tell us more.' Merrit carefully settled the pitcher and leant forward. He turned back to John. 'That's quite a story,' he remarked coolly.

John grinned. 'Now don't go thinking that I've made

that up just to entertain you; I haven't got that kind of imagination.' He sat back and stared into the fire before suddenly snapping his fingers as if a thought had occurred to him. Reaching into his pocket, he drew out a small white figure. 'I quite forgot to thank you for the hunk of ivory you brought last time you were here. I've found a fellow in one of the villages who has a fair hand at carving and he's made me a number of these.' John held up the ivory figurine. 'I've sold a fair few of these lucky charms of late. People are ready to part with good money for a token if they think it's going to turn away bad luck,' he said flippantly. 'That's where I got the goblets.'

Rollo picked them up and looked at the pewter and the rather strange design on the metal. Feeling somewhat slowed by the wine, he examined the figures and realized they weren't of men at all but of all sorts of creatures: the warriors of Ash, the long-limbed hobs, the small and nervous kobolds and the stocky dwarves. The metal was finally wrought, the balance of the design perfect and the figures beautifully formed. Rollo had never knowingly seen the work of a dwarf but he guessed that this was probably an example of it.

'Where did the man find these goblets then?' Merrit asked. Clearly, he had drawn the same conclusion as Rollo about their origins.

'He was a strange fellow. He didn't eat too much but asked too many questions. And he kept coming back to the movements of the hobs and the mammoths and dragons. And as if I'd know such things! He was wondering if any of the old priories or the druid's schools had gone into hiding in the woods. He was convinced that there was some learned sect of people hiding somewhere in one of the old forests of Jotunn but I told him there were none that I knew of. Who's got time for that sort of thing in these troubled times? All people want nowadays is lucky tokens, not knowledge and religion. Anyhow, he left on his fine horse, determined to search the Oldhart Forest though

I warned him against it.' John sighed and there was a lull in the conversation.

Quinn, however, who had looked lost in thought, suddenly filled the silence with a hoot of delight. 'If those pilgrims were still alive then so is Guthrey! I know he is and it's not too late! And you said they were all heading for Nattarda?'

John shook his head. 'Anyone would be a fool to chase after such a creature. You don't put your head in the mouth of a lion now, do you, lad?'

'Not unless it's swallowed your brother whole and you hope to pull him out again. What are we waiting for? You must tell us where the creatures were taking their victims.'

'Lad, I don't know. I only hear tales that travellers bring me and, like as not, they're tales exaggerated in the telling long before they get to me.'

'Wiglaf's lands, you said?' Quinn slurred, leapt up and immediately staggered back and sat down again. 'Isolde, we're leaving right now. Which way?'

Isolde looked up at the sky and the evening sunlight slanting in through the trees. She stepped slowly round. 'I don't know. The world won't keep still.'

Rollo groaned. His friends had sipped but half a goblet of wine each but they were drunk.

Chapter 27

'Leaf!' Caspar called out into the mist.

Uncaring that he was cold, wet and exhausted, his only thought was to find the little girl.

Leaf's voice came to him muffled through the mist. 'Spar? Where are you? I could see you a moment ago. I could see the river and I was walking towards you but now I can't see anything. Where are you?'

'Over here!' he called. 'Over here. The river swept me over the dam.' He took a step towards the sound of her voice.

'The mist is getting worse. I can hardly see a thing.' Leaf's voice sounded frightened.

'Keep talking. I'm coming towards you,' he told her, trying desperately to stop his teeth chattering so he could make himself audible.

'I'll try,' she called back bravely and continued to call his name at regular intervals.

He didn't think they could be that far apart but it seemed to take an age to find her. Inch by inch, he worked his way forward. All the while, her cries seemed lost and distant and so it came as a surprise that she was suddenly there before him, a dark silhouette in the white of the mist.

'Oh Spar! I thought I'd lost you.' She hurried forward and flung her arms around him, her hands slapping against his wet clothes. She pulled away and stared at him in alarm. 'Get those wet things off at once!' she demanded as if she had been a child's nurse all her life. 'Now, now, now!'

Caspar could not keep his chattering teeth still long enough to allow him to smile and only managed to grunt.

'You should know better than to stay in wet clothes,' Leaf continued to berate him.

She dragged at his sleeves and he knew he must try and obey her. It was quite incongruous that this girl, who could be no more than eleven or twelve, was ordering him, a man of thirty-six, around with such authority but he obeyed her without question. His cuffs seemed to have stuck to his skin and his sleeves dragged against his wet flesh but, eventually, he had his shirt off and Leaf sacrificed her own comfort to throw her woollen cloak over his back.

He rubbed himself vigorously and soon was feeling very much better. He didn't bother to take off his breeches but only pulled off each boot to tip the water out. He wrung out his socks and replaced them onto his white wrinkled toes before searching deep to find the strength to pull his boots on again.

The young girl was tutting and staring perplexedly at the amulet. 'It was working. I could see clearly all about me . . .,' her voice trailed away as if she were thinking, 'until I started walking towards you. Of course! It's so obvious. The amulet doesn't work for you; it works only for me.'

Caspar thought that was partially good news. At least one of them would find a way out of there. Leaf sat down firmly on the ground and stared at the gold pendant. 'It must have been specifically designed for the people of my mother's household or perhaps for anyone of our hidden realm. Now our problem is how we work with that information.'

'Could we not alter the amulet?' Caspar suggested. He didn't want to be left here alone in the mist while she tried to find a way out of here before coming back for him – or not as the case maybe.

'But I don't know what all the sigils mean,' she said in defeat. 'If I did, it would all have been obvious to me from the start but I don't. Oh Spar!' She fell against him and hugged his numb body. 'What are we to do? Perhaps a long piece of thread between the two of us? I could go on ahead and you could follow the thread.'

'And have it snap just as we got to the difficult bit? Let me have a look.' Caspar held out his hand. It was trembling and it was only through sheer force of will that he managed to make his chilled fingers uncurl.

Leaf raised an eyebrow, evidently sceptical, but, nevertheless, gave it to him. He frowned at the interlinked patterns; there had to be a way.

'Silas managed it,' he said thoughtfully. 'Silas brought us all through the shrouding curtain that protects your lands. I should have looked more carefully.' He cursed himself for not taking more notice of Raven's headcollar and the runes marked upon it. He should have memorized them. Perhaps one or two of the marks on this amulet looked familiar and the same as the one on Raven's browband but he wasn't really sure.

'Of course,' he exclaimed with hope. 'Now bear with me on this, Leaf. We don't need to know what these runes mean or how they are formed; we simply know that they work for you. Could we not just add to them to make them work for me too?'

'That's so simple,' Leaf laughed delightedly. 'Too simple! And I cannot believe you thought of it before I did.' Suddenly her face fell as if another thought had occurred to her. 'Perhaps . . .' Her face wrinkled into a frown and Caspar read the look of self-doubt. 'Perhaps it's happening already.'

His muscles still shaking violently, the Baron took her hand. 'No, don't think that. You said yourself that you were too young for the disease to affect you. All that's happened here is something that happens more often than you'd think with clever folk; they all too easily underestimate the intelligence of others.'

She grunted in acknowledgement though seemed less enthusiastic about his idea. 'Well, I guess it's worth a try but, if it fails, we may ruin the amulet altogether. We have to consider that possibility.'

The thought quelled Caspar's confidence for a moment and his teeth even stopped chattering for a second. Then he braced his shoulders and raised his head. It had to be the right way. He gritted his teeth. 'Sometimes, Leaf, one has to go on instinct. There is no way to solve this problem logically because we simply do not have enough information. What we need now is faith and a little luck.' Kneeling down, he pinned the amulet against the hard ground and took out his knife from his boot. With the tip of his knife, he scratched the first line of the rune that Morrigwen had bestowed on him: R Rad, the rune of the seeker.

Carefully scratching the last mark, he closed his eyes and willed the rune to work, not daring to raise his eyes in case his one plan had failed. He was too scared to look until Leaf laughed like a child who had just been given a birthday present.

'But that's wonderful!' She kissed him on the nose. 'Absolutely wonderful. How did you know?'

'I didn't know,' Caspar told her, gazing round at his surroundings. Swallowing hard, he couldn't speak for what he saw. They were not sitting on the edge of a riverbank, as Caspar had assumed, but were on a long thin island, the raging river gushing by to one side and a sluggish dark channel on the other. Leaf had reached the island via a marshy peninsula, which looked like the remnants of a damn that had collapsed into the water. They were, in fact, extremely lucky that they had not fallen into deeper water. The turbulent whirlpools in the otherwise sluggish channel showed Caspar where there was a large underwater drain running under the island, carrying water back to the river. If he had fallen in there, he would never have got out again; there was absolutely no question of that. He shuddered. The river itself was high from winter rain, engorged with mud and not even the strongest of swimmers would have had any hope of crossing it.

Through the sparkling haze, which a moment before had looked to them like a blanketing fog, they could see the lone poplar some way upstream and, beyond that, a hamlet, which appeared to be at the far edge of the crystal curtain. It was quite extraordinary; what had once appeared to be an impenetrable mist had become a mass of tiny sparkling shards of crystal, which parted before the eye. Caspar held out his hand and caught one of the minute crystals. It was quite beautiful, as perfect as a snowflake.

'We must go back the way you came and cross back along that marshy peninsula until we reach firm ground again. Then we'll have to work our way along the riverbank until we find a bridge. Or . . .' He looked back down to the tip of the long thin island and the narrow point of the river where the water bowed in a silver stream over the weir. 'There was something in the water there, just where the river narrows above the weir. I pulled myself out by means of what must have been a thick pole or beam. We could perhaps bridge the river with that and then walk across to the other side. Come on; it's worth a try.'

They ran to the point where Caspar had hauled himself out of the river and there, indeed, was the long slippery length of wood that looked as if it had been a beam from a truss of a barn, or something similar, before being washed into the river and becoming jammed against the bank. His hands numb with cold, Caspar dragged at the beam to try and pull it free of the water but he simply couldn't keep his grip on it.

Leaf looked at him sideways. 'Just stop and think,' she protested at his actions. 'You need to cover your hands so that you can grip the beam. And it's heavy, so you only want to move it once.'

Caspar looked at her, awaiting her plan.

She looked the beam up and down. 'If you wedge another piece of wood under it just on the bank here it will become a seesaw. Then all you have to do is put your weight down on the near end and you'll be able to swivel it into position.'

Caspar grunted and immediately set to work, thinking how ridiculous his own plan had been compared to Leaf's. He had thought to drag the entire beam out of the water, stand it on end and let it topple over, hoping that the far end would land safely in place on the opposite bank of the river.

It did, however, still take a great deal of effort to swing the beam clear of the rushing water and, pressing down with all his weight, he pushed the shorter end around, swivelling it on the piece of wood that was acting as a fulcrum beneath. Once the longer end was free of the water and pointing up into the air, he only had to position it and the let it drop down into place.

'Well done,' Leaf praised him coolly. 'You have it in place but we can't possibly cross on that. The log is smooth and slippery and the river is too dangerous. It isn't worth the risk.'

'We'll manage,' Caspar told her confidently, refusing to become irritated that she had waited until after he had gone to so much effort to voice her doubts. It would be quite possible to walk across the beam so long as one didn't focus on the force of the river below. He doubted very much that she had ever played such games as damming streams and scrambling through woods though he and Hal had attempted much more fearful feats in their childhood. He scooped Leaf up and marched firmly toward the river.

'You're not going to do it! No, Spar, no! We'll die! We'll both drown!'

'Only if you wriggle and squirm like this,' Caspar scolded her. He was, in fact, quite confident. He had spent his youth climbing and scrambling over the battlements of his home. Born and bred in the mountains, he had no fear of heights. Leaf went limp in his arms and then clung on, her eyes tightly closed. Caspar stepped up onto the beam, his head level and his eyes fixed firmly on a point on the far bank. The beam was slippery, as were his boots, but at least Leaf kept perfectly still. Biting his tongue, he took positive steps forward, placing

461

his feet toe first, the sole of his foot as sensitive as a palm as he eased his weight down with each new step. In ten heart-stopping seconds, they were across.

'There!' He put Leaf down onto the damp grass. 'That wasn't so bad.'

She glared up at him, lower lip trembling, and quite unexpectedly kicked him on the shin. 'I wish I had left you in the mist to rot. How could you do that to me?'

'Because we could spend all day looking for a way to cross and, every second that passes, Silas's trail is growing colder. I have to find Brid.'

After crossing the river, it was not very long before they reached the far side of the crystal curtain. When Caspar looked back, all sign of the river and the haze of crystals was completely gone. Instead, he could see only forest. He turned his back on it and looked for the way forward.

Ahead was the hamlet they had seen from the riverbank. The buildings were of wattle and daub construction topped with turf roofs. About the perimeter of the hamlet was a ring of hazel staves stuck into the ground, forming a very tight and high fence.

'Let's hope there's someone at home,' he said brightly.

They found out the answer very quickly as they were immediately met with the sound of angry shouts.

'Get away from us, you pixies!' were the first words they could understand and someone was scared enough to fling a stick at them. 'We don't want you demons here. Stay away!'

'We are ordinary people; we mean you no harm,' Caspar shouted, somewhat taken aback at the reception though he realized he was stretching the point to call Leaf an ordinary person. He dismissed the matter, knowing that she did look normal. He wondered why the villagers were so afraid of them. 'We wish no harm. We are wet and cold and are in need of a fire to warm ourselves. Please can you help us?'

There was whispered argument from within the compound and then silence. 'Who are you? Where are you from? How do we know you're not pixie people trying to trick us?' a male voice asked.

'Because we are shivering with cold. We're lost. Please help us.'

'Go and take a closer look at them, Gart,' one man urged from within.

'No, you go and take a look,' a young man's voice disrespectfully retorted, 'since you're so bothered about them.'

'Do we really look that frightening?' Caspar asked. 'I only wish to dry my clothes. Can you help us or not?'

'Not!' one of them grumbled.

Then a rather shrill voice belonging to a woman scolded, 'What's the world coming to if we can't help a fellow man in distress. Look, it's just a man and a young girl. What harm can they do to us? Look at them. They look half frozen with cold? Now, let them in at once.'

It seemed the woman had some authority because the rather makeshift gate of roped logs was eased open a crack and they were beckoned forward. Just as they arrived at the opening, a spear with a crooked shaft was thrust forward and prodded at Caspar's belly.

'Any weapons you have just put them down here at the gate,' a young man ordered.

'We have none,' Caspar assured him, thinking it unnecessary to admit to his knife sheathed inside his boot. He held his hands up and slowly turned full circle to show he was carrying no blade or bow.

'See! They're not dangerous at all.' An old woman shuffled forward and looked them up and down. 'Bless my husband's old boots, you're near drowned. The both of you. Gart, put some logs on the fire. We've got to get these two warm.'

Caspar was deeply relieved to feel the warmth of the fire on his skin and to have a dry blanket thrown over his shoulders. Shivering and wide-eyed with nervous energy, Leaf pressed close to him and he remembered that she had never been beyond the bounds of her hidden realm before.

The people of the hamlet brought out cups of warm acorn tea, which tasted unpleasantly bitter though the warmth was very welcome indeed.

The Baron looked up at his hosts and, for the first time, realized that there was something curious about them. At first glance, they were simple woodsfolk with grubby hands and uncut hair, their clothing ragged from wear and tear. They lived in poorly constructed houses, the walls of the wattle already sloping outwards where it had splayed under the weight of the turf roof. He looked again at their appearance; their clothes, though grubby, were also brightly coloured and there were traces of fancy trimmings.

Bright brass buttons still brightened Gart's doublet though one or two had popped off and been replaced by wooden toggles. Another man was wearing glasses, which would be hard to come by in so remote a village.

'Thank you for your hospitality,' he told the old woman as she offered him bread and cheese and some hazelnuts.

'It is a pleasure to meet such fine folk. It has been a while,' the woman admitted. 'We have little contact now with the outside world.'

'What brought you to the woods?' Caspar asked. 'Surely, it is not safe here.'

'Safer here than in the towns.'

'Really?'

'Oh yes! If it wasn't bad enough that the hobs had attacked us three winters running, the young knights, lords and squires saw fit to fight amongst themselves for land and power. They set the example and, once started, everyone else followed. There's nothing now but looting and pillaging within our once proud towns. My family owned a granary. We had a good supply of grain and would have shared but in the feuding someone set light to the stores and the lot went up in smoke. We fled Faronshire and went north with others who saw no gain in the fighting. It seemed lovely at first, with the shallow stream and the green fields and the abundance of nuts and berries and all was well until . . .'

Caspar nodded, politely waiting for the old woman to continue.

'We set to exploring and lost three of our number in the direction from which you came.' She jerked her head towards the hidden realm of which there was now no evidence. 'One minute they were there and the next they had ambled out of sight beyond a tree and we never saw them again. We never go that way now. We've even seen strange sights there; pixies at night appear out of the very heart of the trees themselves but we never go near. It's a cursed place.'

'Oh, Mother, stop being so hysterical!' Gart chided her. 'Pixies indeed! There has to be a rational explanation. We might live like woodsfolk but we're not daft like woodsfolk.'

Caspar found that a very ignorant remark but said nothing.

'You explain how these people came to us all wet yet we know there's no lake or river in these woods only our little stream' the old woman complained. 'Look at the man; he's half drowned, water still dripping from him like he's been swimming. You can't tell me that anyone is fool enough to get wet like that in our little brook. It would be easier to drown yourself in a bucket.'

Caspar was not concerned about their dilemma. 'You say you've seen people coming out from that area of the forest; have you seen a man on a black horse? He has long hair, is well-armoured and his horse is powerful with an elegant, high-stepping gait – quite unmistakable?'

'We don't look at the apparitions. Pixies don't like to be stared at!' the old woman said emphatically.

'But they always take the same path,' young Gart said more calmly. 'They head straight out to the forest track and then turn for the road heading east.'

'How do you know?' the old woman demanded anxiously.

'I have followed them,' the young teenager said brightly. 'I'm not afraid.'

465

Caspar smiled at the youth's cheeky grin.

'The trouble with these old folks here,' Gart told the Baron, 'is that they're still unhappy that there are no cobbles beneath their feet. Even after all this time, they wake with a start at the sound of an owl or a nightjar. Well, I followed them. I'm not spending my life trembling at the thought of pixies. I wanted to know what they were doing. And they certainly don't look like pixies to me!'

'Gart, I'm shocked. I'm appalled,' the old woman exclaimed. 'You promised me! You solemnly promised me that you wouldn't go near them. You're not to be trusted. I don't want you going outside the compound for a week, do you hear?'

The youth grinned. 'Nope!' He put his fingers in his ears to emphasize the point.

Caspar chortled to himself; it pleased him greatly to know that all parents seemed to have trouble controlling their children. And why indeed should they be controlled, he asked himself philosophically? The answer was all too painfully obvious. His son had paid not the slightest heed to him and ended up lost, probably stolen by hobs. Children needed to be protected from themselves.

Gart was still keen to tell Caspar more and sat down next to him. 'But before they head east, they meet up with dwarves. Would you believe that?'

'Dwarves!' the old woman echoed in horror. 'You've been near conniving dwarves?'

The boy smiled dismissively at this and turned back to Caspar. 'Mother does fuss so but she is a woman and I suppose it is to be expected.'

'Go on,' Caspar urged quietly since he did not wish to offend the woman who was their hostess. 'Tell me more about this man on the black horse.'

The youth smiled, perhaps pleased at being taken so seriously by an adult. 'Well, about five miles along the track, there are a number of huge pits and the man you spoke of stopped by one of them. I tried to get closer but

I think he heard me so I had to come home,' he admitted almost as if acting prudently was somehow a failure.

'That's where he will have taken her. He didn't have time to go further,' Leaf said quietly, her usual confident manner somewhat suppressed in front of strangers. 'He uses the pits to catch the mammoths. If they are deep enough for a mammoth, they'll be deep enough to hold Brid.'

Caspar nodded and watched the steam rising off his clothes. He wished he had time to wait for them to dry. He wished he had time to wait for a good meal and a rest but he did not. Almost regretfully, since he was so near to exhaustion, he began pulling on his boots. 'Well, lad, can you show us the way?'

The woman sprang up. 'Gart, you're not going off alone with these strangers. You're not going anywhere near those pits or meddling with stuff that dwarves have dealt with. I've lost my beautiful home, lost my business, lost all the good clothes I had on my back but I shan't lose you. You're not going!'

The youth patted his mother on the head. 'Dear old woman, you do fuss so!'

'Gart, keep an eye on Leaf,' Caspar ordered as he stared into the deep black pit. It was the third pit that the youth had lead them to and he was despairing of ever finding Brid. 'And, Leaf, you stay with Gart this time and stand back by that tree. Don't move one foot from there. I don't want you falling in. The place is pocked with them.'

Tentatively, Caspar inched forward to the edge of the huge hole and stared down, being careful not to stand too close to the edge for fear that the side might collapse. Twenty foot below in the gloom, he could see a horse lying down on its side, panting in distress, it's leg strapped to a splint.

'What kind of a bastard leaves their horse to suffer like that?' Gart complained at his side. Evidently the youth had disregarded his order.

'There's no kindness in trying to save a horse with a broken leg.' Caspar fingered his knife. In any other circumstances he would have immediately climbed down and ended the horse's suffering but now he had no time. He peered down at the horse; it seemed strange that someone had gone to the effort of bandaging its leg only to leave it to die. He squinted at the bandage and thought he could see a pattern of runes daubed onto the cloth. His heart missed a beat. Instinctively, he associated the runes and the bandage with Brid.

Knowing he had to investigate more closely, he examined the wooden shuttering that lined the pit. It was no use; he could never climb out even if he managed to get to the horse without breaking his neck. He was shaking his head in exasperation when Gart dropped a rope on the ground beside him.

'It was lying behind one of the trees over there. I saw the dwarves use it.'

Caspar knotted the rope to the nearest tree and, taking the other end, prepared to lower himself into the pit. The end of the rope dropping into the pit frightened the horse and it began thrashing with its back legs in an attempt to get up. But Caspar was confident that he could calm the animal and was about to lower himself down, when a growled threat stopped him short.

'Touch her and you die right there!'

The middle of his back prickled and Caspar sensed that a knife was aimed at his spine. He turned slowly.

It wasn't a knife but a double-bladed throwing axe. The man holding it was both tall and broad. He wore a metal breastplate over a heavy gambeson, moulded to give the impression of bulging chest muscles. The leather covering his upper arms had rounded to his heavy musculature and his sharply defined jaw twitched. His thick neck was ridged with tendons and he wore a heavy cloak, adding to his bulk. All in all, he bore an impressive demeanour of strength.

Unbefitting his warrior-like appearance, his hair straggled

out from beneath an impressive horned helmet covered in leaf mould and burs as if he had been crawling through the undergrowth. But the strangest thing about him was his squinting eyes, frantically scanning the clearing. They passed over Caspar but never saw him, and he became quite positive that the man was at least partially blind.

He was leading a draught horse harnessed with a heavy collar and chains. Its ears were laid flat but it obeyed as the man urged it forward.

Caspar eyed the axe in the man's hand and noted uncomfortably how the stranger's head flitted about at the slightest sounds and even jerking towards Leaf when she whimpered.

'Steady, there,' Caspar said in a reassuring tone. 'She's only a young girl so let's not do anything hasty.'

Instantly, the man turned back to Caspar. Though his sight was obviously impaired, his ability to sense sound was apparently most reliable. There was also a hardness to the man's broad jaw that indicated that he might throw the axe without further provocation and Caspar wasn't prepared to test how good his sightless aim might be.

'I'm not going to hurt the horse; I promise,' Caspar soothed, rising slowly.

'Just get away from the pit,' the man said with taut restraint, his accent strange and most definitely not Belbidian.

Caspar stared into his bloodshot eyes for a long moment and then stepped slowly back from the edge of the pit, still watching the man's face for any warning that he might attack.

In response, the man stepped forward uncertainly, feeling his way by brushing his toe through the crisp leaves piled deeply about the pit and keeping a wary distance from the Baron. But oddly, once in sight of the horse, his hesitant movements altered dramatically and he snapped his head up to look Caspar confidently in the eye, as if appraising him for the first time. More hastily, he cast his eye over Leaf and the young lad, Gart.

469

'I need your help. It's taken me three days to find this horse.' He jerked his head at the draught animal. 'And with your help, I'll get her out.' He nodded down at the animal in the pit.

'I doubt you'll drag her out alive,' Caspar cautioned, staring in amazement at the change in the man's behaviour. 'If she's been down there three days, she'll be very weak.'

'She'll live,' the man retorted sharply, though he peered forlornly down at the horse, his eyes flitting between the drop and the draught horse. 'I've returned to water her regularly and she has a strong heart. I would just be grateful for your help now, that's all.'

Caspar nodded. He had no time to waste, yet he sensed that, once this man was free of the worry over his horse, he might be able to help them. He must have seen, or heard, something of Brid. Surely it was she who had bandaged his horse and daubed the runes of healing onto the cloth. He prayed with all his heart that it was so and that she was safe.

The man nodded back in gratitude, gripped the rope tied to the draught horse, and lowered himself into the pit. A moment later, he hurled up another length of rope that Caspar also harnessed to the horse before peering into the pit to watch the man's progress. The stricken horse was on its side but struggling to rise; clearly, the task was not going to be easy.

The man looked up. 'Can you give me some help down here?'

As agile as an elf, Caspar slithered down the rope and alighted on the firm bottom of the pit. The warrior was trying to wrap the rope around the horse's belly and chest but needed Caspar's help to pull the rope under her girth as he shoved it through from the far side. Caspar looked the beautiful chestnut mare over, pausing on the bite marks on her rump.

'Hobs,' the man told him laconically.

Once the rope was fastened tightly and the man had given his horse a reassuring stroke on the muzzle, he called up to Gart, 'There's a lad, now loop the rope around the tree to act as a pulley and guide the horse back towards the pit. That'll ease the strain. Then we'll heave her out.'

Caspar watched as the ropes snapped tight, creaked and inched forward. The warrior was doing his best to support the horse's head and he could hear Gart urging on the draught horse above. Eventually the mare was on her feet.

Caspar spotted something lying on the earth. He was staring at a ring of small white stones. Giddily, he bent forward and took careful note of them before hastily pocketing them and moving to snatch at the warrior's arm.

'She was here! Brid! Brid was here with your horse! Very small and slight with coppery-brown hair and the greenest eyes you've ever seen. She was here. Look at me!' Caspar's voice rose as the warrior ignored him, reaching up for a rope that Gart was lowering. He grabbed the man's hand. 'Forget the horse and answer me!'

The man turned round slowly to face him. 'What?' he asked as if it were incredulous that anyone would be thinking of anything other than his horse. Without answering, he hauled himself up the rope. Caspar followed hastily.

By the time he reached the top, the man was heaving the animal up and out of the pit and leading her to a soft piece of grass away from the edge. He soothed her head and examined the chestnut mare for further signs of injury. She was trembling but was able to put weight on her bandaged leg. Caspar slid his hand over the injury and felt the swelling and heat within the binding. Leaf had stepped bravely closer and was looking on curiously as the warrior removed the leather straps that held two wooden splints in place and began replacing the bandage.

The man nodded in satisfaction. 'It's much better; the swelling's all but gone. I suppose we were lucky that it was dislocated and not broken but I've never seen an injury heal so well.' The stranger beamed at his horse and affectionately stroked her velvet muzzle. The mare raised her head to nibble gently at his ear.

Caspar examined the bandage more closely. He had been right; they were indeed runes of healing.

'Brid!' he croaked, panting slightly from his effort of hauling himself up the rope. 'She was here. She even bandaged your horse's leg for you.'

The warrior barely looked up. 'Oh Sorrel,' he purred at the animal. 'I thought I had lost you.'

'I'll kill her myself if you don't answer me!' Caspar threatened through gritted teeth, his hands trembling with emotion.

He didn't have time to reach for his knife. The man had taken his threat seriously and sprang at him, pressing him to the ground, twisting his neck painfully sideways and pressing his large fist on Caspar's windpipe. Though the man was considerably heavier than Caspar and well armed, Caspar was not without experience. With great agility, he kicked his legs up and forward and hooked them around the man's neck, pulling him backwards. The warrior responded by somersaulting backwards onto his feet and snatching up a long sword that was just within reach, strapped to the horse's side.

Bellowing and roaring, the warrior swung his sword in a wide arc, the glimmering metal cutting through the air barely a hair's breadth from Caspar's chest.

Prudently, Caspar retreated to the safety of a tree. 'Now steady there! Is this the thanks I get for helping you?'

'I have no wish for more killing,' the man said, his composure returning. He lowered the tip of the blade.

Caspar was glad of it. Even if he had been armed, he would have doubted his skill against the strength of this sturdy warrior. 'I simply need to know about the woman who was here,' he repeated his demand. 'I am sure she helped you and it would be scant payment for the service we have done you if you denied my request.'

At last, the man seemed to hear his words and nodded. Caspar felt his heart plummet; there was regret in the warrior's eyes.

The stranger hung his head and looked down at his black boots. 'The little woman. She was in the pit when we fell in. She was in a bad way already but still managed to help my Sorrel.'

'What happened?' Caspar asked, fearing to hear the answer.

'I was bending down over my horse. The woman was standing up over me. She screamed and I looked up to see a great claw grip her tight and snatch her away.'

Caspar's arms dropped weakly to his sides and he sagged forward, his hands clutching at the bare earth. 'No! No!' he breathed into the dirt. 'Great Mother, you would not let this happen to Brid.' Hot tears pricked at his eyes.

Leaf knelt beside him and placed her small hand on his shoulder. 'Spar, hush. Brid is alive.'

Pushing himself up until he was sitting, he stared at the child. He was mad to listen to her yet he could not stop himself from clutching at any hope. 'How do you know?'

She did not answer but instead, turned to the warrior. 'Tell me again, what snatched the woman away?'

He sighed. 'I could do nothing to save her. It grabbed her and all I could see as I stared up into the sky was her tiny kicking body hanging from the great talons.'

'A dragon?' Leaf queried.

The man nodded. 'A huge she-dragon, a golden dragon.'

'The great golden dragon that Silas feeds with his offerings. She enters the crystal realm to frighten my people so that Silas can win their trust,' Leaf asserted. 'He deliberately left Brid in this pit because he knew that the dragon would come for her. If he wanted her dead, he would have killed her himself. Silas wanted her alive, and the dragon has simply taken her some place at his command.'

Caspar found it extremely difficult to follow this argument

but he was prepared to hope. The warrior was staring at Leaf, his eyes wide.

She drew a deep breath, met the warrior's gaze and then looked up at the sky. 'The question is; which way did they go?'

Chapter 28

Rollo snatched the pitcher out of Quinn's grasp. 'You've had enough.'

'You can't tell me what I can and cannot do!' Quinn unexpectedly exploded. 'You can't! Guthrey's always doing that to me, isn't that so, Issy?'

Rollo placed the pitcher down on the table. 'Have you forgotten? We need to get home.'

'Home? No, not home, not anymore.' Quinn rose to his feet but was swaying and beginning to look a little green. 'We're not going home; I've got to find Guthrey. You'd never give up on your brother now, would you, Rollo?'

'I haven't got a brother and you're drunk.'

'He's alive.' Quinn spread his arms wide, spun round, tripped and slumped forward to his knees until he was hugging the ground. 'He's alive. Alive, you hear? All we have to do is head towards Wiglaf's and we're sure to find word of these ravenshrikes. He's alive.'

'It's been too long; he will have certainly perished in this time. Forget about Guthrey and let's get home,' Rollo said unkindly.

The slackness in Quinn's face stiffened. 'Forget? Forget about my brother? You don't care. Why should you? Guthrey is no one to you. But, he's *my* brother. Or perhaps that means nothing to you. Have you no loyalties? Or are you like your father, capable of turning his back on his duty for fifteen years, hiding on the other side of the world?'

Rollo could take no more. He had thought Quinn to be

generous-hearted; he had liked him but, now he was just as full of hatred towards him as Hal and all the rest of the Torra Altans. Fists clenched, he flew at the youth.

The wine had made Quinn remarkably strong. He punched back hard, his long wiry arms having no difficulty over-reaching Rollo's attack. But Rollo was not going to give in. He was younger and a little shorter but he had fought in more scraps than most boys his age and had learnt well from his few defeats. Quinn's upright stance left his injured knee within easy striking distance and Rollo kicked hard. But not even the sight of the Torra Altan youth crumpling to the ground could assuage the red cloud of anger that stormed into his brain.

As the rage claimed him, he became unaware of Sara's squeals or the little child's cries of terror only of his own wordless yelling at Quinn. He tried to scream that he, Rollo, had killed Guthrey, that he was a murderer, but the words would not form and a moment later the red anger seeped from his darkening mind and he sagged to his knees.

He was floating softly back down to earth, falling, falling and then, with a thud, his forehead smashed into the ground. He was vaguely aware of a moist trickle running down the back of his neck. Remotely, almost carelessly, he wondered when Quinn was going to kill him but it seemed the Torra Altan wasn't being given the chance.

Someone dragged Rollo by the heels and thrust his head into the water trough. The horse squealed in alarm.

'Don't . . .,' Rollo spluttered. 'Don't! Stop it!' he tried to shout as his head came clear of the water before being stuffed back under. He couldn't breathe. Panic was racing through him as he was plunged in and out of the water, gasping for breaths. No, he must not panic! 'Please sto—' he gurgled, bubbles bursting from his mouth as he was forced under again. He knew what would happen if he panicked. It was too much. He couldn't bare the sickness and the unbearable pain in his head that came with the seizures.

His brain snapped and sizzled, jagged beams of light flashing before him. His muscles jerked and a salivary froth bubbled from his mouth. He didn't know what was happening around him, only that he was now clear of the water, immersed within his own small world of misery. His tongue swelled and he could barely breathe, the sound of his gasped breaths screeching in his ears. He wanted to tear out his tongue, his fat slippery tongue, but he could not will his hands to his mouth. His backbone arched and he thumped his head, time and time again, against the floor, trying to be rid of the raging pain within his body.

It seemed an eternity before the fit passed and, when he came round, he found himself lying face-down on the ground. At first, because it was so silent, he thought he was alone but then felt a soft touch against his cheek.

'Hello,' Isolde murmured. 'Don't worry! It's all over.'

Rollo turned away from her and retched, blood coming up in his vomit.

'Devil,' Sara shrieked. 'A devil in my home. He's a hob in disguise!'

'Now, don't be silly, Sara,' John soothed. 'It may be the wine. The youngsters aren't used to it. Really, it's my fault, there's no need to get upset; there's no harm done.'

'No, just a broken bench that you'll never get round to mending and my child half scared to death. That youth is a monster.'

Rollo pressed his face into the earth. Sara was right; he was monster. He didn't deserve to live.

'Sara, what can I say?' Merrit apologized. 'I am responsible. I would not have brought them here if I had known they would behave so badly. What can I do to make it up to you?'

'Don't worry, Merrit, I don't hold you to blame. You've always been good to us and it's nice to know that you seek us out on your travels but these three are no longer welcome.'

'Regrettably, I can't see how I can possibly get them out

of here tonight for you. I'll get them to sleep in the shelter back there near the horses where they'll be away from you and your young ones.'

'Well, so long as you watch over them. I don't want any disease that the red-haired one is carrying being passed onto my boy now. I should have known they'd be trouble; I've never seen such a queer lot. Imagine wandering about in the middle of winter all bare foot just because you want to listen to the trees!'

'Don't worry, Sara, I'll watch them very carefully. I told you, I feel personally responsible for them. And I'll mend your bench,' Merrit promised.

'Well, that I would appreciate,' the woman said a little more softly. 'John's too busy selling his carvings and wine nowadays to help about the house.'

Even in his drained state, Rollo thought Sara sounded ridiculous. How could she call this shabby collection of huts a house?

It took the strength of both John and Merrit to move him and Quinn into the shelter farthest from the sleeping quarters. Though he tried, Rollo could not find enough sense in his legs to walk and he slumped gratefully into a heap of moss and wood-shavings. Quinn was thrown down beside him. The youth was snoring loudly and Rollo was shocked to see the bruising to his face and neck. He looked at his own knuckles and saw that they were split and bleeding; he hadn't even remembered hitting Quinn in the face yet he must have done. He closed his eyes in shameful regret. Why this, just when he was beginning to like him? Always that was the way. Sooner or later, he lost his friends.

Isolde stooped over him and pulled up his eyelid to look into his eye. 'Are you with us yet?' she demanded. The shock of the events had quickly sobered her up.

Rollo groaned, feeling too ill to reply. But he was grateful when Isolde pulled his cloak up and tucked it round him for warmth. Through the gaps in the side of the simple shelter, he gazed back at the fire around which Sara and her husband were still seated. He blinked and a tear slid from his eye across his cheek. It was followed by another but before the second tear had finished its meandering journey, he was fast asleep.

It was probably the effect of the wine as well as the fit but, as he slept, he dreamt of Torra Alta. In his dream the skull of the dragon hanging above the door pulled itself free from the wall and began to chase him around the room, the great jaws snapping at his spine.

He awoke covered in sweat. It was dark, and the fire had dwindled to a quiet glow. He could hear Merrit talking to Isolde. He could not hear their words but her tone was unmistakably apologetic. They were walking as they talked and, as their silhouettes moved nearer to the shelter, their voices gradually grew louder and their conversation returned to one they had touched on earlier in the day.

Merrit was questioning her. 'How do you know so much about the trees and plants? Is it that, perhaps, you have had training?' Merrit asked, in Rollo's opinion, a little too intently.

The thought of Isolde chatting to Merrit brought him instantly to his senses. He groaned loudly, trying to distract her from answering without actually shouting out that she must be cautious. He could not believe that these Torra Altans were so trusting and naïve.

His plan must have worked because she immediately excused herself and was soon crawling through the straw to him, peering into his face. 'Are you all right?' she asked. 'Do you want some water? Or maybe I can get you some valerian to ease your sleep?'

Rollo grunted dismissively. 'Just don't talk to Merrit,' he whispered. 'He's asking too many questions. We need his help, but the less he knows about us the better.'

Isolde nodded. 'I wasn't going to tell him anything. Why does no one trust me?' she protested. 'I was beginning to think you were different.'

Rollo sighed in exasperation. 'Just stop talking about trees and symbols. Ordinary girls don't do that sort of thing.'

'What do you know about girls?' Isolde snorted.

'What do you know about ordinary people?' Rollo retorted, trying to be cutting though he only succeeded in making Isolde laugh.

She stroked his brow. 'A sight more than you do, that's for sure.'

Merrit coughed insistently outside the shelter. 'Isolde, I have a splinter in my finger from that bench. Do you think you can help me with it?' He enticed the high priestess back outside and towards the light of the fire. Rollo tried to grip her hand and hold her back but, too easily, she slipped through his fingers to obey Merrit's request.

'Where? I can't see it,' the girl complained.

'It's there,' Merrit insisted. 'So tell me, do you believe that hobs and dwarves hold the same beliefs about the trees?'

'Well, of course . . .,' Isolde began quite enthusiastically but then coughed. 'Of course, I wouldn't know anything about that. Oh look, here's that splinter. Don't move. Got it!'

'They say that the hobs speak to the trees,' the man continued.

'That's just . . . Oh, do they really?' Isolde said flippantly. 'If you'll excuse me, I must get some sleep. We've had so little rest in the past days.'

'It's early yet,' Merrit cajoled. 'Besides, I think I have another splinter.'

Rollo cringed at Isolde's innocent reply. 'I need to look in the light of the fire. You'll have to sit back down.'

Rollo crawled out from his snug nest to see what was going on. Isolde was sitting before Merrit, her head tilted up, and she was looking at him thoughtfully.

The long-haired foreigner coughed. 'It is very kind of you to help me, young lady.'

Isolde hastily returned to examining his finger. 'No, no. It is you that has been kind to us, giving up so much of your time to help us when you are already helping so many others.'

'As I said earlier, I feel responsible,' he said, smoothly dismissing his actions before pulling away from Isolde to reach for the pitcher of wine. He poured some into a small shiny brass cauldron, which he set to warm over the fire. 'There's nothing like a spot of mulled wine to help one sleep.'

As the pot began to give out a warm vapour, Rollo was pleasantly soothed by the smell wafting towards him but craned his neck forward, puzzled to see the man adding sprigs of honeysuckle to the brew. The flower could bloom early in the year, and the honeysuckle buds were just appearing.

He coughed loudly and began to moan, 'Isolde, I have a pain in my stomach, please . . .'

He was relieved to see her quickly jump up and hurry back to the shelter. When she saw him sitting up, watching for her and in no apparent discomfort, she put her hands on her hips, pursed her lips and shook her head at him.

'I thought you said you were ill,' she complained.

'I thought you needed rescuing,' Rollo responded quickly.

Her manner relaxed and, shrugging, she knelt down and crept through the straw to lie close against Quinn. Rollo growled in his throat; she had been gentle and sweet to him, and he did not like having to share her affection with Quinn.

He tried to sleep. Soon the shelter was filled with the comforting sounds of Quinn and Isolde's easy breaths, which persuaded him that they were both asleep. Noises without, however, kept him awake. Merrit and John were still fussing over the fire and Rollo strained to listen to their conversation.

'I was working on how to improve your brew, John,' Merrit spoke from his seat beside the fire.

'I thought it was quite good enough.' By the sharp sniffing sound, Rollo guessed that John was unenthusiastic about the additional honeysuckle.

481

'Ah, but warm wine needs to be sweet,' Merrit argued his case. 'Taste a drop and see what you think.'

'I think I've had quite enough for one day,' John laughed but, clearly drank some of the adulterated wine as, a moment later, he sighed and smacked his lips. 'It was good before but this is excellent. If I had made that brew when we were back in Bleham, I'd have been the richest man in the town rather than the most overworked.'

'Come now! Lawyers are never overworked.'

'Oh, they were in Bleham. It was always land disputes – always. The land was rich and grew such plentiful amounts of grain it may as well have had gold beneath the soil. And where there is value there is dispute. But land is tricky stuff; the maps in many of the deeds went back hundreds of years, the boundaries clearly marked along hedges, roads, rivers and streams. But rivers and streams shift their course. Did you know that? I didn't believe it at first when I moved out from Farona to Bleham but it's as true as my nose. It's very hard to claim ownership of a piece of land when the boundaries keep changing.' He yawned. 'Well, it's been a hectic day. I'm off to bed.'

'Honeysuckle,' Isolde sighed in her sleep. 'Honeysuckle . . . Secrets,' she sighed. 'Secrets. Nobody wants to have secrets.'

Rollo closed his eyes. He no longer felt the cold nor was he troubled by any eerie sounds of the night. The jarring calls of the nocturnal birds were silent; no taurs grunted in the groves and the wind was still. His aches were eased by the effect of the wine. He sighed; it was a welcome change. Normally, every inch of his body ached after a seizure. The fits made his muscles jerk rigid and pull against each other. At this moment, only his neck muscles and tongue throbbed, and even those pains were beginning to lessen.

Rolling over, he tried to sleep, but was still distracted by the activity around the fire. Merrit was still up, stirring the pot. Dreamily, he wondered about the man's horse. Could a man be genuinely kind if he were so brutal to animals?

He could hear the horse kicking against an empty water butt. He knew he would not sleep for the noise and thought to rise and give the animal water himself only Merrit got up and he heard the sharp crack of a whip followed by a squeal.

'Silence, you idiot horse. That noise is enough to wake the dead or bring the knockermen. And *I'm* not going to stop them chewing on your hide when they come.'

The horse shrieked as if she understood the man's words and ceased her kicking. Rollo's head thumped, still preventing sleep, and he was aware of the bubbling thrum of the small cauldron. How strange, he thought, that Merrit would retire to bed and leave the wine boiling. Come morning, it would be a crisp caramel at the bottom of the pot.

Pulling his cloak over his head and groaning inwardly, he reflected on the day. How could he have come so close to blurting to Quinn that he had killed Guthrey? What if, in one of his fits, he did actually confess his crime? What would he do then? Try and make his way home? But would he be welcome in Artor? Word of his crime would spread rapidly; his father would send word to Imogen and, though she had always been his friend, she would believe Caspar. The girl was like their father. It was ironic that she had inherited their mother's gift when she was so like Caspar. Ursula had been wild, daring and confident. Imogen was quiet and sensible.

Trying to blank his mind and think nothing but pleasant thoughts, Rollo screwed up his eyes and tried counting sheep but in his imagination each one turned to him with the face of Guthrey.

A sound like the scratching of rats made him suddenly blink his eyes open. When the scratching turned to a rattle and a tap of wood against metal, he thought that Merrit had returned to the cauldron. Mumbling, he rolled over to peer at the fire through the gaps in the boarding. With his eyes barely open, he looked through the feathering of his eyelashes and nearly yelped in surprise at the sight of the thing stirring the pot.

A small figure was standing up on a stool and leaning over the brass cauldron that Merrit had filled with wine. The little figure looked feminine, he thought, judging by the tiny waist and the long curling hair. It was beckoning to something in the shadows beyond the glow of the fire and soon another figure approached. This one was just as short though it moved a little more awkwardly and was not quite so thin.

With great difficulty, it dragged another of the stools closer to the pot before scurrying back into the shadows. Soon, it reappeared, staggering under the weight of an urn. Grunting, the creature heaved it up onto the stool and, with the help of the first tiny creature, sloshed the contents of the urn into the cauldron. The first figure with the long curling hair began to stir vigorously.

Rollo laughed nervously to himself. This was just as ridiculous as the sheep with Guthrey's face; he was simply dreaming. The vapour from the cauldron was moist and sweet as it drifted into the open shelter and soon he believed he was floating. Of course he was dreaming, and it was a most luscious dream, as if he were lying on a feathered bed surrounded by peaches and marchpane. He hadn't eaten such luxuries since he had left Artor and he missed the sweet foods of his warm homeland.

His dream took a strange turn as the creatures crept into the shelter, carrying a lamp that they swung into his face. One lifted his eyelids and he stared straight into the face of the tiny creature with the long hair. Apart from her large eyes, she had minute features and the tips of two filmy wings protruded above each shoulder. Her ears were pointed and her nose sharp and she smelt as sweet as the honeysuckle itself.

Most unexpectedly, she kissed his nose and he felt quite extraordinarily light-headed. How could he have dreamed up such a thing? The delicate creature then breathed into his nostrils before spinning around in delight, her wings spreading out and brushing his nose. The touch sent a shiver right through his body and he suddenly felt completely vulnerable.

'You are a wicked boy,' the fairy whispered in his ear and laughed. 'Wicked! We know you are awake. We know your secrets and you will do as we bid you. What would they do to you if they found out? You are wicked boy.'

Rollo cringed back into his cloak. He wanted to cry. His hands were trembling and a cold sweat prickled his body. A dream had not so disturbed him for a very long time. He tried to run but, as was the way in dreams, his legs were like lead.

A rattle of trotters made him swivel his eyes around. He wanted to scream as he now had too close a look of the second figure that had crept out of the night and entered the shelter.

The fairy turned to greet it. 'A wicked boy,' she repeated. 'Isn't that right, Bibo?' She turned back to Rollo. 'Bibo's a vine imp, you know. And vine imps always get to the truth.'

The other creature was far less graceful than the first. Having the body of a miniature man, it strutted forward on tiny goatlike legs. In one hand, it carried a small pitcher filled with some of the brew taken from the cauldron. The vine imp looked at Rollo and glared hard into his eyes before sticking out its tongue and laughing.

'Lonicera says you'll do as you're told,' he taunted, 'because you've been a naughty boy. If you're going to be bad, human child, you should learn not to regret it. Your guilt is a sharp tool and Lonicera knows all your secrets.'

Rollo wanted to crush Lonicera although the idea was ludicrous because she was only a figment of his weird dream. Yet, it felt utterly real. Everything was happening in the right timescale and he had seen no strange images of Guthrey or his mother. The dead always haunted his worst dreams.

'Come on,' the fairy hissed at Bibo, her little wings beating faster and drawing her up into the air. 'She's over here.'

Rollo knew he should get up. He should do something to

help Isolde even if this were only a dream. But his body would not move.

'Ready, Bibo?' Lonicera asked.

The little imp nodded. 'I'm always ready.' He leant over Isolde and sniffed her breath. 'This shouldn't be hard. She has had enough of the brew already.'

'Wait, before you wake her,' Lonicera insisted. She bent close to Isolde's face and also sniffed her breath. 'She is very sad and carries a burden of secrets as weighty as an adulteress.' The little fairy let out a long slow sigh. 'But they are complex and deeply buried in her long past. So sad.'

'So what?' the vine imp grumbled. 'If you can achieve nothing, stand aside and let me have my turn. She must know something. From what we've learnt, she's either mad or driven by fervid religious compulsion. And religion means learning. She's too pretty to be mad, therefore, she can help us.'

The creature placed its hand on Isolde's lips and began to press them open before dribbling a few drops of liquid into her mouth from the small jug. He waited half a moment and then shook her vigorously.

Isolde blinked, stared at them for a second of horrified amazement and then let out a low moan. The noise woke Quinn, who staggered up onto his knees but was still swaying and grunting and apparently without the balance to rise further. His eyes fumbled for the pitchfork leaning up against the wall of the shelter beside him but he clearly didn't have the strength to reach it.

'Rollo! Rollo! Do something,' Quinn was slurring.

Lonicera flitted to Rollo's ear and whispered. 'Move a muscle and I'll tell them everything. Now, don't worry, we're not going to hurt the girl. We just need to know a few things.'

'Rollo!' Isolde implored as another five little creatures similar to Bibo trotted into the tent.

He wanted to help her but, before he could try to react,

they were on him. One of them clenched his nose so he couldn't breathe and he was forced to open his mouth. It was then that the liquid was poured into his throat. It tasted like bad wine and he wanted to be sick. Immediately, his head was spinning and he could not focus. The sides of the shelter seemed to bend away and then back toward him as if they were the restless waves of the sea.

One of the creatures nudged Quinn and snorted derisively as the youth swayed and toppled. Within seconds, five of the little goat-men were on top of the Torra Altan and forcing liquid down his throat.

Rollo wasn't entirely sure what happened after that. He was aware of being dragged and propped up against Quinn but it was Isolde who held the little creatures' interest. They slapped her cheek to revive her. She groaned miserably.

'Girl! Speak!' A torch was thrust into her face and Rollo saw how her eyes were glazed. Quinn broke free and flung himself at the creatures, crashing to the floor where he lay moaning, his hands clawing at the ground in a pathetic effort to move. His legs kicked feebly.

One part of Rollo urged him to try and do something to save the girl but another part told him that he was as useless as Quinn. He wished he could think more clearly. What on earth these creatures wanted with Isolde he could not possibly imagine. Two of them held her head back while another one leapt in front of her.

'Vine imp!' Isolde spat the words in disgust.

The creature before her bowed. 'There's not many of your kind that know us by name. Perhaps you've reached the bottom of the barrel a few times before now.' He pirouetted before her, waggling his stumpy little tail and then bowed low, his screwed up little face laughing merrily. 'Usually, the sad ones welcome me. You should welcome me. I offer ease. Unburden yourself; speak your inner thoughts. There's none to listen but me.'

'Vine imp, I have nothing to tell you!' Isolde slurred, 'Nothing! I have done nothing.'

'Believe me, she has dark secrets,' Lonicera assured her accomplice. 'She wants no one to know. Just like the youth here.' The fairy pointed her twiglike arm at Rollo.

'Lonicera, we're not interested in their secrets. Don't you want the haven? Do you not want happiness for your daughters? Focus on the matter at hand,' the imp snapped at her and stamped his cloven hoof.

'Very well! Very well!' Lonicera conceded and began to scratch a picture in the loose earth floor of the shelter.

Rollo let his head loll to one side as he puzzled over the sketch. Lonicera appeared to be drawing a row of nine circles but, as she added to the design by drawing a stem on the top of each dimpled circle, he saw they were pictures of apples. Below that she then drew a row of trees, differing in height and finally a wandering line that snaked around the apples and through the roots of the trees. He looked at the last bit and puzzled over it as Lonicera drew the crude form of a human hand whose fingers closed about the snaking line. She worked on the picture for a few minutes more and Rollo decided that the line was either a snake or a piece of thread.

The colour drained from Isolde's cheeks.

'She knows!' Lonicera declared. 'She knows of these symbols. She has seen them. She knows! We shall be well rewarded.' The little fairy leapt up into the air and somersaulted three times before alighting back down and standing just on the very tip of one toe. 'I have always wanted to live in the haven and now is my chance. It's no good, human child, trying to hide your secrets from me; I know you know what those symbols mean.'

'Of course, I know what they mean,' Isolde snapped. 'The apple represents choice. That middle tree is the ash and gives us understanding of how all things in the universe are linked. The one on the left is a birch representing cleansing and new beginnings and the one on the right is an oak, representing both protection and the gateway to all mysteries.'

Lonicera cocked her head on one side, evidently a little puzzled. 'Bibo, she speaks too easily. I had no idea your mead was as powerful as that.'

'Mead!' Bibo seemed outraged by the word. 'Mead indeed. Only the finest wine is good enough for my craft. Only the finest grapes ripened and fermented by vine imps could make such wine. But she has told us nothing we don't know already.' On his hairy legs, he strutted in front of Isolde. 'You have not told all that is in the picture? What does the hand symbolize?' he demanded.

She looked at it sideways. 'Sewing, I would think. Yes, definitely sewing.'

'But why? What's the significance of that?'

Isolde's mouth worked up and down and she looked helplessly at Quinn. 'I can't tell you.'

'Can't or won't?' The vine imp pressed its nose close to her face. 'No one will blame you. It won't be your fault if you tell us. No harm can come of this. None at all.'

'I don't know,' Isolde stammered. 'You're a vine imp. You're not to be trusted.'

'Of course I am to be trusted; I am the bringer of truth. Freed from your responsibilities,' he lifted a goblet to indicate the heady brew, 'you speak the word of truth. No, I trust Lonicera when she tells me that you truly know what the picture means. You have seen it before and understand its subtleties.'

Isolde was nodding.

'Where have you seen these symbols?' the vine imp asked very slowly, his eyes watching her all the while.

'Books . . .,' Isolde, said at length. 'Books, of course.'

'And from what source are the drawings copied?' the imp persisted.

Isolde was turning slowly green and Rollo thought she might be sick at any moment. She stuttered and stammered and finally the words fell out from her mouth. 'The Chalice, I believe.' Her head flopped forward and the imp prodded her sharply. When she did not respond, he lifted her head by pulling back her hair and held a finger up before her swivelling eyes until she focused on it.

'No harm will come to you by unburdening yourself of this truth but, if you do not speak, Lonicera will look for your secrets and she will tell! Where are these symbols from? Where have you seen them?'

'I told you; the Chalice. I may have actually seen it once myself, but that was, so long, long, long ago.' She spread her arms wide to indicate the passing of many years.

'But, what does it mean?' Bibo emphasized.

'Mean?' Isolde looked at him as if she were on the point of madness. 'I told you, the apple represents choice—'

'Think, girl! Think. What is the significance of the choice?' his eyes flitted to the fairy and Rollo had the sudden hope that the vine imp was losing confidence. 'Lonicera, are you sure she knows what it means?'

The fairy stared into Isolde's red eyes. 'Little human, your kind has done me so much wrong. My daughters are poisoned and my men hounded from the hunting fields. You have wronged us but you can put things right by helping now.'

'Why would I help you?' Clearly, Isolde found it impossible not to speak her thoughts out loud.

'Merrit! John!' Rollo managed to squeeze the cry through his throat. 'Merrit, you must help us! Help!' Why wouldn't they wake up? 'Merrit!' he yelled once more only to find a pitcher of Bibo's brew thrown into his face and more forced down his throat. The burning liquid punched into his belly, making him choke and gasp for air.

'What do the symbols mean?' Bibo demanded of Rollo this time. 'You tell us, boy!'

'How would I know what they mean? I'm not a priest; I know nothing of these things.' He couldn't help but let his eyes stray towards Isolde.

'Tell us more,' Bibo cajoled.

Rollo couldn't help himself. Somehow, the thoughts in his head worked their way straight to his mouth. 'I've said too much. Oh, Isolde, what can I do to stop saying things? How can I not tell them that you are a priestess, that Quinn's mother is a priestess.'

'And what's her name?' Bibo's eyes swirled before him, the hypnotic effect eroding his will to resist.

Rollo screwed up his eyes and clenched his teeth shut, desperate to say nothing more. Bibo held his nose and Rollo twisted, trying to swat at the creature. But it clung on and would not let go until Rollo was forced to breathe. Again the liquid flooded his mouth and poured down his throat. Almost immediately, he felt his stomach bunch as if he were about to vomit.

'Tell me!' Bibo bit his hand but Rollo could barely feel the pain. The creature then shrieked in frustration and ordered Lonicera to bring more wine.

Unlike the elderberry wine, this liquid had a deep golden colour and was almost viscous. Rollo's head was held and the liquid sloshed down his throat until he thought he would choke. It tingled on the tongue and then, like fire, tore down into his body. He jerked, suddenly fortified by the energy in the wine. He didn't know from where he found the strength but he leapt up and ripped Bibo from his face and began to throttle him. Lonicera whacked him hard on the nose and the other creatures left Quinn and began scrambling over Rollo to try and prise his hands away from Bibo's throat.

'Bibo, don't worry. Don't worry! I'll save you!' Lonicera swam before Rollo's eyes, throwing dust into them. 'The raw liquid should have either loosened the boy's tongue or knocked him out completely. But now he's like a demon,' Lonicera was squealing.

Like a rabid dog, Rollo tried to snap at her with his teeth. Their eyes met and she looked deep into them and suddenly he felt the strength draining out of him.

'You killed him!' she said coldly and then yelled more loudly, 'You killed him!' Her eyes slitted in concentration, she said, 'Your friend? Your brother? No!' She pointed at Quinn who was staggering to his feet, trying to kick at the vine imps that were swarming over Isolde. 'No, no! His brother. You killed his brother!'

Rollo sagged to his knees, felt his fingers slip from the vine imp's neck and looked down at his hands. 'I didn't know what I was doing. I couldn't help myself. It was the rage within me, the black rage. I could not even see what I was doing,' he tried feebly to excuse himself.

Quinn no longer seemed to notice the creatures in the shelter. He was staggering to the pitchfork and found the strength to grip its handle and point its twin tines at Rollo's chest.

Rollo turned to flee. Head down, he ran from Quinn and the vine imps, which dragged about his ankles and thighs. He fled through the mouth of the shelter only to crash into the rocklike chest of a man, standing feet astride and braced to catch him. Quinn was still after him but the man deftly raised his staff, deflecting the pitchfork, and struck Quinn on the shoulder, sending him sprawling to the floor.

Merrit looked at him and laughed. 'Poor fool, your petty secrets are of no concern to me. You don't even need to tell me your mother's name. I had it from her very own lips. She pleaded with me. "Don't do this. My sons Guthrey and Quinn are missing and I am their greatest hope. I would do anything for them. Please do not leave me here to die," she begged when I chained her within the pit in readiness for the dragon.' He nodded in satisfaction. 'And now I have her son . . .'

On her knees beside Quinn, Isolde looked up at the hunter. Her eyes narrowed. 'If you have harmed Brid in any way you will . . .'

Rollo groaned at his own idiocy. He had felt that Merrit was not to be trusted yet had ignored his instincts. He staggered towards Merrit, scooping up the fallen pitchfork as he went.

The sound he made was fleeting, barely enough to warn Merrit, but the man outmanoeuvred him and ripped the weapon from his hand. The last Rollo remembered was trying to duck as the handle of the pitchfork was swung through the air towards his head.

Chapter 29

Rollo felt sick. A vile smell swirled through his nostrils and white lights flickered behind his eyelids. His head was spinning as if he were reeling within the bowels of a ship tossing on a violent sea; it took him many moments to realize that it was the movement of a horse's swaying gait beneath him that produced this unsteady motion. Yet, he remembered nothing of mounting a horse . . .

They were no longer in the woods. A bright clear sky was all about them. His hands were tied and lashed to the front of the saddle on which he sat. The horse was bay in colour and its black mane tickled his face and the backs of his hands.

Feeling unutterably sick, he let his eyelids sag again; he could not muster the energy to work out any more of his situation. In an attempt to control the nausea, he concentrated on the strange stench that assailed his nostrils. The more he dwelt on it, the more he realized that it was the smell that had brought him to this uncomfortable state of consciousness in the first place. Pungent, it kicked at the back of his nose.

Opening his eyes again and looking ahead at the area framed by the horse's neat ears, he saw a man in a long cloak, the hem of which trailed in the mud. Rollo immediately recognized him as the cloaked figure he had seen at the mill; it wasn't a man at all. And it was from this figure that the vile smell emanated.

Rollo jerked back involuntarily as the figure turned to face him. Dry and flaking, the hob's skin was a brownish green hue, and its nostrils were cut high on its thin nose revealing the pink gristle beneath. Large, red, slanted eyes glinted over broad cheekbones and small pricks of ears pushed through the ragged slime that sprouted from the sides of its scalp. The hob smiled, revealing angry canine fangs behind his thin, fleshless lips.

Though dazed and still unaware of his surroundings, Rollo's reaction was immediate. He stabbed his heels into the horse's sides and rode the animal straight at the hob, at the same time yelling the ululating battle cry of his homeland that was designed to put fear into the stoutest of hearts. The horse's head, however, jerked sharply to the right and the animal twisted and stumbled. The sudden change of direction unseated Rollo and, with his wrists still tied to the pommel, his body was flung from the saddle. His arms twisted painfully in their sockets and he dangled from his wrists, his face pressed up against the horse's shoulder.

Someone hauled him back into the saddle and brought his chin up smartly with a stick. A dribble of bloody saliva ran from the corner of his mouth. Rollo wiped his mouth against his shoulder and stared down into Merrit's face. Slowly, the curious memory of the tiny creatures and the taste of sweet wine came back to him. His eyes swivelled to take in the full scene around him. A rope attached to his horse's bridle was secured to the saddle of Merrit's mare.

The two tiny creatures were perched on the back of the black mare's saddle, chattering away in excited argument with one another. Being pulled dejectedly along behind by ropes about their wrists were Isolde and Quinn, trudging on foot.

Rollo sought out their gaze. Isolde stared blankly back at him, her eyes dead. Quinn, however, glared back with a look of unspeakable hatred and then turned his head to the side and spat in an unmistakable expression of contempt.

'Murderer!' the fairylike woman perched on the black mare's withers taunted Rollo. 'Murderer!'

The scrawny imp beside her cackled, 'Have you know, the truth will out. The truth is always there to be found.'

All that had passed came back to Rollo in a deluge of distress. He remembered the fairy creature riding high on Merrit's horse, her name was Lonicera. Once drenched in the imp's wine, he had listened to her soothing song and, seeking her forgiveness and release from the torturous guilt, had revealed his foul secret. He looked back at Quinn with remorse.

'It wasn't my fault! Quinn, you have to believe me,' he implored.

Quinn raised his chin and stared back defiantly, his thick brown hair falling back from his taut face. 'You vile snake! You tried to make me your friend; you smiled into my face; you offered me hope yet, all along, you knew he was dead. You killed my brother!'

'But I didn't mean it to happen,' Rollo tried to explain, knowing that his words sounded lame. 'He attacked me. We were fighting and when you were not—'

'You didn't have to kill him!' Quinn roared. He charged forward to the extent of his tethers, his arms twisted round behind him in an effort to get at Rollo. 'You knew he was dead. That was why you wanted to return to Torra Alta so that we would never uncover your vile crime.'

Spit spluttered from Quinn's mouth. His wrists were white where the rope cut into his flesh and strangled them of blood. Wrenching at his bonds, he made determined but futile efforts to break free so that he might attack Rollo, who stared glumly back, his mouth slack and his brain numb. He had no answer to the truth. What else could he say other than all of it was true? He was that vile human being.

Quinn was making a strange strangulated sound as if a demon within him were trying to crack open his body in order to be free to attack Rollo. Merrit blocked his way, putting his hands on the Torra Altan's shoulders and jerking him straight.

'Now, lad, there's a good chap, we want you looking at your best. I can't have you damaging yourself, young fellow. I need your mother to see you looking fit and well.'

Rollo admired Quinn's spirit: even though he was tied at the wrists, he lashed out with his feet and butted with his head. Merrit, though quite a big man, had no trouble leaping back out of reach. He then smacked the rump of the mare to make her move on more quickly and, when Quinn again tried to kick Merrit, he stumbled in the process. Sprawling to the ground, Quinn was dragged along by the horse. It was a minute before the youth could get a foot underneath himself and struggle up, his face muddied and grazed. After spitting out a mouthful of earth, he stared sullenly at Merrit who walked on with an easy stride several paces in front of him.

'That's better! Just you keep calm and quiet now. Your mother spoke most highly of her boys, a twinkle of love bright in her eye. She will do anything I ask to save you, I have no doubt.'

Quinn laughed coldly. 'You don't know my mother. She will do only what is right. And, if that means sacrificing those she loves, then that is what she will do.'

From the horribly triumphant way in which Quinn bragged, Rollo was quite certain that the youth was right; Brid would not save them.

He wondered what had happened for Brid to be somehow held by Merrit but knew that it would be best if he did not ask; he had caused enough trouble and to ask after her would only anger Quinn more. Still feeling sick, he turned his back on his comrades and slumped down into the folds of his cloak, doing his best to stop himself from shivering. He knew he should think of some way to escape. They were held only by Merrit and a single hob and there must, surely, be something they could do; but he could not think straight as his mind persisted to pick and worry at the memory of his crime.

All he could think of was Guthrey and feeling his sword push into his flesh, and the sudden jar of the hilt in his hand as the blade shuddered and halted against bone. The vision of Guthrey lying still, crushed beneath the weight of his toppled horse, swam before his eyes. He could even feel the warm blood on his hands. He wanted to scream but gave out no more than a wretched whimper.

The hob turned and stared at him, its pointed dark-red tongue flickering out from its tight mouth in a hideous gesture of threat. 'Vile little human, you, too, are someone's son? And for your sake, they'd better be someone important; I've grown bored with horseflesh and am in need of sweeter victuals.'

Rollo did not care for the menace in the hob's eyes.

The giddy minutes dragged into a long cold hour as they trudged across the open terrain. The grass about was cropped by cattle and Rollo had the realization that, in this region, man was still in control. He looked from the cows to the hob: this was very odd indeed. A hob leading a motley band of roped humans boldly through open countryside without fear of discovery by man? It didn't seem possible.

He twisted his hands but the bonds securing his wrists remained tight. There was no way he could get free. Feeling ill and drained from the effects of Bibo's brew, he let his head flop down to rest on his chin and, after a few more minutes, he was asleep.

Many hours later he awoke. The sky was violet, a single evening star bright in the heavens. Behind him, a molten sun sunk into the charred black of the earth, the last orange rays warming his back and creeping beyond to touch the tip of a ring of giant standing stones.

As they approached, a circle of fires sprang up around the stones that became bathed in a glow of liquid orange. Thirteen dark figures arose out from the peaks of the granite obelisks and stood tall, arms upstretched and spread wide, revealing the ugly silhouettes of their scrawny female hob bodies. A single barking cry rang out from one hob throat followed by a cackling chant and a half-musical moan. Rollo felt his blood run cold.

Looking behind him for Isolde and Quinn, he saw that they were now both mounted on Merrit's horse. Isolde was slumped against Quinn who, in turn, was swaying precariously. Like himself, Quinn was only held in place by his wrists that were tied to the front of the horse's saddle and his legs strapped to the horse's girth. He was half-glad to see that his two companions were sleeping since it freed him from their loathing and accusations. Yet, he missed them and the fragile friendship he had so easily shattered.

Most of his life, he had felt alone and a failure. With Isolde and Quinn he had felt, for the first time in his life, that he was part of a team, joined in spirit and purpose. But now that was gone.

Merrit drew his horse to a halt and snapped at the lead rein attached to the bridle of Rollo's bay. The sudden jolt roused him from his melancholy thoughts. It was fully dark now, the moon flitting out between rolling clouds.

Turning his attention to the megaliths before him, he saw that the stones did not form a full circle but were open at one end. Nearest them, at the closed end of the circle, two of the largest stones stood close together, supporting a third recumbent stone to form an impressive portal. At the far side, the circle opened into a channel that slanted away. The hob women standing on the stones now swung torches around and around, creating circles of light that sprayed out sparks.

As Merrit and his captives passed beneath the stone arch, the hobs above them abruptly ceased to whirl their torches and stood perfectly still. The sudden hush was broken only by the hiss and crackle of the red torches whose flames lapped upwards into the gloom. A cold gust of wind blew between the stones. The hairs on the back of Rollo's neck prickled and the spinning in his head slowly steadied. Perhaps it was the cold night air but he was rapidly coming to his senses.

A bright moon slid from behind scudding clouds. As they came to a halt and were helped to dismount, the hobs set up a low hum. The simplicity of that single note and the menace that underlay the unity of voices quite terrified Rollo. The sound pierced through his body as if it were a long needle. Quinn groaned softly and Isolde took in a sharp breath.

'Great One! Wise One!' the hobs began to chant as Merrit and the cloaked hob beside him swept forward into the heart of the arena.

Jerking his head about, Rollo searched for any means of escape. Directly ahead of them was a low stone set into the ground and shaped like a giant arrowhead. Beyond that was another low, pointed stone and, beyond that, another.

Each giant granite arrowhead was set into the earth of a sloping channel. At intervals of thirty paces, other partially buried megalith stones pointed the way down through the cutting. With the chanting hobs now at their backs, they advanced below the half-circle of stones into the cutting. After perhaps a hundred paces, the channel opened into a deep amphitheatre hollowed out of the earth. To the east above the steep, tiered sides of the arena, set back upon a rising mound, was a lone megalith.

The very bottom of the amphitheatre was flat. The sides were terraced with row upon row of stone seats from which hundreds of red-eyed hobs stared down expectantly. Three other entrances led into the arena; two to the left and one to the right of their approach. However, these portals were not open to the sky but were dark burrows, filled with heavy iron gratings set into vertical stones.

Rollo's gaze was drawn to the very centre of the arena; a large flat circular stone lay in the raked sand, thin slabs radiating out from it like rays around the sun. A female hob, wearing a skirt and bracelets of feathers about her waist, wrists and ankles, shuddered and jerked before them. She wore a head-dress of antlers, which cast long shadows by the light of the moon.

At once, braziers were lit all about the arena, giving out a hungry roar that made Rollo jump. In their orange light he could now see what held the hobs' attention. The dancing hob-witch had in her grasp a human hand that dripped blood. Pegged out at the centre of the stone sunburst was the unmoving body of a young man who had either passed out or was already dead.

With the sound of metal grating on stone, another prisoner was dragged from one of the dark tunnels. The hob-witch gyrated towards him, pointing a staff at his throat. 'Tell me of the Chalice. Tell me what you know of its power and how to wield it. Tell me with what phases of the moon each ingredient should be blended to the brew within the cup. Tell me otherwise you will lose your hands and then your feet.' She stuffed the severed hand into her mouth and shook it as if she were a dog with a rat before spitting it out into the face of the prisoner. The man squealed uncontrollably.

Merrit drew to a halt. A smile lifted his thin lips and he observed the display with apparent amusement. He inclined his head towards Isolde, who was closest to him and was staring on, swaying slightly on her delicate feet.

'Hobs are such fools. They look at a human and see only a human. They do not see a farmhand or a kitchen boy, dairymaid or queen. I set them gathering humans from around the environs of Torra Alta in the hope they would find someone with knowledge and understanding of the Chalice. They have brought me back hundreds of villagers and, fervently, seen them tortured and slaughtered. But, bar keeping the hobs excited and happy, it has accomplished nothing. Eventually, I knew we would find someone useful to us but never did I think that, with all the hundreds of hobs assigned to the task, I would have to find them myself.'

He sighed to himself as if the hobs were naughty school children. 'They did find Brid first, of course, and just when I was beginning to give up on them. The moment I saw her I knew she was no dairymaid and I was deeply perturbed that she was in their hands. As you can see, hobs are not famed for their subtle approaches. Although they are eager to take captives, they are not so good at keeping them alive. For every three they take, two will die before the end of the first day. It's a wonder they managed to bring any back. Look at that man whose hand that hob has torn off. She will have been in such a frenzy that she won't have heard anything he might have said before he bled to death. I couldn't let them waste Brid, so I took her myself.'

Merrit looked at Isolde to check that she was concentrating on his words. 'She was very ill when I found her so I saw to it that she was healed by the learned physicians who hide so secretly in their quiet world and, then, I had her brought here. It was such a clever plan.' He preened himself and smiled at Bibo and Lonicera. 'And you two know how I like to be clever.'

Bibo nodded and chortled. 'To have her frightened by the old queen was a masterful plan, I admit. But, just when she believed that the dragon was not set on killing her, delivering her into the clutches of the ravenshrikes was a stroke of genius. After such treatment there's no human alive that wouldn't tell all to her rescuer. And at the same time you could still go back to Zophia to make sure you still had her trust.'

'Ah, yes, Zophia,' Merrit sighed. 'Luck has been with me but I still have use of her.' He grinned hideously at the three youngsters. 'I thought to trick Brid, seduce her into spilling the knowledge by arriving here as her rescuer but I am no longer forced down such a clumsy complicated path.' He flicked his hands at Bibo and Lonicera as if dismissing their usefulness. He snorted derisively at their alarmed reactions and jerked his head at Rollo, Quinn and Isolde. 'Now, you see, I have you three, you sweet children of Torra Alta. Ha!' He threw back his head and roared with laughter.

He laughed until his face was puce before stopping abruptly. 'Hob-wench, cease!' He raised his hand to stay the creature. Her new victim fell from her, shrieking and trembling in panic. Leaping onto the stone, Merrit wrenched the hob's long staff from her crooked fingers. He rapped the ground with it and then pointed it at the large male hob who had brought the prisoner from the tunnel.

'You there, get these three seated,' he pointed at Rollo, Isolde and Quinn, 'and see to it that they remain so until I need them.'

With flaring nostrils that revealed the throbbing black blood vessels within, the hob snorted his assent and shoved Rollo, Isolde and Quinn forward and down onto one of the terraces. Pressure from the creature's bony fingers forced them to sit. Two more hobs lurched closer, sniffed at the humans and then stood guard to either side of them, Rollo pressed up uncomfortably close to Quinn.

'You are a vile murderer,' Quinn hissed in his ear. 'If we are ever free, I will see to it that you have your comeuppance.' The Torra Altan's eyes were tight with menace.

'I . . .,' Rollo began and then wondered what the point was. How could he defend the indefensible? Yet he had to say something and so continued, 'I didn't mean it. I meant only to scratch him to make him know that I wasn't someone to be trifled with. But then he sneakily crept round the back of you and attacked when we were both distracted. He was not fighting fairly; I was enraged. I could no longer see for my anger and I attacked without knowledge of my actions. It was only when I felt my blade jar against bone that my vision cleared. I saw him pinned beneath his horse, which must have lost its footing in the mêlée.'

'It was not a mêlée; it was murder,' Quinn said icily. 'And don't forget, stranger, that I am waiting only for my moment.'

'Stop it, Quinn!' Isolde snapped at him unexpectedly.

'Why should I?' the Torra Altan youth retorted. 'Why? Guthrey was my brother.'

'Hush, Quinn,' Isolde persisted. 'It is Brid you should be worrying about now not revenge. Guthrey is dead and nothing can alter that fact. Hurting Rollo won't help.'

'No, but it'll help me.'

'But it won't help Brid,' Isolde said softly. She nodded towards the centre of the arena.

A hush filled the amphitheatre. For Rollo, the silence was so intense that he thought that he would explode. The very air seemed to throb with the pulses of the hobs all around him.

'Mother!' Quinn croaked the word.

A small, bent-over woman with a chain about her neck painfully stumbled out from one of the tunnels, her eyes blinking in the sudden light. A long-legged, almost fleshless hob snapped the chain taut and jerked her forward. Rollo would never have recognized the woman; her clothing, or what was left of it, was in rags. Her feet were still clad in good strong riding boots that stopped at the knee but her gown was ripped and shredded, the tattered skirt stopping at her slender, muddy and bruised upper thigh. Her long hair was partially tied at the back of her neck but, otherwise, hung down like a mare's matted tail. She no longer had the rounded belly of a woman with child but looked thin and, even in the imperfect light cast by the braziers, her skin was unnaturally wan.

'Mother!' Quinn repeated, gasping in shock. 'Isolde, what have they done to her?' He moaned softly, twisting his wrists within his bonds until his fingers went white. 'How could this happen? This is all your fault, Rollo, all of it. She would never have gone out looking for us if it hadn't been for you.'

'I—I—,' Rollo stammered, feeling anger, pity and understanding all at the same time. He wanted to express his sorrow but his pride and anger got the better of him. 'I'm less to blame than you!'

Quinn paid him no heed. 'Issy, I can't let them use me against her. Is there nothing in your herb scrip that might see to it that I have a swift finish now rather than a slow torture before my mother's eyes?'

Quinn's voice turned to a throttled snort as the hob

behind him yanked him back. 'Do you think we have waited this long, come this far to waste an opportunity now?' He closed his fingers tightly about Quinn's neck until the youth's breaths came in strangulated gasps. His eyes bulged as he stared at his mother who was dragged onto the central stone.

Although Brid had not raised her gaze in their direction, Rollo sensed that she knew they were there. She had lifted her heavy head to look in every other directions but seemed to take great pains not to look towards them.

After ordering the gory bodies to be removed, Merrit leapt up onto the stone sunburst, a corner of his cloak in each hand and his arms spread wide like a monstrous bat. 'Woman, tell us what you know.' His words carried easily throughout the arena; even his breath was loud.

'I know of many things.' Brid's voice was weary yet rich with disdain. Clearly she had suffered a great deal recently yet showed no sign of breaking. She looked the man in the eye. 'You! I remember you now, Silas, you wretch, you treacherous wretch! You will not prosper from this!'

Rollo glared at the man, unsurprised to hear that he went by another name.

Silas smiled at Brid, satisfied with the passion he had induced. Without taking his eyes from her, he clicked his fingers at the cloaked hob who, in a long-legged lope, made his way to Silas's horse and unbuckled the small pack covered in wolfskin. With an ugly grin, he brought out a bundle wrapped in red silk cloth that he carried to Silas. His eyes black with anticipation, Silas reverently unfurled the cloth. A warm glow lit his face as the light from the torches glinted off the burnished metal of the cup cradled in his hand. Even Brid visibly started.

'You had it all along!' Her words croaked from her dry throat. She stood tall before him and, though she barely came up to his chest, her presence overshadowed him. 'You vile thief! You are a traitor to your race!'

He shrugged. 'That's really of no concern now, is it? All I want to know is that you can make it perform its deeper magic.' He sighed. 'We took swords of the crudest metal and, with the Chalice, made weapons with edges to cut diamond, and hearts strong enough to shatter rock. But no more than three could we forge before the magic was lost and, of those three, all were clumsily mislaid.' He looked accusingly at the assembled hobs. 'Either the Chalice will only pass on the power held within its cup three times or something went awry with our methods. We require more of such swords and have no doubt that now we will get all that we desire.' He looked knowingly at Brid.

She smiled at him. 'And you think I will help you?' She laughed. 'Even if you could kill me a thousand times, you would never break my will.'

Rollo frowned. Perhaps his eyes were deceiving him but he was sure he saw a violet halo about Brid's head. He certainly believed every one of her determined words, knowing that she had a greater will than any there that night. The man he knew as Merrit but whom Brid had addressed as Silas knelt down and dipped his head towards the woman. He cupped her chin in one hand and she stared back defiantly into his eyes.

'You will tell me,' he demanded.' You will make the Chalice work for me.'

Brid laughed and eased her head aside from his grip. 'You only succeeded in making those weapons in the first place because a great runesword blessed by the Mother herself was placed within the Chalice long before you attained it. How you spoilt the spell I do not know but it cannot be recreated. Even if someone showed you the correct manner in which to use the Chalice, you cannot infuse your hobs' crude weapons with the deadly power of a master sword if you lack such a weapon in the first place.'

His lip curled up into a triumphant grin and he snapped his fingers. All stared as, out from another tunnel came the hearty figure of a dwarf. This dwarf was more smartly dressed than any of the ruffian band that had taken Rollo, Quinn and Isolde prisoner. He had a red tunic covering a suit of glimmering mail. Brightly emblazoned on the garish red of the tunic was a sunburst surrounded by images of the moon in its different phases. His hair was long and grey, combed and tied low down his back; similarly, his long beard was neatly groomed. Reverently, he carried a black sword. As he stepped out into the open arena and the firelight fell on it, there was no bright glint off metal; the blade was like a slice of night in his hands.

'Madam,' Silas addressed Brid with feigned obsequiousness. 'Here is such a sword.'

Solemnly, he took the blade from the dwarf and ran the tip of his index finger down the grove of its fuller from hilt to point as if he were tracing the line down the centre of a maiden's bare navel. His hand trembled and a leer drew back his lips. Returning down the length of the blade, his hand folded about the hilt and he swung the black steel up in an arcing circle about his head. Instinctively, all those near him, save Brid, shrank back.

'A beautiful, clean, pure weapon,' he breathed.

Like a cat, he sprang at the nearest hob, raising the sword ready to smite down at the creature. The hob lifted his own sword to block the blow but the dwarf blade cut clean through the weapon, severing through the creature's upper shoulder and cutting half its torso away in one smooth blow. The hob fell to the ground, its ribcage pared open, the heart visibly pumping within.

Breathing heavily with excitement, Silas wiped the blood from the blade and held up the unmarked edge for Brid to examine. 'Not a nick, not a blemish,' he boasted. 'The alchemists of northern Athell have been working on it for three years. I must add that they have been working only under the light of a waxing moon to regulate the consistency of the metal and avoid all impurities that the moon's pull drags out from the rough ores. The hobs need thousands of such swords. It takes their smiths a week to make one of their wretched blades. But with the Chalice, we can give the hobs' crude weapons the refinement and strength of this sword. All I need is your help.'

'And that you are not going to get,' Brid said clearly.

'Ah, but I am. You will tell me of the symbols. You will tell me the phases of the moon, the ascension of the sun, the purity of the water and anything else required to unlock the power of the Chalice.'

'Not even if you start by cutting off my toes and end by plucking out my eyes will I tell you what you wish,' Brid gave her rebuttal calmly.

'But what if I do that to your son?' Silas threatened with a smile of triumph.

There was just a fraction of a pause before Brid's reply. 'You do not have my son.'

Silas snapped his fingers and Quinn was dragged to his feet. Rollo and Isolde were also hauled after him and led to the centre of the amphitheatre.

Silas triumphantly took Brid by her shoulders and swung her round until she was facing Quinn. 'Here is your son. What torture would you have him suffer? Losing his ears perhaps? Or his nose? What first?'

The hob holding Quinn added weight to the threat by producing a knife, which he held against the youth's ear.

Chapter 30

Brid's eyes gazed studiously on Quinn's face but no smile broke her pale lips.

'That is not my son.' The corners of her face relaxed and she smiled at Silas as if she were a young pupil who had proved her tutor wrong. 'You thought to confuse and trick me. Why would I jeopardize all my people for a single life? I have witnessed the slaughter of many over the past few days; one more will make no difference.'

Silas's eyes flitted between Quinn and Brid. It was only then that Rollo noticed that Brid's left hand was splinted and bandaged in dirty strips of ragged cloth. The man's lip twitched. Then he laughed a little more lightly. 'You are telling me that this youth is no more than a kitchen boy?'

'I doubt it. By the look of him, he's a youngster that's lately begun to train as one of Torra Alta's archers. Is that not right, young man?' Brid coolly addressed her son.

Quinn smartly nodded.

Silas chortled at their charade. 'Your self-control is impressive.' He placed the Chalice down on the large circular slab of stone and then produced from within his jacket a small dagger. With half an eye on Quinn, he said very calmly to Brid, 'I have no doubt of your mettle, lady. And believe me, I hold it in the highest regard. However, your son, here, is young and there is fear in his eyes.' With one deft lunge, the man snatched up Brid's hand and pressed the knife across her fingers. He turned and glared at Quinn. 'One slice and she loses three fingers in one go.'

Quinn went white. 'Leave her alone! Don't you touch her!' His voice was hoarse and throttled as he struggled against the hob's restraining grip about his throat.

Silas slowly loosed his hold on Brid and let her hand slip through his fingers. 'Well, now there, Quinn, it didn't take too long to establish that this woman is very dear to you. Don't even begin to think you can outsmart me.' He swivelled on his heel and spat his words at Brid. 'Now, woman, tell me of the Chalice of Önd, otherwise your *son* dies!'

'Very well, you are right, but it is but a half-truth,' Brid continued in her smooth tone. 'He is my son but only a bastard and so of no account. I would not exchange the safety of my people for a thousand such as he.'

Rollo did not listen to any more of the exchange; his whole attention, every sense in his body was drawn to something high up in the darkness beyond the confines of the arena.

Silas waved the priestess's words aside as if they were of no consequence. 'Shall we start again? I must make it quite clear that you can make life a lot easier now by just abandoning your stand against me. Bastard or not, you love him; I see it in your eyes. You will do as I say or Quinn will suffer – truly suffer.'

The priestess did not reply and was no longer even looking at the man. She had her head twisted round and was staring behind her; she too sensed that something was coming.

From out of the black sky came the sound of beating wings. Isolde gave out a little moan as a giant ravenshrike swept down and landed before them. It strutted on its long legs, its giant claws raking the ground. Stretching up its neck, it screeched into the night as another seven of the giant predators alighted. Each bore a man on its back who tapped the bird's shoulders with a short thick stick to direct it. Speedily, they took up posts around the edge of the arena, anxiously flapping their wings. The riders on their backs fixed Silas with their gaze, waiting for his command. When he clicked his fingers, one of the riders tapped his ravenshrike with his stick and the monstrous bird strutted to the centre of the arena. Wings spread out and curving downwards like skirts, it stood over Quinn.

'One signal from me and its beak will bore into his skull as easily as if it were an egg,' Silas threatened.

Brid looked up at the ravenshrike and back at Silas. 'You must feel very small indeed to require the presence of such large pets!'

Rollo glowered at the man on its back, hating him for allying himself with these fearful creatures. What madness had driven Silas and his minions to turn against their own kind?

'Well?' Silas demanded, ignoring Brid's taunt.

She looked at him, glanced towards her son and then down at her feet. She twitched the grit on the surface of the stone with her boot and then finally brought her chin up to stare Silas boldly in the eye. Her hands were held up in defeat. 'I will tell you what I know,' she murmured weakly.

'You will do more than that,' Silas assured her. 'You will perform the magic. You have power and knowledge; the magic will work all the better being conjured by your artful hand.'

Brid nodded. 'Very well. But only with the guarantee that you release all the people here. Get them out from the dungeons and have them ready.'

Silas tilted his head to one side. 'You are a clever lady indeed. But there is no point in me releasing them since, then, you would simply refuse to do as I say. But I will meet you half way. The prisoners shall all be brought out into the open so that you can see them while you perform the rite. Once I am satisfied that you have performed your end of the bargain, I shall have no further use of them and they will be freed.'

Brid nodded in agreement. Rollo could not believe she could be so naïve. Silas would never let any of them go. It didn't take a genius to predict that, once Brid had done his will, his first act would be to test the swords.

Silas nodded at two huge hobs that approached and indicated the barred tunnels. 'Get the prisoners out into the arena,' he ordered.

Rollo had never seen such giant hobs. Their huge bones pushed up out of their stretched skin, long arms dangling from angular shoulders. The guards loped off down into the tunnels, their barks echoing from the dark, leaving the ravenshrikes and their riders to guard the three youngsters. Rollo could not stop his teeth chattering in fright as he felt the breath of the ravenshrike on the back of his head, wafting his hair. Whimpering, Isolde pressed close to Quinn.

It took many long minutes before the wretched prisoners were dragged out of the tunnels. The women were whimpering and staggering, children shrieked in terror and men flung themselves at the great hobs only to be beaten down with whips and sticks. They were all shoved forward to be corralled by the seven ravenshrikes who stood at the perimeter of the arena and used their savage beaks to peck at the unfortunate prisoners. The men on their backs thwacked at the captives' heads with their barbed sticks until all were cowed.

Brid cast her eye into the throng of wretched life that limped into the light but hastily looked away as if the shock of seeing them might weaken her powers. Rollo noted, however, that her bandaged hand was trembling very slightly and that she bit her lip.

'Is that every last one?' she solemnly asked Silas.

He nodded dismissively, his mouth wide with pleasure.

The priestess looked him in the eye. 'You give me no option but to trust you.'

Rollo thought to himself that there could be another thousand men and women hidden behind the walls of the amphitheatre but he sensed that Brid was satisfied.

Silas took a step back to study Brid and Quinn together. 'Well, who would have thought that one bastard would make all the difference to my plans?' he sneered. 'I had planned to pose as your rescuer, delivering you from the ravenshrikes and the hob-witch in order to seduce you into freely giving up the Chalice's secrets but that would never have worked. And see there.' He nodded at Bibo and Lonicera, whose little forms sat alone, crouched high up on the terraces, staring down at the scene. 'I even brought along the vine imp and the fairy. They have their own subtle ways of extracting knowledge. But who needs subtleties when I've been handed a hammer.' He nodded as if in gratitude towards Quinn. 'How fortune has smiled on me today! You see, I deserved this moment. I have worked so hard for it.' His eyes sprang onto the golden goblet that glowed pale in the moonlight. 'Now, woman, do your work!'

Brid glanced up at him, her tired eyes calm and her mouth still. Quinn was looking on with hope and love touched with dismay. Clearly, he had not believed that his mother would help the hobs and Silas. He did not believe she would help bring about the downfall of her own kind to save him. Rollo could not believe it either yet there Brid was, preparing her sanctified setting for the casting of her magic.

'The moon is high and strong. Her light will feed the spell.' The priestess spun around, her arms stretching up into the night. She then thrust them out at Silas and the vulture-like hobs that stood at his back. 'First, you must stand well back from the stone,' she demanded. 'Every one of you.'

Obediently, they paced back and watched in silence. Silas stood as rigid as rock, a bead of saliva forming at the corner of his mouth.

'This will take some while,' Brid informed them with unnatural calmness. 'The magic itself must be performed at first light. But first, I must prepare the circle. I shall need buckets of fresh water drawn from a well or spring but not a stream. It must come directly from the belly of the Great Mother. Also, I want a cauldron in which to prepare my brew and a centre for my rite.' She looked about her and then down at the great round slab of rock on which she was standing. She stamped down the heel of her boot. 'This circular stone will suffice, but it must be cleansed of all impurities and the imprint of the atrocities that will have been absorbed into the fabric of the rock.'

Silas nodded, pleased by her co-operation. 'You will need apples then.' He displayed his knowledge grandly and with pride. 'I have them in readiness. It was one of the things that was plain from the Chalice; apples and ash sprigs. Apples seem to be a ridiculous ingredient but, nevertheless, I can see for myself that they are required.' He gestured towards the Chalice and the depiction of apples around the rim.

Brid shook her head at him. 'Your knowledge is that of a child who, still unable to read, believes they have the content of the book from its pictures alone. The essential magic, the preparation and the channelling of the energies of the Great Mother is not just a simple mixing of ingredients as if one were making a cake.' She paused, head bowed in deep concentration before continuing. 'I shall need rowan sprigs with berries, and leafed oak twigs bearing acorns. But, first, I need birch to cleanse and prepare a sanctified area. It is important to remove anything that would ruin the spell.'

The High Priestess worked on through the night, using juice crushed from the birch stems and water drawn from a spring to scrub the stone. When the stone was clean, she withdrew from her herb scrip a small sickle no larger than her palm with which she halved five apples through their girth to reveal the pentagram formed within their core. Nine apple halves she placed around the Chalice, each displaying the pentagram. When a hob eventually arrived with a large spray of rowan with a few withered autumn berries still clinging to the stem, she nodded in tempered satisfaction. Carefully, she selected nine berries and placed them base-up between the apples.

Silas bent over her work and examined the rowan berries. 'Ah, I see the significance now. Most berries have a dimple at their base but the rowan bears a little brown pentagram.'

Brid nodded. 'It wards off adverse magic from the spell

but, if you continue to interfere, these powerful symbols will not be enough,' she warned. Turning back to her apples, she took the remaining apple half and used the juice to polish the Chalice before using it to scrub the blade of the dwarves' black sword.

'Why are you doing that?' Silas asked suspiciously, ignoring her warning.

'Apple represents choice. The energy intrinsic to the sword would remain within the metal but the application of the juice from the apple facilitates a choice to remain where it is or for the energy to flow out into the brew within the cup. Now stand back and stop breathing on my work. I told you, there must be no contaminants,' Brid emphasized. 'If there are, it will be their properties that are transferred rather than those you desire.'

When the hobs returned with pitchers of icy water drawn up from a clear spring, Brid imperiously ordered them to be tipped into the cauldron that they had provided. Hastily, they lit a fire beneath the pot and set it to boil alongside the central stone. Within the waters, she began to prepare her brew, tossing in sprigs of rowan and ash and carefully consulting the symbols on the Chalice.

'Acorn from the oak to open the doorway for the natural magic in the ether to enter the prepared womb of spellwork,' she muttered. Her finger ran around the rim of the Chalice, hastily brushing over the symbol for fire and tapping on the depiction of the moon. She raised her head, checking the moon's position and nodding to herself as if noting at what point each part of the rite must be performed.

Rollo began to lose interest in this long process and turned his attention onto the sorry group of men and women guarded by the ravenshrikes. Beneath the shadow of the ravenshrikes' great wings, they were shrouded in darkness and so it was impossible to see more than the points of their cheeks or noses flashing white in the firelight. He could hear the moans of their prayers; one or two cried out to the Great

Mother while others called to Brid, thanking her for saving them. However, she did not break her concentration to look up at them but maintained her intense focus on the cauldron and Chalice. Repeatedly, she muttered a chant evoking the powers of the moon and the energies of the earth to influence the magic within the Chalice.

When the moon reached its zenith, she had the fire beneath the cauldron extinguished with sand. Using a hollowed out apple to form a small cup, she carefully spooned the infusion from the cauldron into the Chalice that she then placed centrally on the circular stone. 'I want cold pure water for the cauldron so that I can use it to set the magic once it has passed to the hob swords,' she explained. 'Lift the pot and move it just a little way from the heat of the ashes so that it can cool. Place it down right here, right by the stone,' she ordered, pointing to the opposite side of the now sanctified stone. 'When it is cold, fill it with fresh water from the spring.'

After looking to Silas for approval, two of the large hobs carried out Brid's instructions.

As the night wore on, Rollo, Isolde and Quinn sank to the ground and stared on forlornly while Brid continued to make her preparations. Several hobs now crouched about them, their red eyes watching every move to ensure that they could not escape. Rollo grew more exhausted with each passing hour and inadvertently slumped sideways against Isolde, who pointedly pushed him off. Cradling himself in his arms, he listened to Isolde's quiet gasps of despair.

'I cannot believe she is doing this. I am the Maiden of the Trinity and, though I am still unschooled in many of the old ways, I am sure that this is wrong,' she whispered to Quinn.

'Hush,' Rollo advised, noting that the sly hob that had accompanied Silas on their journey here was now close behind them.

Quinn cast Rollo a contemptuous look. 'Hold your tongue,

murderer, what right do you have to say anything here? All of this is your fault.'

Isolde put a hand on Quinn's. 'That is not fair, Quinn. Many things have happened and they have not all been triggered by Rollo.'

Quinn stood threateningly over Rollo until one of the largest hobs pinched his shoulder and shoved him back down to the ground. 'Just sit there, boy. No one is going anywhere until this is over.'

Rollo had already decided that none of them would be going anywhere anyway. Surely, Brid knew that, so why was she making this treacherous yet futile gesture of complying with Silas's demands? Since it was obvious that she could not possibly hope to save them as individuals, why was she going to such lengths to betray all mankind?

Again, Silas approached the circle and nodded at the array of artefacts and herbs, and at Brid, who was now burnishing the black blade of the dwarves' sword with the juice from the ash tree. But he was not altogether satisfied.

'The thread? Why is there no thread?' he demanded suspiciously, pointing towards the Chalice. 'I can see it clearly, a hand holding a thread. Surely that means that some thread is essential to permit the transference of energy from the sword to the Chalice?'

Brid sighed in exasperation. 'Your meddling and doubt interferes with the preparations. If you must know, no thread is needed when the artefact in question is metal since there is an easy interchange of energy in such materials. You must surely know that metals heat up very quickly and that the heat is quickly passed to another object; it is all the same principle. The thread is needed for an altogether different category of transference,' she explained haughtily.

'What?'

'Teaching you the basic principles of elemental lore is not a part of our bargain and, if I am to perform this spell for you, then you must cease to interfere for dawn is now

517

fast approaching. Moreover, your criticism will be having an adverse effect on my preparations,' she warned him.

Nodding in apparent accord, Silas took a step back in heed of her words and grumbled quietly to himself, but it seemed he could not hold down his concerns for any great duration. 'Still, I see no fire. I know there must be fire. I have read the symbols on the Chalice time and again and the symbol of fire is unmistakable,' he insisted.

'Ah, but it is just a symbol. Just as the image of the moon here represents silver and not actually the moon, the emblem of the fire does not mean that I must apply fire. It is no wonder that you have been unable to discover the correct methods to use the Chalice.'

Silas thoughtfully tapped his staff on the ground. 'So what does the emblem of fire represent here?'

'I thought you merely wanted me to perform the rite. I've told you; I can not teach you all the things it has taken me a lifetime to learn in just one night.'

'No, but you could tell me that one thing,' he said with remarkable smoothness. Rollo was not surprised; he knew to his cost that the man was capable of being calm, polite and even affable when he chose.

Brid sighed in resignation. 'It represents the heat created by the exothermic reaction within the Chalice. Once dipped into the special potion within the Chalice, the two metals become heated, the elements within each vibrating and generating a freer flow of the very matter itself within its form and so allowing the essential energy trapped within the particles to be released. This energy is held in the medium of the potion ready to pass to the next artefact dipped into the Chalice.' She drew a deep breath since she had been speaking quickly and without pause. 'The symbol of fire simply represents the heat generated during the spell.'

She nodded at her words, watching Silas's expression to see whether he had absorbed them and then, hastily, looked to the layout of her consecrated scene before turning her gaze upward at the sky, nodding at the position of the stars. 'We have only a few minutes more before the very first threads of dawn will be upon us. Bring forth your swords and have them placed about the central stone,' she ordered. 'All one hundred must point inwards towards the hub of the stone.'

In remarkable silence, since the hobs were generally noisy creatures, they carried out her instructions as if awed by her mystical presence. Once all were in place, Brid turned her face towards the east.

Her fingers trembling, she slowly raised her hand. Huskily she murmured, 'We await the dawn.'

Rollo wished for the night to last forever since morning would not bring the warmth and light of new beginnings; this dawn heralded darkness and despair. He swallowed dryly, horrified that Brid had fulfilled Silas's wishes. This was not the Brid his father has spoken of with such reverence; just as Isolde was not the brave and happy child that Caspar had reminisced about.

Every inch of Rollo's body cried out against the act as Brid solemnly placed the tip of the dwarf-crafted sword so that it pointed towards the pale grey of patch on the eastern horizon. The thin and ravaged body of the high priestess stood astride the sword, her arms upheld as she waited for the dawn and the coming light.

A hush clamped down upon their world. The fiery ring of beacons that flickered high around the amphitheatre began to dwindle. On the distant megalith on the mount along the channel to the east of the amphitheatre, a hob rose up from where it had been hunkered down on top of the stone. With a booming cry, the figure hoisted a staff topped with a golden ball that caught the very first rays of the sun.

The hush was broken with gasps of, 'The sun.'

One hundred blades radiated out from the centre of where Brid stood, one hundred crude, long-handled hob blades. Rollo felt quiet sick at the sight. *Please, Brid don't do it*, he silently willed her. *You must not do it.*

Silas looked anxiously back and forth between the swords, the Chalice and Brid. 'She is too bold,' he grunted and snapped his fingers at the cloaked hob who had ridden with him to the amphitheatre. 'Gobel,' he commanded the attention of the hob who had helped him escort his three young prisoners through Nattarda.

The hob loped to the side of long-haired man and drooped his head as Silas whispered something in his tiny pricked ear. Gobel sprang away. Brid flinched for a second, her head jerking round to watch the hob's sudden flight, but she kept her hands upraised.

'No! You must not!' a muffled cry broke out from the midst of the wretched knot of captives penned in by the barrier of the ravenshrikes' wings.

Quinn stiffened. 'It can't be,' he murmured as if he had recognized the voice.

The great birds standing over the chained men and women spread wide their wings and flapped them vigorously, sending up great vortexes of dust into the air while the riders on their backs thumped their barbed clubs down on the heads below.

Brid lowered her hands. 'Harm but one of these people and I shall nullify the spell.'

Silas raised his staff at the men riding the birds. 'Cease!' he cried.

But the shrieks from the group of captives would not stop and, a moment later, one of the group was doing his best to fight his way free of the rest though several of the men were struggling to hold him still and force him to be quiet.

Rollo pressed down on Isolde as he craned up to see. Though it was impossible, instinct told him that it was Guthrey. The Artoran's hands were shaking; could it be that he was not the out-of-control murderer he had believed himself to be? He had seen the flash of black hair and the viciousness with which the figure punched and fought at those trying to hold him back. The blood throbbed through

Rollo's head and his lips went dry. He could not believe it! He was not a vile murderer. And it was no wonder that Brid had insisted that the human captives were brought out into the open; she had known that Guthrey was amongst them.

'Be still!' the priestess commanded the struggling figure. 'I command you not to interfere!'

'Mother, it's me!' the youth cried. 'Mother, you must not do this. For the good of us all. Quinn, you must not let her,' the voice cried out from the moaning knot of humans shrouded beneath the spread of the ravenshrikes' wings.

Silas tapped a hob's shoulder and the creature rushed to the group of humans, dragging Guthrey, kicking and screaming, back to the stone walling at the perimeter of the arena where he locked him in chains. The other humans were driven back against the wall where they were more easily controlled.

'Cowards! Cowards, the lot of you,' Guthrey roared. 'And a curse on you, Mother, if you betray us all.'

Brid did not so much as flinch but turned smoothly to Silas. 'I still have much to do here. You must see to it that under no circumstances will that youth come to any harm. See that he is kept quiet but keep him where I can see him.' She waggled an imperious finger at the man. 'Do not forget I have the power to remove the strength from the sword your slave-dwarves have taken a year to make. I can undo all of that just as easily as I can transfer its power to the lesser weapons.'

Silas jerked his head up and back in alarm and blinked at her, astonished that he had not thought of such an eventuality.

Brid gave Guthrey the barest glance before fixing her piercing eyes back on Silas, glaring at him long and hard.

'Guthrey . . .,' Quinn expressed the name with a heavy, disbelieving breath. He turned on Rollo. 'You evil trouble-maker, you told me he was dead.'

Though perplexed by Quinn's attack, Rollo felt an over-whelming sense of relief that, terrible though things were, at least he had not committed such a heinous crime as the murder of his cousin. He was not a murderer. Isolde's hand slipped into his and squeezed it firmly though she said nothing and did no more than flash him one brief look, her eyes forgiving.

Quinn continued to glower at him. 'I cannot believe you made me think Guthrey was dead. I cannot believe you put me through that.'

'I thought it was true,' Rollo stammered, his voice as thin as air. 'I felt the sword penetrate flesh; it struck against solid bone and even knocked off the tip of my blade. I felt it and then I saw Guthrey, still and pale beneath his horse.'

'Clearly Guthrey was unscathed. Perhaps your sword jarred against the breastbone of Guthrey's mount,' Isolde suggested

'I was aiming for Guthrey,' Rollo admitted his treacherous intent. 'I was mad with rage and was aiming for him.'

A low groan emerged from Brid's throat. Despite being chained and under the scrutiny of the hobs and ravenshrikes, Guthrey continued to struggle and shout in protest at his mother. But the priestess did not once look at him, instead concentrating only on the sunlight and the golden sickle in her hands. She used it to deflect the first rays of the sun so that they plunged down to light the water within the Chalice. Her song was beautiful and intense and Rollo could feel spikes of energy sparking out from her and radiating across the amphitheatre. She began a low drone, the rhythm of her strange words repeated over and over until suddenly she stopped.

'It is ready,' Brid said determinedly. 'Now set every human here free. I will not continue otherwise.'

'No,' Silas argued. 'I will have my swords before I release a single one.'

'I cannot trust you,' Brid reasoned.

Isolde twitched. 'She does not mean to do it; I am certain. She is still merely trying to buy our freedom. She is trying to see to it that we are set free with the promise that she will then perform the rite once we are safe. But she will not do it and there will be no way for her to escape.'

Again, Brid began a slow chant and Rollo wondered at the meaning. He understood so few of the words as she spoke of runes and invoked the power of plants but intermingled with these words were other strange phrases that made little sense. With a suddenly shrill voice, she beseeched the wolf to listen with pricked ears and then followed with the strangest invocation to the Great Mother. 'When I invoke you, Great Mother, take a rune for life and safety and pluck from it the strength of the horse so all may be well.'

Isolde's grip was suddenly tightening about Rollo's wrist, her nails biting into his skin. She bent her head towards Quinn and murmured, 'She means for us to make a run for it.'

'How do you know?' the youth demanded.

'I have learnt *some* things over the past years. She spoke of the wolf, meaning me since she knows how close I am to them. Then the rest of what she said was by no means a spell. And since she knows full well that I have failed to learn the magical properties of each rune, she has given me no more than the basic letters to work with.' Isolde's voice was high and strained with excitement. 'That nonsense about a rune and the horse is really very simple. Ehwaz is the rune for the horse, which transliterates into the letter E. If I take that letter from the word rune, it spells run. She is telling us that when she invokes the Great Mother, we are to run.'

'But we will not be able to get her free,' Quinn protested. 'And what of Guthrey? She will not leave Guthrey.'

'She may have to,' Rollo said slowly. 'This way she gets you and Isolde free. But what can any of us do to rescue Guthrey now that he is chained?'

'I won't leave my mother or Guthrey,' Quinn stubbornly proclaimed.

Isolde drew in a deep breath. 'We should do as she says. If Guthrey had obeyed her and kept quiet, she may have had a chance to set him free but not now. Still,' the young priestess's eyes fixed on Brid. 'I would never abandon her. She means everything to me.'

Rollo had no wish to appear a coward but, in all honesty, they had made so many mistakes by listening to their own youthful counsel. For once would it not be better to heed the advice of those wiser than themselves and make a run for it?

'The moment is nigh,' Silas bellowed triumphantly.

Hearing a soft hissing sound, Rollo watched as, circling up from the brew within the Chalice, there arose a haze of vapour.

'The potion is set. She has actually done it,' Isolde choked. 'I did not believe that she would.'

Silas stood tall and looked on Brid with contempt. 'You thought that you, who has known so little of life, struggled so little for your knowledge, could outwit me. You can no more imagine my—' His words were drowned by a sudden shrieking of fear from his horse. Even the ravenshrikes drew back and dipped their heads as the ground shuddered and quaked.

'Now!' Brid shouted. 'Now! It is set. It is done, in the name of the Great Mother.'

'That is the signal,' Isolde murmured. All eyes were turned towards the approaching sound. All were distracted. They had a chance to slip through the fingers of their captors but Isolde did not move a muscle. Her eyes were fixed on the Chalice.

Silas stood with a contemptuous smile on his face. 'You said the reaction would create heat but it has produced no more than the merest breath of warmth. You gave in to me too easily, woman. I knew you would resist to the bitter end and try to outsmart me, but it is I who have outsmarted you,' he told her smugly. 'See! I bring you the intense heat needed to trigger the transference of energy. I bring fire.' He thrust his staff up as, over the rim of the amphitheatre, appeared a vast head armoured in golden scales. At the end of its long snout, two red nostrils flared and smoked. 'Dragon's fire!'

He swung on his heel and snapped his staff round to point at Brid. 'Hold her!' he ordered the hob-guard as Brid lunged at the Chalice to topple it; but she was too late.

His mouth dry and his heart racing, Rollo's entire vision was filled by the terrifying sight of the dragon. Feeling elated and fearful all at once, he was aware only of the creature's flaring nostrils and the flicker of fire within. He could smell her sweet steamy breath. He could hear the double thump of her vast hearts.

Snaking her neck from side to side, she spumed a dense cloudy vapour over the hobs, making them cringe in fear. Ponderously, she descended the terrace, her scales like liquid amber in the early light. Though enormously heavy, she moved with a fluid grace, the power in her muscles easing her footfall so that she now approached with stealth worthy of a lioness.

Rollo felt the sweat on his brow as it trickled from his forehead and down to sting his eyes. Completely transfixed by the sight of the dragon, he could think of nothing save that she was more powerful and more beautiful than anything he had ever seen in his life.

The vast beast drew in a deep breath, swallowing it back into her belly and, with his own breath held in awe and alarm, Rollo knew that she was preparing to spit fire, granting the heat that Silas had said was essential for the spell. Brid had indeed lied and Silas had known that all along. He had seen to it that the intense energy would be provided and, presumably the words he had spoken to Gobel had been a command to summon the dragon. But Rollo could not allow the spell to be completed by the flame. Now that Brid had so punctiliously demonstrated the methods required, those one hundred blades would soon be a thousand and then a thousand thousand and that army of swords would fell them like wheat before the scythe.

But what could he do? His eyes were still transfixed by the sight of the dragon and, looking up at the awesome beast, he remembered how his sister, Imogen, had said that she felt deeply awed and excited at the sight of a great bear. She had said how they stirred her heart and made her tremble with their energy. This was how he felt at the sight of the dragon? Could it possibly be that, though he had failed to inherit his mother's wondrous gift to talk to the bears, he had, after all, been blessed with an even greater power?

Just as the dragon began to fill the great bladder at her throat in readiness to blast out her flame so, too, did Rollo draw in a deep breath. Without thinking, he gave out a cry that came right from his gut, the sound deep and bestial, ululating out as if it were the primeval song of his soul.

At once, he felt giddy and his sense of smell was suddenly overwhelming. He could feel the breath of the dragon on his cheek as she was immediately drawn to his extraordinary cry. He could taste her spit as she drooled over him. He could even hear the faint click and rasp as her golden scales slid one over another. Her big eyes blinked just above his face as she fixed her beady gaze on him. But, her breath was held, the ball of fire already in her gullet there to be spat, its furnace-like roar filling the arena.

But something distracted her and, Rollo turned his head to see three hobs loping towards him, their swords drawn in attack. The dragon lashed out, sending one hurtling into the terraces with the force of the blow. With a single snort of flame, she shrivelled the other two like parchment in the flame of a candle.

'Queen! Great Queen,' Silas was shouting. 'I need you here; I need your fire for the Chalice.'

The dragon slowly swung her armoured head towards the long-haired man and roared. Her neck stretched out long and low, skimming over the ground. A thin jet of controlled flame spurted from her mouth, sending the ravenshrike guarding the three young humans into a state of alarm. Despite its rider's best efforts to control it, the giant bird made a stab at the dragon before fleeing to join the rest of its kind.

Rollo stared up at the magnificent dragon, only vaguely aware of the activity around him. While the hobs were distracted by the panicking ravenshrikes leaping back to avoid being trampled by the dragon, Isolde snaked her way between the hobs' legs. Quinn, too, had disappeared from sight.

Rollo had no opportunity to see where Quinn went because, at that moment, the beast scooped him up in one of her great claws. Though gripped by fear, he managed to stay conscious and maintain the ululating cry that, somehow, had caught the dragon's attention and distracted it from fulfilling Silas's command. Although he was beginning to feel disorientated, as if he were about to suffer one of his crippling fits, he stayed in control by focusing on the mesmerizing jet of flame blasting from the dragon's maw. It fascinated him; he wished he could roar out with such dreadful effect, so that all fell before him as the hobs cringed before the dragon. How he wished he could spit fire like this magnificent monster.

His body shook with an excess of fear and elation and his voice trembled and cracked, yet he knew that, he alone, held all their hopes for life. He was somehow affecting the dragon and preventing her from doing Silas's will.

The golden monster swirled round and swatted a group of skulking hobs behind her with a single blow from an outstretched claw. Her sudden spinning motion half-dragged Rollo's cry from his throat but he continued with renewed concentration as he saw Brid struggling vainly with the great hob.

And there was Isolde! She was running back between the scattering hobs straight toward the central stone where the glinting Chalice sat serenely amidst the surrounding shrieks and chaos. In an instant, she was on the stone. But rather than grabbing the Chalice as Rollo had expected, she snatched up the prized, dwarf-crafted blade just as a hob leapt up from the far side to oppose her. With a shriek of determination, the scrawny girl dragged the blade across the bare skin of her left forearm. The hob snatched at her but she was too quick; jabbing the sword at his neck, she drew blood.

The hob's long fingers went to his throat to press at the bleeding wound and Isolde used that moment to grasp the Chalice. With a shriek of victory, she plunged her bleeding wrist into the cup. Then the hob was on her, struggling for the golden prize.

Yelling in attack, Quinn leapt forward and, snatching up one of the many hob blades, thrust it into the belly of the creature holding Isolde. In his next movement, he wrenched the master dwarf-blade from Isolde's grip and hacked it down on the hob's neck to be certain that he had killed the wretched thing. The hob fell with the Chalice still grasped in its dead hand.

Rollo did not care that the dragon held him. He was staring at the spilt cup.

Isolde had done it! With her own blood, she had contaminated the cup and so destroyed the spell. In his amazement and relief, Rollo forgot that he must keep singing and, in that instance, the dragon's snout was suddenly up against his. He stared along the nodular ridge into those dark golden eyes.

The beast stared back with the strangest look as if, somehow, she were trying to penetrate his eyes to reach his soul. But another yell from Silas drew her attention. She snapped her head round to focus on the man, who was now yelling at her to destroy every human within the amphitheatre. Instead, she seemed intent on fulfilling his initial demand to blast the Chalice with intense heat. With menacing concentration, she swung her head round to stare at the Chalice. With the sound of a storm whistling through a pass, she sucked in air ready to release the furnace-hot flame from her belly. All looked towards the dragon in fearful amazement save Quinn who fell on Isolde, dragging her back.

'No, no! We must have the cup,' she yelled, a trail of blood smearing the stone as she was hauled back. She wriggled free and, again, made an attempt to lunge for the Chalice.

Watching her actions, one of the hob guard sprang forward. In a moment of transient glory, it grasped the Chalice and held it high just as a huge fireball exploded from the dragon's mouth. Too late, the hob looked up as the storm of flames engulfed him and the Chalice. Within the second, the gold of the cup absorbed the intense heat and was aglow. The hobs burnt-away hand tumbled from the shimmering air, the charred fingers still locked about the stem of the Chalice.

Leaving a golden spray of fire as it fell, the cup splashed into the cold waters of the cauldron. The sudden and tremendous heat of the metal set up a sizzling hiss of steam and there was a resounding crack as the cauldron split. Boiling water and the golden cup tumbled out onto the sunburst pattern of stones. A jagged crack sundered the bowl of the Chalice.

Remembering himself, Rollo continued to croak out his cry. The cup was broken. Silas was defeated. The devious traitor could no longer wield his power against man. Surrounded by a hundred hobs and a flock of ravenshrikes, and gripped in the claws of a vast queen dragon, he saw no way of escape; but it did not matter. Though they would surely fall, they had thwarted Silas. The day was theirs.

Chapter 31

Leading his horse on a loose rein, Arathane strode east towards Baron Wiglaf's lands and the Barony of Nattarda.

Caspar followed behind, tugging on the lead rope of the amiable but ponderous draught horse that bore Gart and Leaf on its broad back. They had been travelling together some while but he had failed to learn much about this man other than his name was Arathane and that his reason for being in this area of Belbidia was that he was also hunting Silas – though for what purpose the Baron had been unable to fathom. Although Arathane had grumbled bitterly about the hobs and how they had managed to get close enough to inflict a nasty bite on Sorrel's rump, he said nothing more about himself. Caspar was still very puzzled about the man's initial sightlessness but he did not feel it was appropriate to ask about it.

Gart had followed them, refusing every argument Caspar could provide to make him return to his family. What the youth's mother would have to say on the matter, he could only imagine. But at seventeen years of age the boy was eager for adventure.

Miraculously, Arathane's horse was barely limping now. The warrior had, that morning, ridden her for a short time with no ill effect but, for the moment, still preferred to walk by her side and so burden her as little as possible.

The stranger looked round at Caspar. 'This woman of yours; Brid. She is very skilled. I have never seen an animal heal so fast. The heat is all but gone from Sorrel's leg.'

Caspar smiled at this. 'Oh yes, she is indeed skilled and many more things beside. But she is not mine,' he added hastily. 'She is but a dear friend and my uncle's wife.' He swallowed hard, praying that she was safe and wishing that they had a faster means of finding her instead of plodding into the growing dark. If Arathane were wrong about where the dragon had taken Brid, what would he do then? Once again, he questioned the man on the matter. 'Are you sure this is right? If it was the golden dragon that took her, wouldn't she return to her home in the Yellow Mountains east of Torra Alta?'

Arathane took a while to consider the question. At length he shook his head.

'Home? No. I have observed her movements for several weeks. She scours these curious dwarf-made mammoth pits, then flies away to the south-east. I often saw her take the things she caught within the woods in that direction. I know Silas has something to do with the huge pits in the woods; his telltale signs are everywhere. I have found bolts from his crossbow and seen his tracks in the earth.' A look of disgust hardened the lines of the warrior's mouth. 'And since the dragon also patrols the pits, I know she is involved with the foul man. The territory to which she flies in the south-east is overrun with hobs; it is there we shall find Silas and your unfortunate Brid.'

Caspar nodded, absorbing his words. 'I suppose it is a reasonable assumption.'

Arathane nodded. 'It is indeed reasonable and, believe me, everything to do with Silas is driven by reason. If the dragon is in league with him, as the girl believes, then I am sure I know where she has taken her; I'll bet my staff on it. To the south-east, there is a curious earthwork alongside some huge standing stones and I have watched the dragon drop to the ground and disappear into the mound. I could not get closer than perhaps a thousand yards for the number of hobs lurking thereabouts; they were very nearly the death of me. I was hoping the dragon would lead me to Silas but I have yet to spy the man himself though, as I said, I have seen signs of his presence all about the mammoth pits and the mark of his horse's hooves in the ground.'

'I told you,' Leaf murmured, her eyes blinking fractionally open. 'Spar, didn't I say he is in league with the dragon?'

'Yes, child,' Caspar agreed warmly, 'you did.'

By the evening of the third day, Arathane's mare was quite capable of bearing the warrior's weight. Sitting comfortably in the saddle with Leaf before him, he soothed the girl's head as she slept against his chest. Her hair lifted and fell to the rhythm of the horse's high-stepping gait as Sorrel covered the ground in floating strides. Caspar and Gart took unequal turns to ride the draught horse. The Baron soon discovered that, though the young man was very keen to offer his help and did his best to keep up when on foot, he quickly tired and frequently stumbled during the dark of their night marches. They therefore made better time if Caspar strode alongside.

The draught horse plodded on, content to follow Arathane's beautiful chestnut mare. Seeing that Arathane was beginning to nod in the saddle, Caspar quickened his pace to march alongside the mare's head and guide her along the way. But Sorrel, paced nobly on and soon Caspar realized that she had no need of direction.

'There's a girl,' he crooned to her. With Leaf and Arathane now asleep and Gart some distance behind, he and Sorrel marched on together. He had managed to grab a few short unrestful naps lolling in the saddle but preferred to keep marching as it made him feel that he was doing more to help sort the disasters that had befallen his kith and kin. In the space of a few days, his family had been torn apart and his world destroyed by the vile creatures of the dark world. If he could not find Brid and, worse, if he could not find his son, what more did he care?

He sighed heavily. But, in truth, he did care. Even though he might perish from a broken heart if he lost his son and

Brid, he would want Isolde to continue and, someday, to find happiness; he would want Hal and his offspring to flourish. But, most of all, he wanted his dearly beloved daughter to be safe and happy; he prayed for her as he had every day since they had parted. He hoped that all would be well with Imogen. Ursula had taught her daughter well and she had many faithful followers and was well-loved by all throughout the Kingdom of Artor.

His wife had done a good job and, when she had died, she left her kingdom intact and in faithful hands, her people cared for. It was he who had failed; he had failed his son. It was true that the boy had a difficult nature but he had failed to provide the right support and comfort after his mother's death. Perhaps if he had grieved less himself, he might have stopped the boy from retreating into such a cruel world of isolation and distrust. He had brought him to Belbidia in the hope of restoring his faith in life, certain that Keridwen and Brid would know how to ease the boy's distress and help him to find himself.

The horse nudged him in the back as if offering her support and Caspar reached up to tug at her forelock and gently stroke her velvet ears. 'You are a fine lady,' he whispered to her.

He stroked her again but she did not respond. He had grown accustomed to her gentle supportive company. Now, he was surprised when she threw up her head. Her mane and tail were lifted by a breeze, which was swelling out of the rolling plain they were just entering; her nostrils flared. Dawn would soon be on them; Caspar could smell it on the breeze; a subtle change as the light touched the earth on the unseen horizon to the east.

'Steady there!' Arathane was instantly awake, his arm about Leaf to stop her sliding from the saddle as Sorrel stamped her feet and crabbed sideways.

The eyes beneath the horned helmet that he did not remove even as he dozed, were immediately alert, searching around him. They had trudged through endless scrubland and were now on an open plain that was gnawed by the black-faced cattle of Jotunn whose white bodies were luminous in the last of the moonlight. He looked about him at the dark hump of a low rise to his left and smartly turned Sorrel's head, ripping the bridle from Caspar's grip.

It took a moment for Caspar to spring up behind Gart and urge the cumbersome draught horse to follow the sleek charger as Arathane made for the higher ground to ascertain what had startled the mare. The draught horse grunted with the effort and it was several minutes before Caspar caught up with the warrior and Leaf. The powerful charger was stamping and twisting and, clearly, even Arathane's strong hands were having trouble holding her. She half reared and Leaf gave out a squeal of alarm.

'Hush, child,' Arathane warned her in his deep, steady voice. 'Listen, I can hear something; a distant shriek.'

'It's a ravenshrike,' Caspar interrupted, his head tilted to one side as he listened. 'But what is that other noise? I can hear something more, a faint hum.'

'Hobs! The drone and chants of many hobs.' Arathane pointed and, in the far distance, Caspar could make out a ring of fire, whose flames gave off wisps of smoke that circled up into the first ragged tatters of a grey dawn. His heart stopped in his mouth and he froze. He had heard another cry. Blood racing, his heart pumped into his mouth; it was the ululating cry of command that his wife and then his daughter had used to control the giant bears of Artor.

The warrior looked across at Caspar and pointed to a group of holly trees half way to the ring of stones. 'Quick! Make haste!'

Caspar dug his heels into the draught-horse's ribs and made a stoic but futile effort to keep up with Arathane as they cantered across the open ground. As they drew closer, Caspar could see the tall standing stones and a bank of rising ground from which came roars, smoking tongues of flame and the intermingled cries of humans and hobs. Arathane reined in, waiting for Caspar to draw level. The Baron swung himself down to the ground and held up his arms to take Leaf from the lone warrior.

'Hide the girl,' Arathane commanded. 'Leave Gart with her.'

Caspar accepted his words of command without thought. He looked around and picked a holly tree with a thick covering of spiky leaves for their hiding place. If the hobs came this way, it was still possible that they might smell them out but he couldn't very well fight with a child and an inexperienced youth at his side. It was the best he could do.

'Keep very still,' he told them. 'I'll be back soon, I promise.'

Leaf's lips were trembling but she managed to raise a smile. 'I shall be fine with Gart. Go and bring back the woman. Find Silas and his dragon. You are strong and brave and I believe in you,' she said with confidence and a courageous spirit.

Caspar nodded grimly. It was a terrible to leave Leaf with only Gart to protect her but he had no option. Clamping his jaw tight on his fears, he hurried back to Arathane.

The foreign warrior was tightening his girth and adjusting the buckles on his horse's harness to make sure that all was secure. Mounting, he took up a mace for one hand and a spear for the other. The Baron considered the draught horse and decided he would fare better on foot than riding into a fearful pit of screaming hobs on an untrained horse. However good his horsemanship, the cumbersome animal was not trained for warfare and would be very unlikely to do his bidding.

'What is your choice of weapon?' Arathane asked.

Caspar nodded at the warrior's sword. 'After the bow, my skill is with the sword.'

Arathane unsheathed the weapon and offered it, hilt first. It was heavy in Caspar's grip but it was well-balanced and the feel of it gave him immediate confidence. By agreement, they approached the lee of the circular earthwork, south of the half-circle of giant stones. As the smoke from the hob torches blew into their faces, Arathane soothed Sorrel's arching neck and Caspar sniffed the air. His nostrils stung with the foul smell of warm, decaying vegetables mixed with rotten eggs. He was certain that the pungent stench was that of a mature dragon.

Just as he began the steep climb up the high earthen bank, a figure burst over the top. He braced himself but, seeing that it was a young man, his face white with fear, Caspar lowered his sword.

'Run!' the man shouted. 'Run!'

Undaunted, Caspar let the man race past and turned his attention to the climb. Together, he and Arathane scaled the outer rise of the rampart, Arathane keeping a little distance behind on his horse while Caspar stealthily crept ahead until he reached the summit. Head pressed low against the earth he realized that this was not a fortification but the outer earth wall of an amphitheatre. Though it was still only early dawn, there was enough light to see clearly. He took in a sharp steady breath at the sight below and waved Arathane back.

Below him, all was chaos. Immediately, his eye had leapt to the vast dragon whose sinuous body and tail lashed back and forth, slamming against human and hob alike. Bursts of flame jutted from the beast's nostrils. The Baron took in every detail: Silas, hobs, humans in cringing groups penned by flapping ravenshrikes, and Isolde, Brid and Quinn. Frantically, his eyes searched on through the milling chaos as the distinctive, ear-splitting cry of command rang out again. His breath caught in his throat; there, at last, was Rollo.

'Rollo!' he breathed in relief and terror. He couldn't believe it; that alarming cry of command was singing out from Rollo.

He could hardly trust his eyes; it seemed that the dragon was responding. It could so easily have killed his boy but, instead, was standing over him, keeping the hobs at bay and protecting him.

'Give me your horse,' he hissed at Arathane. 'Give her to me. My son is there; I must pluck him out from under the dragon. I cannot do that without the weight and strength of a war-horse and there's no time to go back for the draught horse now.'

'You cannot have Sorrel,' Arathane refused. 'I cannot fight without her and the two of us together will have a better chance of helping those poor people down there than you would alone.'

Caspar decided that Arathane was right; he needed the warrior's skill and thunderous power to throw the hobs into disarray, which he could not achieve if he charged in alone.

'On my lead,' Arathane ordered.

Caspar nodded, readying himself into a crouched position from which he could sprint forward, every one of his muscles aquiver with adrenaline.

Sitting deep down into his saddle, reins knotted, his weapons high in both hands, Arathane charged down into the fray like a bolt of lightning parting the night. Caspar ran in his wake, shrieking out his own war cry that pumped his veins full of courage. His hand jarred as his blade hacked into the lower back of a hob, the metal sticking between the vertebrae. He twisted his weapon and swung the blade round blindly, only just in time to see it smash into the jawbone of the next hob that was on him. But he was lucky. He would not have stood a chance against so many hobs except that they were fleeing from the dragon. They fell on him in panicked surprise as they ran from the terror of the golden fire-breather.

In the thick of the panic-stricken hobs, Arathane was amidst the tallest of their number, cutting left and right and searching all about. Men and hobs were running in wild panic in all directions, scrambling for the heights of the amphitheatre and only fighting when their paths crossed.

For a moment, a way opened for his line of sight through

537

the fighting and Caspar saw Quinn wielding a black-bladed sword, slashing back and forth, its keen edge severing arms and legs and necks from hobs' bodies as easily as if they had been made of soft clay. The hobs that remained were disorganized and uncertain and none had set upon the humans with any determination since all were most concerned by the dragon whose flame was spraying about the arena. He ducked as a sheet of flame burst over his head and swept the lower edge of the terraces behind him. Ravenshrikes screamed and several flapped awkwardly into the air, tattered and charred feathers tumbling down as they beat their massive wings in an effort to flee the monster's wrath. Men on their backs shouted in panic.

For the moment, it was impossible to reach Rollo. Extraordinarily, that ululating cry coming from his son appeared to be having a remarkable effect on the dragon, who turned her fire only on the hobs and spared the humans. But to rescue his son, Caspar knew he must wait until the dragon had exhausted herself. In the meanwhile, he must use her angry flame to his advantage and reach the others. Brid was lying on a stone slab set into the surface of the arena. Quinn was standing over her, protecting both her and Isolde who had, with considerable wherewithal, snatched up one of the hob's own weapons and was striking anything that came within her reach.

'Arathane, to me!' Caspar yelled, trying to attract the warrior's attention. If they could stand together as a unit, they could use Arathane to open a way for them to escape the arena.

After bringing his mace crashing down onto the back of a hob and simultaneously spearing another through the throat, the warrior glanced over his shoulder but, rather than come to Caspar's call, he saw his own quarry. Wheeling his horse, he burst through the line of hobs in pursuit of Silas.

Running low to avoid the flame and struggling through the charred and smoking bodies of hobs that littered the ground,

Caspar ran for Quinn, again yelling for Arathane's help. But Arathane was focused only on Silas, who was standing at the opening of a dark-mouthed tunnel, bellowing at the hobs before him in attempt to marshal them into some form of order.

'Stand! You wretches! Kill all those on the sacred stone,' Silas yelled, pointing at Quinn and the two women.

'Silas!' Arathane roared. His horse reared and then plunged forward into the thick of the hobs, the ground shaking beneath her pounding hooves.

The mammoth-slayer jerked his head up at the sight of the mounted warrior charging towards him and then ran. At first, Caspar thought that he was running to flee Arathane but then he saw Isolde. The young priestess had broken away from Quinn and was sprinting for all she was worth with something golden glinting in her grasp. It took Silas only seconds to catch her. With one brutal shove, he knocked her down into the swill of blood and mud, kicked the object from her grasp, snatched it up and sprinted on.

Desperately, Caspar tried to cut his way towards Isolde but a huge rangy-limbed hob barred his way.

'We've come this far,' the hob snarled in his face. 'Do you think, we'll stop now?'

Clumsily, it swung its sword at him. Blocking the blow and turning the hob's weapon aside, Caspar saw the hob's elbow burst through the blackened, charred skin of its arm. The hob's forearm twisted round at an unnatural angle and Caspar used his blade to cleave through the remaining ligaments that held its arm in place. But the act of disabling the hob had slowed him down. As the creature fell away, writhing in agony on the floor, he saw that Silas had what he wanted and was still running, now with the golden object grasped in his hand.

Isolde did her best to struggle up and leap after him but was immediately caught by Quinn who had sprinted after her. The hobs around him turned from his cruel weapon to follow Silas, who was already mounted on a sleek black horse.

Sorrel was doing her best to crash through the ranks of running hobs, Arathane swinging his mace and bellowing. But Silas's horse was also fast and the running hobs slowed Arathane. Nevertheless, Arathane closed the distance, circling his mace about his head ready to smash it down with all his might. Silas's black mare wheeled and reared, her head coming into line with the sweep of the warrior's blow.

Caspar knew the rules and tricks of mounted warfare: disable the horse and you have the man. But Arathane stayed his blow to save the sleek black mare. His own chestnut mount stood on her hind legs and screamed, her great hooves lashing the air as a burning ravenshrike flapped between the adversaries.

The moment was enough and, before Arathane could rejoin his attack, Silas had ridden his horse into one of the dark tunnels in the side of the arena and disappeared from view. Arathane swore loudly as the iron grid within the tunnel's mouth crashed down and barred the way. For a split second, his weapons sagged in his hands as if he were vanquished. Then, he snapped upright, used his armoured boot to kick at the nearest hob and charged into the subterranean world of the next nearest underground passageway.

Caspar sprinted the last few paces to the centre of the arena. With Silas gone, the hobs were leaderless but there remained the dragon and the ravenshrikes to contend with. The hobs about the central stone had fled and there were just the number guarding the other captives left; but they would have to wait. His thoughts were only for his son. He was finding it hard to think for that screeching song coming from Rollo, though he hoped that, so long as those notes were ringing out, the lad was safe. But how was he going to get his boy away from the dragon? What if the dragon suddenly took to the air still holding him?

The monstrous lizard stared at them and then crooked her

neck round at Rollo, her great snout touching his cheek. At that very moment, Rollo saw his father and his mouth stopped open, his song suddenly silent. The dragon tilted her huge head to one side, and nudged at him, as if to test his responses.

Caspar held his breath, fearful that such an action would terrify the life from his beloved son. Clearly, the dragon was becoming confused and disorientated. She had bellowed out so much flame that her inner core must be already dangerously chilled, she would soon be exhausted. The ravenshrikes must have come to a similar conclusion because two of them suddenly leapt into the air and dived at her.

The men on their backs beat at the giant birds' heads in an attempt to regain control but it seemed that the creatures were too incensed by the dragon to respond. One rider tumbled from his position about the ravenshrike's neck and ran after the hobs. Once one rider had deserted, the others followed.

Swiftly, the golden dragon thrust Rollo down and pinned him beneath her tail so that she could rear up onto her hindlegs and rake the giant birds out of the sky with her claws. One of the ravenshrikes caught her cheek, its iron-hard claws ripping away her golden scales to reveal pulsating, pale white flesh beneath. With Rollo still pinned and frantically struggling to free himself, Caspar leapt forward, his only thought to reach his son.

But the golden queen had seen him make his move. Like an eagle swooping out of the sky, her head swept down and forward to block his path. The Baron froze, utterly aware that he was at her mercy.

The golden queen drew back her neck like a monstrous cobra but then screams from the captives snatched her attention. As if furious at this intrusion into her thoughts, she lumbered forward. Now riderless and with no one to command it, a ravenshrike was doing its murderous best to savage the remaining captives, keeping them penned at the stone edge of the arena and thwarting any attempts they made to flee. The sight of the ravenshrikes' frenzied movements seemed to enrage the dragon further.

A whistling roar of air was drawn down her throat into her belly as she prepared to blast out her flame, this time her mouth aiming for the ravenshrike, which was stabbing its great beak at the cringing knot of humans. The few remaining hobs turned and stared in alarm, aware of what the giant lizard was about to do. They scattered wildly, enabling a few of the men and women to break away, tripping and scrabbling to be clear of her fire. But a poor unfortunate few were still trapped, held against the stone by the ravenshrike.

'No!' Rollo cried. 'No! Not Guthrey! He's chained. He can't run!'

Caspar seized his opportunity to sprint forward to try and pull his boy free but Rollo had already managed to twist and wriggle and, with one last burst of effort, squeezed out. Instead of running to his father's arms, he scrambled away over the dragon's raised spines, which jutted up along the length of her tail, and began to run for the ravenshrike and captive humans, skipping between and over the charred bodies and diving beneath the ravenshrike's snapping beak.

Immediately, Caspar sprinted after his boy, his view of him now blocked by the ravenshrike's dark body and flapping wings. He had to get past the dragon who now lowered her neck and spewed out a broad sheet of flame that swept low over the ground. Again and again, she blasted out her fire to left and right.

The Baron flung himself down behind the fallen body of a large hob that shielded him from the blast, tucking down his head to protect his face. The heat sucked away the oxygen but he held his breath, knowing that to breathe was to draw in death, as a lungful of air scorched by a dragon would burn him from within.

He looked up as the roar from the blue sheet of flame silenced. The air about him was being buffeted as the dragon's

542

great wings flapped vigorously, the wind knocking the Baron to the ground. Her great bulk was momentarily lifted from the ground, jets of thin flame still bursting out from her maw at anything that moved. Surely, soon her energy would be spent.

Caspar knew that his ancient ancestors had only managed to defeat the dragons that had inhabited the hollow rock of Torra Alta because the act of spitting flame soon depleted the dragon's strength. The art of the dragon-slayer was to provoke the dragon into spitting flame whilst managing to shield themselves from the blast of its furnace. The great beasts could only bellow out so much flame before they became exhausted and so they would turn away from attack before they reached this perilous situation. If they were provoked into exhaling fire beyond that point, taking them beyond the limits of their stamina, they could be felled.

Stumbling on a fallen hob, he looked up in horror to see his son, running ahead of the dragon's flame. Recklessly, Rollo flung himself into the midst of the screaming people who were fleeing the ravenshrike and the stabs of its beak.

'No!' the youth yelled.

Caspar was on his feet and could see that all the captives had managed to flee bar one. Rollo was covering the remaining captive with his body, arms wrapped about him and still continuing to shout, 'No!' at the dragon.

The ravenshrike flapped above him but Rollo stood firm, his arms spread wide. In the same moment that the dragon was about to release her flame, he found again his note of command and cried it out.

The golden beast spat the flame harmlessly into the air, her head swivelling like a hawk's as if she were scanning the ground for the source of the sound, but she overlooked Rollo and evidently didn't see him up against the rock because of the ravenshrike barring the way. She seemed panicked, a thin cry of distress wailing from her throat; perhaps her vision was shot with blood. Unfurling her wings, she spread them wide to balance herself.

The ravenshrike took heed of the dragon's weakened state and flew up at her face. The dragon slashed with her claws, knocking the bird to the ground; but the other ravenshrikes had seen her distress and closed about her.

Still with the ball of fire held glowing in her throat, she flung her neck back, her head skywards, releasing the flame in a belching, roaring column. Her great body crouched and, with visible effort, she sprung up into the air. With tired, irregular flaps of her wings, she climbed high into the golden haze of the morning, the ravenshrikes mocking her.

Exhausted and confused, the few remaining in the arena raised their heads and watched in stunned silence until she and the black specks of the pursuing ravenshrikes were finally lost amongst the clouds of the distant horizon.

Chapter 32

Exhaustion flooded through Rollo's body. His knees sagged and, feeling the stone of the arena wall at his back, he slid down until he was sitting. Vaguely, he was aware of his father beside him, removing the fastenings of Guthrey's chains. Not far away a dying ravenshrike gave several feeble flaps of its wings and then lay still; a maimed hob scurried away into the darkness of one of the tunnels.

Wisps of smoke drifted about the bowl of the now silent stadium. Silas and his hobs were gone and with them all sense of threat. Shaking with fatigue, Rollo dropped his head into his hands and closed his eyes for a long moment.

It was the sound of fresh voices that roused him. A young girl and a youth were anxiously calling out to Caspar as they picked their way through the carnage towards the Baron and all those of Torra Alta, who stood together close to the centre of the amphitheatre. Rollo's father gave their names as Leaf and Gart as he introduced them.

Brid acknowledged them with a weary smile and a rather formal handshake as did the others of her household with the exception of Isolde who looked up shyly before hurriedly averting her gaze. The young priestess was quivering and seemed to be in pain, clutching her arm to her body.

With an open smile, the girl whom his father had called Leaf took Isolde's hand and offered to tend her wound. Immediately, Isolde tried to pull herself away but was unable to deter the girl and with a sigh, gave in. Leaf began the slow process of cleaning, stitching and dressing the cut on Isolde's forearm. Isolde was silent but it was clear to everyone that she was distressed beyond the effect of the wound and finally her quivering lips opened to let out the sobs that she had retained so stoically.

'He got away.' The sobs racked her body and her shoulders heaved as she gasped for breath. 'He has the Chalice,' she cried, shaking her head violently, and looked up with tears streaming down her cheeks at those around her. 'I tried and failed. I ruined everything.'

Brid soothed her hands through the girl's tangled hair and wiped the tears gently from her eyes. 'The man has gone, child, and the Chalice with him, but you saved us. You have saved every one of us.' She spread her arms wide to indicate the expanse of humanity. 'You broke the spell with your blood and the Chalice cracked when it tumbled into the sudden cool of the cauldron. Silas can't use it now. We are safe from its powers. You acted bravely and you did what you thought was right; no one could ask more of you.'

Isolde gave Brid a faint smile.

Rollo sat and watched, noting how intent they all were on each other. He tried to catch Quinn's eye to share a moment of elation but Quinn's attention was focused only on Isolde and Brid.

It was Guthrey's inquisitive eyes that turned first from the closeness of the group. Slowly the boy looked about the stadium until his gaze stopped on Rollo where he still sat at the edge of the arena. He stared without smiling at him for a long time before he broke away from the others and crossed to him.

'Rollo!' Guthrey looked down at him, offering his hand to help him to his feet. 'Quinn was just telling me how you thought you had killed me.' He paused and frowned. 'The truth is I was trying to kill you; and I would have done, if you had not struck my horse down from under me.' He drew in a breath and flicked back his hair, fixing Rollo firmly in the eye. 'I have had time to think on my actions that night and I know now I was wrong. Can you accept my apology? Can we not begin again?'

Rollo could see that Brid was observing them. Evidently Guthrey's words had carried across the arena. She pressed her hands to her abdomen as if her son's confession had deeply pained her.

'Guthrey is right; it is best to leave such struggles behind that we may all focus more clearly on the future.' She took Quinn's hand. 'We must send word to Hal that we are safe.'

Rollo let his eyes rest on Quinn a moment. But when the youth caught his gaze, he stared back fleetingly without raising a smile. Rollo was deeply saddened that he had lost his friendship, but for now, like Brid, he was too tired to deal with such problems and there would be time on the journey home to make amends.

Home, the word mulled through his mind. Without answering Guthrey, he let the youth's hand drop from his. Turning, he climbed the tiered stone steps to the rim of the amphitheatre and looked out across the land. The thought of Torra Alta atop its high tor stirred the embers of a fire deep within his soul. The Artoran prince lifted his head, gazing at the vortex of pink clouds where he had last seen the golden dragon. She was gone and his stomach tightened at her departure; his moment of glory was gone with her.

He allowed a faint smile to stretch his mouth and drew in a deep breath at the thought of what he had done. All had done their part, but it was he and the dragon that had saved them. What did it matter what Quinn or anyone else thought of him? No longer would he be a prince who could never be king, a humiliated youth plagued by shameful fits; he had set his will to control a dragon and had won!

A light touch on his shoulder made him snap his head round and he looked into his father's sky blue eyes that were like the height of the heavens on a crystal-sharp day. The Baron of Torra Alta gripped both Rollo's hands tight and looked him up and down, nodding in satisfaction.

Rollo smiled back, acknowledging his father's emotions of relief and love. But what really touched him was that his father's honest eyes beheld him with pride.